THE LAST CONFEDERATE

HEROES

THE FINAL STRUGGLE FOR SOUTHERN INDEPENDENCE

&

THE ASSASSINATION OF ABRAHAM LINCOLN

By

William L. Richter

Edited with an Introduction by

J. E. "Rick" Smith III

Laurel, Md. Burgundy Press, copyright 2008

In Memory of

General William A. Tidwell;

The man who figured it all out.

TABLE OF CONTENTS

Book 2

The Assassins

PART I

REGROUPING (1865)

I have decided long ago, that I cannot allow myself be kept a prisoner in the White House to suit the convenience of my enemies, North or South. Nor can I prevent any determined man from killing me, especially if he is willing to lose his life in taking mine.
--Abraham Lincoln, April 5, 1865

Harney is missing, probably captured and held in the Old Capitol Prison. There is no time to contact Richmond--indeed, Richmond has been abandoned by a government (dare I think it?), perhaps too cowardly to fight on. It remains but for me and mine to carry out Harney's Gunpowder Plot singly by assassinations of Lincoln, Johnson, Seward, Stanton.
--From the missing pages of John Wilkes Booth's *Diary*, April 12, 1865

1. Lincoln on Black Confederate Soldiers

As Booth belatedly found out, Abraham Lincoln did not visit Campbell Hospital to see E. L. Davenport and his friends put on the play, *When Still Waters Run Deep.* Oddly enough, he went to Booth's rooming house, the National Hotel, down on 6th Street and Pennsylvania Avenue, to participate in a small ceremony, dear to the hearts of all politicians. He was to witness representatives for the 140th Indiana Volunteer Infantry Regiment, still serving in the Carolinas, present a fallen Rebel flag to their state's Governor Oliver Morton, a staunch, albeit hard to get along with, supporter of the Union war effort.

The usual political folderol was engaged in to entertain the crowd of 2,000 interested spectators. The United States Marine Band played a selection of spirited patriotic songs, until shortly after 4 o'clock, when the presidential carriage drove up. President Lincoln emerged (or, rather, he sort of disentangled his ungainly, tall body from the confines of the carriage) to the loud and prolonged cheers of the crowd. Mr. Lincoln took off his characteristic stovepipe hat and acknowledged the crowd's accolades with a bow. He then went inside the hotel lobby to meet with the guests invited to share the day's glory.

Soon the whole party emerged to the applause and renewed cheers of the on-lookers. President Lincoln and Governor Morton came out arm-in-arm, followed by Colonel W. T. Dennis of the War Department, who would act as master of ceremonies.

"Ladies and gentlemen," Colonel Dennis said, holding up his hands for silence. "Please, ladies and gentlemen." He smiled officiously as the crowd grew silent.

"Ladies and gentlemen!" It was obvious why Colonel Dennis had been selected for this assignment. He had a voice that carried effortlessly up and down the street and a style of speaking that mimicked a sideshow barker or a circus ringmaster.

"We have with us today several prominent people as guests on the veranda here of the National Hotel," Colonel Dennis began. "We are especially honored by the presence of our great leader at this time of strife, a man who has been the nation's savior--I give you the supreme captain of the Union, his Excellency, the President of the United States, Abraham Lincoln! (The crowed cheered and applauded).

"And the scourge of the Copperheads; Governor of that great state of our sacred Union, Indiana, whose troops are universally feared throughout the so-called Confederacy, Governor Oliver P. Morton! (More cheers and applause).

"Here are four of the brave soldiers from the 19th Indiana Volunteers, part of the famous Iron Brigade of the Army of the Potomac, men captured by the Rebels on the first day's battle at Gettysburg, as they stoutly defended the Union against the invading Rebel hordes, and recently back from twenty months suffering in horrible Confederate prisoner of war camps!"

As the four heroes stepped forward and stood at attention, the crowd roared. Despite the brilliance of their spanking new uniforms and distinguishing black hats, these men looked especially lean and haggard, their faces burnt by overexposure. As the cheering and applause died down, the crowd began to notice their emaciated condition and a murmur of sympathy swept up and down the street.

"And now, the spokesman of these gallant soldiers, Captain George W. Green!" The captain stepped forward; he carried a folded flag under his left arm.

"President Lincoln, Governor Morton, Colonel Dennis, ladies and gentlemen!" the Captain's sonorous voice echoed down the street. "I have the honor, on behalf of Colonel Tom Brady and his command, the 140th Indiana Volunteer Infantry, of presenting to your Excellency, Governor Morton, a rebel garrison flag, captured at Fort Anderson, in the Cape Fear country below Wilmington, North Carolina. Please accept it and give it such a place in the records of Indiana as it may deserve."

The crowd yelled their heads off as Governor Morton stepped forward and took the flag offered by Captain Green and his companions. Morton took hold of one corner and unfurled the folded banner with a flick of his arm. Captain Green and his men grabbed onto the flag and extended it full length so the crowd could see it. It was of the variety known as the "Stainless Banner," a pure white field with the Confederate battle flag as its union. Colonel Dennis stepped forward and conferred briefly with the soldiers. The Rebel banner was collected together and carried up to the roof of the entrance portico where it was suspended the long way over the railing. But it was fairly large and unwieldy in this manner of display and hung up on the gilt eagle that graced the veranda roof's railing.

Colonel Dennis sought to make light of the difficulty. "I guess that *this* flag is not accustomed to flying over the eagle."

Several in the first several rows of spectators chuckled.

President Lincoln interjected a little humor of his own." Well, Colonel," he said in a fairly audible voice, "*I* reckon the reason for the difficulty is that the *eagle* objected to have the flag put over it!"

This time, those close enough to hear, laughed appreciatively. People who heard the exchange repeated it for those in the rear. The laughing rippled through the crowd with the story. After the flag was hoisted from the veranda, Governor Morton spoke to the assemblage.

"Ladies, Gentlemen, honored guests. I would like to take this opportunity to thank the valiant men of the 140th Indiana for their bravery and sacrifice in capturing this flag from a dangerous Rebel bastion. That I am especially proud of these troops from Indiana goes without saying. But I would also extend our thanks to all the brave men of Indiana who have born such a gallant part in the defense of our nation. In the South, East, and West, Indiana troops have sustained the honor of their State and Country, and the people of the State are proud of their conduct. (Applause).

"They are also proud of their state as a part and parcel of this great Nation. (Applause).

"I state here and now, as I have ever held, that I recognize but one nation and one people and repudiate the bloody heresy of State Sovereignty or State Rights. (Applause).

"We are *one* people and, although divided into States, our national unity is not thereby destroyed. (Applause).

"I congratulate you here and all Americans on the speedy end to this Rebellion. I have seen the dark hours, but my faith in the success of the cause has never been depressed. I believe that God is just, and will aid the right. We have numbers on our side and, if rightly used, cannot help but be successful. . . . I now have the honor to present to you the President of the United States, whose purity and patriotism has been confessed to [by] all, even among his most violent opponents. (Applause).

"His administration will be recognized as the most important epoch of our nation's illustrious history. It struck the death blow to slavery, (applause) and built up the Republic with a power it had never before possessed. If he had done nothing more than put his name to the Emancipation Proclamation, that act alone would have made his name immortal. (Applause)."

President Lincoln then came forward, bowed, and addressed the crowd:

"*Fellow citizens*: It will be but a very few words that I shall undertake to say. I was born in Kentucky, raised in Indiana, and live in Illinois (laughter), and I now am here, where it is my business to be, to care equally for the good people of all the States. I am glad to see an Indiana regiment on this day able to present this captured flag to the

Governor of the State of Indiana. (Applause). I am not disposed, in saying this, to make a distinction between the States, for all have done equally well. (Applause).

"They are but few views or aspects of this great war," Lincoln said, "upon which I have not said or written something whereby my own views might be made known. They is one: The recent attempt of our erring brethren, as they are sometimes called (laughter), to employ the negro to fight for them. I have neither written or made a speech upon that subject, because that was their business and not mine; and if I had a wish upon the subject, I had not the power to introduce it or make it effective.

"The great question with them was, whether the negro, being put into the army, will fight for them. I do not know, therefore I cannot decide. (Laughter). They ought to know better than we, and do know. I have in my lifetime heard many arguments why the negro ought to be a slave; but, if they fight for those who would keep them in slavery, it will be a better argument than any I have yet heard. (Laughter and applause). He who will fight for *that* ought to be a slave. (Applause).

"They have concluded at last," Lincoln went on, "to take one out of four of the slaves and put him into the army; and that one out of four, who will fight to keep the others in slavery, ought to be a slave himself, unless he is killed in a fight. (Applause). While I have often said that all men ought to be free, yet I would allow those colored persons to be slaves who want to be; and next to them those white people who argue in favor of making other people slaves. (Applause). I am in favor of giving an opportunity to such white men to try it on for themselves. (Applause).

"I will say one thing with regard to the negro being employed to fight for them," Lincoln continued, "that I *do* know. I know he cannot fight and stay home and make bread, too (laughter and applause), and as one is about as important as the other to them, I don't care which they do. (Renewed applause). I am rather in favor of having them try them as soldiers. (Applause). They lack one vote of doing that, and I wish I could send my vote over the river, so that I might cast it in favor of allowing the negro to fight. (Applause).

But they cannot fight and work, both," Lincoln opined. "We must now see the bottom of the enemy's resources. They will stand out as long as they can, and if the negro will fight for them, they must allow him to fight. They have drawn on their last branch of resources (applause), and we can now see the bottom. (Applause). I am glad to see the end so near at hand. (Applause). I have said now more than I intended to, and will, therefore, bid you good-bye."

As the cheers and applause of the crowd competed with the Marine band for volume, the President retired to the lobby of the National Hotel. Governor Morton stepped forward, and waved the throng quiet.

"We have all seen the Rebel flag. Now I propose that each and every man in favor of the perpetuity of this great Union take off his hat and give three cheers for the Union flag!" The crowd obliged with great enthusiasm.

Colonel Dennis, not about to let the Department of War be outdone by civilians, Secretary Stanton would not cotton to that eventuality, called out:

"Three more cheers for President Lincoln!" The crowd yelled even louder.

Then Dennis yelled:

"Three cheers for Governor Morton!"

The crowd responded, but by now was a mite worn down by speeches and yelling, so the response was considerably of a lower key. But Morton lost no chance to bask in the limelight. He removed his hat and grinned widely, before he and the rest on the veranda followed the President into the lobby. The Marine band struck up "Yankee Doodle," and the crowd began to melt away. Lincoln, Morton and, to their discomfort, the four soldiers of the 19th Indiana, shook hands with select members of the crowd for a while. Then Lincoln went out to his carriage and drove off, as cheer after cheer followed him down C Street onto the Avenue.

Oddly, the whole affair had been announced in the *National Intelligencer* earlier that day. Booth, distracted by the conversation in Matthew's room and pressure from Sam Arnold and Mike O'Laughlen to do something soon, had simply failed to heed the morning newspaper. He probably considered Davenport to have the most recent and intimate information on Lincoln's day over the newspaper and its overnight deadlines--an unfortunate slip-up for the success of the would-be kidnappers.

2. A Pair of Slippers

"Mr. Weichmann? You and John will have to move up to the attic again. Mrs. Slater is back for the night, and a lady of quality deserves to have the best room in the house. When you have finished, please come down to the street and carry Mrs. Slater's things up to her room."

"Yes, ma'am, Mrs. Surratt."

When Lou Weichmann got to the street, he found that Mrs. Slater had her usual full veil and dark clothes on. It was 8 o'clock p.m., so he could see but little of the mystery woman. But she sure did *smell* good. "It was that way all the way up from Port Tobacco," the young man who drove her said as Lou collected her baggage. "Ain't she just ever so dee-vine?"

"Yeah," Lou agreed absentmindedly. He took her things up to his old bedroom and then looked in on the parlor below to tell Mrs. Surratt everything was arranged. But the French Woman was no where to be seen—probably freshening up, as Mrs. Surratt demurely put it.

When Weichmann awoke the next morning, March 12, 1865, he discovered that his room mate, John Surratt, had already gone down. He hurried down to the floor-level dining room, but he was alone at the table.

"Everyone else gone a' ready," the black cook said, as she dished out grits and eggs and poured the coffee.

That evening, Lou was more determined than ever to find out additional facts about the mystery woman, especially after he moved back into his old room and found a new resident--a pair of Nettie Slater's "dainty slippers," left behind by mistake. Since John had taken Mrs. Slater to New York City, Weichmann turned to the font of all knowledge at the boarding house, Mary Surratt.

"Well, about all I can tell you is that she is from New Bern, North Carolina. Her husband, Rowan Slater, was a traveling dance master, who later enlisted in the army. The rest you probably know from Mr. Spencer. The most interesting thing about her is that she can claim the protection of the French counsel, if she is imprisoned by the Yankee authorities. This makes her a most valuable courier, almost immune, as it were, from retribution."

For the next week, John Surratt was too busy with Booth and his gang, including the Reverend Mr. Paine, to have much to do with inquiries from Lou Weichmann. There was the incident of Surratt and Paine playing on the attic bed with their assorted revolvers, knives and spurs, the borrowing of Lou's beautiful military cape for a night out with Surratt and the young ladies of the house at the play *Jane Shore*, followed by the secret meeting at Gautier's, the abortive kidnap plot and the scattering of gang members to the winds, fearing (uneccessarily) Union penetration of their plans and ultimately arrest.

But on March 21, John opened a letter he had received from Mr. R. D. Watson, supposedly an agent for DeMille & Co. of New York City, but really a cover for a key operative of the Confederate underground between Washington and Montreal--and a former resident of Charles County, Maryland. It read:

New York
March 19th 1865
Mr. John Surratt
Dear Sir:
I would like to see you on important business if you can spare the time to come to New York.
Please telegraph me immediately on the reception of this whether you can come or not & oblige.
Yours &
R. D. Watson
P.S. Address care of Demille & Co. 178 1/2 Water St.

Surratt was off to New York and returned by March 25 with the ubiquitous Nettie Slater in tow. At least that is what Weichmann saw from the dining room window as he came down at 8 o'clock a.m. from his morning toilette. Out on the street, just leaving the curb, were Mrs. Surratt, Mrs. Slater in the usual heavy veil, and John Surratt, driving a four seat rig pulled by two white horses. As nothing had been done about moving him into the attic, Weichmann wondered where she and John had spent the night. Probably at a hotel to confuse the police that Mrs. Surratt seemed to think were always watching the house.

"It was awful, Mr. Weichmann," Mary Surratt said when she got back from Surrattsville, alone on the stage. "When we got out to Surrattsville, Mr. Lloyd informed us that Gus Howell (in her anxiety, she slipped up and called Spencer by his correct name, Weichmann noticed without comment) had been arrested the night before by some of that devil's cavalry. Colonel Baker's that is. Imagine what would have happened had they waited until we got there the next day! And people think I worry *too* much. I lay some do not worry enough!

"So I came back on the stage coming out of Leonardtown, while John was to take Mrs. Slater down to Port Tobacco and get her across the river. Fortunately, he took along Mr. David Barry, a neighbor, because John had to keep going all the way to Richmond, no other courier being available to escort Mrs. S. across the river. But I noticed on the way down that he was quite smitten by her. A mother notices those kinds of things, you know. Mr. Barry was kind enough to tell me about everything and return the horses and rig to Mr. Brooke Stabler over at Howard's Livery around the corner."

William L. Richter

When Barry turned in the team and rig, unknown to Mrs. Surratt, he had handed Brooke Stabler this note, which confirmed Mary Surratt's surmise about her son intentions:

March 26, 1865
Mr. Brooke:
As business will detain me for a few days in the country, I thought I would send you your team back. Mr. B[arry] will deliver in safety and pay the hire on it. If Mr. Booth, my friend, should want my horses, let him have them, but no one else. If you should want any money on them, he will let you have it. I should like to have kept the team for several days, but it is too expensive, especially as I have women on the brain, and may be away for a week or two.
Yours respectfully,
J. Harrison Surratt

"It is these constant delays, Mr. Weichmann," Mrs. Surratt groused on. "These boys are way too complacent about this matter. I have had to push them along, constantly. I have just given Mr. Booth and his drunken, idiot minion, Port Tobacco, a good talking to."

And so she had, being most concerned that if they were to hesitate much longer, all their plans would be for naught.

"Time is of the essence, gentlemen! Get on with it! If y'all wait much longer, there will be no more war and Mr. Lincoln's dictatorship will be a fact for the Confederacy as well as the Union. The whole continent will be under the despot's heel, just like Maryland--my Maryland--has these past four years. We must *move*, Mr. Booth, posthaste. I warn you, sir!"

'I am off, dear lady," said Booth, "to New York City to effect just *that*, I assure you. We will move again, when John returns. I cannot be expected to act without my right-hand man, your capable son. Soon . . . I promise you upon my word of honor, soon."

With that, he touched the brim of his hat in a salute that was topped off with one of his most brilliant smiles, and smoothly strode off down H Street, where he turned right and headed toward the Avenue.

3. A Room for James C. Kinchloe

Lou Weichmann and John Surratt met each other in front of the post office on Seventh and F Streets quite by accident. Weichmann was on his way home from work. Surratt was there to pick up a letter.

"James Sturdy," Surratt told the clerk. He was back shortly with a letter that was written in a very bad hand.

"Who is James Sturdy?" Weichmann asked naïvely.

"You are looking at him," Surratt said, tearing open the envelope. He handed it to Weichmann. It had a New York City post mark near the stamp. Weichmann would later claim that he did not see the contents, just the signature, James Wood. But he heard enough from Surratt to have implicated him later.

"Is that the Wood who stayed at your mother's--the one who later called himself the Reverend Paine?"

"Yes. He went to Baltimore, after leaving here, to see his girl and warn her father that our plot to kidnap the President had failed. They are continually under scrutiny of the local Provost Marshal's office. So Wood went to New York City shortly after. Keeps the Federals off their guard, don'tcha know? He expects Booth any moment, now. A new scheme is being cooked up against the Federal high command. We still hope to use the information you have given us on the numbers and locations of Confederate soldiers in Federal prison camps to win the war."

"You mean the stuff that *you* took from my office during off-hours?"

"Lou, old boy, you are in this as deep as anyone. If you do not believe me, go ask Secretary of War Stanton. You will still be protesting your innocence as they slip the noose around your neck, I allow."

Several days later, Weichmann was scribbling away on a report at his desk in the War Office Building, when to his surprise, Mrs. Eliza Holohan came in, looking very puzzled and overawed by the scale of things at the Union War Department.

"Oh, thank God! Mr. Weichmann, I have a telegram for you--at least, Mrs. Surratt says it is for you."

"Really? I am not expecting any telegrams." He opened it and found the message read:

To Wickmann, Esq., 541 H. Street,
Tell John to get the number and street at once.
J. Booth

Damn it. If I am going to hang with these bastards, the least our irreverent leader could do is learn to spell and pronounce my name correctly, Weichmann thought. "Thank you Mrs. Holohan," he said aloud. "You have done the right thing."

Later, Weichmann gave the telegram to John in their room.

"What does it mean?" Lou asked.

"Do not be so damned inquisitive," John snapped.

"We have to be that careful in our contacts, huh?" Weichmann countered. Surratt merely stared at him with a fed up look on his face.

"You may as well take a walk with me after supper, Lou."

Later the two went down to Tenth Street and turned towards Ford's. But they stopped a block and a half short of the theater at St. Patrick's Catholic School. There Surratt inquired for Miss Annie Ward, an old family friend, who was a teacher there.

"What did Mrs. Murray say?" John asked her.

"She said that she would have a room whenever you all needed it. Go on down, she is expecting you."

"Thanks, Annie. You are a real doll." Miss Ward blushed demurely.

"C'mon, Lou." The men walked down F Street to Ninth. Here, on the southwestern corner, was the Herndon House, one of innumerable boarding houses in Washington. This one was a going business, not a come-as-you-may operation like Mrs. Surratt's.

"Mrs. Murray, please," John said to the mulatto servant at the door.

When Mrs. Murray came out, John asked to speak with her privately.

"Privately? What for?"

"Perhaps, Miss Annie Ward has spoken to you about . . . about a room? Did she not speak to you about engaging a room for a delicate gentleman, who was to have his meals sent up to him? We need it for Monday the 27th this instant."

"Oh! Miss Ward! Yes, she was here. Your room will be ready at the appointed time. Send the gentleman over, no problem."

It did not take long for Weichmann to put two and two together and come up with the suspicion that the "delicate gentleman" was none other than that very indelicate bruiser (for that is how Weichmann saw him), Lewis Paine, or Wood, or whatever he was being called now. Actually the name on the register read, James C. Kincheloe, one of Powell's fellow Mosby raiders from Prince William County, Virginia.

A few days after, Weichmann was walking back from Lenten mass at St. Patrick's with Mrs. Surratt, Anna, Cousin Olivia Jenkins, and niece Honora Fitzpatrick. As they passed the Herndon House, Mrs. Surratt told the young people that she had business inside.

"Why do y'all not perambulate around the square, and I should be finished when y'all return."

Sure enough, Mrs. Surratt was waiting when the city block had been traversed by Weichmann and the girls. Later, Weichmann accosted the black waiter at Herndon's and asked him if he had been carrying meals to a tenant on the second floor.

"Yessir, I sure has."

"Is he a delicate eater?"

"Why bless your heart, sir," he smiled, "I think not. Why, if I had served a young pig to him he would have eaten it, sir, bones and all!" Not wanting to be slipshod, Weichmann asked Atzerodt, who confirmed that the mysterious lodger was indeed Paine. When Weichmann triple checked his theory by asking Mrs. Surratt if that were not true, she appeared very angry that the secret had been revealed.

Meanwhile, as Weichmann was playing detective in the District, Booth was trying to re-establish his contacts in Baltimore through Mike O'Laughlen:

Get word to Sam. Come on, with or without him, Wednesday morning. We sell that day
sure. Don't fail.

J. Wilkes Booth

O'Laughlen came in, but Arnold was absent. Booth told him that a new scheme was coming up, and that he needed to have him ready to move at a moment's notice. O'Laughlen said that he was still game, and that he would try and sell Arnold on it, too. With that, Booth went back to Washington City.

After picking up a letter from the front desk, Booth went back to his room at the National. It had a Baltimore postmark. Maybe it was from Powell, although Booth thought him in New York City by now. He tore open the envelope carefully, because it was part of the letter, itself. Damn it! Booth thought. It was from Samuel Arnold, still dragging his feet and second-guessing everything I want us to do:

Hookstown, Balt[imore] Co.
    March 27, 1865

Dear John:

Was the business so important that you could not remain in Balt[imore] till I saw you? I came as soon as I could, but found that you had gone to W[ashingto]n. I called also to see Mike, but learned from his mother that he had gone with you and had not returned. I concluded, therefore, that he had gone [to Washington] with you.

How inconsiderate you have been! When I left you, you said we would not meet in a month or so. Therefore, I made application for employment, an answer to which I shall receive during the week. I told my parents I had ceased with you. Can I, then, under existing circumstances, act as you request?

You know full well that the G[overnmen]t suspicions something is going on there; therefore the undertaking is becoming more complicated. Why not, for the present, desist, for various reasons, which, if you look into, you can readily see, without my making any mention thereof.

[Neither y]ou, nor anyone, can censure me for my present course. You have been its cause, for how can I come now after telling them I left you? Suspicion rests upon me now from my whole family, and even parties in the country. I will be compelled to leave my home any how, and how soon, I care not.

None, no[,] not one, were more in favor of the enterprise than myself, and today would be there, had you not done as you have--by this I mean, manner of proceeding. I am, as you well know, in need. I am, you might say, in rags, whereas today I ought to be well clothed.

I do not feel right stalking about with means, and more from appearances, a beggar. I feel my dependence; but even all this would [be] and was forgotten, for I was one with you. Time more propitious will arrive yet. Do not act rashly or in haste. I would prefer your first query [to be], 'go and see how it will be taken at R[ichmon]d,' and ere long I shall be better prepared to again be with you. I dislike writing; would sooner verbally make known my views; yet your non-writing causes me to thus proceed.

Do not in anger peruse this. Weigh all I have said, and, as a rational man and a friend, you cannot censure or upbraid my conduct. I sincerely trust this, nor aught else that shall or may occur will ever be an obstacle to obliterate our former friendship and attachment. Write me to Balt[imore], as I expect to be in about Wednesday or Thursday, or, if possible, you can possibly come on, I will Tuesday meet you in Balt[imore] at B[arnum's].

Ever, I subscribe myself,
Your friend,
Sam

Booth looked at the letter again, folded it up and placed it in his trunk. It would be found there, when police broke into his room after the assassination, and lead to the quick arrests of Arnold and O'Laughlen.

4. Tying Up Loose Ends

"Mrs. Surratt! I was worried," Louis J. Weichmann exclaimed, as his landlady walked into the parlor on the second floor of the rooming house on H Street. It was April Fool's Day, 1865. "You were here at breakfast, but missing when I came home from work. No one seemed to know where you were."

"Good evening, Mr. Weichmann," Mary Surratt said. "Not to worry. Everything is fine. I was down in the countryside with Mr. Stringfellow. He was going back to Virginia and I felt obliged to go along and vouch for him with John Lloyd down at the tavern at Surrattsville. That is where he will spend the first night."

"I thought after Gus Howell's arrest that Surrattsville was a mite risky for agents to spend the night?"

"That was *luck*, Mr. Weichmann. The Yankees rarely demonstrate *skill* in their work. They probably will not be back for weeks. That has been their pattern."

"By the bye, just who is this Mr. Stringfellow?"

"He is one of our best agents. Once was a cavalry scout for Jeb Stuart, but now works clandestinely. Actually, he is a lieutenant, I think. He had a plan last fall to capture that Union cavalry general, that German fellow who was tearing up the Virginia Peninsula back then. . . ."

"Oh, yeah, August Kautz. The 'pushy, young hero of the hour' is what Port Tobacco calls him."

"I do not know how you keep up with those *foreign* names, I do declare! . . . Well, nothing came of it. I do not know why. Tried again back in February this year, proposing to kidnap U.S. Grant. Took it to Jeff Davis right personal-like, so that it would not fall through the bureaucratic cracks in the War Department. He arrived right after the Kilpatrick-Dahlgren raid, when Davis was hopping mad. Davis said, 'if you want to kidnap somebody, why not Lincoln?'"

"I thought *we* were assigned to kidnap Lincoln?"

"To keep suspicions down, Lieutenant Stringfellow was assigned the task of scouting out Lincoln's daily habits and such to confirm what Captain Conrad had found out last fall. He came up the mail route disguised as a dental student. He was such a good one, that he passed the licensing examination in four weeks study! Had false papers that made him out to be a Union Maryland soldier; the real one was securely locked up in Belle Isle, doncha know."

"So that is how we found out so much about Lincoln's habits."

"Certainly, such information doesn't grow on trees. Got to dig for it. Tipped us to look for a trip out to the Soldiers' Home on Seventh Street. He was in direct conversation with an officer occupying a very important position, I hear, in the President's *own* house. Mr. Stringfellow often stays at the Kirkwood House, the exact same place as Vice President Johnson lives. Can you beat that? But with the failure of the kidnap attempt a couple of weeks ago, Richmond has decided to send us this Sergeant Frank Harney to blow up the White House."

"Blow up the President's own house? With everyone in it?"

"That is what they say. Our people up here are to figure out how to get into the White House basement and help Harney set the powder train and he will fire it by some machine device that he sets, ahead of time. Sounds fantastical to me, but I am merely a woman. I do not comprehend this so-called scientific knowledge."

"So Lieutenant Stringfellow is no longer needed up here?" Weichmann said aloud, while wondering to himself if he ought not to approach Major Gleason, again. Nah! He would not listen, I have cried "wolf" too often.

"That is right. So I took him down to Mr. Lloyd. I had the buggy driven back here by my brother Zadoc, who is over getting it returned now. Do you think that you could get one of John's horses for him to ride back down country on?"

"Of course. I will get right on it."

Weichmann came back an hour later.

"Get the horse?" Zad Jenkins wanted to know.

"No. It was very frustrating. I told Brooke Stabler, the manager at Howard's, that John's own mother wanted to use the horse for a day or two, but he had a note that said no one except Mr. Booth could use them. Then Atzerodt came up and said the horses were really Booth's property. Said he would check with the Reverend Paine, you know, that fellow, Wood, over at Herndon's. Booth has left town and the horses were to stay put until he got back."

"Oh, for crying out loud," Jenkins growled, "I can go shank's mare and make it in three or four hours, and I reckon I will. Be there by midnight."

"In the dark?" Mary Surratt wailed to her brother.

"Hell, I ain't afeared o' man nor beast."

As if to emphasize his point, Zad lifted up his coat and revealed a Remington .44 caliber revolver in his waist band.

"No, Zad, you shall stay here. We can go to Mass tomorrow and, if Mr. Atzerodt does not come through with a horse, you can walk back on Monday, during the day."

Jenkins looked into the determined face of his sister and knew that it was not worth the argument. Besides, a little vacation would not hurt. So he stayed the weekend, but not an hour more. First thing Monday morning he kissed Mary good bye and thumped out of the house and down the outside stairs and disappeared around the corner. Atzerodt had checked with Lewis Powell and both agreed that Zad should get no horse that belonged to Booth. They were reserved for more important business.

5. John Surratt Goes to Montreal

Louis J. Weichmann sat in Kloman's Oyster House opposite Johnny Surratt the night of April 3. It was just like the old days. Surratt and he; he and Surratt. No interference from John Wilkes Booth or that ersatz preacher man, Lewis Paine or Wood or whatever his real name was, or the inane prattle of Davy Herold, or the Pidgin English of Andrew Atzerodt that was delivered with that incomprehensible German grammar. The two men sat over after-dinner drinks and cigars. Neither really smoked, but it presented a sophisticated air that each liked to think himself capable of, so they put on a good show for the public and themselves.

"You should have been there, Lou," John said. "It was like something off the far side of the moon. You ever look up there in a spy glass and see the craters on the moon? It was like that only there was no light. Every so often a rocket would shoot off or a mortar shell would loop skyward with a sputtering trail of fire in its wake only, and hesitate at its apogee only to fall earthward and hit with a big flash and a loud thud that reverberated through the night.

"All night long, flash-thud, flash-thud, flash-thud," Surratt continued, absentmindedly, staring deep into his snifter. "Way off in the distance down toward Petersburg or the Chickahominy. Out where the men had fought in 1862, where Bobby Lee had made his reputation driving Little Mac and the Army of the Potomac away from the city to Harrison's Landing. It all seems so long ago. Back when we were winning the war."

"How different it is now," Weichmann agreed. "Grant must be close to victory. The newspapers are acting that way. Lee's last attack has failed. General Phil Sheridan has brought thousands of Yankee horse soldiers in from the Shenandoah. It is enough to make your heart break."

"To think that we might be whipped by that uncouth, damnedyankee log-splitter from Illinois. He and his arbitrary arrests, unconstitutional acts like freeing the slaves, illegal acts like confiscation of property, illegal appropriations of all kinds without the prior sanction of Congress, policing the polls with soldiers to intimidate the voters. And they used to gripe about the plug uglies in Baltimore. Damn! It is one thing to be confronted by a street hooligan, quite another to face a squad of soldiers and bayonets."

"Did you have an enjoyable trip with the French Woman?"

"Yeah, if you consider smelling her heavenly perfume a nice trip. I could not get her to take the bait. I tried to get her interested all the way down to Port Tobacco. O' course, I had to shut up in the boat with Andrew Atzerodt. A body does not flirt with a lady when another is present. Damned if I did not sit in that rig with her all hot and bothered all the way to Richmond and she never let on. I could barely get out without announcing my intentions to the world. Thank God, the whorehouses are still the only things functioning smoothly in Richmond, huh?"

"Well, what is the news from Richmond, about the military campaign of 1865, not your amorous adventures? I trust Lee is doing better against Grant than you were with Mrs. Slater?"

"It is all there, Lou. It is in place. I talked to Sergeant Brogden, Assistant Secretary of War Lucius Quinton Washington, Judah P. Benjamin, and Jeff Davis, himself. The notion is that Lee can move faster on the railroads to unite with Joe Johnston in North Carolina, than Sheridan can push his cavalry through the mud to cut him off. Lee will tear up the tracks behind him. While Grant flounders in the mud, Lee and Johnston will join to defeat Sherman coming up from South Carolina. Then Lee will turn to hit Grant's army, strung out in pursuit. He will occupy the central position, able to turn and feint at will, while the Bluebellies will be unable to respond fast enough to save the day. That is a Napoleonic position, in the middle between the enemy's two forces, or so President Davis said."

"That is where *we* come in?"

"Yeah, Harney will blow up the White House during a cabinet meeting. That will destroy Lincoln and the government's ability to control and coordinate the Yankee response. The Radical Republicans will be so caught up in their desire to take over the government by electing a new Secretary of State, so the plan of succession will get under way, that they will just spin their wheels like a railroad locomotive on ice. And no one will be willing to back down, to throw sand on the tracks, so to speak, and to get everything moving again, until it will be too late."

"How come you are going to Canada?"

"I got to deliver dispatches and bring the Montreal group up to snuff. We are staying over at the Metropolitan Hotel, me 'n' dear, sweet Miz Nettie. In two different rooms, damn it, on different floors, to boot. We thought we ought to avoid the National and the Pennsylvania House-- too well-watched by Baker's men. I feel I cannot sleep at home--Ma says that the detectives have been around asking the house servants about me. She don't trust that new one--Susan Ann Mahoney, she calls herself. Kind of a fancy name for a black maid, huh? I met her earlier, and I do not trust her much, myself."

"Oh," Surratt said, suddenly changing the subject, "I told Atzerodt that I had not seen Booth since the failed kidnap attempt a couple of weeks ago, that I was going north with Nettie. He knows her as Kate Thompson or Kate Brown--I left it thataway. Hell, some of the big-wigs in Richmond think she is Mrs. Howell, or Howells, as Mr. Washington put it. Nettie just smiled when he said it. I told Andrew I did not know when Booth would be back, and that he should just go home and find some work.

"Nettie and I leave tomorrow," Surratt went on. "I think I will suggest that she stay in New York City with her mother and sister. I can go through to Montreal myself, alone on the cars. I got ten $20 gold pieces from Benjamin. I exchanged $40 with Mr. Holohan, Ma's boarder, for greenbacks when I got a clean change of clothes. They spend with less fanfare. We came up on the Leonardtown stage, you know--caught it near Chaptico. No rigs to rent and trace thataway. Made good time--got here in only two days. Took us just over three to get down to Richmond."

"Being all hot and bothered must have been what slowed you up on the way down," Weichmann mused.

Surratt laughed.

"But it seems that the timing of the campaign is already fouled up," Weichmann probed, taking Surratt back to the spring campaign. "Richmond has fallen and Petersburg, too. We are nowhere ready to act. What's his name . . . Harney? . . . has not shown up, yet."

"Yeah, it sure don't look good," Surratt admitted. "Davis and Benjamin swore that they would hold on as long as they could. Harney is supposed to be with Mosby and come in across from the Virginia shore. He left a couple of days ahead of us. The damned weather has been too dry. That bodes ill for Lee, if Sheridan's cavalry can move rapidly to the south of him to cut the rails at Amelia Court House."

6. The Confederate Sympathies of Dr. Mudd

"I reckoned I heard a horse come up," John H. Downing said to one of his guests, Daniel J. Thomas.

Thomas raised up in his chair, leaning on one elbow, and looked out the window of the parlor which gave him a view of the front lawn.

"Well, it is Dr. Sam Mudd."

Downing got up and went to the door. He opened it and admitted Mudd into the comfort of the parlor.

"Come in, Sam. You know these men."

Thomas, Benjamin Gardiner, and Jerry Dyer, the brother of Mudd's wife, all stood and shook his hand.

"Sit down Sam," Downing said. "I will go into the kitchen and bring out some refreshment for all of us. And a little wood for the stove to warm this place up a mite."

"We have been reminiscing about the course of the war and how things have changed here since Lincoln's unconstitutional administration was forced upon the South," said Dyer.

"Remember when Marse Robert gave them Hell down on the Rappahannock at Second Manassas back in '62?"

"Oh, yeah," Mudd said with a smile.

"You were down attending to my wench; you know, the light, bright, damned near white one married to Willie Marshall, when I bumped into you down by the slave quarters. We said, 'howdy.' Then I says, 'damned if Ol' Stonewall ain't the best part of the devil--I do not know what to compare him to.' And you says, 'he is quite a smart one.' Then I says, 'Now he has gone up toward Maryland and he is going to cross at Point of Rocks, or somewhere. And I will not be the least surprised if very soon after this he will be down here and take the capital of Washington and soon have Ol' Lincoln burned up in his house.' And you says, 'I would not be the least surprised, either.'"

"I 'low that check Little Mac gave our boys at Sharpsburg was quite a disappointment to you all then?" Thomas inquired.

"I'll lay!" Mudd said. "Gardiner was so disappointed that come next tobacco planting time, he ups and says, right out of the blue, 'Abe Lincoln is a damned son of a bitch and ought to have been dead long ago.' O' course we was working in the fields like a couple of slaves at the time. It was so hot that I says, 'that was much of my mind, too!' Wished we had done for him in '61 when he come through Baltimore. Too much procrastination and he sure did fool us dressed in women's clothes, or whatever that disguise was."

"That battle on Antietam Creek is what give us the Emancipation, damn him!" Gardiner exclaimed.

"Well, the war will soon be over," Thomas opined. "Our army is defeated. South Carolina has fallen to Sherman's bummers and Richmond will soon wind up in Grant's hands. Then we will have peace."

"Peace?" Mudd interjected with disbelief. "Abraham Lincoln is an *abolitionist*. His whole cabinet is such. I do not believe that the South will yield to advocates of abolitionist doctrine. This war is far from over. Besides, Lincoln, his cabinet and other Union men in the State of Maryland will soon be killed--within six or seven weeks, I will lay."

"Oh, come on! Lincoln is so well guarded that no plot against him will succeed. What you suggest is so without sense as to be laughable," Thomas asserted.

"I am not laughing, I assure you," Mudd said firmly.

"And who will kill Union men like me? Surely I have nothing to fear from the likes of you!"

"I am not your problem. The Rebel raider, John Boyle, has just shot a Union man in this area. You had better watch your back and your tongue, Thomas. He might think you to be an abolitionist jackass, incapable of doing your job as Federal detective, just as I do."

"What do you mean?" Thomas demanded.

"I think Daniel, I am much better educated than you are, and I do not think I am capable of filling that office myself--and I do not think you are. . . ."

From his place in the kitchen, Downing coughed and shook his head, unseen by Thomas, indicating that he did not want the harsh words to lead to a fight.

"No offense, Daniel," Mudd concluded, acknowledging Downing's preference.

"Come, now, Mudd," Thomas persisted in his role as *agent provocateur*. "You took the oath of loyalty to the Union in order to vote on the new State Constitution last year, did you not? The one that abolished slavery in Maryland. You cannot say such things about Lincoln and his administration, or any loyal man, after taking such an oath. Do you not consider it binding?"

"No, I do not consider it worth a chaw of tobacco. It was given under an aura of compulsion. If a man is forced to take such an oath it has no effect. It cannot be held binding."

"Bah! No one would kill you for *not* taking the oath. It was not compulsory. It was purely voluntary."

"If I wished to exercise the rights of citizenship, rights fully available before the war without such an oath, I was forced to compromise principles that the Founders called inalienable. That means that we cannot be forced to give them up, oath or no oath. Hence, I consider it compulsory."

Downing came in to feed the fire in the stove.

"Downing, you have been a justice of the peace," Thomas said. "You know something about the law."

"Yeah, just a *little*," Downing affirmed with a wink. "What is the problem?"

"Do you consider the oath we all took to vote in the election for the State Constitution last year binding? It pledged our fealty to the Union, did it not? To the Lincoln administration? Did you not take that oath?"

"I took it alright," Downing admitted. "But I am no more loyal to the Union now than I was before I took it. I have been a loyal man from the beginning of the war, you all know that. But I am a States' Rights man under the Constitution as it was in 1860, as regards political philosophy. One can take the oath and still disagree with the Republicans as to political philosophy and policy. But the manner in which that oath was administered had a feeling of compulsion to it, I am afraid. No less a constitutional lawyer than U.S. Senator Reverdy Johnson from our own great State of Maryland says so. That oath cannot be considered morally binding."

"Well, what do you think, Jerry?" Mudd wanted to know. "You even went to Richmond in 1861."

"Yeah, I did," Dyer said. "That was when we all were afraid that General Sickles and General Hooker were going to arrest all of us for being in the home guard militias. But they were all set up before the war. They sort of kept the blacks overawed and from acting on the abolition promises of Yankee agitators."

"Were you not part of a secessionist unit?" Thomas asked.

"Not really," Dyer responded. "I mean, I suppose that if Maryland had passed an Ordinance of Secession we would have all been in the Rebel army. But I did not join to aid or advocate secession. It was to protect hearth and home. Hell, Governor Hicks, the one who kept Maryland in the Union after Lincoln's election, was the fella who set us up, originally. We all broke up after the war started. Some of the men did go to Richmond and sign up. I went with them to keep from being arrested. I got tired of living in the woods behind your place, Sam. Me and the Gwinn boys. Andrew was the only one who stayed to enlist. I come back when I was sure I would no longer be thrown into Old Capitol Prison."

"You took an oath at that time. Did you not?" Thomas wanted to know, seeking support for his original position, no doubt.

"Sure, I took the oath, *then*," Dyer explained, "but I suppose that my sympathies deep down remained with the Confederacy. But I never went back over the lines after that. And I discouraged several others from doing so. I have never violated my oath. What I mean to say is, I have nothing against *Union*, but I object to *emancipation*. Like Sam says, Lincoln and his government are nothing but abolitionists. Abolition is wrong; I 'low there is no way around that. A body can disagree as to politics and not be disloyal, I reckon."

"Yeah, 'specially because of abolition," seconded Downing. "We cain't get a damned thing done down here without paying the blacks two or three times what they are worth. If it was not that they stand the climate and diet better, I would ship the whole lot, *instanter!*

"At least they are working," Mudd said. "I have great apprehensions from the idle, roving, and lawless Negroes that roam unrestricted through the country."

"You been over to Benedict lately?" Downing asked. "That whole lowland before you get into town is covered by a Federal post called Camp Stanton. Since last fall. It is a place to train colored soldiers! Can you beat that? At least four thousand of them there." Downing shook his head in disbelief. "This is the stupidest war a man ever fought--two groups of whites killing each other over a bunch of damned black people!"

"You know," Mudd commented, "it is bad enough to be made virtual prisoners in our own homes, land, and State by Yankees, but to be lorded over by a set of ignorant, prejudiced, and irresponsible beings of unbleached humanity is more than we should have to submit to."

"You have experienced your share of the alleged benefits of that 'New Birth of Freedom' that the Tyrant in the White House so proudly dispenses, haven't you, Mudd?" Downing asked.

"Yessir, you might say that. My brother, Jeremiah here, had to come down from Baltimore to help out when thirty or forty of the hands got freedom fever and walked off," Mudd said. "Went to the City, I reckon, to see the elephant. We nearly lost the whole crop. That was when I gave Mary Simms 'a touch of the cat,' as Navy men like to say. Just after her brother, that worthless Elzee Eglent, sassed back at me when I told him to go to work. O' course, some of the other hands got infected with the 'slows,' too. I told them that that fella, Turner, was taking recalcitrant slaves to Richmond to build fortifications under Rebel military supervision. They was under contract to work and they was going to do it, willingly here, or by force in Richmond. Hell, I can get eleven dollars a month from the Confederate government for every slave I send. It is the law since last March."

"Which ones was it that dragged their feet along with Elzee?" Dyer asked.

"Oh, le's see--Elzee, his brothers, Frank and Sylvester; and the two Douglas boys, Dick and Lou. Well, all of them started to move to the fields 'cept Elzee. He just did not get the message, I reckon. So, I told him to git moving or I would shoot him in the hind parts. I had my shotgun with me. He dared me. So I shot at him to miss but he took a buckshot in the thigh. I doctored him up and told him to get back to work. Bad move on my part--near forty hands lit out the next day. So much for the management of freedmen, as the Yankees call the slaves after emancipation."

"You are lucky that the army did not come down and arrest you for interfering with black rights--they got so many now, you know," Downing said. "You need to be more careful."

"Prob'ly. . . . Well, I am going up to Giesboro on Thursday to look at the government's horse sale. Any one care to come along? How about you, Ben?"

"No," Gardiner demurred. "But I 'low that Llewelyn might like to. I will tell him, if'n you like."

"That is all right. Thanks, but I will ride over there myself on the way home. Well, good day, gents."

Downing followed Mudd outside and said, "Sam, dammit, you and Gardiner ought to be more careful in front of Thomas. I know that he always tries to be casual, perhaps too casual, but he is a federal detective and a deputy provost marshal."

"Aw, Hell! So are my brothers, Jerry and George," Mudd responded, "as well as several other neighborhood men. These are *supposed* to be undercover appointments, but everyone knows of them."

"Unlike the others, however, Thomas takes the appointment seriously. The others will never inform on any local man, but Thomas will. Mark my words!"

"To the Devil with him," Mudd replied. "Ain't no one who will listen to him, anyway. And if he should attract attention, we all can stick together and call him a liar with a twisted mind. Even his own brother thinks *that*."

As Downing feared, Thomas' testimony, and that of Mudd's abused ex-slaves, would go a long way to help send the doctor to a lifetime's misery on the Dry Tortugas. Liar or not, the Federal military court would believe Thomas. After Mudd's arrest, he would ask a reward for being the first to recognize Mudd as a Confederate agent. He was probably as close to right as anyone else in this, but he was in competition with *real* Federal agents by then, and they were not inclined to share.

7. Mudd's Trip to Giesboro

"Mighty disappointing that the horse sale was changed to next Tuesday," T. Lewellyn Gardiner said, as he and Dr. Samuel A. Mudd stepped off the porch at Martin's Inn in Uniontown on the south bank of the Eastern Branch of the Potomac River at the foot of the Navy Yard Bridge. "I was looking forward to examining some of the stock."

"Typicall of the government--they can never keep a schedule. Besides, we probably would not see much anyway. You know how the Yankees use up their horses and mules."

"So that there is very little left of them, I reckon," Gardiner hazarded.

"Yeah. Been chasing after Mosby and Fitz Lee too long to be worth much. They ride the dickens out of them, put them up wet, let them loose on cold water, and then wonder why they founder. You know, I was told in 1862 that the whole horse herd of the Army of the Potomac was foundered all at one time--must have been 10,000 or 12,000 animals. Right after Jeb Stuart rode around the whole Yankee army, the second time."

"What a waste. Wasn't Ol' Jeb a corker, though? Sure made fools out of the Yank cavalry. Too bad he got gunned down at Yellow Tavern last year."

"Well, Fitz Lee ain't nothing to sneer at," Mudd opined, "neither was Wade Hampton. He sure tore them Yanks apart at Trevilian Station, didn't he?"

"Yeah. . . . But Fitz Lee ain't Jeb Stuart. Neither is Hampton, nor our own Bradley T. Johnson."

"Well, le's walk across the bridge to the Navy Yard," Mudd said, ending the discussion. "We can catch the street car there. No need to take our horses over to the City. The livery prices are too costly and the stables overcrowded. No telling what disease our mounts might find over there."

"Hope we can find a wagon or two, second-hand," Gardiner muttered.

Gardiner's worry proved to be prescient. The two Marylanders went to several carriage shops and a couple of livery stables. Nothing seemed to satisfy them. By five that afternoon, they were ready to call it a day. They went across the putrid drainage canal into that part of Washington City that lay between the ditch and the Potomac called the Island to visit a friend and find lodging for the night.

Both Mudd and Gardiner tried to hold their breath as long as possible while crossing, but their physical activity used up oxygen faster than they had anticipated and both men had to inhale deeply before they cleared the aromatic environ of the canal. The result was much wheezing and coughing, as they vainly tried to expel the noxious vapors from their bodies.

"I do not know how Alex Clark and others live in this hole," Gardiner said with a curse, blowing the mucus out of his nose, *sans* handkerchief. He wiped his still-wet fingers, that had alternately blocked each nostril, on his pants' leg.

"Hopefully, we will not have to cross it again 'til morning," Mudd prayed aloud.

The doctor's wish turned out to be a pipe dream. Alexander H. Clark proved not to be home from his shop. So Mudd and Gardiner risked the miasma emitting from the swampy ditch a second and third time as they went down to Clark's place of business and back home with him for tea--actually, more of a light supper--after he closed.

"I am going over to Allen's office for a game of cards. We meet each week at this time," Clark said at the end of supper. "Why do y'all not come with me? A couple of fresh players are always welcome, if they are gentlemen, like you all are."

"Fresh players or fresh fish?" Mudd wanted to know, using the popular army term for gullible new recruits.

"I am sure, Mudd, that you and your friend will not be out-classed. After all, I have seen you play before, and you took me for a few Secretary Chase notes. Easily, I might add."

Dr. Charles Allen's office proved to be a crowded house. There were perhaps ten to a dozen men present, and the rooms reeked of cigar smoke that broke up the light of the oil lamps so much as to make their gallant efforts to brighten up the scene quite dim. Mudd, Gardiner, and Clark quickly added to the card room's pollution as they lit up cigars of their own.

After introductions, the two Maryland farmers were seated apart at different tables for a night of penny ante draw poker. Playing quite skillfully, Gardiner came out ahead. Mudd, however, became everyone's favorite, as he lost pot after pot. His mind seemed elsewhere. Abnormally, he even failed to keep up with the pro-Confederate political views and casual banter of the other players.

They played cards, smoked, and swilled various liquors for four hours or more. It was well after midnight before they broke out into the night air, still fouled by ill-smelling fragrances from the cross-town drainage canal. But the men's nostrils were so overlayed with cigar smoke, that the coolness of the evening was more refreshing than odoriferous. The visitors from the country could not imagine how residents of the island --indeed, the whole city--put up with the effluvious emissions not only of the canal but from the filthy streets. In the fashion of the time, Mudd and Gardiner slept in the same bed in a spare room up in Clark's attic.

The next morning, after breakfast, Mudd and Gardiner walked back across the canal a final time, headed for the capitol building. They were off to see the display of oil paintings hanging in the rotunda. At least that is what they told anyone who would listen. After crossing the canal, the two pedestrians soon separated.

"I am off on my errand to see a gentleman at the National Hotel," Mudd explained. "You go on down to the capitol and I will meet you there in an hour or so. Then, we can catch a car down to the Navy Yard, and go over to Martin's for dinner. He puts on quite a spread, you know. We can ride home after that."

"You going to see that Booth feller?"

"Yes. I must find out what has happened with the plot to capture Lincoln. I am tired of this waiting in the dark."

Gardiner waved and Mudd headed up the tree-studded north side of Pennsylvania Avenue. It was a pleasant morning and a slight breeze kept the scents of the canal and the dust of the many horses and carriages and wagons to a minimum. When the doctor passed opposite of Marble Alley, a strip known for its fine selection of whorehouses, a six-gun light field artillery battery came thundering by, spraying mud all directions in its wake. As Mudd and other passers by brushed the filth from their clothes, he could hear the young soldiers laughing. He looked up the street to see the several caissons flying past the sidewalk in front of the National Hotel and spray its noted patrons and loungers with muddy water. Several well-dressed ladies screamed, their gowns ruined for the day.

"Damnyankees!" Mudd barked, not realizing how loudly he had spoken. Mudd looked around, expecting rebuke. But no one contradicted him. Indeed, several other victims of the battery's passage had a few choice epithets of their own to deliver, one man shouting his at the top of his voice for naught.

Mudd entered the hotel lobby, stepping aside as several high-ranking Union officers rudely pushed by in a body. "Common bastards," Mudd said quietly. He crossed the lobby, passed the front desk and took the stairway to the second floor. Booth's room was at the end of the hallway. Without knocking, Mudd opened the door and strode in.

"Booth, I . . . ."

A strange man sat at the desk, looking quite shocked, pen in hand. Mudd had so startled the man that he had allowed a blotch of ink to fall on his letter.

"Oh!" Mudd exclaimed, quite as disturbed as the man he addressed. "I . . . I seem to have made a mistake. Please accept my apology."

"Whom did you wish to see?"

"Well . . . I . . . ah . . . Mr. Booth."

"Sorry. I am Marcus P. Norton, Esq., sir, attorney at law, of Troy, New York, practicing before the United States Supreme Court this session. Perhaps your Mr. Booth has a room on the floor above?"

"No . . . I have simply made an unfortunate mistake. Excuse me, please, sir, forgive the intrusion. I must be going."

Mudd quickly backed out of the room and turned to go down the stairs. Behind him he heard the door hinges squeak. He took the stairs rapidly, stopping to look back up at the first landing. There, quizzically staring after him was the stranger in Booth's old room.

"Mr. John Wilkes Booth, please," he said to the desk clerk.

"I am sorry, sir, Mr. Booth checked out a few days ago. No forwarding address, I am afraid."

"Thank you, sir," Mudd replied.

Where the Hell was Booth? Who was that Marcus P. Norton, Esq. Was he really an attorney? Or perhaps a government spy? Had the plot already been executed? No, no! It could not have or the whole town would be abuzz with Lincoln's disappearance or Booth's death or capture.

Mudd pondered these and other questions as he hurriedly marched down the Avenue toward the glistening capitol building on the hill in front of him. He looked backward, checking the road behind him for anyone who might be following him. Nothing. No one. At least, he could *see* no one suspicious. He came into the legislative halls of the federal government from the back way and climbed to the rotunda. There was Gardiner, making much of being a *faux* art critic.

"Ah!" Gardiner said, looking up at the sound of Mudd's foot steps approaching.

A pulsing tension was building pressure in Mudd's brain. His boots seemed to call out as he strode, click, click, click, I am a traitor, look at me, click, click, click, I am a traitor, look at me.

"In the name of Our Lord, what is wrong?" Gardiner asked. "You look the very picture of death warmed over."

"Booth was not there--there was someone else in his room. I barged in without knocking. It was all ever so embarrassing. You will tell anyone who wants to know that I was here with you, won't you?"

"Sure, Sam. You can count on me. And the men back at Allen's will swear to your being there, too. Do not worry a body so. You will have a fit of apoplexy, if you are not careful. Calm down!"

"Le's get out of here! We can catch our car at the block below the Old Capitol Prison."

As Mudd and Gardiner walked out of the capitol building, Mudd looked across the way to the foreboding walls of the infamous jail that housed those who would compromise the Union war effort. Those held without charges were a majority of the internees--suspected Confederate sympathizers, outspoken newspaper editors from all over the North and occupied South, actual spies, along with captured Confederate soldiers awaiting their transfers to places like Fort Delaware and Point Lookout, unseen men and women with whom he suddenly felt a strong kinship.

And in the valley beyond were the dregs of the war, the former slaves and white refugees, living in a rotten slum called Swamp Poodle. Mudd shuddered that he could be in the one place and Frankie and the children wind up in the other, all because he had agreed to the absurdities of that infernal, now missing actor, John Wilkes Booth.

But, damn it! It was all for The Cause, for slavery of the black and freedom of the white, for constitutional government, for limited government and the rights of states and localities, for the insults and injustices Maryland has had to endure for its Southern way of life. Mudd drew a deep breath and bucked up against the pressure. Like the troops in the field, the boys in gray, he too must soldier on.

As he and Gardiner stepped on to the street car steps, Mudd smiled. His hands shook no more, his mind cleared, and he felt buoyant in spirit. He found that deep down he was proud of his small role in saving the South from the domineering New England codfish aristocracy and its mantra of centralized, national governmental tyranny and race amalgamation. This was no time to falter. Yes, by God, he would go the whole hog!

8. Aboard the *Malvern*

"Mr. President? Sir? They is a gentleman to see you, sir. It is General Ripley, the Commandant of Richmond, sir--ours. He has a 9 o'clock appointment. He is the one who wished to see you last night, only we put him off."

"Thank you, Sergeant," Abraham Lincoln said, untangling his legs from the table top upon which they rested. He checked his watch. Nine o'clock in the morning, straight up. "Please, show the very prompt General Ripley in."

Lincoln was in Admiral David Dixon Porter's stateroom of the *Malvern*, a 1,500 ton side-wheel steamer upon which he lived, while at City Point, Virginia. The *Malvern* had been a very fast, ill fated blockade runner. During a storm, she sought shelter in a North Carolina inlet. The next vessel to come in for the same reason was a Union warship, which forced her to heave to. Outgunned, the *Malvern* surrendered after a short fight.

As she was a vessel with big, comfortable staterooms, the *Malvern* became part of the North Atlantic blockade squadron, generally used as a headquarters ship. Today it was sort of a mobile White House. The *Malvern* was safer than a land berth; at least Lieutenant General Ulysses S. Grant had thought so. The Rebels had shown much imagination during the Siege of Petersburg and Richmond. Rebel cavalry had stolen the Army of the Potomac's beef herd right out from the midst of the quartermaster's supply officers. Nothing was truly safe, not even the city that boasted General Grant's headquarters.

Grant's headquarters town, City Point, was a Yankee creation--a gigantic city constructed for the supply of men and materiel for Grant's whole collection of Union armies that had once invested the Confederate capital. City Point was a fine tribute to Yankee ingenuity--it had its numerous docks and storehouses behind the siege lines connected by its own private railroad. It was also a fine target of opportunity for the Confederate clandestine apparatus. The port had to be built twice. Once, at the beginning of last summer, and again after a pair of operatives, John Maxwell and R. K. Dillard, from the Rebel Torpedo Bureau, had blown a large part of it to Hell on August 9, 1864, by touching off an ammunition barge using a horological explosive device designed to look like a piece of coal.

But nothing could turn back the inevitability of Union victory. It took from June of the previous summer to April 3, 1865, but Richmond had fallen. Just as Grant had promised it would. It just had taken a little longer than he and Lincoln had expected. What was that Grant had said last year? "I propose to fight it out along this line if it takes all summer." Lincoln chuckled. He liked Grant, because Grant delivered--no matter how long it took. He was the proverbial bulldog. He just latched on to his opponent's leg, while Major General William T. Sherman and the others gutted the South alive, taking heart and all.

The South knew it was finished. Lincoln's old friend from his congressional days in the late 1840's, Alexander Stephens of Georgia, now Vice President of the Confederate States of America, had come down in early February to talk peace for the last time. But the Rebels still did not understand. They wanted independence in exchange for stopping the fighting. Lincoln wanted Union and Emancipation. In the end, there had been nothing to talk about. And the war *went on*, to paraphrase his Second Inaugural speech.

"Howdy, General," Lincoln said to the man who entered the room, ducking through the door. "Watch your head, sir. I have bumped mine a lot on that headpiece. I reckon some folks would wish that such a good crack might knock some sense into my mule head."

"Brigadier General Edward H. Ripley, sir, originally of the 9th Vermont Volunteer Infantry." The two men shook hands.

"Vermont is a beautiful place, I hear. I have never had the privilege of seeing it, myself; but my son, Robert, tells me so. He is a Harvard man, you know. And to think his Pa learned all *his* schooling in the light cast by the logs of a cabin fireplace. How times have changed. . . . Well, General, sit down, take a chair. What is so all-fired important that you need to see me right off?"

Lincoln sat on a long sofa that ran the length of the state room. Ripley sat opposite him in a hard wood chair. Suddenly, Lincoln's overindulged son, Tad, entered the state room with a yell and a rush, crawled up on the sofa and began to run its length, back and forth, making childish noises of cheer, crawling over his father's back each time the boy passed. It was very annoying to Ripley, who had to talk over the boyish exclamations.

"Sorry to intrude, sir. I know all commanders relish their few private moments," Ripley said. His statement came out a mite more icily than he anticipated. Lincoln did not appear to notice; or, if he did, he did not appear offended. "But I have an urgent mission, sir. I hope that it will save your life."

"Have you checked with Congress, General? I have reason to suspect that quite a few of *them*, some from my *own* party, might like you to reconsider." Lincoln's Upper South drawl contrasted markedly with Ripley's clipped, and obviously well-educated, flat, New England accent. Lincoln grinned amiably as he spoke. Tad crawled over his shoulders, once again.

Ripley did not grin at all. Indeed, like many sober people, he mistakenly saw the President's attitude and speech as quite flippant. "This is quite serious, sir. I would wish--no, sir, I *insist*--that you talk to a man I have outside. He is a Rebel soldier, name of William Snyder. He is an enlisted man. His last duty station was in Richmond with Brigadier General Gabriel Rains' Torpedo Bureau--the same people who blew up City Point last year. It is part of the Rebel Secret Service. They were the ones who tried to set fire to New York City in November, and free Confederate prisoners held in our camps up North, like Camp Douglas and Johnson's Island. I understand they tried to spread smallpox and yellow fever in some of our port cities."

"I am quite familiar with the infamous operations of that nefarious institution, General. They have been devilishly impudent and quite clever in their activities for some time." He reached up and pinched Tad on the bottom as he passed over his shoulders. The boy squealed with delight.

"This fellow, Snyder, says that the last party dispatched from General Rains' headquarters, before Richmond fell to our arms, was an assassination team. They are going to join up with Mosby and he will infiltrate them into Washington, D.C."

"Yes, Colonel Mosby. . . . He has made himself quite a nuisance for the last couple of years. Go on with your story, General." Lincoln had been seated behind the table. He now placed his head in his hand, supporting his chin, as if he were too weary to sit upright. Tad had more room and passed by in a flash, missing his father's groping hand. Ripley quickly moved to finish his report. The childish hub-bub annoyed him.

"Sir, the head of this latest group is a powderman named Thomas F. Harney. As I understand it he is originally from Missouri. He was captured and exchanged, and wound up with General Rains. His mission is to assassinate you, sir. Perhaps blow up this ship, or even the White House! At least, that is what we think. The Torpedo Bureau missions are highly secretive. Even Snyder does not know Harney's actual mission. Sir,

I must emphasize the man's sincerity and good faith in coming forward voluntarily. May I read his statement, given to my adjutant last night?"

Lincoln shook his head affirmatively, and Ripley read the statement from a piece of paper that he took from his coat. It basically repeated what he had already told the President, orally. Tad continued to interrupt Ripley's concentration, although the President seemed not to notice the boy's competing for his attention.

"Do you know how many warnings or threats of this kind I have received during my four years in the White House?" Lincoln asked when Ripley had finished. "I would guess about eighty--at least, those are the ones that *I* know of. Well-wishers often mistakenly censor what I receive in these matters. I have most of them rolled up like a tube and tied with a ribbon, stored in a cubby hole in my desk. They distress Mrs. Lincoln to such an extent that I keep them hidden from her.

"General," Lincoln continued, "I have decided long ago, that I cannot allow myself be kept a prisoner in the White House to suit the convenience of my enemies, North or South. Nor can I prevent any determined man from killing me, especially if he is willing to lose his life in taking mine. Ever since I *stole* into Washington in 1861, I have determined never to permit myself to be made a fool of, as I was on that unfortunate occasion, or to demonstrate a lack of courage. I have had my hat shot off, been cursed and threatened, and plotted against. I know that."

"But you must take *some* precaution, sir. For your safety and that of the gloriously restored Union. Please, Mr. President . . . at least *talk* to Snyder. He is outside. The Marine guards will not allow him in."

"No, General Ripley. It is impossible for me to adopt and follow your suggestions. I deeply appreciate the feeling which has led you to urge them on me, but I must go on as I have begun in the course marked out for me, for in all honesty, I cannot bring myself to believe that any human being lives that would do me harm."

"Mr. Lincoln . . ." Ripley remonstrated. But the President cut him off.

"General, surely you are aware as commandant of the City of Richmond, that I toured the city yesterday with a small guard of sailors. They were armed of course. Spencer carbines. Fine weapon, the Spencer. I shot it once, myself. Anyhow, I went through the streets, entered the Confederate White House, and, just for fun, sat in the same chair, behind the same desk that Jeff Davis had sat behind and worked from some hours before. Even met and talked with Judge John A. Campbell--he was once a *United States* Supreme Court Associate Justice. We spoke of reconstructing the Virginia state government, bringing it back into the Union formally, beyond the military fact of conquest.

"Well, sir," Lincoln went on. "Many of the whites stared at me with venomous looks. More simply went indoors and closed their shutters against seeing my promenade. I suspect what really amazed--no, angered--them, was the conduct of their former slaves, now freedmen. They soon realized who I was and thronged into the streets by the hundred. They cried, sang, and cheered me politely. Everyone wanted to touch me. Many knelt before me, supplicating for my blessing, comparing my arrival to the Second Coming, I swear. I was most gratified and even more *embarrassed*. My Emancipation Proclamation, that so many in the North erroneously honor, really freed none of them, but the coming Thirteenth Amendment to the Constitution will. So, I asked them to rise and be free, bowing and kneeling to no man.

"When I was but a young man, I took a flatboat down the Illinois to the Mississippi clean to New Or-leens. That was the first time I really encountered slavery. It was an eye-opener. To think that anyone could hold his fellow man in bondage! I vowed then and there, that if I ever could, I would strike this evil *hard*, in any way I could. I have been granted an answer to that prayer. We now, or soon will, have a Union of *free* men for the first time. I am consoled by this idea, one that confounded the Founding Fathers, whenever I view the destruction of this war.

"No man can hurt me, General Ripley. Should I be taken at this hour of our national triumph, I die knowing that I--all of us--have strengthened the *imperfect* edifice of government built by the Founders and that we have brought about a New Birth of Freedom, as I call it. We have torn out the rotten foundation of slavery and rep!aced it with the solid foundation of all men, free and equal, for the *first* time in our brief history as a country. I hope to be present for the continuance of this great event, but, should I perish, I die knowing that I in some small way, I have saved this great nation from the tyranny of bondage. Thank you for coming, sir; but go now remembering, that I fear nothing, nobody. A greater power than you or I will determine my future and the future of our reunited nation. We can but acquiesce.

"Besides, General," the President chuckled and stood up, "what do they wish to kill me for? If the kill me they will run the risk of getting a worse man!"

Ripley arose as the President did. Lincoln offered his hand, which Ripley took and shook firmly. Then the General stepped back and snapped to attention and saluted. Ripley realized that here was nothing flippant about this man with his countrified manners and speech. More than anyone, the President knew the direction in which he wanted this war to go and why.

9. Mrs. Surratt's Trip of April 11

"As you may be aware, Mr. Weichmann," Mary Surratt said to her erstwhile boarder, "one of the biggest financial obligations my late husband left me with is the money owed to the Calvert estate on the land upon which sit a tavern and residence at Surrattsville. I paid a large sum on it last January, and I have rented the property to John Lloyd, which will go far to relieve me of the debt.

"But Mr. Lloyd's rent is insufficient to cover the whole amount owed, and the Calverts have been pressing me for the whole amount. If I can get Mr. John Nothey to make good on what he owes me for property he bought from Mr. Surratt some years back, it would go a long way to satisfy the Calvert note, about half of it, should I hazard a guess. So I have to ask of you a great favor . . . as John is out of town, would you be able to take tomorrow off from work and drive me out to the crossroads, so that I might try and come to some kind of agreement with Mr. Nothey?"

"By all means, Mrs. Surratt. I think a drive in the country would be most welcome. My office at the War Department is getting a bit stuffy, anyhow."

"Perhaps we can borrow the horse and carriage Mr. Booth owns. Could you go over to the National Hotel tomorrow morning early and see to it?"

Weichmann was off on his assigned task the next morning after breakfast. By 9 a.m., he was back, with horse and carriage.

"Wait a minute! That is not Mr. Booth's horse and carriage," Mrs. Surratt said, when she came out on the front walk.

"Nome," Weichmann admitted. "Mr. Booth said that he had sold off both horse and carriage and he insisted in giving you $10 to offset the costs of a rental from Howard's Stable and any inconvenience he may have caused. Strange, I always thought the horses belonged to John."

"Oh, no, they were always Mr. Booth's--John just took care of them. What a gentleman Mr. Booth is! He is correct to a fault."

Indeed he was, as his friends well knew. But to a stodgy military board, two months later, he would appear to have had an ominous, ulterior motive in assuring Mrs. Surratt's arrival at Surrattsville that day.

Weichmann clucked the horse into a sharp right turn so that the carriage wheel would not snag Mary Surratt's dress. Then he climbed down and helped her aboard. The weather was inclement, beginning to drizzle, and Weichmann had already put up the convertible top.

He took the reins upon climbing aboard, and turned the rig to the east and south, headed for the 11th Street Bridge at the Navy Yard. They crossed the bridge, after a rudimentary inspection by the guards, and turned up Harrison Street toward the slope of Good Hope Hill.

"Hold up!" Mrs. Surratt said, placing her hand on Weichmann's arm. "Is that not Old Black drawing my carriage from Surrattsville?"

"Yes, conveying a gentleman and a lady."

"Whoa!" she shouted." Mr. Lloyd! Hold on, there!"

The approaching carriage came to a stop three or four yards past them. Lloyd got down and walked back toward them, turning up his collar and pulling down his hat against the damp. He stood, with his hat on and hands in his pockets, preferring warmth to social proprieties. That was no way to address a lady in the nineteenth century.

"Mrs. Surratt. I thought it was you. Are you perchance on your way to see me? What might I do for you?"

"Yes, I am on my way to Surratt's, but not to see you. I am out on business concerning the debt owed me by Mr. Nothey. I hope to see Capt. Bennett Gwinn, my representative in this case."

"Well, I am on my way with Mrs. Offutt into the City."

Emma Offutt was Lloyd's sister-in-law, as Mary well knew. Mrs. Lloyd was an invalid, and her sister came over to Surrattsville often to help out. But neighbors noted that she came as much when Mrs. Lloyd was in Allen's Fresh, visiting her family, as when she was at the tavern-residence. Word was that Mrs. Offutt and John Lloyd had something special going on the side. Having been a victim of such rumors herself, Mary Surratt did not bother to credit them publicly, even though she believed them. Her tenant and his helpmate were awfully friendly, touchy-feely friendly, that much she *did* know.

"Heerd anything about Gus Howell?" Lloyd's question brought Mrs. Surratt out of her reverie.

"Hmm? . . . Oh . . . he is in the Old Capitol. He will not take the oath of allegiance. Cain't say as how I blame him, but the war is over for all practicality. The *oath* ought not to bother him, if that is *all* they want to hear. I am thinking of going to see Judge Turner and see if we cannot strike some sort of deal. The Yanks did not find those shooting irons when they arrested Mr. Howell? "

"Nome, they never even bothered to look. They was too thrilled at getting their hands on a real *spy* that they trussed him right up and rode right off to report their great deed to the higher ups."

"I allow I am glad to hear *that.*" She laughed heartily.

"You ain't the only one, I'll lay! I would hate to have to join him in jail. I have half a mind to bury them things, the guns and all, they scare me so. If the Yanks find them there. . . ."

"No, no. Do not do that. The shooting irons will be called for soon, in a matter of days. You get them ready, you hear? You will be shuck of them real soon."

"Yes'm. By the way, did you hear about Stringfellow? He escaped from the Yankees who took him near Port Tobacco. "

"That is good. I heard that, after he left the tavern, he had been captured down in Charles County and taken to Port Tobacco for questioning."

"He is either hiding in the swamps or already across the Potomac. The soldiers said that they want your son John for going to Richmond."

Mrs. Surratt laughed. "Come, come, sir. One would have to be very clever to accomplish *that* trip in these days, for sure! John is far, far north of the wiles of Yankeedom."

"Well, then, ma'am, I reckon we will be going. Best of luck on the intention of your trip. I hope the weather holds for both of us."

Lloyd tipped his hat to Mrs. Surratt and Weichmann and strode back to his rig. Mrs. Surratt leaned out of her carriage and shouted, "Hello, Mrs. Offutt, so nice to see you!"

Emma Offutt looked back, a mite too red-faced to suit Mrs. Surratt (she *has* been servicing more than the after dinner dishes, I reckon), and waved, self-consciously. Yep, *I* know the signs, Mary said to herself, smugly, reckon I *ought* to!

It was just before noon when Weichmann drove Mary Surratt up to the faded red building in the southeast quadrant of the crossroads at Surrattsville. Joseph Knott, the barkeeper, saw her coming and stepped out on the porch to meet her. He took her message for Mr. Nothey to meet her at the tavern at 2 p.m., and promised to deliver it, right off. Mary and Weichmann then drove to Captain Gwinn's, about a mile southeast, and graciously accepted an appreciated invitation for dinner. Gwinn followed them back to the tavern to mediate the talk with Nothey, who was awaiting them in the barroom.

"Good day, Mr. Nothey."

Out in the hall, Mary could hear them talking through the door, as she headed for a seat in the parlor.

"Captain Gwinn! How are you, sir?"

"Tolerable, given the state of the weather--hurts my joints, doncha know? Would you be so kind as to step into the parlor and meet with Mrs. Surratt?"

"Certainly, lead the way. . . . Mrs. Surratt! You are looking mighty fine today! I do declare!"

"Mr. Nothey. How are you and yours?"

"Right as rain--which I see we are getting off and on today."

"Please sit down," Captain Gwinn said, "and le's get down to business. I hate to be short, but Mrs. Surratt has a long drive back to the City and my wife feels poorly."

"Fine. I am worried about your note owed the Calverts," Nothey said." I fear I cannot receive a clear title until you are clear with them. Are you prepared to hand me over the title to my farm? I shall pay you the amount due on my note then."

"Oh, no, sir!" Mary Surratt insisted. "You must pay me first, then you shall receive clear title. I shall bring out all the relevant papers on my next visit."

"If I might interject here," Captain Gwinn said, "why do we not arrange for Mr. Nothey to pay the Calvert estate directly? That would guarantee that the title would be clear and take care of your note, Mrs. Surratt, without having to go through an extra step."

"That would be fine with me. Then it is agreed upon? We will begin to settle both accounts through the one payment."

The two men shook hands. Mr. Nothey was a bit hesitant to offer his hand to a woman, especially one who could read and write (he could not), but Mary took care of the potential problem in etiquette by offering hers.

"Thank you, gentlemen. Now, I am on my way back to the City. I shall bring out the documents after Easter, and you can pay off my account with Mr. Calvert."

10. Lincoln Confiscates "Dixie"

"You should have seen it, Johnny," David Herold bubbled over to Booth and Powell in the latter's room at the Herndon House on the morning of April 11. "People marching all over the streets, some groups with bands and others not. I came up with the crowd that formed at the Navy Yard yesterday morning."

"I suppose you are going to tell me of how Lincoln gloated over the South's destruction. My God! I cannot bear it. But I can see you want to tell me all of it. Go ahead! My day, my week; no! My *life* has been completely ruined by these latest horrific events. I fear that God wishes to press me down with it all repeatedly, until finally, my very soul is crushed beneath the weight."

"We came up the avenue," Herold went on, "the *Intelligencer* estimated that there were at least 3,000 people. I reckon they was right, the whole street was filled as far as I could see. We had two or three bands playing. Everyone ignored the rain and mud--you know how bad the city streets get, especially those off the Avenue."

"Get to the point, Dave," Booth interjected impatiently. "What about Lincoln--what did he say?"

"Hold your horses, John, I am getting to it," Herold said. "Well, we marched to Secretary Welles' house--he is the Secretary of the Navy, you know, and no one was to be seen. So the crowd trudged over to the War Department. They had a Veteran Reserve Corps band, composed of disabled soldiers. They played real good, but Secretary Stanton refused to appear. The crowd yelled and yelled for him. Nothing happened but more music. Just like at Welles'. Then the band began to march over toward the President's House, and we all followed."

"No doubt the War Department used the band to get rid of you. The crowd moved just like sheep, I'll wager," Booth noted sourly.

"We got over to the north side of the White House--it is really gray, sort of, wonder why they call it white? Well, anyhow, we all got there and Lincoln's son, the hare-lipped one, Tad, I believe they call him-- he was running around waving a captured Rebel flag. I hear Lincoln asked the army to send a few of them over for him to play with."

"What a disgrace! Our sacred symbol reduced to a child's plaything!"

But Herold ignored Booth and rattled on, Powell seemingly hanging on every word. "Then, all of a sudden, Lincoln stepped out on the second porch where his boy had been running. Of course, everyone cheered (Booth bristled and scowled at the word, 'everyone') . . . except me and a few others. He said that he would make a formal statement tonight and that he hoped that we--the crowd, that is--would not try to make him dribble it all out of him. Honest injun! Them's his very words, 'dribble it out of me.'"

"I see his grammar and diction are up to the usual ignominious colloquial standard," Booth grumped.

Herold thought a moment about what in Heaven's name "ignominious" or "colloquial" might mean, but gave up on it. Typical Booth, he thought, always using them fancy, big words from all them plays he did.

"Then he said that the Yanks had captured the song, 'Dixie,' fair and square, and asked the band to play it."

"What?" Booth appeared incredulous.

"Here it is, Cap," Powell said. He read laboriously from the newspaper:

I have always thought 'Dixie' one of the best tunes I have ever heard. Our adversaries over the way attempted to appropriate it, but I insisted yesterday that we had fairly captured it. (Applause). I presented the question to the Attorney General, and he gave it as his legal opinion that it is our lawful prize. (Laughter and applause). Now I ask the band to favor me with its performance.

"That is what he said," Herold confirmed. "It was followed by 'Yankee Doodle.' Then everyone, except me and some others, of course, cheered General Grant and his army, and the Navy. Lincoln asked us to," Herold said defensively, in reference to Booth's glower.

"I reckon he was doing that all day," Powell said. He had been reading Washington newspapers with great interest, ever since that attempt to kidnap the President had failed from the lack of concern about newspaper statements. Here is what the *Daily National Republican* said about a similar speech to another crowd at 6 that evening: "My Friends: I am informed. . . ."

"Let me see that," Booth said, not about to listen to Powell's slow rendition of something that he could dispense with in a quick reading. His sonorous voice was undoubtedly in sharp contrast to Lincoln's thin, high-pitched delivery:

I am informed that you have assembled here this afternoon under the impression that I made an appointment to speak at this time. This is a mistake ("Hell, his whole administration is a mistake," Booth muttered parenthetically). I have made no such appointment. More or less persons have been gathering here at different times during the day, and in the exuberance of their feeling ("the damned bastards"), and for all of which they are greatly justified ("what crap!"), calling on me to say something. I have from time to time, been sending out what I supposed was proper to disperse them for the present. ("Laughter *and* applause, humph!").

I said . . . ("uh huh, uh huh, uh huh") . . . I would much prefer having this demonstration take place tomorrow evening, as I would then be much better prepared to say what I have to say than I am now or can be this evening. ("look at this, some cretin said, 'And then we will have heard from Johnston,' meaning his surrender, I surmise. More crap!"). . . . Everything I say, you know, goes into print. ("Laughter and applause. These controlled newspapers always think that everything he says is so damned funny or of such import!")

"Well, he *can* be a funny man," Herold opined.

"Yeah, he is a real laugh," Booth said. "Just ask the half million dead from his beloved war for the damn Union! Even Lincoln knows he is responsible for this, deep down, he knows. His face has aged several score years with the burden of it. Look at him! Compare his photographs from four years ago with how he looks now! . . . Here! Listen to the rest:

If I make a mistake it doesn't merely affect me nor you, but the country. I therefore, ought at least try not to make mistakes ("then some jackass has the gall to yell, 'you have made no mistakes, yet.' He has made 500,000 of them, you ignorant sycophant!").

If then, a general demonstration be made tomorrow evening, and it is agreeable, I will endeavor to say something, and not make a mistake, without at least trying carefully to avoid it. ("Laughter and applause.") Thanking you for the compliment of this call, I bid you a good evening.

"You know," Booth said, suddenly, "I believe that *we* will compliment Lincoln with a little call and attend that demonstration tomorrow night. See what that son of a bitch has to say. And afterward we can have a drink or two until late and scout out the White House basement again for Harney. See if we can still get in the basement without notice and look for a place to put those explosive devices George Sanders bragged about the last time I was in Montreal. . . . That's right, boys--this war isn't over yet!"

11. Lincoln's Final Speech

Booth was in a foul mood by the time he, Powell, and Herold got to the circular drive that led into the north portico of the White House from which Lincoln was to give his speech. Everywhere they passed there were reminders of the Confederate defeat in Virginia. Buildings were covered with red, white, and blue bunting and flags flew from improvised poles that hung out over the sidewalks. The major Federal offices had illuminations in their windows and on walls facing the streets. "God Bless Our Soldiers and Sailors";"Lincoln, Grant, Victory";"Union Forever";"Union, Liberty, and Equality";"U. S. Army, U. S. Navy, U. S.

Grant" were among the many sentiments guaranteed to make the hyper-sensitive Booth touchier than ever. Banners proclaiming similar feelings, and so long as to be carried by as many as a half dozen people each, festooned the White House lawn.

Crowds gathered and cheered on every street corner, some honoring passing troops, others hailing important dignitaries, a few yelling merely for the sake of it. Often the patrons of saloons and hotel bars ran out to cheer for Lincoln, Grant, Sheridan, Sherman, and such oddities as women with red dresses, women with no dresses or, in one case, the man who could drink the most beer from a schooner without pausing for breath. The hero in the last case simply fell into the gutter amidst the horse leavings to the accompanying laughter of those who saluted him.

Here and there, large crowds of Negroes sang the *Year of Jubilee*, *the Battle Cry of Freedom*, and *Kingdom Coming*. Powell had to forcibly restrain Booth from assaulting one black baritone who was entertaining a crowd in front of the Treasury building with a rousing version of the early war song; *We are Coming Father Abraham, Three Hundred Thousand More*. Booming cannon sounding from the forts and the Navy Yard gave special resonance to the Union military power that had ground Dixie down. The non-ideological Herold actually seemed to be enjoying the evening, much to Booth's growing disgust.

"Damn their impudence!" Booth snarled, calling Herold back to the intent of conspiracy.

"Come on, Cap," Powell said, as he hustled him down the walk," we have more important things to do. Remember Harney. . . ."

It was well after dark before Lincoln stepped out onto the north portico. The crowd, which had been chanting for his appearance for hours, broke into impromptu cheers. Lincoln acknowledged their plaudits as he tried to solve the practical problem of holding a candle and the unwieldy pieces of foolscap upon which the speech was written; the one he had promised the crowds several times in previous days. Finally, he had Noah Brooks, a journalist, friend, and supporter; hold a lamp off to one side. So as not to detract from Lincoln's presence, Brooks stood concealed behind the curtain to the door through which Lincoln stepped. Tad Lincoln was not so circumspect. He ran and crawled about on the porch, picking up the pages of the speech as Lincoln finished with them and dropped them to the floor.

"Throw me another!" he implored at regular intervals, much to the crowd's glee, whenever his father seemed to linger on one page too long.

As the crowd quieted, Lincoln's drawling voice penetrated out to the street. Booth and his comrades stood near a lamp post under a tree and listened as well as they could hear. The President's high, thin voice fairly screeched into the night air:

We meet this evening, not in sorrow, but in gladness of heart. The evacuation of Petersburg and Richmond, and the surrender of the principal insurgent army, give hope of a righteous and speedy peace whose joyous expression cannot be restrained. In the midst of this, however, He, from Whom all blessings flow, must not be forgotten. A call for a national thanksgiving is being prepared, and will be duly promulgated. Nor must those whose harder part gives us the cause of rejoicing be overlooked. Their honors must not be parceled out with others. I, myself, was near the front, and had the high pleasure of transmitting much of the good news to you; but no part of the honor, for plan or execution, is mine. To Gen. Grant, his skillful officers, and brave men, all belongs. The gallant Navy stood ready, but was not in reach to take active part.

By these recent successes the re-inauguration of the national authority--reconstruction--which has had a large share of thought from the first, is pressed much more closely upon our attention. It is fraught with much difficulty. Unlike the case of a war between independent nations, there is no authority organ for us to treat with. No one man has authority to give up the rebellion for any other man. We simply must begin with, and mould from, disorganized and discordant elements. Nor is it a small additional embarrassment that we, the loyal people, differ among ourselves as to the mode, manner, and means of reconstruction.

As a general rule, I abstain from reading the reports of attacks upon myself, wishing not to be provoked by that to which I cannot properly offer an answer. In spite of this precaution, however, it comes to my knowledge that I am much censured for some supposed agency in setting up, and seeking to sustain, the new State Government of Louisiana. In this I have done just so much as, and no more than, the public knows. In the Annual Message of December 1863 and accompanying Proclamation, I presented *a* plan of reconstruction (as the phrase goes) which, I promised, if adopted by any State, should be acceptable to, and sustained by, the Executive government of the nation. I distinctly stated this was *not* the only plan which might be acceptable; and I also distinctly protested that the Executive claimed no right to say when, or whether members should be admitted to seats in Congress from such States.

This plan was, in advance, submitted to the then Cabinet, and directly approved by every member of it. One of them suggested that I should then, and in that connection, apply the Emancipation Proclamation to the theretofore excepted parts of Virginia and Louisiana; that I should drop the suggestion about the apprenticeship for freed-people, and that I should omit the protest against my own power, in regard to the admission of members to Congress; but even he approved every part and parcel of the plan which has since been employed or touched by the action of Louisiana.

The new constitution of Louisiana, declaring emancipation for the whole state, practically applies the Proclamation to the part previously excepted. It does not adopt apprenticeship for freed-people; and it is silent, as it could not well be otherwise, about the admission of members to Congress. So that, as it applies to Louisiana, every member of the Cabinet fully approved the plan. The message went to Congress, and I received many commendations of the plan, written and verbal; and not a single objection to it, from any professed emancipationist, came to my knowledge, until after the news reached Washington that the people of Louisiana had begun to move in accordance with it.

From about July 1862, I had corresponded with different persons, supposed to be interested, seeking reconstruction of a State government for Louisiana. When the Message of 1863, with the plan before mentioned, reached New Orleans, Gen. Banks wrote me that he was confident the people, with his military cooperation, would reconstruct, substantially on that plan. I wrote him, and asked some of them to try it; they tried it, and the result is known.

Such has been my only agency in getting up the Louisiana government. As to my sustaining it, my promise is out, as before stated. But, as bad promises are better broken than kept, I shall treat this as a bad promise, and break it, whenever I shall be convinced that keeping it is adverse to the public interest. But I have not yet been so convinced.

I have been shown a letter on this subject, supposed to be an able one, in which the writer expresses regret that my mind has not seemed definitely fixed on the question whether the seceded States, so-called, are in the Union or out of it. It would perhaps, add astonishment to his regret, were he to learn that since I have found professed Union men endeavoring to make that question, I have *purposely* forborne any public expression upon it. It appears to me that question has not been, nor yet is, a practically material one, and that any discussion of it, while it thus remains practically immaterial, could have no effect other than the mischievous one of dividing our friends. As yet, whatever it may hereafter become, that question is bad, as the basis of a controversy, and good for nothing at all--a merely pernicious abstraction.

We all agree that the seceded States, so-called, are out of their proper practical relation with the Union; and that the sole object of the government, civil and military, in regard to those States is to again get them into that proper practical relation. I believe it is not only possible, but in fact, easier, to do this, without deciding, or even considering, whether these states have been out of the Union, than with it. Finding themselves safely at home, it would be utterly immaterial whether they had ever been abroad. Let us all join in doing the acts necessary to restoring the proper practical relations between these states and the Union; and each forever after, innocently indulge his own opinion whether, in doing the acts, he brought States from without, into the Union, or only gave them proper assistance, they never having been out of it.

The amount of constituency, so to speak, on which the new Louisiana government rests, would be more satisfactory to all, if it contained fifty, thirty, or even twenty thousand, instead of only about twelve thousand, as it does. It is also unsatisfactory to some that the elective franchise is not given to the colored man. I would myself prefer that it were now conferred on the very intelligent, and on those who serve our cause as soldiers. Still the question is not whether the Louisiana government, as it stands, is quite all that is desirable. The question is 'Will it be wiser to take it as it is, and help to improve it; or to reject, and disperse it?' 'Can Louisiana be brought into proper practical relation with the Union *sooner* by *sustaining*, or by *discarding* her new State Government?'

Some twelve thousand voters in the heretofore slave-state of Louisiana have sworn allegiance to the Union, assumed to be the rightful political power of the State, held elections, organized a State government, adopted a free-state constitution, giving the benefit of public schools equally to black and white, and empowering the Legislature to confer the elective franchise upon the colored man. Their Legislature had already voted to ratify the constitutional amendment recently passed by Congress, abolishing slavery throughout the nation. These twelve thousand persons are thus fully committed to the Union, and to perpetual freedom in the state--committed to the very things, and nearly all the things the nation wants--and they ask the nation's recognition, and its assistance to make good their committal.

Now, if we reject, and spurn them, we do our utmost to disorganize and disperse them. We in effect say to the white men, 'You are worthless, or worse--we will neither help you, nor be helped by you.'

To the blacks we say, 'This cup of liberty which these, your old masters, hold to your lips, we will dash from you, and leave you to the chances of gathering the spilled and scattered contents in some vague and undefined when, where, and how.' If this course, discouraging and paralyzing both black and white, has any tendency to bring Louisiana into proper relations with the Union, I have, so far, been unable to perceive it.

If, on the contrary, we recognize, and sustain the new government of Louisiana, the converse is made true. We encourage the hearts, and nerve the arms of the twelve thousand to adhere to their work, and argue for it, and proselyte for it, and fight for it, and feed it, and grow it, and ripen it, to a complete success. The colored man, too, in seeing all united for him, is inspired with vigilance, and energy, and daring, to the same end. Grant that he desires the elective franchise, will he not attain it sooner by saving the already advanced steps toward it, than by running backward over them?

Concede that the new government of Louisiana is only to what it should be as the egg is to the fowl, shall we sooner have the fowl by hatching the egg than by smashing it? Again, if we reject Louisiana, we also reject one vote in favor of the proposed [Emancipation] amendment to the national constitution. To meet this proposition, it has been argued that no more than three fourths of those States which have not attempted secession are necessary to validly ratify the amendment. I do not commit myself against this, further than to say that such a ratification would be questionable, and sure to be persistently questioned; while a ratification by three fourths of *all* the states would be unquestioned and unquestionable.

I repeat the question. 'Can Louisiana be brought into proper practical relation with the Union *sooner* by *sustaining* or by *discarding* her new State Government?

What has been said of Louisiana will apply generally to other States. And yet so great peculiarities pertain to each state; and such important and sudden changes occur in the same state, and, withal, so new and unprecedented is the whole case, that no exclusive and inflexible plan can safely be prescribed as to details and collaterals. Such exclusive, and inflexible plan, would surely become an entanglement. Important principles may, and must, be inflexible.

In the present *'situation'* as the phrase goes, it may be my duty to make some new announcement to the people of the South. I am considering, and shall not fail to act, when satisfied that action will be proper.

Lincoln dropped the last page of the speech within range of Tad's grasping hand. The crowd cheered him and applauded vigorously--all except three men on the periphery.

"By God!" Booth cried. "That means n----r citizenship!" He turned to Powell, who seemed puzzled at the sudden outburst. Booth grabbed the big man by the arm. "You have your pistol?" Powell nodded. "Well, shoot him! Here and now! Shoot him where he stands!"

Several nearby onlookers were transferring their interest from Lincoln, who was still receiving most people's appreciation from the portico, and Tad, who had sorted the pages of his father's last public speech, to this disturbance in front of Lafayette Park. Powell was made uneasy by Booth's verbal explosion and the attention he was drawing to them. He swung his arm in a circle, breaking Booth's hold on him, and turned away, walking eastward down the street. Booth followed, cursing and fuming. Herold looked around at the spectators, shrugged his shoulders quizzically, and ran after his companions.

"That is the last speech he will every make!" Booth vowed to Herold as he caught up. "Now, by God, *I'll* put him through!"

12. The Meeting at the Herndon House

A couple of days later, John Wilkes Booth entered the National Theater, also known as Grover's, from the street side, where Pennsylvania Avenue crossed E Street, on its way to the Treasury Building.

"Going to illuminate tonight Hess?" he asked the theater manager, C. Dwight Hess.

"Certainly. At least to some extent. But I reckon I will save most of my effort for tomorrow night."

"Good Friday?"

"No, no. It is the day the Fort Sumter fell in 1861. There will be a big celebration there in Charleston, the raising of Old Glory for the first time since the war started. Lots of dignitaries and such. General Robert Anderson, he was a major in command of the fort in '61, you may recall, will raise the same banner he struck, when he surrendered the fort four years ago. Precisely at noon, so they say."

"You thinking of inviting the President tonight?"

Hess was concentrating on materials on his desk. He did not see the inquisitive, or was it more a devilish, arching of one eyebrow, as Booth spoke? Nor did he see those famous eyes, which glowed menacingly, fairly spitting fire and conspiracy, as if Booth were portraying malefic Richard III or, perhaps, the wicked Duke of Alva from the *Apostate*.

"Yes!" Hess sat up and snapped his fingers. "That reminds me, I must send that invitation."

Booth bade Hess a pleasant good-bye and went upstairs to Deery's Tavern over the theater lobby for his first drink of the day. Then he walked over to Ford's Theater. Edward A. Emerson, one of the stock actors, was standing in front of the main doors, when Booth approached. As was his wont, he grabbed Emerson's cane playfully and placed it over his shoulders behind his neck, holding it by both ends.

"Hey, Ned. Did you hear what that old scoundrel did the other day?"

"What old scoundrel are you talking about? There are so many of them."

"Why, that old scoundrel, Lincoln. He went into Jeff Davis' house in Richmond, sat down and threw his long legs over the arm of the chair and squirted tobacco juice all over the carpet. Somebody ought to kill him."

"For God's sake, John, stop right where you are! I am going to quit you. Lincoln always sits like that and he does not use tobacco in any form. You ought to know that."

With a cruel look, Booth drew both hands down and forward, splintering the cane into several pieces. He left it lying on the walk and went in to check his mail.

Booth went back to the National to see if Andrew Atzerodt was there. The night before, he had asked him to come around, wanting to talk to him about his excessive drinking. Booth knew he had little room to criticize. He himself drank too much, but Atzerodt was becoming so debilitated as to be utterly useless.

Atzerodt was in the bar--of course. Booth paid his tab and they went up to Booth's room together.

"Andrew, I tell you as a friend, you got to go easier with the bottle."

"*Was?*"

"For crying out loud, speak English! You are crocked out of your ever-loving mind most of the day. I need you for important work tonight. I cannot have you so drunk as not to be able to function."

"What do you by that mean?"

"Oh . . . tarnation! Never mind. I want you to do something very important. Think you can handle it?"

"Ja, sicher."

"Go over to the Kirkwood House and rent a room. They are expecting you. Tell the clerk that you come for the room that Mr. Booth wanted. It will be Number 126. Then go down to Mr. Andrew Johnson's room. It is on the floor directly below your room. Get us a pass to allow us to leave the City at any time. Tell him it is for J. Wilkes Booth--we met in Nashville. He will remember me. Show him my card. It has a message on the back. Can you do all that?"

"Sicher. 126. Tell clerk it for you is. Johnson is direkt darunter. He will me a pass for you give. You know him aus Nashville."

"Perfect. Here is my card and I paid for the room for two nights. You may as well stay there as anywhere else."

"Fantastisch! I do that. Und danke! Thank you!"

"And Andrew--go *easy* on the booze today." Booth gave him six half-dimes, hoping that six drinks would hold him until that evening.

Atzerodt did as Booth ordered. The actor, meanwhile, went out and encountered Davy Herold on the street.

"Le's go down to Deery's and get a drink."

Herold did not need a second invitation. He eagerly went with Booth, happy to be seen in such auspicious company, even if he had to walk fast to keep pace him. It was almost as if Booth wanted Herold to walk a step or two behind, like a valet. And that is exactly what John Deery thought he was, when Booth introduced him.

"This is my friend, David Herold, John. Set us both up. He will have a whiskey and I will have my usual brandy."

Deery set the drinks up. He marveled at the amount of brandy that Booth could hold in a twenty-four hour period and still negotiate about town appearing sober. He had downed a quart of the stuff in less than two hours the night before. It was getting to be too regular a thing to be good for him.

"Hey, John," Booth said, after swilling his brandy right down. "Please set me up another, and how about sending a table boy down to reserve me a box for tonight?"

"What? Downstairs? Why do you want to pay for that box? You can have it by going to Len Grover."

"He is away."

"Well, then, Dwight Hess will let you have it on the house. I am sure of it."

"I do not care to accept any favor from the house. I do not wish to be beholden to anyone."

"Go on down to the box office, Jimmy, and reserve Mr. Booth a box."

"The same as on the President's side, if possible. Here is a greenback or two for the cost."

The boy was back shortly with an order for the box. Booth and Herold left soon after. Booth headed for Powell's secret room at the Herndon House. He sent Davy Herold to bring Andrew Atzerodt to the rendezvous. Atzerodt was running short on cash that evening, so he had gone out and taken supper at a small restaurant across Pennsylvania Avenue. When he came back to the Kirkwood, Herold was waiting for him in the lobby.

"Hey, Andrew," Herold called out as he entered. "Booth wants to see us, right off."

The two men went out and down the Avenue. Evidently, Booth did not make it clear where Herold and Atzerodt were to meet him and Powell. They turned on Louisiana and stopped at the Canterbury Music Hall. No Booth. They next tried the National Hotel, but the clerk said Booth was out.

"Look," Herold said. "You wait here and I will find Booth and come fetch you."

Atzerodt sat and waited in the National Hotel's plush lobby a while, but Herold did not return. Many of the tonier types who regularly stayed at the National began to look at him curiuously. Atzerodt grew nervous. He decided to go to where he was more acceptable. He began the trip back to the Kirkwood, stopping at several lower-class restaurants and drinking establishments along the way. When he returned to the Kirkwood, the bell man said that a young man had come in asking for him. Atzerodt sat in the lobby and waited.

"I found Booth," Herold said, when he came back in. "He and Wood want to see you, right quick. You got your room key?"

Atzerodt took it out of his pocket and Herold put his finger over his lips and whispered conspiratorially, "Le's go to your room. I got something to show you." In the room, Herold drew a large pistol from his belt, and a Bowie knife out of his boot. He laid them on the bed. They left, locking the room after them. Herold took Atzerodt to the Herndon House. They entered through a side door and took the stairs up.

"Come in, boys," Booth said, as Herold led Atzerodt into Powell's secret Washington hideaway. John Surratt was there, too. Herold and Atzerodt looked at Surratt a bit surprised. He was supposed to be away in Canada. "Sit down and listen up. I have news. . . . I have heard that there was a clash between Mosby's men and the 8th Illinois cavalry a couple of days ago at Burke's Station, down in Virginia."

"Uh, oh," Powell interjected. "They are one tough outfit. We always hated to mix with them boys."

"The Yankees think that it was a typical Mosby horse and mule raid," Booth continued, "but I suspected that it involved our man, Harney, and his escort. So I went over to the Old Capitol prison this morning and bribed a guard with a bottle. He said that several of Mosby's men were there, recent arrivals. He did not know Harney's name, but he did think that one of the Rangers was an ordinance man. He said that Colonel Wood, the prison commandant, was very suspicious, but that no one had talked yet. Everyone claimed that it was just an ordinance delivery that got out of Richmond before it fell.

"I stopped at Ella's sister's place on the way back. Met an Illinois officer fresh in from the Eighth, relaxing with a drink after a satisfying visit with one of the girls. Nice, lose-mouthed feller. I chatted a bit with him about the war. Then, I asked how he and his boys were faring. He said that his Illinois boys had scattered a Mosby party at Burke's. Picked up a loose pack animal with twenty-five pounds of black powder on his back. There was a slew of the stuff along the road, and another mule with busted packs. Now, if that don't smell like Harney, I am a monkey's uncle!"

"That means that we the White House will not be able to blow up?" Atzerodt asked.

"What it really means is that we will have to carry out Harney's mission for him," Booth explained.

"Andrew is right, though. We cannot blow up the White House!" Herold exclaimed. "We lack the talent to set off such an explosion without killing ourselves in the process."

"Right," Booth said, in a very matter-of-fact tone of voice. "That is why we are going to assassinate the whole Union government individually, with the result having the same effect of Harney blowing up a cabinet meeting."

13. The Aborted Attempt of April 13

Herold and Atzerodt sat dumbfounded with amazement. Blowing something up was fun--it was not murder, except in a sort of a detached manner. A body did not have to look his victim in the face, risk opposition. Instead it was just bang! And the whole matter was taken care of cleanly, except for the disintegrating carcasses of the victims, but then no one really *saw* that. It just happened. But a knife or a pistol was downright personal.

"We are going to do what?" Surratt said, as surprised as his compatriots at the turn in events.

"So what is the plan, Cap?" Powell asked.

It made no never mind to Powell if the victim was one, ten or a hundred feet away. Fighting on a Civil War infantry firing line did that to a man. Powell had wiped the gore and brains of many a companion or opponent off his tunic between Williamsburg and Gettysburg. One more time would not make any appreciable difference to him.

"Always to the point, Wood," Booth replied with a smile. "Now, here is the lay of the political land. What remains of the Confederacy is hanging on out there, somewhere in the Piedmont of North Carolina. The government is probably around Danville, just north of the Virginia line. Johnston's army was near Goldsboro, the last I heard. Lee surrendered, true, but he had only 25,000 men with him. Where are the rest?"

"I bet they all ran away--deserted," Herold said gloomily.

Booth ignored him, oblivious to the youth's accidental wisdom. "I put it to you that they are on their way to Johnston right now. That means that the Union government and its communications and leadership, right here in Washington, are still a prime military target. I have it on good word that General Grant has come to the City to regale Lincoln and his cabinet. What an attractive target this presents!"

"Wood, you must get into Seward's house," Booth continued, his eyes blazing with excitement. "That is our biggest problem. He has a grand old house of three floors, maybe an occupied attic on top of that. The old Decatur place--you know, that Navy officer from the War of 1812 who was shot dead in a duel."

"I thought it vas the 'Club House' called," interjected Atzerodt. "Outside vere that congressman, the one who vas a general, that man, Key, he killed."

"General Sickles," Booth said. "He was the one who shot Philip Barton Key for bedding his wife. Right outside where Seward lives now. And that slimy shyster, Stanton got him off. Called him 'temporarily insane'."

"The biggest laugh was that Sickles took his wife back after *she* was the one doing the running around. Remember how angry every one was?" Herold laughed.

"Of course," Booth said. "It proved him a cuckold rather than a rightfully indignant husband."

"I never heard of none of that down in Florida," Powell said. He was amazed at the close manner in which Washingtonians followed the events of their city. He puzzled over that word, "cuckold." He had never heard *that* one before. Just like Booth to use a hundred dollar word. He was not the kind to give a body the short end of the horn, when it came to speechifying or play acting--or assassination.

"Do you think you can get in?"

"Sure, why not?"

"Good. I will personally take out Lincoln and Grant at the National. Andrew, you will shoot Vice President Johnson."

"No! I did not for that come. I am not willing to kill, a person to murder."

"Will you assist us then? All you have to do is show us the road to Indiantown in the dark. If you are unwilling, it will go bad for you."

Booth and Wood both gave Atzerodt a hard look. He quailed under their gaze.

"I will all I can on the road to do."

"Then, get yourself a horse and ride out to Benning's Bridge and wait for us. We will go to Surrattsville and then around Piscataway through Tee Bee to Bumpy Oak. Herold does not think he can find the road after dark. Can you?"

"Ja. I do it. Maryland Point and the Nanjemoy are on the most direkt weg nach Virginia."

"All right, then, Herold will take out Johnson . . . right, Davy?"

Deep down, Herold was no more enthusiastic than Atzerodt to kill anyone. He had great doubt he could do it but, after Booth's threatening tone with the German, he feared to tell his revered pal, Johnny, otherwise. He hated to show cowardice, especially in front of the stolid, brave man he knew only as "Wood."

"Sure, Johnny," he gulped, wide-eyed.

"No, no, I was just teasing. Surratt will do it, right Johnny?"

"You can count on me, Pet," Surratt assured him with an easy smile and a wink. He understood that Booth was openly displaying his contempt for the weaklings, Atzerodt and Herold.

"Davy, I want you to go out to Huntt's place down to Tee Bee, and pick up our horses there. We will stop for you after we strike Lincoln and the others. We will stop and get our stuff from Lloyd--you need not bother."

"What if Lincoln don't cooperate. You know he don't keep your appointments. We have missed him two or three times already, you know."

"Do not be such a pessimist. He would not dare miss this engagement, being with General Grant and all."

"But. . . ."

"All right! All right! I tell you what. If we do not show by midnight, we will not need those horses any longer. You can bring them into the District, tomorrow. I have already got a buyer for the bay, anyhow--Mr. Greenawalt," Booth said in answer to Herold's look of inquiry. "He offered me a fabulous $140--and I think that Judge Parker will take the other two.

"We must all be ready at 8 o'clock tonight," Booth went on. "If all goes right, Wood will check with me and I will estimate the proper time to shoot. Sometime after 8 o'clock. You, Davy, may as well leave for Tee Bee right now. We will meet you at Huntt's store, not Thompson's like last time. Huntt has the horses. Well, now, le's get cracking!"

"Do you have your key?" Herold asked, as he and Atzerodt left the Herndon House.

"No, at the hotel it is. Why?"

"Nothing, it is not important. See you later."

Back in Powell's room, Booth issued his final instructions. "Gentlemen, I am going out to change into riding clothes. I will come back and pick you all up and show you, Wood, where Seward's is. Then, I will meet you, and we can ride out of town, together, after the deed is done."

"All right, Cap."

"I sure am glad that you got back, John," Booth said, earnestly. "I really need an extra hand I can rely on. Johnson will be over at the Kirkwood House, but meet me here with Wood, so we can coordinate times together."

"Right, John."

Booth shook his hand firmly, gripping Surratt by the elbow. He then did the same to Powell. The actor went over to the National Hotel and up to his room. He very carefully dressed in his black riding clothes, put his slouch hat on the table, and sat down. He took the small pocket diary he had been keeping out of his coat pocket and pulled the little pencil stub out of its loop holder inside the crease. He turned to the next open page. It was dated for Sunday, June 12, 1864. Booth scratched out the printed material. He wrote under it:

April 13
The Ides

Then, Booth stopped. No, he would wait until the deed was accomplished. There was plenty of time for brag, later. He put the little pencil in its loop and stuffed the notebook back in his inner coat pocket, over his heart, and walked out of his room.

"I am going over to Stanton's," Booth overheard a Union major say, as he and his companions walked out of the hotel bar into Booth's path.

"Excuse us, sir," the rearmost officer, a lieutenant, said. Being last in line, he had nearly bumped into Booth.

"Certainly, Lieutenant. Nothing too good for our men in uniform. Big doings at the Secretary's?" Booth asked, politely.

The lieutenant smiled, relieved that Booth was not one of those fellows who liked to start fights over an accidental jostling. "Yes, sir, General Grant is going to appear for the evening. We are on his staff, in fact."

"I thought the General was going to accompany the President to Grover's National Theater tonight?"

"Where did you hear *that?*"

"Oh, the usual rumors. The City is full of them, you know."

"Yessir. That is what we heard, too. No, the General is not going to the theater. He will spend the evening among old army friends, and various governmental officials at Secretary of War Stanton's."

"All the boot-lickers he can employ, huh? No offense meant to you and your fellows, Lieutenant."

"None taken. I know what you mean."

"Will the President be at the theater or at the Secretary's house?"

"Oh, I hear that either he or Mrs. Lincoln is not feeling well. I believe that he will be staying in tonight. Perhaps we will send a delegation to wait upon him."

"How thoughtful. Well, thank you, Lieutenant. I guess that I will forego the theater tonight, especially as 'Our Beloved Guardian of the Union' will not be there. Disappointing."

Booth walked out of the National Hotel and crossed C Street. Jim Pumphrey, the stableman, waved. "I have got a good mare for you, Mr. Booth," he yelled over.

"Thanks, not tonight, Jim."

Booth jog-walked the five blocks to the Herndon House in quick time. Powell was standing on the walk out front, holding the one-eyed brown horse that Booth had bought down at Dr. Mudd's neighbor's late last fall. Armed to the teeth, Surratt rode up, a few moments later.

"Give me your horse, Wood. You all can go back to your rooms. Plans have changed. Lincoln and Grant will not show tonight. I will call on you all tomorrow."

"All right, Cap."

"Where you off to now?" Surratt asked.

"I reckon I ought to call in Andrew. No need to leave him out alone. He might get real angry or real drunk and start blabbing everything." He mounted the brown. "Damnation!" muttered Booth. "If this is not just dandy, I do not know what is. Foiled, again! That damned Lincoln is getting to be downright unreliable in keeping his--my--appointments."

14. Booth Spends a Night with Ella Starr Turner

After the failure of the Ides of April attempt on Lincoln, Booth did not return to the National Hotel. Although he normally stabled his horse at Howard's, after he brought in Atzerodt, Booth turned in his horse at Naylor's (all the city stables had reciprocal arrangements with each other and it was not unusual to see strings of horses being moved from one to the other by hostlers). He strolled down to the honkey-tonk and brothel district southeast of the White House known as 'Hooker's Division'. He entered at number 62 C Street, the whorehouse-home of Molly Turner, the sister of Booth's favorite sporting girl in the District, Ella Starr Turner. Here he hoped to find the solace he sought and needed so desperately. He had come to the right place. Ella met him at the door.

"Oh, John," she said, as he drew her close to him, their lips meeting in a lingering kiss.

"Ella, I am so down, really blue. So help me, I cannot for the life of me figure out how Lincoln manages to avoid every rendezvous for execution I set up for him. Sometimes I almost fear that God, Himself, is protecting that scoundrel of a tyrant. Yet how can that be? If God is truly just, that Robinarch cannot continue to avoid the vengeance of the people and the judgment of history."

As he ranted, Ella guided Booth down the hallway to her room. It was not one of the little cribs that her sister's whores used to pleasure Yankee soldiers and government officials out of their pay, but a real room, in which Ella lived in relative luxury. She got her money in the same manner as the others, but she reserved her favors only for special men, like Wilkes Booth. She was a freelancer, not an employee.

Whether Booth ever stopped to consider who might have enjoyed Ella's charms before him was doubtful. She treated him (and each them) as if he were the only man she ever spent time with. But she loved only one--John Wilkes Booth. She would try to commit suicide when she heard of his death, an overdose of chloroform. She would fail. But tonight, she would excel in that which she did best.

"Tell me all about your miserable day," she said, as she began to slowly undress him, kissing him as she went on every new place laid bare by the skillful probing of her fingers. Soon, Booth forgot about his complaining and began to pay attention to Ella. Now, both unclothed, they tumbled into her bed, caressing and kissing, panting and moaning in sensuous ecstasy. But no matter how long they sparred, Booth could not get aroused--he was still possessed by the desire to end Lincoln's life, rather than satisfy Ella's growing passion.

"John, you must forget this evening's problems and concentrate on the joy I can bring you."

"I cannot, for some reason, I cannot."

"Lie back and close your eyes. Let Ella take you to Paradise."

Later, as they lay entwined, Booth again ungallantly turned his thoughts from the masterful Ella to the *real* matter of importance, the liquidation of Lincoln, the destruction of the American Robinarch and his cabinet. At the next opportunity, he would steer the pursuit (surely there would be a vigorous one, mounted by all the police and soldiers available) into Southeastern Maryland, into the confusing, interlocking swamps, woods, and rivers of the Lower Peninsula. He hoped to leave that impression by planting implicating items, especially his bankbook, in his coat in Andrew Atzerodt's room.

Then, while Atzerodt became the focus of wasted pursuit, Booth, Herold (he knew all he roads), Surratt, and Powell (the man Booth still knew only as Wood) would ride north to Relay Station and take the last train to Baltimore and beyond to New York City. Powell and Herold would hide out with the Baltimore connection, people like the Bransons, Heim, and Parr. Booth, disguised by a false beard, and Surratt would continue on to New York City, hiding with others there, until it was safe to cross into Canada and catch a ship to Europe.

He already had his accomplice ready to receive him, a woman fully as capable, in her own way, of replicating Ella's skills with the human body. She had pledged her fealty, although he would never receive her letter:

New York, April 13th
Dear Wilkes
I received your letter of the 12th (stating that you would be in this city on the 16 inst.) this morning, and hasten to answer it. On account of a misunderstanding between my Landlady and your humble servant, I have

been obliged to leave her hospitable mansion, and am now for the time being, stopping at the New York Hotel, after your arrival, should you not approve of my present location, it can be easily be changed to suit your convenience.

Yes, Dear, I can heartily sympathize with you, for I too, have had the blues ever since the fall of Richmond, and like you, feel like doing something desperate. I have not yet had a favorable opportunity to do what you wished, and *I* so solemnly promised, and what, in my own heart, I feel ought to be done. I *remember* what happiness is in store for us if we succeed in our present undertakings, therefore, do not doubt *my* courage, have faith, 'for even as you put your faith in me, so will I in you' and Wilkes hath said *vengeance* is mine.

My removal has consumed the means you gave me when we parted, take this as a gentle hint and bring a good supply, 'for money makes the mare go' nowadays. I do as you desired and keep as secluded as a nun, which is not agreeable to me as you have found, but ere this, but anything to oblige you, darling. If anything *should* happen (as I trust there will not) to prevent your coming to the City, please let me know, and I will join you (as agreed upon) at the house of *our* friend A[nnie']s. 'Don't let anything discourage *you*.'

    believe me *yours*
and *yours* only
    Etta
    P.S. Annie who is acting the maid to perfection, wishes to be remembered to her dear ahem!! Sam.
    Au revoir
    Etta.

Then there was the unfinished matter of Lucy Lambert Hale. What to do with Lucy? Her father would soon take the whole family to Madrid, where he had been appointed United States Minister to Spain. Booth liked Lucy's quick wit and intelligence, although she was admittedly not very pretty when compared to Ella or Etta or many of the theater women he knew. Actually, the problem was that Lucy did not use her God-given looks to her best advantage, being very plain in make-up and hair style. He might be able to use her when he arrived in Europe.

No! He would ask her to *marry* him--not because it was something he thought might happen or that he *wanted* to happen. Hell, her parents would never allow it to transpire. But she would say, *yes*; Booth just knew that in his heart. It would needle the tarnation out of her parents, those stuck-up Yankee bastards. Best of all, it would prove to him that *he* was the superior man to Bob Lincoln and cut that smug, little pseudo-soldier-boy, that Harvard College brat, out of the race. Booth smiled and tuned back to Ella. She giggled and happily accepted his renewed interest with abandon.

15. Herold Stays Overnight at Huntt's

After he left the Herndon House, Davy Herold cut out for the Maryland countryside southeast of Washington City, as quickly as he could. Herold would not come back in until after daylight tomorrow, so there would be no problem passing the Navy Yard Bridge guards, in either direction. After crossing the Eastern Branch of the Potomac, he took the Upper Marlboro highway up Good Hope Hill outside Uniontown. At the top of the ridge, he turned to the southeast, taking the rougher, less-maintained mail road that would pass through Surrattsville. He would not stop tonight. He wanted to get to Tee Bee before it got too late.

He was headed for the home of Joe Huntt, where Booth and Johnny Surratt had stored three horses since January, as relays for the abduction plot. He was to pick them up. Booth said that they would no longer be needed. But Davy had no idea why. He did not know that Booth figured that he could ride his own rented animal all the way to Baltimore. Or that Booth would have left him hanging at Tee Bee, had the assassination taken place, as planned on, the night of the 13th.

As Davy crossed the Piscataway-Woodyard road, the warm lights of the old Surratt Tavern beckoned. The night was damp and cool, and Davy needed warming. One little drink would not hurt. He pulled up to the tavern entrance and tied up to a porch support.

"Well, well. Look who is here," John Lloyd said, coming in from the center hallway, and closing the door to isolate the rest of the house from the bar. No one else was around.

"Got rum?" Herold asked.

"Nope. Just whiskey."

"Well, pour me a shot. It is getting nippy out."

"What are you doing out this late? Thought a young swell like you would be in bed with one of Washington's finest, by now."

"Aw, I am off to see Joe Huntt about some horses. I cannot stay but for one drink. I need to get down to Tee Bee before he turns in. Here is a bill--I will pick up my change some other time. Booth is expecting to pick up the guns and ropes tonight."

"I wished he had said something. I would like to clear the missus and her sister out before that happens. Damn it! Nobody tells me anything in advance."

"Well, this is your advance," Herold mumbled, saluting him with a full shot glass.

After downing his drink, Herold mounted his horse and kicked him into a ground-eating lope, heading down the road that led a half dozen miles to Huntt's Store. He got there just as Huntt was about to blow out the lights. It was pouring rain.

"What is up Davy?" he asked. "Kinda late to be out in the middle of nowhere, ain't it?"

"I have brought you good news. You know those three horses that have been eating you out of house and home? Booth has sold them."

"I wondered when y'all would get back to me. Reckon there ain't no need to kidnap Lincoln no more. War is about over. Who is the buyer?"

"Well, they is two, I reckon. Mr. Greenawalt, the proprietor of the Pennsylvania house took the one, the bay, for $140. I ain't sure about the others. He reckons that Judge Parker might take them. At least, Lewis Gregory says so, I hear tell."

"Is he the Gregory that lived at Piscataway till recent and now runs an oyster house over at Upper Marlboro?"

"Yes sir, the very same. Say, mayn't I stay the night? I kin stay here and sleep on the floor by the stove. It is mighty late and I *am* bushed. I am expecting Booth to show up during the night."

"Sure. Come on over to the house after you tend to your horse."

"But Booth wanted me here. . . ."

"Hell, he ain't coming out in this downpour--no one in his right mind would. Come in and sleep comfortable, ya hear?"

Returning from the barn, Davy shed his wet cloak as Huntt met him at the door. "You can use the room in back. If Booth shows, he can roust us out."

Huntt pointed to the rear of the first floor. Davy went in and shut the door. He removed his wet clothes and took his nightshirt out of the saddlebags. Actually, it belonged to John Surratt, even had his name inside the collar. He and Booth and the others would be along shortly, anyhow.

The next morning, Herold woke up to the smell of bacon, eggs, grits, and coffee in the air. Davy got up, dressed, and slipped outside to relieve himself. In his hurry, he forgot to pack Surratt's nightshirt, leaving it to lie in a wrinkled pile on the floor, to be found later. It would stay in the possession of the Huntt family for generations, finally winding up on display at the restored Surratt Tavern, now a museum and archive dedicated to telling the history of the Surratt Family and of their participation in the Lincoln abduction and assassination plots.

As Davy came into the kitchen, he was surprised to see another familiar face.

"Hello, Ed Henson, what is new?"

"Hey, yourself, Davy Herold. Joe tells me you have turned horse dealer."

"Only for the time being. I was supposed to meet Booth here, but he never showed--as usual. I am on my way back to the District to see what has happened."

"I am headed that way myself. Mind some company?"

"Not in the least."

"Why don't you boys take those three horses of Booth's in when you go," Huntt said. "No need to have to come back for them."

"You got that right!" Herold said. "Besides, that is what Booth wanted me to do, anyhow."

The Huntts and their guests ate a leisurely breakfast. Then, Davy went out and saddled his horse. Henson's was all ready to go, as he had been riding since daybreak.

"There are supposed to be five of us, headed into the District. We have been given orders to contact your Wilkes Booth for orders. Something about blowing up the White House during a cabinet meeting. Know anything about that?"

"Sure, I am in on it at the center. I am Booth's *right-hand* man, doncha know? You can come in with me, and I will get you to him. But ain't you heard?"

"What is that?"

"The blowing-up has been canceled. The powderman got hisself captured and is in the Old Cap. We are onto a new plan, now. Reckon we can use you, though."

"What is the new plan?"

"We are going to *kill* Lincoln and his whole cabinet, one by one, all at the same time!"

"No kidding? That is unbelievable!"

"It was supposed to happen last night, but I guess something must have come up, because Booth never made it to Tee Bee, like he said he would. Well, I will let Booth set you straight. I call him *Johnny*, you know. His chief assistant, *I* am."

Right, thought Henson, but he kept it to himself. He knew that no one in his right mind would trust the likes of Davy Herold, for anything important, unless no one else was available. Hell, all he knew was Southeastern Maryland. Maybe that explained it. He might be Booth's right-hand man after all, if they were to escape in that direction. He knew everybody and everybody knew him, or his old daddy.

As the two men came over the brow of Good Hope Hill and began the descent into Uniontown, a familiar rider approached. It was Booth.

"Hey, fellers," he said, as he reined in.

"What happened last night?" Herold asked.

"Nothing. Another false alarm," Booth said. "Glad you came in. We can take the horses over to Greenawalt's, now."

"I hear you are going to do in Old Abe," Henson said.

"Yep, tonight, most likely. Want in on the play?"

"Not really. Me and my boys have to live here and do not cotton to being hanged. But I tell you what we will do. We will spot for you, so long as we can melt into the crowd afterwards."

"That is a deal. How many are coming?"

"Five, but I doubt that we can rely on but one more than me-- James Donaldson. The rest will not show, or will cut when they hear the plan."

"I reckon that is all we will need," Booth said as they turned their horses off Harrison Street and headed for the Navy Yard Bridge. "C'mon, fellows, I want to make the last breakfast call at the National."

PART II

THE ASSASSINATION (1865)

Fortunately Surratt came in. With Arnold and O'Laughlen
doubtful, I am thrown back on the weakest of my men, Port Tobacco and
Herold. Of Wood, Surratt, and myself, I have no doubt. If only the others
had *half* the courage of *Mrs.* Surratt.
--From the missing pages of John Wilkes Booth's *Diary*, April
13, 1865

Tyrannicide is the public duty of all good citizens. The only
inconvenience is that all depends upon success, and he who tries is the
worst of villains if he fails; and at best may be deprived of all by the same
means he employed to gain it.
--John Wilkes Booth's Letter To My Countrymen, April 14, 1865

1. Booth's Friday Morning

John Wilkes Booth walked up Tenth Street towards Ford's Theater on Good Friday April 14, 1865. It was a morning ritual. He received his mail at Ford's, a service that allowed him to move about without worrying about using a general delivery address or losing letters during his constant travels from town to town. As usual he was immaculately groomed, just having had a precise shave and haircut from barber Charlie Wood at Booker and Stewart's tonsorial parlor on E Street. Several men who knew Booth, including John Surratt and Mike O'Laughlen, had been present and a general, good natured ribbing had taken place.

"Say, Wood, have you noticed a scar on Booth's neck, when you put the chair cloth on him?" O'Laughlen asked, seriocomically.

"Yes, now that you mention it, I have," Wood said.

"They say that it was a boil that had to be lanced," Surratt chipped in. "But I have it on good word that it really was a pistol shot."

"No! He must have got a little too far up front that time."

"Why, look at it!" Surratt urged. "He near lost his head!"

Booth laughed heartily with the others.

Freshly-shaved and groomed from the barber's chair, he cut a fine figure of a man as he strolled. He wore a dark wine-colored suit coat, with black velvet collar, lapels and trim and carried a light camel-color overcoat over his arm. His contrasting, buff trousers had stirrups that encircled the vamp and arch of his block-toed, patent-leather walking shoes. His black silk top hat was tilted jauntily to one side. His gloves were a fashionable yellow kid, and he cockily twirled his gold-headed, ebony cane on occasion, as he perambulated along so smoothly, he fairly seemed to glide.

Booth mulled over the events from the day before, oblivious to the half dozen people who turned to stare twice at this magnificent specimen of American manhood as he passed. Chagrinned by his failure once again to successfully neutralize Lincoln for the Confederate cause, he had been forced to admit to Herold that the night had been a failure. He had ridden back into town with Herold and Henson, and they agreed to turn his horse in at Naylor's Livery. Booth stopped at the National to have breakfast. Indeed, he had been the last person served in the dining that morning. He had been offered a place at a table of late-eaters that included Miss Carrie Bean, an attractive young lady from a successful Washington mercantile family.

His breakfast, consisting of ham, eggs, grits, and several cups of real coffee, full-bodied and coal black with flavor (not the ersatz, watery, army stuff less tonier establishments served in this fourth year of the war) had revitalized his spirits. Everything was made complete, when Lucy Hale had emerged from the lobby to say, "Hello," to Carrie. Booth's polite greeting had been surprisingly well-received, and he promised to join Lucy and Mrs. Temple's Circle at dinner that evening. Good meal, good haircut, Good Friday! Booth began to feel, down deep in his soul, that the day would live up to its religious title. It would be a day that history would never forget. He smiled and nodded as he encountered other pedestrians, politely touching the tip of his hat with his cane in salute.

"Here comes the handsomest man in Washington City!" Harry Ford greeted him, when he arrived at the theater Ford owned and managed with his two brothers.

"Say, Wilkes, have you heard?" Ford casually handed Booth a letter as he spoke. "The President will be here tonight with General Grant. They have got General Lee a prisoner. He will come, too. We are thinking of putting him in the opposite box."

"Come on, Harry!" Booth scoffed. "They have not got Lee a prisoner. They certainly would not bring him to Washington."

He sat down on the steps and read his letter, smiling and laughing, off and on. He looked at the back of the last page and, finding nothing more, folded the note up and replaced it in its envelope.

"Harry, are you for certain that old scoundrel Lincoln and his chief minion, Grant, will come out *here* tonight?"

"Oh, yes. It is a benefit and the last appearance of Laura Keene in *Our American Cousin*. They are surely coming. I have Mrs. Lincoln's acceptance right here. He patted a folded piece of paper in his waistcoat pocket, triumphantly. I am going to have Spangler and Burroughs fix up the box--turn the double into a single so the whole party will fit. . . . You know, John, I would not talk about the president that way if I were you."

"But you are not." Booth turned to walk into the theater.

"Hello, Mr. Booth." It was Harry Hawk, the male lead in the night's production, one of the few actors really loyal to the Union cause, earning him the nickname, "Yankee."

"How are you, Mr. Hawk?" Booth said, respectfully, and with feeling.

He stopped a moment and watched the rehearsal going on stage at that moment. Booth knew that a comedy like *Our American Cousin* had several big laugh lines. One that never failed to draw a great laugh occurred in Act 3, Scene 2. Harry the Yankee would utter the line and be alone on the stage when he did it. If Booth shot Lincoln at that moment, most of the audience would have no idea what he had done, until it was too late to stop him. Few actors or stage hands would be available to stop him. Behind the scenes, they would have even less chance to comprehend what had happened, until it was too late. All he needed was to have a horse at the back stage door, and he would be out of there in nothing flat.

Booth quickened his pace to the front of the theater. Once mounted he could outrun any pursuit, which would take at least thirty minutes to an hour to get organized--at best. Confusion would probably give him more time. He had two routes of escape to choose from. He could go north east to Baltimore or beat the pursuit to the Relay House for the last train to New York City. Canada beckoned from there.

Or he could go southeast into the Maryland Peninsula and cross the Potomac into Virginia and what was left of the Confederacy. Better yet, he would fake the trip south as far as Surrattsville and then swing north. It could be done by a skillful horseman, who knew how to get the best out of his mount. What he needed was the password at the bridges. Or a pass signed by someone important.

Who did he know that could sign a pass? His pass from Grant might do the trick, but it was getting old and had been signed out in the Western Theater of war. But there was Andrew Johnson down in the Kirkwood House! Atzerodt had failed to find the Vice President, so far. Booth decided to try in person. Johnson might give his old sporting companion from Nashville free passage, so to speak. Booth stepped out of Ford's and dug in his heels for the three block walk to Johnson's hotel.

Booth entered the Kirkwood House within the quarter hour. He walked up to the desk and asked for the Vice President. Actually he asked if *Governor* Johnson was in. Vice President was such a nothing position comparably, its only obligation was to preside over the U.S. Senate and vote to break a tie. The clerk said that he thought Johnson was out--he believed that Johnson had a meeting scheduled at the White House with President Lincoln.

Booth took a card from his waistcoat pocket, and turned it over. Using the desk pen, he wrote:

Don't wish to disturb you; are you at home?
J. Wilkes Booth

The bell man was back in minutes. No one answered the knock at Johnson's door.

"Would you like me to put it in his box?"

"Yes, either his or William A. Browning's--you know, his personal secretary."

"Right." The card wound up in Browning's box. Later, it would lead many to suspect Johnson had something to do with Lincoln's assassination. Mary Lincoln was particularly incensed by its discovery:

"[T]hat miserable inebriate, Johnson," she said afterward (referring to his appearing drunk at the inaugural), "had cognizance of my husband's death. . . . [He] had an understanding with the conspirators & *they* knew *their man*. . . . No one ever heard of Johnson regretting my sainted husband's death, he never wrote me a line of condolence, and behaved in the most brutal way."

But casting suspicion on Johnson was not Booth's intent. He had simply hoped to get a pass from the Vice President to cross the Navy Yard Bridge that night. Disappointed, Booth left the Kirkwood House and walked over to the National Hotel. Mrs. Surratt! She and that Nancy-boy, Weichmann. Maybe one of them could get the *password* for the bridges tonight! Yes, that would do, just fine. But first to check out the dining room at the National. Ah! There were Mrs. Hale and Mrs. Temple.

"Good day, ladies!" Booth called out.

"Mr. Booth, how good to see you!" Mrs. Temple said. Mrs. Hale's greeting was quite perfunctory, as usual. She was not enamored of John Wilkes Booth, especially after his quarrel with Lucy.

Booth did not see Lucy anywhere. After a few platitudes about the weather, how pretty the ladies looked, and the dinner menu, Booth decided to leave.

"Please excuse me, ladies," he said with a bow. "I need to go down to Ford's to witness the rehearsal for the play, *Our American Cousin*."

"We have been considering taking in the show this evening. Is it going to be well-presented?"

"Oh, I would strongly advise *against* it. It is Good Friday, and few will attend. I fear the play will drag horribly. As you know, ladies, theater is a civilizing process. An enthusiastic audience is part of the entertainment; it has to work as much as the actors on stage. The play deals with ideas the audience must comprehend and respond to. The crowd responds to the actors as much as the players react to the audience. It is a living experience, as it were. That is the theater's appeal as a form of entertainment. It is escapism with a purpose. It gives one a glimpse of how beautiful, poetic, and meaningful life can be."

"Well, what do you think? Perhaps we should postpone our attendance until tomorrow night?" Mrs. Temple looked at Mrs. Hale. She agreed.

"Won't you enjoy supper with us tonight, Mr. Booth?" Mrs. Temple asked with a smile. Booth could see the displeasure writ large in Mrs. Hale's face.

"Delighted!" Booth said. "Thank you so much for the invite."
He had a lot to say to Lucy Hale, before he finished his planned activities with Mr. Lincoln. Booth smiled that thousand dollar smile of his. One could always count on Mrs. Temple for doing the socially proper thing. Booth ran upstairs to his room to pick up a pair of binoculars. He obtained some wrapping paper and string from the bell man, and made a nice package of the field glasses. Then he opened the window and looked over to the stable below across C Street. Booth put his fingers to his lips and whistled loudly. James Pumphrey looked up and waved. Booth indicated that he would be right down. Descending the stairs, he came out on C Street, crossed over, and entered the stable area.

"You got my sorrel, Jim? I need her to go overnight into the country."

"No, sir, Mr. Booth. She was rented already, early this morning."

"Damn! I want her badly. She was nice--active and high-spirited. Will she be back by early this evening?"

"No sir. But I can reserve you one just as nice."

"As good as the sorrel?"

"Certainly. I have a pretty, little, dark bay mare. Seven years old. Small, only eleven hands or so. A little wound up but you can handle her. Wanna take a look?"

"No, you know your animals. I will take your word. Have her ready around 4:30 today?"

"Guaranteed."

"Buy you a drink down at Willard's?"

"No, sir. No one else to watch the place. Dinner hour, you know. Maybe later, if you are so inclined."

Booth shook Pumphrey's hand and turned back towards Sixth Street, then walked west to Pennsylvania Avenue.

2. A Fateful Letter and a Pair of Binoculars

After her return from Surrattsville on April 11, Mary Surratt had concentrated on devoting the next two days to preparations for Easter Sunday. She went to Mass daily, accompanied by Louis J. Weichmann, Honora Fitzpatrick and, of course, Anna. The only event that seemed out of step with the season was at Thursday Mass, when Anna got off her knees in a huff to keep from kneeling next to a Yankee officer in full uniform. Mary scowled at Anna, but the look was lost on her. The officer saw it, however, and hid his smile with the back of his hand.

On Good Friday, Mary Surratt and Louis Weichmann went to early Mass at St. Patrick's. Then after a hearty breakfast, Weichmann was off to his office on the other side of the White House. But he had hardly got there when an acting assistant adjutant general, one of those uncounted myrmidons that daily clogged the halls of the War Department offices with their officious wanderings, came in and read a circular letter from the Secretary of War. In it, Mr. Stanton gave the rest of the day off to all of those whose religious denominations had regularly scheduled services on Good Friday. During the Civil War in Washington, D.C., that included just about the whole population.

Weichmann and everyone else in his department left immediately. Weichmann went to St. Matthews Church and heard Dr. Charles I. White preach the sermon before going home. Weichmann visited with a few friends and arrived shortly after noon. He ate a quick lunch and retired to his room to lounge on his bed with a good book. Just after 1 p.m., there was a knock at the door. It was Mrs. Surratt and she held a letter.

"Mr. Weichmann I have a letter here from Mr. George Calvert. It seems that our negotiations with Mr. Nothey have fallen through. In any case, I must go back to Surrattsville and see about my debt. Would you oblige by driving me down?"

The weather was much nicer than last Tuesday, so Weichmann readily agreed, took the tenner he was offered and skipped jauntily down the stairs to go and hire the same old rig at Howard's around the corner.

"Great Scott! Mr. Booth! You startled me," Weichmann said as he opened the second floor main door to be confronted by the actor just in the process of pulling the bell cord. He held a package in his left hand.

"How are you, old man?" came the reply. "Here, take my hand in friendship and excuse my silent approach."

Booth went inside and Weichmann descended the outside stairs thumping his feet louder than necessary and whistling a little tune. Booth closed the door and turned to see Mrs. Surratt coming down the stairs.

"How Providential! How are you, dear lady?" He took the proffered hand and brought his lips to it, tenderly.

"Oh, Mr. Booth! I do declare! My day has just gone to the dickens--before your entry, not because of it, I assure you."

"What is it? Perhaps I can help."

"It is this letter."

She handed it to him for his perusal:

Riversdale, April 13th, 1865
Mrs. M. E. Surratt:

Dear Madam:

During a late visit to the lower portion of the county, I ascertained of the willingness of Mr. Nothey to settle with you, and desire to call your attention to the fact, in urging the settlement of the claim of my late father's estate. However unpleasant, I must insist upon closing up this matter, as it is imperative, in an early settlement of the estate, which is necessary.

You will, therefore, please inform me, at your earliest convenience, as to how and when you will be able to pay the balance due on the land purchased by your late husband.

I am, Dear Madam,

Yours Respectfully,

Geo. H. Calvert, Jr.

"I met Mr. Nothey three days past and assured him that I was willing to settle. Indeed I asked him to pay what he owed me directly to Mr. Calvert, and he has let me down. I am quite angry. I am about to leave on another journey to Surrattsville to settle this matter, once and for all. I have a mind to settle with Mr. Calvert myself and sue Mr. Nothey for his part."

"I understand you viewpoint. Actually, the solution of your problem might be the answer to one of my own."

"How is that?"

"I plan to move against Lincoln tonight. Could you deliver this package to Mr. Lloyd and tell him to have the carbines ready to go? And perhaps a bottle or two of whiskey? I have a feeling we all shall be in need of some stimulation by the time we reach the crossroads. I also need the password and countersign for the Navy Bridge."

"What is in here?" She turned the package end for end, examining it carefully. It was about eight inches square.

"It is a field glass, the kind the armies use. You will guard it carefully? And mayn't I leave my pistols here until later?"

"Certainly, Mr. Booth. Dan! Oh, Dan!" The mulatto came quickly--Mrs. Surratt was no one to play his hesitation games with. "Put these over on the sideboard, downstairs in the dining room. . . . Ah! They is Mr. Weichmann, all ready for travel, coat and all, out at the front door. I shall deliver your package and the message to Mr. Lloyd."

"Thank you, dear lady. You are more helpful than I can say."

Booth turned and went out the main door and down the steps, his walking stick under his arm as he pulled his gloves on. He saw Weichmann holding the horse and carriage, waved him a good-bye, and turned west along Avenue H. Mrs. Surratt was close on his heels. But as Weichmann turned to help her climb into the rig, she said, "Stop! Let me get those things of Mr. Booth's."

She returned shortly, carrying not only Booth's package, but one of her own. It was a packet of all the papers relevant to Mr. Nothey's land purchase, title and all. She placed the wrapped items carefully on the floorboard and climbed into the seat.

"We must be careful. This is glass," she said, picking up Booth's package and cradling it in her lap. It was 2:30 p.m.

3. Booth's Friday Afternoon

Coming back from Mrs. Surratt's, Booth stopped at Ford's again to check out the stable he rented down the back alley. He told Edman Spangler that he would be using the stable later that day. Spangler and Johnny Burroughs were removing the partition from the President's Box. As Booth walked through the theater, players were on stage rehearsing their parts for the night's performance. Others were off to one side singing patriotic songs that would round out the night's program.

Then, he stepped out the back door and took a look at the alley. Nothing had changed. It was clear of any obstruction, the Negro shanties off to one side. From the porch of one, a comely quadroon, Mary Jane Anderson, took in the pale Apollo outlined in the theater door.

"My, my, ain't he *pretty*," she said quietly to no one in particular. She felt a warm desire surge through her lower body. She stared at Booth licking her lips, hungrily, swaying her hips provocatively. Her frank testimony of her prurient feelings for the self-styled Prince of the South would be a thigh-slapping crowd-pleaser at the trial of Booth's cronies, some two months later.

Walking back into the National, Booth stopped in at the Kirkwood, once more, to see if Vice President Johnson had returned. He saw Andrew Atzerodt in the bar.

"Is Johnson back?"

"Nein, still is he gone."

"Listen, I saw Davy Herold outside. He will be in soon. Take him down to Naylor's and rent a horse for tonight."

"Ja." Atzerodt looked at Booth intently. The actor reached into his pocket and pulled out a coin. He flipped it on the counter, where it rattled to a stop. "Have one on me," Booth winked. Atzerodt smiled through his stained, food encrusted teeth, and slapped a big paw on the half-dime, the price of a cheap shot of whiskey in those days. Booth went back to the National.

Halfway through the Good Friday afternoon, Booth came down the stairs and walked over to the registration desk at the National Hotel. He had changed his attire to what would have been called a plain black business suit; with sack coat, double-breasted waistcoat, slouch hat, and riding boots that reached up over his knees almost to his hips.

"Merrick," he called to the clerk on duty. "Mayn't I have a piece of paper or two and an envelope?"

"Certainly, Mr. Booth. Right away."

Henry Merrick brought the required writing materials to the actor. The clerk also pulled out a bottle of ink and a pen, kept on hand for such ocassions as this. Booth carefully pulled the stopper off the ink bottle and dipped his pen. He wrote a few words. Then he looked about somewhat nervously, as if the coming and going of others was disturbing his reverie or perhaps compromising his privacy. Carefully, Booth picked up his writing materials and edged over to the door of the clerks' office.

"Say, Merrick. Would it be permissible for me to come in and use the desk?"

Ordinarily, Merrick would have directed a customer to the lobby where several writing tables had been set up. But Booth was no ordinary customer. Besides, he was of the habit of buying the clerks a round or two at the bar, now and then.

"Come in and sit down, sir."

"Thank you. You are most kind." The chair scraped across the floor as Booth pulled it up and sat. "Merrick, is the year '64 or '65?"

"You are joking, John." He used the more familiar form of address because he and Booth were out of the public eye, so to speak.

"Sincerely, I am not."

"It is '65."

"Thank you."

Merrick went about his business. Something was wrong with Booth, he thought. He was not his usual jovial self. Too serious. Too nervous. Must be thinking about the damned war, again. Booth looked into space, thought a moment, said to Hell with the year, and began to write:

April 14, 2 [p.m.]

Dearest Mother:

I know you expect a letter from me, and am sure you will hardly forgive me. But indeed I have nothing to write about. Everything is dull; that is, has been till last night (the illumination).

Everything was bright and splendid. More so in my eyes, if it has been a display in a nobler cause. But so goes the world. Might makes right. I only drop you these few lines to let you know I am well, and to say I have not heard from you. Excuse brevity; am in haste. Had [a letter] from Rose. With best love to you all, I am your affectionate son, ever,

John

Sealing the letter, Booth smiled at Merrick and left the hotel. Merrick noted that Booth seemed at peace with himself now. He was whistling a merry tune, as he tipped his hat to the ladies and gentlemen in the lobby and strode out on to C Street. He turned right toward Pumphrey's stables.

"I am a little early, Jim, am I not?" Booth called out as he walked into the barn.

"No problem. I have her ready, Mr. Booth. I will go down and see she is saddled."

As Pumphrey went down the alleyway, Booth walked over to some men standing in the doorway.

"Hello, Cobb," Booth said to one he recognized as an old friend and schoolmate, C. F. Cobb, who had served in the Union army. "Did you, perchance, hear that dirty little tailor from Tennessee speak in front of Willard's the other day?"

"How is it going, John? No, I did not hear the Vice President speak, but I read his remarks in the *Washington Chronicle*."

"That stinking bastard has fallen for the Lincoln line. He is as much a dictator as that dumbbell from Illinois. Another Black Republican revealed. He is a disgrace to the country. If I had been there I would have shot the reprobate! Right off the porch."

An old man who was chewing tobacco spat loudly to gain Booth's attention. "Sonny boy," he said, "you might ought to have joined the Southern army. I lay you would have got your fill of shooting by now."

Booth turned to him, ready with an angry response, but heard Pumphrey leading his mare up the alleyway. Clip-clop, clip-clop, her measured gait sounded out on the floor bricks. Booth left the men standing and went over to inspect the mare that the stableman had picked out for him. She opened her eyes wide as Booth approached and shied back on the reins a little. She was a dark bay, alright; almost black. The white star on her forehead flashed in the half light of the stable interior.

"She has spirit," Booth said. "Well, Jim, if she is as good as my sorrel, I reckon we can dicker. If she is not, we will not deal."

"Fair enough. Try her out. Ride her up and down C Street, if you like."

Booth got up on the saddle and took her out in the street. He jogged east a half block and turned to come back. The street was clear, so he put the spurs to her. The little bay mare jumped ahead and about ten feet sideways, fighting the bit all the way.

"Hold on, Mr. Booth," Pumphrey called out. "She don't need spurring. Just talk to her."

Booth calmed the mare and pulled up outside the stable entrance. "You got a tie rein for her? I want to go over to Grover's and write a letter."

"No. You do not want to hitch her. Get a boy to hold her."

"That is a mite inconvenient!"

"They is always a bootblack around who will hold a horse for a dime."

"Well, Grover's has a stable out back. Say, what is the best ride one might take out of the City?"

"You know more about that than I do, sir."

"I am thinking about Crystal Springs."

"I dunno. It is a mite early in the season for that."

"I will try it out as soon as I write my letter. Put it all on my tab, Jim."

With that Booth remounted, after putting his spurs in his coat pocket, and moved off westward.

4. The Letter to the *National Intelligencer:* Booth Opts for Assassination

Grover's National Theater was on E Street, roughly where it crossed Pennsylvania Avenue. On the second floor up front was a bar and billiards parlor kept by John Deery, a one-time champion of the game. Although he was known for his fine billiards tables and liquors, Deery's also had some of the finest victuals available, free to those who drank and played.

Deery knew Booth well, especially his penchant for drinking. What Deery marveled at was that Booth could consume prodigious amounts of liquors of all kinds, and rarely get drunk. In the parlance of the times, Booth could "drink square." He maintained all the amenities and acted the role of the gentleman. Deery believed it was a hard matter to provoke Booth into a quarrel, but noted that he was more edgy than usual when he stopped by for a brandy that afternoon.

After downing his drink, rather quickly, Deery thought (one really ought to savor such a hearty concoction, not toss it off), Booth went downstairs to the theater manager's office. Paper and ink were handy, and Booth sat at the desk, selected a piece of paper and a pen. After he sat for a pensive moment, Booth began to scratch at the papers, dipping his pen in the ink regularly:

Washington, D.C., 14 April 1865
To My Countrymen:

For years I have devoted my time, my energies, and every dollar I possessed to the furtherance of an object. I have been baffled and disappointed. The hour has come when I must change my plan. Many, I know--the vulgar herd--will blame me for what I am about to do, but posterity, I am sure, will justify me.

The principles secured by the Founding Fathers through the American Revolution are that all white men are created equal; that just government rests on consent of the governed; that government is instituted among men to secure the indefeasible rights of human nature; that one of these inalienable rights is the right to revolt against despotism. Indeed, rebellion against tyranny is not a crime but a benefaction.

This right of revolution is governed by two principles: when the Executive desires or attempts to govern arbitrarily and not by law or constitution, and when the Executive seeks to exercise a power that the Constitution does not grant him. By doing both, President Lincoln seeks to replace freedom of consent and law with force and slavery. The exercise of power beyond right is Tyranny.

In certain circumstances, such as those we live in now, only the force of violent revolution is capable of ensuring that the power of the president is limited and exercised according to law and not will. Any president who so acts may be resisted by the common citizen, or a combination of many citizens, just as he resists an invader of his property. A Tyrant replaces law with force and institutes a war between people and government, as President Lincoln did in 1861, by refusing compromise on the issue slavery in the territories. And he had the temerity to assert in his Second Inaugural Address that he sought to *avoid* war.

Moreover, this so-called Executive, with the connivance of his party, seeks to free the slaves through executive proclamation, then by a constitutional amendment, passed through a Congress absent the representatives of very people whom the amendment would affect. It is the only manner in which he could gain the votes necessary. He cares nothing for the future of the black people, slave or free, replacing the security and benevolence of slavery with nothing but exploitive freedom that leaves them drifting in a hostile white society with no future.

President Lincoln allows the corruption of our government by jobbers and cronies and justifies all as wartime measures necessary to defeat the Confederacy. He has instituted the unconstitutional, thieving economic program of the discredited Henry Clay, the Corrupt Bargainer of 1824, who sought to keep the great Andrew Jackson from power after he was fairly chosen by the American people. This includes high tariffs, to destroy the cotton exports of the South; controlling national banks, to destroy access of the common man to easy money; internal improvements, to the benefit of his section alone; homesteading, which squanders our national legacy in the West, to attract immigrants who defile our culture and will be taught to vote Republican; bounties for railroads, to link the North to the West at the exclusion of the South. All of this is financed by the highest taxes in American history, including an unconstitutional direct tax on personal incomes, designed to stifle the natural incentive of the American industrial and agricultural communities.

Worse yet, the President has *illegally and unconstitutionally* expanded the powers of the executive beyond the limits of those imposed on the office by the Founders. He summoned the militia, a right of Congress; expanded the size of the army, again a prerogative of Congress; decreed an illegal blockade, since he refused to recognize the independence of the Confederate States, against part of his own nation; arrested unoffending citizens, denying their rights to assemble and discuss political issues of the day; refused to honor the writ of *habeas corpus* and defied his own Supreme Court, particularly its Chief Justice, when asked to show where in the Constitution his power of arbitrary arrest lay; illegally transferred thousands of dollars appropriated for specific purposes by Congress to his own pet projects; and pledged the honor and credit of the United States without authority. The only thing that makes this American Bastille more bearable than the French Revolution's is the *absence* of mass executions.

He put domestic priorities of creating an *infernal Republican political machine* ahead of preserving the lives and well-being of American soldiers in the field. His political considerations brought forth hundreds of incompetent officers, many of them generals, for party patronage. Each time peace has been in the offing, he has *refused* to consider it. He prefers to continue the bloodletting by raising new terms or objections or stalling and refusing to negotiate in good faith. The latest of these outrages was the Hampton Roads Conference a few days ago. And why not? He *started the war* by refusing to accept fair payment for Federal installations in the South and forcing the South to fire first to preserve its own national integrity, when he tried to succor and reinforce his garrison. He *continues it* through the offices of General Useless Grant and his subordinates, *traduced* by the promise of future Republican political rewards.

The general revolt of all or a part of this Nation against these Republican travesties cannot be called the *War of Rebellion*, as Lincoln and his minions maintain. Indeed, the term Rebel ought to be applied to the tyrant Lincoln, not those who *resist* his unlawful and unconstitutional application of power. But to resist a tyrant one must have exhausted all other forms of legal resistance. It should only be resorted to after a pattern of abuse has been established. That is, there must be more than ill-administration but actual malice in the president's actions. I was a Cooperationist in 1860, wishing to see for myself the evils this barbarian would institute. I can no longer be anything but an Opponent, a Secessionist. President Lincoln has forfeited his trust and, say I, by needs be, his life.

One might argue, it is one thing to destroy the tyrant, but *quite another* to destroy the tyranny. Mere removal of the president will leave the constitution intact with all the weaknesses that led to his rule in the first place. All constitutions are subject to corruption over time. But the American government was *not* ill-constituted, the defects more lately observed proceeding from the change of manners, and the corruption of the times, the desire of Lincoln and his Black Republicans to meddle with the best system of government created by man.

The purpose of this so-called Rebellion is to restore the rule of law. The Union as it was and the Constitution as it is. Constitutional government and the separation of powers were designed to facilitate this restoration by checking corruption, facilitating change, and advancing the public interest. We have always governed ourselves, and we always meant to. Lincoln did not mean that we should. Proclamations are not laws, they are merely the opinion of the President.

It has been hitherto thought, that to kill a King or a President was a abominable action. They who did it, were thought to be incited by the worst of passions that can enter into the hearts of men. But if Algernon Sidney can be credited, under the current circumstances, it must be rather the most commendable and glorious act that can be performed by man. I say, death to tyrants, by any means and in any way. Tyrannicide is the public duty of all good citizens. The only inconvenience is that all depends upon success, and he who tries is the worst of villains if he fail; and at best may be deprived of all by the same means he employed to gain it.

The success of the South has been dear to my heart, and I have labored faithfully to further an object which would more than have proved my unselfish devotion. Heartsick and disappointed, I turn from the path I have been following into a bolder and more perilous one. Without malice I make the change. I have nothing in my heart except a sense of duty to my choice. After all, as Tertullian said, against men guilty of treason and against public enemies, *every man* is a soldier.

If the South is to be aided, it must be done *quickly*. It may already be *too late*. When Caesar had conquered the enemies of Rome and the power that was his menaced the liberties of the people, Brutus arose and slew

him. The stroke of his dagger was guided by his love of Rome. It was the *spirit and ambition* of Caesar that Brutus struck at.
Oh that we could come by Caesar's spirit,
And not dismember Caesar!
But, alas!
Caesar must bleed for it.
We answer with Brutus:
Men who love our country better than gold or life.
John W. Booth
John H. Surratt
Lewis Payne
David E. Herold
G. Andrew Atzerodt

5. Booth Prepares for His Biggest Role

A short while later, John Matthews, a boyhood friend of the Booths up in Baltimore, and now, a fellow actor who had refused to join in the kidnapping of Lincoln from a theater stage earlier that year, encountered Booth riding up Pennsylvania Avenue. Matthews was on the triangle across from Grover's National Theater, between 13th and 14th streets.
"Ho! John!" Matthews called out.
Booth skillfully guided the horse over to him, avoiding a slow moving carriage and a drayman's cart.
"Johnny!" Booth struck out his hand. Matthews warmly shook hands with his friend.
"A fine day, is it not?"
"Yes."
The conversation was interrupted by the shout of commands and the trudging of many feet. A military unit swung into view. It was a bunch of Confederate prisoners of war. Several Union infantrymen and a few mounted cavalry rode on their flanks, keeping them separated from the people on the street.
"Have you seen the prisoners?" Matthews asked. "Lee's officers--just brought in from battlefields near Appomattox."
"Yes, Johnny. I have seen them. They have been passing all day."
Booth placed his hand on his forehead, brushing his hat back so far, it nearly fell off. He seemed to reel in the saddle, most unusual for so experienced a rider at rest. He became quite jittery--pale and agitated.
"My God! I have no country!"

"John! How nervous you are. What is the matter?" Matthews almost regretted calling Booth's attention to the Rebel prisoners.

"Oh, no, it is nothing." Booth struggled to regain his composure." Johnny, I have a little favor to ask of you. Will you grant it?"

"Why, certainly, Johnny! What is it?"

"Perhaps, I must leave town tonight, and I have a letter here which I desire to be published in the *National Intelligencer*. Please attend to it for me, unless I see you before 10 o'clock tomorrow. In that case I will see to it myself."

Booth handed the envelope over to Matthews, who slipped it into his inside coat pocket.

There was a creaking of leather, the ring of harness chains, as two splendid black horses passed drawing an open Phaeton carriage.

"Look!" Matthews cried. "There go General and Mrs. Grant. Headed to the railroad station, I would guess, judging by the luggage on the boot rack."

"Where?" Booth exclaimed.

Matthews pointed into the street, his finger following the carriage as it headed toward the Capitol.

Booth sat upright, then leaned over and squeezed Matthews's hand, and very gently put heels to his mare, who now responded without shying.

"You will not forget me, will you?" he called over his shoulder as he moved off at a lope.

Matthews waved to reassure him.

Booth moved his little mare down the Avenue and level to the Grants' carriage. She took off so fast that a less alert rider might have wound up in the dirt behind her. He marveled at her speed and quick response. Booth peered into the Grants' vehicle and stared with his evil Richard III look. Mrs. Grant openly shuddered and pointed him out to the General. Booth snickered to himself. He had done the same thing to her at dinner in the dining room, as she and her friends ate at Willard's, during the noon hour.

Pulling up the mare (she fought the pressure from the snaffle, wanting to run more), Booth turned north on Tenth Street, heading for Ford's Theater to stable the mare for the night's coming events. Damn that Grant! He would not be at the rendezvous with fate in the Presidential Box. But Lincoln would. He must prove reliable, at last. After all, Mrs. Lincoln had *promised*. As he rode, he surely hoped that Matthews would prove more reliable than either the Grants or the Lincoln had been heretofore. He probably would not prove to be.

"Drat! I am surrounded by idiots, allies and enemies alike!" Booth muttered.

As Booth feared, Matthews would forget--until Booth had shot Lincoln. Then Matthews remembered the letter in his coat. He pulled the envelope out and tore it open. To Hell with privacy! He read the missive a couple of times hurriedly. He read it once more slowly. My God! If he delivered this to the newspaper or gave it to the authorities he would hang with Booth! If he were *lucky*. The crowd outside Ford's was crying for the lynching of all actors. He grabbed the stove door, shaking his hand violently from the pain of the heat burning his flesh. Then Matthews stuffed the offending letter and its cover deep in the box, and watched with relief as it turned to ash. That evil Rebel playactor damn near did me in! And I had told him *no*, as far back as January!

After he left Matthews with his letter rationalizing Lincoln's impending death, Booth decided to try and find John Surratt. He jogged the little mare east on E Street. He was about to turn north on 6th Street toward the Surratt House when he spotted John Surratt on the curb.

"John!" Booth called out. He pulled the mare up and leaned over toward Surratt. "Listen, things are coming rapidly to a head. Grant has just passed heading to the B & O Railroad station. Can you get over there posthaste? I hate to let him get away."

"You want me to shoot him at the station!?"

"No, no. Follow him on the train and wait 'til around ten or 10:30 tonight. Do him in at an opportune spot. Then keep going north, I will meet you at St. Albans on Saturday or Sunday night. I think the train out of New York City is called the Midnight Express."

"I know it. I will get on it, right off."

Booth turned his horse about and headed for Ford's Theater, confident that Grant would not live out the night. If anyone could do the job, it was the intrepid Surratt.

Surratt made it to Grant's train all right, and climbed aboard. But at the appointed time that evening, he found the vestibule door to Grant's car locked, and the window blocked by a curtain. He quietly stepped back into the public cars and then continued on to Philadelphia, New York City, and St. Albans, where he waited for Booth. He lost his handkerchief as he slept in the station, finally going on to Montreal, after hearing of Lincoln's death and not encountering Booth by the night of April 16 as planned.

In the wake of the hunt for Booth's co-conspirators, John Surratt was at the top of the National Government's arrest list. He hid among friendly Catholic prelates for weeks, until he could secure passage to Europe. Although he was revealed to United States authorities in England, he seemingly managed to escape into oblivion. Finally, Henri Beaumont De

Ste. Marie, the man Surratt had met with Weichmann during their Easter trip to Little Texas, Maryland, chanced to recognize the fugitive in Rome in 1867 in the uniform of the Papal Guards. Seeing him as a liability, the Vatican ordered his arrest and extradition. Surratt made a daring escape, leaping over the wall of the citadel he was being held in and dropping to land on a shelf of rock thirty feet below, thereby gaining his freedom, only later to be cornered in Alexandria, Egypt. Federal authorities returned him to Washington, where he was arraigned and tried in front of a civilian jury for treason. The jurors could not make up their minds as to his guilt, voting on a strictly sectional basis, Yankees and immigrants seeing him guilty, Southerners, not.

But all that was in the future. As Booth approached Ford's, he saw James Mattox, the property man for the theater, taking a smoke on the walk, just north of the theater in front of James P. Ferguson's restaurant.

"Hey, Jim," he called out, "Look at what I have here!"

"Whoa! That surely is a sweet-looking little mare. Love that white star on her forehead. Is she yours?"

"Just a rental from Pumphrey's. Did Spangler tell you I would be using that stable in the back alley?"

"No, but that should be all right. She is kind of charged up, ain't she?"

"You bet. That is the way I like them. Got to have a little spirit or they are not worth putting a saddle on them."

At that moment, Ferguson came out of his restaurant, wiping his hands on a towel.

"See what a nice horse I have got, Jim. Now watch; she can run just like a cat."

Booth spurred the bay and she tore down the street. Then he pulled her up fast, shifting his weight as he did, forcing her to tuck her rear end under her body. Booth shifted his weight again, and laid the reins over her neck, causing her to roll over her left haunch. He gave her the spurs and tore past the restaurant. At the end of the block, Booth turned once again, slowed the mare to a walk, and brought her back to the hitching post where Maddox and Ferguson stood in wide-eyed amazement.

"Amazing, John," Ferguson remarked. "How fast will she go?"

"I have not had the room to open her full out, yet. Hell, I am the only rider who has learned how to *spur* her. She shot so far sideways the first time I tried it, that she nearly dropped me into the street."

"Her hind end is going faster than her fore. Look at the way she side-passes down the street at a walk," Maddox said.

"She is a cat all right," Ferguson said. "But I tell you, I had an army officer inform me once that a friend of his, a major, had a horse like that--

a real fast, beauty--and she took him clean into the Rebel lines. He could not stop her. The Rebs could not, either, but they sure shot the Hell out of that major. You better be careful or she will have you in a wreck."

"Bah! I have been training them since I was knee-high to my old Da. Say, go in and have Spangler meet me in the alley, will you?"

When Booth got to the alley, he rode up to the stage door and yelled, "Ned! Ned! It was open to create a draft inside to air the place out."

"Ned is busy, John. I will help you." It was Jacob Ritterspaugh, another theater employee.

"Bring a halter, Jake."

They took the mare down to the stable and shut her in. Ritterspaugh moved in to remove the bridle and saddle.

"Never mind," Booth said. "I do not want it off. Let it and the bridle remain. Put the halter on over the bridle, army style. Watch it! She is a bad little bitch," he said as Ritterspaugh jumped back from a nip at his arm.

"Who is inside?"

"Oh, me, Maddox, Peanut John, and Spangler, and the call boy, Willie Ferguson."

"Why do we all not go over next door to Pete Taltavul's Star Saloon and have a drink before supper, on me? After we feed and water my little four-legged princess, here."

"Le's go and get a drink, boys," Maddox said, when they came in.

"We are already on our way," Booth retorted with a smile. "You all come--I am paying. I reckon I will not drink--I have a touch of pleurisy--but I will walk over with you all and buy a round."

At Taltavul's, Booth reconsidered and had a glass of ale. Young Ferguson had a sarsaparilla, proud to be associated with the greatest actor of the day and the rest of the theater men. Booth left shortly, and the others went out front and over to Ferguson's (no relation to Willie) café for supper. Booth went back into the theater.

Booth looked around and listened carefully. The building was empty. He moved up the stairs to the second floor dress circle and over to the south end of the theater. He picked up the shaft from an old music stand and entered the hall that separated the President's Box from the rest of the dress circle. Taking a small gimlet tool from his pocket, he was surprised to find that a hole had already been made in the inner door that would be directly behind Lincoln's head. Unknown to Booth, it had been drilled there some time earlier to permit presidential guards to check up on Lincoln and his guests during a play without disturbing them. Booth, ever the opportunist, shrugged his shoulders at his good luck. Putting the gimlet back in his coat, the actor opened his pocketknife and widened the hole so it revealed a better view of the scene in the box. Then Booth opened the inner door--as Powell had noticed several weeks earlier, its lock was broken from some time before and never fixed--so that the light from outside would illuminate the little hallway. He shut the door to the dress circle, and put the shaft from the music stand behind the door to wedge it closed. Because the door made an acute angle with the wall, a rough triangle was formed between the door, wall, and the wooden shaft. All Booth had to do to make it perfect was cut a bit of plaster off the lath to fit the shaft's end into the wall.

His job completed, John Wilkes cleaned up all the plaster and wood detritus, wrapping it in a pocket handerchief and putting it in his pocket. He closed all the doors as before, placed the shaft in the corner, and calmly walked out onto the street. Hum-m-m. Getting late. Almost time for supper! He whistled a little tune as he walked:

The n----rs we will sell,
And the Yankees we will send to Hell. . . .

6. Meeting at the Canterbury Music Hall

"Wood!" There was a knocking at the door of Lewis Powell's room at the Herndon House. "Wood! Open up!"

Powell knew that voice. He went over to the door and opened it. There was Davy Herold, all out of breath from running up the stairs.

"Booth has called a meeting over at the Canterbury--you know, that music hall over on Louisiana Avenue?" Powell had a blank look in his eyes.

"Lou-ees-ee-ana Av-e-nue?" Herold said the syllables slowly, hoping to make them more intelligible.

"Oh, yeah," Powell acknowledged. He never could get the hang of all these streets with their fancy names. He was more used to one-horse towns and geographic markers.

"I got your horse out front. Le's go!"

Outside, Herold mounted a red roan, while Powell got up on the large brown horse with the cloudy eye on the off side. They rode down and stopped at a stable behind the National Hotel. Dismounting, Herold handed the two animals over to M. P. Poe, the livery owner.

"Please, hold them for a couple of hours, Mr. Poe," Herold said jovially. "We will be back for them, then."

"Sure Davy," Poe responded, signaling for a hostler to come and fetch the horses to a stall. Every stable owner in the City knew David Herold on sight. He was well-liked, even though most of them thought him a mite irresponsible and flippant. More to the point, they envied his ability to come and go, as he pleased, when he pleased. He was like a schoolboy playing perpetual hooky. Hunting, drinking, whoring--anything, but working. They wondered where he got all his money, not realizing John Wilkes Booth was his benefactor, as well as friend.

Herold and Powell walked inside a building two blocks down gaudily marked "Canterbury Music Hall." It was a popular haunt of the City's lower class, and all those toney types, such as Booth, who liked to hob-nob with the "ordinary people." The bar was full and the piano was tinkling some little ditty that Powell had heard of before. Standing besides the upright, a used-up-looking woman of questionable virtue--at least she was dressed in what society women would have called a "scandalous outfit;" fishnet stockinged legs, short dress cut off outrageously above the knee with a risqué décolletage that left very little of her ample bosom to the imagination--was singing a jaunty, raunchy song slightly off-key and out of sync with the piano player.

The song was an old favorite of the period called "John Harrolson." It was the story of a Confederate officer who went from town to town collecting Southern belles' urine or "chamber lye," as it was called then, in large tanks, mounted on wagons or rail cars. The purpose of this seemingly strange activity was to extract ammonium nitrate for use in making gunpowder, the Southern nitrate mines ordinarily used for such substances being tapped-out by the exigencies of the war effort. Or so the story went. Herold and Powell looked around. There were several dance hall girls-- some mingling with the crowd, hustling drinks, while a couple of others danced, or tried to dance, with a couple of tipsy customers at the back of the room.

"Herold!" Booth called out from a table in the midst of the crowd. Even using all of his acting talent to project his voice, he could just barely be heard over the din of the joy makers. He waved a bottle and several glasses. Sitting with him was Andrew Atzerodt, loaded to the gills, as usual, but giving the outward appearance of total sobriety. Herold and Powell elbowed through the crowd.

"Sit down, men, Booth ordered, have a drink. Pour your own." He slid the bottle and two glasses over to the newcomers. "Hold it, Andrew! Let the new arrivals get theirs first. Otherwise there will be none left after you get yours." Booth winked.

Everyone laughed. The glasses clinked as the neck of the bottle hit them, but it went unheard in the noisy room. Herold noticed it was brandy. He preferred whiskey but, Hell, Booth was buying, that was the most important consideration. The girl at the piano droned on in her sultry voice, lubricated by the cheap liquor she swilled, as she sang. The noise from the patrons, the piano and the dance hall girls covered their conversation, so much so that Booth wound up actually shouting. God help us, Powell thought, if suddenly all the ruckus stopped at once. Booth would probably be revealed yelling something about killing Lincoln to the whole world!

"Andrew found out something very interesting last night. Benning's Bridge is closed and locked by dark. It is surrounded by a stout fence. We will be unable to use it. I propose that we use the Navy Yard Bridge. Mrs. Surratt is checking it and the road south to Surrattsville, now. I will get the lay of the land and the passwords later tonight. "

"Why not go straight to Baltimore on the main road to Relay Station, where the Washington railroad branch meets the cross-country line?" Herold asked.

"We will go south to Surrattsville to pick up whiskey and long guns, but mostly to mislead the pursuit in to thinking we have gone south into Lower Maryland. It is a feint, in military parlance."

The bar vocalist screeched out another verse of her ditty, interrupting the intense topic at the table of the co-conspirators. "Do you reckon she will ever finish?" Booth wondered aloud.

"Last verse, Cap," Powell reassured him.

There was a monstrous laughter and cheering as the singer finished her ballad and bowed low, her dress dropping from the weight of her pendulous breasts. The crowd cheered in appreciastion.

"Grant and Lincoln were to attend the play at Ford's tonight, but something has come up and our general of the hour left on the train for the North. I have sent Surratt to intercept him on the cars and snuff his lights out."

"You did not know?" It was Atzerodt, suddenly come alive again.

"What?" Booth said.

"It vas in the newspapers. Maybe two veeks ago. When Lincoln was the soldier boys to visit. Mrs. Lincoln and Mrs. Grant hate themselves. It had something about a military review at City Point to do. Very bad." Atzerodt tilted the bottle. It was empty. He idly banged its neck back and forth in his glass, as if somehow the ringing would magically distill a new flagon of *eau de vie*.

Booth waved. He took the empty bottle from Atzerodt and handed it to the waiter. "More of the same."

"Now look. We are going to do it better, this time. I asked O'Laughlen to come down and take care of Secretary of War Stanton. He has already scouted out his place a while ago. Wood will do in Seward; in lieu of

Surratt, Andrew can kill Johnson. I, naturally, get Lincoln, and Herold can coordinate. I will use a Derringer. One cannot carry a revolver into Ford's without drawing too much attention."

Powell jerked his head toward the approaching waiter. Booth took the bottle and dropped a gold coin on his tray. "Thank *you*, sir!" the waiter said as he went on to the next table and out of earshot in the din.

"What was this you said?" Atzerodt asked, so astonished that he did not pour himself a drink. He set the bottle down and squinted his eyes to concentrate on the conversation at hand.

"I will kill Lincoln, O'Laughlen will do in Stanton, Wood will take Seward, and *you*, Andrew, will kill Vice President Johnson."

"Nein, nein! I kill nobody! I told you last night." All of a sudden, Atzerodt was stone cold sober.

"Shut up!" Booth snapped. "You will do as you are told. You already have checked into the Kirkwood House right above Johnson's room. All you have to do is walk up to Johnson's door and knock on it. When he opens it, you pull the trigger. It will be as easy as pie. Bah! Do not argue!"

"I kill no one," Atzerodt mumbled, returning to his bottle. "Kidnap, ok. Cross the Potomac, ok. I am good blockade runner--best on the river. But kill another man, I do not do." He swilled the full glass before him, but no one was listening or watching.

"Herold will coordinate with O'Laughlen and Wood. Because we have to kill Stanton and Seward at the same moment, I have asked that another couple of men help us on the outside. Davy got them to come in last night, when he went down to Tee Bee. We must all be ready at 10 o'clock tonight. If all goes right, Herold will check with me and I will estimate the proper time to shoot. Sometime after 10 o'clock. . . . How can we get Wood into the injured, immobile Seward's presence?" Booth still puzzled aloud. "I do not know what to say. . . ."

"I have it!" Herold popped up like the proverbial jack-in-the-box. Literally jumped up in his seat. "Look! Like you said, Johnny, Seward was badly injured in a carriage accident a week or ten days past. He has to be getting medicine from his doctor, a man named Verdi, I think. It was in the *Intelligencer*. Ma's still got it at home, if she don't throw it out before I get there. I can fake a medical prescription for you. All tied up pretty with a bow, a letter, and everything. I have done that many times when I was a pharmacist's clerk. Mosby takes the package to the door, the servant answers, he says he has to give it to Seward personal, explain instructions or something like, and he is in and led to the proper room in a matter of a few minutes."

"That is not bad!" Booth said. "Davy, with a mind like that, you ought to think about writing plays. I may have underestimated you! What do you think, Wood? Can you handle that?"

"Well, I guess so. What is a perscipshun?"

"*Pre*-scription," Herold said, yelling above the din of the crowd. Several drinkers looked over, but when it looked like no fight would erupt (Herold smiled boyishly), they went back to their drinks and conversation, albeit disappointedly. "I will set you up later tonight, never fear," Herold promised Powell.

"Good, that is settled. Wood, go over and pay off the Herndon House. Get something to eat. Where will you be until 10 o'clock? So Herold can pick you up with the horse."

"Right here, Cap. On the front porch."

"Well, gentlemen, it is nearly dinner time. Let's get cracking! Here is where you all pay me off for supporting you with drinks, food, and women all this time."

They all left the Canterbury Music Hall together, Atzerodt last, still muttering to himself, "I ain't about to kill no one, for nobody, for nuttin'!"

"Well, I reckon I will stay here a while," Powell said. He turned back into the music hall.

"C'mon, Andrew," Herold called, "ride this horse back to Naylor's for me. You know, Johnny, Fletcher said I cannot have it after nine. We need to stay away from *him*, I lay."

Booth smiled absent-mindedly and crossed the Avenue engrossed in his own thoughts.

He was humming quietly.

'In 1865, when Lincoln *shan't* be king!'

7. Booth's Friday Evening Dinner

Booth walked south on Tenth Street to Pennsylvania, turned left on the Avenue for a couple of blocks, and then east on C Street. He walked rapidly and arrived back at the National Hotel at the dinner hour. He waved to the desk clerk and went upstairs to the parlor where he knew that The Circle, as Mrs. Temple called her brood, would gather before ascending to the hotel's main dining room. Booth could hear the bantering voices and laughter of The Circle long before they appeared in his view. The usual members were there--Mrs. Temple; a woman he had not met before; and the Hales, Lucy and her parents. The only one missing was Mr. Temple, who was out on business, his absence being satisfactory to both men, since he and Booth loathed each other.

"Ladies and gentlemen--oh! . . . *gentleman*--how are you all this fine evening?"

"Why, Mr. Booth! Where have you been keeping yourself all this time?" Mrs. Hale's tone was a bit dismayed, as if she had hoped that Booth might never show up again. Booth noticed her intent but smiled broadly, anyway.

"Senator and Mrs. Hale, my compliments."

He shook the senator's hand firmly, then took Mrs. Hale's hand graciously with his left and deftly transferred it to his right, bowing until his lips met the back of her hand, ever so gently. Before the still-surprised Mrs. Hale could respond, Booth bowed ostentatiously to Lucy and, with a wink, was off to Mrs. Temple, knowing that she was the queen bee of this little hive.

"Mrs. Temple, I have been away far too long and without explanation. Please accept my most humble apologies. Business of the most pressing nature called and I own that I am guilty of being most unfeeling of the needs of others--and who is this beautiful lady?"

"Oh, go on, Mr. Booth!" Mrs. Temple dismissed his alleged omissions with a half-hearted wave of her hand. "We are all so happy to see you, again!"

Mrs. Temple had noticed Lucy's fluttering heart and the excited look in her eyes when Booth had winked at her. The plot thickens; the romance is not dead, oh! She was still enamored with this loveable rapscallion! Wonderful!

"Mr. Booth, may I present a new visitor to our little group, Mrs. Whipple from England?"

"Mrs. Whipple, I am charmed. It is always a great pleasure to be introduced to anyone so fair from the land of the Noble Bard."

"Thank you, Mr. Booth. I have hoped to meet you. What would the world be without the inspiring words of our Sir William?"

"I cannot speak for the world, but I can guarantee you that I, my whole family, and the English language would be at a loss without him--a dreary thing indeed. And now, with her parent's permission, and my pardon to you all, I would like to speak with Miss Lucy privately--say, over in the corner on that little settee? And perhaps I could join you all for a light supper, later?"

Lucy arose and looked anxiously over to her mother. She knew better than to let the Senator rule on a matter of this import. Mrs. Hale smiled, half-heartedly. What could Booth do within sight and ear-shot of Lucy's parents? He would dare nothing in Mrs. Temple's presence.

"Will you all excuse us a moment, then?" Booth said, leading her by the hand, as if they were about to enter a dance floor.

"Lucy, I own myself a complete ass, a fool, and a prating cockscomb," he said as they sat, she on the settee, he on its arm, close to, but towering over her, a subtle psychological advantage in the conversation that followed. "Can you possibly forgive me?"

"Well, I do not know, Johnny. Perhaps I should. You have changed much in the last weeks. Mrs. Temple has told me about you."

"You asked about me?"

She blushed, lowered her eyes shyly, and said in a very low voice, "Yes."

"Oh. Lucy! I knew that you still cared, as do I for you. I have learned to control my feelings, to change from a jealous, ranting boy to a cool, composed, rational man."

"I know Johnny. I can sense it now."

"I treated you so unfairly after that ball in March. I had no right to be angry with you for dancing with Robert Lincoln. In my absence, you could not be expected to sit as a wall flower. And that episode with the book, a couple of days later. What was I thinking?"

"When you came into Mrs. Temple's parlor and just sat there, *pretending* to read." She giggled.

"Yes, I thought that Robert Todd would never leave. It took an hour!"

"I believe that he is a bit afraid of you. You have quite a reputation as a duelist. He feared you might *challenge* him."

"I was a mite afraid that I *might* challenge him. That would have been a stupid thing to have done."

"Especially since you have him beaten at the starting gate."

"You mean that you do not love him?"

"No, you silly goose! I *like* him, as I do many men. But I do not *love* him. That is reserved for someone very special--you!"

Booth leaned toward her slightly.

"No! John! Not here! My parents would be positively *mortified* if you were to hug or kiss me in public!"

The smile in her eyes belied her words, but Booth knew that this was neither the time nor the place.

"Methinks thee dost protest too much," he teased.

"Wait a minute, what about all of those horrible things you said to me in Mrs. Temple's parlor after Robert left?"

She leaned back, reasserting her personal space. Her black silk dress was set off fashionably by the red velvet of the settee. Her bosom rose and fell alluringly. She smiled, her teeth flashing prettily, her tongue played along her lower lip, coyly.

"I apologize for all of them."

"Even for calling Robert a 'damn Yankee pimp?'"

"Oh! Especially that!" He laughed and she giggled in return.

"Well, maybe he *is*." She had a devilish look in her eyes.

"Listen! It is quite possible that I may be in Europe sometime soon. Perhaps I can visit you in Spain. Your father is still to be American minister there, is he not?"

"¡Sí que sí!" she said. "See? You like my Spanish?" She did not tell Booth that she practiced her language lessons daily with the hated Robert Lincoln and his friend, John Hay. After their linguistic gymnastics, the two males usually visited one of the better Washington whorehouses, for a gymnastics contest of another kind, something Lucy would not have fathomed, even had she known. "I am ready to leave at once. I would love to see you in Spain."

"*See* me, nothing! Lucy, I want to *marry* you."

"Oh, John! Yes, yes! But my father. . . . I need time to prepare *both* my parents for this."

"I will meet you in Spain a year from now and we will be wed, with or without your father's permission."

"No! I will come back to you here, with or without my father. That is my promise to you. We must keep it secret until I am ready to confront my parents."

"You have my word on that."

On the other side of the room, Mrs. Temple listened half-heartedly to the conversation around her, all the while keeping a weather eye on the handsome young couple across the room on the settee. Oh, she wished that she could hear what they were saying. She tried to read their lips, to no avail. She ought to practice *that* art, she thought, it might come in handy some day. Lucy was listening to Booth intently, her soul in her face, so to speak. He seemed to be inspired; the musical murmur of his voice was mesmerizing.

Mrs. Temple could make out nary a word. But Lucy sat spell-bound. His beautiful language, his tender ways, personal beauty, rich voice, and magnetic presence were all calculated to make him a romantic maiden's ideal. They stared at each other like moonstruck calves. Their eyes glistened with an unnatural luster and were softened with unutterable longing. There sat John Wilkes Booth with Lucy Lambert Hale, the only woman he ever really loved! Then Mrs. Temple blinked her eyes with a perceptible start. Reality intruded. Was she crazy, or was all of this quite one-sided? Was Booth merely putting it all on and only Lucy being sincere? He was not *that good* an actor. Surely not!

"Come, children," Mrs. Hale called out, interrupting Mrs. Temple's doubts and the young pair's doting, real and feigned. "It is time for supper!"

Everyone stood and the older members of the party walked into the hallway, followed by Booth with Lucy hanging on his arm.

"Ah! Lucy! Lucy! Can I trust you utterly?"

"Even as Ruth said, so say I--even unto death!" She would later be mortified at her own unanticipated prescience.

In the dining room, they took their seats--Booth next to Lucy; Mrs. Whipple; Mrs. Temple; and then Senator and Mrs. Hale, in that order around the round table. The meal went pleasingly well. The food was excellent, and Booth was most entertaining, his clear laugh often drawing glances from others nearby. It would be his last meal in Washington.

Finally, Booth stood and pulled out his watch. "It is after 8 o'clock; I fear I must go."

"Oh, John! So soon?" Lucy lamented.

He looked down at Lucy, smiled broadly, his white teeth framed by his coal-black moustache, and spoke the witches' line from *Macbeth*, "When shall we three meet again?"

"When the hurly-burly's done," Lucy took up the line, "When the battle's lost and won." (Act I, Scene 1)

"Hark! I'm called," Booth responded (jumping text to Act 3, Scene, 5). "My little spirit, see! Sits in a foggy cloud, and stays for me!"

Booth then made a sweeping bow, and retreated to the door, amid the polite applause of his entourage and an unusual "bravo!" from the Senator.

Booth turned to step out the door, when suddenly he whirled and came back in, narrowly missing a couple leaving behind him. He apologized gracefully, tipped his hat, and returned to the dinner table. He looked Lucy deeply in the eyes, and spoke a couplet from *Hamlet:*
"Nymph, in thy orisons / Be all my sins remembered." (Act 3, Scene 1)

He took her frail hand and gazed at her in one long, loving look. His whole personality shone, his lips quivered, and that smile! . . . Then Booth dropped her hand as suddenly as he had taken it up. She let it fall lifelessly into her lap, staring at him lovingly in the eyes all the time. He shook his head, as if he had more to say but did not dare. But he thought it.

Well, I have done for Bob Lincoln, the little son of a bitch--now, for his Old Man, the Robinarch!

Booth turned and departed without casting a backward glance and disappeared into the lobby and out the main door. None of them ever saw him alive again.

8. Mrs. Surratt's Trip of April 14

Through the City, across the Navy Yard Bridge, over Good Hope Hill and through the dales and hills that followed, Weichmann's rented rig carried Mary Surratt and her precious packages southeastward. Just beyond the District line, they were surprised to see a platoon of cavalry lolling about in the grass. Their horses had wandered about grazing and flicking a few flies and other insects their pilgrimage rousted out of the early spring field. Mrs. Surratt asked Weichmann to stop.

"Sir!" She hailed an old farmer. "Who are these soldiers and what are they doing here?"

"Calvery picket. They keep watch for strange riders who might be carrying the Rebel mail and such."

"Will these poor boys have to stay the night? It gets so cold this time of year after dark."

"Nome, they leave about 8 p.m."

"I am glad to know that!"

"They will be back tomorrow at first light though, I reckon."

"Come, Mr. Weichmann. We have a far piece to go. Will you permit me to drive a spell?"

Weichmann surrendered the reins and Mary Surratt urged the horse on, cheerfully commenting on the beauty of the day and the countryside that was beginning to submit to the encroaching spring. The two travelers arrived at Surrattsville about 4:30 that evening. Mrs. Surratt went inside to sit in the parlor, while Weichmann drove the horse around a while to cool him off. Then in response to a rap on the window, Weichmann tied up and went inside. Mrs. Surratt was in the parlor with her brother, Zad Jenkins. The one package was broken open and its contents of legal documents lay on the center table. The other was still wrapped up and lying on the sofa.

"Mr. Nothey is not available," Mary groused. "I will have to write him. I am not happy with this business."

"I have seen the two judgments that Mr. Calvert got against John H. Surratt, Sr., in the county circuit court some time past," Jenkins said, "and I have figured the interest on each so we can pay it now."

"I will have to get Captain Bennett to carry it on down," Mary went on. "Would you be so kind to write the letter for me, Mr. Weichmann? You have such a legible hand. Mine is so cramped and scraggly. And I seem to have forgotten my eye glasses."

Weichmann smiled and sat down. He took pen in hand and wrote at Mrs. Surratt's dictation:

Surrattsville, Md., April 14th, 1865
Mr. John Nothey
Sir:
I have this day received a letter from Mr. Calvert intimating that either you or your friends have represented to him that I am not willing to settle with you for the land.
You know that I am ready and have been waiting for these last two years; and now, if you do not come within the next ten days, I will settle with Mr. Calvert and bring suit against you immediately.
Mr. Calvert will give you a deed on receiving payment.
M.E. Surratt
Administratrix of John H. Surratt

Zad Jenkins examined Weichmann's handiwork. He had Weichmann add the words "have been" to the second paragraph. He nodded his agreement with the finished product. About that time there was a ruckus out in the yard, and Captain Bennett Gwinn drove up. He had been in Upper Marlboro for court day.
Jenkins stepped out on the porch. "Hey! Gwinn! Ben Gwinn!" He waved him to come over.
Gwinn got down from his carriage, and walked over. "Hey, Zad. What is up?"
"Come inside. Mary has to rattle Nothey about this land deal. He has welched on everything y'all did last Tuesday."
"Oh, dear, no!"
Mary showed the legal papers and the reply to Captain Gwinn and asked him to carry it all over to Nothey and read it to him. The papers could be transferred to Calvert and picked up by Nothey with a deed when he paid.
"I will do it, but not until Monday. My wife is more unwell than ever and I must attend to her. But you can rely on me. Please, allow me to help you to your carriage."
Weichmann went out and turned the carriage fifth wheel so that Mrs. Surratt could get her skirts past the road wheel.
"Hold on!" Gwinn said. "Look at that spring. It has pulled loose from the axle. I am glad we caught that. Y'all could have had a nasty accident going over all those hills and hollows on the way back to the City. Joe Knott!" The barkeep was coming across the road from the barn." Get a shank of light rope. We have a spring to tie."
Knott waved and went back to the barn. He returned with the rope. Gwinn began to tie the spring to the axle, carefully weaving the rope over and over itself.

"See how this is done, young man?" he said to Weichmann. "You finish it and tie it off with a couple of half-hitches. I am going home to sit with my wife. Good day, all." He touched two fingers to the brim of his hat, mounted his gelding and was away.

A few minutes after Gwinn left, in drove John M. Lloyd. The carriage skidded and fishtailed as he brought the speeding horse to a stop. He never applied the brake and nearly flipped the rig over. But it righted with a bang, after balancing a precarious moment on two wheels. He leaped down with a whoop. He was obviously very drunk.

"Mr. Knott, do you know how to tie this off?" Weichmann asked.

"Sure, sonny, let me have the rope and I will fix it so you can get back safely."

Weichmann walked over to the house, carefully cleaning his hands, rubbing them together without benefit of soap. He hated to be unkempt. Behind him the wind picked up. It was cold and smelled wet. It would storm before they got back tonight, Lou opined.

He went into the house. Although there were as many as ten to fifteen men in and out of the public barroom and sitting on the north porch, the parlor on the private side of the house was empty. Lou went to the back and looked in the attached kitchen. No one there but Mrs. Offutt. She walled her eyes when Weichmann passed. Outside, John Lloyd was trying to sing, as he clumsily brought baskets of oysters and fish around from the carriage in the front yard to the stoop in back. He had got them at Upper Marlboro. Tiring of his inept musical attempts, he began to rant and rave to no one in particular.

"I got stabbed I did, some time ago by *Mister* Edward Perrie. I will be dammed if they did not hear the case. Now that is *justice*, ain't it? Perrie got it put off 'til November session. What a damned, foul-up court! You call that *justice*? I never see'd such a court!"

"Well, well, well. Speak of the Devil and his Imps will appear."

Lloyd turned on his unsteady legs, nearly falling over. "Sh-h-h-!" he said upon seeing Mrs. Surratt standing there. He put his finger to his lips--or he tried to and hit the side of his nose, instead.

"Mr. Lloyd, sir! You are drunk. I do not abide drunkards, sir. My late husband was one, you know! Now you attend to me, sir! There will be some parties that come by tonight and pick up those shooting irons--you know? The ones in the storeroom?"

"Yes'm," Lloyd said, suddenly cold sober. He shivered in the approaching storm's cool wind.

"And furthermore, sir, I have another item in this package you are to give out tonight, too! And have a couple of bottles of whiskey handy. It looks like a cold night to be out in."

"I-I-I am mos' sorry, Mrs. Surratt. Truly I am. Why do y'all not stay for dinner? It promises to be a good'n; fish an' ersters."

"No, thank you, sir. I must be going. Do not forget your responsibilities tonight, y'hear?"

"Yes'm, yes'm, yes'm," he began to sing his answer, grinning and winking at his departing landlady. "Her old man was drunk all the time, too, eh?" he mumbled to himself as he turned once again to his fish and oysters. "Hell, I bet she drove him to it, the sanctimonious old shrew. She plays with them church beads so intensely! I bet he did not have an understanding sister-in-law like me, either, to hone them horns down. I 'low I would not know what I would do without Emma."

Ignoring Lloyd's mumblings, whatever they were, Mrs. Surratt met Weichmann at the back door, which he politely held open for her to pass through. They said their good byes to Mrs. Offutt at the kitchen door and went out into the back yard. The rope repair to the axle completed, Lou escorted Mrs. Surratt back to the carriage and they drove off into the rain and headed for the nation's capitol.

"You know, Mrs. Surratt, Mr. Booth does not appear to be with employment, lately. Do you reckon he will act, again?"

"Oh, no, Mr. Weichmann. Mr. Booth is done with acting. He is going to New York very soon, never to return."

"In truth?"

"Yes, sir. Mr. Booth is quite crazy on one subject, and I 'low as how I am going to give him a good scolding the next time I see him."

"What. . . ?"

"Drive on, Mr. Weichmann. We must try to get home by 9 o'clock. I have an appointment."

"Who is it with…? Mr. Booth?"

"Now, now," Mrs. Surratt said soothingly, patting his arm, "that is my affair, no one else's."

Just before reaching the forts at the top of Good Hope Hill, they were passed by the cavalry pickets, coming in as the old man had promised. Weichmann reached out and gently stroked the horses' rumps as the mounted men passed.

About a mile from the City, just past the forts, the full glory of the capital burst forth, a flash of light in the dark night, made more so by the illuminations celebrating the final Union victory in the East.

"Is this not fantastic?" Weichmann exclaimed.

Mrs. Surratt threw up her hands. "I am afraid all this rejoicing will be turned into mourning, and all this glory into sadness."

"What do you mean by that?"

"After every day of sunshine there comes a storm. I fear that our people are too proud and licentious. God will punish them as a just retribution for their sins."

They recrossed the Navy Yard Bridge a few minutes after the cavalry, just after the 9 p.m. curfew. But not to worry, Weichmann knew the password and counter sign--Tee Bee, Tee Bee Road.

"We are coming in from Tee Bee," he said to the guard's query. "By the Tee Bee Road."

Mary Surratt made a note of the passwords and how they were used. Mr. Booth and his people would have need of them later.

9. Booth Arrives at the Theater

As Booth came away from Mary Surratt's Town house, he had just enough time to get back to the theater to coordinate the assassination. Her trip had proved vital to the success of the night's events. The guns and the field glasses were ready, Weichmann had revealed to her the passwords for crossing the bridges that night, and she had discovered from that talkative farmer that the stationary and roving patrols would be withdrawn by 8 o'clock. With this bit of information, he would to be able to clear the City and, with Herold's help, get all the way to Baltimore, perhaps even New York City, by morning. Herold would bring Paine along. But if they got separated, Paine would have to be sacrificed, just like Atzerodt. But he had to have Herold. Only he knew the roads.

Booth knew that Atzerodt would not kill Johnson. Even if he got a shot off, chances were that Johnson would simply knock him down bare-handed and sit on him until the police arrived. More than likely, the little German would sit in a bar, befuddled, doing nothing. That is why Booth had pulled Herold over after the Canterbury meeting and asked him to plant an item in Atzerodt's room. It was Booth's black overcoat with a bank book in his name showing a balance of $445. Let Atzerodt explain how these items were not his and he did not know how they got there. Booth even told Herold to keep Atzerodt's key, to limit his access to the room.

"It will be our little joke," Booth assured Herold, with a wink.

Then he went to dinner with Lucy and the rest of her National Hotel entourage. On his way out of the National Hotel, he deposited his room key with the desk clerk, George W. Bunker.

"Are you going down to Ford's Theater tonight?" Booth asked him.

"No, sir. I reckon not."

"You ought to go. Take my word for it, there is going to be some splendid acting there tonight."

Booth walked down to Ford's, took his horse out of the make-shift stable and rode over to Surratt's. When he arrived, he hallooed for the mulatto half-wit, Dan. He might fool that idiot Weichmann, Booth thought, but he knew that Dan was as good an actor as there was off the stage. Dan took the mare's reins and Booth went up to talk to his mistress, Booth's most important informant.

Fresh from Mrs. Surratt's, in possession of the passwords for crossing the Navy Yard Bridge, Booth walked his horse into the L-shaped Baptist Alley off F Street, that led to the stage door behind Ford's. The mare was still traveling sideways, her rump threatening to pass her front. Booth straightened her out, stopped her, and slid to the ground. The mare shied back a little as Booth threw the reins over her nose and led her forward.

"Ned!" he called. "Ned Spangler!"

An actor, J. L. Debonay, appeared.

"Tell Spangler to come out and hold my horse."

"Hey, Johnny," Spangler said from the doorway as he stepped into the dim light shooting out from backstage into the alley. The former carpenter, who had helped to construct the Booth's Tudor Hall, was a jovial, eager-to-please, red-headed man of middle height, sporting perpetually unshaven whiskers that never seemed to grow into a beard.

"Will you help me, Ned?"

"Yes. I will get some one to hold your horse. I am too busy with the stage production. Get Peanut John for me will you, Mr. Debonay? I have no time. Mr. Gifford is out front of the theater and all the responsibility of the scene lies on me." Debonay disappeared into the darkness of the theater.

Booth followed Debonay into the theater a step or two, still holding the reins, nearly bumping into John Burroughs coming out in response to Ned Spangler's call.

"Hold Mr. Booth's mare, Johnny, like I told you earlier." Burroughs hesitated and looked back at the door. "Do not worry. If there is anything wrong, you can lay the blame on me."

Burroughs took the reins. He was worried. Earlier that afternoon, as he and Spangler had worked on removing the partition from the Presidential Box, Spangler had, out of the blue, exclaimed, "Damn the President and General Grant!"

"What are you damning the man for--a man that has never done any harm to you?"

"Hell, he ought to be cursed--both of them--when they got so many men killed for no good."

And now Burroughs was holding a horse for a Rebel like Spangler. But Ned was mild compared to Booth; that much Burroughs knew. He sat on the carpenter's bench beside the rear door. No need to stand. He could be there a while. The mare nipped at his sleeve and he slapped her sharply on the snout. She backed up several feet, but Burroughs got her to step forward again so he could sit. She nuzzled him some, but she did not try to bite him again.

Inside the theater, Booth asked Debonay if he could cross the stage.

"No, John. It is the dairy scene. It runs clear back to the rear wall. You will have to use the tunnel under the stage."

Booth went down the stairs, crossed under the stage, and came back up on the other side. He went out the side door into the Star Saloon. Sitting near the bar were Frank Burns, Lincoln's coachman, and Charles Forbes, a White House valet-messenger. Across the table from them sat John Parker, the president's body guard. Many have found Parker's absence from the door outside the President's Box outrageous, but in those days during the Civil War, security, both in closeness of mouth and personal protection of governmental officials, was in its infancy. Parker really had no duties from the time Lincoln entered the box until he emerged after the play.

"Brandy!" Booth yelled over the din of the intermission crowd. He shouted so forcefully that many thought him drunk. He was merely throwing his voice. Booth might be in liquor, but he was sober enough to handle the task at hand. Booth downed his drink quickly in a gulp or two. He looked at the clock over the bar, and waked rapidly through the front door to the street. Lincoln's presidential coach was parked down the block. Booth walked over to the front door of the theater. The doorman, J. E. Buckingham, was standing in the doorway, facing toward the lobby. His right arm blocked entry from the outside.

Booth playfully grabbed a couple of Buckingham's fingers and shook them. "You will not want a ticket from *me*, will you, Buck?"

Buckingham looked back over his shoulder and smiled. "I guess not, Mr. Booth."

Booth entered the lobby and looked at the clock. Thirty minutes or so to go. He checked out the stairway to the dress circle. He would have to go up and pass behind the audience all the way across the room to the hallway entrance to Lincoln's box. Booth went down the stairs, nodded to Buckingham, and walked out to the curb. He saw Henson and an accomplice. Booth walked up to them and smiled.

"Everything is set. Le's get to it." Henson called down the street, "ten o'clock!" Off on the corner of Tenth and F another man waved and flashed a hooded lantern toward the Treasury building.

For the next twenty minutes, this procedure of Henson, checking the time and calling it out to his accomplice who relayed the message down the street toward the west, continued. Booth meanwhile, his nerves strung taught, tried to appear calm, far too calm, while awaiting the hour to strike. He walked up to Buckingham, borrowed a chaw of tobacco, talked to Henson and his friend, asked Buckingham the time and checked it out against the theater clock, threw his chaw into the street way too soon for the flavor to have been exhausted from it, refused an offer from Mounted Police Captain Willie Williams (who would later be one of his more active pursuers) for a free drink at Taltavul's, only to show up in the bar by himself a while later, drinking and checking the clock in the saloon.

"Here is to the greatest Shakespearean actor in America," said one patron, recognizing Booth as he stepped up to the bar.

"You mean Edwin Booth?" joshed another.

"Oh, Hell no," came back the first. "I mean Junius Brutus Booth, Sr."

"You know that I am J. Wilkes Booth," an irritated Booth snapped.

"Oh, really? Well, whoop-dee-doo. You will never be the actor your father was, sonny boy."

Booth got a grip on his temper and down his whiskey in one swallow. "When I leave the stage, sirs, *I* will be the *most famous* man in America-- you can *lay* to that!" He stormed out onto the boardwalk.

"Twenty minutes past ten!"

Booth walked past Henson towards the theater. He nodded his head. Henson did the same. Then Henson turned and, with his friend, disappeared forever into Clio's ethereal pages.

Without looking back, Booth walked into Ford's, past doorman Buckingham. He winked. Buckingham remembered that he was humming a little tune. Inside, he softly sang the words:

'In 1865, when Lincoln shall be king!'

10. Lewis Paine Prepares for the Fray

The piece of paper read "Mary J. Gardner, 419."

She and her sister were billed as singers and dancers at the Canterbury Music Hall. Powell had caught her eye while he, Booth and the others had plotted to do in the important members of the Lincoln government. She had been *real* appreciative to the tall Floridian when they spoke and mentioned that if he would come around to her room at the Lichau House later that evening, say after 5 o'clock, they could have an especially enjoyable time. Powell reckoned that she would charge a fortune for such "private entertainment," but she ought to be worth it. Hell, it was Booth's money, anyhow.

After he had arranged his rendezvous with Miss Gardner, Powell had walked back up to the Herndon House to close out his account.

"Hello, Mr. Kincheloe," Mrs. Martha Murray, the owner's wife and erstwhile manager had said. She was one of hundreds of Washingtonians who covertly supported the Confederacy. In her case, it was by quietly arranging for a night's--or a week's, or a month's--stay for a multitude of suspicious people, men and women, who seemed to be traveling a lot between unknown destinations. They would stay a few days, disappear for a while, and return, always asking for a room. She kept several rooms empty to be ready for these unexpected guests, and was paid a bonus by the grateful travelers for her trouble. Just like the Branson's up in Baltimore and, to a lesser degree, Mrs. Surratt's in the City.

"I am here to close my account, ma'am," Powell said.

"Oh! Well, now, Mr. Kincheloe, we will be mighty sorry to lose you."

Mrs. Murray meant that. Powell was a quiet, clean tenant, who never complained. He was on time for meals and knew the Surratts and Miss Anna Ward. These were good recommendations. All fine Christian people. Fine Southern people. Which meant loyal, *Confederate* people to Mrs. Murray.

"I must leave for Baltimore tonight, ma'am. I will clean out my possibles now and leave as soon as I can partake of supper. If that is permissible--I mean, can I be served earlier than the rest?"

"Certainly, sir. I will step into the kitchen and arrange it immediately. When you return from collecting your belongings you can eat it right here in the dining room, if you do not mind eating alone."

"Thank you, ma'am," Powell said as he left to go up the stairs.

Mrs. Murray stared at his back a while and decided that she would have to deny that she knew the Surratts and Miss Ward. Had never seen any of them. As for Mr. Kincheloe, whoever he really was, he sat in his room and had no visitors. Not even that actor fellow, John Wilkes Booth. My! But was he a caution! He made a woman's heart flutter so. Always said the right thing, just so correctly that it made you wonder why you wasted all your life with other cruder, less attentive men. Reckon that ought to satisfy the prying Yankee provost marshals and Mr. A. C. Richards' City Police. It was always wise to plan ahead for the ultimate interrogation. She looked at the clock. The police always liked to know the time things happened. She once heard one detective call it, "tying up loose ends." He was looking for Mr. Howell, I believe. Or was he calling himself "Spencer" then? Oh, well! Mrs. Murray smiled and went to the kitchen to find Mr. Kincheloe's supper.

Powell dismissed the thoughts of his dinner and room check-out from his mind as he climbed the stairs to room 419. Fortunately for the success of the evening, Mary Gardner would see his heavy Whitney revolver and "sure 'nuff" Bowie (the latter having engraved on the blade, "The Hunter's Companion--Real Life Defender") as phallic symbols, rather than the potentially dangerous weapons they really were. He spent the next four hours literally in the lap of luxury, as Mary Gardner skillfully took him to heights of ecstasy in a multitude of ways he had never experienced before.

At just after 10 o'clock that night, Herold and Powell reined in their horses opposite 17 Madison Place, then popularly called $15^1/2$ Street, across from Lafayette Park, guarded by the bronze equestrian statue of Andrew Jackson.

"Now, Mosby, you know what to do?"

"Yeah," Powell said. "I go up and give the package to the doorman after he lets me in."

"No, no!" Herold remonstrated. "You tell whoever answers the door that you have a prescription from Dr. Tullio Verdi, their family physician."

"Who? What kind of a name is that?"

"Oh, Hell! Just say 'Dr. Verdi.' You can remember *that*, cain't you?"

"Dr. Ver' dee," Powell repeated, trying to instill the name in his mind.

"Dr. Ver' dee. I have a *pre*-scription from Dr. Verdi."

"Right! But be sure *not* to give the servant the package. You must give it to Seward personal. Why?"

"Because it has instructions I have to say to him, myself."

"Good! Now can you remember all that?"

"Yeah, I got it. How am I to find the right room?"

"Come on! The servant will *take* you there to give the oral instructions."

"Oh! . . . Yeah! Well, here goes nothing," Powell said with a grin, as he tossed Herold his reins.

The big man ambled loosely across the street and up the walk to the front door. He twisted the bell handle that was embedded in the center of the oak portal. Silence. Powell rang again. This time he heard footsteps coming inside. The door opened to reveal a small black man, smartly dressed in a dark suit and matching neck tie.

"Yes, sir?" William Bell asked.

"I am from Dr. Verdi. I have a *pre*-scription for Mr. Seward."

"Thank you, sir. I will take it up." Bell reached for the package.

"I reckon *not*." Powell drew the package back with his left hand. His right hand was in his coat pocket, gripping the handle of the Whitney revolver. "I have to give it to him personal-like. I must give him particular instructions face-on. I must go up."

"Well, sir, Mr. Seward is asleep, now. He cannot be disturbed. He is injured, as you know."

"I must see him. Dr. Verdi said I must do it personal."

"I have my orders, sir. I cannot admit anyone. If you would give me the medicine, I will guarantee Mr. Seward will receive it when he wakes. You can give me the instructions and I will tell him for you."

"That will not do. I am going up!"

Powell boldly strode past Bell in the open doorway. In the entry hall he could see the ornate stairwell to the upper floors. He started for the stairs. Bell quickly moved around the big man and tried to block his way. But Powell kept moving forward, causing Bell to mount the stairs in front of him. He went up backwards, keeping his face on the intruder.

"I am sorry, sir. I hope I have not offended you." There was no way to stop Powell, and Bell now sought to protect himself from any repercussions. A black man could get in a heap of trouble contradicting a white man, no matter the justice of his case. Bell had been at this job only three months. He liked it and did not wish to loose it through some unintended indiscretion.

"That is alright," Powell said kindly. "I know you are just doing your job."

"Please, sir," Bell remonstrated. "Please walk lightly. You stomp the stair too heavily. We do not wish to wake Mr. Seward. He sleeps so lightly and not often enough. He hurts so."

Powell tip toed up the next flight, headed for the third floor. When they reached the landing, a tall, fairly thin man with bushy side whiskers confronted Powell.

"I am Fred Seward. What do you want here?"

"I need to see Secretary Seward. I have medicine for him."

"You cannot see him," Seward said firmly. "He is asleep. Give me the medicine and I will see that my father receives it."

"That will not do," Powell said. "I must see him."

"You cannot see him."

"But I must see him. I have instructions."

Suddenly a door opened a crack. Fanny Seward, the Secretary's daughter looked out. Fred Seward and Powell looked over at her, Powell standing at Seward's right hand, nearer the banister. She stared at Powell, a handsome stranger with black hair, dressed in shiny new boots and a light hat and linen duster overcoat.

"Fred," she said quietly, "Father is awake now."

Fred gave her a pained look, one that puzzled, and then alarmed, Fanny.

"Is the Secretary asleep?" Powell asked. The tone of his voice seemed harsh and full of unnecessary determination to Fanny.

"Almost," she muttered.

Fred grabbed the door handle and pulled it to. Quickly, way too quickly. That *had* to be Seward's sick room.

"You cannot go in," Seward insisted. "Leave the medicine and the instructions with me. If you cannot leave it with me you cannot leave it at all. I am in charge here."

"Very well, sir," Powell said. "I will go."

Powell sighed, seemingly resigned to leave. He turned on the landing and began to descend the stairs. Bell was already on the stairs in front of him, intent on escorting him back to the front door.

"Please, do not walk so heavy, sir," Bell warned, once again.

Powell had taken perhaps three steps, when he turned and charged up at Fred Seward, the Whitney revolver in his hand.

"Damn you!" he shouted. He put the gun to the astonished Fred Seward's head, and pulled the trigger. Nothing happened! The gun had dry-fired. Seward reached for Powell, fully intending on pushing him down the stairwell. Powell, not trusting to pull the trigger again, struck Seward on the head, bringing the barrel down again and again with vigor. Seward staggered and fell, blood gushing from his head, his skull cracked open. Bell took one look over his shoulder and ran down to the first floor and out the front door. He never even saw Herold as he ran past him, headed for the provost marshal's headquarters a block away.

"Help!" he screamed. "Help! Murder! Help!"

Herold panicked. Already soldiers were looking his way. He got down and tied the big brown to a tree limb. Then Herold sprang up onto his steed's back, and kicked him in the sides. Mosby would have to fend for himself! He cut around two sides of the treasury building and turned onto Pennsylvania Avenue. Herold was admiring the smooth single-foot gait of his red-gray roan. He liked his unpretentious name too, "Charley." Suddenly, his reverie was disturbed by a sharp voice.

"You there! Get down off my horse! You have ridden him long enough!"

"Well, for crying out loud," Herold said softly to himself. "Fletcher! Standing in the middle of the whole damned street, just like he owns it!"

Herold pulled Charley to the left and thundered up to F Street. There he turned right, leaving a winded Fletcher in his wake. He was headed to rendezvous with Booth at Mrs. Surratt's.

"Damn! Herold shook his head. What a mess!"

He kicked Charley into a ground-eating, racking lope, nearly crashing into Booth and his flighty mare as they came charging out of Baptist Alley.

11. Booth Kills Lincoln

Booth took the stairs to the lobby of the dress circle two at a time. He felt good, light-hearted. The hour had come, all that he had worked for so long. He and he *alone*, would now strike the most important blow for the Southern cause ever struck during the whole war. It would be a victory that would surpass all that General Robert E. Lee had ever accomplished during years in the field. Booth would not kill or wound thousands of Yankees, as had Lee and his army. Booth would fire but a single shot from his Derringer pocket pistol at one man. It would be the most important bullet fired in the whole war.

That one bullet would destroy the heart of the Northern tyranny that Abraham Lincoln represented. It would be vengeance for all those who had died or were maimed wearing the gray; for all those mothers, widows, and orphans who had lost their sons, husbands, and fathers; for all those innocent persons whose property had been illegally seized by Lincoln's crooked government jobbers or destroyed by his marauding armies; for all those civilians arrested and held without charges, who had rotted illegally, in violation of their constitutional rights to free speech and assembly, in the infamous Yankee Bastilles; for all the men and women of the two nations, North and South, who suffered at the hands of the greatest miscalculator ever to hold the office of the American Presidency.

The Robinarch had called the South's bluff. He had thought they would not fight. Well, they had showed differently. And now Booth would fire the only shot that should have ever been fired. The one that should have been fired at Baltimore in 1861, the one that would have prevented it all from happening, this whole damned, worthless war that this two-bit shyster railroad lawyer had wanted all along as an excuse to install Henry Clay's constantly rejected "American System," to free the enslaved and enslave the free as a part of his so-called "New Birth of Freedom." This was his "more perfect Union," the one that would condemn the newly liberated slaves to live in perpetual second-class freedom, as hirelings on a land still owned by their masters and destroyed by Yankees. But those masters would be controlled by Northern invaders by granting the ex-slaves the right to vote and thus limiting Southern white political control.

Booth walked rapidly to a point where he could see the whole dress circle. No one noticed him. All eyes were focused on the stage. He would have to sidle along the rear wall behind the seats. Actually, the seating provided for patrons of nineteenth century theaters was mostly various styles of moveable chairs. The back row was a luxury for long legged men. They could push their chairs back into the aisle behind them and tilt the chair backs against the chair rail along the wall. Booth politely excused himself as he moved along, headed to his right, always closer to the little door that led into the hall behind the Presidential Box.

As he moved along, Booth could hardly believe his eyes. There was no one blocking the entrance to Lincoln's box. No guard, no aide, no one at all! Booth stepped down to the door.

"Who are you, sir?" The voice came from Lincoln's valet, Charles Forbes, recently returned from his intermission drink and sitting on the end of the nearest row. He rose to confront Booth.

Booth flashed his million-dollar smile and handed Forbes his card d'visite. "Wilkes Booth. I have been asked to join the President and his entourage in their box to enhance their enjoyment of the play. I provide a running commentary, you know, being an actor and all."

Forbes looked at the card and puzzled a moment. No one had said anything about visitors, but he knew Booth and. . . . He handed the card back to Booth and waved him on. Booth smiled again. As he did, a few favorite lines from *Richard III* raced through his mind:

Why, I can smile, and murder whiles I smile,
And cry 'Content' to that which grieves my heart,
And wet my cheeks with artificial tears,
And frame my face to all occasions. . .
And set the murderous Machiavel[li] to school.

Booth opened the door to the hall behind the boxes casually, stepped in, and closed it. He reached down into the corner behind the door and pulled out the modified music stand leg. He jammed it into place. Now he was locked in. No one could interfere with the task at hand.

The hallway was as black as a tomb at first. Booth stood a moment and let his eyes grow accustomed to the dark. When they had adjusted, the glow that filtered in through the hole he had widened in the door to the box proper appeared like a beacon. Booth crouched, drew the Derringer out of his waistcoat pocket and peered through the hole. Lincoln was directly in front of the door, blocking it. Booth could see the back of his head over the rocker in which he sat. Next to him was Mary Todd Lincoln in a straight backed chair. They were holding hands. But the door to the other side of the box was open!

Booth shifted to his right, still in the hall. Over on a settee against the far wall sat Clara Harris, next to her was Major Henry Rathbone, her fiancé, an adopted member of the Harris family, who had been raised as her step-brother. Booth could not see him, just the extended blue trouser and boot that represented his right leg. They had been last minute replacements for General and Mrs. Grant--no one else of higher social standing would accept an invitation from Mrs. Lincoln-- this night. Her repute for having a nasty temper had preceded her.

Booth fingered the Derringer and listened. A woman's voice floated up from the stage. It was Helen Muzzey in the role of stuck-up, money-hungry Mrs. Mountchessington. It was her daughter whom she hoped to marry off to the wealthy American Cousin, Asa Trenchard, played by Harry Hawk. He had just revealed that he was stone broke, having given all his money to the heroine, played by Laura Keene. This fact altered his reception by the Mountchessingtons, considerably for the worse.

"What!" The marriageable Mountchessington daughter yelped. "No fortune!"

"Augusta! To your room!"

"Yes, Ma. The nasty beast!"

"I am aware, Mr. Trenchard, that you are not used to the manner of good society, and that alone, will excuse the impertinence of which you have been guilty!" She flounced off the stage after her daughter, all in a huff, leaving Hawk standing alone. The scene was ready. Booth was about to alter the text of *Our American Cousin*, for all time. Hawk gave the line for which Booth waited--the last words that Lincoln would hear in this life.

"Don't know the manners of good society, eh?" Hawk bellowed. "Well, I guess I know enough to turn *you* inside out, old gal--you sockdologizing old man trap!"

The audience roared. Lincoln laughed along with them. So did the rest of the parties in the box. Booth could hear them over the merriment of the crowd.

Now! Booth slid through the open door and to the left. Major Rathbone saw him out of the corner of his eye, but was momentarily transfixed by the rapidness of Booth's unexpected move. Booth extended his arm. The pistol was less than a foot behind the President's head. Lincoln turned his head to the left, as if he felt Booth's presence. There was a report, dull and hollow-sounding. The box filled with black powder smoke. Big bullet;

small charge; maximum damage. Lincoln's head dropped forward and he rocked in the chair from the sharp impact of the .44 caliber lead sphere. The President was mortally wounded, the ball tearing through his brain, coming to rest behind his right eye.

"Sic semper tyrannus!" Booth shouted.

He used his best stage voice, and the words drifted over the stage and into the audience. Like Rathbone, the crowd sat there, unsure of what was happening, some thinking it was a part of the play. Booth dropped his Derringer, useless now that its one shot had been expelled, and drew his double-bladed knife. Rathbone was the first to recover. He leaped at Booth. The actor raised the dagger high above his head and brought it down at the major's chest. Rathbone parried the blow, but the long blade gashed his arm from elbow to shoulder. Rathbone staggered and reeled away.

Booth rushed between the Lincolns to the front of the box and forked over the rail. As he did, Rathbone grabbed his coat tail, ever so briefly. But it was enough. Booth lost his balance; his spur gouged the picture of President Washington and then got snagged in the Treasury Guards Flag that adorned the center of the box opening. As he descended, his black slouch hat fell from his head and lay on the boards. What should have been an easy drop to the stage, one he had made many times before in countless plays, became a dangerous fall. Booth landed hard, falling to the stage on all fours.

Something snapped in Booth's back, a searing pain ran along his lower spine and across his hip. But there was no time for pause. He rose up, chagrinned at his clumsiness, and staggered to the front of the stage. He raised his arm high, theatrically, still holding his knife, red with Rathbone's blood.

"The South is avenged!"

"Stop that man! Catch him!"

It was Rathbone shouting from the edge of the box. Mrs. Lincoln's screams punctuated the major's plea.

"My husband has been shot!"

Some in the crowd began to move. John Wilkes Booth broke to far side of the stage, headed for the prompt entrance and the passageway to the back door. There beckoned his fiery mare and freedom.

In Booth's wake, Ford's Theater was in pandemonium. Men shouted; women screamed; children cried.

"What?"

"Stop that man!"

"The President?"

"No, no. It was part of the play!"

"Well, then, down in front! Just sit down!"

On the stage, Harry "Yankee" Hawk stood paralyzed at the events that unfolded before him. Booth came tumbling out of the Presidential Box and fell on his hand and knees. Then he got up and faced the audience, and uttered what Hawk thought was, "The South shall be free." Booth then turned toward Hawk, knife in hand. Hawk recognized Booth immediately. He did not wait. Booth had once threatened to kill him over Hawk's sparking of Booth's whore, Ella Turner. To hell with their earlier handshake. Hawk wisely turned tail and ran off stage to a stair well and thundered up it. Booth swept by without a second look.

"My God!" Hawk gasped in astonishment, "that is John Booth!"

Booth waved his left arm frantically signaling Laura Keene and William J. Ferguson, who stood blocking the prompt entrance, to get out of his way.

"What is John Booth doing on stage in the middle of our American Cousin?" Keene wanted to know.

Before Ferguson could pull her out of the way Booth swept between them, so close that Ferguson could feel his hot breath, bumping Miss Keene's hand as he passed, yelling, "I have done it! The Robinarch is dead! I have done it, *at last!*"

Out front, the audience finally realized what had happened. It cried for vengeance. "Kill the actors!"

"Kill the goddamned Rebels!"

"Kill the traitors!"

At last, Laura Keene, not only the starlet of the play but the head of the company of players, came forward to the footlights. "Ladies and Gentlemen, please." Some of the crowd simmered down to hear, shushing the rest. "Ladies and Gentlemen, the President has been shot! For God's sake, have presence of mind and keep your peace, and all will be well!"

With these words, the riot was on again. Keene hurried to get water to take to the President's box, as requested by Clara Harris. Several men in the crowd came up on stage. One of them, Joseph B. Stewart, a tall, burly man (the kind that Sam Arnold and Mike O'Laughlen had always warned Booth might interfere with any plot carried off in a theater), ran off through the prompt entrance in pursuit of the man who had jumped from the President's box.

By now most of the stage crew and actors knew that it was John Wilkes Booth who had addressed the crowd and fled. Many in the audience had recognized the prominent, athletic actor as the man who had jumped out of the President's box and addressed them from stage center, hand and arm raised with bloody knife brandished; point downward, in a classical fashion, before he fled.

"Which way?" Stewart yelled to Jacob Ritterspaugh, who had just been bumped out of the way by Booth.

"This way!" Ritterspaugh pointed down the aisleway, kept open so that actors might go between the stage and their dressing rooms or the green room.

Later, Ritterspaugh claimed that Edman Spangler, Booth's friend and drudge, slapped him in the mouth and muttered, "Do not say which way he went."

"What do you mean by hitting me?"

"Oh, for God's sake." Spangler shook his head in disgust. "Shut up!"

Out in front, they could hear the cry," Kill him! Kill him!"

Others yelled, "Burn the theater!"

After Booth barreled past Laura Keene and Willie Ferguson at the prompt entrance to the stage, he ran down the aisle. Orchestra leader, William Withers, stood in his way, angry because he and Miss Keene had had a tiff over when his specially-composed patriotic song was to be sung. Withers had been put off to the end of the production, instead of performing between acts, as once promised.

"Let me pass!" Booth shouted. "Let me pass!"

Withers had heard the shot that felled Lincoln, the thump as Booth leaped to the stage, and the shouting that followed. He was puzzled and still fuming over his exclusion from the between act performances. He stepped out of the way, but too slowly for the quick-moving Booth. He and Booth collided full force, spinning Withers around and around. Booth waved the knife at Withers, who took the blow in the left side of his coat. Booth swung at him again, this time the knife hit Withers in the neck.

"Damn you!" Booth shouted. He grabbed the cringing Withers and threw him mightily to the floor. Withers rolled out of the way past a stage flat.

Why in the world would Wilkes Booth want to kill me? What have I done to him? Withers wondered, bewildered. Examining his shredded coat, he noticed blood. The neck wound stretched for six inches along his shoulder. In years to come, he would be able to forecast the weather with ease, as his old wound throbbed with each rise and fall of the barometer.

Booth ran up to the back door into the alley. It had been opened, but now it was shut. He deftly felt for the door latch and pulled it open. He thought he heard someone running down the aisle past where Withers lay.

"Stop that man!" Stewart shouted.

"I think he has a horse at the door!" came another voice.

Booth leaped into the alley and slammed the door shut. On the far side, Stewart was at the door. Unfamiliar with the theater backstage, he felt for the latch in the dark, and wound up with the hinge side. He ran his hand over to the other side of the jamb and finally found the latch. Through the door, as he fumbled, he thought heard voices and the clatter of horse's hooves on cobble stones.

PART III

TENUOUS ESCAPES (1865)

I am pretty certain that we have assassinated the
President and fixed off Secretary Seward.
--John Wilkes Booth to John Lloyd, Surrattsville, April 14, 1865

All those God damned Booths are crazy!
--Fellow Actor Edwin Forrest, April 14, 1865

Oh, Mrs. Surratt, that vile woman! She has ruined me! I am
to be shot! I am to be shot! If the Surratts had not brought me
down here to run the tavern, I never would have
gotten into this difficulty!
--Tavern Keeper John Lloyd to his Captors, April 17, 1865

1. A Quick Stop at Mrs. Surratt's

Booth grabbed the steel stirrup and placed his left foot in it. As he reached for the saddle with his right hand, he saw that Peanuts had not yet released the reins.

"Give me that horse!" he snarled.

With his left hand he hit Peanuts in the solar plexus with the knife hilt. Peanuts dropped the reins. But the slashing motion had startled the bay mare, which immediately went white-eyed. She began to walk out to her off side away from Booth, threatening to drag him to the ground with his foot still stuck in the stirrup. He grabbed her mane and reins with his left hand and pulled himself upright, struggling to turn the animal to the left, which would help throw him into the saddle.

The mare responded and Booth got his seat. But the mare continued to spin around, as Booth kicked with his right leg and foot, trying to find the off stirrup. In the process, he accidentally kicked Peanuts, who had blundered into the mare's path, still gasping for air from the first blow Booth had given him. The circling horse threw rocks and gravel all over Peanuts and Stewart, who had just emerged from the theater.

Fortunately for Booth, Stewart had been delayed as he felt for the door handle on the wrong side in the dark entryway and came up with the hinges. Then he tried to push the door open, before realizing that it had to be pulled inward. Now Stewart leaped into the alley and reached for Booth's reins. The bay shied and backed into a corner made by the theater and another building. Booth spurred the mare forward. She made one last attempt to spin around and bumped Stewart away with her rump as she stamped past. Stewart turned to avoid her flying feet and Booth urged her forward and into the clear.

Booth charged down Baptist Alley and turned left out onto F Street, nearly colliding with another rapidly-moving horseman.

"Look out! . . . Davy Herold! What the Hell are you doing *here?*"

"Running from Fletcher, the stableman at Nailor's!"

"What? Where's Paine?"

"Who?"

"Mosby. Wood."

"I don't know! We went over to Seward's . . . ."

"Never mind! Follow me!" Booth kicked the little bay mare into a fast lope and cut up 9th Street, past the massive block of the Patent Office. His sleek black locks flew wildly in the wind.

Where the Hell is he going, now? Herold wondered to himself. We need to get out of town fast, the Feds are sure to close off everything mighty damned quick!

Up ahead, Booth could hardly contain himself. I got him! If the others play their parts as well, the whole Yankee government will be in a shambles for weeks! The Confederates can defeat Sherman in that time and turn on Grant before anything like equilibrium is restored to the Yankee command system. Dammit, I do not need any help or to be a subordinate part to anyone else's plan. I did it myself, all alone! I was the star, as usual! Top billing, again, for Mr. J. Wilkes Booth!

Booth turned his mare to the right and headed east on H Street. Herold knew where they were going. It had to be the Surratt boarding house, dead ahead. Booth pulled his mount up sharply, bucking to a rough stop in front of the three story gray house that he had been in so many times before. Herold's pacer calmly slid to a smooth stop behind him. Both men got down.

"Here, hold my mare," Booth said, throwing the reins to Herold. "She will not tie."

The door to the English basement opened up upon their arrival. The shadowy figure of Mary Surratt was visible inside the hall, next to the dining room.

"Come in Pet, but be very quiet," she whispered. "One of my servants sleeps in the kitchen. Lette, go in and check on Susan. See if she is still asleep." Olivia Jenkins left the room through the rear door.

"Who is this man?" Booth whispered with a snarl.

"He is one of us. This is Mr. Smoot. He is here seeking money for his boat. It is the one that you are supposed to use to cross the Potomac. Mr. Smoot, this is our agent, name of Pet."

Booth and Smoot shook hands. Booth decided to sell the idea that he was going south to the Potomac to Smoot and the Surratt household, beginning now. "I am in great need of your boat tonight, friend. Where exactly is it now?"

"I believe that it is still on King's Creek, a tributary of the Nanjemoy. The best place to get to it is from Colonel John Hughes' place off Nanjemoy Creek. It is called Indiantown."

"Indiantown...I know it! Herold can find it, I am sure. He is outside with the horses. Thanks, Smoot. Mrs. Surratt, is there a spare hat of John's around? I lost mine in the theater."

"I will see." She left by the hall door. Booth went to the sideboard and grabbed his pistols and holsters, which he buckled around his waist.

"Susan is still asleep, Auntie," Olivia Jenkins said, returning from the kitchen. "Auntie?"

Coming in from the hall, Mrs. Surratt held up her index finger to her mouth. "Thank you, dear. You may go up to bed, now." Lete quietly left by the hall door. "Mr. Booth, here is one of John's hats off the cloak hooks."

"Well, then we are off. Mr. Smoot, you are from Southern Maryland, I presume, so you might not wish to go back across the Navy Yard Bridge. That is where we are headed."

"I can go through Alexandria by way of the Long Bridge and take the ferry tomorrow."

"Godspeed, gentlemen," Mrs. Surratt said. "Now go!"

Outside, Herold could neither hear what was said nor who said it. But Booth was back in a flash, wearing one of John Surratt's slouch hats on his head, and sporting two holstered horse pistols about his waist. He took the reins from Herold and mounted the mare with some difficulty, as she skittered off to one side.

Once mounted, Booth looked about. "All right, Davy," he said, "le's hear it, all of it. Quick-like!"

"It was like I started to say, we went over to Seward's and I stayed outside holding the horses. I didn't dismount, just like you told me. Mosby knocked on the door and a black man answered. They went in and a couple of minutes later the servant came running back out screaming, 'Murder, help, murder.' So I got down and tied Mosby's horse to a tree and lit out past the President's house. You know, ol' Fletcher tried to stop me right on the Avenue. Claimed I had Charley here out past time."

"Did he?" Then Booth returned to the point at hand. "You abandoned a comrade, Davy?" Booth sounded incredulous.

"You bet I did! That little doorman ran straight to the provost marshal's house. They was soldiers coming from all over the place. But, I tell you, Johnny, he had to have killed Seward. They was so much noise and folderol that he had to have done it! I had to leave, lest they pick me up. Soldiers all over the place! How'd you do with Lincoln?"

"He's dead. I shot him right in the back of the head. The gun was not more than a foot away from him when I fired."

"That's grand, Johnny! You really done the job up right, just like you said you would. What about Plug Tobacco?"

"That coward," hissed Booth. "Somehow I bet he will not be coming. Or Mosby, either. Now, the password is Tee Bee and the countersign is Tee Bee Road. You got it?" Herold nodded his head affirmatively. "You give me five minutes head start and follow me to the

Navy Yard Bridge. Do not stand around here. Take another route than me. I am going to cut down to the Avenue on 6th and take the road past the capitol building on the south side. See you in Surrattsville. Le's skedaddle!"

Mrs. Surratt silently stood in the door, watching the two riders disappear in the dark, each in a different direction. Then she signaled Smoot the coast was clear. After he slipped out west down H Street, she closed the door and slowly climbed the stairs to the next floor. She entered her bedroom and sat in the fashionably cushioned boudoir chair. She stared into the darkness, random thoughts running through her mind. Booth had done the job. He had not kidnapped Lincoln, but he had taken revenge upon that Devil for all he had done to the nation the last four years. The burning, looting, arresting, of innocent civilians, the stealing of the slaves, the destruction of the old Union for something his advocates called the New Freedom.

Freedom they call it! Bah! What a country! Emancipating the black people to enslave the whites. And they call it *freedom*. The South had suffered grievously, under Lincoln's tyrannous rule, but Maryland had suffered even more. Four years under the boot heel of the Yankee army, becoming a laboratory for every idiot reform that the North had bred the last forty years, from abolition to sinful communal living to a half dozen no-account religions to Sylvester Graham's supposed extra-nutritional crackers. Where had the Founding Fathers and their Constitution promised we had to abide all that?

Well, Booth and his hangers-on might be able to run, but *she* could not. Where would she go, anyway? No doubt the authorities would be along soon, sometime tonight, or tomorrow at the latest. Booth had to be known as a visitor to their house. Then, it would be prison or the rope for all of us. She put her head into her hands and began to cry softly. She cried for the destroyed South, the reconstructed Maryland, the other conspirators, her children, herself. But she did not cry for President Abraham Lincoln. He got what he deserved, damn him!

Mary Surratt would not go to bed that night. She stayed up waiting in the dark for the police, fully dressed, sitting in her chair. At least she would go to her fate like a Southern lady, dressed properly, with grace, admitting nothing; in short, with style.

2. A Busy Night at the Navy Yard Bridge

It had begun to spit rain intermittently, but no one was in his way. Booth headed south, rapidly cutting down 6th Street, gaining the

Avenue at the National Hotel. Everything was quiet. Turning left again, Booth spurred his horse into a full gallop. He circled the Capitol to the south and took New Jersey down to Virginia Avenue. A few blocks later, he turned right into Eleventh Street and slowed his thundering steed as he approached the Navy Yard Bridge.

"Halt! Who goes there?" The voice of the sentry rang out loudly.

Thanks to Mrs. Surratt's previous journeys, Booth already knew that these men were from of the Third Massachusetts Heavy Artillery. The "Heavies," as the other soldiers called them, were special, extra large regiments of nearly 1800 men (as opposed to a normal regiment's 1000) trained to do double duty. As infantrymen they carried muskets and as artillerists they manned the big guns of the sixty-eight forts that surrounded wartime Washington. They lived a soft garrison life, slept in real beds, hardly marched at all, ate full rations, got lots of leave to visit the City to partake of its various vices and pleasures, and never had to fight the Rebs.

The other troops, especially combat veterans, hatefully envious of their soft billets, called them "Band Box" regiments, "Paper Collars," and "Abe's Pets." They were smugly arrogant in their superior position and they often got slipshod about rules and regulations. After all, constant guard duty was pretty boring, and besides the 3rd Massachusetts had political connections right up to one of Stanton's assistant secretaries of war to cover up mistakes. Indeed, like every other Confederate agent, Booth was counting on their lackadaisical attitude and a judicious use of the proper password supplied by Weichmann, through Mrs. Surratt. The key was to act commonplace. The war was practically over, anyhow, at least here in the East.

"Who are you, sir?" It was the sergeant of the guard, Silas Cobb of F Company, who spoke.

"My name is Booth." He gave his real name to draw the inevitable pursuit south while he fled the opposite direction to Baltimore and then by railroad to Etta in New York City.

"Where are you from?"

"From the City," Booth replied. The mare stamped her feet and threw her head in protest to the lengthening pause in her trip.

"Where are you going?"

"I am going home," Booth said. Now that was a nothing answer, Cobb thought. The mare shook her head as if to agree.

"Where *is* home?" Cobb pressed Mr. Booth.

"Charles," came the cryptic answer. The mare stamped impatiently, reflecting Booth's own inner testiness. These damned

Yankees! Every one acted snotty--like they all came over on the *Mayflower* in 1620, even this obviously Irish sergeant of 1848 genre. Of course Booth ignored his own heritage and did not apply his standard to himself. He acted as if his heirs had come over with the *Susan Constant* in 1607, not in 1821. But Booth kept a calm exterior. Twenty-seven years a bluenosed, native American did make.

Cobb assumed that Booth meant Charles County, Maryland, but wanted to know more.

"What town?"

"I do not live in town."

"But you must live in some town."

The sergeant was from Massachusetts with its numerous small towns. He never quite comprehended the Southern fashion of ignoring specific towns for the more vague county address. Although Cobb's education was too meager to express it in so sophisticated fashion, what he meant was that the South lacked civilization in the classic Roman sense of *civita*s or city dwelling. Everyone down here lived all by himself on his own little farm or larger plantation. If Booth were not in so big a hurry and could have read the sergeant's mind, he would have set Cobb straight, perhaps with a Shakespearean flourish, to boot. As it was, he settled for the sergeant's more mundane preference.

"I live close to Beantown. But I do not live in town."

"Why are you out so late?" Cobb wanted to know.

Booth was getting a bit perturbed at the sergeant's stubbornness. Would this damned fool never stop asking ignorant questions? The mare agreed. She snorted and shook her head trying to free the reins. Viscerally Booth hated the sergeant's Irish brogue modified by a down east, clipped, nasal accent, all of which lacked the beauty and unhurried roll of a Southern drawl. But Booth held his temper and displayed his well-known charm masterfully.

"The rule is that no one passes after nine o'clock."

Cobb's statement of rules jerked Booth back to the situation at hand.

"That's news to me," Booth said, acting puzzled. "I had somewhere to go in the City, and the night is dark, so I thought I would await the rising of the moon to light my way home. It came up about ten, you know. Surely, Sergeant, a man of your obvious qualities as a leader can make an independent judgment here. I am but a harmless, loyal Union man like you and the war is all but over. I wish to go to Beantown via Tee Bee."

Cobb chewed over Booth's words slowly. Ordinarily, no one would have been allowed to cross, but Booth was right. Lee's surrender had caused rules to be relaxed. At least Cobb thought so. Cobb often permitted persons to pass South across the Eastern Branch of the Potomac River. As Mrs. Surratt and her driver Weichmann had discovered but hours earlier, some guards even let people into the City against explicit regulations, especially if one of a carriage's occupants were female--be she pretty and young, or charming and matronly--or if one had a proper code word. Cobb's notion was that no one leaving could do much harm, but those coming in might still be Confederate agents or persons who hoped to cause some sort of mischief. But women he exempted. Nothing like a touch of gallantry. Hell, he's right, Cobb concluded, I am in charge here. Screw officers and their regulations. Besides he had the correct password.

"How did you say you would travel?"

"Tee Bee Road." That clinched it for Cobb--password and countersign.

After musing a little more over this calm man and his very nervous horse, Cobb waved and stood aside. "Go ahead."

"Thank you, sergeant." Booth touched heels to his mare and held her to a controlled trot as they entered the bridge. Cobb watched horse and rider disappear into the darkness.

Judging from the approaching clouds, it was more likely to rain than show the moon tonight, Cobb thought. That dandified idiot was no better than most officers. Didn't know enough to come in out of the rain. Never catch an enlisted man riding out in weather as doubtful as this. He'd better be careful, that fella Booth. That mare was a real handful, and would be even worse on a stormy night like tonight on a wet road--or what passed for roads in Maryland. Nothing like Massachusetts. Why we have roads that. . . .

"Halt!" The sentry had stopped a second horseman. "Hey, Sergeant, lookee here! This one's hardly old enough to ride without his momma." The others in the guard house laughed.

"Who are you, boy?" Cobb asked, trying to sound very gruff and official.

Davy Herold, seated on his red roan, which was old enough to seem much grayer in the light of the rising moon, decided not to use his real name.

"My name's Smith." The whole squad laughed.

"It *is*," Davy insisted.

"All right, *Mister* Smith," Cobb intoned in a bored fashion, "where are you going at this late hour?"

"I am going home--I live at White Plains."

"Come on over in the light of the guard house door, sonny, I want to take a better look at you." Well, thought Cobb, as he examined "Smith's" youthful face, at least he knows what a town is. But Cobb could not place this White Plains.

"What are you doing out at this late hour, anyway? I am not supposed to pass you after 9 p.m."

"How long has that rule been out?"

"Some time, ever since I have been here."

"Aw, fellas, c'mon."

"Why were you not out of the City earlier?" Cobb insisted.

"I been out with some bad company." Herold seemed to blush, visible even in the poor light of the door and the just-past full moon, as it peeked in and out among the passing rain clouds. "I wanted to get laid before going back to the country. You know." As Herold quietly mumbled the reason and his voice fell away, the squad could not hear.

"What'd he say?"

"He's been to get laid!" the sergeant repeated *sotto voce*, grinning widely.

One of the guard house privates called out, "he looks more normal than most--at least his story is!" The rest laughed. "Hey, Sergeant! We want to go and get laid!"

"Shut up!" Cobb snapped at the kibitzers." Where is this White Plains? How are you going? Which way?"

"By way of Tee Bee," came the reply, "on the Tee Bee Road."

"Yeah," Cobb agreed, turning back to Herold. "Go on through, sonny. *We* won't tell on you!" The squad laughed again. Herold laughed with them. So did Sergeant Cobb. Where *was* White Plains, anyhow? Huh! It was down near Beantown. Sure! He and that Booth were practically going to the same place. Odd. I wonder why. . . . But they had the password and countersign.

Still grinning, Davy Herold clucked Charley forward, distracting Cobb's thought. Instead, the Sergeant noted that the red-gray roan horse was not hot-blooded as the first man's bay. It also moved in a smooth, racking motion, sort of a single foot gait. Not the hot trotting gait that threatened to spring into a gallop at any moment, as Booth's horse had been. Gelding. Cutting them nuts deep always produced a better controlled animal, Cobb thought. A stallion was too hot for normal use. Gotta cut 'em deep. Brain surgery--right between his legs. Hell, a mare like that other fella's--what was it, oh yeah, Booth, he called himself--his mare was not much better than a stud, especially if she was in heat. . . .

"Halt!" The sentry's sharp voice brought Cobb out of his reverie.

What, again? Cobb mused. Awful busy tonight.

The new rider said he was John Fletcher, a stableman from the City, looking for a roan horse ridden by a very young man. A red roan, almost gray. The mane was black, with yellow highlights, and the body a steel reddish gray.

"Yeah," Cobb said, "the young fella--he passed through about ten, twenty minutes ago. Headed for White Plains. Racking out rather slow."

"Reckon I can catch him and be back in an hour or so, if I push it."

"If you pass, you cannot come back until daylight," Cobb warned. He had to enforce regulations sometime. That young boy was all right, Cobb thought silently. Give him a break.

"What?"

"I can let you out of the City but you cannot come back until after dawn. It is regulations, you know."

"What stupidity!" Fletcher hissed. "That man has stolen my horse! And the army worries about dumb rules. Hell, the war is over. Lee has surrendered, or don't you know?"

"*I* know, mister, but the muckety-mucks up on top don't care. Go track him down, if you please, but do not come back with him until dawn. Not unless you give the password."

"Password! What password? This is downright rediculous! I do not wish to be out all night!"

"Why don't you go to the police? Report it to them and let them hunt him down for you. When he comes back to town, they'll arrest him."

"Well, I might just *do* that," Fletcher growled. He turned back toward Washington and loped off. Cobb smiled and winked at the squad. God, but they loved that man. He always stood up for the young bucks that might get into a little, innocent trouble. Good ol' Sergeant Silas Cobb!

3. Carnage at Seward's

Even though Lewis Powell had pistol-whipped Fred Seward within an inch of his life, Seward would not release his grip on his assailant. The two men spun around, crashing into the banister, then the walls, in the process breaking the barrel latch that held the Whirney's rammer in place. The ramrod dropped down of its own weight, so that the next time Powell tried to thumb back the hammer, it fed into the revolving cylinder, effectively disabling the weapon. Powell could have disengaged the rammer--if he had had time to think. But he did not.

Finally, the two combatants slammed into the door of the elder Seward's sick room, sending it crashing from its hinges. Fanny screamed. All she could see was two shadows, one of which she knew to be her brother. The other flung Fred to the floor along with the disabled Whitney and drew a massive Bowie knife from his belt. It flashed in the dim light of the night lamp.

"Don't *kill* him!" Fanny yelled. At the word, "kill," the elder Seward awoke from his dozing sleep to witness the horror of the attack. It was as if some sort of ghost-like banshees were flying across the room in front of him.

Private George Robinson, a male nurse who was sitting up with Fanny as she watched over her father, ran to impede Powell's progress toward the bed, in which the stricken Secretary lay. Powell smashed him on the forehead with the knife butt. Robinson fell back tripping across Fred's outstretched legs. Powell leaped for the bedstead, shoving Fanny aside--he had not the heart to use the knife on a woman--straddling the Secretary of State. He stabbed at him several times. But the rush of the fight and the dimness of the room caused him to misjudge the location and size of the body. Each knife thrust missed its target, slashing Seward's cheek and neck, breaking the hematoma the doctors had been afraid to lance for fear of striking an artery. Blood flew all over the room, the victim, and the combatants.

Because of the carriage accident, Seward wore an immobilizing cast of hardened leather around his neck. Sparks flew in the dark as Powell's knife struck and slipped off of the leather apparatus and its metal stiffeners. Flying pillow feathers now added to the eeriness and gore of the slaughterhouse atmosphere of the room. By this time, Robinson was up again and on Powell's back, pulling him away from Seward. The Secretary either slipped intentionally, or was inadvertently dumped, on the floor on the far side of the bed. Powell put an elbow into Robinson's guts, freeing himself one more time from the nurse's grasp. He slashed at the gasping nurse, driving the knife into his arm twice, both times to the bone.

Meanwhile, another shadow ran into the room. At Powell's later trial, it was claimed that this man was Major Augustus Seward, Fred's older brother. But in reality, it was a State Department messenger,

Emerick W. Hansell, there by chance, on Department business. Powell saw, or rather felt, his presence and met him with a Bowie thrust to the rib cage. Hansell screamed and fell, choking on his own blood. He was luckier than he could have hoped. The knife had missed both lungs and his heart. He would bleed much, but recover, in time.

Attracted by the ruckus, particularly Fanny's screams, Major Seward now entered the room. Robinson, wounded but game as ever, had once again come to grips with Powell. Gus Seward could not believe the scene before him. In the dim light, he somehow figured that Robinson had gone berserk and was attacking his father. Gus Seward grabbed both Robinson and the strange shadow he did not recognize and shoved them both toward the door.

"For God's sake, Major," Robinson gasped out, "let go of me and take that knife out of his hand and cut his throat!"

Easier said than done. The mighty Powell twisted around with all his strength, dumping Robinson, striking Gus Seward on the head with his knife, and then nicking him in the arm. By this time, Powell found himself closer to the door than any of his assailants, most of who were in a pile on the other side of the room. He spun out the opening and thundered down the stairway, a little worse for wear, but lucky not to have more than a mild scratch or two on him.

At some time during the fight, a sobbing Fanny Seward had stumbled past the combatants into the hallway. She was in a daze, not fully comprehending the events she had witnessed. As Powell shot out of the room, she stood there, flanked by her equally astonished mother and sister, and watched him pass. Then the defenders of the Secretary of State, all except Hansell who lay in a pool of blood, stumbled out, one by one. Each was dripping blood and too exhausted to pursue.

"Is that man gone?" Fanny asked between her tears.

"What man?" Her mother replied, still not understanding what had happened.

"Where is Father?" Fanny rushed into the room and found the elder Seward lying on the other side of the bed, where he had fallen early in the struggle.

"Oh, dear Lord!" she screamed. "Father is dead!"

"No," William H. Seward's weak voice hoarsely rasped back. "I am not dead. I am alive. Close up the house--send for a surgeon! Get the police!"

Seward would survive his attack, his face and neck horribly mutilated. Hereafter, he would always sit for portraits showing his undamaged left side. But his wife, Frances, and the daughter named for her, Fanny, were not so lucky. Both would be dead within a year and a half, their physical declines spurred on by the psychic trauma of that horrible night.

Outside, Powell ran across to the big brown horse Herold had left tied to a tree. He paused, hunched over, hands on his knees, gasping for breath.

"That's him!" William Bell shouted. "He is getting on a horse!"

Powell untied his steed and mounted very slowly. The Bowie fell into the gutter with a clang. It would be found by a passer-by the next morning. Powell could hear feet, running boots, crunching in the gravel of the street. Soldiers! The provost marshal's guard. Coming to arrest him! Powell clucked to his horse and started off north, away from Bell and the soldiers.

"Stop!"

"Murderer!"

"Thief!"

"Stop that man!"

Voices came from all over Lafayette Park, people out for a late walk, now witnessing the end of the affair at the Seward home. William Bell was out ahead of the others, running for all he was worth. Powell finally realized the closeness of his escape. He put the spurs to his mount and racked up $15^{1/2}$ Street and onto Vermont Avenue. Bell stopped his pursuit at I Street, where Vermont began, too fatigued to take another step. Lewis Powell had disappeared in the darkness.

For generations, historians would claim that the rural-born Powell got lost in the confusing streets of Washington. But he did not. He was headed for Baltimore and the Confederate underground there. It was now too late to try and follow Booth to Surrattsville. He rode northeast on Vermont Avenue until he came to M Street. There he headed east to the Boundary Road, the last street on that side of the City. He passed the dozens of military hospitals and camps on the outskirts of Washington, headed out past Fort Bunker Hill, where he shed his blood-soaked linen duster without slowing. It would be found two and a half days later by a soldier of the 3rd Massachusetts Heavy Artillery.

Powell spurred his horse on, headed for the Bladensburg Road and the highway to Baltimore. But the big brown horse was growing weary. Powell was a heavy load, and the brown was not used to going full-out. Mudd's neighbor Gardiner had been a light-use rider. Powell was pushing him on like a well-conditioned cavalry mount. It was too much. In the dark, the pot hole was not visible. The brown's fore foot literally fell out from beneath him and down he went, throwing Powell into the drainage ditch. The big man hit the ground hard, cracking his head on a mostly buried rock, bared over the years by passing waters flowing over it.

Both horse and man lay there a while, too stunned to move. Finally the horse struggled into a sitting position and regained his feet with difficulty. Limping because of his sprained tendons and with a swollen fetlock joint, the one-eyed brown horse stumbled back to Washington, looking for home. The provost marshal's guard found him an hour or so after midnight, lathered in sweat, grazing near the Lincoln Barracks on the east side, at Capitol and 15th Streets, about half way to the stables he sought. They took him in with several other stray mounts and tied him out back of General Augur's headquarters, about a block from where his wild ride with Powell had begun. A short time later John Fletcher arrived, angrily muttering about horse thieves.

Powell lay in the ditch for some time. He was not unconscious, but he was not himself. His head spun around with vertigo. When he tried to rise, his stomach rebelled, and he dry-heaved. He had a hard time trying to think clearly, but he knew he had to get out of the road and under cover. He crawled over an old stone wall and collapsed prostrate under the meager shelter of a nearby tree. The rain began to come down in a light mist. He slept until the chirping of the birds and the warmth of the morning sun awakened him. He lay under the tree and tried to contemplate his situation. Across the field was a farmhouse with smoke issuing lazily from its chimney. He thought to go there but he could hear dogs barking. Were these people trustworthy? Would they turn him over to the provost marshal?

Out on the road, Powell could hear the approach of a cavalry patrol. Horses feet thudded rhythmically against the ground, accompanied by the creaking of leather, and the clanking of sabers, picket stakes, and tin cups. Yankee Cavalry always carried too much superfluous gear, he thought. Moved too noisily. Mosby always warned about loose gear rattling against the saddle. One could hear it for miles, especially at night or in the still of an early morning. Powell crawled into a furrow in the ground, where the farmer's plow had passed around the tree's roots. He lay flat, watching the patrol thunder past. Then the nausea and dizziness overcame him again. He lay there and fell asleep, the sun baking him dry after the previous night's sprinkling precipitation.

Late in the day, Powell awoke again. So far no one had seen him. He knew that he was not well. The dizziness had dissipated some, but he could rise only with difficulty. He had to find a friend, someone who he could rely on. Someone who would help him get away. Someone who could hide him from the Yankees. There was no way he could get to Baltimore in his condition. He would have to return to Washington. To the Surratt home on H Street. Mary Surratt would shelter him. She knew how to pass him along to other safe houses. She would help him get away. Powell looked pretty battered. He would have to pass as a laborer looking for work. He pulled off his coat, waistcoat and shirt. He cut a sleeve from his undershirt and made it do for a stocking cap. Powell struggled to his feet. It was getting dark. Perhaps he could keep to the shadows. He needed to find something to eat and drink. He splashed water from the ditch in his face, but he did not drink. Water had to be running or it would make you sick. That is what he was taught as a boy. He needed some clear water. He needed some food. He needed Mrs. Surratt.

4. O'Laughlen Misses Stanton

I gotta be crazy, Michael O'Laughlen thought to himself as he walked up 14th Street past the Willard Hotel. Sam is right; this whole project reeks with incompetentcy. Probably has no sanction from the Confederate government, either, no matter what Booth says. Hell, Sam had been right all along. First the theater botch up, then the mess on Seventh Street at Campbell Hospital. But I gave Booth my word of honor to help him nearly two weeks ago, on a moment's notice, when I came down and he proposed my part in this whole deal. Johnny Surratt and that woman that goes with him, Nettie Slater, passed through to tell Canada what was going on. I tried to get Sam to come along, then, but he was on his way to Fortress Monroe, to be a clerk at the sutler's there. Said he would write Booth and give him his feelings, as if Booth cares much about anything that Sam says.

So me'n three others, Bernard Early, Edward Murphy, and Ensign Jim Henderson, come on down on the Thursday evening train to see the illuminations. It was Henderson's idea, he was Yankee to the hilt, being in the U.S. Navy and all. Got here on that 3 o'clock train out of Baltimore. Went up to Rullman's Hotel, or the Lichau House, as some others call it. Henderson sat for the barber, while I went up to the National to see Booth. Early came with me, while Murph stayed with Henderson. Left Early in the lobby of the National to see the others did not pass by without us.

But at the time, I thought that we were to be the assistants to this Harney fella, the powderman from Richmond. He was going to blow up the President's house, lock, stock, and barrel. It was a project developed by Reb agents in New York City. Then Booth tells me earlier this evening that Harney was taken prisoner and that we have to do his project *for* him, *individually*. I have to shoot Secretary of War Stanton, while he takes care of Lincoln, Powell gets Secretary of State Seward, and Surratt kills Vice President Johnson. And we are all supposed to do it at the same time, around ten tonight.

O'Laughlen pushed his way through the boisterous crowds, stopping once to take a drink from a bottle shoved at him by a very persistent stranger. Well, it was getting chilly, anyway. He pushed on towards Stanton's house on Franklin Square, around Lafayette Park from Seward's. He thought of looking to see if Powell were already in place, but Powell was of the type who would be too inconspicuous to be seen, so he moved on towards his goal.

Rats! The Stanton house was lit up like the Canterbury Music Hall. Hordes of people were milling about. What had happened? Did somebody beat me to it . . .? No . . . it was nothing. These people were mere celebrants. Happy over the defeat of the Confederacy . . . well, General Lee's army, anyhow . . . the bastards. They was a military band playing various patriotic songs. This was not going to be an easy job, O'Laughlen thought as he entered the yard. He looked at his watch. It was only 9 o'clock. He would have to waste an hour without becoming a suspicious character in the process.

A sergeant was standing on the top step of the front porch, watching the illumination. But he had been distracted from the fireworks, and was now looking at O'Laughlen. The Marylander would have been positively terrified if he had known that the sergeant was from the Adjutant General's Office, and Stanton's personal aide. Here goes nuthin,' O'Laughlen said to himself.

"Say, you would not happen to know if General Grant is in, would you?"

Sergeant John C. Hatter looked at O'Laughlen for a moment. "Yes, he is. Why?"

"I would wish to see him."

"This is no occasion for you to see him. If you wish to see him, step out on the pavement or on the stone where the carriage stops, and you can see him."

O'Laughlen stepped back towards the street. Hatter could not make out what he said, probably just as well.

"What a damned mess," O'Laughlen muttered. "Booth can never get anything to hook up right."

The would-be assassin stood around a while, mingling with the curious. Suddenly, there he was, there they *all* were; General Grant, Mrs.

Grant, Secretary Stanton, his daughter, Surgeon General Barnes, and three small children. Booth would probably rush the crowd and start shooting, yelling something Shakespearean or profoundly political. O'Laughlen chuckled to himself and moved into the yard. The sergeant was gone. But now, at the bottom of the stairs, was a Major, leaning against the balustrade. O'Laughlen stepped over beside him.

"Is Mr. Stanton in?"

"I suppose you mean the Secretary?"

"Yes, I am a lawyer in town; I know him very well."

Major Kilburn Knox, a War Department staff officer, looked at O'Laughlen. As an army man, he was quite familiar with men slightly under the influence of liquor. This man was not drunk, but he was tight. And he was no lawyer. He was not a gentleman, but a well-groomed mechanic of some kind, the Major would hazard.

"I doubt that you can see the Secretary right now," Knox said.

O'Laughlen stepped to the other side of the step and waited, feigning to watch the illuminations. Five minutes later, he was back.

"Is Mr. Stanton in? Oh, excuse me. I thought that you were the officer on duty here."

"There is no officer on duty here."

O'Laughlen nodded his head and mounted the stairs to the porch. The party of the Secretary and General Grant had gone inside some time ago, and O'Laughlen was trying to muster up the courage to enter the open front door. O'Laughlen entered the front hall and stood there.

Major Knox collared David Stanton, the Secretary's son. "Do you know that man?"

"No, sir, I do not."

"He says he knows the Secretary very well, but he is right smart for liquor, and you had better send him out."

"Excuse me, sir," young Stanton said, as he walked up to O'Laughlen. "What is your business here?"

"Where is the Secretary?"

"He is standing right in front of you."

O'Laughlen stood there silently a few moments.

"Excuse me, sir," David Stanton finally said. "I think you had better leave. Would you follow me, please?"

O'Laughlen walked behind the Secretary's son to the front door. Then he turned and walked off. Booth will have to do without this part of his plan, I reckon, O'Laughlen decided. Well, I will join the others on the Avenue around 9th Street. They said that they would cover for me, if necessary.

O'Laughlen joined his companions, and they proceeded to have a good time. They went to the Canterbury, Lichau's, and a half dozen bars and saloons. Booth came by Stanton's a short while later, to call O'Laughlen off. Not seeing him, Booth rode out to Benning's Bridge to fetch in Atzerodt. It was 2 a.m., before O'Laughlen's party arrived at the Metropolitan Hotel and registered their names. Early, Murphy, and Henderson got a room with three beds, and O'Laughlen, the last to register, slept in a room by himself.

The quartet of revelers got up around 8 or 9 o'clock Good Friday morning. Initially they were to go home that day, but Henderson wanted to stay one more night. O'Laughlen and the others agreed, enthusiastically. After breakfast at Welker's, the men went down the avenue.

"Say, fellers, there is the National," Early said. "Will y'all wait while I use the water closet?"

"Yeah, sure," O'Laughlen said.

When he got back to the lobby, O'Laughlen was gone. "What happened to Mike?"

"He is gone up to see Booth," said Henderson.

They waited forty-five minutes and then decided to walk down to a restaurant, strategically located across from Marble Alley, a well-known red light area. O'Laughlen found them there.

"Will you boys vouch for me again tonight? I have another errand to run." The other three said they would.

After supper again at Welker's, the men sat around drinking, mostly in the vicinity of Lichau's. At 9 o'clock, John H. Fuller, a former employee of Mike's brother, Will, came in. He had just escorted a lady friend back home, and was ready for a night on the town.

"Le's you and me go out a while," O'Laughlen suggested.

Out on the street, O'Laughlen and Fuller walked rapidly over to Stanton's, as O'Laughlen explained what was up.

"What time you got?" O'Laughlen asked.

"Looks like 9:30," Fuller said, tilting his watch to catch the light of a nearby lamp.

"Le's walk slowly over to the other side of Lafayette Park. When we get there, we can sit on a bench and wait for 10:30. Some one will flash a hooded lantern, when it is time. Then I will go up to the house."

"Can you answer me a question?" Fuller asked as they sat.

"Sure."

"You said that Booth wanted to strike last night on the Ides, to commemorate Brutus' killing of Caesar."

"Yep. He said it is a sympolic sort of thing," O'Laughlen explained.

"Right. Then what about tonight?"

"Huh?"

"Look! Last night was Maundy Thursday, commemorating the Last Supper. Tonight is Good Friday, Mike--will not all this make the assassinated Lincoln seem more like the crucified Christ than a Roman tyrant?"

Before the thought fully filtered through O'Laughlen's mind, Fuller punched him in the arm. "Look!"

Eastward on I Street and 15th, two men on horseback stopped. Although he could not tell at that distance, O'Laughlen knew they were Davy Herold and Lewis Powell. There was a flickering of light a block or two to the east. Herold waved in O'Laughlen's direction. The horsemen walked on south towards Seward's.

O'Laughlen got up. "Well, here goes nothin'!"

Fuller remained on the bench. O'Laughlen walked over to Stanton's house across the street, mounted the stairs quietly, and pulled the bell cord. Nothing happened. He pulled it again and listened. He heard neither the bell nor anyone inside. It must be broken, O'Laughlen thought. Maybe I ought to knock.

Suddenly, someone ran out of Seward's across the park, shouting at the top of his lungs.

"Help! Murder!"

He ran down Pennsylvania towards the Provost Marshal's quarters. People began milling around; loungers, strollers, couples out sparking each other, and such, puzzled at the ruckus. The Provost Marshal's guard came out of their quarters with a bang, as their doors opened wildly. They began running down toward Seward's, feet crunching in the gravel. By now O'Laughlen had recrossed to Fuller in the park.

"What do you reckon we ought to do?"

"Did anyone see you?" Fuller asked.

"No, I do not think so."

"Then, le's run across the park like everybody else. Shout 'murder' and 'thief.' Blend in with the crowd. When we get over there we can walk quietly away, no one the wiser."

"They is Wood, now," O'Laughlen said. "Why don't he take off? Look how slow he is!"

"Murder! Thief! There he goes!" Fuller shouted and pointed. O'Laughlen joined him. "Murderer! Stop that man!"

O'Laughlen and Fuller ran to Madison Street, and then slipped out of the crowd and went back to Rullman's and sat around with O'Laughlen's three companions, Washington City friends John R. Giles, Daniel Loughran, and Henry E. Purdy, the manager of the house. They said nothing about their experience. Soon, a cavalry sergeant rode up, horse all in a lather.

"Have you heard?"

"What?" Purdy called out.

"The President has just been assassinated."

"No! Who done it?"

"It was that actor feller, John Wilkes Booth."

"Well, I will be damned," O'Laughlen said slowly. "Can you beat that?"

The next day, the quartet from Baltimore set out for the 11 a.m. train. But after purchasing tickets, they decided not to leave just then and stayed until 3'oclock. The got back to Baltimore in a couple of hours. On the way home, O'Laughlen's brother-in-law, P. H. Maulsby, told him that the police had been looking for him that morning in connection with his friendship with Booth and his so-called oil business. O'Laughlen went home to see his ailing mother, and left immediately afterwards. He did not want his fragile mother to witness his imminent arrest.

5. Booth Breaks a Leg

Booth cantered across the lengthy Navy Yard Bridge only to see that the gates on the south end were closed—just as Surratt had warned.

"Halt! Damn you! Walk that horse or I will fire at you!"

Private George Drake leveled his 58 cal. Springfield at the horseman, who pulled up quickly.

"Where are you going?"

"Out into the country," Booth replied.

"What country?"

"Tee Bee by the Tee Bee Road. Say, soldier, has anyone passed across before me?"

Corporal Thomas Sullivan answered, "No."

"My friend is a damned pretty fellow. Well, I cannot wait."

Squad leader Sullivan turned to another soldier, "Demond, help me open the gate."

Booth came off the end of the Navy Yard Bridge and entered Uniontown, a small settlement still within the boundaries of the District. He loped through town taking the first left turn onto Harrison Street. After riding the length of a couple of blocks he was back into the country and ascending Good Hope Hill. He passed by three massive Yankee earthworks, whose soldiers, more 3d Heavies, were safely in their billets, as Mrs. Surratt had promised they would be. Two men on a wagon appeared headed in the opposite direction.

"Gentlemen, has another rider passed on ahead of me?"

"We ain't seen no one," came the reply

"I am looking for the road to Upper Marlboro," Booth hollered back. "Do I take the right fork out of the junction up ahead?"

"No, sir," came the reply, "keep straight ahead on."

Booth had hardly broken stride as he fired his questions. He soon reached the ridge, spurred the mare to full speed, and passed into Maryland by the right fork, known locally as the Brandywine Road.

Meanwhile, Davy Herold reached the south end of the Navy Yard Bridge. The gates had closed after Booth's passage.

"Halt!" cried Private Drake. "Walk your horse."

"Has a man on a flashy bay mare just passed?"

"Yeah." It was Corporal Sullivan again. "He called you a damned pretty fellow to be late. Where are you going tonight?"

Herold was through with the play-acting. He would leave that to Booth.

"Tee Bee. Up the Tee Bee Road."

Huh! Thought Sullivan. There was that countersign that Lieutenant David H. Dana, their commanding officer and the bridge provost marshal, had told them to use tonight. He waved to Demond and the two men opened the gate and watched Herold single-foot smoothly through into Uniontown.

"This whole thing stinks," he said to his comrades, "but orders are orders."

Polk Gardiner and George Doyle, the two men Booth inquired of about the road did not think much of the incident, until Davy Herold came out of Uniontown just as they reached the bottom of Good Hope Hill, and passed a group of government teamsters, who were stopped in the road to one side. At the top of the hill, these teamsters had tied extra wood spars between the wheels under their heavy freight wagon beds to lock the wheels for the steep ascent. Now they were releasing these temporary brakes for the rest of the way into Washington.

"Has another horseman passed ahead of me up the hill?" Herold shouted at the teamsters.

"Maybe five or ten minutes ago," came the reply.

Gardiner turned to Doyle and laughed. "It looks like them two is just wearing out horses chasing after each other."

Doyle laughed back and shook his head side to side in disbelief as Herold kicked Charley into a full gallop. It felt good to laugh, Gardiner thought. Been thinking of daddy lying there in the City too much lately. Getting close to death. Could really get to a son--seeing his old man dying inch by inch. A little laughter helped lighten the load of life, when it threatened to get too heavy.

As Gardiner and Doyle passed into Uniontown, it began to rain in earnest, soon turning the dust-filled ruts, still damp from the winter's constant precipitation, into mud bogs. Down in Maryland, Herold slowed the pace, lest Charley slip and go down. At the foot of Soper's Hill, about eight miles out, Herold saw something big and dark that did not rightly belong in the road up ahead. Oh, oh! It was Booth's bay mare. She neighed and moved aside, limping on her near front leg.

"Davy!"

It was Booth. His voice sounded pained and lacked in its usual sonorousness. Herold pulled Charley into a sliding stop and jumped down. Booth lay on the side of the road, resting on one elbow, unable to rise.

"Give me a hand up, Davy."

"What happened Johnny?" He put an arm about Booth and helped him stand. Booth winced in pain and appeared out of breath with the exertion.

"That . . . damned . . . mare . . . slipped . . . and fell. He breathed heavily and the words came out in partial phrases, punctuated by breaths. Was going too fast . . . and the ground gave way, or . . . something. . . . she's pretty . . . skittish."

"Well, she sure has had the gumption taken out of her in that fall. Can you put weight on your leg?"

Booth stepped down and sucked his breath heavily as a sharp pain came up his leg.

"No. . . . You'll have . . . to help me . . . mount."

"Well," Davy said, "you better get up on old Charley. He rides much better--single foots, you know. I'll try that jumpy mare of yours."

Herold walked Booth over to Charley. "Mount him from the right so's I can throw you up by your good leg."

"Let me lean . . . over his back . . . first, then . . . give me a hand up." Booth gritted his teeth to keep from crying out as Davy hoisted him up and onto the saddle.

As Booth mulled over his predicament, Davy caught up the mare and examined her carefully. She was covered with mud, but he could see the darker wet where her leg was cut and feel the swelling in her left shoulder. The rest of her limbs were sound. Her shoes were on tight.

"I reckon we can make it to Lloyd's, if we take it easy. But we better get moving before she stoves up. Too bad about your leg, though."

"And . . . too bad we . . . brought in those horses . . . from Huntt's . . . this morning!"

Davy mounted the mare and led the way. "Can you make it?" he asked Booth.

"Yes," came the reply, "I will make it . . . or die trying." There was some of the old Booth in the ring of his voice.

Herold smiled. Leave it to Johnny, he said to himself. He'll make anything sound heroic. The two riders turned back into the road and headed to Surrattsville for succor from the bottle and to retrieve the carbines and field glasses stored there. Let Plug Tobacco and Mosby catch them there--if they came on at all.

6. On to Surrattsville

As Booth and Herold cleared Soper's Hill, they came upon another pair of men, whose wagon had broken a wheel. The two were an adult black men, Henry Butler, who worked for Dr. Joseph Blandford, and a teenaged white boy, George Thompson. They had spent the better part of the night unloading the wagon's cargo and were ready to switch wheels.

"Kin you men get down and help us hold up the bed, so's we kin change the wheel?" Thompson asked, earnestly.

"I am afraid I have broken my leg," Booth said, "and we are in some haste, but my companion will assist, if you work quickly, in exchange for some information on the road ahead."

"Fair enough. Here mister, you and Henry hoist the bed with your backs. I will pull the wheel as soon as you steady the bed. The hub nut is off already."

Herold and Henry Butler lifted the wagon up a few inches and Thompson pulled the broken wheel and put the spare on the hub. The men lowered the wagon onto the new wheel.

"Henry will grease and set the hub nut," said Thompson. "What is it y'all need to know?"

"Where is the fork to Upper Marlboro?" Booth asked

"Take the left down a piece. If you get to Surratt's tavern, you have gone too far. But you can pass left there and head over to the Wood Yard. It all comes out to the same place in the end. The first left is shorter, tha's all."

"Thank you, young man." Booth politely cut off their conversation. "Mount up Davy. And as for you, uh, *gentlemen*, I hope your trip will be better on the morrow than tonight. We would help you with your lading, but I need to seek a doctor quickly to tend to my leg."

"Ol' Doc Blandford is down to Piscataway, but you all is going the other way," Butler ventured. "But there are quite a few others in the area, like Doc. . . ."

"Many thanks, Uncle," Booth cut him off. "I have a different sawbones in mind. Good night!"

About fifteen minutes later Booth and Herold passed the Marlboro turnoff.

"My leg is terribly painful," Booth sighed as they rode on. "We will have to seek a doctor as soon as we pick up our equipment at Surrattsville."

"Like the freedman said, I bet they is a dozen good doctors in this area," Herold proffered.

"Indeed, I daresay you are right, Davy," Booth answered, "but I have one special man in mind for my treatment. And he is down near Beantown."

"What about Baltimore?"

"Our plans have to change with the circumstances we face. My leg. . . ."

"But we are riding the same way you wanted to send the Bluebellies. All the stuff I put in Port Tobacco's room. . . ."

"There is no choice. We have friends on this route, too. The Yankees do not. Besides, if these teamsters and the ones back at Uniontown talk, the Federals will be confused or head for Upper Marlboro and give us time to get away."

Lord, I hope so, thought Herold. Sure don't want to tangle with Yankee cavalry.

"Let us ride on!" Booth snapped impatiently, spurring Charley's flank with his good leg. Herold thought he sounded a bit too pompous for the occasion, but he urged the bay mare on, too.

Meanwhile, down the road at their immediate destination, the Surratt Tavern, John Lloyd was getting ready for his expected visitors. He was still drunk, or right smart for liquor, as they said in those days. But he was not as drunk as he had ever been. He could still function, after a fashion. He went into the secret attic at the back of the Surratt Tavern and hauled out the two carbines from between the floor joists. He also had a monkey wrench and a coil of rope downstairs from the aborted Lincoln kidnap plot.

Wonder what she wants me to do with those, he thought. Mrs. Surratt said the shootin' irons, them fancy French spyglasses, and some whiskey. But she did not say nuttin' about the rope and wrench. Damn women! They always leave something out and then yell at a feller when he didn't do it up right. Good thing the missus and her sister, Emma, was off to Allen's Fresh. They would never take to this sneaky stuff.

Well, dammit, Mrs. Surratt said only the carbines and the booze. Nothing to do about the whiskey--there was plenty of it in the barroom. But he would take the Spencers to his bedroom, if he could make it that far. He struggled out of Anna's old bedroom with the weapons, stumbling against the door jambs. Then Lloyd staggered across the hall and fell into bed, hugging the two carbines like a child cozying up to a favorite rag doll. Lord! He was tired.

The clock struck midnight. Lloyd vaguely heard it chime. He started to drop off again when he heard hoofbeats out in the yard. "Lloyd! Lloyd!!" The half-sleeping barkeeper snorted awake. "Lloyd!" Then he remembered. The men must have come for the guns. And the field glasses. Where in the Hell were those damned Frenchy glasses? Lloyd stumbled around until he found the field glasses on a table. Wait a minute! What if they were Federal soldiers? Lloyd stumbled down the stairs empty-handed. No need to have to explain those brand new Spencers to a bluecoat.

"Lloyd!" It was Davy Herold. "For God's sake, make haste and get those things! "

Lloyd opened the door and stared at Herold dumbly. Then something clicked in his mind. He turned and laboriously climbed back to his room. Herold made himself at home at the bar with a bottle of whiskey and a glass. Before Lloyd got to the top of the stairs, Herold took the opened bottle out to Booth, who still sat, gasping and writhing in pain, on old Charley. He took a swig of the rotgut and then guzzled it deeply. The pain seemed more bearable, now. He drank deeply, again. And again. How he wished it were brandy!

Back in the bedroom, Lloyd put a box of cartridges in his pocket and looked dumbly at the two carbines and the glasses lying on the bed. Three items. Two hands. What to do? Lloyd sighed heavily, picked up the binoculars and one of the carbines and took what he neatly saw as a full load clumsily down the stairs. Righting himself with exaggerated dignity, Lloyd looked about carefully for lurking soldiers, as if he could have saved his skin after standing there in the exposed doorway with a light at his back with a carbine and field glasses in his hands. He saw only Herold and a stranger sitting on a reddish gray roan. He went out into the yard and gave the two items to Herold. Next he handed up the cartridge box. Lloyd then remembered the other carbine. He belched loudly and, signaling with a raised finger for his visitors to wait, turned to go get it. Davy handed his carbine up to Booth, who hefted it briefly and handed it back.

"It will not work, Davy. It is hard enough to balance myself without it. I cannot carry it. I am sorely wounded and will need both hands to help maintain my seat."

"Hold on, Lloyd!" said Herold. "We only need one gun." Herold broke open the cartridge box and dumped the contents into his coat pocket. He mounted the bay mare and rode over to Lloyd, between him and Booth, and offered him the nearly empty whiskey bottle. "I owe you a couple of dollars. Here." He handed a bank note to the rumpled barkeeper.

"I will tell you some news, Lloyd, if you want to hear it."

It was the man who rode with Herold, the man whom Lloyd thought he had never seen before. But that voice. Lloyd knew it! It belonged to John Wilkes Booth. He had come through here a couple of times last winter.

Herold had moved the mare to one side--she was already impatient to move on--so Booth could see Lloyd. Herold wound up across the road before he could bring the bay mare under control, so he did not hear the rest of their conversation clearly.

"I am not particular, Mr. Wilkes Booth," Lloyd said dismissively, belching air involuntarily. "Use your own choice about telling news."

Booth was a dandified smart-ass, anyway, and Lloyd was in no mood for his damned mind games.

"Well," Booth said, looking very much like a child about to divulge a delicious bit of gossip, "I am pretty certain that we have assassinated the President and fixed off Secretary Seward."

Lloyd stared at them silently as they rode off toward Tee Bee, too dumbstruck to reply, too drunk to panic, but oddly aware that he was going to be in one heap of trouble. Damn Mrs. Surratt and her Rebel friends, anyway, and damn me for going along with them. Lloyd stumbled back into the tavern and closed the door.

Mrs. Surratt has ruined my life. She and the stinkin' Kunfedracy. Lost the dam' war, they did. They was supposed to win. Shot Lincoln--I thought they was going to kidnap him or blow him to Hell! Not Booth. What was the name of that feller? Varney, Harney, or something. He never showed. And now this with the war about over, anyway! Couple of dollars, my ass! Hell, that little rat, Herold, gave me but one! They drank more booze than that. Damn! Too stoned to go up the stairs, Lloyd fell exhausted onto a front room couch, broke wind indelicately, and was soon lost in a dreamless, alcoholic sleep.

7. John Fletcher Identifies a Horse

John Fletcher, the foreman at Naylor's Stable who had been turned back at the Navy Yard Bridge, rode back into the City still disgusted by Sergeant Cobb's obtuseness. He had made good time pursuing Davy Herold, but now he rode back at a walk, thinking. Maybe he had gone off half-cocked. Perhaps his red roan had been turned in at another stable. The various stables received each other's horses regularly, exchanging them in the next day or so. He would try Murphy's at Fourteenth and E Streets. That was near the President's house and in the area he had last seen Herold. He looked at his watch in the glow of a street light. It was lacking ten minutes to midnight. He cut up Third Street to E and then rode west to Fourteenth.

"Dorsey," he called out to the foreman, who was still up. "You seen one of Mr. Naylor's horses--the red roan with a steel gray hue and black points?"

"Hey, Fletcher," Dorsey answered. "No, I ain't seen no horse like that. Say, you had better keep in. President Lincoln is shot and Secretary Seward is near dead. People acting like idiots all over the place."

"When did that happen?"

"About 10:30 this night, over to Ford's Theater."

Fletcher returned to Naylor's and put up his horse. It was 1:30 a.m. People were all over the streets and sidewalks, just like Dorsey said, talking about the night's events. Fletcher perked up his ears when he heard several people talking about how the assassins were mounted men. Fletcher thought about how Atzerodt was out so late and Herold's failure to return his horse at all. He walked out into the night. A light rain was beginning to fall, borne on a chill wind.

Fletcher pulled on his hat against the weather and turned up his collar. As he walked down E Street toward Fourteenth, again, he saw a cavalry sergeant leading several horses.

"Sergeant, have you picked up many stray horses tonight? Where might I check them out?"

"Yes, sir," the soldier said. "These two and several others. I reckon that you ought to check with the police office over on Tenth Street."

Fletcher retraced his steps. At the police station he saw a detective standing outside, watching the storm come up.

"Where would I go to check on stray horses picked this evening, sir? I am missing one from the stable where I am engaged to work, Naylor's."

"I am Detective Charlie Stowall," he said sticking out his hand.

"John Fletcher."''

"What kind of horse are you looking for, Mr. Fletcher?"

"A red-gray roan with black points."''

Well, we do not have any, but there are probably some up at the Provost Marshal's headquarters. Horse got loose, did it?"

"More'n likely stole," Fletcher said glumly.

"Who did it?"'

"A little rat named Davy Herold, I reckon."

"Oh? . . . I tell you what . . . I will walk over to the Provost's with you if'n you do not mind. Maybe you can tell me about this Herold feller as we go."

"Well, he is probably not yet twenty, short and stocky, but not too stocky, likes to talk a lot about nuttin'. He come in and took my roan out until nine o'clock. Never came back. I caught him out on the Avenue and tried to reclaim my gelding, but he spurred off too quick. Chased him clear down to the Navy Yard, but the guard would not let me cross the bridge, and then come back."

"Le's go to General Augur's office; he is the Army's big shot around here, y'know, and take a look."

Major General Christopher C. Augur was more than a mere Provost Marshal; he commanded the whole Department of Washington. A veteran of the Mexican War and several Indian campaigns, he had once been the Commandant of Cadets at West Point. During the war, he commanded several brigades, division and corps-size organizations, principally under Major General Nathaniel Banks. Together they had *nearly* whipped Stonewall Jackson at Cedar Mountain in 1862, and captured Port Hudson, Louisiana, in 1863, just after General U.S. Grant had taken Vicksburg. Of course, Grant had received all the glory. Augur, troubled by a wound he had received during the Second Bull Run Campaign, had been recalled to Washington to serve on investigative boards and command the garrison. He was not a man to be taken lightly.

Augur scowled at the two men before him. Normally, he had not much use for civilians or detectives. But Fletcher's story interested him. The stableman had just finished talking about Herold when he spied some familiar pieces of tack on the General's desk.

"Where did you get that bridle and saddle?"

"Have you seen them before?" Augur asked.

"Yes. They belong to the man who came with Herold, who rented my roan. I have saddled his horse many a time with them."

"What kind of horse?"

"It was a big, heavy brown animal. Blind of one eye. Heavy tail. Kind of a pacer. Single-foot rack."

"What is this man's name?"

"I do not recollect, German sounding, but I have a card on him at the stable."

"Mr. Stowall, would you and Mr. Fletcher go out back and identify a horse we have there? If he is the same brown, the one Mr. Fletcher knows, go down to his stable and bring me that card back."

An hour later General Augur received Fletcher's registration card. It read: "George Atzerodt, Port Tobacco, Maryland."

8. The Boardinghouse Search

"Who is there?" Louis J. Weichmann finished buttoning up his fly of his hastily-drawn-on trousers as he stumbled down the stairs. The door bell to the main entrance on the second floor jingled violently. Some one was pulling the bell cord without let-up.

"Who is there?" Weichmann asked again, hesitant to open the door without some form of identification. He feared that perhaps some drunk or a body up to no good was trying to get in the house. He walked into the parlor. For Pete's sake, it was 2:30 am! At least the coals of the dying fire made the clock face *look* like 2:30 a.m. He looked outside. At least four men were on the landing. One of them was trying to peer into the parlor window as Lou looked out.

"Officers of the Government!" came the reply.

"What?" Weichmann came back into the hall.

"Detectives! We have come to search for John Wilkes Booth and John Surratt. We want them to surrender, if they are here."

"They are not here," Weichmann yelled back, still refusing to open the door.

"Let us in, anyhow. We want to see the lady of the house and search the building."

"Mr. Weichmann!" It was Mrs. Surratt calling from her room down the hall.

"Here, Mrs. Surratt. There are men claiming to be detectives, who have come to search the house."

"For Heaven's sake! Let them come in. I expected the house to be searched."

Puzzled by her reply, Weichmann opened the door, clad in nightshirt, his trousers and stockings. He had left his slippers in his room. Embarrassed, the fastidious Weichmann retreated up the stairs to tidy up his attire and comb his tousled hair.

Leaving two men in the front hall, Officers James McDevitt and John Clarvoe went upstairs to the attic where Anna and her cousin Lete Jenkins were sleeping. Anna said something that no one could hear below, but from the tone of her voice, she was not pleased by the intrusion of strange men into her bedroom. Neither were the Holohans across the floor from Weichmann. The policemen soon confronted Weichmann in his room.

"Gentlemen, what is the matter? What does searching this house mean?"

"Do you pretend that you do not know what has happened?" Asked Clarvoe.

"I have heard nothing. I have no idea what has occurred, I assure you."

"Well, then, I will tell you. John Wilkes Booth has shot the President and John Surratt has assassinated the Secretary of State." Clarvoe drew a black cravat out of his pocket." Do you see the blood on that? That is the blood of Abraham Lincoln!"

Weichmann threw up his hands. "Great God, I see it all," he mumbled to no one in particular. "But gentlemen, John Surratt is in Canada. He cannot have acted in committing any crime here tonight. Why, we have just received a letter from him this evening, written on the 12th instant."

"Perhaps everybody ought to assemble in the parlor below," McDevitt suggested.

Weichmann followed the two officers down the stairs. They met Mrs. Surratt just coming out of her room.

"Mrs. Surratt, what do you think, these gentlemen say that Mr. Booth has murdered the President."

"My God, Mr. Weichmann. You do not tell me so!"

"Are you Mrs. Surratt?" It was Clarvoe.

"I am Mrs. Surratt."

"I have come to see your son, John."

"My son is not even in the City, sir! He has not been here for two weeks. Why, sir, I received a letter from him in Canada just today."

"Have you been here all evening?"

"I was down in the country earlier. Mr. Weichmann drove me."

"You tell her, Mac." Clarvoe went back to searching the house, headed for the basement.

"Mrs. Surratt, your son, John, is wanted for the murder of the Secretary of State."

"My son would kill no one, sir!" Mrs. Surratt said coldly and firmly.

"Please, could we see this letter from Canada?"

"It is in here somewhere," Mrs. Surratt said. She went around the room, but no letter could be found. Anna and Nora helped. Finally, Weichmann and the police took a turn with the same result. No letter could be located. None ever was, even after an exhaustive police search of the whole house a week later. For all practical purposes, it was as if the letter had never existed.

Convinced that neither Booth nor John Surratt were present, the officers excused themselves ("by your leave, ma'am," they said to Mrs. Surratt on the way out) and left the premises.

"This is indeed a great crime," Weichmann opined.

"They is no use of your going on so, Mr. Weichmann," Anna said curtly. "Surely the death of Mr. Lincoln is no worse than that of the meanest n-----r in the army."

"That is not so," Weichmann insisted. "The repeated visits of Mr. Booth to this house will probably cause official inquiry."

Anna watched from the window to be sure the police had gone. As the police carriage pulled away, she turned into the room ashen-faced. The full import of what had just occurred finally hit her.

"Oh, Ma! What if Mr. Weichmann is right! Just think of that man having been here an hour before the assassination. I am afraid it will bring suspicion upon us."

"Anna, come what will, I am resigned. I think that Mr. J. Wilkes Booth was only an instrument in the hands of the Almighty to punish this proud and licentious people."

"Did you *expect* these men, Mrs. Surratt? You said. . . ."

"Indeed, Mr. Weichmann. In fact, Mr. A. C. Richards, Chief of the Metropolitan Police, has been here only an hour or so before making the same inquiries. He got his information from a saloon keeper named Ferguson, he said. He had seen Mr. Booth in John's company and so Mr. Richards came here. He informed me of the President's shooting and I told him John was not present.

"I also had heard of the incident earlier from a couple of noisy soldiers, after you all had retired for the night. They shouted it up from the street when I asked them what all the ruckus was around 11 o'clock. Now le's go back to bed and make the best of what is left of this tragic night."

Everyone returned to their rooms, but there was very little sleep to be had the rest of the night. Damn it, Weichmann thought, Mrs. Surratt was fully dressed. She had never gone to sleep the whole night. She had been sitting in a darkened house, waiting for the police. She must have seen Booth earlier.

But the caller at 9 p.m. was not Booth. It was a man named Scott, carrying items for Lete Jenkins. At least that is what Anna said at the time. And she had answered the knock by going up the stairs from the street level dining room to the front door. He must have come after everyone else was asleep, just like the soldiers and Police Chief Richards.

And the letter. Weichmann had seen it at dinner. Annie Ward had brought it over. True, Lou had not *read* the letter, but Anna had. It was full of general stuff. He was at the St. Lawrence Hotel, he liked Montreal, he had seen the old French cathedral, he had bought a pea jacket for $10 in silver, and that daily board generally cost an outrageous $2.50 in gold! With such expenses he expected to remove to a private boarding house soon.

He was also glad that Lou had been able to drive his mother to Surrattsville on the 11th of April. Wait a minute! How could John Surratt hear of the April 11 trip and write back already about it? In only three days? He had signed the letter with his pseudonym, John Harrison. Anna had giggled at that. Where was that letter? Surely Mrs. Surratt would not have destroyed it. But Lou never really *saw* it. What he saw was a piece of paper with writing on it. Maybe there was no letter--it was a ruse to make it appear John was in Canada. Then, where *was* he on April 14?

9. Booth Finds a Doctor

To this day no one knows which route Booth and Herold took out of Tee Bee. Legend has them passing through Brandywine and Horse Head, but modern authorities believe that they veered on to the right fork below Tee Bee, and took the old way south. It was closer to the Potomac crossings and, more importantly, it led nearer to the home of Booth's old Rebel contact, Dr. Samuel Mudd. Booth's leg was causing him a great deal of pain. As Herold had surmised, gone was the idea of beating the Federal pursuit to Baltimore. Now Booth was actually travelling on the approximate route he had told Sergeant Cobb at the Navy Yard Bridge. But instead of it being a ruse as planned, he had inadvertently brought the

Yankee pursuit down upon himself, his partner, and the Confederate operators of the old Secret Mail Line.

About 4 a.m. on April 15, one of those Confederate mailmen, Dr. Samuel Mudd, heard knocking at his front door. He had not been feeling well and, as he lay in bed listening to the rain tickling the window pain sounding like the ticking of an irregular clock, a wave of nausea swept over his body. The banging at the door took on a new urgency.

"Frankie, why don't you go out and answer the door?" he mumbled to his wife.

"I would rather you would go and see for yourself," she replied, uneasily. "One never knows who might be abroad at this hour in these times."

"I really do not feel too well."

Mudd rose up in bed and suppressed a mild desire to throw up. He put on his robe and stumbled still half asleep out of his first story bedroom in the darkness. The banging at the door began again. Frankie was right, no telling who could be out there. He would later tell the Yankee policemen that he was afraid of Confederate guerillas that infested the neighborhood; but Mudd knew that he, of all people, had nothing to fear from Rebels. Not in *that* neighborhood.

Mudd peered out of the parlor window next to the door and saw two men in the misty, pre-dawn darkness, one on foot at his porch and another mounted, holding on to a riderless horse. They were soaking wet. Mudd opened the door a crack.

"What is the matter? Why do you wake me in the middle of the night?"

"My companion has fallen with his horse and needs a doctor's help. He might have broken his leg, we don't know. Cain't you look at him?"

"Well, I am a physician, not a surgeon." Mudd was half tempted to send the two strangers on when the man on the horse spoke up.

"Mudd! I need your help. I am badly injured."

The voice sounded familiar. Mudd turned up a lamp in the parlor. He then entered the yard and looked at the horseman in the light emanating from the doorway. Fortunately, it had stopped raining except for an occasional misting, here and there. But the air was humid and cool.

"Booth?" He squinted at the sodden form on the red-gray roan. "It *is* you Booth! What are you doing here?"

"We were on our way to the City and my horse fell on me and pinned my leg. I require medical assistance." Booth spoke carefully, between his clenched teeth, as if the slightest movement would cause excruciating pain.

"Help me," Mudd turned to Herold. The two men lifted Booth from Charley's back and the three stumbled into the parlor. Booth fell onto a settee, crying out softly in agony as he breathed out heavily. Mudd turned to see Frank Washington, a black employee who had been awakened by the noise.

"Frank, would you put up and feed these men's horses at the barn? They are ground tied outside. Maybe you can brush some of the rain off of them, too."

"Yessir, Mister Sam," Frank said unenthusiastically. He walked gloomily into the wet darkness.

"Wait here," Mudd said to Herold.

He went into the bedroom and saw that his wife had lit a candle.

"There are two men out front," Mudd said. "One of them is John Wilkes Booth who visited us last winter, while looking for land and horses. You remember him? The man who said he would buy our land and then backed out?"

"That horrible man who left that evil letter behind? Does he want it back, *now?*"

"No, no. Booth has broken a leg, I believe. Please tear some bandages so that I might fashion a splint and tie any wounds he has. I will take them to the extra bedroom upstairs. He will not be able to move and will have to stay here for a while, I suspect." He visibly grimaced a bit at the thought, as did Frankie. She *really* disliked the womanizing actor.

In the parlor, Mudd lifted Booth's left leg carefully. Booth sucked in wind, but did not cry out.

"I am going to try to remove the boot," the doctor said. He began to pull on the boot heel.

"No, please, stop!" Booth had tears in his eyes from the pain.

"Young man," Mudd turned to Herold. "You will have to help me get him upstairs to the spare bedroom. Mrs. Mudd will light the way."

Frankie appeared at the foot of the stairs with her candle and guided Herold and Booth after they ascended the stairway, a task in itself. Booth hung onto Herold's shoulder and pulled himself up by the railing. Mudd hoped that the railing would hold up to such vigorous work, but his doubts proved unnecessary. He helped the two men into the bedroom, led by Frankie with her candle. Booth slumped into the near bed. It was the same room he had occupied in happier times, some five months before.

"I will have to cut off your boot," Mudd said. He took a sharp knife and slit it down the seam from the top of the vamp and then along the foot past the instep. Booth, resting on his elbows, dropped full length into the bed and writhed in agony as the boot came off. With a move the doctor would later forget and then regret, because Federal detectives would find it had the name "J. Wilkes" in it, Mudd casually kicked the knifed boot out of the way and under the bed as he felt along Booth's lower leg for the broken bone. "There!" It was a clean break of the fibula about two inches above his ankle.

"I will have to splint your leg, Booth." Mudd broke up a band box and tied it in place with the bandages that Frankie brought in.

"Good! I guess we can move on by daybreak," said Herold eagerly.

"Oh, no!" Mudd looked up rather surprised. "This is a painful break. Although not serious, as it is not a compound fracture, it will be two weeks or more before he can be moved. Now, Booth, you must stay here and rest. It is the best medicine I can provide you--nature's own remedy."

With that Mudd covered him with a quilt, turned and left the room. He descended the stairs and went out into the early light of the farm yard to supervise his hands, black and white, at their chores. Booth sank into a stupor of exhaustion and pain. Davy Herold sat with him briefly and then went down to the barn to check on the horses. Later, Herold returned and lay down on the other bed in Booth's room.

10. All Those God Damned Booths Are Crazy

The Temples and other usual Booth hangers-on at the National Hotel turned in for the night at their customary ten o'clock bed time. But within minutes after falling asleep, something awakened Mrs. Temple. At first, she could not make out what it was. She listened more intently. Then it came to her. Doors were being slammed shut throughout the hotel. Voices murmured along the hallways, but none seemed clear enough to give an indication as to what was happening.

"Henry," she called to her husband. "Humph?" Having come in late, he was still asleep. She shook her husband. "Wake up! Something is going on."

"What is it?"

"Doors banging all over the house," she replied, using the common name for any building, including business establishments and residences, at that time.

"Perhaps some has taken ill. They are merely sending for a doctor."

"No! Do not fall back asleep, Henry." She shook him again. Men were so unimaginative at times like this.

Henry Temple rolled over into a half sitting position, resting on his elbows. Is it a fire, possibly? He sniffed the air. Nothing but stale carpet and the usual unwashed bodies. He thought to rise and throw open a window, but the canal was but a block away, and the streets' normal odor of horses and their leavings did not appeal to him at this hour. But his wife got up and committed the deed for him. They could hear the sound of many horses coming and going at a run, but no alarm bells.

"Reckon the Rebs have stormed the City?" Mr. Temple asked as a battery of artillery passed noisily down the avenue.

"Well, I am getting my wrapper on," Mrs. Temple said. "I will not meet the Confederate army half-dressed. I am going down to the parlor. Get dressed and follow me!"

"Oh, Hell....all right." Henry Temple grumped, as he absentmindedly scratched himself. Just like a woman. Never let a man get his rest. No wonder he slept half the afternoon all the time. And she just thought him lazy.

Mrs. Temple hurried down to the parlor on their floor. It was empty. But there were the sound of voices coming up through the stairwell. She followed them down to the main floor salon. The grand parlor was crowded with people and abuzz with talk, most of them half-dressed, *en dishabille,* as they said in those days, just like Mrs. Temple.

"What has happened?" Mrs. Temple inquired.

"Horrible things," came the reply. "Mr. Lincoln . . . oh! It is just too horrible to contemplate. Mr. Lincoln has been shot by that actor, J. Wilkes Booth! Right in the Presidential Box at Ford's Theater!"

"By Booth? By *our* John Wilkes Booth? Oh, no! That is impossible!" Mrs. Temple was adamant. She had never failed to underestimate anyone's character before. No, no. Not now!

Others in the crowd confirmed her worst fears; it was J. Wilkes Booth, the great Shakespearean tragedian, the most popular thespian of the day. Then Mrs. Temple saw *her* coming-- Lucy Lambert Hale. Before Mrs. Temple could get to her, she heard the news. With a shriek, she fainted dead away, and fell full length upon the floor.

"Lend a hand here!" Several men carried the prostrate young woman up the stairs to her room.

Meanwhile, Mr. Temple and many others arrived. No one gave any thought to going back to bed. Everyone sat or stood where they were in a state of shock; aghast, dazed and dumb-founded. Finally, Mr. Temple and several other men, all fully dressed, got their coats and went out into the night to see what had transpired. The women sat clustered together for warmth and mutual support until the first gray light of dawn spread down Pennsylvania Avenue. It was some little time before the men returned from their scouting trips. Henry came back with a couple of others about 8 o'clock in the morning.

"President Lincoln is dead," he said somberly. "He died about a half hour ago. He had been taken across the street to a place called the Petersen House. There a death watch was maintained all night. Mrs. Lincoln, Robert, several cabinet officers, doctors, and a preacher or two were there. And did you hear? The vile assassins had attacked the William H. Seward house across from the White House at Lafayette Park. I cannot be sure, really, but we heard that the Secretary and several of his family were dead or dying. Army and detective units are going out now, hoping to capture all those involved. Yes, my dear," Henry said softly, "your favorite, Wilkes, is among those being sought. I am sorry. I know you loved him dearly."

The Temples went up to their room and tried to get some sleep. As soon as it was possible, Mrs. Temple attempted a visit to Lucy Hale, who was being kept in seclusion in her room. But no one was allowed in but her mother and a physician. Several days later, a rumor that Booth had been taken circulated around official Washington. Mrs. Temple was startled by the appearance of Lucy Hale caming into her room.

"M-M-M-Mrs. T-T-Temple." Her voice shook almost as much as her body.

"My dear! Please come and sit beside me." Mrs. Temple put her arm around the shuddering, shrinking figure who, just days before, had been the vivacious, ever-popular young woman, the envy of the community. Now she felt like a pariah.

"They have f-found John! Mrs. Temple, I d-d-do not know w-what to do. I feel so a-a-ashamed. We w-were to be married within the y-y- year. I was to come back from Sp-Sp-Spain, with or without f-father's p-per-permission."

"Now, now, my child, it is not your doing that John committed that evil act. You knew nothing about it beforehand."

"I t-tell you, Mrs. T-Temple, I tell you a-a-alone. I still l-love John, in spite of what he is s-s-said to have d-done. I w-would marry h-h-him on the sc-sc-scaffold."

Lucy broke into tears. The normally proud, haughty, even (at times) cold, young woman had lost complete control of herself. Lucy would recover, in time. At least she would be able to function in the real world. But she seemed to *exist*, rather than *live*. Even the trip to Europe, where she remained for five years, did little to help. The fair, sweet face was drawn with pain. Her eyes appeared hollow, her smile patient, but melancholy; her visage haunted those who had known her through happier times. Ultimately, she would marry her girl-hood sweetheart, a successful corporate lawyer, raise a son, and die in obscurity a decade and a half after the turn of the century.

"Were I to write Lucy's future," Mrs. Temple would say, in the heady years after the end of the war for the domination of white America, "I would simply call it, *A Dead Woman's Life*."

Booth's friends and fellow actors always maintained their collective shock at his greatest and most infamous deed. All but one, old Edwin Forrest, for whom the Elder Booth had named Johnny's older brother, Ned. While he might on occasion praise their acting abilities, Forrest viewed with never-ending distaste the Booth eccentricities, committed by father and sons, alike.

"Oh!" Forrest would pontificate foully, when asked about his most worthy theater competitors. "All those God damned Booths are crazy!"

11. Lafayette C. Baker Takes on the Pursuit

Lafayette C. Baker was colonel of the 1st District of Columbia U.S. Volunteer Cavalry. It was an interesting regiment. It had four companies, or troops as the cavalry called them, raised in the District, no mean task in this bastion of Confederate or, rather, Southern cultural support. The other eight companies were down-east men from the state of Maine--a series of independent companies arbitrarily joined together to give Baker military rank and an independent power base--on paper, anyway. But in reality, he had a more important job--he was head of the National Detective Police, a sort of personal gendarmerie of Secretary of War Edwin McMasters Stanton. But that was on paper, too. Baker had essentially turned his National Detectives into a personal secret police force dedicated to ridding the Union of suspected and actual Rebel sympathizers or, at least, collecting bribes and payoffs from them.

Baker had been with the National Detective Police since 1862, when the unit was an adjunct to William H. Seward's State Department. It was this unit to which the Secretary referred in his memorable conversation with Lord Lyons, the British Minister to the United States, who sought the release of a British citizen jailed without benefit of habeas corpus, in an alleged plot to kidnap President Lincoln in 1862. In response, Seward pointed to a bell that stood in a prominent position on his desk.

"My Lord," Seward had boasted, "I can touch this little bell with my right hand and order the arrest of a citizen in Ohio. I can touch it again and order the arrest of a citizen in New York, and no power can release them. Can the Queen of England do as much?"

Seward agreed to free the British citizen in question, George A. Mason, as a personal gesture to Lord Lyon and British sovereignty, under the condition that Mr. Mason would not travel south of Philadelphia during the war's duration.

There were other intelligence agents in Washington, every department had at least one such person, it seemed. But Seward knew that he and Lincoln (early in the war Seward often got the hierarchical order of the Union government mixed up, until Lincoln subtly straightened him out and Seward became the President's most reliable man in his cabinet) needed someone loyal to them, to the administration, no questions asked. Lafayette Curry Baker was that person.

A former San Francisco vigilante during the turbulent gold rush years, Baker had already conducted behind the lines spying missions and a more open one into the southeastern peninsula of Maryland, designed to curtail Rebel activities. There, he met a certain Mrs. Mary Surratt at her tavern home. He knew well the disloyal people of Port Tobacco, and had been all the way to Leonardtown, arresting and harassing suspected Southern leaning newspaper editors and any others holding anti-Union views.

When Stanton became Secretary of War in January 1862, Seward sent Baker over to him, with the admonition to use the agent's talents fully. Stanton did not let Baker's peculiar genius grow rusty with inactivity. He turned him loose on the entire nation. Baker sought out Rebel spies, often turning them against their former masters at the threat of a slow hanging. He cleaned up the corruption in the Treasury Department, where employees stole old bills instead of destroying them, funneled the special bill paper to counterfeit rings, and kept notoriously poor records. In the process, Baker ran afoul of Congressman (and future President) James A. Garfield, who was in on the take and nearly got Baker fired through a congressional investigation of his unwholesome methods of intimidation, arbitrary arrests, and use of female informants of doubtful sexual morality.

Baker also *tried* to clean up houses of prostitution and gambling in the City--after all, there was a limit on anyone's success here, soldiers' appetites being what they are-- but Baker settled again for using the corrupt of both genders as informants. He was more successful exposing civilian and military friends of President Lincoln and General Grant, who were getting rich off of illegal sales of seized and smuggled Southern cotton. He got away with it because he was so important to the war effort in other areas, as when he penetrated the Confederacy's Northwest Conspiracy with his spies, male and female.

Of course, he formed "Baker's Rangers," as he liked to call the 1st D.C. Cavalry, and filled its staff with relatives; cousins L. Byron Baker as adjutant, J. Stannard Baker as company commander, and Ray Stannard Baker as Major. He armed his men with Henry carbines, an early version of the late nineteenth century Winchester lever-action series. Even Mosby's men knew better than to try and stand up to Yankees with such rapid-fire weapons. Led by Lt. Colonel Everton Conger, whose brother was a U.S. Senator from Michigan, the regiment cut its combat teeth during the Confederate retreat from Gettysburg.

When Booth shot Lincoln, Baker and his right-hand man, Cousin Byron, were cleaning up the Bounty Jump scandal in New York City. This involved men who would join Union regiments to collect the enlistment bounty and then desert and repeat the process all over again. Large rings organized these men and managed the process as a big business, with important politicians in on the take. The "Great Barbecue" of theft and greed did not limit itself to the later Grant Administration--it began prior to Lincoln's presidency, in the 1850's--and Baker suspected that the President, while not making money on the deals any more than Grant would, turned a blind eye to them and let the perpetrators run amok with the public's money.

But then, Baker never went broke during the war either. His personal reputation for bribery and corruption was as widely known as was his nickname, the "human ferret." And, to their joint credit, Lincoln and Grant never stopped his investigations or their results, beyond allowing a friend or two to escape with a resignation instead of a jail sentence.

Like his superiors, Baker knew well the necessity of keeping up appearances. He wore his simple motto emblazoned on a silver medallion hung around his neck for all to see."Death to Traitors," it read, and he lived by it and everyone knew it. Hence, when a hotel employee came in at four in the morning to awaken Lafayette Baker, he felt no trepidation. He knew Baker would be angry only if he were *not* awakened.

"President Lincoln has been shot!"

Baker went into the room next door and shook Byron awake. They went out on the streets and read the newspaper headlines and the false and exaggerated stories that followed. Lafayette Baker did not believe the rubbish he was reading, but Cousin Byron was convinced that the headlines were true, even if the stories that followed were not.

"Lafe, don't you think we should put up some expression of our feelings at headquarters?"

The building a 12 Vesey Street quickly was covered in black crepe, the first display of mourning in the whole city. All day, the Bakers discussed the assassination, for it was soon revealed that Lincoln was truly dead, and continued to read more newspapers. By nightfall, Lafayette Baker decided that he and Byron would return to Washington City and help pursue and arrest the suspects. As they walked out of the hotel with their bags, the bellman handed them a telegram from Secretary of War Stanton. It had been delayed by the great traffic over the wires all day:

WASHINGTON, April 15, 1865
COLONEL L.C. BAKER:
Come here immediately and see if you can find the murderer of the President.
EDWIN M. STANTON, *Secretary of War*

12. Breakfast at Dr. Mudd's

Frank Washington brought Davy Herold down the stairs shortly after the breakfast horn had sounded at 7 a.m. Herold was about to follow him into the kitchen, when Dr. Mudd bade him to take a place at the family table in the dining room. Herold sat, and then noticed that the Mudds were still standing. After an uncomfortable moment he rose and stood behind his chair, too.

"In the name of the Father, Son, and Holy Spirit," Mudd intoned as he and the others at the table, two women, one a sister-in-law (the four children having eaten earlier), crossed themselves.

Mudd intoned a few words of prayer and everyone crossed themselves again. Then the whole gathering sat down. Unused to such regal treatment, Davy sat at one side of the table between Dr. and Mrs. Mudd with as much deportment as possible. But he could not restrain his mouth, and he prattled on incessantly, giving lie to his nervousness at being treated as an equal by those so obviously superior to him in birth, manner, culture, and religion.

"Do you know many folks in this area?" he asked Dr. Mudd.

"Not really," Mudd said thoughtfully. "I have a tendency to keep to myself and my kin hereabouts. I do not practice much medicine except betwixt me and mine. Plantation life can be quite lonely, restricted to family and labor, you know."

"Well, sir," Herold bragged, "I knock about quite a bit. I am passionately fond of partridge shooting, you know, and every fall I often take two or three months for that purpose. I was fox hunting lower down in the county and banged up my ankle jumping a fence. But I am alright now."

Herold dug into the grits, eggs, and ham on his plate with obvious relish. And just a little too exuberantly for the more restrained and mannerly Mudds.

"I know quite a few folks in Charles and Prince George's and St. Mary's. (He shoveled in some eggs and ham and chewed). You know Mr. Walter Edelin? No? [Swig of coffee. Davy started a bit--it was *real*, not fake! And this late in the war with the shortages and all]. I also helped Mr. James R. Burch as a clerk when he sold his place over on Piscataway Branch. How about Mr. Walter Griffin, or Mr. John Jarboe--he lives up toward the City some distance from here? [More grits and eggs are forked. Frankie made a slight face behind her napkin at the boy's poor table manners. He talked with his mouth open and chewing]. And of course, Mr. Philip Beale, Mr. John Steed, and Mr. John Roberts. [Coffee]. Down closer to Port Tobacco, o' course, there is Mr. Peregrine Davis. [He shoved in little bit of everything on his plate. That boy must not have eaten in a week. What an appetite, thought Frankie]. I have hunted that region for years. Perhaps Mr. John Hughes, son-in-law to Mr. Davis? His house overlooks some of the best marshland shooting grounds on the Potomac."

Mudd nodded, "Oh, yes, I know Mr. Davis some." He did not tell Herold that he knew every secessionist along the Secret Mail Route, including most of those he mentioned and many more besides. But Peregrine Davis was known to everyone in Southern Maryland. No harm in admitting the Mudds knew the Davises. At least not to this young blade.

"Well, then," Frankie interjected, "do you live here in the county?"

"Nome," Davy said (swilling more coffee), "I live in the City, but I have been playing around in this neighborhood for the past six months or more."

Frankie thought this impetuous young man a mite immature and irresponsible. She could not resist giving him a mild rebuke. "All play and no work makes Jack a bad boy. Your father ought to make you go to work." She smiled. "Sarah, give the young gentleman more coffee."

Herold took no offense. Indeed the whole criticism sailed right over his head, as the black woman obligingly filled his cup. "Pa is dead," he said. "And I am way ahead of the Old Lady. But I have been in the drug business in the City."

Mudd looked up. He wondered if this meant as a druggist's assistant or one who illegally supplied Confederate hospitals. "The drug business, eh?"

"Oh, yes sir. Eleven months with T. S. Ward's. Lived in with him and his family. And before that with William S. Thompson. [Davy cleaned his plate up one more time. Oh, Blessed Lord, Frankie prayed, do not let him lick it clean]. I even carried prescriptions to the President's house. [Davy arched his back a little and sat proudly to indicate his self-inflated importance. Frankie noted that he actually sipped his coffee politely, for a change]. Why, before I hurt my ankle in the fox hunt I was going to clerk with Captain Burrill for the base hospital of the Army of the James. But I was in bed two weeks and never got down there. [More coffee]. Someone else had the job by then."

Frankie seemed pleased he had at least tried to work, no matter how haphazardly. For, in truth, this boy seemed to have not a care in the world. She smiled, in spite of herself.

"Say, Doctor," Davy interjected as the conversation lagged and victuals and coffee had been consumed, "Booth and me wish to go down to the river and take a steamer home. It would mean much less movement for his leg after we got there. How close is the Potomac, anyway?"

"Eighteen or twenty miles. Since breakfast is finished, perhaps you could step outside and I will show you a shortcut through the Zekiah Swamp."

Herold sprang to his feet, feeling much more comfortable in the outdoors than in the Mudd home with its toney atmosphere; at least that is how he saw it, now that he was well-fed.

As he left the dining room, Herold turned to Dr. Mudd and asked for the loan of a razor, soap, and water so that Booth might remove his key physical identifying feature; his moustache. Mrs. Mudd said they would be ready when he came back from the road tour.

"By the bye, I have an old carpet slipper for Booth's injured limb," Mudd said as they stepped outside. "And I will have my English tenant, John Best, construct a pair of crutches from some spare barn lumber. That should help Booth move around more easily. But he must stay off the injured leg as much as possible. They is your road, young man," Mudd waved his hand westward. "Now I must get to work."

"Thank you, sir," Herold intoned absently, as he examined the terrain with the practiced eye of the hunter. Mudd's road was little more than a trail, he thought. Then aloud he said, "I think I will go up and grab some shut-eye, myself." The two men parted; Mudd to the fields and Herold to Booth's bedroom.

13. Lloyd Misleads the Pursuit and Cuts a Deal

Just about noon the day after Booth and Herold had picked up their weapons and the binoculars, John Lloyd came to the barroom porch of the tavern at Surrattsville. He was drawn there by the noise of many hooves coming up the road. He looked out and saw a Metropolitan police posse led by Detective John A. Clarvoe, guided by Louis J. Weichmann, and accompanied by John Holohan.

Encouraged by reports that the killer of the President was John Wilkes Booth and that he and another man had already crossed the Navy Yard Bridge, Detective Clarvoe's boss, Superintendent of Police A. C. Richards, organized Clarvoe and a dozen men to follow up this lead. The posse was to ride into Southern Maryland, as soon as they could get cavalry horses to ride. The City police normally walked or utilized carriages for their work and had no riding steeds of their own available.

There had been a long delay in getting started, as the District's Provost Marshal, Brevet Major General Christopher C. Augur, did not initially want to lend horses to a competing department to follow up clues his men were not privy to. But Richards was persistent and finally got the animals from Naylor's Stable, where a still-angry John Fletcher was foreman. Meanwhile, Clarvoe had led the search party to Mrs. Surratt's boarding house, on the grounds that John Surratt was a known drinking companion of Booth.

It was there that detectives ran into boarder Louis Weichmann. Under pressure from fellow boarder John T. Holohan, Weichmann came into police headquarters. Detective James McDevitt took Weichmann up to Richard's second floor office and he was waiting there when Richards showed up for work, Saturday morning. After a brief introduction, Weichmann spilled his guts to the Superintendent; giving names, dates, and details of everything he knew; except for anything that might have implicated himself.

Richards, who had witnessed Lincoln's assassination, knew that he had hit the jackpot. He immediately took Weichmann under his personal care, even holding him at the police station without charges, feeding him at home, and having him sleep Saturday night at the station. Sunday morning, after the trip to Surrattsville, he would send him off with McDevitt on a lengthy trip to Baltimore and then Montreal, looking for the missing John Surratt. Richards was damned if Secretary of War Stanton or his lackey, Lafayette C. Baker, would beat him out of this boon. In his defense, Stanton would have done the same to him, but it was a wonderful example of inter-departmental rivalry, rather than cooperation. On Saturday, both Weichmann and Holohan agreed to ride with the posse and lead it to Surrattsville.

"Hello, John," Clarvoe said, upon dismounting. He was very stiff from the ride and could barely walk without groaning and grimacing in pain.

"Clarvoe! Good to see you," Lloyd said. He and Clarvoe knew each other from the old police department before the war; before it had been purged of secession sympathizers like Lloyd. "How are things at the nation's capital?"

"Bad, John, real bad. You have not heard?"

"No," Lloyd lied, "tell me."

"The President has been shot. He died this morning, just before we left."

"No! So late in the conflict? Why? Who done it?"

"We figure it was a last-gasp plot out of the heart of the Confederacy, ordered by Jeff Davis and his minions. The shooter was a well-known actor, John Wilkes Booth. Maybe you know him?"

"An actor? I never did cotton to play-acting much--even when I lived in the City." Weichmann started to say something, but thought better of it. He stepped back and merely listened.

"You ain't seen two men come thisaway, have you?"

"No, cain't say I have and I was up the better part of the night."

Clarvoe lowered his voice. "You know there is enough money in this for both of us, if you but tell what you know."

"I am unable to tell you anything, I swear." Lloyd shrugged his shoulders.

"Which would be the most likely way someone would go from here. How about to Beantown?

"You might better try the west fork--goes by way of Piscataway."

It did not take Clarvoe long after finding no trace of Booth or Herold to suspect that Lloyd had misled him. Unfortunately, the posse had bigger problems than Lloyd. They had ridden their horses too hard and barely got them back to Washington that night. But Lloyd was not out of trouble yet. He had merely gotten rid of the City authorities. He still had to face the provost marshals.

The Federals were on their way, slowly but inevitably. Unknown to Lloyd, his barkeeper, Joseph T. Knott, had been conversing with a customer later that Saturday about how he had heard from two assistant provost marshals in the District that John Surratt was suspected of being the man who had so brutally attacked the Seward family.

"Where do you reckon Surratt is now?" Edward L. Smoot asked, as Knott poured the whiskey, acting in the self-assumed role of *agent provocateur*.

"I reckon he is at least to New York City by now," Knott surmised, corking the bottle.

"How so?"

"My God! John knows all about the murder. Do you suppose he is going to stay in Washington and let them *catch* him?"

"Is that so? He knew *all* about it?" said Smoot, feigning surprise.

"It *is* so, by God! I could have told you that Lincoln's murder was coming to pass six months ago." Knott put his hand on Smoot's shoulder, and lowered his voice. "Keep that in your own skin, my boy. Do not mention that. If you do, it will ruin me forever. Excuse me, here are some more customers. Remember, mum's the word," Knott whispered with a wink.

A Loyalist, Smoot immediately went to Washington and reported the whole matter to Provost Marshal General Augur. The following day, Monday, acting on Smoot's statement, Detective Captain George Cottingham, his partner, Lieutenant Joshua Lloyd, and six cavalrymen under Lieutenant Alexander Lovett arrived at Surrattsville to talk to John Lloyd once again. They encountered a terrified neighbor, Andrew Kallenbach coming from the barroom.

"Lieutenant, I have just been threatened by Zadoc Jenkins. He said that if I persisted in talking against him or his family he would horsewhip me within an inch of my life and send me to Hell."

"That is the damn truth. If he ever says anything against my sister or my nephew again he is in for a hurting."

"Who are you, sir?"

"I am Zad Jenkins."

"The brother of Mary Surratt, gentlemen, mother of John Surratt." Kallenbach threw in as an aside.

"Why do you two not give it up?" Lieutenant Lovett asked.

"Go home, the both of you, said Cottingham. Mr. . . . . ah ["Kallenbach, sir"] . . . Kallenbach, why do you not start off first. I will keep Mr. Jenkins back for fifteen minutes or so. You can get a head start then. What have you got Josh?"

Lieutenant Lloyd came down off the barroom porch, holding John Lloyd (no relation) by the arm. The tavern keeper had just brought his wife home from her several days' stay in Allen's Fresh, which kept her ignorant of any of the goings on of that weekend. "This is the man we are looking for."

"Place him under arrest. Le's take him down to Robey's store. Witnesses tend to be more *loyal* there."

"Wait! You cannot arrest me. I have done nothing."

"That is a most damnable lie, sir. I suspect that you assisted in the escape of John Wilkes Booth, murderer of President Abraham Lincoln. You had better come clean, or you will face the rope."

"But I know nothing."

All the way to Robey's, John M. Lloyd held to his story. Finally, in a handy dale, Cottingham permitted the cavalrymen to interrogate him, the army way. The troopers threw some heavy twine over a tree limb and hoisted Lloyd up by his thumbs, his toes just touching the ground.

"I am perfectly satisfied that you know what we want to know," Cottingham said. "It must be a heavy load on your mind, concealing a murderer, and the sooner you talk and unburden yourself, the better."

After an hour or so, when the blood trapped in his thumbs began to throb unbearably, he began to crack. "Oh, my God!" Lloyd wailed. "If I was to make a confession, they would murder me!"

"Who would murder you?"

"Those parties that are in this conspiracy."

"Well, if you are afraid of being murdered, and you let those fellows get away, that is your business, not mine. Of course, you will look mighty funny, trying to keep them away from you and yours without any thumbs."

"No, no! Wait! I will tell it all." Cottingham motioned for the troopers to cut him down. "It was just like Kallenbach wanted to say; only Jenkins said he would send him to Hell if he did. Mrs. Surratt come down on the evening of Good Friday about four or five o'clock. I had just come in from Marlboro. It was court day, doncha know, and I had a feller up for knifing me a while back. But they postponed the case. By that evening, I was right smart for liquor. Me 'n a couple of fellers had been drinking all the way home. They turned off earlier.

"Well, I pulled in and was unloading fish and oysters I brung for dinner. Mrs. Surratt come up with this package and told me it would be called for that night. I was to have the shooting irons ready. Them's her exact words, I tell you. 'Have them shooting irons ready!' Well, Herold and Booth did call; I did not know it was going to be them. Herold got down, they took a drink and I give them the stuff. But Booth said that he could not carry the carbine. His leg was broke.

"When they was leaving, Booth said to me, 'I have murdered the President,' and Herold said, 'I have fixed off Seward.' I did not know they was going to kill Lincoln, I swear it. Please do not hang me. I will tell everything I know, just do not let them shoot me!"

"Where is the extra carbine?"

"It is down between the studs in the kitchen wall. You can get there through the old storeroom. I will show you."

"Lieutenant! Mount up the patrol and let's go on over to Surrattsville. Lloyd can show us the carbine and we can carry him in--to the Old Capitol."

"Please, Captain," Lloyd begged plaintively. "Can I say good bye to my wife? She is an invalid. I do not know what she is going to do without me. And my prayer book. I want to take my prayer book!"

With that, Lloyd broke into tears and sobbed all the way home. "Oh, Mrs. Surratt, that vile woman! She has ruined me! I am to be shot! I am to be shot! If the Surratts had not brought me down here to run the tavern, I never would have gotten into this difficulty!"

At Surrattsville, Cottingham found that the carbine had somehow slipped from the cord that held it up between the wall studs. So, assisted by Andrew Kallenbach, who had returned, he took an axe and cut the plaster and lath away from the dining room wall, revealing the weapon later presented in court. Lloyd kept his word and turned state's evidence. More than anyone else, even Louis J. Weichmann, he placed a rope around Mary Surratt's neck.

But that was not all. After the trial and his eventual release, Lloyd had the gall to bill the Federal government for damages allegedly suffered when a battalion of the 6th West Virginia Cavalry passed through Surrattsville, following Booth's likely trail down the old secret mail line. In a go-to-hell report, Major Thomas E. Day admitted that his men had confiscated twenty-five bushels of corn (Lloyd said it was twenty-five barrels), for which he had given Mrs. Lloyd a receipt, but denied that any of the other twenty items listed had been touched. Seven months later, Day wrote a full explanation, obviously disgusted he had to bother:

The whole thing is trumped up, and Lloyd perjures himself when he swears to it. At the time of the alleged taking, Lloyd was in *prison* at Washington. How does he know who took the food or whether they were taken at all? Instead of being *paid* for anything, he should be sent to keep Mrs. Surratt company.

Day astutely ignored Lloyd's mention of various stolen horse shoeing tools, shoes, nails, and nail rod and bar steel that would have kept his unit on the road for weeks. After all, a good commander in the field often had to supplement the shortcomings of an overworked quartermaster's corps to keep his men properly outfitted. Who better than a traitorous Reb to make up any shortfall? But Day did have one point. Why would his mounted men have removed 300 pounds of old junk iron and several horse harnesses? What in Heaven's name would cavalry do with it, while pursuing John Wilkes Booth? Maybe they just threw it in the swamp as a lesson to the man who got Mary Surratt hanged.

14. Looking for a Conveyance

It was dinner time before the Mudds saw either of their guests, again. At the sound of the horn, Herold came down and took to the noon meal with his usual relishing appetite. His nervous banter had slowed since breakfast, much to the delight of his hosts. He actually tried to be a polite, urbane visitor and even improved some on his table manners.

As the meal ended, Herold asked, "Is there any place nearby that we might borrow a carriage? I think that Booth will do much better if he don't have to mount and ride a horse."

Well, Dr. Mudd replied, "I am going into Bryantown to get the mail and see some sick. You could come along with me to the village. Perhaps you can get a carriage there. It would be better for him not to have to ride in the saddle. Let me go up and check on Booth, before we leave."

Mudd quietly ascended the stairs and opened the door to the extra bedroom. Booth lay there, dinner tray on the small table by his bed untouched. He had shaved off his famous trade mark moustache and his face looked eerily pale. Booth did not appear to be awake. Mudd left the room, closed the door, and descended the staircase.

"Sam, do you think it would be alright if I went up to see Mr. Booth?" Frankie asked.

"Of course, dear," the doctor said. "Yes, certainly you can. It might be good to have some feminine attention given to him. Come, Herold, let us go to the barn and start our trip into town."

They made a fine-looking, well-mounted pair, the good doctor and his young companion as they jogged along at a slow trot. Herold rode Booth's rented bay mare to see if she could take some exercise without being too lame. Frank Washington had put a home remedy on her cuts and bruises. She responded to the movement along the roads well, especially after she warmed up a bit. Mudd was on his favorite bay filly, a spitting image of Herold's mare in everything but manners. It was a sunny day and the Maryland countryside was cloaked with the promise of spring.

Mudd decided to take Herold over to Oak Hill, his father's plantation. Mudd knew that they had a carriage or two, but when they arrived they found one was out of commission and the other consigned to family use for Easter Sunday church services. Mudd led the way to the Bryantown road, winding his way through a maze of plantation paths to get there. As they traveled, Herold carefully checked landmarks so he could find the way back.

No problem, he thought. Besides, the doctor would be with him.

Suddenly, Mudd pulled up his filly. "Herold, they is a federal cavalry outpost in front of the town. Maybe you ought to go back and let me scout out the area alone. You being a stranger and all."

"Good idea," Davy answered. He had no desire to meddle with soldiers if he could help it. Besides he had left his carbine at the Mudd house.

"Turn and ride back slowly, so as to not attract attention. I will see you and Booth later this evening."

Herold did as he was bid, and after the sentry disappeared from sight, he kicked the bay mare into ground-eating canter. As he passed the coach house at Oak Hill, it crossed his mind that he might be able to steal the carriage Booth needed. Herold turned in toward the prized carriage.

"You looks a mite lost, Massa." The voice startled Davy. He looked over to the side and saw a black man standing with his hat in his hand.

"Yes, Uncle, I reckon I am," Davy said, deciding it was smart to feign confusion. In reality, the boy rarely got lost for more than five minutes, anywhere. "I am looking for Dr. Mudd's."

"Well, sir. Does you want Dr. George Mudd or his cousin, Dr. Sam Mudd?"

Crap, Davy thought, what was Dr. Mudd's name? Then he remembered. Mrs. Mudd had called him "Sam." "It is Sam" he said aloud.

"You takes this path right here to the edge of the woods yonder," said Electus Thomas, a former slave." Then you heads along the woods and takes the first road through the woods. It ain't very wide there. You can see through the woods. The Dr. Sam Mudd place is on the other side. Cain't miss it."

"Thanks, Uncle. I rarely lose my way, but it can get confusing for a stranger about here."

"Yessir, Massa, it sure can, even for those borned and raised here." Thomas watched him go, convinced that there was more to that boy than met the eye.

Davy turned the mare down the indicated pathway and soon came through the woods to the hill. He gave an audible sigh and turned for Mudd's house, more determined than ever to get Booth out of there before the Yankee soldiers found them, carriage or no.

15. The Uncommunicative Patient

Betty Washington had been a slave until the 1864 Maryland state emancipation. Then she left her old mistress and elected to hire on at the Mudds as a paid servant. She had been there since Christmas 1864, the holiday period from then to New Year's being the traditional hiring and contracting time for blacks since time in memorial. Evidently she either liked her employers or feared reprisal, because when federal detectives questioned her, she would maintain adamantly that she had never seen Booth at the Mudd house, and Herold only once, briefly, at a distance. Both statements were false.

As part of the kitchen help, Betty worked closely with Mrs. Mudd, and Frankie treated her well. At breakfast, Frankie had Betty set up a tray of food and coffee and carry it up to Booth.

"Just put it on the little table beside the bed, Betty. No need to awaken the gentleman or feed him. Come right on down after you are finished and serve breakfast in the dining room."

"Yes, ma'am, Miz Frankie," said Betty. She went up the stairs and found Booth lying with his back to the door, acting as if he were asleep. Betty put the tray down quietly and left it there as instructed.

At dinner Frankie had Betty prepare another tray. Soon she was back in the kitchen with both trays, none of the food having been touched.

"I done like you told me, Missus, but he told me to get out. He don't want no food, he say."

"Very well, Betty, prepare a special tray of cake, maybe a couple of oranges, and a decanter of red wine. I will take it up myself. After all, an injured man must eat to keep up his strength."

Frankie entered the spare bedroom and found Booth lying with his back to the door. Although she could see only a bit of his face as he looked to see who had entered, what she saw had a ghastly pallor to it.

"How are you feeling, Mr. Booth?"

"Not very well, ma'am. My back pains me dreadfully. I must have hurt it when my horse fell and broke my leg."

Frankie was about to suggest that he remove the two revolvers, the butts of which protruded from beneath his coat and the blanket, but something told her it would be wiser to hold her tongue.

"Perhaps a little refreshment will help. I have brought you some cake, a pair of nice oranges, and a bottle of wine. Will you not take some cake and wine?"

"No, madam," Booth said firmly, his face turned to the wall. Suddenly he moved his head toward her again. "By any chance do you have any brandy in the house?"

"Oh, no," said Frankie. "But we do have some whiskey. I would be glad to get you some."

"No, I think not."

"I guess you think I have very little hospitality--you have been sick all day and I have not been up to see you."

Booth made no answer.

"Is there nothing I can do for you?" Frankie persisted.

Booth still said nothing. Frankie sighed, slowly picked up the tray, and left the room. Not only was that man suffering the pain of a broken bone, Frankie realized that he was experiencing a debilitating alcohol withdrawal. Downstairs, she went to the kitchen to assist Betty Washington and the others in preparing tomorrow's Easter dinner. Some time later, there was a sudden tapping at the kitchen window. It was Davy Herold, grinning widely. Frankie pointed to the front of the kitchen and went around to let him in.

"Have you procured a carriage?" She inquired, as she opened the door.

"Oh, no, ma'am," Davy said. "We stopped over at the doctor's father's and asked for his carriage, but tomorrow being Easter Sunday, the family had to go to church, and he could not spare it. I rode some distance down the road with the Doctor, and then concluded to return and try the horses. Excuse me ma'am."

Herold left the kitchen, went around to the house's front door, and bounded up the stairs. "Come on, Johnny," he called out. "Let's try those crutches!"

Frankie called after him, "wait a minute! The doctor said Mr. Booth is not to be moved. Do you hear me?"

Scraping footsteps indicated her words were to no avail. Men! Why does a body even bother? They never listen to common sense, anyhow. Frankie threw up her hands as if to be rid of the whole project and went back to the kitchen.

16. Dr. Mudd at Bryantown

After Davy Herold had turned back, Samuel Mudd urged his bay filly into a slow trot and boldly rode up to the sentry on the bridge at the edge of Bryantown.

"Hold on, sir."

"What is going on? Why are you soldiers down here?"

"You have not heard?" the cavalryman queried. "The President has been killed and Secretary Seward and his whole family assaulted. His son is believed dead and the secretary is feared dying. We are in pursuit of the assassins. Troops are scouring the countryside in all directions looking for them."

"Who are you looking for? Who are these assassins?" As he asked the questions, Mudd began to have a queasy feeling in his stomach. Deep down he knew that part of the answer was back at his house.

"Sir, you will have to ask Lieutenant Dana, I really do not know. He told me to watch this road for anyone suspicious, but how do I know who is suspicious or who lives around here? Just like the army. Hell, he don't even command us normally. We are of the 13th New York Cavalry, and he is some fancy officer from the 3rd Massachusetts Heavies, with a brother or a cousin in the War Department or something. Everything is all fouled up."

"Well, I am a country doctor from a few miles north of here on the way to do some shopping and visit a few patients." He showed the soldier his medical bag." Would you like to examine it?"

"No, sir, that is good enough for me." The boy evidently did not realize that half of the spies in the South were country doctors. Visiting patients, real or imaginary, made for a good cover.

"Thank you. I shall go forward, then." Mudd sighed inwardly in relief. The bag contained not only medical instruments, drugs and home-made remedies, but a half dozen letters to various Confederate agents that would have been hard to explain, if examined.

Mudd rode into E. D. B. Bean's general store and deposited the latest letters from Virginia that had been sent up to him by way of the Secret Mail Route. Bean would send them on as ordinary mail, as indicated on their cover envelopes. The recipients would open them and find envelopes addressed to the real parties for whom the messages were intended, and mail them again. To cover the operation from snooping Federal soldiers, Mudd asked to look at some calicoes just arrived from the North. Fortunately, the Yankees were too much *men* to think why would a wife trust her husband to buy cloth that was obviously for her?

"Have you heard the tragic news?" Bean said it loudly enough for the Yankee lieutenant to hear.

"Yes, I am sorry to hear it." Mudd turned to Lieutenant David D. Dana. He was a Heavy Artillerist, all right. Just too much spit and polish for a combat leader. "The trooper at the edge of town told me of the assassination. Who perpetrated this foul deed upon our beloved President?"

"A sad day indeed," Dana intoned solemnly. "We are looking for Edwin Booth."

"The tragedian?" Mudd had been preparing for the answer ever since the bridge. He managed to converse calmly, showing concern, but without a hint of the real agitation going on inside his body and mind.

"The same, sir. We have been sent here to look for him and take him and any associates back to the City."

"I'll take five yards off this bolt, Mr. Bean. Please put it on my bill," Mudd said, turning to the storekeeper. *Edwin* Booth, my ass! He said to himself. It has to be John Wilkes. It all makes sense now. Going *to* the City. . . . Hell! They were *fleeing* the City. And they are hiding at my place right now. By God, Mudd thought, I ought to turn Booth and Herold in right now. No, no, I cannot. The soldiers would ride out, Herold would see them coming, and that show-off braggart, Booth, would go down in a gun fight. Frankie and the children, all of the servants. . . . Even if no one got hurt, Booth and Herold would implicate him, for sure. He had no desire to hang for the President's murder. Kidnapping was one thing but. . . . maintain your composure now, Sam. Then he looked back at the lieutenant.

"I wish you luck in your mission, sir. I must be going to visit a few patients. I am a country doctor, you know."

"Thank you, sir. Always a pleasure to talk with Union men. I am expecting reinforcements momentarily from Chapel Point, below Port

Tobacco. They will search the west side of the Zekiah and we will do the east."

Mudd took the cloth, bade everyone a good day and went out to his horse. He looked over to Pete Trotter's blacksmith shop where about a dozen troopers were passing the time of day, watching him shoe a horse. Then Mudd headed east out of town, opposite the way he came in. When beyond the sentry he kicked the filly into a quick lope. He was off to the next safe house on the way south, a small place ensconced in a hollow, owned by William Bertle. He needed to get ready to move Booth and Herold on to the Potomac before the whole area was shut off by Union patrols. Damn that Booth! He has really gotten everyone into a fix this time!

17. Dr. Mudd Confronts Booth

Returning from Bertle's, Mudd cantered down the road toward his anticipated showdown with Booth. He was not going to let him off without a good tongue lashing. Bertle told him to give him a few choice words from him, too. Mudd was about to cut cross country when he remembered another chore he had to complete. He must check on some fence rails he wished to purchase from John F. Hardy, a neighbor. This meant using the main road and taking a half hour more. But he needed those rails, and Booth ought not to be out in broad daylight . . . too risky, and not just for that damn Booth!

Then, as he cantered by Frank Farrell's place, he heard shouting. "Mudd! Mudd!"

It was Hardy. Mudd turned the filly and rode into Farrell's yard.

"I needed to see you, Hardy. In fact, I was headed to your place just now to inquire about those fence rails."

Hardy looked slightly embarrassed. "Mudd, I am truly sorry. It has been so long since we last spoke that I thought you were no longer interested in the rails and I sold them to your cousin, Sylvester."

"You are right, Hardy, I should have acted quicker. No offense taken, none meant. . . . But to change the topic, have you all heard? President Lincoln was killed on Good Friday eve. They also killed Secretary Seward's son."

"Good news, indeed! They finally got that son of a bitch. Farrell! Come out here! Our black Republican President is dead!"

"*Your* black Republican President, you mean," said Farrell as he stepped from the porch with a grin. "I 'low he was not *mine*. What happened? How did it occur? Tell us, Mudd."

"I do not know much. Rumor in town has it that the guerrilla Boyle killed Seward and Lincoln was shot by a man named Booth."

"Wait a minute," Hardy puzzled. "Wasn't that the name of that feller we all saw at church last year?"

"I reckon," countered Mudd, "but I am not sure. There are several men named Booth, all from that acting family. . . . Well, I must be going if I am to make it home by dark. If I see anyone, I will be sure and tell how grieved we all are."

"So will we." Both Hardy and Farrell laughed, and bantered back and forth.

"Damn! Old Abe is dead!"

"Can you beat that?"

"After all the suffering and tragedy he has brought the country!"

"Damn good riddance!"

"See you later, Mudd!"

"Come back when you have more good news!"

It was pitch black when Mudd turned into his plantation, but he could see activity up at the house by the glare of light thrown from the windows. As he rode up, he saw Booth hobbling out with John Best's rude crutches under his arms, and Herold tending to the tack on the horses.

Frankie ran up. "Oh, Sam. I told them to wait for you. Mr. Booth ought not to be traipsing around in his condition. They want to leave on horseback. Did you find a carriage?"

"There will be no carriage. They could not make it with one, anyway. The cavalry would be on them by daylight. Booth! You scoundrel! You did not tell me about Lincoln. You have endangered my family and all my people with your reckless behavior!"

"What are you talking about, Sam?" Frankie asked puzzled. "They have acted as perfect gentlemen here."

"I am not talking about that. You want to tell her, Booth? No? Well, my dear, you are looking at the assassins of the President of the United States, the *former* Abraham Lincoln. What happened to cause this? Did Richmond's plan failed and you decided to do it alone?"

Booth looked up sharply from where he was leaning on his crutches, staring at the ground.

"That's right," Mudd continued. "I know about blowing up the President's house during a cabinet meeting. You two get the Hell out of here and do not come back for any reason. They is cavalry all about Bryantown and, I daresay, you cannot head west over the swamp, as they are probably at Beantown by now, too. So, I will tell you how to circle Bryantown to the east and pick up assistance from another man, name of

William Bertle at Hagan's Folly. He will send you south to get you accross the river. For the sake of me and mine I hope you make it, but, by God, you deserve to hang for endangering all of us.

"Now look and listen well. Bertle knows of a Confederate mounted unit in the area. It was supposed to ferry Harney across, you know, the man who was to blow up the President's house? They will carry you all to Virginia, if you can find a suitable meeting place and make contact with them in the midst of all the Yankee patrols. Bertle will know." And with that Mudd took a stick and began to sketch the route to Bertle's farm, Hagan's Folly. He fairly snarled the instructions and muttered a good bye ("Go on, git, git.") then shooed them away with both hands as one might do to chickens pecking in the garden.

Before they left, Herold told Mudd that if he were contacted by Federal authoritires, he ought to identify them as Henson (Herold) and Tyson (Booth), and state that Tyson wore a false beard. Then, the younger man silently pressed a few bills into the doctor's hands. Mudd unwrapped the notes and found twenty five greenback dollars. Treason comes cheaply nowadays, he thought. Iscariot got *thirty* pieces of silver. Mudd shook his head and turned to Frankie.

"Come, my dear," he said. "We have to agree upon a good story as to what happened here this last sixteen hours that will make sense to the Yankees and keep me from hanging and the rest of us out of prison." That "good story" would keep Dr. Samuel Mudd from the hangman by one vote. But it threatened to send him to prison for life, until he was pardoned by Lincoln's successor, Andrew Johnson, three and a half years later, as a slap at Congress' strict Reconstruction policies, passed over his veto.

18. Seeking William Bertle

Booth looked at the road junction. It was the usual rural Maryland crossroads, surrounded by copses of cedars, sweet gums, tulip poplars, and white oaks. If he could have distinguished between the black shadows up on the ridges, he would have seen hundreds of pines standing guard over the hollows like massive armies awaiting the dawn. In this light, or lack of luminescence, one branch of the junction looked as good as the others.

"Well, Davy, which fork is it? Right or left?"

Davy looked at the moonlit heavens. "By the Dipper I say right. But if we want to stay clear of the soldiers, left seems safer."

"Wait!" Booth looked intensely off to the east." Did I see a light over yonder? Let us ride a bit that way and see if we can get some directions to Bertle's."

A few hundred yards brought the two riders to a small cabin. Herold hallooed and after a brief wait, Joseph Canter came out. He carried what people of the time would have called a "squirrel rifle."

"State your business," he said.

"Sir, there is no need for suspicion," Booth said. "We merely seek direction to Hagan's Folly, the home of William Bertle. We have lost our way in the dark."

"Yeah, that is easy to do around here. You are on the correct path, all right, but you ain't gone far enough. You need to go a couple of miles south east on what they call hereabouts Cracklin' Town Road, and then turn east."

"We though the right fork would take us back to Bryantown," inquired Booth casually.

"All rights but this one will. This one goes straight south to Bertle's place. Two miles, second road to the left for city boys," he said looking at Booth." That's more or less east to country folk," he said looking at Herold.

Thanking Canter, Booth and his companion rode south. Suddenly, Herold grabbed Charley's halter and spurred the bay into a copse of woods.

"What in Hell?!" Booth felt like his leg was being jerked off his torso. He stifled a cry of pain and struggled to keep astride old Charley as his leg shifted position.

"Ssst!" hissed Herold, riders coming. "Yanks, I think."

The clanking of sabers and the creaking of leather soon confirmed Herold's assessment. In the gloom the two fugitives could make out the forms of a Union cavalry officer followed by four troopers, cantering two abreast. Herold waited a few minutes to be sure no one else was coming and then led Booth out of the trees and onto the road.

"We better ride cross country, keeping along the woods as much as possible," he said.

Booth thought to demur, feeling that they might get lost without the landmarks offered by the road network, but for once he held his tongue. He did not want to blunder into a Federal patrol any more than Herold. They rode some time in silence.

"Davy, did you hear popping noises off to the south?"

Both men pulled up. "There! Hear it?"

"Yeah," Davy said. "Let's go back and find Bertle. We are hunting blind and the Bluecoats are trigger happy."

"Davy, I do not think we can find our way."

"Sure we can, Johnny." Davy dismissed Booth's doubts too casually to suit Booth.

Booth's fears proved prescient. The sky had clouded over hiding Davy's markers, the stars. They rode back and forth in the area for two or three hours. But they could not find the correct side route or their pathway back. Davy opined that they had missed it in the thick underbrush. They would have to find someone to ask for instructions again.

"This time, we find someone who will take us to Bertle in person," Booth said. His leg was bothering him again and his temper was growing short. "Offer them cash."

19. Oswell Swann Guides Booth to Captain Cox

Finally, the two fugitives struck a well travelled road road. Herold, seeing a light in the near distance, turned off the road to the right into a narrow, sandy lane and rode up to a cabin standing in a small clearing. "Hello, the house," he called out.

The door opened a crack. "Who there?"

"Just a couple of travelers. We are lost." It was Booth who spoke, hoping that his more polished English would be more amenable to the still hidden cabin dweller. "We seek the house of William Bertle. Do you know where it is located?"

Out of the now fully opened door stepped Oswell Swann, adjusting his galluses. He was a free man of color, that is to say, he was free-born before the war, one of many such people who lived mainly in the Border South, (especially Maryland, where they comprised nearly half of the black population), but could be found in all Slave States. Like many considered to be of African descent--in most states, North or South, it only took one great-grand-parent to be legally "black"--Swann was a mixture of African, Native American, and white ancestry. His yellow skin and high cheek bones told the story. But it was too dark for Booth or Herold to draw such fine distinctions. To them, Swann was non-white, or as Herold and most other Marylanders indelicately put it, he fell under the category of Negro and was treated as a second class being. But he owned quite a few acres of land and knew the countryside, as only a native of the area could.

"We will give you two dollars to take us to Bertle," Booth said. "Do you have a horse?"

"Yessir," Swann admitted, "he ain't worth much. But I go get 'im." Two dollars was a nice piece of change to a one-horse farmer like Swann, who rarely saw much money at all, except in the late fall when he sold his tobacco crop.

Swann bridled his horse and rode bareback. He headed to the right out of the farm lane and onto the main road. After a few minutes travel, Davy Herold began to recognize that they were headed the same way as the Yankee cavalry they had tried to avoid earlier that evening.

"Say, *boy*, how far is Bertle's place, anyhow?"

"Maybe a mile or two. Now, you'uns gentlemen *did* promise me two dollars, didn't you? I take you'uns at your word, now. You'uns is *honorable* gentlemen, ain't you?

"What is the matter Davy?" Booth wanted to know.

"We are spending two dollars for an awful short ride. Besides it is leading us right into the teeth of Union patrols. I recognize this piece of ground. This is where we got lost in the first place. See? We went through the woods over there. We need to put the swamp between us and the Yanks, *tonight*. There are only two crossings. One in this neck of the woods and the other up near Mudd's."

"You are right," Booth commented. "Uncle," he said turning to Swann, "do you know the way to Captain Samuel Cox's?" Swann nodded. "I tell you what; we will give you five dollars more in Yankee greenbacks to take us there. It is across the swamp, is it not?"

"Yessir," Swann said, "but it is a mite far for this time of night. . . . It is so cold and all."

"How about *ten* dollars more," Davy Herold interjected.

"All right," Booth said dejectedly, seeing Swann's hesitation as a subtle form of blackmail.

Swann smiled politely to the rumpled, but well-dressed, man on the red-gray roan. Twelve dollars! Now that was more like it, he thought.

"We gots to turn around, then, gentlemen."

As Swann led them down the road, Herold sidled up to Booth. "Who is this Cox? I do not recollect him, except as a busted tobacco planter with some good hunting land. Did he not kill one of his slaves for tipping off the Yanks about hidden guns and powder on his place?"

"That is right," Booth said quietly, so Swann would not hear. "Early in the war. The slave fled to the Union camp for protection but a higher officer turned him over to Cox as a runaway. Was a year before Lincoln's idiotic Emancipation Proclamation. Cox took him home and whipped him to death, of course. His plantation is called 'Rich Hill.' And it was once, but he has gone broke with the emancipation. He has a son or two in the Confederate army, I hear. He raised a company of Secesh militia in 1861, but he has kept his nose clean lately after the beating incident--except for helping with the secret mail."

It was well after midnight before the trio reached the gate way of Rich Hill. Swann's horse was pretty slow, and Booth's leg complained much less at the slower gait. Only Herold fussed a bit, having to hold back the bay mare, as usual.

"You stay here," Booth told Swann, "if you want your money, that is. Davy, go knock on the door and wake up Cox. I'll wait here with our guide."

20. Trying to Fool Swann

Cox was slow to rise from his bed and slower still to make his way downstairs through his hallway and to the front door. He was a reserved old man with the overbearing manner that characterized men who had been in business for themselves all their lives. "What is it that you want?" He demanded gruffly. He held a candle in his hand. His other was in the pocket of his dressing gown. Herold suspected it held the butt of some sort of pocket pistol.

"Are you Samuel Cox, sir? If so, the gentleman at the gate would like a word with you. It is very important--a matter of life or death."

"Yours or mine. The life or death, I mean."

"We mean you no harm, sir." With that, Cox followed Herold to the gate.

Booth moved his horse up to Cox. "May I have a word with you, sir, privately?"

"Certainly," Cox said. "Hey, Swannie," he said in passing to the guide. The two moved away from Herold and Swann.

"You are Captain Samuel Cox? I am John Booth, the tragedian. I have played in Washington, Baltimore and Richmond. You may have heard of me as 'Dr. Booth,' or just plain 'Doctor.'" Cox nodded knowingly at Booth's reference to drug running. "I was one of those who sought unsuccessfully to capture President Lincoln, and bring him through here to Richmond." Cox nodded again. "Well, I have assassinated President Lincoln two days ago." Cox's jaw dropped. "My companion and I are on the run from Federal cavalry and we need a place to hide until we can cross the river into Virginia. I have broken my leg in a fall with my horse and the need to rest is of the utmost importance. I know you are loyal to The Cause."

Cox recovered from his initial shock at hearing Booth's tale. He began to wonder if this were not some sort of diabolical plot to implicate him in pro-Confederate activities by disguised operatives of the Union government.

"You can identify yourself?"

Booth reached out his arm and showed him the India ink tattoo in the web of his left hand. It was faded, as if from years of wear. Exactly where Thomas Harbin had once told Cox it was to be found.

"Come inside. Leave old Swann outside. We can use him later for an alibi."

Cox was a gracious host. His fourteen-year-old black cook, Mary Swann (an odd coincidence, she was no relation to Oswell), once a slave and now his employee, spread the table with ham, bread, and fruit. Soon a fire was going and hot coffee boiling. Booth and Herold ate voraciously.

"Can we trust your Negress?" Booth wanted to know.

"Better than you can trust that boy who brought you here," came Cox's sharp reply. He was worried. They would have to devise a stratagem to fool Swann into believing Cox had not been too friendly, lest he tell inquiring pursuers what really happened. As for his cook, Mary, Cox would buy her off with a house and a plot of land. She loved intrigue, anyway.

While they ate, Booth and Herold then told Cox their whole story. Resting his leg on a chair allowed Booth to relax a little, and the tang of the coffee soon allayed his pain. Cox offered him a little whisky to sweeten the coffee. They talked and laughed for nearly three hours. Swann, meanwhile, sat outside near the gate, shivering. He wondered how long he would have to stay. But he was damned if he would leave without his ten extra dollars. After all, they had promised him. But deep down, he figured that the white men would come out and tell him to cut without paying him a dime, beyond the two dollars he got at the trip's beginning.

As dawn was breaking, Booth and Herold came out, looking disgusted. "I thought you said Cox was a reliable man," Herold said.

"Damn him," muttered Booth, limping uncomfortably on his crutches. "I *thought* so. I was told he was. Let us mount and get away from here, before I lose my temper. He looked at Swann. You still here? Give him his money, Davy, so he can go home. At least he was more loyal than that bastard Cox."

Herold handed over ten dollars in greenbacks and Swann thanked them profusely. He helped Booth get on his horse and tipped his hat as he rode off toward the swamp.

"Don't you say anything, boy," Herold called out after him. "If you tell anybody, you will not live long!"

Swann looked back and waved. He saw the two white men turn their horses out of Cox's yard onto the road and head off in a southerly direction. Swann had a notion to nose his way back through the underbrush and see what they really did. But, in light of the threat he already received, he thought better of it and kept on going. Cain't trust white men, no how, thought Swann, except to keep their threats. Had he stayed just awhile longer, he would have seen Herold, Booth, and Cox headed back into the house arm in arm, laughing together over how they had pulled a fast one on Swann.

But, in a way, the guide would have the last laugh. A few days later Swann would blurt out the story to a white friend, who took him to Federal detectives. Samuel Cox spent many a hard day and night as the Union soldiers beat him to gain a confession. Cox was smart enough to admit that two men had come to his house. But they rode right off, he insisted. His black serving girl, Mary, lied and backed up his story and received the promised pension from a grateful Cox, who escaped further prosecution and a hanging. The Yankees simply did not know how to handle blacks (they assumed erroneously that they would always tell on their employers) who would willingly protect their masters.

But cooperation did not always pay off. Stanton's prosecutors threw poor Oswell Swann in jail for three weeks after his coming forth with key evidence, just in case they had need of his services in the near future. His Yankee jailer--who clearly understood the new order of Union and freedom without equality, which would doom the so-called Reconstruction that was to come--dismissed the wrongful incarceration, later: "Aw Hell, he was nothing but a colored boy, anyhow."

PART IV

FIRST ARRESTS (1865)

I have not seen Arnold for some time, but saw O'Laughlen on
Thursday evening, on the Avenue at a saloon near the U.S.
Hotel. He told me he was going to see Booth.
--Confession of Andrew Atzerodt, May 1, 1865

God bless you, my dear friend, for all that
you have done for me. Good bye, old fellow.
--John Wilkes Booth to Thomas Jones, April 21, 1865

Did your son, or Mr. Booth, or Port Tobacco ever tell you
that they had engaged in a plot to kill the President? Never in
the world, if it was the last word I have ever to utter.
--Col. H. S. Olcutt's interrogation of Mary Surratt at Carroll
Prison Annex, April 27, 1865

1.   Tom Jones Takes Over

Thomas A. Jones was Samuel Cox's foster brother. He was a widower, who lived a short distance from Rich Hill above the Potomac at a place called "Huckleberry." He looked like a very slow-thinking, not-too-bright farmer, an impression furthered by a full drooping moustache, dull gray eyes, and a very slow gait. But Jones' exterior concealed one of the sharpest minds in the county, and an exciting wartime career as a Confederate agent. Huckleberry was a new house for Jones. He had spent the war at another place nearby, strategically situated on an eighty foot-high bluff above the Potomac. Jones could look out his windows and see about ten miles up river and as far as weather would permit to the south. It was only two miles across the Potomac, one of the narrowest points in either direction from Washington to the coast. And the convenient drainage of Pope's Creek on one side of his property made for a perfect landing point. One could hide a boat or two in the creek and sortie out after the Union patrol boats passed. It wasn't difficult. The Yankees kept a pretty certain schedule, usually.

Jones was well-known to the people of the neighborhood as the chief signal officer of the Confederate army. He was the man who coordinated the pick-up and forwarding of the mail from Richmond to places north. The drop spot was the fork of an old tree. He also helped people make the proper contacts to cross the river into Virginia. He was, moreover, well-known to the Federal soldiers and detective police. In fact, he was so well-known to the Yankees that he spent six months in the Old Capitol Prison for anti-Union activities in 1861.

But he did not impress his captors as worth much; dimwitted, they thought; and Jones smiled smugly to himself when he left for home, where he went back to clandestine activities. He was more secure than ever, and more dedicated. His wife, Jane, Tom Harbin's sister, had died shortly after he was released from his incarceration. Both men were determined to even that score with the Yankees. The mail was never kept in Jones' home; numerous, intermittent searches by Federal agents turned up nothing. The operation was so successful, that during the war's duration, not one letter was lost.

In 1862, Confederate signal officers paid Jones a visit and set up a permanent signal station. Using the home of a neighbor, even better situated than Jones' house on the bluffs, operatives would hang a black curtain in an upper window when it was unsafe to cross. Most crossings were done in the twilight hours, when shadows along the shore and the glare of the setting sun made visibility next to impossible. But, from the houses on the bluffs, one could see the exact location of Union gunboats and the black signal curtain.

Early Easter morning, right after breakfast, Jones saw Samuel Cox's adopted son, Samuel Cox, Jr., ride up to Huckleberry. Sam called out, "Uncle Tom, Pa needs to talk to you about getting some seed corn, as soon as possible. Can you come right over?"

"I'll get Kit saddled and we'll be on our way." As they passed out through the gate, young Sam said quietly, "Some strangers were at our home last night." They rode in silence; Jones having an uneasy feeling that he knew what was up.

Jones had heard about Lincoln's assassination the day before from some prowling Union soldiers. "Whose boat is that down in the creek?" they had asked.

"Mine," Jones had said.

"Well, you had better keep an eye on it. There are suspicious characters in the neighborhood who will be wanting to cross the river, and if you don't look sharp you will lose your boat."

"Indeed," Jones replied, thinking to himself that the only suspicious characters he had seen in days were the two Yankees. "I will look after it," he promised. "I would not like to lose it, as it is my fishing boat and the shad are beginning to run."

The two Yanks conferred to one side a moment. Then one asked Jones, "Have you heard the news?" Jones had not. "Then I will tell you," the soldier said. "Our President was assassinated at ten o'clock last night."

Jones was truly stunned. Of course he knew about the various kidnapping and assassination plots--they had been current throughout the war. Some he knew were real, others merely rumors. But this late in the game?

"Is it possible?" he exclaimed in shock.

"Yes," the soldier said, "and the men who did it came this way."

It was a bright spring morning, and Jones was lost in his thoughts about the day before. He was unresponsive to young Sam's attempts to talk. He saw Sam, Sr., at the gate in front of Rich Hill. His foster brother indicated that young Sam ought to take the horses off a piece and let them talk in private. Cox walked out to the middle of a plowed field, looking about intently, as if someone might be lurking to hear. Hell, Jones thought sourly, we could holler our heads off and no one would hear us out here.

Cox thought a few moments, and then he spoke. "Tom, I had visitors at four o'clock this morning."

"Yeah. That is what Sam, Jr., said. Who were they? What did they want?" Jones asked.

"It is Lincoln's assassin, Wilkes Booth, and a companion, Davy Herold. They want to get across the river." Cox's voice dropped to a whisper. "Have you heard that Lincoln was killed Friday night?"

"Yes, I have heard it." He told Cox about the two Yankee soldiers the night before.

"Tom, we must get those men across the river." He proceeded to tell Jones the whole of the night's events. Then he repeated, this time throwing the whole burden on his foster brother, "Tom, *you* must get them across. Can you do it?"

"I will see what I can do," Jones said with obvious reluctance. "I have to get Stringfellow across, too. He has first rights to cross. Now, with Booth down here, the whole Yankee army has to be avoided. Damnation! This is a real mess! Now, Sam, I must see these men. Where are they?"

"In that thick pine copse about a mile southwest of the house. Frank Robey," Cox said, referring to his farm manager or overseer, as they were called then, "guided them to the spot. You remember that signal we used to whistle when we were hunting in the woods as boys? I taught it to them. Take care how you approach them, Tom. They are heavily armed and rather jumpy. Might shoot by mistake."

Jones rode over to the pine thicket and dismounted. He saw a loose bay mare with full tack on, grazing in a small clearing made for a tobacco bed. Jones caught her up and tied her to a nearby tree. The mare was skittish, but not anything like she was the night of Lincoln's shooting. That she allowed herself to be tied was evidence of that. But she would break away again before the hour was out. Jones then went farther into the thicket. He whistled. Nothing. He whistled again. Davy Herold came out from behind a tree, carbine cocked and ready for action.

"Who are you? What do you want?"

"I come from Cox. He told me I would find you here. I am a friend. You have nothing to fear from me."

Herold looked Jones over a moment. Satisfied he was safe, he nodded, "Follow me."

Thirty yards later Jones stood before John Wilkes Booth. He was lying on a blanket, on his left side, his head cradled in his hand. His knife and pistols lay before him. Behind him lay his crutches and hat. He was partially covered by a second blanket. His dark clothes heightened the paleness of his skin; his face bore the unmistakable traces of his suffering. Right then and there, Jones knew he would do all that he could for these men, even at the cost of his life. So did Booth.

"Good day, sir," Booth said politely. Jones marveled at his still good looks and his polite manner and courteous speech.

"This friend comes from Captain Cox," Davy said.

"Sir, I am Thomas Jones. I will do all that I can for the both of you. But we must be cautious. For the present, you must remain outdoors and endure the elements. It is a dry place which Mr. Robey--he is the man who brought you here earlier--has led you to, the best in these woods. High and out of the swamp. Well drained and the sand will be warmer than lying on dirt. I will bring you food, and eventually, when the pursuit lessens sufficiently, I will get you over to the Virginia shore."

Booth extended his hand. "Thank you from the bottom of my heart. As you undoubtedly know, I am John Booth, the assassin of the President. My companion is Davy Herold. I know the government at Washington City will use every means in its power to secure my capture. But John Wilkes Booth will never be taken alive!"

Booth's flashing eyes were enough to convince Jones that he meant what he said.

"Now, le's get down to cases," Jones said. "They is a spring about thirty or forty yards that way you can use for water. Be cautious using it. Others, especially local servants, use it at times. Also, I saw a bay mare when I arrived here." Booth indicated the animal was his. "You will have to get rid of the horses--I assume you have one, too," he said looking at Herold, who nodded in affirmation. "They will betray you for sure. Besides, it will prove impossible to feed them, and we cannot take them across the river. I will tell young Cox, to help you get rid of them. You boys keep a cold camp--no fires for any reason. Someone might see or smell the smoke. I will return sometime tomorrow with something to eat and drink, and more blankets."

"Many thanks, Mr. Jones. Would you be good enough to please bring some newspapers also?" asked Booth. "And whiskey," chimed in Herold. Jones promised, then turned and walked back to his horse, and rode home.

2. Baker's Handbill

"Well, Baker, they have performed what they have long threatened to do. They have killed the President."

Secretary of War Stanton was physically ill from the ordeal he had suffered during the past thirty-six hours. His eyes were filled with tears. He turned to wipe his eyes. Baker was so moved that he, too, felt his eyes begin to well up. He fought back the urge to cry.

"All we know for certain," Stanton said when he regained his composure, "is that John Wilkes Booth killed the President. We have a description of the man who wreaked havoc in the Seward house. We know that Booth fled south across the Navy Yard Bridge, followed by an accomplice named David E. Herold. Got that from a liveryman who rented him a horse. We also believe that a George Atzerodt was involved, possibly to kill Vice President Johnson. But Atzerodt has disappeared. I have just been informed that Provost Marshal James McPhail up in Baltimore has a line on two of Booth's friends, Samuel Arnold and Michael O'Laughlen, and is in the process of running them down now. Would you believe that one of his detectives is Atzerodt's own brother?"

Baker shook his head in disbelief. "Has anyone secured tintypes of them or other suspects, Mr. Secretary?"

"No, no," Stanton sighed. "No likenesses have been assembled. No organized effort is under way."

"Who is out looking?"

"Well, there are the local detective forces from New York, Philadelphia, Boston, Baltimore, and other cities, and of course, the whole military force under General Augur. I have word that probably 10,000 soldiers and 500 civilian detectives are in the field. You know some of them from New York City. Colonel H.S. Olcutt, the Provost Marshal--remember him?--is among them. Came with Police Superintendent Kennedy's best men. There are at least seven major groups like that out looking for John Wilkes Booth."

Baker stood there, momentarily stunned. This was a complete muddle.

Stanton looked at him and read his mind. "Go to work Baker! Go to work!"

Baker arrived at 217 Pennsylvania Avenue half an hour later.

"How did it go?" Cousin Byron inquired. Baker related his conversation with Stanton.

"Looks like we are not much needed."

"Like Hell! These army provosts and half-baked civilian detectives are not going to find Booth. *We* are. But they are going to do the dirty work. We are going to put an agent in each group to keep track of its progress. Then we will step in at the right moment and garner the credit and the reward!"

"Huh? What reward?"

"They isn't one yet. But you and I are going to start the ball rolling. We are going to print up broadsides, offering a preliminary reward. Then others, not to be outdone will add to it. I bet it will reach at least $100,000 dollars--maybe a half million! And we Bakers are going to collect it *all*. As God is my witness!"

"What are you going to use for money?"

"I will put up $10,000 of my own and add $20,000 of the District of Columbia's money. I have written up a description. Get it to a printer and then have half a dozen men put them up all over southeast Maryland. I think that is where Booth has gone. You know, Byron, I think this is the first time such a handbill will have been circulated nationally. It is a fine idea, even if I say so myself. We will mail them out all over the place. Booth and the man who tried to kill Seward won't have a chance to get away."

"How did it go at General Augur's headquarters on the way back from Stanton's?"

"All the provost marshals; Colonel Olcutt, Colonel Foster, and Colonel Wells; were meeting when I showed up. I offered to work with anyone or under anyone in any capacity, but they told me to butt out--in a friendly way, mind you. But they were on to me. Augur said the army could handle it all. They are afraid we will do exactly what we will do-- cut them out of the glory and reward."

"And with the head of the Metropolitan Police force, A. C. Richards?"

"I tried out a different approach on him. I knew that his men had several items of evidence from Ford's Theater and the rooms of various co-conspirators. So I walked in as if I owned the world and asked him to turn it all over. But he is hiding something or someone; a witness; I know it! It is rumored that he has one of the roomers at Mrs. Surratt's house on H Street in tow. Has sent him with a detective to Canada. Looking for Mrs. Surratt's son, John, a man I have been watching for years, ever since I went into Maryland in 1862 to unearth Rebel supporters."

"What are we going to do, then?"

"First, let us make up the reward handbills and distribute them. Then we will round up a likeness for everyone on this list--he handed Byron a piece of paper. We are going to get Stanton to offer a big reward, say $50,000 for Booth, $25,000 for Herold, and another $25,000 for John H. Surratt. And we will put their pictures on the poster! That *is* a first. Then we will round up everyone we can who was working at Ford's the night Lincoln was shot. They are all a bunch of Reb sympathizers, anyhow. A little time at the Old Capitol will soften them up, I reckon. And a Provost in Baltimore is sending two of Booth's cronies down in a few days. We will grill them, too. Meanwhile let's get a man in every group going into the field. We need information!"

3. The Confederates Withdraw from Maryland

After their run-in with the small unit of Union cavalrymen at Mechanicsville (thus the popping noises that Booth and Herold had heard while trying to avoid the same patrol) Lieutenant W. Garland Smith and his Confederates fell back toward Newport. Smith was confused as to how many men he had confronted in the dark. He believed that caution was the best policy until things shook themselves out. He came up on the porch of Adams' Tavern and met Thomas H. Harbin and his telegrapher, Private Joseph Baden (pronounced "Bay' den").

"This is getting a mite perplexing to me, Harbin. First, my men and I are ordered to provide support to John Wilkes Booth in his plan to kidnap Lincoln, which never happens. Then, we are supposed to provide escort back to Virginia for Lieutenant Harney and his explosives team, who were to have blown up the President and his cabinet. But Harney disappears and no explosion occurs. Then, we are to help this Lieutenant Stringfellow, the spy who escaped from Port Tobacco, but he is no where to be found. Finally, we are to meet Booth tonight, this time at the academy in Charlotte Hall, and instead, run into a Yankee ambush at Mechanicsville. We cannot find this Bertle fellow who is supposed to guide Booth to us, nor can we find Booth. If the Yanks hold Mechanicsville that means we probably can no longer get to Charlotte Hall to meet Bertle, and through him, Booth. They control the high ridge between the Patuxent at Benedict and the Potomac at Port Tobacco."

"That is the least of our troubles," Harbin said. "Baden has been listening in on the Yankee telegraph with his field unit. The whole country is crawling with Bluebellies, looking for Booth and two others wanted for killing Lincoln. More and more troops are pouring into this part of Maryland. If the telegraph is correct, by morning, we will be outnumbered by a thousand to one."

"I think Booth will have to fend for himself," Lieutenant Smith said. "It is too dangerous to be nosing around here much longer. Booth will have a better chance if we disperse. Besides, if the Yankees hold Mechanicsville, the citizens there can no longer feed and shelter us. Not without exposing themselves to possible retaliation."

"We are in agreement, Lieutenant. I will take Baden across the river tomorrow at the Banks O'Dee to Sergeant Brogden's old camp at Oak Grove. I suggest you disperse your men and cross the river in small groups, beginning tonight. The Marylanders amongst you can just go home. We will wait Booth's appearance on the Virginia shore at Mrs. Quesenberry's, if he makes it."

"You are right," Lieutenant Smith said, "no need to waste valuable men, especially since General Lee has surrendered." He gazed into the darkening night. "We will scatter tomorrow. . .Where in the Hell do you think Booth is?"

The Lieutenant was not alone in puzzlement. Although it would not be found until May 1, and turned over to Federal authorities only sometime after Booth's death, an interesting letter, misdated April 15, 1865, turned up floating next to a pile-driver at Morehead City, North Carolina. It was in code. But the operators at a nearby military telegraph post found it easy to decipher:

Dear John--

I am happy to inform you that Pet has done his work well. He is safe and Old Abe is in Hell. Now, sir, all eyes are upon you. You must bring in Sherman. Grant is in the hands of old Gray, ere this. Redshoes showed a lack of nerve in Seward's case, but fell back in good order. Johnson must come. Old Crook has him in charge. Mind well the brother's oath, and you will have no difficulty. All will be safe and enjoy the trust of our leaders.

We had a large meeting last night. All were bent on carrying out the programme to the letter. The rails are laid for safe exit. Old L----, always behind, lost the list at City Point. Now, I say again, the lives of our brave officers and the life of the South depend upon the carrying of this programme into effect. Number Two will give you this. It is ordered no more letters shall be sent by mail.

When you write, sign no real name, and send by some of our friends who are coming home. We want you to write us how the news was received there. We are receiving great encouragement from all quarters. I hope there will be no getting weak in the knees.

I was in Baltimore yesterday. Pet had not got there yet. Your folks are well and have heard from you. Do not loose your nerve.

O. B. No. 5

Booth and Herold were safe for the time being, but already the network protecting them was beginning to unravel. They were not headed for Canada, but deeper into the Yankee-occupied South. It might have been better had this letter shown up sooner, to turn Federal attentions away from the southern peninsula of Maryland, which the first arrests failed to do.

4. O'Laughlen Turns Himself In; Arnold Is Captured and Confesses

The carriage pulled up at the nondescript, multi-storied, red brick town house on High Street in Baltimore. It was the morning of April 17. Inside, three men sat and talked. One was Philip H. Maulsby, brother-in-law to Michael O'Laughlen. The other two were civilian police detectives, William Wallace and James S. Allison, in the employ of Baltimore Provost Marshal James McPhail, the latter of whom had known the O'Laughlens for nearly thirty years.

"You are sure this is going to work out?" Wallace wanted to know. "We have been looking for O'Laughlen for two days, to no avail."

"Everything is going to be fine," Maulsby said. "He *wants* to turn himself in. He has nothing to fear. He never was in the plot to assassinate the President. The only reason that you have been unable to find him is because of mere coincidence. He never got back from Washington City until late Saturday evening, after you all had called. When he learned from me that you all had been to his home inquiring about him, he went into hiding to give himself time to think things over a while.

"This is a big step," Maulsby went on. "You all cain't expect a body to just throw himself into the arms of the law. He was very worried that any arrest at home, if front of the family, might adversely affect his mother, who is not well. When you all came back again Sunday, I told him, and he agreed to be here this morning to surrender--on neutral ground, so to speak. How did you all connect him to Booth and the killing of Lincoln, anyway? And so quickly?"

"The boys down in the District found a letter signed, 'Sam,' out of Hookstown in a trunk in Booth's room at the old National Hotel," Wallace said. "Provost Marshal McPhail had two men, Eaton G. Horner and Voltaire Randall run it down. Just went out to Hookstown and found that the only Sam worth taking note of was Arnold, your brother-in-law's close friend. It did not take much from there to get to Mike O'Laughlen. We then decided to move and telegraphed the War Department for confirmation. They said bring them in. But we were way ahead of those idiots in the Lunatic Asylum, as they call the War Department nowadays."

"Well, you all stay in the hack. I will get down and go in to get Mike."

"We are not going to have to worry about trouble. He ain't going to come out shooting?"

"Naw. Mike O'Laughlen is an easy-going feller. If he says he will give up, he will do it, with no trouble at all. He was mild mannered even as a boy. I just cannot believe that he is in any way involved with this. I mean, I know he was in the Rebel army, but he came home in 1862 just before Sharpsburg, sick as a dog. He has lived with me and his sister most of the time since. He had his fill of the war."

"Well, let's get on with it."

A few minutes later, Maulsby was back with O'Laughlen. Introductions were made, but the conversation in the cab back to headquarters was practically nil. In front of McPhail, O'Laughlen said that he had numerous witnesses to give him a complete alibi for his time in Washington over the past weekend.

Meanwhile, tipped off by some fine detective work by Lewis Powell's Baltimore nemesis, Lieutenant H. L. Smith, Provost Marshal McPhail had sent another team, Detectives Horner and Randall, to round up Sam Arnold at his place of employment, "Wickey" Wharton's Store at Old Point Comfort, Virginia. The store was sort of a sutler's business, or general store, selling goods to the soldiers at nearby Fortress Monroe. An old brick and earthen structure held by the Union army throughout the war, it was from Fortress Monroe that the Federal forces had launched their advances that had led to the battles at Big Bethel, the 1862 Peninsular Campaign, the Wistar raid on Richmond, and the disastrous campaign on the Bermuda Hundred in 1864. Nearby, out in Hampton Roads, the U.S.S. *Monitor* had fought the C.S.S. *Virginia* to a standstill in 1862, saving the integrity of the Union naval blockade.

The store owner, J. W. Wharton, showed the detectives to where Arnold slept in a back room.

"Wake up, Arnold!" Horner said, cocking a pistol in Sam's ear. Arnold was up like a shot, but remained sitting on the edge of the bed, offering no resistance.

"My God!" he exclaimed. "You near scared ten years off my life!"

"Sorry. But we have to be careful in cases like this. I am going to have to put the irons on you. Search him and that carpet sack over yonder, Randy."

Randall checked out Arnold's pockets, he slept in his pants and underwear, but came up with nothing but a small, folding Barlow knife. In the carpetbag the detective found a change of clothes, some letters, a few papers, a box of paper cartridges, and an 1851 Colt's revolver, capped and loaded. Randall stuck the pistol in his belt, after jotting down its serial number in his pocket notebook.

"What is this all about?" Arnold asked.

"You know very well," Horner responded. "Did you ever engage in correspondence with John Wilkes Booth? You probably have heard; he killed President Lincoln last Friday."

"I have never written to Booth."

"Are you sure? You had better come clean. Or those ten years of life I scared out'n you will not matter much. This is treason, doncha know? That's a swinging crime. Besides, Marshal McPhail says that they have a letter from you to Booth up at Washington City. Found it in Booth's trunk, left behind in his hotel room."

That dirty, rotten scoundrel! Arnold screamed deep inside himself. The detectives saw him wince. Horner handed Arnold a letter from his father, asking him to cooperate with the authorities to try and save his life.

"All right," Arnold admitted, after he put the letter down with a clank of his chains and thought a minute, "you got me, fair and square. I did write a letter to Booth. But you all must know that I have been down here clerking since the first of the month. I got this job because my father knows Mr. Wharton, the storeowner. I did not kill the president or help anyone else to do it, either."

"Want to tell us about it?"

"Yeah," Arnold said in a very resigned tone of voice. "Pa says I should cooperate. I was in on a plot to kidnap Lincoln--no murder was ever spoken of-- and carry him to the Confederate lines to exchange him for Reb prisoners of war held in the North. It was back in March. I have been in contact with Booth since last year. We were boyhood friends, you know. Mike and I hauled some gear back to the City for him, once. We met at a place one evening. . . . Me'n Mike O'Laughlen, Booth, John Surratt, George Atzerodt, a feller named Mosby, and another . . . I cain't remember his name, now. A young feller, always talking nonsense, telling jokes.

"Booth said he had letters of introduction to a Dr. Mudd and a Dr. Queen," Arnold continued. "I never saw those gentlemen, though. But we could not come to an agreement--Booth was crazy in his recklessness and got pissed off when I objected. So, Mike O'Laughlen and I took a walk. Went back to Baltimore. We ain't been near Booth since. At least, *I* have not. I came to work down here on April 1."

"Where did you get the arms to kidnap President Lincoln?"

"Booth provided everything; guns ammunition, money, you name it. That revolver is one of them. I have a Bowie and another pistol up to home."

"Are you willing to make a written statement?"

"Sure. Just give me a paper and something to write with."

"We will save it for Marshal McPhail, Eee Gee," Randall suggested to Horner. "It will hold 'til we get back to Baltimore. Let's go over and pick up Stanton's minion, John Potts."

"The War Department clerk? Yeah, I guess we have to take that little jerk along to keep the evil eye on us, lest one of the big wigs in Washington City blows a gut. But he is going to blab everything we do, good or bad, from here to the District, I will lay. We can catch the evening boat outta here, I reckon."

5. Edman Spangler, Fall Guy

After Booth ran out of the theater, Edman Spangler just stood off to one side and wept. He was dismayed at what had happened, in spite of his voiced hostile opinion of the Lincoln Administration, something that was pretty common, not only in Maryland, but throughout the North. But most of the people who spoke out against the policies of Lincoln did not take the extra step of wishing him dead or attempting to assassinate him. Lincoln, himself, seemed to realize this. It may have been part of what historians generally attribute to his "fatalism" on the numerous threats he received against his life. Only a very few went beyond private talk or anonymous letters.

Spangler came from York, Pennsylvania. His family was among the town's founders, and was well respected. His father served as sheriff for several years. Ned was born on August 10, 1825, the last of four children. His mother died shortly after his birth. His father remarried when Ned was five, and sired four more children. Ned was a well-liked fellow. He was described as good-natured and dependable by all who came into contact with him throughout his life. He was also the only one of the defendants in the assassination trial to be found not guilty of murdering Lincoln, but culpable in Booth's escape. He was given a sentence of six years at Fort Jefferson on the Dry Tortugas as a result.

A carpenter by trade, Edman Spangler was already skillful in woodworking by his late teens. In the early 1850's John Wilkes Booth came to York to attend Bland's Boarding Academy. Just how and when young Spangler met an even younger Booth is not known, but by the end of 1853, Spangler was working on the building of a new house for the Booth family, Tudor Hall. His supervisor was James J. Gifford out of Baltimore, an architect and builder, and later supervisor of the carpenters and scene shifters at Ford's Theater in the District.

Spangler followed Gifford back to Baltimore after the Tudor Hall job and the Monument City became his home. He worked as a carpenter, and also did odd jobs. Among the latter was assisting behind the scenes at the Front Street Theater and the Holiday Theater. Spangler met and married Mary Brasheare, ten years his senior, in the summer of 1858. Perhaps she was the mother figure he had needed in his life.

The outbreak of the Civil War saw John T. Ford expand his theater empire by refurbishing the Old Tenth Street Baptist Church into what became known as Ford's theater. Ford hired Gifford to supervise the work, and one of the men hired to do the carpentry was Ned Spangler. Both men stayed on to form part of the stage crew after the remodeling, Spangler working as a part-time scene shifter. As such, he and others like him were critical employees, working between scenes to move the flats and create the proper atmosphere for the plays. Ford was so pleased with his work, that in 1863, he made him a permanent worker.

As stage productions were not presented during the stifling summer months, Spangler would then go back to Baltimore. He seems to have spent much of his free time crab-fishing. He often invited his fellow stage-hands to go out with him, in the hope that they would enjoy themselves as much as he did. But in the summer of 1864, disaster struck in Ned's life. His wife died. She was only forty-nine years old. He buried her in Baltimore Cemetery and went back to Washington.

Because Spangler had a home in Baltimore, he made do while working in Washington. He boarded at Mrs. Scott's at Seventh and G Streets, a popular place among the stage crew at Ford's. But unlike the others, Spangler only ate at the Scott Boarding House. He lived at Ford's and slept there. Ford did not seem to mind, having a man on the premises after hours gave a measure of security. Spangler's worst habit was a common one--he drank too much. And with the absence of his wife in late 1864, his drinking only increased. At times, he would become so inebriated as to be incapable of working. But he was still the affable man everyone liked when sober.

In the end, Spangler's worst vice proved to be his friendship with John Wilkes Booth. He did all sorts of odd jobs for the actor, pleased to do anything his friend asked of him. His most obvious job was re-constructing the shed that Booth rented in Baptist Alley a hundred yards or so behind the theater. Spangler raised the roof a couple of feet and repaired the walls. After that, Booth paid him to care for his horses and carriage. When the kidnap plot fell through, about which Spangler was ignorant, Booth had Spangler dispose of the horses and carriage at auction.

"Will you help me?" Booth had asked him the afternoon of the assassination at the back door to Ford's.

"Oh, yes." Spangler had responded.

Since the shooting of Lincoln followed shortly, most, especially the trail judges and prosecutors, assumed he meant, "Will you help me get away?" But not a soul really knew that--they just assumed it. After all, he was a friend of Booth. The same might be said of another incident, the slapping of co-worker Jacob Ritterspaugh in the mouth, when Ritterspaugh identified the fleeing man as Booth. This face slapping incident may or may not have taken place--no one else saw it happen--but Spangler was Booth's friend and everyone believed it.

Besides, he did set up Joseph "Peanuts" Burroughs to hold Booth's horse. In popular parlance, Booth's horse-holder has been Spangler for ever after. And who assisted in changing Ford's Theater boxes seven and eight into the double Presidential Box the afternoon of the assassination? Surely Spangler drilled the hole in the door which was directly behind where Lincoln would sit, jimmied the door latches, and provided the modified music stand to bar the entrance to the hallway outside of the Presidential Box, and scraped a niche out of the plaster in the wall to hold the bar and make the door secure. This, even though Henry Clay Ford believed that Spangler had done little of the work, apart from merely pulling the partition out and handing a hammer and a few nails to him. The door latches had been kicked open months earlier by a theater employee who could not find the key and needed to admit a party with reserved seats. Worst of all, for the government's case, Spangler worked on the opposite side of the theater from the back door from which Booth fled--and he was at his post when the shot bored into Lincoln's head.

Ned slept in Ford's theater the night of the assassination, but he was too afraid to stay there any more. There had been too much loose talk of burning the place down. He went to his co-worker, Louis Carland and asked if he could not sleep with him at Scott's. And that is where a detective and the provost marshal's men found him on the night of April 17, between 9 and 10 o'clock.

"Does he have any personal belongings?" Detective Charles H. Rosch asked, after the other officers had hauled Spangler off in chains.

"Only this carpetbag," Carland said.

Rosch looked at it. He hefted it. It was heavy.

"Is there a key? It is locked."

"Here, try this one," Carland said.

Inside the opened bag, Rosch found eighty-one feet of rope, some blank paper, and a dirty shirt collar. Not much evidence to the uncultivated eye. But the rope could have been used to trip up pursuing cavalry horses--at least the trial judges suspected that, with proper coaching from investigators. In reality, Spangler was like most employees--he picked up anything of use that the employer might not miss or no longer needed. Some thought that he might have used it as a main line in his crabbing hobby, with trot lines branching off it. The rope was most likely the same as dozens like it used in the theater for holding up or suspending scenery flats.

But the court was geared to convict suspects, not turn them loose. Spangler received a six year sentence, which, according to guards, he endured with much less trouble than his co-conspirators. He was pardoned in 1869, along with Mudd and Arnold, O'Laughlen having died during the yellow fever epidemic of 1867. He was unceremoniously dumped on the Florida mainland stone-broke, and had to work his way back to Maryland. He finally wound up at the home of the Mudds. In one of the most selfless acts of the whole kidnap-assassination episode, Dr. and Mrs. Mudd took him in. He paid his way by doing numerous odd jobs on the farm. He died February 7, 1875, after being caught out in a vicious winter storm. He was forty-nine years old--the same age as his wife had been when she passed on years before.

6. The Arrest of Mary Surratt

"We got a tip from a neighbor that Mrs. Surratt's servant girl heard some men come into the basement the night of Lincoln's murder. This Surratt family is known to have had connections with Wilkes Booth. So, Colonel Olcutt wants us to take possession of the house, seize all papers and items that might be used as evidence and arrest everyone there. Detective Rosch, you stay here and prevent anyone from leaving the premises. The rest of you follow me."

The man who spoke was Brevet Major Henry Warren Smith. He was out of the provost marshal's office in Washington and one of hundreds of officers called in to beef up the provost's units in Washington in the aftermath of the Lincoln assassination. Like all Stanton-inspired arrests, this one was accomplished after dark. Around midnight, when the parties least expected to be disturbed, Smith quietly led Captain W. M. Wermerskirch, Lieutenant John W. Dempsey and Detective Eli Devoe up the outside stairs of the gray brick building at 541 H Street. Smith pulled the bell cord.

"Is that you Mr. Kirby?" The voice came from a window over the stairway.

"No, Ma'am. I am Major Smith of the provost marshal's office. Open the door, please. At once!"

A lady of forty some odd years opened the door. She was attractive, fairly tall for a woman of the time, full figured, with a round face, auburn hair, and piercing gray eyes.

"Are you Mrs. Surratt?"

"I am the widow of John Surratt."

"And the mother of John H. Surratt, Jr.?"

"I am."

"Then I have come to arrest you and all in the house, and take you for examination to General Augur's headquarters. Detective Devoe, go downstairs and round up the servants. Mrs. Surratt, could I trouble you for your keys?"

Mrs. Surratt handed over the house keys to Smith, who gave them to Wermerskirch for use in conducting a full search of the house.

"Who are these ladies?"

"This is my daughter, Anna; my niece, Lete Jenkins; and Miss Norah Fitzpatrick, who boards in my house."

Eliza, Charles, and Mary Holohan had already left the day before, tired of the police raids and the rowdy crowds that often gathered in the street. John Holohan, of course, was with Lou Weichmann and Detective McDevitt, looking for John Surratt in Canada.

"Sit down ladies, please." Major Smith motioned to the sofa. Suddenly the bell rang. Wermerskirch went out to see who was at the door. After a few moments, he came back in with two other men.

"Major these men are Detectives Sampson and Morgan. They were sent to give us a hand, if we need them."

"Fine. Sampson, you go down the inside stairs and relieve Mr. Devoe. Tell him to report back up here."

When Devoe arrived, Smith told him, "Go out and find our carriage. Bring it up about half a block off. We do not want to excite suspicions."

"Yeah, let these Rebel women walk. It will be good enough for the likes of them."

"Sir," Mary Surratt spoke to Major Smith, "since you are in charge, I will inform you that I expect these women to be treated with the courtesy and deference due them as ladies."

"Madame, I will accompany you to get the cloaks and such that you will need. It is a cold, damp night for travel. Captain Wermerskirch, entertain these young ladies while I am gone. Allow no communication between them."

Mary Surratt and Major Smith soon returned laden with wraps. Mary had also brought a special pair of warm shoes for Anna. She knelt to put them on. The import of the moment hit Anna hard and she began to weep.

"Do not behave so, Baby. You are already so worn out with worry that you will make yourself sick. The officer who has arrested us is a gentleman and will treat us kindly."

"But, Ma! To be taken there for such a thing!"

"Hush, child, hush! Major Smith, are we allowed a moment of prayer?"

"Certainly, Mrs. Surratt. Take your time."

Mary and the girls all knelt around the seat of the melodeon, under the crucifix on the wall. As they prayed (or merely put on a good show, as the skeptical Captain Wermerskirch maintained), Smith stepped into the hall and called Detective Morgan upstairs to the parlor.

"Now listen, you men. Anyone who comes here is to be treated as a suspicious person and taken into custody. No exceptions. Let anyone in, but no one gets out. Clear? Where is Devoe with that carriage? If he doesn't get back soon, someone will have to fetch him."

There was the sound of footsteps on the stairs outside. Smith looked puzzled. It was too quiet a tread for Devoe. He loosened his revolver and motioned Morgan and Wermerskirch to answer the knock on the door. Strange; no ringing of the bell. Just a quiet, but firm, knock. Whoever it was, it most certainly was *not* Detective Devoe.

7. The Arrest of Powell

Historians have spent one hundred and forty-odd years describing how Lewis Powell blundered around, desperately trying to find the Surratt home on H Street, after being dumped by his horse. But, in fact, he had no trouble at all in finding the boarding house. He knew the geography of Washington. It was not that difficult to learn. His real problem was the fact that he was suffering from a concussion that befuddled his thought processes. It was difficult enough to walk the distance that he had to cover without being physically and mentally less than one hundred per cent.

Travelling mostly at night, sleeping in a field the next day, he managed to arrive at his goal, the house on H Street, just past 6th. He had confiscated a pickaxe that had not been put away at a building site he passed. Made his laborer story look that much better. As near as Powell could guess, it was Monday April 17, around 11 p.m., when, through the shadows, he approached the building. He was aided by a foggy mist that drifted in and out of the streets. At times he could see only a few feet ahead.

"Whoa! Lewis ol' boy," Powell said to himself. "Just set tight and take a look-see."

Nothing. He looked again and listened carefully. He would probably hear danger before he could see it, anyhow. The street was deathly quiet. Probably too quiet, but Powell was not himself. Satisfied with his scouting, he boldly strode across the street and up the steps. The wooden stairs thudded under each step.

"Please, sir," came a quiet voice out of Powell's recent memory. "Please walk lightly. You stomp the stair too heavily. Please, do not walk so heavily, sir!"

Powell paused in his mounting of the staircase. He looked around and back down to the street. Nothing. Yet the voice seemed so intense, so close, so *real*.

Powell continued his ascent. He tip-toed. That was better! Less noise. "We do not wish to wake Mr. Seward," the voice in his mind whispered once more.

Down below, hidden in a doorway next door, a shadow moved slightly. Powell did not see it. The dark form belonged to Officer C. H. Rosch, a special policeman attached to General Augur's provost guard, who had arrested Edman Spangler, a couple of blocks away, a few hours earlier. Powell had approached with such cat-like steps that Rosch had not seen him until he heard the first clunking footsteps going up to the Surratt's front elevated landing, to the outside door on the first story above the street level basement. Then he spied him, a giant of a man, ascending ghost-like, now making no sound at all, almost like the angels going up Jacob's Ladder.

"Nie Engel sondern Bengel," Rosch muttered in his family's native German. Not an angel but more of a rascal.

Well, Rosch surmised. No harm done. My orders were to prevent anyone from *leaving*. Anyone going up was alright. As long as he did not come back down and get away. Rosch checked his pistol, just in case. He looked up and down the street to see if the stranger on the stairs had any accomplices. But the fog that concealed him from Powell, and initially Powell from him, blocked any visual reconnaissance.

Powell stood on the landing. He thought he heard something, someone, move inside. He listened again. Nothing. He knocked on the door quietly, but firmly. The door swung open. Morgan and Wermerskirch stood there, staring at Powell, who had the appearance of a lost soul, and a rough looking soul at that. His lower pants legs and boots were covered with dried mud. His head was swathed in his undershirt sleeve, which he had earlier torn off after losing his hat, and he was now wearing it like a turban or a nightcap with a tassel hanging down. Had the officers looked out past Powell down the stairs they would see a trail of fallen crumbs of mud that had dropped off of him at each step.

"I . . . I guess I am mistaken," Powell stammered out. Who in the deuce were these men? He wondered silently.

"Who do you want to see?"

"Mrs. Surratt."

Major Smith stepped forward, drawing his 44 caliber Remington revolver and cocking it, loudly.

"No, sir, you are not mistaken," he said. "Step right on in."

In a benumbed stupor, Powell stepped over the threshold. The door and all hope of easy escape clicked shut behind him. The inside lights seemed dimmer than he remembered them. The words from Dante's *Inferno*, read to him by his mother in a time long ago now rose up and struck him hard, "Abandon all hope ye who enter here."

"Put the pick down, slowly," Smith said. Powell set it in the corner of the hall, next to the front door. Morgan stood between Powell and the door. He, too, had drawn his pistol to prevent any escape.

"Take him to the back of the foyer," Smith ordered.

Wermerskirch pushed Powell into a solitary dining room chair up against the wall near the stairwell which led up to the bedrooms. Smith and Wermerskirch stood and looked at this strange man who had intruded at such a late hour. Powell faced their scrutiny in silence. He was dressed in his gray coat and vest, black pantaloons and mud-caked boots. Superficially, he looked like a laboring man. But his clothes were much too fine for such a person. And his hands! Even from a distance, the officers could see that they were relatively clean, uncalloused, and even well-manicured. And those boots! They were downright expensive, with a hand-tooled, red Moroccan band around the top of the stovepipe. Indeed, further examination some days later would reveal they once had the name "J. W. Booth" inked inside. Booth evidently had tried to destroy the name with acid before he gave the footwear to Powell, but a chemical analysis would bring back most of it, "J. W. B---th," in time for the trial.

"Why are you here? At this odd time of night?" Smith asked.

"Mrs. Surratt hired me to dig a gutter, out back, I think."

"At 11 o'clock? After dark?"

"Oh, no! I met her on the street today. I am a poor man and asked her for work. She took pity on me and engaged me for the job. I have come here to inquire as to when I should start to work in the morning."

"She just picked out a strange man on the street?"

"No, no. I have been working around the neighborhood. She found me there."

"What is your name?"

"I am Lewis Paine, of Fauquier County, Virginia. Here are my papers." Powell pulled out the oath of allegiance he had taken in front of another Smith at Baltimore, six weeks before. Smith scanned the document and noted that there had been an unsuccessful attempt to erase the restriction to stay north of Philadelphia. He could still read its outline on the oath.

Major Smith went to the parlor door and called out, "Mrs. Surratt. Can you come in here a moment, please?"

Mrs. Surratt and the girls had just risen from their knees, having completed their prayers. She stepped hesitantly through the parlor door. She had recognized the voice of her one-time boarder and co-conspirator, and wondered what he was doing there. She silently steeled herself for the ordeal she was about to face.

Smith looked at her as he pointed toward Powell.

"Do you know this man? Did you hire him to dig a ditch for you?"

Mary Surratt squinted in Powell's direction. The detectives stood him up, under the only lamp in use. She leaned her head forward, as if to gauge the correct distance for her myopic eyes, even though Powell stood merely five feet away.

Mary Surratt looked at Powell intently, and then threw up her hands. "Before God," she vowed, "I do not know this man. I certainly did not hire him to dig a ditch!" Sorry Mr. Wood, or whatever your name is, she said to herself. You are on your own. God help us all!

There was thumping outside on the stairway. The door flew open and officer Rosch came in.

"The carriage is here for the ladies," he said.

Major Smith indicated to the ladies that they should go on down. Mrs. Surratt, Anna, Olivia Jenkins, and Honora Fitzpatrick each followed an escorting officer to their fates. As they passed Morgan at the door, Mrs. Surratt turned toward him and whispered very loudly, "I am so glad you officers came here tonight. I fear this man came here with a pickaxe to kill us!" She sounded almost conspiratorial, but much relieved.

Major Smith was not fooled by this play-acting between Powell and Mrs. Surratt. Pieces of this plot against Lincoln were falling into place, as far as he was concerned. And Smith was not the only one to feel so. Officer Thomas took one look at Powell and immediately saw the man in Colonel Lafayette C. Baker's wanted poster. He began to grill the would-be laborer.

"Where have you been working?"

"Different places," Powell hedged.

"What wages do you usually get?"

"From a dollar to a dollar and a quarter a day." Powell knew that his duds belied his wage scale, but he kept on. "I have got no money. How can I get money when I work for a dollar a day and have to pay any lodging and board out of that?"

"Do you have steady work?"

"No. I only get jobs now and again."

"Can you give the names of any persons you have worked for?"

"No. I cannot give any names."

"Can you take me to their places?"

"No."

"Do you know the names of the streets?"

"No."

"Would you know the street if you were in it?"

"No. I know nothing about it."

"Where is your boarding house?"

"I have not got any."

"Where is the balance of your clothes?"

"I have got all my clothes on."

"Where did you sleep last night?"

"At the railroad depot."

"Where did you sleep last Wednesday night?"

"I do not know."

"Thursday night?""

I do not know."

"Friday night?"

"At the depot."

"Saturday night?"

"I do not know where I slept."

"Well, where did you sleep last night?"

"I have been walking about so much that I do not know where I slept last night." The detectives looked at each other. A few minutes ago he had answered the same question with "at the railroad depot."

By that time, the carriage had returned from delivering the Surratt residents to General Augur's office. Officers Sampson, DeVoe and Rosch, the burliest of the troop, sat in the carriage with Powell as they were driven to Augur's headquarters. They all carried pistols to enforce their authority, if needs be. But Powell was so exhausted from three nights without food, constant wandering, and the effects of the concussion from his fall, that he offered no resistance.

At the Provost Marshal's, the detectives searched Powell's pockets thoroughly. They found quite a list of items. Unfortunately for Powell, none of them appeared normal for a poor, day laborer. There was a packet of pistol cartridges, unopened; a pocket compass, so much for the idea he was lost; a needle case with various shades of thread; a small hair brush and bottle of hair pomade, a folding comb and *two* toothbrushes, which made his unkempt appearance truly an anomaly; a small penknife; a Webster's pocket dictionary, perfect for Confederate secret service decoding; two fine white handkerchiefs, one of them a woman's, probably from Mary Gardner; and a pocketbook with some American pennies, a few Canadian coins, scraps of paper, postage stamps and, worst of all, twenty five Yankee dollars, all of which made him a well-heeled, well-traveled man. Of course, there was his oath of allegiance, illegally tampered with, that would send investigators to Baltimore and the other Provost Marshal, also named Smith, after the Bransons, posthaste.

"Have you heard the news?" Officer Sampson asked Powell after the search.

"What news?"

"The assassination of Mr. Lincoln and the attempted assassination of Mr. Seward on Friday night last."

"I have heard nothing."

"Why, it is all over town here--and even in New York!"

"I believe I heard something about it the next day," Powell lied.

"Can't you read or write?"

"No," Powell lied again. It was a misconception that he played upon all the way to his death. That he was ignorant, uneducated, confused, and incapable of rational thought. And the Yankees were smug enough about their supposed superiority to Rebels to let it ride. But he would not be granted an insanity plea, temporary or otherwise, that had allowed Congressman Daniel Sickles escape punishment for the murder of Phillip Barton Key, even though Powell's lawyer gave it a good try.

"Where did you get all that money?"

"I worked for it."

"At a dollar a day? What about room and board? A man must eat, even if he sleeps under the stars."

"Well, I allow as how you are right," he said. "I reckon I found it."

By now the officers were fully satisfied that Powell was the man who attacked the Seward house. But they pulled out their trump card before dawn. They left Powell sitting in the anteroom at the provost marshal's office. He sat there almost half an hour. Then there was a commotion as several people entered the room.

"Come on, Paine."

Powell entered an interrogation room. The light had been dimmed. It looked just like the light in the upstairs hall of the Seward house, Powell mused.

"That is him! I know his mouth! He has holes in his cheeks when he smiles." Powell grinned at William Bell's characterizations. "See! Look at him! I know him; that is the man!" Seward's house servant had just made the most positive identification of a suspect the detectives said that they had ever heard. He would repeat it as a star witness at Powell's trial a month later.

8. Mary Surratt in Jail

"That is *him*, Ma! That is Mr. Wood!" Anna pointed at the figure in the receiving room at General Christopher C. Augur's headquarters, as she whispered earnestly to her mother. Mary Surratt had hurried into the room upon hearing Anna's scream. She was followed by the general and his adjutant. Anna had been sputtering at a soldier on guard over her, Honora Fitzpatrick, Lete Jenkins and a newcomer, Lewis Powell, better known to the young ladies as "Paine" or "Wood."

"This *man*," Anna said indignantly, the only way she spoke to Yankees, especially those in uniform, "has just suggested that this *ugly* thing (pointing at Powell) is my brother." She shrugged her shoulders. "I just let him know that he was no *gentleman* to have said such a thing."

"She is correct," Mrs. Surratt said to the general, "this man is not her brother, my son, John H. Surratt, Jr."

With that, General Augur gave an admonition to the soldiers to keep their thoughts to themselves and behave properly in front of the young ladies. Powell was taken to another room to await proper identification from the Seward servant, William Bell. Mrs. Surratt was escorted back into General Augur's office for her preliminary interrogation before she would be taken down to Duff Green's Row, now the Carroll Annex of the Old Capitol Prison, where females, suspected or convicted, were kept in Federal custody.

"Now, Mrs. Surratt, where was I?"

"We were asking about her son, sir," said the adjutant, checking his stenographic record, ." . . his relationship to the villain, Booth."

"Ah, yes. What was the bond that brought your son and John Wilkes Booth together? And you said that you supposed it was made as any gentleman would meet another. And then you claimed that Booth had made no political statements. I find that interesting, as he is known nation-wide for his outspoken sentiments for the so-called Confederacy. Did your son say where he was going when he left you?"

"He did not."

Mary told Augur that she reckoned that it all had to do with the military draft. She had wanted John to pay the $50 exemption fee to a broker to hire a substitute, an entirely legal process at that time. He had disappeared after having supper out with her boarder, Mr. Weichmann. She assumed her son was in Canada.

Augur did not believe that. John Surratt had exchanged too much gold for greenbacks. That pointed to his staying in the States.

"No man on the round earth believes that he went to Canada," Augur grumped.

"*I* believe it!"

Augur scoffed at her. Then the conversation degenerated into the mechanics of crossing the Potomac, how long it would take, how wide the river was, how long it might take to go to Richmond and back. Mrs. Surratt looked at him wide-eyed and professed her ignorance of any of this, having crossed the river at only one place, Alexandria, and never having been south of there. The exasperated general then tried a different tack.

"Don't you know of his making the acquaintance of a Mr. Atzereodt? What sort of man was this Atzerodt? What colored hair had he? Did he stoop a little?"

All Mrs. Surratt could remember was that Port Tobacco--she did not respond well to the name "Atzerodt"--was German, maybe had dark hair, probably a moustache and side whiskers, and some times rode a dark horse. She could not recollect much more.

"He remained only part of a week, until I found some liquor in his room; no gentleman can room with me who keeps liquor in his rooms, and I told my son he could not stay--that I could not board him."

"Before he left your house, your son went with him when he went to get board at the Pennsylvania House?"

"I do not know anything about that; I only know that I told my son *I* would not board him."

Augur asked about another young man who came and stayed a while. She remembered two or three such persons, one of whom was called "Wood." Although she identified Booth by his photograph, she denied ever knowing David Herold and could not identify his picture when shown one. Augur was astonished.

"He is a very intimate friend of your son's!"

"Well, sir; I assure you he is not a visitor to our house, on the honor of a lady."

Augur then delved into the story Susan Ann Mahoney had told about three men visiting the boarding house shortly after the Lincoln shooting. He did not reveal his source, and Mrs. Surratt was completely mystified by what he meant.

"You cannot remember anything about it?"

"I do not remember anything of three *gentlemen* coming into *my* house."

Augur began to parse his phrases with the precision of a lawyer. After all, Mary Surratt was doing the same. "Of these three persons, there was not a gentleman among them."

"I do not remember indeed."

"There were three gentlemen though."

"No; not to my knowledge. . . ."

"Now, I *know* they were there."

"Well, sir; if *you* do, *I* do not."

Mary did concede that Weichmann, Holohan and Detective James McDevitt were there Sunday morning, but denied saying any more than good morning--or was she at church when they came? She really did not remember. Nor she did recall that Mr. Booth's name was ever mentioned by any of the three men—if she saw three men at all. They did speak of John Surratt, but not in relation to anything concerning Booth. Of course, John Surratt had nothing to do with Lincoln's shooting. Mr. Weichmann and the other two did say good morning as they left.

General Augur then showed Mrs. Surratt a letter signed, "Kate" (Mrs. Slater was also known as Kate Brown or Thompson). She did not recognize it, adding, "[m]y eyesight is not very good; is it in pencil?"

"Yes," Augur said eagerly hoping for a break in this repartee or some real information.

"I do not know it," came the firm reply.

She admitted that she owned a farm (Surrattsville) and that there had been some livestock on the place, but it had been reduced by the fortunes of war to a big black horse and an old cow. Then she skillfully led Augur on a wild goose chase about the black horse, which he seemed to think was the one-eyed horse Powell had ridden to the Seward house. Then he returned to Lewis Powell, or Paine, or Wood.

"Did you meet this young man arrested this evening within the last two or three days and make an arrangement with him to come to your house this evening?" Augur probably was referring to the time a few weeks past when Mrs. Surratt had gone alone into the Herndon House, while an obliging Lou Weichmann squired the young ladies around the block.

"No, sir. The ruffian that was at my door when I came away? He was a tremendous fellow with a skull cap on, and my daughter commenced crying, and said these gentlemen came to save our lives. I hope they arrested him!"

"He tells me now that you met him in the street and you engaged him to come to the house."

"Oh! Oh! It is not so, sir; for I believe he would have murdered us; everyone, I assure you."

The army did not learn much from Augur's interrogation of the wily landlady. After her transfer from the provost marshal's headquarters to Carroll Prison Annex, Augur sent Colonel H. S. Olcutt down ten days later to try it all again. But prison had not softened Mary Surratt one bit. She had not seen her son since the beginning of April and did not know where he was. She remembered that Atzerodt *did* have a bay horse--at least he rode one. She admitted to the two trips out to Surrattsville, but recollected little beyond her business dealings with John Nothey, mostly transacted through Captain Bennett Gwinn. "Oh, yes, Mr. Lloyd had invited me to a fish fry and oyster bake." She had declined so as to get home, because, "Mr. Weichmann had to have his bread and butter," so she said.

Oh, yes, Mr. Weichmann was there, but she did not know where he was now. She remembered a Baptist minister, Mr. Wood. He stayed a few days, she did not know why, and she presumed that he knew of her place as it had been advertised in the newspapers. She neglected to say the advertisements had appeared two months earlier, and Olcutt missed his chance to challenge this seeming aberration. She had no idea why Mr. Wood came to Washington, he did not say and she did not ask. Was the man who came to the house while the police were there Mr. Wood? You don't say! The only three men who came to her house about the time of Lincoln's assassination were Mr. Weichmann, Mr. Holohan, and Detective McDevitt.

Then Olcutt got to the point. "When did you get acquainted with Mr. Booth?"

"Some three months ago."

"Who brought him to the house?"

"He came to the house and asked whether my son was in. We always found him pleasant. His visits were short. I never knew anything about his private matters at all."

"Were his visits always visits of courtesy?"

"Yes, sir."

"Any business discussed?"

"No, sir; not political affairs. I do not think that his longest stay was over one hour."

"What part of the day did he used to come?"

"Sometimes in the day and sometimes in the evening."

"Did not an attachment spring up between him and your daughter?"

"Not particularly I should suppose; not that I knew of."

"He was a handsome man?"

"He was a handsome man and gentlemanly; that is all I knew of him. I did not suppose he had the Devil, which he certainly possessed, in his heart."

"I should suppose from the papers and letters that Miss Surratt thought favorably of him?"

"If so, she kept it to herself. She never corresponded with him."

"Did he pay particular attention to any one of the young ladies?"

"No particular attention. We were in the parlor together and he did not pay particular attention to any one."

"How long has your son known him?"

"Ever since he came to the house. I do not know whether he knew him before or why he came there. I only know Mr. Weichmann was with my son when they met at some hotel, the National, I presume, and there made his acquaintance."

"Mr. Weichmann was well acquainted with Mr. Booth before they came together?"

"I do not know. I think Mr. Weichmann was with my son when he was introduced."

"Your son never went to college with Mr. Booth?"

"No, sir. He went with Mr. Weichmann to St. Charles at Ellicott's Mills, some three or four years."

"Did your son, or Mr. Booth, or Port Tobacco ever tell you that they had engaged in a plot to kill the President?"

"Never in the world, if it was the last word I have ever to utter."

And as far as the official record went, it pretty much was. Mary Surratt had spoken a tragic truth, at last.

Olcutt stared at her.

"So help me Heaven, I don't know anything about it," she insisted, withering under the colonel's gaze, "and so help me Heaven, I do not tell untruths, for I never have told a lie in my life."

"Mrs. Surratt, it matters not to me what you desire to reveal or not reveal in this matter. But I can say it will go far better with you to come clean with me."

"Why, sir," she replied indignantly, "what on earth could you all do with me if I knew anything and did not cotton to say naught to you about it?"

"Why," Olcutt assured her, "in case you prove to be implicated as much as I am afraid you are, you may fairly well be hanged."

"Posh! Justice should be tempered with clemency as President Lin—"

"Ah, yes, my dear madam, but you forget that the clemency man is dead." Olcutt called for the guard.

As she returned to her cell, she considered it all in silence. *Mr. Lincoln has been killed. Thank God! I am not glad. But somehow I cannot be sorry. I truly believe it was the judgement of Our Lord!*

9. New Home in the Swamp

"What a slough of despond this place is," Booth grumped.

"You think so? Let me tell you," Herold asserted, "it is the best spot for miles. This part of the country is filled with swamps, Allen's, Jordan's, Atchall's, Scrub, Zekiah . . . all part of the Wicomico River above Allen's Fresh. You hain't ever seen so much dense growth of grape and bittersweet vines, red bud, dogwood, gum, poplar, sycamore, and beech. Nothing but sluices and bog. Lots of deep ponds that have no bottom. As for people, few to none live here; just vile, crawling critters. Some lizards, but mostly snakes. Full of cotton mouths, copperheads, and six-foot canebreak rattlers as thick as your arm. We are lucky it is still so cold that the snakes have not come out, yet.

"And we are fortunate that Cox knows of this spot," Herold continued, "one of the few dry ones in the whole region, his man Roby says. Look at the white oaks, green holly, cedar, and pine. In the swamps, even the clay is treacherous and quicksands abound. The Yankees will never find us, even if someone leads them here. It is too scary for words. *I* would not like to sweep this place searching for someone. Better chance with a needle in a haystack. This is a great place to hide. And do a little wing shooting. Too bad we cannot. Now, if you only would just set yourself down, enjoy life, and not get up at the butt crack of dawn all the time. . . ."

A whistle rang out in the morning air. A few moments later, Tom Jones came into the camp, carrying a basket of corn.

"Corn? Parched corn? Is that all you have to feed us?" Booth was acting a mite touchy, but Jones paid him no heed. He knew that Booth's leg was talking, not the man.

"Relax, boys. The corn is a disguise. If Federal detectives or soldiers come up on me sudden-like, I can tell them that I'm calling hogs. Here's the real stuff." With that, Jones set down the basket of corn and pulled two massive slabs of ham and a couple of chunks of bread out of his right pocket, and a flask of coffee out of the other. "Pays to wear a coat with big pockets," he mumbled, in his inoffensive, slow-witted manner that had fooled so many over the years.

As Booth and Herold eagerly gobbled up the modest repast, Jones went on. "I got this colored boy working for me, good feller, name of Henry Woodland. Wunst was my slave, now a freedman and employed by me under a contract supervised by the government. That's what they replaced slavery with last year, don'tcha know? Well, I got two boats out on the river, and I figure the Bluebellies will confiscate everything that can float. They already been nosing around, looking for y'all for days. They was the ones that told me of Lincoln's shooting. So ol' Henry is going to go fishing every day, all day--the shad are about to run, don'tcha know--and he will bring the boat he uses back to Dent's Meadow, below my place and hide it each night. Did you know that our Maryland Dents are related to the Missouri Dents from which the Yankee General Grant's wife hails? Small world."

Jones paused and grabbed a deep breath. He rarely talked that long over anything.

"Dent's Meadow is a lonely spot above the Potomac about a mile off the public road and with no dwelling in sight. A sort of a valley leads down to the river--steep cliffs, heavy timber, and covered with laurel. A body can hardly get through it, lessen you know the way. Nice little creek leads to the big river."

"When can we cross?" Booth wanted to know.

"Don't rush things, now, boys. This country is got more Yanks crawling through it than snakes in summer. Y'all will. . . . Hark! Did y'all hear something?" Jones put his finger up to his mouth and motioned

Booth and Herold to lie low. Soon they could hear the thud of hoofbeats, clanking of sabers, and squeaking of leather as a Federal cavalry patrol passed just beyond sight.

Someone cursed, "Damn Maryland's rain, swamps, and Secesh sympathies."

"Aw, Hell, Whitey, you. . . ." The voices trailed off, followed by laughter.

They waited a few minutes and Jones got up and spoke again. "That is what I mean about using that spring yonder. See? Y'all gotta wait. Patience."

"Yes, of course," Booth apologized. "I leave it all in your hands, Mr. Jones."

"My nephew-in-law, or whatever his relation is to me since his daddy is my step-brother, young Sam Cox, picked up your horses and has taken them over east to Newport, a place called Adams' Tavern. Austin Adams is another Confederate contact around here. They have been colored up and their markings clipped with a scissors so as to look different and are pastured with his horses. Other times they are stabled in his barn."

"Best way to hide things is in the open, you know. No one figures to look there, leastwise not Union soldiers and detectives. After court day, as soon as the Yankees thin out a bit, I will bring them horses back and carry y'all over to the inn where Mrs. Adams will feed y'all some hot food and let y'all sit on the porch each day a while. But y'all must still sleep in the woods every night with a cold camp. Cain't risk an early morning raid by detectives or soldiers picking y'all up. When it is safe, Young Sam will carry y'all down to me at the Potomac to cross. That's the plan.

"Yep, gotta be careful around here. Few come in over here, but some do go by on the path beyond the spring. I am going back now to find my horse. There might be a Yank or two waiting for me there. Oh, I forgot. Here is a newspaper from the City. *Daily National Intelligencer.* Jones reached inside his coat and handed it to Booth. Pays to have lots of pockets," he winked and smiled. Then he got up and disappeared into the woods, calling his nonexistent hogs as he proceeded, slow and dim witted as ever.

Booth looked on with admiration. "There, Davy, that man has the makings of a first-class actor in him!"

10. Tom Jones Meets Billy Williams

The next day, after feeding Booth and Herold, Jones rode up to Port Tobacco. Tuesday was court and market day and there were a lot of local citizens who had come in from nearby farms to tend to business. And lots of Union soldiers and detectives. At least in the bars. Jones got down and passed among the little groups of local men and soldiers in the town square. Everyone was discussing the assassination, the probable whereabouts of Booth, and what the incident boded for the reconstruction of the nation. Jones said very little. He just sort of ambled around, looking as inoffensive as possible. Most of the Yankees did not even see him as he stopped to pack his pipe bowl or strike a phosphorous, listening for the slightest clue as to what was going on. He soon was satisfied that everything was surmise, very little was factual. About all everyone agreed on was that Booth had not yet crossed the river.

Jones went up to the Brawner Hotel to check on the Union officers and detective police. They did not patronize the grog shops Port Tobacco had in profusion for so small a place. That was for the enlisted men. Nothing but the best for those who took Lincoln's shilling, so to speak. The men with the shoulder straps drank with several prominent, local citizens, including James Brawner, the house proprietor.

"Say, Jones," Brawner called out, "this here's Captain Billy Williams. He runs the men hunting for the presidential assassins. Captain, Mr. Jones here is a reluctant expert on the Old Capitol, having been a resident there at public request in 1861."

The crowd laughed. Jones did, too.

"Hello, Jones, have a drink." Captain Williams seemed awfully friendly for a Federal officer. The hair was standing upright on the back of Jones' neck. This man was trouble, for sure.

"Don't mind if'n I do." Jones took up the proffered glass.

Jones was about to down the drink, "here's mud in your eye," when Williams said, almost too casually, "I will give one hundred thousand dollars to anyone who will give me the information that will lead to the capture of the President's assassin."

Jones drained his glass without emotion or hesitation. He had long ago become practiced in the art of not showing his feelings. The death of his wife while he had languished in prison, the ruination of the Old South, the management of the Secret Mail Line, and six months in the Old Capitol had given him steel nerves. And it helped that the Brawner House served very fine whiskey. Anything less and he probably would have choked, as he figured Williams wanted him to.

He kept his face turned from Williams. "That is a large sum of money and ought to get him, if money can do it."

Jones knew that no sum of money would entice him to betray Booth and Herold. He would be violating what he saw as a trust. He lived on land owned by Cox, had few prospects, and his beloved Confederacy had gone down in defeat, but to have given up Booth would have taken from him something more important than monetary wealth. It would have cost him the one thing he was born with and would carry to his grave--his honor. That was something the money-grubbing Northerners never seemed to understand. It was why the South continued to fight, long after there was any real chance of success. It was why the South had left the Union four long years ago. It was why Jones delivered the Confederate mail and risked capture every time he crossed the Potomac. A man's honor, the keeping of his word, being true to a cause; these things mattered.

He turned to the Yankee Captain attired in civilian clothes. "No offense, Captain Williams, but y'all keep a lousy jail up there in the City." The patrons at the bar stood spellbound. Men had been arrested for saying less in this war.

But Williams kept his good humor. "I know, Mr. Jones, but remember, it is still taking on boarders. We never run out of room."

Jones knew it! Williams suspected that he knew something. Jones still maintained his outward equanimity and Williams kept his. They continued jostling each other, like two dogs circling stiff-legged with hackles raised just before a fight.

"That is indeed a shame, Captain. All the same, I will pass the opportunity by, today, I reckon," Jones said.

"Always another day," Williams smiled and chuckled. You will be there, he thought to himself, sooner than either you or I think, *I reckon*.

Jones excused himself, went to a store to purchase a few items, and left town the way he came. He spent the next two days uneventfully, if enduring numerous searches of his house and farm by different Federal officials and soldiers can be called uneventful. But he knew that he received no special attention. Everyone else's farm was pretty well pried into, as well. They even interviewed Henry Woodland, Jones' former slave and present employee. Woodland could tell them nothing because Jones told him nothing.

But Woodland suspected something was up. He bided his time and went fishing every day, all day. The weather was cloudy, cold and damp but, fortunately for the men in the woods, it did not rain more than every other day or so. There was little to make their days pleasant, and

Booth's leg appeared to grow worse each day. Tom Jones visited the small hamlet of Allen's Fresh across the Wicomico from Newport daily to keep up with the news and avoid Captain Williams over in Port Tobacco. Out on the Potomac, Henry Woodland caught a lot of fish. But the Yankees came up empty handed in their search for the fugitives or Thomas Jones' fishing boat, which Woodland faithfully hid every night below Dent's Meadow.

11. The Arrest of Andrew Atzerodt

George Andrew Atzerodt was no killer. He was, if anything, an abject coward, when it came to shooting. But he was one Hell of a riverman. He could get a boat across the Potomac, right under the noses of the Federal navy. So he had a different kind of courage--one not needed for Booth's assassination schemes to succeed. He could be real handy when it came to escaping over the tidal waters into Virginia.

After leaving the Canterbury House on Good Friday, Andrew Atzerodt turned to the only friend he had left--booze. He turned his horse in at Naylor's and offered to buy the ubiquitous John Fletcher a drink at the Union Hotel, next door.

Atzerodt said, "If this thing tonight happens, you will a present get."

Fletcher did not understand. He wanted to know about Davy Herold. "Your acquaintance is out late with our horse."

"Ach! He will after a while back be," Atzerodt reassured him.

Then Atzerodt rented another animal and rode back to the Kirkwood House--for another drink. Fletcher followed him on foot, hoping to see Herold and collar Charley, his rented horse. Atzerodt went into the dining room. The only other patron was Andrew Johnson, having an early supper. Now was the chance! Just walk over to him and his black servant to shoot! But Atzerodt's nerve failed him completely. He left the hotel and turned in his horse at Kellner's Stable at E and Eighth and walked toward the Avenue. His jaunt included most of the bars on his route, until he finally got tired of walking and boarded a horse car bound for the Navy Yard gates.

Then, Atzerodt decided to turn in for the night. He asked Washington Briscoe, a fellow passenger and an acquaintance of some years, if he could sleep in his store. Briscoe said, "No." Atzerodt reboarded the next horse car and rode back to Sixth Street and Pennsylvania. He walked around the block and got a room at the Kimmel House--otherwise known as the Pennsylvania Hotel, where he commonly stayed while in the District. He had to share a room with another man, Samuel Thomas, who entered the hotel about the same time as he. Atzerodt had tried to go up without registering at the front desk.

The Negro bell man saw Atzerodt about dawn, walking west toward Sixth Street. "What brings you out so early this morning, sir?"

"Well, I have business got," was the reply. The bell man did not know that Atzerodt had just walked out on his bill.

He would go to his boyhood home near Germantown, now owned by his cousin, Ernst Hartmann Richter. He walked to Georgetown and pawned his revolver for $10 with clerk John Caldwell at Matthews & Company's general store. Flush with funds, he took breakfast with an accommodating widow. Next, he went to the Cunningham Tavern, and the stage stop for Germantown.

At Tenallytown, all the highway traffic stopped. Up ahead, a picket post was examining everyone, looking for the assassin of Lincoln and the assailant of the Sewards. Atzerodt bade his stage driver good-bye, and walked forward along the line of horses and vehicles. He was naturally gregarious, and stopped often to chat with all sorts of people he did not know. When he reached the picket post, Atzerodt began to talk to the soldiers and drink a little hard cider with them. Then he got up on a wagon and rode through the inspectors, everyone waving him on. After all, they now *knew* him. He rode into Gaithersburg and took a drink or two at John Mullican's groggery and blacksmith shop.

By 11 o'clock p.m., he had reached the Old Clopper Mill and stopped for the night. The miller, Robert Kinder, really did know Atzerodt and the Richters. The next morning, Easter Sunday, Atzerodt was off early, but he stopped at the home of Hezekiah Metz for Easter dinner. The Metzes knew him as Andrew Atwood. He spoke about the assassination with the others at the table

"Are you the man who killed Abe Lincoln?"

"Ja, ja." Atzerodt laughed. Everyone else did, too.

"I want to know the truth of it. Is it so? Was the President assassinated?"

"Ja, es ist wahr. The President died yesterday about 3 o'clock a.m."

"Was Secretary Seward's throat cut?"

"Ja, Mr. Seward was stabbed, or rather, at the throat cut. But not killed. Two of his sons were stabbed auch."

"And General Grant? Was he assassinated the same night?"

"If the man that was to follow him followed him, it was likely so. Ach, du Lieber! What a trouble I see."

"Why? What have you to trouble you?"

"More than I will ever shut of get."

Atzerodt seemed to know too much. One of the other dinner guests turned out to be a Yankee military informer. He went straight to his superiors. By mid-afternoon, Atzerodt had reached the Richter farm. They were glad to see him. He could stay, so long as he worked for his keep.

For three days, Andrew Atzerodt lived with his cousin and his family. But on Thursday morning at 5 a.m., he was awakened by Sergeant Z. W. Gemmill and a six-man patrol from the 1st (Union) Delaware Cavalry. Gemmill arrested both Atzerodt and Hartmann Richter. Soon, they were on their way back to the District, Atzerodt knowing why, but Richter wondering what had happened to cause an innocent farmer like himself so much grief. At least they went in style, on a Baltimore and Ohio passenger train.

12. Boredom in the Swamp

Booth sat on the blankets, shivering in the bone-chilling dampness of the fireless camp. He reached into his coat pocket and pulled out the memorandum book that served as his diary--his recorder and confessor. He opened the book to the next blank page and pulled out the precious little piece of pencil from its loop. He had dated it earlier during the day before the assassination, but no entry had been made. Booth altered the printed date on the page of "Tuesday, June 14, 1864," and penciled in the date of the murder, even though he actually was writing on April 17. He kept "the Ides" for effect. He *was* Brutus or, at least, following in the noble footsteps of him for whose antecedent his father and brother had been honorably named. After all, as any good thespian knows, one has to think and act grandly for posterity. Booth did not intend to lose distinction in this matter, as his enemies wished. Thus, the entry fluctuated between reality and fiction, as if he were writing an historical play and editing the facts to make a better story.

"Well, if it did not happen exactly this way, it should have," Booth reasoned aloud.

He began with a half page ungrammatical, anonymous assertion of his love, "Ti Amo," for his mother--or was it Lucy Hale, or Ella Turner, or . . .? Then he wrote in his pinched cursive script:

April 13th 14

Friday, the Ides

Until today, nothing was ever *thought* of sacrificing to our country's wrongs. For six months we had worked to capture. But our cause being almost lost, something decisive & great must be done. But its failure is owing to others, who did not strike for their country with a heart. I struck boldly and not as the papers say. I walked with a firm step through a thousand of his friends, was stopped, but pushed on. A Colonel was at his side. I shouted 'sic semper' *before* I fired. In jumping broke my leg. I passed all his pickets, rode sixty miles that night, with the bones of my leg tearing the flesh at every jump. I can never repent it, though we hated to kill: Our country owed all her troubles to him, and God simply made me the instrument of his punishment. The country is not what it *was*. This forced union is not what I *have* loved. I care not what *becomes* of me. I have no desire to out-live my country. This night (before the deed), I wrote a long article and left it for one of the Editors of the National Intelligencer, in which I set forth our reasons for our proceedings. He or the Government . . . .

Evidently something distracted him from the erstwhile effort-- Booth never finished his thought on paper. But he never stopped wondering, what had happened to the letter he had entrusted to Matthews? Four more days in the swamp with an occasional jaunt to Adams' nearby roadhouse did not improve Booth's humor any.

"It is *not* here, Davy. My letter is not here! I have read every newspaper from Friday to now and it is not even hinted at. That damn Matthews did not deliver my letter---no, no, he *did* deliver it, but the stinking government would not let him publish it. Yes! That's it! They do not dare let my letter be seen, lest it cause an immediate challenge to their concept of the 'Dying God,' Lincoln."

"Yeah, to publish your letter now would be tantamount to sneaking out a fart in a crowded church, all right," Herold opined.

"Dying God, my ass! Those bastards raped the whole country when they forsook the Constitution for their own sordid ends. Listen to this drivel! 'Perhaps the crime committed last night in Washington is the worst committed on any Good Friday since the crucifixion of Christ. It was not only assassination, it was parricide; for Abraham Lincoln was as a father to the whole nation.' What crap!"

"What is that fancy word . . . par . . . parri . . . oh, whatever?"

"Parricide-it means killing one's own father."

"Oh. Humph!" Herold shook his head in disbelief at the fancy, big words some people had to use. Why in the Hell did they not say what they meant in simple terms a body could understand?

"But look at this! The only men they mention by name are John Surratt and George Atzerodt. There has been an arrest and confession up in Baltimore. That must be O'Laughlen or Arnold, maybe both. And they found Arnold's letter to me in my room. Hell, let those wretches explain away their own problems. They deserted me--I mean, The Cause--in my--its--time of need."

"Well, they sure were not there the night we could have used them," Herold agreed.

"At least they got my 'To Whom It May Concern' letter from my sister Asia's safe. That will help if it is not hidden away from the public, too. And look at this. Southern generals lauding Lincoln--the man who caused this war! It is all enough to make me sick at heart--to vomit my very guts out! Instead of calling for me to come forth as a hero, like William Tell or Marcus Brutus, they allow Marc Antony to speak instead."

Booth continued, after some thought, "How right Shakespeare was (*Julius Caesar*, Act 3, Scene 1) in putting into the mouth of Caius Cassius: 'Know you how much the people may be moved by that which he utter?' I was a fool to rely on weaker spirits to present my reasons, leaving the field to the Republican-controlled press. I should have stayed. . . ."

"Stayed?! Are you crazy?" Herold interjected. "You would have been hanged on the spot. Not even *your* silver tongue could have saved you from that crowd at Ford's."

Herold's lack of sophistication proved much more practical than Booth's ranting romanticism. And Booth knew it. But he sulked and groused, nonetheless.

"They is the whistle," Herold exclaimed, relieved to be able to change the subject. "It must be Jones."

"It is about time," Booth growled, "I am going to give him what for. Keeping us out here in the cold and damp. My leg is killing me."

"Hey, boys," Jones said, using the familiar Southern greeting between friends, "how y'all doing?"

"Mr. Jones," Booth began somewhat patronizingly, "we have been out here in these God-forsaken woods for nearly a week, it is cold enough to freeze the balls off a brass monkey, and it rains every other day! When may we next go down to that Adams' place?"

"Five days, Mr. Booth. This is the fifth day. I know that the weather has been frightful for men sleeping on the ground. But it beats the accommodations at the Old Capitol. I'll lay to that from personal experience."

The prison reference cooled Booth down. The old man had risked a lot to be here each day. Jones began to hand over the tedious daily ration of cold ham, bread, and coffee.

"Oh, by the way, I have brought a cheese to vary your diet. Ham and bread can get on your nerves, day after day, but it is about all that keeps well in our climate. Except for cheese. I reckon it's especially rough on a man like you, Mr. Booth, who is accustomed to finer fare in the City than an old tobacco farmer like me."

"We *must* move on Mr. Jones. Can you not see that? Can you not do something?"

"Well," Jones scratched his moustache thoughtfully," it is not me who determines what goes on in southern Maryland. There must be close to 10,000 Bluebellies looking for you in this state. They is sure a passel of Yanks down in *this* county, alone. All I can do is keep an eye on them. First chance I get, you will be moved on to Austin's for some shelter and a hot meal, I promise you that, sir. You have my word on that."

Jones decided not to mention that Stringfellow was waiting at Dent's Meadow to cross ahead of them. In the mood he was in, Jones knew that Booth was not about to take second billing to anyone.

"I know Mr. Jones," Booth stated resignedly. "You have been more than generous with us, risking your very life fighting the imposition of Yankee tyranny over men as patriotic as ever served the South. But my leg is killing me and the boredom is most irksome. Even the newspapers no longer help."

"You mean the ones that call you an infamous murderer of the noblest man God ever created?"

"You have read them, then?"

"Oh, yeah," Jones said. "I would not put much stock in that stuff. They could not publish if they did not print the usual Yankee drivel. Lots of good men and women in jail for not paying heed to their mouths and pens. But the local folks down here are with you, boys, I assure you. No one has turned you in and many of the rumors of your presence are planted by our own agents. Best to keep the Yankees hunting. Cannot let them stop to think, you know."

"Now, I am agoing into Allen's Fresh," Jones continued, "a small place at the southern end of the Zekia--where it turns into the Wicomico River. Been going in there every evening to sound out the situation. You boys be patient. And above all, lay low! I'll get you to Ol' Virginny as soon as it can be done. You can lay on it."

"Don't worry, we will be here when you return, just agigglin' and awhittlin'," Herold promised jovially.

With that, Jones picked up his basket of parched corn and ambled off, calling his ever-absent hogs. Reckon I sure better go into town again, today, he thought. Those boys are going a mite crazy out there in the trees, all alone. Well, Herold ain't. That boy is like a pig in mud out here in the woods. But Booth. . . . He just scribbles in that little book of his'n and fights it all the way.

Back at the camp, Booth opened "that little book" to where he had left off writing. He did not finish his broken sentence. The thought had left him. Instead, he turned the page sideways and drew a makeshift calendar across the bottom two-thirds of the page. He began with Monday, April 17, and optimistically continued through Sunday, June 18, when he ran out of space. Hereafter, he would cross out each day as it passed.

13. The Arrest and Statements of Dr. Samuel A. Mudd

It was not that Dr. Samuel Mudd was the *only* liar who faced the inquisitors investigating the Lincoln murder; it was simply that he was the *smoothest*. Davy Herold was too blatant to be respected. Atzerodt and Arnold pretty much told the truth. O'Laughlen successfully concealed his true role with the help of his friends' alibis. Mary Surratt admitted to nothing at all. Powell said nothing at all. Spangler did not know what to say; he had done nothing, except that he had known Booth from his childhood. Everyone else said what the government men told them to say to save their own skins. But Dr. Mudd backed and filled like an expert. He even lied to his own attorney. Mudd trusted no one but himself. All in all, it probably was not a bad move—he eluded the hangman by one vote.

Mudd's wife Frankie allegedly was too afraid to be left alone on Saturday night. She feared that Booth and Herold might be watching from the woods to see if Sam went in to tell on them. Then they would take their revenge on her, the children, and other residents of the Mudd farm. But Sunday was another matter. The Mudds all went to Mass at St. Peters, and there Sam disclosed to his cousin, Dr. George Mudd, a devout Unionist, the events of his harrowing Saturday, which had begun before dawn and did not conclude till dusk.

George Mudd had already met Lieutenant Dana, the Federal troop commander at Bryantown, and told Sam that he would inform the Yanks as to what had happened. Some one had to do it and Sam was still hesitant, unsure of what he ought to divulge. On Monday, Dr. George Mudd rode into Bryantown and cornered Lieutenant Dana.

"Lieutenant, my cousin had two strangers show up at his place on Saturday. He was afraid to inform on them for fear that his family might be hurt in an exchange of gunfire. One of the men had a broken leg, suffered in a riding accident during the early morning hours of that same day."

"Thank you, sir; we shall get right on it."

Samuel Mudd waited all day Monday for the troopers to come out. Nothing happened. Finally, at noon Tuesday, one of the white servants, John Davis, came out to the tobacco fields and said that Federal authorities were waiting to see him over at the house.

"Who is there?"

"Well, sir, they are Dr. George, and four detectives--least that is what they says. They ain't dressed like sojers, just like us. But they calls each other 'Lieutenant' and 'Captain' and such."

Mudd went in. After introductions, Lieutenant Joshua Lloyd asked, "Have you heard of the President's assassination?"

"Oh, yes," Mudd said, "it was all about at Mass, day 'fore yesterday."

"Have you seen two parties pass, say, on Saturday morning?" asked Billy Williams.

"No."

"You have not seen John Wilkes Booth, David Edgar Herold, or John Harrison Surratt?" It was Lloyd, again.

"No."

The detectives looked at each other. In the later words of Lieutenant Alex Lovett, Mudd was pale as a sheet of paper, blue about the lips, and extremely nervous. He was obviously hiding something. Lovett took over the questioning.

"No one *passed?*"

"No."

"Did anyone *stop* here and *come in?*"

"Yes, two men. It was early Saturday, before dawn, about four o'clock. One stayed on his horse and the other rapped at the door."

"Now we are getting somewhere. That is what Lieutenant Dana told us. What did *these* men look like?"

"One was older, in his twenties, and had a broken leg. The other was younger, around eighteen. He helped me get the hurt man in and I set his leg. We took him upstairs to a bedroom there."

"How long did they stay?"

"Most of the day. They left around dusk."

"Which way did they go?"

"They asked about the way to Allen's Fresh, but then wanted to go across the swamp to Parson Wilmer's (the parson was a Unionist whom Mudd disliked--let him explain why Booth wanted to come his way). I showed them the road." Mudd pointed it out with a sweep of his arm.

"What did they do while here?"

"I had my man make a set of crutches. The younger fellow and I went around looking for a carriage they might borrow, but came up empty. Next day was Easter, you know. Everyone needed theirs to go to church with. The younger led the older man across the swamp on horseback. The younger man walked, led his own horse, too."

"Did the man with the broke leg just sit around?"

"He lay in bed. Oh! He shaved off his moustache. Asked for a razor. The rest of his face was covered with a full beard."

"Ain't that mighty suspicious?"

"Indeed. That is why I talked to my cousin about it the next day."

The detectives thanked Sam Mudd and left. But Friday, they were back again. This time they were accompanied by two dozen heavily armed cavalrymen.

"Dr. Mudd," Lovett said, "do you happen to have the razor the older man used to shave off his moustache? We are going to have to search the house."

"That will not be necessary, gentlemen. Frankie will bring it out. By the way, we happened to find the boot the injured man wore. I had to cut it off to set his broken bone. I thought he had carried it with him when he left. But Frankie, my wife, found it under the bed while cleaning it after you all left the other day."

"Great Scott! Lovett, lookee here!" Billy Williams said.

Inside the boot were the words: "J. Wilkes. Henry Lutz, Maker, 445 Broadway, New York."

"Do you not think this refers to John Wilkes Booth?" Lovett asked Mudd.

"No. The man was bearded and. . . ."

"Show him the tintype."

"I *know* the man in the portrait," Mudd admitted. "He was down here last fall, looking for land to buy. Mr. Thompson introduced us. He bought a horse off my neighbor, Squire Gardiner. But the man I treated Saturday had a full beard. They are not the *same*."

"Are you sure?"

"Well, something about the forehead and eyes *is* familiar."

"Were these men, the ones that stayed here on Saturday, armed?"

"Well, the one with the broken leg carried two horse pistols under his coat. I do not know about the other."

"Get your gear, Doctor. You must come with us and answer a few questions for Colonel Henry Wells, the local provost marshal in charge of this case. You may have to stay over night."

At the Bryantown Tavern, the same place where Mudd had introduced John Wilkes Booth, the man he now claimed he did not know, to Thomas Harbin, during a visit that he would never admit took place, Mudd was held for the next three days. While there, Mudd wrote in his own hand a voluntary statement of facts to Colonel Wells, which he signed. Then Wells came back and interrogated Mudd verbally. The next day he handed Mudd a second statement, written out by a clerk and asked him to sign it.

In the voluntary statement Mudd said little more than he had told the detectives, except that he inserted a statement that he was and had always been a loyal Union man, even though he was not a Lincoln supporter. He thought that the names the two visitors used were Henson, for the younger man, and Tyser or Tyson, for the older. He mentioned his neighbors, John F. Hardy and Frances Farrell, as character references. They were the first he told of the strangers' visit, even before telling it to Cousin George.

In the second, or what is now referred to as the Wells' statement, Mudd admitted that he had met Booth the previous fall through an introduction by J. C. Thompson, the son-in-law of Dr. William Queen. Booth had stayed overnight at the Mudd home and went next door to the Gardiner place to buy a horse. He had never seen Booth since. He had sent the strangers over the swamp to Parson Wilmer's.

Wells smelled a large rat. He informed Mudd that he would have to go to Washington under arrest as a suspect after the fact for assisting in the murder of Abraham Lincoln. On Monday April 24, an officer and three soldiers escorted him home to pack for the trip. Mrs. Mudd, who had remained stoic until this moment, broke down and cried. She would not see Sam again for four hard years.

"Do not grieve," the officer in charge said, "I will see that your husband returns to you." Later, Mrs. Mudd wished that she could remember the man's name. He was the only Federal official who showed "some heart."

Sam might have thought he was going in merely for further questioning. Frankie was wiser. Something was very wrong. She did not know what; it was a woman's intuition. Sam would soon find out that she was correct. For if John M. Lloyd had the story that would do in Mary

Surratt, then Louis J. Weichmann had the tale that would nearly get Samuel A. Mudd hanged.

14. Baker's Pictorial Reward Poster

"Well, Byron, here we are!" Lafayette C. Baker entered his office at 217 Pennsylvania Avenue in grinning triumph. "Look! The reward now totals $100,000, half of it for Booth, and the rest split evenly between John Surratt and David Herold. And there is another $25,000 for George Atzerodt."

"The photographs really set that poster off from others. First time it has ever been done."

"Right! Another Baker innovation!"

"Too bad that Atzerodt has already been taken, by some Delaware Cavalry up in Montgomery County," Byron said. "Arrested his cousin, too, at whose farm he was staying."

"Hell! He is small potatoes. What we want is Booth. That is where reputations and money are to be made. Now let us see where we stand this Friday of April 21, 1865."

"So far," Byron Baker intoned, reading from a set of carefully kept notes, "the Provost Marshals and the Metropolitan Police have done the most. Evidently this Fletcher, the livery stable manager, reported a horse stolen by David Herold. This led him to Police Superintendent Richards, whose detective took him to General Augur's headquarters, where Herold was connected to George Atzerodt. The latter had ridden a horse, blind of one eye, which was later found over near Lincoln Hospital. Out at Fort Bunker Hill was the coat worn by the man who tried to kill four men at Seward's, including the Secretary and his sons."

"Right. Meanwhile," Lafayette Baker chimed in, "Richards got wind that Herold was a friend of Booth and John Surratt, whose mother ran a boarding house on H Street. He sent a squad over, but they found none of them. The next morning, however, two residents of the Surratt House come in to Richards and one of them, a Louis Weichmann, tells of all sorts of plots to kidnap President Lincoln and the fact that Surratt and Booth are close companions. Stories since confirmed by one of Weichmann's fellow workers over at the office of the Commissary of Prisoners. At different times, the Army and the Metropolitans searched the rooms of Atzerodt and Booth, and we are kept in the dark about what was found."

"As usual!" Byron Baker exclaimed. "Then Richards sends detectives out with Weichmann and Holohan, another boarder at Mrs.

Surratt's, to a tavern in Surrattsville now rented by John Lloyd. On the road the soldiers at the Navy Yard Bridge said Booth and Herold used the proper password and countersign night of the murder. Lloyd says he has heard and seen nothing. But an enterprising officer named George Cottingham, this time from the Provost Marshal's headquarters, picked up the bartender, Joseph T. Knott, and he knows all about a plot to kill or kidnap the President and says Surratt is in on it. But the Metropolitan police ruin their horses with too much activity and drift back into the City, leaving the field open to Augur's men, the Army provost marshals. Weichmann is held off limits to us and Richard's detectives take him to Canada to try and find Surratt. We will arrest him and take him from Richards when they return, probably empty-handed. Stanton has already promised to back us up."

"Good!" Lafayette Baker exclaimed. "The army's detectives return to the Surratt House on H Street and arrest all left there, Mrs. Mary Surratt, her daughter and a couple of boarders. As the women are about to leave, in walks Lewis Paine, who fits the description of the man who assaulted the Sewards to a Tee. He is identified at Augur's headquarters by Seward's black servant. Augur also sends units down to Surrattsville and on to Bryantown. Lieutenant Alexander Lovett arrests John Lloyd who then implicates Mrs. Surratt."

"And now for my favorite part," Byron interjects. "Dr. Mudd's own *cousin* reported him to Lieutenant David Dana, the brother of Assistant Secretary of War Charles Dana, a special friend of ours through Stanton, and he and Lovett and others go out to interview the doctor and he feeds them a line of bullshit a mile long. Finally, the provost marshals go back and find Booth's boot under a bed, yesterday, and arrest Mudd on the spot."

"But the best part," Lafayette Baker said, "is that Major James R. O'Bierne, who I thought would be the most dangerous man to our cause of getting the reward money, has been to Leonardtown. I suspected that O'Beirne was close to finding Booth. So I connived with Eckert over at Military Telegraph to send Grant's own telegrapher, Captain S. H. Beckwith to Port Tobacco to contact O'Beirne and find out what he is up to. It has already paid off. O'Beirne was holding out on the fact that Booth had broken his leg, confirming the evidence found at Dr. Mudd's. And Beckwith is sending us every bit of information O'Beirne developes before O'Beirne knows its significance."

"What about that Dr. Coombs?" Byron asked. "The one who claimed that he knew where Booth and Herold had to be hiding--the only place they could--the only dry spot in the whole swamp? He seemed to be pretty certain. Pointed the finger right at Dr. Staughton Dent, Samuel Cox and old Tom Jones. You know we have suspected them for years. Jones has even served jail time on suspicion."

"Bunk!" Lafayette Baker snorted. "All he wanted to do was get cut in on the reward. And he had the nerve to call *me* a $200,000 man! The cavalry has scoured that swamp from stem to stern and found not a trace. O'Beirne would have them in custody already, if Coombs had told the truth. He went right over to Augur after he left us."

15. Jones Moves Booth and Herold to the Potomac

After noon dinner on Saturday, Jones told everyone at home that he was off to Allen's Fresh. He mounted his old nag, Kit, and rode over to Colton's Store. It was the best grog shop for miles, and Union soldiers and detectives had been keeping Colton in more cash than he had ever seen or expected to see. It was getting along near dusk, when a troop of Federal cavalry rode in led by John R. Walton, a local man, as guide. The troopers all called for whiskey, and Colton brought out his best watered stock. Hell, Jones understood, a good barkeep never served the real stuff to the damned Yankees.

Suddenly, there was a pounding of booted feet on the porch boards and the bar room door was thrown open. It was Walton. "Boys, I have news that they have been seen in St. Mary's!"

The Yankees all cheered. Some washed their drinks down in one gulp. Others tipped their glasses over in the hurry to mount up. But large numbers of them left full glasses on the tables and bar, which Jones helped Colton pour back into the bottle.

"Never pays to waste whiskey," Colton chuckled, "even if it *is* watered down."

Jones helped himself to one of the watered whiskeys at Colton's suggestion. It was weak--very little kick at all. Jones smiled to himself as he sat back down and waited. Outside the Yankees were storming over the bridge headed to St. Mary's County further down the peninsula. Well, well, Jones mused, one of the false leads had finally paid off. He waited a quarter of an hour. More cavalry passed through Allen's Fresh from the direction of Port Tobacco.

This was it, all right; the Federals had bought it good. It was now or never. This is my chance, Jones reasoned. Jones got up ever so slowly and went over to the bar to pay his tab.

"Good luck, Tom," Colton said, quietly.

Jones said, "Thanks," without any emotion, and went out to mount Ol' Kit, his flea-bitten gray mare. It was growing dark. He pulled up to let another troop of cavalry pass. Jones shook his head in amazement and slapped his thigh. Lookit those suckers run! They sure have been sold!

Jones crossed the bridge and turned in at the Adam's Tavern at Newport. A white fog was rolling in, ghost-like at first, and then becoming a dense, thick cloud. Good, in one hour it would be difficult to see much over a hundred feet. Jones stopped at the tavern, and hailed his nephew, Sam Cox, Jr., who came out on the porch.

"Let's do it now!" Jones said

Sam got on his own horse and rounded up the disguised bay and the red roan. Then he disappeared into the woods nearby. He had never been into the camp at night before, or on horseback. Cox gave the signal further out than usual. He rode right into the woods, and gave the signal again. He hoped that the fugitives would listen and not shoot first. He whistled and walked the horses into their camp. Booth was lying on the ground, pistols drawn. Herold was nowhere to be seen. He soon stepped out from behind a tree. He had been covering Booth from Cox's rear.

"The coast seems to be clear," Cox said, "and the darkness and fog favors us. Uncle Tom says le's make the attempt."

Herold quickly packed up their few possibles and was ready to move out.

"This is what we will do," Jones instructed, when they met him on the road in front of the tavern. "I will scout the path ahead on Ol' Kit for about fifty yards or so. If it is clear, I will whistle. Y'all come up to me at a walk and stop, and we repeat it all over again. If I fail to signal in a reasonable amount of time, you two get out of the road, with as little noise and as quick as you can. Hide and wait until you hear from me."

Jones figured the whole trip was six miles or so. The worst part would be on the public road to Huckleberry. Not only might someone accidentally stumble into them, but they had to pass the home of a freed man and his family, whose children played outside at all hours, and a white hunter, who had a pack of coon hounds.

The trip ought not to take more than an hour and a quarter under normal conditions, but Jones had to move quietly along the road, stopping to evaluate each sound and shadow that seemed unusual. He was soon perspiring, even though the night was cold enough as to cause him to wear a heavy coat. Indeed, the air was so saturated with moisture that, although it had not rained, dew dropped from the leaves in a constant patter, as though the very trees felt the anxiousness of the men who passed below.

Herold and Cox, too, were on tenterhooks, waiting for Jones' signals and then moving cautiously forward. Davey rode with the butt of his carbine resting on his thigh and on half cock, his finger held lightly on the trigger, thumb on the hammer, ready for immediate action. Only Booth and the horse seemed oblivious to the danger. Booth was in too much pain to care. And Jones' Ol' Kit really did not sense anything noteworthy about the trip, except the numerous stops, which she appreciated after the fast run from Allen's Fresh.

The dampness of the night solved the problem of Sam Thomas' numerous children. It was too wet to be out, unless one had something secretive in mind, as did the four men passing by quietly on the road. Evidently, not even a good dog wanted to be out in the murky dampness. Jones whistled Herold, Booth and Cox past John Ware's kennels without a response from the hounds. Jones allowed himself a self-satisfied smirk. Just like a coon dog, always barking when unneeded, and never awake when suspicion called for it. Funny how a domestic animal often cooperated exactly as it should, if a body just expected it. True of dogs and horses alike. But not cats. They had minds of their own. Impenetrable. Kinda like women. Jones turned into Huckleberry with relief. Now they could travel on his land, actually Cox's, with little chance of being observed. About forty yards short of the house, Jones stopped the cavalcade under a pear tree near the stable.

"Oh," Booth pleaded, "can I not go in and get some of your hot coffee?"

A pang of guilt swept through Jones' very soul. He could feel the attraction of his warm home, the beckoning light, and warmth of the fire. How much more of a draw it all must have for Herold, even accustomed as he was to the woods. As for Booth, it must have been momentarily more agonizing than even his swollen leg.

Jones put a hand gently on his good leg. "My friend, it would not do," he said softly, with feeling. "Indeed it would not be safe. There are servants in the house who would be sure to see you and then we all would be lost. Remember, this is your last chance to get away."

Fortunately, it was too dark for Booth and Herold to see the sympathetic tears that welled up in Jones' eyes. But his voice quavered ever so slightly, betraying his true depth of feeling. Even in the midst of his agony of suffering, a man as sensitive to stage nuances, as was Booth, did not miss this plaintive note. He knew that Jones was not merely a good man, but an exceptional one.

16. Booth and Herold at the Potomac

"I will go ahead, you follow at my signal," Jones said as they went by his house quietly.

About three hundred yards before the river a split-rail worm fence crossed the path. It separated Cox's land from Dr. Stoughton Dent's. Jones and Herold lifted Booth out of the saddle and left the horses with young Cox. He would take them all back to Adams' place and ride Ol' Kit home to Rich Hill.

Meanwhile, Jones and Herold helped Booth down the narrow draw to the river. It was a slow, laborious job, sort of like going down Dr. Mudd's narrow steps, only much more arduous. Every pace was pure torture. Once Herold slipped and rolled down the trail, but Booth and Jones stayed upright. Fortunately, Booth did not further damage his leg, and Herold bounded up unharmed, but the exercise became more torturous the longer it lasted. All three were panting heavily and drenched in sweat by the time they reached the bottom.

"What if the boat is not here?" Herold's inquiry caused a chill to pass through Booth and Jones, so much so, that they both shivered in unison.

"I will hide y'all in the laurel and go get the other boat, hidden in another cove. Then we will cross tomorrow night." Jones stated his plan firmly, to quell any fear in the hearts of his two charges.

"Ha! There it is!" Jones spoke in triumph, as he stepped into the shallows to drag the dozen-foot-long skiff closer to Booth on the bank. It was tied on a long line to allow for changes in tide. It was painted a dull gray. The same color as used on ocean-going blockade runners, Jones chuckled at the two landlubbers, who gazed upon their means of salvation with less than complete confidence. The little craft had two seats, one in the stern and another athwart amidships, and one oar and a canoe paddle.

"Let me rig a spring line to keep her steady. Here, Mr. Herold," he said, throwing Davy a rope tied to the stern. "Tie this to that sapling over there. Pull it snug. Tie it like you would a horse--so it will hold but come undone easily when we want it to. Now help Mr. Booth to the gunwale--I mean, the edge of the boat. All right, Mr. Booth, turn with your back to the boat and sit in the stern--I'll catch you from the rear as Mr. Herold lowers you. Grab hands, now!"

Booth sort of fell into the boat with a solid thud. The boat rocked and bobbed sideways, despite Jones' effort to steady her. But Booth took his seat without hurting his leg, and without ducking Jones in the water. Herold crawled in front, and Jones came out on dry land to hand over their possessions; blankets, the carbine, and a small box compass. Then he rigged a sort of shield from one of the blankets.

"All right, Mr. Booth, you are the helmsman. Steer with the oar. Mr. Herold will paddle." Jones pointed a scrawny finger, crooked from years of hard work, to 195° on the compass. "Keep to that and it will fetch y'all to the opposite shore around Persimmon Point. It is about two miles off. You cannot see it through the fog. When you get to the Virginia side, Mr. Booth, stay parallel to the shore line and keep southward to the first inlet. That is Gambo Creek. Go up the creek till you come to a bridge and tie up there. Confederate Navy partisan rangers used to have a camp there, in an old log house put up by the first agent operating on the Virginia side, name of E. Pliny Bryan, but he is dead now. If you get into a fix for any reason, go to the second inlet. That will be Machodoc Creek. The first house on the right or north bank is Mrs. Quesenberry's. If y'all tell her you come from me, I think she will take care of you. Gambo comes up about a mile behind, or this side of Mrs. Quesenberry's. Mr. Herold can go overland straight south to get help from her. You can wait by the boat. Leave the boat with Mrs. Q., when y'all are done with her.

"When you get started, light this little candle and stick it on the compass case so you can see your heading. Pull the blanket over you so the light don't show. A light travels awful far out on the water, so be careful. Good bye, boys." Jones left unspoken the rest of his thought— "good luck, you'll need it."

Booth grabbed Jones by the arm. "Wait a minute old fellow. Let us pay you for all you have done." Jones refused. "Then let me pay you for the boat."

Now, that was not a bad idea, Jones thought. He would never see it again. "I will take eighteen dollars, Mr. Booth. That's what I gave for her in Baltimore last year." Booth remonstrated with Jones to take more. Jones again refused.

In a voice choked with emotion, Booth croaked out, "God bless you, my dear friend, for all that you have done for me. Good bye, old fellow." Jones stepped to the lines and set the little craft free and watched as Herold paddled into the stream. The fugitives soon disappeared in the darkness and fog. He could hear the sound of the paddle strokes long after the boat was lost from sight.

Jones felt as if a great burden had been lifted from his shoulders. The next morning Sam Cox, Sr., came over to tell him their worries were over, the Yankees had gone down the peninsula and that they ought to get Booth and Herold on their way.

"Didn't Sam, Jr. tell you? They're already gone," Jones explained, "I put them across last night." Cox burst into joyous laughter and clapped him on the back.

"Good job!" He exclaimed. "No wonder Sam was out all night."

"Reckon he slept at Adams' last night. It was a long one."

They did not even begin to realize how fortunate they were. That evening, the Yankees came back from their wild goose chase into St. Mary's County, more attentive than ever. Soldiers asked to see his boat, but Jones told them it had been stolen. Why, you could even see the keel marks in the sand bar, where the thieves had crossed into Pope's Creek. Henry Woodland, Jones' fisherman, knew the boat was gone, but he was not sure why. If he had his suspicions, he kept them to himself. Jones had gotten Booth and Herold out through the only available window in time.

17. Booth Detours to Indiantown

Davy Herold dug the canoe paddle deep into the river. If he and Booth were to reach Persimmon Point before daylight, he would have to do much good work against the flood tide that Thomas Jones had forgotten to warn them against. Suddenly the skiff began to heel over and change course. Davy switched sides of the boat with his paddle, trying to battle the change in course. It did not help.

"Johnny, I cannot hold her," he whispered as loudly as he dared. Like light, sound traveled far on a body of water at night.

"It is not your fault, Davy, I have steered a new course. We are going back to Maryland at Nanjemoy Creek. We will pass north of the lightship at Cedar Point in the shallows."

"Why? . . ." Herold cut off the conversation. He would have to hear about the reasons later. At the moment, he had his hands full.

Booth and Herold now were going upriver with what little tide there was. About midnight it would begin to recede, and they would have to fight the ebb tide until they reached their goal.

Soon, the two men could hear the pounding of the engines and churning of the paddlewheels on the USS *Heliotrope*, a river gunboat on patrol, headed on a parallel course in the same direction.

"Duck!" Booth rasped, "Do not look at them, or they will see our faces!"

He blew out the candle; they would not need a course to run parallel to the shoreline anyway. Then Booth pulled the blanket over himself. Herold stopped paddling and looked toward the Maryland shore, presenting his dark hat brim to the *Heliotrope's* watchmen. He was never much for praying, but he murmured a plea for Divine help now. The ship went by midstream in a flurry of foaming water, thrashing paddle wheels, steam engine hissing, sounding ever so much like some gigantic, monstrous snake. Its twin stacks belched smoke and sparks which, spraying high into the air, cascaded into the river like a million shooting stars, their dying embers quickly extinguished by the vast river.

The fugitives' little boat bobbed up and down like a cork. The prevailing breeze swept suffocating clouds of coal smoke over them. Both men choked on the dense vapors. Herold coughed violently, the paroxysms of his body shaking the little skiff. Then, Herold began to paddle again and Booth steered a course parallel to the Maryland shore. The broken shore line concealed their silhouette from the view of gun boats in midstream. The wind rose up from the South and helped counter, at least psychologically, the ebbing current. But it was many hours before they rounded Blossom Point and rowed into Nanjemoy Creek.

In the half-light of dawn, Herold now knew where he was, at the shore of Indiantown Farm, owned by his old hunting friend, Peregrine Davis. But Davis lived inland. The farm was taken care of by his son-in-law, Colonel John J. Hughes. Booth waited by the boat, nursing his injuries, while Herold, much exhausted by his night's work, slowly made his way up to the main house to awaken Hughes. A quiet but insistent rapping on the panels soon brought a half-dressed Hughes to the door.

"Colonel Hughes, my apologies, sir, for getting you up so early, but we are down by the creek and need assistance--a place to stay and something to eat and drink."

"Who is 'we', young man?" Hughes inquired with some reserve.

"I am David Herold--I was up last fall, to do a little wing shooting with Mr. Davis's permission?"

"Oh, yes, I do remember seeing you. Please, do not tell me. Your companions are Mr. Booth and Mr. Surratt, the assassins of the President. I have read the newspapers, you know. Somehow, I half expected--feared--that you might pass this way."

"Just Booth, sir. No one else is with us."

"Go back down to the creek and I will be along presently."

About forty-five minutes later, Hughes came along the creek, looking ever so much like a prosperous farmer out surveying the condition of his property before breakfast, shotgun under his arm.

"I have brought you some bread. I have little more available."

"Might we have some whiskey?" Booth asked.

"No, sir, I do not provide spirits. But if you will hand me up that flask, I will have it filled with milk and returned. You men are not to come up to the main house. You should pull your skiff upstream a bit and stay in the small boat house there. Do not go outside, lest Yankee patrol boats see you. Pull up some weeds to cover the outline of your boat. Why did you come *here*, anyway?"

"You were one of many on the mail line who agreed to help us in the kidnapping. We stashed a large craft and a smaller one near here."

"Yes, but that was some time ago, and certainly *did not* involve *killing* Mr. Lincoln. Besides you already have a boat. The Federals have been scouting the banks, looking for any boat. You would waste much time trying to find another craft as good as the one you have now. The closest boat I know of is in Goose Bay in the next inlet south of here. That is where Port Tobacco River enters the Potomac. It would cost you another night finding it--if it is still there--and a second night in crossing."

"Well then, in that case, we shall cross this night to Virginia and land at the Confederate signal camp, if you can set us a course."

"The course is straight south to Dr. Stuart's summer house at Cedar Grove. Then you go downstream a mile or so to Lieutenant Cawood's camp. Or you can go upstream three times that distance to the tower in the trees at Captain Conrad's former camp near Boyd's Hole. But Tom Conrad and Frank Dade have already been arrested earlier this week. Up at George Carpenter's around Maryland Point--that is the next point north on our side of the river. I do not know if Lieutenant Cawood is still there, nor could I direct you to his camp. I do not know its exact location. And Dr. Stuart is still at his winter house some miles to the south, inland. It is called Cleydael. No one has been over on the Virginia side, since before Lee's surrender."

"We cannot cross without Conrad. Only he knows the way amongst the torpedoes," Booth said.

"Maybe we can float over them--the rowboat don't draw much water," Herold suggested hopefully.

"It would make little difference," Hughes said, "they will get you anyway. Actually, this route was a route to move mail--Lincoln was to be a major exception, for obvious reasons. The camp further south under Sergeant Harry Brogden at Oak Grove was the route to move people. Came over and up the Wicomico to Allen's Fresh. There is probably no one down there now, either. But you men would be well advised to go downstream and strike for Machodoc Creek. So you need to go southeast across Mathias Point and avoid trying to land directly south of here. Find the Machodoc. The first house on the north bank of that stream is 'The Cottage.' It belongs to a Mrs. Quesenberry. She can get someone to move you further south."

"Yeah," Herold interjected, "we know of her."

"Then, I suggest that you two eat, rest and leave at dusk, when it is hardest to see a small boat. Go at an oblique angle toward Mathias Point on the Virginia side. I do not know where the torpedoes are. There were, at one time, torpedoes laid across the whole river, between here and that point. The deep channel is open now, pretty much. But the Federal navy is still shy of going into the shallows, so you ought to be, too. Go southeast across the point. It will give you *some* protection from interception. I will bring you more vittles some time later, after dinner."

Herold rowed the boat upstream to the boat house, camouflaged the craft, and helped Booth get inside. It was a dusty old one room frame building, really not suited for sheltering men, but better than the piney woods they had lived in for five days. At least it was dry and had a roof. Booth sat up against a wall and took out his little notebook. He began to write, mistakenly dating the entry a day earlier:

Friday 21--

After being hunted like a dog through swamps, woods, and last night being chased by gunboats 'til I was forced to return wet, cold, and starving, with every man's hand against me, I am here in despair.

And why? For doing what Brutus was honored, for what made Tell a hero. And yet, I, for striking down a greater tyrant than they ever knew, am looked upon as a common cutthroat. My action was purer than either of theirs. One hoped to be great himself. The other not only had his country's, but his own, wrongs to avenge. I hoped for no gain. I knew no private wrong. I struck for my country alone. A country that groaned beneath this tyranny and prayed for its end.

Yet, now, behold the cold hand they extend to me. God *cannot* pardon me if I have done wrong. Yet, I cannot see any wrong except in serving a degenerate people. The little, the very little, I left behind to clear my name, the Government will not allow to be printed. So ends all.

For my country, I have given up all that makes life sweet and Holy, brought misery on my family, and am sure there is no pardon in Heaven for me since man condemns me so. I have only *heard* what has been done [in the slaughter at Seward's] (except what I did myself) and it fills me with horror. God try and forgive me and bless my mother.

Tonight I will once more try the river with the intent to cross, though I have greater desire to return to Washington and in a measure clear my name, which I feel I can do. I do not repent the blow I struck. I may before God, but not to man.

I think I have done well, though I am abandoned, with the Curse of Cain upon me. When, if the world knew my heart, *that one* blow would have made me great, though I desire no greatness.

Tonight I try and escape these bloodhounds once more. Who can read his fate? God's will be done.

About mid-afternoon, Hughes returned with hot food and more milk. As they ate, Booth and Herold listened to their last instructions from him as to their journey.

"Now remember, go southeast from here. Depending on where you strike the Virginia side, the first stream this side of the point is Chotank Creek. Cross its mouth and keep going down river. Do not go up any of the little inlets. They are still full of torpedoes. The shallows have less tide action and the wind will be lessened if it is still coming from the South. But you will have to avoid the shallows until well after Chotank Creek. It will be a hard pull for you across the wind and tides. Watch for little eddies just below the surface. They can be treacherous and sling you right back where you came from. I see you are ill-equipped with oars-- there are some more in the back of the shed here. I suggest you, ah . . . *borrow* . . . them when I leave.

"You will have to go around Mathias Point into the wind. You will know you have done that when the light ship disappears. Now, the Machodoc is the only really large inlet you will come to--almost like a gulf--as big as this one here at Nanjemoy. If you have too little light to make it, drift up into Gambo creek about a mile short of the big inlet. It is the only obvious inlet you will pass going into the Machodoc. If you go into Gambo Creek, it is a real twisty stream, go in as deep as you can till you come to a bridge and tie up there. The Cottage is a mile south overland.

"Leave nothing behind, when you depart here," Hughes cautioned. "You will not see me again. Good bye and good luck."

Hughes scurried back to his home without a backward glance. But he was not totally oblivious to his plight. The very next Monday he went into Port Tobacco to consult his attorney, Mr. William Wilmer. Lawyer Wilmer wrote a letter to the Federal military authorities about an anonymous informant seeing two men in Nanjemoy Creek, one of whom looked like John Wilkes Booth. But it was April 27 before Lieutenant O'Beirne received this information, and by then Booth was dead and the episode at Indiantown forgotten. Hughes was safe.

18. The Confessions of Andrew Atzerodt

No one wanted to tell the authorities the truth more than George Andrew Atzerodt. In fact, he was the *only* one of the plotters, with the possible exception of Sam Arnold, who did. But his testimony was very disjointed and confusing. Unlike Herold, who told nothing but intentional gibberish; Dr. Mudd and Mike O'Laughlen, who told less than they knew and obfuscated their roles otherwise; and Mary Surratt and Lewis Powell, who admitted to nothing, Atzerodt was misunderstood through two unfortunate factors: he was German to a fault, hence neither spoke nor could be understood in anything but the simplest English, and he was so seedy as to make anybody look respectable by comparison. The smug Yankee interrogators never would believe what he said and valued his statements too little to call in a German-speaking officer, who might have cleared it all up. In short, Andrew Atzerodt epitomized all that was wrong with the South in Yankee eyes; seemingly both mentally stupid and socially backward. He was a perfect example of what slavery had done to ruin the white population in the southern half of the country.

Yet Atzerodt was not truly of the South in culture and what he revealed was important, if misunderstood. He exposed *two* Booth assassination plots against Lincoln (the first one, planned on April 13 in the Herndon House and the second, planned at the Canterbury Music Hall, that was actually put into action one night later), told about the failed Harney plot to blow up the White House, and he named names, many of which were ignored because they did not fit the investigators' already-conceived perceptions. He also told the reason why Booth left an innocent, but later-suspicious card, in Vice President Johnson's mailbox, and why Booth was so insistent to go to Indiantown, rather than crossing the Potomac immediately as Thomas Jones had directed.

Because Atzerodt's tale lacked a sense of time, it is very hard to piece together. But strongly suggested is the notion that there were two attempts to kill Lincoln, one on Thursday April 13, and the other, the one known to history, on April 14. Like everyone else, Atzerodt confused them in his vague statements to the authorities. Hence history has the conspirators meeting in the Herndon house after Powell had checked out and left; an unlikely scenario. Actually the Herndon House meeting was on Thursday and, with Lincoln and Grant not going to the theater that evening, the real final meeting came on Friday at the Canterbury Music Hall.

On Thursday night, Atzerodt said, Herold was assigned the task of killing Johnson, but proved to be no more courageous than Atzerodt a day later. In his statement, Atzerodt left out Surratt's presence, to show he was not the only coward. Instead, Herold went down country and set up the escape route, sleeping at the Huntt's and leaving John Surratt's borrowed nightshirt. Atzerodt went to Benning's bridge, to guide the assassins to Herold. Booth admitted to all that "the thing" had failed the night before, because the always unreliable Lincoln did not go to the theater. They would have to try again. At the Canterbury, Booth reshuffled the conspirators' assignments, because Surratt had followed General Grant out of town, giving the murder of the Vice President to Atzerodt and permitting Herold, under the cover of coordinating the program, to set up Atzerodt as the fall guy. After all, Herold knew the escape route to Maryland Point, too.

In addition to the two assassination attempts, there were the "projects," as Atzerodt called them, which the investigators had heard nothing about from the others. They dismissed them way too readily:

They were going to mine the end of the White House, next to the war Department. They knew an entrance to accomplish it through. Spoke about getting friends of the President to get up an entertainment and they would mix in it, have a serenade & etc., and thus get at the President and party.

That sounded a lot like Harney; and Booth's need for a cover like that which Lucy Hale could unwittingly provide, although Atzerodt never mentioned either by name.

In discussing the projects, the number of people that Atzerodt fingered to the Federals boggles the mind. It also makes the testimony of men like Weichmann and Lloyd, just to mention two who got off through their alleged cooperation, seem very inadequate. There were the usual suspects: Atzerodt himself, Booth, John Surratt, Wood (Powell), Arnold, and O'Laughlen. Then, there was the second level of conspirators, Weichmann, Harbin, Howell, and a nice, accurate description of Kate Brown or Thompson (Sarah Slater), with the caveat that young Weichmann knew more about her. But Atzerodt mentioned names that were never brought up in any other context. There was James Hall who ran mail for Lewis Powell while he was hiding out at the Herndon House. And James Donaldson, who sounds very much like one of the men Sergeant Dyer saw calling time at Ford's Theater just before Booth shot Lincoln.

I am certain Dr. Mudd knew all about it [in fairness to Mudd, Atzerodt meant the kidnapping], as Booth sent, as he told me, liquors and provisions for the trip with the President to Richmond, about two weeks before the murder, to Dr. Mudd's.

There was a boatman and blockade runner named Charles Yates, and two mysterious men, Bailey and Barnes, who may have been in on the kidnapping, at least. And, of course the ever-present John "Guerrilla" Boyle, the killer of Captain Watkins and terror of the Maryland countryside. Even Dr. Mudd feared him, according to his testimony. Atzerodt did not forget Smoot and Brawner, who set up the hidden boats. It was he who implicated the chambermaid at the Seward House, the one who gave Booth information of the layout there, and so intrigued the actor that he hoped to see her again under different circumstances. Atzerodt also told of how Herold talked about powders and medicines, his whiskey-dulled mind confusing the Herndon House meeting with that of the Canterbury Music Hall. There was more:

I have not seen Arnold for some time, but saw O'Laughlen on Thursday evening, on the Avenue at a saloon near the U.S. Hotel. He told me he was going to see Booth.

O'Laughlen produced half a dozen witnesses to give himself an alibi for that one, but the court saw through the holes in their corroborative stories.

Speaking of names, Booth's card with the note to Vice President Andrew Johnson, that proved such an embarrassment in 1867 as Congress moved to impeach, was actually quite innocent, according to Atzerodt. Indeed, the whole purpose of Atzerodt in staying at the Kirkwood House above Johnson's room was to get"'papers'" as he called them in one account, or "a pass" in the other.

It seems that Booth wanted to have an alternative to crossing the Navy Yard Bridge, in case Weichmann failed to get the password and countersign, or the soldiers refused to allow him to go by without more identification. Booth told Atzerodt that he wished to appear at the theater in Richmond and wanted the President to authorize his passage south. It was a common ploy used by hundreds during the war. Booth figured that Johnson would do the same for his old peacetime friend.

Booth knew Johnson from Nashville; they had visited "professional" women together in that city, and what was a pass to an old fellow whoremonger? Johnson was not in and Booth left his card, which found its way into the box of Johnson's secretary, instead. Booth never got back to the Vice President and Weichmann's password and countersign worked.

But the real reason Booth wanted Atzerodt as a part of the gang went well beyond the proposed assassination of then Vice President Johnson:

They wanted I should show them the road to Indiantown or Maryland Point. They were to go to Surrattsville around Piscataway and to strike to the Potomac. They were to go through Bumpy Oak. To go to Bumpy Oak, you leave the road leading from Washington to Bryantown at Tee Bee, which is about six miles from Surrattsville. You turn off to the right. It is about 25 or 30 miles from Tee Bee to Maryland Point. The road leading from Tee Bee is not much traveled. I do not know anyone at Maryland Point that would aid them to cross. Nanjemoy Creek runs down to Maryland Point.

Although Atzerodt did not mention it, Goose Bay is a part of the entrance to Port Tobacco Creek on the Maryland Point or upstream side of the inlet, and there was anchored Richard Smoot's boat in readiness for use, since January 1865. But Atzerodt was aware that it was a straight shot south across the Potomac to Lieutenant Cawood's camp and from there, south again, the shortest route into the Confederacy. Burdened by Booth's broken leg, Herold did not take the right fork but continued on toward Horse Head and Dr. Mudd's farm.

But was Atzerodt really necessary to guarantee Booth's escape? If Booth was to flee north through Baltimore, of course not. But even if Booth were to flee south, Herold knew enough to guide them by the correct roads--providing something unplanned and unexpected did not occur--like Booth breaking his leg. Hence Atzerodt could be thrown to the wolves--left behind to take the rap. All Booth had to do was to plant evidence in Atzerodt's room at the Kirkwood House, Room 126, the one directly above that occupied by the Vice President. It was done on Friday evening, when Davy Herold called to take Atzerodt to the planning meeting at the Canterbury Music Hall, although Atzerodt fluctuated between events that occurred on Thursday and Friday in his tale. If the conflicting parts were shuffled about, the real story emerged:

That was Thursday about three o'clock. Herold came there after me. He said that Booth and Wood wanted to see me. . . . Herold went off and said he would find him. We were to wait. I got tired of waiting and left afterwards into Seventh Street and stopped and drank at different restaurants. About half past five or near six o'clock, I went to the Kirkwood House and they told me a young man had called there for me. I took a chair and Herold came in and said Booth and Wood wanted to see me immediately. We went to their house on 9th Street and there they proposed the murder to me. Booth proposed that we should kill the President. Said it would be the greatest thing in the world. . . . Wood was to kill Seward; Booth, the President; and Herold, Vice President Johnson. . . . They said they did not want me to do any act, but only to show them the road into the lower part of Maryland, and if I did not, I would suffer for it.

The next day Herold showed up again to haul Atzerodt to the final meeting at the Canterbury Music Hall:

He then asked me if I had my key. He wanted to go to my room and show me something. We went to the room and he drawed a large knife and a pistol out of his boot and said, 'let's go and see Booth and Wood.' This was about half past six or seven o'clock on Friday, that Wood would go up to Seward's house and kill him. That he and Herold had been and seen Andrew Johnson and found out where he was. He then asked me if I was willing myself to assist them. I said that I did not come for that and was not willing to murder a person.

Atzerodt did not say it, but Herold also left behind Booth's long, black overcoat. In its pockets were a bankbook, showing a credit for $445 to John Wilkes Booth, and a map of the state of Virginia, several handkerchiefs, and three boxes of paper revolver cartridges. Atzerodt was set up to "suffer for it," as Booth had promised. All that remained was for a skeptical barkeep to tell a detective friend about "one suspicious character in Room 126."

But his questioners had already made up their minds--Atzerodt had nothing to say by definition and he was dismissed as too stupid to remember anything of value. Unfortunately, his two statements were taken down by two competing jurisdictions in two separate places. One side was represented by Colonel H. H. Wells out of General Augur's Washington headquarters for the prosecution on April 25 on board the U.S.S. *Montauk*, and the other by Major James McPhail from Baltimore under the influence of Detective John L. Smith, Atzerodt's brother-in-law on May 1 at the Washington Arsenal Prison on behalf of defense lawyer, Captain William E. Doster.

Because of the rules of the military trial, rigidly enforced by Special Judge Advocate John A. Bingham, Attorney Doster's part of Atzerodt's confession was never even admitted in his defense. Worse, this half of Atzerodt's testimony was inadvertently lost for over a hundred and twenty years, mixed in with his attorney's own family and legal papers, until revealed by an heir to the modern-day Surratt Society. Hence, unlike Weichmann and Lloyd, whose testimony was easily understandable, Atzerodt would not be set aside as an informer, but condemned as a co-conspirator and hanged for his own alleged stupidity.

PART V

INTO VIRGINIA (1865)

It is not the substance, but the manner in which kindness is
extended that makes one happy in the acceptance thereof.
--John Wilkes to Dr. Richard Stuart, April 24, 1865

We are the assassinators of the President.
--Davy Herold to Pvt. William Jett, April 24, 1865

I have too great a soul to die like a criminal.
--Undated entry from John Wilkes Booth's *Diary*, April 1865

1. Herold Finds Mrs. Quesenberry

"What time do you think it is, Davy?" Booth looked to the east, where he could see the first light of dawn creeping in.

"Not sure; but we need to find a spot to land, soon," Herold replied. "I am dead tired of rowing all night against the tide. The wind to our backs helped, but I am near all played out. We must have come ten or maybe even a dozen miles."

"I want to try for the Machodoc inlet," Booth argued. "The closer we get to this Cottage place the better it will be for my leg."

"I am more worried about my neck," Herold shot back. "That fire ball ahead ain't the sun. It is another Union gunboat coming in with the tide. We missed one early last night, but this one may be a problem. The wind is pushing us out into the channel. We ought to try for the first inlet we see. Gambo Creek is what Jones called it. Hughes said it was only a mile overland to Mrs. Quesenberry's. There! Just ahead, le's try for that creek and hope it is Gambo."

Booth turned the little craft in toward the shore and headed for the separation in the woods that marked the mouth of a creek. Behind them the Federal gunboat pounded up the main channel. But the dark, shadowy merging of woods and water made for perfect concealment of the fugitives. Herold rowed as far up the creek as he could. "There's the bridge! Up ahead just where Mr. Jones and Colonel Hughes said it would be!" shouted Herold with exultant joy. Booth steered into the creek bank and the boat grounded, finally stopping at a small clearing that had a lone persimmon tree (later chroniclers would describe it as a "monarchial walnut tree") to tie up to and some higher ground for Booth to lie on. Herold steadied the boat as Booth struggled to drag himself out. Having finally succeeded, he then stood up and hobbled on his crutches to a bed of blankets that Herold had constructed. Herold surrounded Booth with their firearms and other implements. Booth then lay down in their pseudo fort, sweating profusely, gasping heavily from exertion and utterly exhausted, while Herold went in search of Confederate partisans.

Herold had the overwhelming feeling that he and Booth were very much alone in these woods. He was making a careful examination of the trees for the growth of moss to find north, when he heard a familiar sound nearby. Ha! Someone was chopping wood. Herold decided to take a chance and followed it to a small cabin in front of which stood an ancient Negro, who appeared to be alone.

"Hey!" Herold shouted to be heard above the sound of wood being chopped.

The old man turned to face him, surprised, axe in hand. "Yessir, young gentleman, what can I do for you?"

"Are you the only one around in these parts?"

"Yes indeed, I am, sir."

"Well then, I am looking for The Cottage, the home of the Quesenberrys on Machodoc Creek. Can you direct me?"

"Oh, yessir, that I reckon I can. You be headed the exact wrong direction. You gots to go back and wade the creek and head straight south for about a mile or so. Her house be the one at the junction of two creeks-- the small one they calls Williams and the bigger one the Machodoc. It flows east to the Potomac, you know."

"The creek I waded is called Gambo?"

"Yessir, you be right! The Gambo it be!"

"What's your name Uncle? They call me Davy."

"I be called 'Old Sic,' Mr. Davy."

"Well thank you, Ol' Sic. I reckon I will be off."

"Yessir. I bet it doan take more'n thirty minutes to get there."

The sun shone an hour past noon when Herold stumbled out of the woods and saw a compact, neat house across the fields. As he ambled up to the structure, a young white girl, seated on the porch, surveyed him with suspicion.

"Who are you, sir? What do you want here?"

"I am an escaped Confederate soldier, out of Point Lookout Prison, up in Maryland," Davy lied. "My brother is off across the country near Gambo Creek, stove up with a broken leg. I am looking for Mrs. Quesenberry."

"She is not here. I am her step-daughter, Louisa. And by the way, she says it Quee'-sen-berry not Cue'-sen-berry like you have done. She is very fussy about it, too."

"I will remember that. Then, this is The Cottage?"

"Indeed, sir, it is. But I cannot help you. My step-mother will have to do it, but she is away."

"Could you send for her? It is a mite of an emergency."

Louisa looked doubtful, but arose from her chair and called out to Miss Julia Y. Duncanson, the 23 year old governess of Mrs. Quesenberry's younger children, who had been in the house. Miss Duncanson came out to the porch whereupon the two young women held a lengthy and very quietly whispered conversation.

When their discussion was finally concluded, Miss Duncanson summoned a lanky, black teenaged boy, who, after a few brief words of instruction, quickly set off down the nearby road at an effortless dog-trot.

Miss Duncanson then grabbed her shawl, stepped from the porch and set off in another direction.

Louisa resumed her seat and spoke to Davy.

"You may sit on the edge of the porch to await Mrs. Quesenberry. But I warn you, I have armed Negroes available should you try anything untoward."

Davy sat down, grinning. Louisa was neatly dressed in clothes that she would have given to the plantation slave children as castaways in better times. She and Herold were separated only by a few feet.

"I will not hurt you," Davy said. "Say, do you like boats? We have a rowboat in Gambo Creek. We crossed from Maryland last night, you know. Dangerous trip. We had to dodge two Yankee gunboats. It was ever so exciting. The man on the Maryland side said that we could give your momma the boat when we had done with it."

"Oh, I love to be rowed in the creeks." As Louisa implied, no Virginia belle worthy of the title would ever row herself--it just would not have been proper, without an escort and all. "But I am afraid of the big water," she said, referring to the Potomac.

"Well, we crossed with no trouble at all. Of course, we had to go against the wind and the waves. I rowed us myself," Herold boasted. Louisa was politely appreciative. The conversation lagged until Davy, exhausted by his efforts of the last twenty hours, dozed off leaning against a roof post. He awakened with a start, suddenly aware he was being shaken by the shoulder. It was the young black who had gone off to fetch Mrs. Quesenberry. She stood a proper distance away, scowling at the uninvited guest. Louisa was nowhere to be seen, evidently having been sent inside.

"Who are you, sir?" Mrs. Quesenberry wanted to know.

She stood there arms akimbo, one eyebrow arched in curiosity and reprobation. She was a grand lady, only two years a widow, now manager of a large estate. Jones had said she came from a prominent Washington City family. One sister had married a collateral descendant of George Washington, and another, a prominent Mexican aristocrat. She also ran a way station for Confederate agents passing between the capitals, North and South, another project inherited from her late husband, along with the plantation.

"Well, young man? Speak up! I am Mrs. Nicholas Quesenberry."

Herold quickly stood up, snatching off his hat and holding it across his chest, looking and feeling every bit the fieldhand.

"Mrs. Quesenberry," he stammered. "I am an escaped Confederate prisoner of war, out of the Union camp on Point Lookout, Maryland. I was looking for a conveyance, a carriage."

"What for, sir? You look perfectly capable of walking."

"My brother ran away with me and he broke his leg in the attempt. We have been running south to escape the Yankees. Last night we crossed the Potomac in a boat and wound up in Gambo Creek. The carriage is for him. Mayn't we borrow a carriage to go up country?"

"No, sir, I do not give, lend, or rent carriages. You need a livery stable. Although, I daresay, there are none around here. And no one has carriage or horse to hire. The armies have taken everything."

"Oh, then what am I to do?" Herold whimpered imploringly.

"I do not know, sir, but you cannot stay here. I have three sick children inside. You had better be off."

"But, please, ma'am, Mr. Jones said. . . ."

"Go, young man!" Mrs. Quesenberry followed the order by pointing her finger back the way he had come.

Herold, his head hung low, hat still in hand, turned away, bitterly disappointed, and utterly dejected. He felt as if he would weep. Jones and Hughes had recommended Mrs. Qusenberry, and she had proven to be a false lead. Now what would they do? Where could they go?

"Young man!" It was Mrs. Qusenberry. "Have you and your brother eaten?"

"Not since yesterday afternoon, ma'am," Davy replied, his expectations cautiously rising.

"Well, you go back to your brother and I will send food and drink out to you by one of my hands. Leave a trail so he can come along directly."

Surely he was dreaming. It was almost more than he could have imagined.

"Yes, ma'am!" Davy hollered back, as he joyously began to trot towards the woods and Booth's hideout on Gambo Creek. "And thank you, ma'am!" he called over his shoulder. "Thank you ever so much!"

As Davy Herold disappeared into the woods, Mrs. Quesenberry turned to a man who had just come out of the house onto the porch. He was holding a Colt's Navy pistol. "Well, what do you think, Mr. Harbin?"

"It has to be them, huh, Joe?"

Private Joseph Baden, Confederate Signal Corps, stepped out of the house.

"I reckon, Tom. No one else would cross the river at this time besides us or them."

"Make up a basket, Mrs. Quesenberry, and I will take it to them and send them on down the line. I have met Booth and will know him on sight." Thomas Harbin, Confederate agent, put the pistol back into its holster. He wore it butt forward on his right hip, army-style. "You stay here and watch for the Quesenberrys' safety, Joe, just in case."

2. Tom Harbin Helps Booth

"What did Mrs. Quesenberry say, again?" Booth must have asked that same question half a dozen times in the last thirty minutes.

Herold walled his eyes to no where in particular. "Doggone it Johnny, I tell you she is safe. She will not turn us in. Besides there is no place nearby to turn us in to."

"Come on, Davy, one more time," Booth insisted.

"She said she did not rent, lend or give away carriages and that soldiers had taken most of the conveyances and horses around here years ago. She will send one of her servants with food."

"That pretty much leaves us stuck here Davy. We can use the food but we cannot go ahead on foot--at least *I* cannot."

"With a little of the Lord's Providence, you will not have to." The voice was one Booth had heard before, but he rolled over with a revolver in hand, nonetheless. Herold reached for the carbine, leaned up against a moss-covered log at his feet.

"Relax, boys. This ol' Reb hain't turned in no Sothron patriots, yet, and don't aim to in the future, neither."

Booth squinted through the confusing shadows and light thrown by the trees and the sunlit open spaces between them. "By God, it is Tom Harbin," he said with a beaming grin.

"The very same. Hold your fire boys, while I advance into your camp there." He strode forward and took Booth's hand in his. "I bet you are happy to see a familiar face. I have been waiting for you ever since that night we missed you after the gunfight at Mechanicsville over in Maryland."

"That seems so long ago. We have been hiding out with Tom Jones for five days and spent another day up at Indiantown Farm. It took us two nights to cross the river. Federal gunboats all over the place."

"Yeah. I hear that they are so thick that they are colliding in mid-stream. My signalman and I left Newport and crossed over on the 16th. Say, who is this young feller?"

"Davy Herold, meet Tom Harbin, one of my first recruits in the kidnap plot. He runs the signal line in this neck of the woods."

"Hey, Herold." Harbin shook hands with Herold. "*Used* to run things. Everything is all muddled up since the break up of the Confederacy. While we are talking, I reckon you all can eat. Davy looks like a slobbering dog, waiting with anticipation. I bet you are every bit as hungry as he is."

Harbin put down the basket. It was a treasure; fried chicken and biscuits. "Damn," Davy said in admiration, his mouth so full he could hardly talk, much less be understood. "This sure beats ham and bread!"

"Listen, boys, I think I can put you in contact with some of the remaining secret agents left around here. All you need to do is sit tight a night or two. We got to clear Stringfellow out ahead of you."

"What?"

"They is another scout running just ahead of you. You did not know that? He has falsely been suspected of helping you. He came through yesterday. You need to wait a bit until he clears the system."

"No," Booth said, vigorously shaking his head back and forth. "I will wait no longer. We have delayed far too long already. I want to go on *now* to Dr. Richard Stuart's. I am most insistant on this point."

"What for? He will not help you much. The war is over for him. He has been arrested too many times already. And his family is coming back from the Surrender. He wants no more trouble. Now look, John, some of Mosby's men are in this neck of the woods. I was working with them up in Maryland that night we missed you last weekend. They can take you direct to a safe hideaway--or start you on your way to Mexico, if you want."

"Mudd told me Stuart was a good contact over here," Booth retorted, "and I need someone to look at my leg. I broke it the night I struck the blow against Lincoln. My horse fell on me. Slick road, don't you know?"

"But a trip west by Stuart's Cleydael will delay you some more. The road south is still open. But it will not remain so for long. The Yankees will come into the Northern Neck, real soon. They have not found out much in Maryland. Besides, the Yanks have arrested Mudd last week and got most of your compatriots in the City, too. You, Herold, and Surratt are all that is left free and clear. No one knows where Surratt is; up in Canada, I guess.

"Listen," Harbin continued, "how about going a little beyond The Cottage to Squire Benjamin Arnold's? He is the key Confederate operative around here. As a matter of fact, he was to have received y'all when Lincoln was kidnapped. His house was where Lincoln was to have been stored overnight after y'all brought him across the Potomac. You two need to get in with those who can help you, like Stringfellow is doing, with men like Arnold. Otherwise, you will be taken for sure."

"I will *never* be taken to be paraded through Washington like some hapless victim of Rome, to be hanged in some ignominious public spectacle, like John Brown, or in mean isolation, like John Yates Beall. I will kill myself first! No, I am going to Stuart's. He will stand by the Stars and Bars, one more time. Can you get us some horses? We have to have *one*, at least. I cannot make any time on these crutches."

"All right," Harbin said, resignedly. "I am against this, but I will get you on your way. . . . They is a white farmer, name of William Bryant, lives near here with a colored woman as his wife. I will show your friend the way. If he balks, offer him a few Yankee greenbacks--you have money don't you?" Booth nodded, yes. "That will put him in a cooperative frame of mind."

Following Harbin's instructions, Herold found Bryant's place just beyond Ol' Sic's on the north drainage of Gambo Creek. After stopping to say a brief "howdy" to Ol' Sic, Herold was back by dusk with farmer Bryant and two horses.

"It's like I told this young feller, your brother, back at my place." Bryant squinted trying to see a family resemblance between Booth and Herold, but found none. "I cain't see why y'all want to go eight or ten miles to Doc Stuart's, when there are several doctors closer. But if'n he was recommended to you and you want to part with ten Yankee dollars, I will do it."

Bryant shook his head over the strange ways of these alleged Marylanders. But, they were from north of the river, and there was no accounting for the ways of others, he told himself. Harbin and Herold helped Booth to mount and then Herold got up behind old Bryant. Harbin watched them leave and went back to Mrs. Quesenberry to report. He would have to try to find Mosby's men or hope that Booth would stumble across them, before he found the Yankees--or they found Booth. If the Federals took Booth, Harbin thought, there might be the need for another assassination. Mosby and his men could handle that. Not much left to do up in Maryland. The pursuit would be along soon, Hell bent for leather, that's for sure.

3. Dr. Stuart's Unexpected Dinner Guests

Guided by William Bryant, the fugitives arrived at Dr. Richard H. Stuart's winter home, Cleydael, at 8 p.m. The house was somewhat isolated, about half a mile off the public road. As Harbin had predicted,

Cleydael was full of relatives and guests, many of them soldiers just home from the war. Everyone had eaten supper and they were gathered about the fireplace talking and joking. The conversation had lagged a bit when a black servant came in and said that there were three men at the door asking for Dr. Stuart.

Upon reaching the front door, Stuart looked past David Herold, who stood on the stoop, to see William Bryant and another man he did not recognize.

"Who are you, what do you want?"

Herold did the talking. "We are Marylanders, recently escaped from Point Lookout prisoner of war camp. My brother has broken his leg. We had it worked on by Dr. Samuel Mudd up in Maryland and he told us you would give us medical help. We also need a place to stay the night."

"I know no Dr. Mudd up in Maryland or anywhere else, sir," Dr. Stuart interjected. "I am a physician, not a surgeon. I cannot help you. My home is already full up. I have no room for strangers."

"Maybe if you knew who we really are. . . ."

Dr. Stuart cut Herold off, mid-sentence. "I do not wish to know *anything* about you, sir." Dr. Stuart had heard about the Lincoln assassination some days earlier, and had a pretty good idea who these men were. But he hoped they would not openly state it for the record.

"But, Dr. Stuart, we. . . ."

"Young man, I have already told you that there is nothing I can do for you."

Herold was nothing if not persistent. "We want to go to Mosby, sir."

"Mosby has already surrendered. You men will be better advised to get your paroles." Dr. Stuart paused and looked them over once more. "I tell you what I *will* do for you. If you are hungry, you may come into the kitchen and have a bite to eat."

"Thank you, sir. We will do that, for sure." Stuart carefully closed the front door and led the bedraggled party around to the kitchen at the back of the house.

Booth dismounted with help, and he and Herold entered the kitchen and sat at a table generally used by the slaves, soon to be called hired help. Booth was visibly angry. He felt that he was being openly, if subtly, insulted. Led to the servant's entrance like a common tradesman, set at a table reserved for n-----rs. Served cold food with very little courtesy. And this man was a known Confederate contact, twice-arrested by the Yankees, and a cousin of General Robert E. Lee, the very soul of the Confederacy!

"Fine treatment for the man who has killed the greatest tyrant in history," he muttered aloud.

Major Robert Hunter was one of the visitors at Cleydael. He was there courting Dr. Stuart's daughter Mary, and had come to the front door to back up the older Dr. Stuart when the conversation with Herold had gotten serious. He now came into the kitchen through the house and heard Booth's remark.

"Great Scott, you *are* John Wilkes Booth!" He shouted in amazement, "Everyone! Here is the man who killed ugly old Abe Lincoln!"

The crowd left the fire in the front room and crowded noisily into the smaller kitchen, all atwitter about their famous, or infamous, guest.

"Yes, indeed, I am he," Booth said grandly, doffing his hat with a flourish from his seat at the humble, rudely constructed kitchen table. "Forgive my not rising ladies, for I have been slightly indisposed. I fear my back is much injured and my leg is horribly broken." Booth's gallant style was duly noted by the appreciative gathering.

"I had the honor to serve with you in 1859, during the John Brown hanging at Charlestown," Hunter said. "You entertained us all with your renditions from the words of the noble Bard. This, sir, is indeed a great pleasure." Hunter and the other men and boys crowded around Booth to shake his hand. The ladies ooed and aahed with admiring stares.

"Tell us of your deeds and travels, Mr. Booth!"

"How came you here to Cleydael?"

"How did you hurt your leg, sir?"

"Please, ladies and gentlemen," Major Hunter interjected, "give Mr. Booth time to eat. I am sure he will regale us with tales of his derring-do in good time."

Good time! Dr. Stuart snorted to himself from his place at the back of the crowd. They were *wasting* good time! Fifteen minutes already. Stuart had no intention of taking the fall for or with the assassin of Abraham Lincoln. He quietly left the kitchen and went back outside. Damn! Where was Bryant? Stuart rushed around the house to see Bryant and his horses disappearing around the road bend and into the woods.

"Bryant!" he shouted. No response. Stuart ran as hard as he could to catch the retreating old man. Good way to bring on a heart attack, he thought, as he pounded down the road, gasping for air. "Bryant!" he shouted again. This time he got results. Bryant pulled up and turned in his saddle. Seeing Stuart, he turned the horses and met the winded doctor half way.

"Where are you going?" Stuart demanded. He was bent over, hands on knees, trying to regain his breath.

"Home, sir, my job is done here."

"No, it is not, sir! I need you to help me with a little favor. I have to get these men out of here, as quickly as possible. Will you take them over to William Lucas's place?"

"The free n-----r?" Bryant asked.

"Yes, the free man of color," Stuart retorted. Like most men of his class, Stuart looked upon the word "n-----r" as being in poor taste, especially when used to describe a neighbor.

"Sure, glad to oblige," Bryant said, oblivious to the criticism. He noted that there was no money offered, but perhaps at a later date he might have a problem that Stuart could help him with. Never hurt to have a good word from a man of his stature.

Stuart and Bryant went back to the house together, where Stuart bade him to wait. Entering the kitchen, Stuart announced loudly above the din of the crowd, "Excuse me ladies and gentlemen!" Then to Booth and Herold he said, "The old man is waiting for you. He is anxious to be off. It is cold and he is not well. He wants to get home."

Booth and Herold could see that Stuart was not to be put off. Gallantly expressing their good byes, both sides parted, the crowd waving from the kitchen entrance. No one went out, nor did Booth expect anyone to. Anyone of culture was well-aware the Southern night air was not good for ladies without wraps.

"Do you know the way to Lucas's cabin?" Herold asked Bryant. "Someone said we might find a place to stay the night there."

"Yeah," Bryant, said, "it is just across the field. But we will have to go around. Get up, boys and I'll take you there--no charge," he chuckled. They gave Booth a leg up and the little cavalcade rode the quarter mile to their promised haven for the night.

4. William Lucas' Two Unwanted Overnight Visitors

"Loo-cas! Wee-yum Loo-cas! Come out here!"

Even before William Bryant had yelled out, Lucas' hounds bayed and pow-wowed, "yow, yow, yow!" The racket was deafening, but Lucas managed to hear everything shouted to him over the din.

"No sir! I ain't acomin' out. No way! Who is you, anyway?"

Lucas had heard of nightriders. He was a free man of color from before the war. He knew better than to step outside in front of a group of whites, especially unknown whites and, more particularly, after dusk.

"Don't you know Ol' Wee-yum Bry-ant, Lucas? I am Ol' Bryant from down the road, eastwards, towards the river."

The door opened a crack and a head looked out furtively. "Yessir! It is Ol' Bryant," Lucas affirmed aloud. "I come on out, gentlemen."

Lucas approached the two strange riders and Bryant, whom he recognized, standing on foot before the horses. The two men got down from their saddles. The younger was quite spry, and went over to the other, who was very slow and deliberate in his movements. Lucas soon saw why--he limped over on crutches.

"We want to stay here tonight." As the young man spoke, the lame man hobbled on by toward the cabin.

"You cain't do it. I am a colored man and have no right to take care of white people," Lucas wailed. "I have only one room in the house and my wife is sick." He did not like these men with Bryant. They had a terrifying manner about them. Like men who would not stand to reason. Men who would not take "no" for an answer.

"We are Confederate soldiers," the lame man said. Lucas could see, even in the darkness of night, that he was a very handsome man with keenly chiseled features. But pale of color, very wan, almost ghost-like, and in need of a shave. And his exquisite facial features were marred, twisted ever so slightly with wrinkles. Like one who had suffered much lately.

"We have been in service three years. We have been knocking about all night, and do not intend to do so any longer. We are going to stay."

All the while he was talking, the lame man continued to limp over to the door. As he finished his discourse, he poked open the door with one crutch and was inside with a bold sweep of both legs. Everyone else followed the lame man in. All except for Bryant. He had his ten dollars, Yankee greenbacks, and was going home, riding one horse and leading the other. He had done as Stuart had asked. He was tired and wanted to crawl into bed as soon as possible. He rode off silently, saying nary a word.

"Gentlemen," Lucas protested, "you have treated me very badly."

The lame man collapsed into a chair at the table--one could hardly say he sat down, for that was much too defined a movement. He crumpled into the chair wearily and, as one would into a place of refuge, with marked relief. He paused, girding up all of his remaining strength, pulled out a Bowie knife and whipped it around, as a man would test a sword. Lucas had seen a man do the same before the war down in Port Conway. It was said that he was a duelist. The lame man seemed ever more skilled than the so-called duelist. Every movement was calculated; but so smooth as to be swift and graceful. Menacing, deadly, but symmetrical. Somehow so very beautiful; and yet, so very evil in its intent.

"Old man, how do you like that?" he growled.

"I do not like that at all," Lucas responded uncomfortably. "I was always afraid of a knife."

Booth, for the lame man was he and the spry young man Herold, grinned an evil grin. One that he had practiced to perfection for his role of Richard III. The same one that caused virile men to cringe, and some women actually to faint, and had garnered him renown from the Atlantic to the Mississippi, from the Gulf to Canada. "We were sent here, old man. We understand that you have good teams."

"You cain't have my team. I have hired hands to come Monday morning and plant corn."

"Well, Dave, we will not go any further, but stay here and make this old man get us his horses in the morning."

Lucas motioned to his wife to get up and go outside on the porch with him. He took some blankets and they spent the night there, wrapped up like a pair of mummies, shivering from the cold, their fear, and his wife from her fever. Neither one got much sleep--it was far too cold, and they were afraid that they might never awaken should they nod off.

"Aren't you going to sleep, Johnny?" Herold asked after Lucas and his wife left the cabin.

"In due time, Davy, in due time. But first I will write a letter to that popinjay, Dr. Stuart, and set him straight."

"Huh? Everyone there liked you, I thought."

"The family and guests lionized me, but Stuart was every part the inhospitable ass. He could hardly wait to be rid of us. And he dared to interrupt my performance as Brutus, the noble assassin who saved his country. And in front of an appreciative audience, no less."

Herold shook his head in disbelief, but held his tongue. Booth had rarely been in a fouler mood during their trying journey than now. He scribbled a while in his diary and then tore out a page.

"What do you think, Dave?" He read his letter to Stuart, with a few dramatic flourishes, for effect:

Dear Sir:

Forgive me, but I have some little pride. I cannot blame you for want of hospitality. You know your own affairs. I was sick, tired, with a broken limb, and in need of medical service. I would not have turned a dog from my door in such a plight. However, you were kind enough to give us something to eat, for which I not only thank you, but, on account of the rebuke and manner in which it was given, to feel obliged to pay. It is not the substance, but the way in which kindness is extended that makes one happy in the acceptance thereof. The sauce to meat is ceremony. Meeting were bare without it. Be kind enough to accept the enclosed five dollars (though hard to spare) for what we have rec'd.

Most respectfully, your obedient servant, etc., etc. . . .

"Boy, you sure can write good," Herold cooed admiringly. "What's that sauce bit?"

"A little Shakespeare--*Macbeth*, Act 3, Scene 4," Booth returned absentmindedly, engrossed in rereading the letter to himself.

"No, no. It is all wrong," Booth grumbled, editing his own work, mentally." I must do it again, more carefully. Besides, the sum given is too high. Not insulting enough." A new page produced this result:

Dear Sir: Forgive me, but I have some little pride. I hate to blame you for want of hospitality: you know your own affairs. I was sick and tired, with a broken leg, in need of medical advice. I would not have turned a dog from my door in such a condition. However, you were kind enough to give me something to eat, for which I not only thank you, but, on account of the reluctant manner in which it was bestowed, I feel bound to pay for it. It is not the substance, but the manner in which kindness is extended that makes one happy in the acceptance thereof. The sauce to meat is ceremony; meeting were bare without it. Be kind enough to accept the enclosed two dollars and a half (though hard to spare) for what we have received.

Yours respectfully,
Stranger
April 24, 1865.

"*Much* better," Booth said triumphantly. He put the rejected original in his coat pocket. "Got fifty cents?" he asked Herold, who contributed a shinplaster from his pocket. Booth then folded the money carefully into the letter, which became a sort of envelope, too. He scribed, "Dr. Richard Stuart," on it.

"I will give it to Lucas, tomorrow before we leave. He can transfer it to his Lord Highness, the Bastard of Cleydael."

The next day, as he promised, Lucas did take the letter to Dr. Stuart, who read it and saw it for the insult it was intended to be. At first, he was furious. Then Stuart caught himself. He carefully preserved the letter and the money. When the Federal detectives came after him, as he knew they would, he showed it to demonstrate his good citizenship. Although Stuart was arrested, for the third time during the war, he did not stay locked up for long. Booth's written "insult" kept him out of a lot of trouble, in the long run.

5.   Charlie Lucas Takes Booth and Herold to Port Conway

The next morning, Monday the 24th, Herold went down to the lean-to that doubled as a barn and rounded up Lucas' horses. He found harnesses hanging on a wall next to a ramshackle wagon. He began to hitch everything up. Booth stood by, leaning on his crutches, hands on the butts of his holstered revolvers. It was obvious that they were going to use Lucas' team and wagon, with or without his permission. Lucas decided to take a chance, and confronted the two white men. He did it with hat in hand, looking at the ground, speaking politely and hesitantly, as befitted a clever black man when dealing with white strangers. One false move now and he might receive a round from one of those big horse pistols carried by the lame one.

"Is you gentlemen going to take my horses without pay?" Booth and Herold ignored him. Lucas tried a different tack. "I thought you be done pressing teams in the Northern Neck since the fall of Richmond."

Booth snapped his head toward Lucas. "Repeat that again," he snarled, loosening a revolver in its holster with his right hand. Lucas backed off, hands silently supplicating in front of him.

Herold finished hitching the horses and looked over at the agonizing Lucas. "What do you get for driving to Port Conway? You know, on the Rappahannock?"

Lucas answered promptly and overly politely. "Well, sir, I generally gets ten dollars in gold or twenty dollars in Yankee paper."

"We might want to go farther. You can drive."

"No, sir, I gots to work all day here. My son, he twenty-one, will drive you to Port Conway. Then he can bring the horses and wagon back. His name be Charlie."

The name struck a tender spot in Herold's heart. Charlie. Just like the old red-gray roan they had left back at Adams' in Newport. It all seemed like a lifetime ago. Herold had liked Charley. He looked over at Lucas' son, a strong, nice-looking, mannerly young man. About the same age as Herold, himself. Charlie smiled and raised his head slightly in recognition.

"What do you say, John?" Booth nodded wearily in agreement. "Get up, Charlie." The youth climbed into the right side seat and Herold handed him the reins. Then Herold helped Booth sit in the back and slide into the bed made of their worn blankets.

"Ah . . . most folks pays in *advance*, gentlemen," Lucas hinted quietly.

Booth sighed and nodded to Herold, again. Herold took the Spencer carbine and walked over to Lucas. Placing the carbine under his left arm, like a hunter would when crossing a field not looking for game, he handed Lucas Booth's letter from the night before.

"Give this to Dr. Stuart. Don't forget now, y'hear?"

"Yessir."

Then Herold dug a twenty dollar greenback out of his pocket and handed it to Lucas.

"Oh, no, sir," Lucas remonstrated, shaking his hand back and forth. "The missus, she take the cash in this family."

Herold chuckled and handed the money to Mrs. Lucas, standing nearby. "Here you go, Auntie," he said politely, but condescendingly, as befitted the spirit of the times. Then he got up on the left side of the seat next to Charlie." Le's go, boy."

It was a two or three hour trip over rough roads to Port Conway, which the party reached around eleven o'clock. Once a prosperous adjunct to Port Royal, the bigger town across the river, Port Conway had fallen into decline during the war, like so much of the South. The buildings lacked paint and were in various stages of disrepair. In fact, it was practically a ghost town; streets still, like a cemetery, each building more like a gravestone than a human habitation. Nearby, on north side of town, was the birthplace of former President James Madison, architect of the U.S. Constitution, chronicler of the debates of its birth, and creator of America's first political party designed to follow its tenets, word by precious word. Unfortunately, Booth had neither time nor inclination for sightseeing nor honoring this original soul-mate in the American theory of limited government.

Charlie Lucas took his passengers right down onto the wharf. Herold got down and helped Booth get out of the wagon bed. The two men sat on its tailgate, where they could see the road through town.

"I am a mite thirsty, Dave," Booth said. "Would you please go up to the first house there and get me something to drink?"

As Herold reached the gate of the picket fence surrounding the yard of the house, a man came out of the door, carrying a fishing net. He was William Rollins, a local store keeper, fisherman and the expediter of secret Confederate mails. He and Herold stared at each other briefly. Rollins also glanced at Booth sitting in the wagon at the wharf.

"Mayn't I have a drink, sir?" Herold queried. Rollins went to the bucket hanging from a porch rafter and filled the dipper. He handed it to Herold. "It's for my brother in the wagon, yonder," Herold said as he left the yard. Booth drained the dipper and Herold brought it back and returned it to Rollins. He replaced it in the bucket and began walking to the wharf. Herold followed, hoping for information.

"Ain't there a ferry at this place?"

"Yep, and I own it. It is over yonder," Rollins said, nodding toward Port Royal across the river. "Be some time before it comes back."

"Would you be aware of where we could get a conveyance around here to Orange Courthouse?"

"Nope, "Rollins answered cryptically.

"Would you perhaps carry us there, yourself?"

"Nope."

"How about only part way to Orange?"

"Well, maybe to Bowling Green. For a consideration."

"My brother has broken his leg. He is the feller yonder, lying in the wagon below us. How much to go to Bowling Green?"

"Um-m-m, ten bucks."

By now the pair had reached Booth in the wagon. He chimed in dryly, probably remembering a similar unproductive conversation with Oswell Swann back up in Maryland a week past: "*How far* is this Bowling Green?"

"'Bout fifteen miles below Port Royal."

Rollins pointed across the river to the town lazily lying along the opposite bank. It had been the headquarters for part of General Stonewall Jackson's Corps before the battle of Fredericksburg in December 1862, and General U. S. Grant's main supply base in May of 1864, as the Union army maneuvered south from Spotsylvania to the North Anna River. But it had seen little of the war since, except for occasional Union naval raiding parties that came up from the Chesapeake, hoping to interrupt the active Confederate mail line that ran through the place.

"Hell," Herold said, "le's give it to him." He reached into his pocket for his rapidly diminishing roll of Secretary Chase's greenbacks.

"Now, mind you, boys, I mean ten dollars in *gold*. No paper, Yankee or Confed," Rollins cautioned.

"That is too much," the man in the wagon said.

"Mist' Bill!" A voice rang out from the riverside of the wharf. It was Rollins' black fishing companion, Dick Wilson, urging him to hurry up.

"All right," Rollins said dejectedly, "I will take greenbacks--but not graybacks. Yankee money only. Now I must go fishing. The shad are running. Yonder, my colored friend awaits me. You all may as well relax for a while. The ferry is over t'other side and will not come over until the tide has run in."

Herold walked toward Rollins' companion and saw he was in a fairly commodious row boat. "Perhaps you could row us over before you go fishing?"

"Nope," Rollins said firmly. "We are going fishing with the tide. And that is now. I will send the ferry over when we come back in." Rollins walked over to the small boat, threw his net in, and went down a short Jacob's ladder to get in. "Ferry cain't run on low water, no how." Rollins and Wilson shoved off with no other comment.

Herold walked dejectedly back to the wagon and sat down next to Booth. "Shit!" They said simultaneously. Suddenly Herold sat upright, worked the lever to chamber a cartridge, and cocked his Spencer.

"What is it?" Booth asked.

"Soldiers," Herold pointed back through town. There were three horsemen riding down a hill to the west. Armed to the teeth.

6. Baker is Put on Booth's Trail

"Lafe," Byron Baker asked, "how in Hell could Booth possibly escape this pursuit? Here we are ten days after Lincoln's murder. There are at least half a dozen major groups out looking for him and Herold, not to mention hundreds of freelancers. In addition, we must have at least fifteen hundred uniformed soldiers combing the swamps in southeast Maryland."

"It is easy, Byron," said Lafayette Baker. "Everything is so disorganized in the field that the pursuers are chasing each other. If you add to that the fact that Rebel sympathizers are intentionally setting up false trails, you have a total muddle. Crap! It is a wonder that our men are not shooting themselves in the dark. That's why we are sitting here awaiting developments."

"You think that Booth has already crossed into Virginia?"

"Yeah, maybe. We already have a report from Stanton's personal informant at Bryantown, Colonel Billy Wood--you know, the Superintendent of the Old Capitol Prison, who stopped our men from exacting deserved extra-legal punishment against prominent Maryland Rebels by seizing their property a couple years ago. That bastard actually had the temerity to jail some of *our* boys!

"Well, he was called in to find Booth about the same time we were. I talked to him the same time I tried to hornswoggle the provost marshals and the city police into 'working' with us. He said he would cooperate by filing his reports with Judge L. C. Turner, and I could pick them up there."

"Is he operating independently from the others in the field?" Byron Baker asked.

"Yeah. He has his own squad of hand-picked men--Wallace Kirby, a friend of the Surratts and Jenkinses (Mrs. Surratt's maiden name, you know); Aquilla Allen, a noted slave catcher from before the war who knows Southern Maryland like the back of his hand, and Bernard Adamson, I do not know him."

"Oh," Byron said. "He is some kid who wants to be a policeman and is tough enough to endure weeks in the field. He is a frequenter of local bars and provost marshal and police stations. A hanger-on."

"Anyhow," the elder Baker went on, "Wood is in the field near Bryantown. He took Olivia Jenkins back to her daddy after she had been in the Old Capitol a while. Got him in with Zad Jenkins and the local Rebs. Wood says that he is certain Booth and Herold crossed the Potomac from Port Tobacco to Mathias Point on the 23rd. We need some confirmation from another reliable source.

"But," Lafayette Baker continued, "I *do* know that there is no place of safety for Booth and Herold on earth, except among their friends in the South. The rebellion is not crushed, despite Lee's surrender. Booth knows it, too. He will try and reach his friends south of the river. His very life depends upon it."

Shortly after 11 a.m. that same morning, Lafayette C. Baker went over to the War Department telegraph office. He had taken to haunting the office, much like Lincoln had during the war, hoping to seize upon the one iota of information that might offer a hint to the whereabouts of Booth and Herold. The telegraph key began to click. Major Thomas T. Eckert, the powerful man whom Secretary of War Stanton had refused to allow to accompany Lincoln (despite the President's request) to Ford's Theater as a bodyguard on that fateful Good Friday, was leaning over the operator at the instrument, listening to a communication from near Chapel Point, Maryland.

"It is from Beckwith, I recognize his hand," Eckert said, as he intently lent an ear to the chatter of the key. "It is in code."

A clerk copied the message for the files, decoding the original Morse Code gibberish into understandable English.

"Great Scott!" Eckert exclaimed, "look at this!" He handed the translated message to Baker. "Major O'Beirne has been across the river on the trail of two men who passed over the Potomac nearly a week ago. He has gone all the way to King George Court House! He wants permission to take a fresh force back and pick up the trail there. Hot damn!"

Baker stood riveted in place. He had a look of incredulity on his face. This had to be it! That son of a bitch, Dr. Coombs, *did* have the information he had wanted all along! Evidently, Booth and Herold had moved over the Potomac before O'Beirne could act on Coombs' story. That was close--too damn close! It had to be Booth and Herold, he thought. This confirmed Wood's report, too. And no one was more credible than Major O'Beirne. Baker knew that he must now act to stop O'Beirne, who was not a Stanton ally like Wood, from getting back into the chase and running down the game. No one was going to collect that reward except Lafayette C. Baker!

"Let me take this in to the War Secretery, before you answer Beckwith," Baker said to Eckert. The clerk made a copy of the decoded message, with Eckert's permission. Baker fairly snatched it from his hand and took the stairs two at a time up to Stanton's second floor office.

"You think it is them?" Stanton grumped. "Harrumph! What do you want me to do?"

"Call O'Beirne off the search. Refuse him permission to recross the Potomac. Then issue an order for, say, a force of twenty-five experienced cavalrymen and an officer of ability and discretion to report to me as soon as possible at my office, No. 217 Pennsylvania, opposite Willard's. I will assign a couple of my detectives to go and arrest Booth and Herold, escorted by this force."

"Consider it done. You may contact Major General Winfield Scott Hancock, using my name as your authority. He will have the cavalry at your office early this afternoon." He smiled smugly as Baker rapidly left his office. Ah, yes, Stanton thought to himself. Greed was indeed a great motivator. Especially where Lafayette C. Baker was concerned

7. The Three Rebels

"They're Rebs!" Herold said jubilantly. He deactivated the carbine. Booth holstered his revolvers, first carefully releasing their cocked hammers. The three Rebel soldiers rode right past Booth and Herold on to the dock. One of them touched his cap brim--how do--as they passed. Another of the three dismounted and put his hands to his mouth.

"Jim Thornton!" Private Willie Jett shouted. "You lazy, black miscreant! Bring that damn ferry boat over here! Thorn-ton! I'll shoot your gizzard out if'n you don't get a move on mighty quick! You know I'll do it, too, boy!"

A voice came back from over the water. It was hard to make out completely what Thornton said, but a hyena-like laugh and the words, "water too low," could be heard plainly. He also waved.

"Humph! He ain't coming over 'til he's durn ready," Willie Jett said.

"Nah, the tide has to turn, Willie," Lieutenant Mortimer Bainbridge Ruggles said. He pronounced Jett's name "Why-lee," in the Southern fashion. Ruggles' father was a general in the Confederate army, hence the commission. He had served earlier with Thomas Conrad's spy group.

"Le's go up to the house and wait, Tibby," Private Absalom Ruggles Bainbridge suggested. He was Ruggles' cousin, hence the informal use of the nickname. After a childhood of growing up together, he was not about to call his own cousin "Lieutenant." Friends called Bainbridge, "Fellow," which sounded more like Fella or Feller, in the typical, soft Virginia drawl.

David Herold sauntered up to the men on the dock, before they could move.

"Gentlemen, which command do you belong to?"

Lieutenant Ruggles paused and answered reluctantly, "Mosby's command."

"If I am not too inquisitive, mayn't I ask where you are going?"

One of the two privates spoke, "Now, that is a secret--where we are going."

Booth got out of the wagon and hobbled over.

The other Confederate private asked, "What command do *you* belong to?"

"A.P. Hill's Corps," Herold still spoke, using a cover story cooked up by Harbin in the woods the day before. "My brother here was wounded before Petersburg. We are Marylanders. I am David Boyd. My brother is John William Boyd."

"Where is he hurt?" Jett inquired.

"In the leg," Herold replied. "Come, gentlemen, I suppose you all are going to the Southern army."

The three Rebel soldiers stared at him in silence, showing no emotion.

"We are also anxious to get there ourselves," Herold said, a little frustrated at the one-sidedness of their conversation, "and wish you to take us along with you."

Again, there was no reply. The three seemed to be waiting for Herold to say something more specific.

Herold tried a new approach. "Come, gentleman, we have something to drink. Get down and le's take a snort or two."

"Thank you, sir. I do not drink anything," Jett stated emphatically. The others agreed.

"C'mon, Fellow." The two mounted men, Ruggles and Bainbridge, turned and rode up to the Rollins house and tied up to the picket fence. One sat on the porch steps, the other sat on the rungs of a ladder leaned up against the house.

"Can we talk privately?" Herold asked Jett, who had seemed the most loquacious. "I take it for granted you are raising a command to go South to Mexico and I want you to let us go with you."

Jett looked at Herold carefully. "Who are you? I cannot go with any man I do not know anything about."

"We are the assassinators of the President." Herold gulped heavily after uttering the fateful words. "Yonder is the assassinator, none other than J. Wilkes Booth, the man who killed Lincoln!"

Jett looked at the two for a moment. Then he grinned widely. "Might I have your holograph?" he asked Booth.

"It is alright, John," Herold said, "I have told him everything."

"It *is* them!" Jett yelled up to Ruggles and Bainbridge. The two men came down to the wharf on foot. Willie introduced himself as *Captain* Jett, Fellow as *Lieutenant* Bainbridge, and Tibby as *Major* Ruggles. Nice promotions all around, designed to impress Booth and Herold. It worked on the latter, but Booth could have cared less. After all, he was *Assassin* Booth. He showed his faded India ink tattoo as a form of identification.

"Booth! How did you get here?"

"How did you remain hidden for so long?"

"We have been looking all over creation for you!"

"Where is the powderman, this Harney feller?"

"You do not need to negotiate with Rollins anymore; we will take care of things from here."

"You can cross the river and ride a ways with us."

"We are going to Richmond to get our paroles, after you are safely gotten away."

"Tell us how you snuffed out Ol' Abe's lights."

Ruggles said, "*Captain* Jett, take Herold and see if you can manufacture a couple of paroles for these men." So while Booth entertained Ruggles and Bainbridge, Jett took Herold into Rollins' house. He asked Bettie Rollins for a bottle of ink and a pen.

"Rollins is a Confederate signalman," Jett explained. "He lives here with his new wife and an old man who helps around the place. The rest of the town is pretty much abandoned. Everyone has fled the war. We learned of you coming this way through my brother-in-law, William Wallace, here in King George County. He lives at Friedland Plantation. He got his orders from Thomas Hoomes Williamson, who is staying with the Taylors at Mount View Plantation and General Lee himself, and the higher command in Richmond. A spy named Harbin told them you were on the way. A Taylor is Lee's adjutant, you know. They all knew you were coming. I do not know how. We are supposed to help you."

As Jett and Herold sought to impress each other with their own pretensions, Jett tried to forge a Union parole. His claim to fame was that he had seen one, once. But he could not get it right. Herold tried a couple of times, under instruction, but he, too, botched the job. Scholars and forgers they were not. Jett looked out and saw Rollins unloading the shad catch. Jett knocked on the open parlor door to get his attention. Rollins looked up and Jett beckoned him to come ahead on. Rollins held up his index finger to indicate he would be along shortly, and finished counting his catch.

Herold and Jett gave up on their inept forgeries and consigned them to the fire. They went out to the street. Thornton's ferry was almost across to the Port Conway side. Booth was standing on his crutches and had dismissed Lucas, who had backed his rig up and turned for home. The fisherman brought his catch up to the back of the house and came around to shut the front door that Jett and Herold had left open. It was still too cold for open doors.

"Wait a minute!" It was Herold. "I have to get my gear."

"I did not know you had any," Rollins said in amazement. Herold came back outside with a Spencer carbine--Rollins recognized it from his seeing the numerous Union Navy expeditions to Port Conway, as sailors and marines always carried the rifle version--a blanket and a box of cartridges.

"I have met with some friends out there," he said to Rollins. "They told me it was not worth while for me to hire your wagon, but we will ride and tie." The latter phrase was reference to the old trick of two men alternatively riding and running along side a horse, while holding on to a stirrup strap. Herold slung his carbine and threw the blanket over his shoulders.

"Nice blanket," Rollins noted.

"Yes," Herold agreed, "a fine lady in Maryland presented me with this." He could not know that Mrs. Mudd would not see her husband again for four long years because of this presentation and other hospitalities rendered earlier.

8. Across the Rappahannock to Port Royal

The Port Conway ferry had been in operation in one form or another since 1726. The service would continue until 1930, when the James Madison Bridge replaced it. The river was only a quarter mile wide and relatively easy to cross, although the tides interfered with ferry operations. When Booth and Herold crossed, James Thornton had two hired hands, to pole the barge by hand. They were Negroes; of course, no self-respecting white man would do such drudgery, especially since the overseer himself was black. Speed was not a factor in crossing the Rappahannock at this spot. People just considered themselves fortunate that they could get across at all. On this day, since there were five passengers and three horses, the barge would be about half full and cumbersome to manage. Because of room and ease of movement, Booth sat on Ruggles' horse for the trip. The others stood on the barge deck. When they reached the Port Royal side, Jett and Herold, who had taken to each other quite readily, would team up on Jett's horse. The cousins, Bainbridge and Ruggles, would share Bainbridge's mount. The idea was to find a safe spot to put Booth up for a few days, until the Confederate underground could organize his escape.

"Hold the boat!" The cry came from a man galloping through town towards the wharf. In addition to shouting, he was waving his hat to draw attention. Booth and Herold stiffened. But Willie Jett shook his head.

"Don't worry, Wellford is a Confederate courier."

Enoch Wellford Mason was the only soldier of his command, the Fifth/Fifteenth Virginia Cavalry, who had been paroled at Appomattox.

The rest had been stationeded in homes scattered across the Northern Neck and on the route to Richmond. All of them were a part of the covering force that was to have expedited Abraham Lincoln and his kidnappers to the Confederate capital. When that fell through, they received the task of helping Harney and his men escape. But now that Harney had disappeared into and out of the Yankee prisoner of war system and General Lee had surrendered, Mason was trying to contact his old comrades in arms to get Booth and Herold out of the country. Barring that, he had orders to kill Booth and Herold, rather than let the Yankees take them alive. His well-trained horse made a perfect sliding stop, hindquarters dropped low, at the dock.

Carrying Booth's crutches, Ruggles went over to talk to him. "What do you have Wellford?"

Mason dismounted. "I received my orders only this morning from Hoomes Williamson. You know, from over at Taylor's. Williamson had received reports from an agent named Harbin that two strangers and Charlie Lucas had traveled to Port Conway early this morning. So Williamson sent me to contact you all and then ride on to spread the word of Booth's coming ahead of us." Mason decided not to tell Ruggles about the kill Booth order just yet. "Is that them?"

"Yep, the *assassinators* of the President, according to the young fella standing over by Jett," Ruggles grinned. "Booth's on my horse. You got your parole, Wellford? We have to be careful to stay clear of roving Yankee cavalry, lest we be arrested and sent to a prison stockade, such as Point Lookout."

"Courtesy of General Grant's provost marshal at Appomattox," he grinned and patted his jacket pocket. "I should be able to travel freely. That is why Williamson sent *me* down. I am supposed to be going to buy a wagon south of here. For the farm, you know. Just like my parole says, going home to farm and be a good boy. Hell, the Yanks even let me keep my horse. Like to wore him out getting here. What are you doing with those crutches? You wounded?"

"Nah. But Booth is. It is in his left leg. I have seen some bad wounds, as have you. I would think he is a good case for an amputation. See what you think, kinda casual like. Well, le's go over all at once. It will take Thornton years to cross, as usual. No need to leave anyone behind for the next run--Christmas will get here first."

Ruggles went aboard, followed by Mason, who led his horse. Thornton said, "Howdy," and adjusted everyone's place to balance the load. Mason wound up standing next to Booth who was mounted on

Ruggles' horse. He spent the crossing with his arm over the horse's neck. No one said much, except Herold.

He sidled up to his new-found friend, Jett. "Your name is Jett, huh? I knew a man in Baltimore by that name. Said he came from Westmoreland County, Virginia. Mightn't he be a relation?"

"Yes, Jett said. He is a cousin."

When they reached the south bank, Mason nodded his head then made a disagreeable face at Ruggles, confirming his analysis of Booth's leg. Then he said, "Goodbye, boys," mounted, and lit out through town at a fast clip. Thornton did not ask for money. He knew it was a Confederate military expedition, "on the house," as there was no longer any Confederacy. Besides, Jett was not joking as much as it might have seemed when he threatened to shoot Thornton some time earlier. Herold went back and gave him a dollar, anyhow.

"Only ten cents a piece," Thornton informed him. "I hain't got no change. No cash around here for months."

"Keep it," Herold said. He walked off to get up behind Jett. As agreed upon earlier, Ruggles was already behind Bainbridge, and Booth rode alone. Ruggles led his horse with Booth on it, leaving the actor nothing to do but keep from falling off--a full time task, given the weakness of his broken leg.

"Why don't y'all stay here at the landing? I'll ride through town alone and see if I can find a safe house to stay in. Save the rest of us unnecessary travel." With that Jett trotted down the street, leaving Herold standing next to the others. Inwardly, Booth felt much relief at his thoughtfulness. The less jogging movement he faced, the better.

Jett was back in fifteen or twenty minutes. "I got you the best place in town. The house of Randolph Peyton. He's an attorney and a planter who keeps a house in town, too. His sister, Miss Sarah Jane says that they will not mind entertaining a Southern gentleman wounded in defense of the Confederacy."

The house was a two story clapboard affair with a long front veranda. The party dismounted. Herold agreed to hold the horses as Ruggles and Bainbridge assisted Booth up the steps, through the front door, and into the parlor. He sat down in a small chair with fine, white lace seat and arm coverings. He was so relieved to get into a real house for a change that he failed to realize that he cut a less than dashing figure. He was unshaven, unwashed, and his clothes were greasy and dirty from a week's continued hard use.

Elizabeth Peyton, the younger sister, managed to swallow her gasp, but Booth and the three soldiers saw her choke. Sarah Jane was also taken aback. This was not quite what she had expected when she had agreed to Willie Jett's request. All of the Confederate officers she had met during the war were well groomed; bathed, shaven or with clipped and styled facial hair, and in clean uniforms. This man looked more like a beggar from the streets of Richmond. He *smelled* that way, too. What would Randolph think--he being away from home for a few days--if he were to come home to this? Worse, what would the neighbors think? This was impossible in a proper Southern home. Surely this man could not be trusted alone with two prim and proper Southern belles, despite their advanced ages. He did not even rise when the ladies entered the room. Certainly he was hurt, but he made no effort at all, nor excused his lapse in manners.

"I do not know, gentlemen," Sarah Jane said. "After thinking it all over, I fear I may have unintentionally misled you. After all, Lizzie and I *are* home alone. Brother Randolph is away for a few days, you know, and it really would not be proper for two maiden ladies all alone to entertain a gentleman visitor. I do declare. . . ."

Booth interrupted her gently. "Excuse us, ma'am, for not having appreciated your situation. We surely did not intend to compromise you ladies in any way."

Ruggles was obviously as embarrassed as Booth and the two ladies. "Our apologies, ladies. Fellow, please assist me."

"By your leave, ladies," Bainbridge mumbled as he helped Ruggles escort an inwardly very angry John Wilkes Booth to the door. But as angry as Booth was at being put off, he understood the etiquette that demanded his leaving the Peyton house. He kept his thoughts to himself, and repeated Bainbridge's apology with a forced smile, "By your leave, ladies."

Jett had meanwhile sought to make the most of the situation by scurrying across the street to the home of George Catlett. He was a reliable Confederate sympathizer. But the black servant, who answered the door, informed the young soldier that the family was not at home. Could the gentlemen wait somewhere else and perhaps come back later? It did not appear proper for men in gray to be standing around the house without the owner's permission. "No, I do not know when Mist' George will return."

Jett crossed back to the Peyton house, where the little cavalcade was mounted up again.

"Oh, gentlemen," Miss Sarah Jane Peyton called out. Then, she hastened over to the little group. "Perhaps, if it is not too presumptuous of me, Mr. Richard Garrett might take your wounded man in. He lives but a short piece out on the Bowling Green Road. You know him, Mr. Jett, do you not?"

"Well, sort of, ma'am, my father and he are acquaintances. But I do know who he *is*," Jett said. "And thank you, ma'am, very much for your hospitality and assistance."

The soldiers all tipped their hats. Herold followed suit and, although in some pain from the lengthy process of dismounting, walking, sitting, rising, again walking, and remounting, Booth managed to sweep his hat grandly and in a voice full of staged drama, proclaimed, "Thank you, ladies, both of you." But inwardly, he was getting a bit tired of being put off by what he saw as "all these stuffy Virginians."

9. Byron Baker and Everton Conger Meet Lt. Doherty

"Byron!" Lafayette Baker cried, as he burst into his office. "Go down to the Quartermaster and get a boat for duty on the Potomac for the next few days. Your authority is the Secretary of War. Make it big enough to carry twenty-five, no, thirty men and their horses. Tell 'em we will meet it at the 6th Street wharf, near the Old Arsenal. Then come right back here. I have a job for you!"

Actually, although none of the Federal agents knew it, the men being persued by Baker were Thomas Harbin and Joseph Baden, returning to Virginia after the skirmish at Mechanicsville had befuddled their attempt to find Booth and Herold. The latter had been ensconced in the pines at Samuel Cox's on the 16th and had just arrived at the Garrett Farm on the 24th, after crossing two days before, unnoticed. But it made no difference. The result would be the same. Baker was hot on Booth's trail, solely by accident. John Wilkes Booth's luck was rapidly running out.

More important to Baker at the moment, as he awaited the arrival of the cavalry and the securing of a steamboat to go south, was how to rationalize how he got the information upon which he was acting. Baker thought a while and then concocted a story that has been passed down in multiple sources to the present as a pure creation of the genius of Lafayette C. Baker. He would claim the information was provided by an old Negro, who would remain nameless to protect him from Confederate retaliation. That would insulate his effort from those already in the field, especially Billy Wood and Major O'Beirne, and secure the reward money exclusively for him and his men. Baker was still rubbing his hands in gleeful anticipation when his cousin Byron returned.

"The tug, *John S. Ide*, has been assigned to us. She will be ready at the 6th Street dock as soon as they restock the wood bunker and get steam up. What do you want *me* to do next?" Byron Baker eagerly inserted himself into any future plans. He was tired of rounding up witnesses, mostly the actors from Ford's, for the Lincoln murder investigation. He wanted to get back into the real field of action that appeared in the offing.

Lafayette Baker took a rolled-up map out of a storage case, and spread it open on the table. It was of the Northern Neck of Virginia.

"Booth and Herold are in this area. . . ." He drew a circle around Port Royal and Fredericksburg.

". . . You got the confirmation!" Byron exclaimed.

"You bet! I have asked for twenty-five cavalry to escort a detective into this area--he drew his circle again--and you are the detective who is going to lead the expedition."

"Aren't you going along?"

"No, I will supervise matters from here. Too much to do. We must protect our claim to the reward money. When you get down river near Fredericksburg, you must act on your own judgment. I want you to take Booth alive. Understand? He must be taken alive so we can hang him publicly in due time. Stanton is adamant about that."

Byron Baker nodded his head in agreement and walked out to the gun rack in the outer hall. He picked up two new Remington .44 caliber Army revolvers. The door squeaked open. It was his former lieutenant colonel of the 1st District of Columbia Cavalry, Everton Conger. He had been wounded through the hips and discharged at the same time as Byron Baker, in early February 1865. Conger was still mending from his wounds, but slowly taking a more active role in the National Detective Police, as was Byron. He limped in and looked at Baker hefting the Remimgtons.

"What is up?"

"After Booth again," Baker retorted. "We have a clue."

"Get me in on the party, will you?"

Baker hesitated. Conger was an able tactician and a bulldog of a fighter. He had Lafe's full confidence. But he still limped. This was going to be a rough expedition. Could he ride all day and most of the night? Should Byron have even said what he was doing? If he went along, Conger would be another claim on the reward money.

"I reckon you think I cannot ride anymore? Well," Conger asserted firmly, "you are badly mistaken."

"No, no. I really could use you along on the ride," Baker said. "I am merely thinking of your own welfare. Are you really strong enough to stand the ride? It will be a long one."

"I want to go. Come on. Let us go in and find out what the Colonel thinks about it."

There was the clatter of arriving horsemen outside. Conger and Baker looked toward the street. The door squeaked open again and a first lieutenant of cavalry walked in. He was proud; spit and polish. He had bushy sideburns that flared into even bushier face whiskers that flowed in a semi-circle over his upper lip. But he had the eye of an experienced combat veteran. Conger and Baker were dressed in nondescript civilian clothes. The lieutenant looked at them and wrinkled his nose ever so slightly.

"Lieutenant Doherty reporting to Colonel Baker. Can either of you gentlemen direct me?"

Conger pointed to the inner office door. "In there."

Doherty walked up to Lafayette C. Baker's door, stood at attention, and knocked firmly. "In!" came the call. He removed his kepi and entered.

"You know," Conger said, after the door closed behind Doherty, "I hate the look of those Burnside whiskers. Ever since Fredericksburg."

Byron Baker chuckled. "I know what you mean. That is quite a soup-strainer he has got there."

After a few minutes, the Lieutenant returned to the anteroom.

"Gentlemen, the Colonel would like you to step into his office for a meeting. By the way, I am First Lieutenant Edward Doherty of the Sixteenth New York Cavalry."

"And I am Lieutenant Colonel Everton Conger formerly of Baker's Rangers." Conger did not like Doherty. Too proper, too cold, somehow. Inflexible. Too *honest*. "This here is First Lieutenant L. Byron Baker, the regimental adjutant and cousin to the Colonel."

Inside, the three officers found Lafayette Baker bent over the same map of Virginia that he had shown Byron Baker earlier. To keep it from rolling up, it was weighted down with a saber and a couple of pistols.

"Now look. Here [he drew the circle with his finger once again] is where you will find Booth. It is a sure thing. You will take the steamer to Grant's old supply base at Belle Plain Landing below Aquia Creek. Disembark there and try and find Booth."

The Colonel continued. "I recommend that Byron and you, Conger, act as fugitive Confederate soldiers without paroles who have been separated from your companions, one of them lame, the other quite young. Doherty and his men will stay in the background out of sight as much as possible, advancing only to protect you from any threat.

"Here is a list of the names and locations of every known Secesh sympathizer between Belle Plain and the Rappahannock." Doherty sucked air. He was truly amazed at Baker's thoroughness. But Conger and Byron merely smiled. Although impressed by the length of the list, they knew that it had taken years to compile and truly reflected the Colonel's value to the war effort and the peace to follow.

"You will call on every one of these Rebels," Lafayette Baker went on. "Tell them you are being pursued and that you have gotten separated from your two friends. Try to get them to tell you if they have seen those men. . . . . Oh! And whatever happens, do not lose that list! It is the only copy I have."

Everyone chuckled. They knew that there were several copies of the list extant.

"Now, Lieutenant Doherty," Lafayette Baker said, "if you will excuse us, I would like to get a photograph of the occasion with my cousin and Colonel Conger . . . looking over the map, I believe, gentlemen. It will be only the second photograph we have posed for--so many from the 1st D.C. are dead or gone." Doherty clicked his heels as he drew himself to attention and left the room. Inside he was seething. However, nobody took any notice of him. He was but an adjunct to a Baker operation.

"Excuse *us*, Lieutenant!" He mimicked to himself in a whiney voice. "Crap!" Another one of those damned escorts of snooty policemen, he thought silently, my men and I do all the work and they get all the glory and lord it over us in the process. But I will not yield command of my column, even if one of them is, or *was*, a lieutenant colonel. Adjutant and cousin--this ought to be a royal pain in the saddle seat, indeed. I bet they try and cut me and the men out of that big reward, too. Huh! Over my dead body!

10. Refuge at Garrett's Farm

Booth, Herold and the three cavalrymen rode off down the Bowling Green Road towards Garrett's farm in the same fashion as before: Booth alone on Ruggles' horse, Ruggles up behind Bainbridge, and Jett sharing his steed with Herold.

"You boys certainly have made good your escape. The Yankees have not been seen in the area since the war's end," said Ruggles, referring to Lee's surrender.

"Hopefully, we have left them up in Maryland, hey Davy?" Booth chimed in.

"I sure was glad to cross the Potomac, I tell you," Herold opined. "Crossing the Rappahannock was also a good deal. But meeting up with real Confederate patriots in gray was the most fortunate occurrence of all."

"I tell you what we will do," Ruggles continued. "You want to go to Mosby, and we are trying to do the same. We will leave you at Garrett's and scout on ahead. Mosby was supposed to come toward Ashland Station, somewhat to the south of here. That man on the horse, back at the ferry, has gone on ahead to alert the countryside as to your presence and also to find Mosby. We will leave you two at Garrett's and go ahead to Bowling Green. It is the junction of many roads. Perhaps we can contact the secret service or send you off toward Orange Courthouse."

"I am safe in glorious old Virginia. Thank God!" Booth exclaimed. It came out more sarcastically than he had expected.

"Do not worry, Booth, we will find a safe haven for you," Jett promised.

"I am in your hands, gentlemen, do with me as you think best."

"Say, John, I am in need of new shoes," Herold said. "These are pretty thin. Cain't I go on to Bowling Green with you all? I might make a purchase there."

"That is a good idea, Dave," Booth said. "One visitor at Garrett's will attract less attention. We can join up in a day or two."

"Where are you thinking of going?" Bainbridge asked.

Booth deliberated a moment. "Well, we will have to leave the country. I had planned to make it to Canada by now and then Europe. But my broken leg prevented that. Perhaps we can get to Mexico by land or to a ship off the coast, either along the Atlantic or on the Gulf."

"There are many Rebel units still fighting in the West, on both sides of the Mississippi River," Ruggles said. "My father knows all about that. He was in Richmond before it fell and he wrote that President Davis hoped to stimulate the continued resistance to Yankee tyranny from somewhere in the West, probably Texas."

"We sure struck a blow against *that* tyranny, huh, John?" Herold bragged. "Especially you, the way you sent Ol' Abe to the Devil. It was a shame the rest of the plan went sour."

"That's nothing to brag about." Booth fairly snapped the words out, indicating that he wanted nothing more said about the failures or anything remotely connected with the assassination. The little cavalcade rode on in silence, covering the three miles to the gate of Garrett's farm in good time.

But it was obvious that the trip had irritated Booth's injury and his soul to an even greater extent. He was not a hero to these Southerners, for whom he had sacrificed everything to kill Lincoln. Instead, he was an embarrassment to be ignored, or sent along the road, if he had enough money to pay. Only the three Confederates in Virginia and Jones, Cox and Adams up in Maryland had assisted them without hope of compensation. And Mudd, but reluctantly, after he heard of the assassination. That burned Booth to the very core of his being.

Did not these damned fools realize the importance of his great deed? The first successful assassination of an American president. The end of the man who had brought four years of unnecessary suffering upon North and South. The man who refused any reasonable compromise. The commander in chief who had sacrificed needlessly the flower of American manhood while seeking a general who could defeat Robert E. Lee *and* destroy slavery (a side issue for Lincoln, at best). A President who--what was that assertion?--had destroyed nine-tenths of the Constitution, that holy document of limited government, to save one-tenth.

And that small part was the ability of the executive branch of government, represented by a President whose grasp for power knew no bonds, to coerce the states and the people to bow to his policies. Lincoln had killed the Ninth and Tenth Amendments to the Constitution, the very core of the Bill of Rights. He had upset the relationship between the States and the National government created by the Constitution and the Bill of Rights. His policy of arbitrary arrests and the denial of the writ of habeas corpus proved how far such a man might go.

And he justified it by referring back to the Declaration of Independence and misinterpreting that document as the primary instrument of American government. What if another more unscrupulous man came along and used these so-called war powers to enhance the central government even more? Then truly all government would come out of Washington City and the idea of the people and the states having sovereignty would be nothing but a farce; a travesty; a mockery.

As Booth mulled what he had done and failed to do, the party arrived at Garrett's main gate. Here it stopped. It was mid-afternoon.

"Well, Davy, I reckon this is where we part company," Booth said. Herold turned to his companion, tears streaming down his cheeks. He and Booth had not been apart for more than a few hours since their meeting at Soper's Hill. They had come far and endured much hardship. He was overwhelmed at the idea of their separation. What would Booth do without his assistance? He tried to put a bold face on matters.

"I will be with you soon, John, depend on it. Good bye. Keep in good spirits."

"Have no fear about me, Herold."

David Herold smiled. For the first time Booth addressed him as a man, as an equal, not a mere boy. Herold was warmly pleased. Booth grinned back and concluded confidently, "I am among friends now." Davy switched horses, riding behind Bainbridge. Jett and Ruggles would take Booth in to the Garretts.

"So long, Tibby," Bainbridge said. "See you on down the road, Willie. And to you, Booth, good luck and Godspeed!" Herold waved as Bainbridge put the spurs to his mount and continued on towards Bowling Green.

"Good bye, Lieutenant," Booth shouted and waved. "Come and see me again!" Booth's gaze lingered until the two men passed beyond the first turn and disappeared behind the trees. It was only then that he slowly lowered his arm, contining to stare fixedly into the distance. "Well," said Ruggles, breaking in on Booth's reverie, "come on, Willie. Le's go introduce the Garrett's to their house guest."

Ruggles led his mount with its precious cargo, the man who killed Lincoln, into the farm yard. Jett rode along to do the talking, being at least somewhat acquainted with the Garretts. As they entered the farmyard, Booth took a look at his new surroundings. The farm was located on the west side of the Bowling Green road, surrounded by pine and locust thickets. It was close to the road, yet the trees and undergrowth were so prevalent that the buildings were very hard to see as one rode by.

The farm road went through two gates. One was right on the highway, while the other marked the edge of the farm yard about a hundred feet farther in. The farm yard itself was surrounded by a split-rail worm fence, inside of which were a tobacco barn, a cow shed, and a couple of corn cribs. The farm road ran straight west to the tobacco barn at the side of the yard. About midway in, a second smaller road branched off to the left. It passed through a picket fence, with its own gate, and led directly to the house.

The farm house was a two story, frame work affair, covered with clapboards and painted white. At the top was a fine attic space which ran the length of the house. It had a tall, narrow brick chimney at each gable end, and a one story high veranda along the entire front side. On the left, as one faced the house from the front, was a single story ell or lean-to, which housed the kitchen. It had its own entrance to the outside, which could be gained by the use of a small set of steps, as well as having access to the inside of the dwelling, and shared the chimney on that side. The cow shed and the corn cribs were behind and to the west side of the house. Farther on were a big tobacco drying barn and behind it, the woods. The fields lay directly behind the house to the south over the split-rail worm fence. The dwelling was surrounded by apple and locust trees, which gave much needed shade from the summer's heat.

In the midst of this domesticated arboreal splendor, Willie Jett dismounted. An older man approached the three strangers with a quizzical look on his face.

"This is Mr. Garrett, I presume?" Jett inquired.

"Indeed, I am Richard Garrett, sir."

"I suppose you hardly remember me."

"No, sir, you have the advantage of me." Garrett was amiable enough in his reply.

"My name is Willie Jett. I am the son of your old friend Jett of Westmoreland County. My companion is Lieutenant Mortimer B. Ruggles [*Lieutenant*? Now Booth got a quizzical look on *his* face, but let it pass], son and aide to the general of that name. And the gentleman on the horse is Mr. John W. Boyd, a Confederate soldier, who was wounded in the battles around Richmond, near Petersburg. He is trying to get to his home in Maryland. Can you take care of him for a day or two until his wound will permit him to travel?"

"Certainly. Nothing is too good for the boys in gray who defended the Cause of the Right. Get down, sir, and welcome!"

"Lieutenant Ruggles and I are on our way to Bowling Green and cannot stay. But we will help Mr. Boyd down so that he may partake of your hospitality, sir."

Ruggles and Jett lifted Booth carefully from the saddle. He winced noticeably, gritted his teeth and audibly sucked in air. Ruggles handed Booth his crutches.

"Welcome to Locust Hill Farm, Mr. Boyd. You seem quite wearied, sir," Garrett said to Booth, "I'll get you some sweet water from the well. Go and take a seat upon the veranda. I'll fetch you a pillow for more comfort."

As Garrett left on his errand, the two Confederate soldiers bade Booth good bye. "We will return when it is safe to move you. Rest and get well," Ruggles said. All three shook hands.

Garrett met Booth as he hobbled to the porch. "Your wound must pain you very much, Mr. Boyd."

"Yes, thank you, sir, for your consideration," Booth responded. "It has not been properly cared for and riding has jarred it so. It gives me great pain. . . . Would you be able to tell me, is Ruggles a lieutenant or a major?"

"Well, he has on the uniform coat of a first lieutenant. But he could be a major, I guess. No one has kept their dress up to date since last summer. So my sons, just in from the army tell me so. He had cavalry markings, too, not those of a staff officer. Why?"

"Merely curious, Mr. Garrett," Booth said absentmindedly.

Garrett went inside and brought out a pillow. Booth placed it in the chair, sat down, and closed his eyes. Garrett could see that he needed rest and not a lot of bothersome questions, so he excused himself and left Booth to doze in the warm afternoon air.

About a half hour later, Mr. Garrett nudged Booth gently and said, "Excuse me, Mr. Boyd. I wish to present my eldest son, Jack, to you. He is just home from the war. He served with General Lee as an artilleryman. No, no. It is not necessary to rise, sir. Hopefully you will get better with time."

"Fredericksburg Light Artillery since 1861," Jack said, "transferred to Lightfoot's Artillery Battalion, Second Corps, and surrendered with them at Appomattox. I was severely wounded in the thigh at Drewry's Bluff last May, so I know how you feel."

Booth looked up and stated, "2nd Maryland, Heth's Division, A. P. Hill's Third Corps. And thank you for your kind consolation." Booth gave an inward sigh of relief. At least Jack was from a different part of Lee's army than the portion indicated by his own pre-planned cover story. But then, maybe Harbin knew few Third Corps troops came from this part of Virginia. Booth said with feeling, "It is indeed a pleasure, sir."

"The pleasure is mine, sir," Jack said. "Always an honor to meet others who have worn the gray. Well, I am on my way over to a neighbor's. I shall see you all later at supper."

Booth sat there a while and pondered all that he endured. He reached into his pocket and took out the little memorandum book. He removed the pencil from the safety of its loop and began to scribble an entry, undated, and yet eerily prophetic:

I have too great a soul to die like a criminal. Oh, may He, may He spare me and let me die bravely.

I bless the entire world. Never hated or wronged anyone. This last was not a wrong, unless God deems it so. And it's with Him, to damn or bless me. And for this brave boy with me who often prays (yes before and since) with a true and sincere heart, was it a crime in him? If so, why can he pray the same? I do not wish to shed a drop of blood, but I must 'fight the course.' 'Tis all that's left me.

With this reference to Shakespeare's cornered king of Scotland (*Macbeth* , Act 5, Scene 7), Booth returned his pencil to its place and closed his little book. The porch empty, he returned to his thoughts to rest and was soon sleeping soundly.

11. Last Night in Bed

As darkness approached, the level of noise at the Garrett house increased markedly. The women and girls were working on supper, and the two older boys came home from their evening visits with neighbors. Booth was soon awake, but he continued to sit on the porch with his eyes closed. He had not felt so safe, and truly among friends, since he had fled Washington City. He felt a gentle shaking of his arm.

"Mr. Boyd, it is time for supper. Please, come and wash up."

Booth came in from the tin wash basin, much refreshed. An open seat at the table was obviously his. He hobbled over to it.

"Yes, sir, please take the vacant chair." Mr. Garrett then proceeded to present his entire family formally to Booth. "You met Jack earlier this evening. These are Mrs. Garrett, and my sister-in-law, Miss Holloway. These are my other sons, Richard, Robert, and Willie; and the girls, Cora, Henrietta, and Lillian. This is Mr. Boyd, Family, a wounded Confederate soldier from the battlefields around Richmond. He is headed home to Maryland."

"How do y'all," Mr. Boyd said, gallantly, if painfully, remaining standing during the introductions and nodding to each in turn. "Thank you all very much for taking me into your home. The reputation of Virginia and Virginians for hospitality is well-acquitted here today--handsomely [he nodded at the men and boys], beautifully [he smiled at the women and girls], and honorably [he indicated the two veterans, Jack and Willie, still wearing their ragged uniforms]."

"Well said, Mr. Boyd," Mr. Garrett rejoined. "Bravo, sir! We are pleased to have with us this night a son of our neighboring state, Maryland, prevented from asserting her true destiny only by the overwhelming force of Yankee military might and unconstitutional and illegal presidential tyranny."

"Well done on both sides, gentlemen. Now, father," Jack said, "with your permission, may I lead those gathered here in our evening communion with God, especially thankful that Willie and I have returned from the war, our lives spared, and that Mr. Boyd is among friends."

And with that the family entered into prayer, thankful that the family was whole again and the farm secure after years of tribulation. Blessing was asked for each at the table, special pleading was entered for Mr. Boyd, a wounded son of the South, and the favorable intervention of the Lord begged for all present, and for friends and neighbors, as well. Then Jack asked that God bless the Confederacy and her government and soldiers still in the field. He closed with a plea that if the South might not win the war, let her be triumphant against her enemies during the peace.

After such lengthy supplications, supper was indeed a feast for the deprived fugitive. And it possessed all the sincere ceremony that a more meager meal had lacked at Dr. Stuart's the night before. Booth was relaxed, happy, and most gallant. The two war veterans regaled the diners with tales of the war, stories of the fabled General Lee and his cohorts, and of battles won and war lost.

Jack told of how General Lee had ridden down the Petersburg lines just before the abandonment of Richmond, without receiving a single cheer from the men." Instead the men began to call out, "General, give us meat." Lee, that noble figure of Southern manhood, stopped Ol' Traveller, both rider and beast as emaciated as the men in the trenches, and spoke with tears running down his beard, "Boys, I have no meat for you." The simple, but adequate, repast at the Garretts appeared fit for a king, Jack concluded, much less soldiers and fugitives. No red meat, but chicken aplenty. Booth applauded with the rest, holding his tongue, beyond crying, 'bravo!' at the end of Jack's story, and letting family members do the entertaining.

After eating, the men went out on the porch. "Might I borrow some tobacco and a fire for my pipe?" Booth inquired. The older boys and Mr. Garrett joined in lighting their pipes. Later Mrs. Garrett joined them in their smoking. The other children and Lucinda Holloway sat quietly, permitting the adult males to talk.

Finally, Booth turned to one of the gray-clad boys about his own size. "Say, young man, Willie, is it not? How would you like to trade my suit of civilian clothes for your tattered and frayed uniform?"

"Surely, Mr. Boyd, you jest," Willie answered. Even through the grime of a week's travel and living in the woods, it was obvious that Mr. Boyd's taste in clothes was superb, and priced well beyond anything the Garretts could afford for themselves.

"No, sir, I am deadly serious," Booth asserted.

"Why would you wish to make such a trade, so much to my advantage, and so little to yours?"

"I will tell you," Booth explained, "I have changed my mind about going home. I am going to make my way to North Carolina and join Johnston's army. Now, as I am still to be a soldier, and your battles are over, I will need a uniform, while you will need a citizen's suit."

Willie Garrett thought a moment. He looked at Booth intently, as if to find some hidden reason behind the proposal in his deep, hazel eyes. Finally he spoke. "No. I will not part with my old uniform. I will keep it for the good it has done."

"I do not know what fancies the rest of you, but I am going to turn in," Jack spoke up.

"Good idea, son," Mr. Garrett said. "I suggest that we all do the same, for it is growing late. Mr. Boyd, after our family's nightly devotions, if you would, please follow Jack and Willie up the stairs. They can share a bed and give one to you. Boys, you will help Mr. Boyd up the stairs. And mind you take care to do it gently, lest his wounded leg be damaged anew."

Upstairs, after the prayers were concluded, Booth took Jack's bed, nearest the door. Booth took off his coat and vest. The Garrett boys eyed the two horse pistols and the Bowie knife strapped around his waist. Then they both looked at each other, as if to say, what do you think of that? Booth removed his belt, the knife in its scabbard, and the two revolvers in their holsters and slung them over a post on the head board. He sat down heavily. The comfort of the rude straw tick mattress seemed like pure Heaven to him after ten days in the wild.

"Jack, would you mind giving me a hand with my boot? Thank you, sir, so very much." Jack pulled off the heavy cavalry boot and set it at the foot of the bed. Booth nudged off the slipper on the injured leg and then slipped off his pants. Jack and Willie could not help but notice the swelling in Booth's injured leg.

"How is your leg doing, Mr. Boyd?" Jack inquired. "Where were you hit? How did it happen?"

"It happened during the evacuation of Petersburg, Booth related. I got hit by a shell fragment. It is not painful, so long as I do not touch it." Then Booth lay back full length with an almost mournful, yet pleasurable, sigh. "Good night, gentlemen," he said with firm finality, putting an end to further talking. All three were asleep within minutes.

12. Looking for Booth Along the North Bank of the Rappahannock

"I am Captain Henry Wilson." These riverboat captains had a different look about them than sea captains. Less salty, so to speak. More of a money-grubbing capitalist air about them. Not very navy-like. But still, in charge.

"I am Lieutenant Doherty. This man is Sergeant Boston Corbett, my second in command. I wish you to read this note and abide by it contents."

"You do, eh? Let me see it. . . . M-m-m-m. . . . It says that *you* command these twenty-five men, not them civilian-looking fellers. Read and noted, Lieutenant." As the two soldiers turned to go aft, Captain Wilson thought, you boys are going to have a *real* enjoyable time of it with that attitude. Hell's fire, not five minutes ago, one of the civilians said *he* was in charge of the whole shebang. They will be pissing on each other's trees the whole expedition. What a life!

By ten that night, the *John S. Ide* docked at Belle Plain's odd U-shaped wharf and disgorged its human and animal cargo. Fearing unseen sunken objects, Captain Wilson refused to pull his boat close into the moorage and docked at the end of the wharf, at the base of the U. Everyone had to walk their horses from there to land along the double, parallel causeways.

The troopers noted that even in the dark, Belle Plain appeared abandoned and in a state of decay. Two years earlier, it had been a bustling place during the Fredericksburg and Chancellorsville Campaigns, and again during Grant's Overland Campaign in 1864, but had since fallen into disrepair. General Grant had preferred to send his supplies farther south up the James River, to keep them from falling into the hands of Rebel raiding parties.

"Keep your steam up and stay here until 6 p.m. the 26th," Byron Baker ordered.

"Whatever you say," came Captain Wilson's ne'er may care response.

"Sergeant, mount the troop," Doherty, ordered.

"Prepare to mount! . . . Mount!" Corbett gave the command.

Baker looked over at Conger. He seemed to be bothered by something. Surely it was not physical. They had not done anything except take a boat ride. Then the adjutant's military mind began to work.

"Colonel Conger, why do you not take charge of the expedition? You have been over the ground before. I want you *not* to defer to me. We are in this together."

"Why . . . thank you, *Lieutenant!*" Conger's tone was truly appreciative. He smiled and waved the column forward. Doherty's command waited until the two detectives had advanced about 400 yards, as ordered. Then, Doherty put his hand up in the air, formed a fist, and brought it down once. Corporals silently relayed the signal back along the column. The cavalrymen moved forward at a walk.

Everyone was a mite edgy, fearing possible ambush. But nothing happened, and soon the men got used to the darkness and the night sounds. Despite the pitch black of night, the troopers could tell that the terrain they passed through was desolate, long-ago stripped by the passing armies. Stone foundations and wrecked shells of former houses dotted the land. Everything that could burn had been consumed long ago.

Broken-down wagons and ambulances lined the road in spots, and the bleached skeletons of draft animals glowed in the dark. Here and there the land fell away from the road in deep ravines that had once temporarily housed Confederate soldiers captured in the fighting at the Wilderness and Spotsylvania, and were collectively known as the "Punchbowl." The ramparts of two abandoned gun emplacements covered what had been a makeshift prison camp.

The column moved as quietly as possible toward Fredericksburg for three miles, skirting the ever-present Virginia tidewater swamp. Then it struck a side road and turned south until it reached the Rappahannock River. There it paralleled the river until it turned onto the so-called Riverside Road. Conger and Baker spent the night rousing farmers and doctors, the people who were on Lafayette Baker's list of names. No one knew anything. When some of them got unpleasant about the questions, Conger called Doherty's column up and the troopers would search the homestead as roughly as possible, turning over beds, smashing in doors, letting livestock loose.

"Ain't this kinda rough treatment?" younger recruits would ask their more veteran companions.

"Don't worry about it," would be the reply. "These Rebs lost the war, anyhow."

By dawn on the 25th, the column was nearing King George Court House, in the vicinity of where Major O'Beirne had quit a couple of days earlier. Ten hours in the saddle overnight to no avail made for short tempers as Conger and Baker rode into the yard of Bleak Hill, the farm of Dr. Horace Ashton.

"Good morning, gentlemen," came the doctor's friendly greeting. "What can I do for you?"

"Have you seen two men? One of them lame the other not yet twenty?"

"No, sir," Dr. Ashton said, "I have not seen anyone like that. Are they friends?"

"We separated during the night. We are all Confederate soldiers without parole. We were going together to get them. The lame man was seriously hurt. We thought he might seek medical aid here."

"Gentlemen, excuse my bluntness, but I doubt your story. I saw the glint off a saber or something like it just beyond the bend. You must be Yankees. You do not have the accent of the South in your words. You say, 'we are all,' instead of, 'we all are.' But, nevertheless, I mean no harm. Please call your men in and we will feed them and your horses, too. You look a mite tuckered out."

Conger waved the column in and the grateful troopers sat on their shelter halves in the yard, after loosening their saddle girths and feeding their hungry horses. It felt good to lie back or walk around, trying to regain circulation in their rumps.

"Heads up," came the call from Private Lewis Savage, near the gate.

Several troopers got up, and one or two produced revolvers. Coming up the road from the highway was a lone Confederate captain, with the buff collar and sleeve markings of a staff officer. He was packing iron, as the troopers would say; a Colt's 1851 Navy revolver stuck in his sash.

"It is all right," Dr. Ashton cautioned. "He is the brother of a neighbor, over at Mount View. Hello, Taylor! Come in and get down."

Conger came up. "Who are you, sir?"

"I am Captain Murray F. Taylor, sir, late of Lt. General A. P. Hill's staff, Third Corps, Army of Northern Virginia. Just in from Appomattox Court House. I am headed to Mount View, my brother's plantation."

God! Conger thought. Just look at the gall of the man. And carrying a weapon, too. "What are you doing with that pistol?" he asked.

"I was allowed to retain a sidearm at the Surrender, as part of the terms." Then Taylor murmured under his breath, but evidently not quietly enough, "What business is it of yours? You damned Yankee!"

"Now listen, you Rebel scoundrel," Conger snapped, "I am going to ask you a question or two, and I want some good answers. And do not give me any of your Secesh sass, or we will stretch your neck, right here!"

"Now, just a moment, sir," Taylor said with much dignity, "I have a parole from the Provost Marshal of the Army of the Potomac. I am to be undisturbed by *your* lot. I have done nothing wrong. I did not even spur my horse away when I saw you were Yankees."

"Lieutenant," Conger said to Doherty, "arrest that smarmy slave-driver. Take his revolver. And do not be too gentle about it, either."

"Gentlemen, I protest," Dr. Ashton interjected. "He has given no offense."

"He is lucky I do not let him stretch a little rope off yonder tree," Conger shot back. "Keep out of this, sir, or you will join him in arrest!"

"Why do you not send for Hoomes Williamson to vouch for him?" Dr. Ashton asked. "We can send a Negro over right now. He is just down the road a piece." Both Baker and Doherty nodded in agreement.

"Oh, all right," Conger growled, "but only because you have been very correct with us, serving breakfast and feeding our horses."

As the black jogged out to the main road, another horseman trotted in.

"Holy Lord!" One of the troopers said prayerfully. "It is a full-fledged Reb General! Lookit them stars and all that gold braid!"

"I am Major General Charles W. Field, gentlemen, formerly of Hood's Division. Is there some problem here?"

"Nothing we cannot handle, sir," Conger said. "This jackanapes has been uncooperative and offensive in his attitude."

"Indeed!" Field said incredulously. "Well, I can personally vouch for his character and honesty. He was one of General Hill's staff, an aide de camp. We both have paroles from Lee's surrender."

"Would you and he be willing to answer some questions, General?" It was Byron Baker, taking this opportunity to let Conger step back and cool off.

"Certainly, sir, if I can."

"Have you, sir, or the captain, seen two men, one young, the other lame, in your travels?"

"Not I, sir," Field answered.

"Nor I," Captain Taylor seconded.

"Gentlemen, here is Hoomes Williamson," Dr. Ashton said. "Williamson, would you be so kind as to vouch for Captain Taylor here to these Union officers?"

"I would be happy to, sir," Williamson said. "I have known him and his family since before the war."

Crap! Conger thought, these Rebels would vouch for the character of Lucifer, himself. Then aloud, he asked, "Mr. Williamson, have you seen two men, sir, one lame and the other about twenty years of age?"

"No, sir, I have not. But if you would be willing to release Captain Taylor to me, I would guarantee to escort him home, where he will stay out of trouble. Perhaps, General, you would like to come have breakfast with us. I see the hospitality of Dr. Ashton has been thoroughly eaten up, so to speak--no offense, gentlemen, I assure you." He smiled.

Damn! Too many teeth, Conger thought. What a sycophant! An insincere grin, if I ever saw one. He waved his hand in resigned assent toward the plantation gate, a sardonic look on his face.

I hope the men Harbin and I sent out earlier have found Booth and his companion, Williamson thought to himself as they rode off, or there is going to be Hell to pay down the road. Those Yankee bloodhounds are hot on the trail. That one detective, the one some of the men called Colonel, is one rough bastard. He is in no frame of mind to show much mercy to the assassin of that wizened old prune, Abe Lincoln.

PART VI

LAST DAY (1865)

Lincoln was elected president under the Constitution in 1860.
After four years of war during which crimes have been committed,
by his permission and with his approval, which would have
disgraced Nero, he stepped into his role as dictator.
--From the missing pages of John Wilkes Booth's *Diary*,
April 25, 1865

Father, Mother, Sisters all / God, and myself, I have lost by my fall.
--From *The Beautiful Snow*, John Wilkes Booth's favorite poem.

Nothing in his life became him like the leaving it.
--From *Macbeth*, Act 1, Scene 4

1. Happy Morning at Garrett's Farm

The next morning, April 25, Jack rose early and went downstairs. Willie arose shortly after and, as he quietly left the room, he collared young Richard on the stair landing.

"Little Brother," he said, "go back into my room and await Mr. Boyd's awakening. He may need help with his clothes and crutches. We will save breakfast for you."

Richard entered the room and sat in a chair. He stared with childish fascination at the belt hanging on the bedstead, the one that held the two Colt's revolvers in their holsters and the Bowie knife in its scabbard. Draped over all of the weapons was a pair of binoculars. Booth himself was a marvel for the boy. He carefully took measure of the man lying there on his back, gently breathing, with one arm thrown above his head on the pillow. Never had Richard seen such alabaster skin, set off by such coal black hair and dark shadow of an unshaven beard, many days old. Strange the boy thought, he is not tanned and leather-skinned like other soldiers who have visited here over the years. He is not weather-beaten like Jack and Willie, who had been in the army--or even Pa, who farmed all day. He looked more like someone who has been attended to carefully and lived indoors. A clerk, possibly, or at least, a city dweller.

Booth soon stirred and sat up. "Morning already?" he asked.

"Yessir," Richard answered. "I am to help you get dressed and onto your crutches."

"How very thoughtful of you," Booth said.

Richard helped him get into his clothes and handed him his crutches. At that moment Jack came up the stairs.

"Breakfast is ready Mr. Boyd."

"Y'all go ahead without me. No need to wait and let it get cold on my account."

"No hurry, Mr. Boyd," Jack said kindly. "We find soldiers to be a privileged class and you may rest assured that breakfast will be available for you at any time you are ready to come down. We are waiting for Willie to come back from taking the cattle out to graze, anyway."

"Thank you, sir. Go on down with your brother, now, Richard. Thank you for your help. I reckon I will go out back before I eat, if you do not mind."

Later, after a huge country breakfast topped off with steaming mugs of ersatz coffee ("do not ask what it is made of or you may not wish to drink it," apologized Mrs. Garrett), Booth went outside on the veranda. He packed his pipe and had a smoke. Then he wandered around the yard, until his throbbing leg indicated he should go back to the porch and rest. Booth lay down on a long wooden bench and took a nap.

After he had awakened and was sitting up, Willie came out on the veranda. Like young Richard, he had noticed the paleness of Booth's complexion and it troubled him. He was no field soldier.

"How do, Mr. Boyd. Feeling better? Are you up to a little conversation?"

"Yes, and certainly," Booth said.

"Where were you wounded?"

"Down below Petersburg," Booth replied.

"What with?"

"It was a shell fragment. It has broken the small bone in my leg. Take a look." Booth pulled up his trouser leg to reveal the ugly, swollen, blackish wound area. "I had planned to go back to Annapolis, my home, after the evacuation of Petersburg, but upon crossing the Potomac I met a cousin. We hired a couple of horses and went on a spree together."

"Oh, yeah," Willie said wistfully, "I feel like one myself, every so often."

Booth smiled with understanding. "My cousin bragged to some Federals in a grog house that we had crossed the Potomac. They informed the local provost marshal on us. As we had no paroles, my cousin and I lit out and decided we ought to re-cross the river to keep from arrest. Point Lookout is not any kind of place to look forward to, don't you know?"

"I hear you," Willie said in sympathy. "I was glad I had managed to get a parole without having to go to a Union prison pen first."

Booth nodded his head in agreement. "But the Yankees were faster than we thought," he continued, "and we had a little shooting scrape with the arresting officers, and had to hide in the swamps. We got down to the Potomac the next day, tied our horses to a couple of pines and tried to cross to Mathias Point. But the weather was too stormy, so we had to try again the next night. Cost us nearly all the money we had to get a boat."

"That is quite an adventure. Well, sir," Willie said as he stretched his arms, "I got chores to do." Mr. Boyd had held to essentially the same story he had told the night before, with some embellishments, thought Willie. No one was going to trip him up with a few questions. Mr. Boyd would have to do that all by himself.

"And I need to exercise by walking a bit," Booth said. He got up from the bench and hobbled out into the yard. He went down the lane from the house to the tobacco barn, took a turn around the barn and stared at the woods. They would make a good hideaway if it ever became necessary, Booth thought. By the time he got back to the house his leg was crying for more rest.

But Booth got little repose initially. Soon the five younger Garrett children began to poke their heads around corners and out of the doors and windows. Booth always liked children and he began to wave his fingers at them and wink and make faces. The children would dart back under cover and giggle, as youngsters do when they shyly test out new people. But curiosity finally got the better of them and they gathered around the stranger to get acquainted.

Booth pulled out his box compass. "Do you all know how to find north?"

"Look for moss on a tree."

"That is one way. This little device tells you how, moss or no."

"Really?"

"Let me see, too," spoke up a younger girl, accidentally excluded from the group crowding around the would-be-teacher.

"Look at the way the colored end of the needle always points the same direction. See?"

"O-o-o-h!"

"I can turn the instrument around and yet the needle always stays the same."

"That's ever so nice," opined one child, politely.

"If I line up the N for north, I always know all the directions. The barn over there is west, the highway is east of here. The house is. . . . "

"That is south," said an older boy with finality." I can tell by the S."

"That's right! Now watch as I take my knife. . . ."

"Ain't that a sure 'nuff Bowie, Mister?"

"You bet it is," asserted another. "I seen one of Jack's friends take one off to the war."

Booth smiled grandly. The children had never seen teeth quite so shiny and white. "Actually, I believe it is more of a variety known as an Arkansas Toothpick . . . Now! . . . Watch how the knife affects the needle. It confuses it, see?"

"Ain't that slick! Look Richard!"

"I see it!" came the reply.

"Let me see," said several others in unison. The older boys stepped aside so their siblings could view the marvels of science as demonstrated by the fancy stranger from Maryland.

Then, Booth pulled out his field glasses, the ones that Mrs. Surratt had taken out to the tavern at Surrattsville that fateful Good

Friday, which now seemed so long ago. Booth had each of the children take a glance out of both ends of the glasses, making things appear closer and larger than life, then farther away and more insignificant. Stage, field, marine . . . position by position . . . closer and farther, each glance a "bewonderment to behold," as they said about such things in those days.

There was a heavy tread upon the veranda, as Mr. Garrett approached. "Children, I suspect Mr. Boyd is a mite tired from his sore leg. Why don't you girls help your mother in the kitchen? You boys come with me. We can clean out the cow shed until dinner time."

Mr. Garrett's orders were greeted by a resounding, "A-a-a-w-w-w," by the whole crowd.

"Le's go now," the elder Garrett insisted, kindly but firmly. The children did as they were told and scattered to their various chores. Mr. Garrett smiled at Booth and left for the cow shed.

Rather than resting, Booth went inside the house and took a long look at a map of the Southern States. Just then, young Richard Garrett passed through the room, headed for the dreaded cow shed.

"Son--Richard, is it not? Is it possible to remove that map from the wall and lay it on the floor?"

"I reckon it is all right," Richard said. He climbed on a chair and carefully removed the map and spread it on the floor. Booth placed his crutches against the wall and using the chair, got down on his hands and knees. He groaned audibly and hit the floor more heavily than he had wanted.

"Are you all right, sir?" Richard said anxiously.

"Yes, thank you. I'll be fine," Booth said. He began to study the map, crawling about its perimeter. After a lengthy examination, he took out his diary and a pencil and wrote a few lines. Then he took the pencil and traced a faint line on the map from Port Royal to Norfolk. Then he made a line to Charleston, South Carolina, and on to Savannah, Georgia.

It was all too much for Richard. He decided to show off geographical knowledge to the interesting stranger. "Where are you going, sir?"

"To Mexico," Booth said without looking up.

"Why, I thought last night you said you were going to join Johnston's army in North Carolina."

Booth looked up quickly, too quickly, thought Richard, and stared at the boy. His eyes fairly glistened with intensity. Richard said nothing more. Then Booth returned to the map and his survey. He marked a line from Savannah around the tip of Florida to Galveston. There he paused, as if he did not know which route he should use to Mexico, land or sea. Years later, Richard believed that Booth really had no plans, and surmised that he could not have been a part of a larger conspiracy involving the Confederate government, because they would not have left him high and dry at Port Royal. But as unfolding events would soon show, Richard was wrong. Certain elements of the disintegrating Confederacy were doing their best, albeit haphazardly, to spirit Booth to safety or, failing that, to permanently eliminate him.

2. The Yankees Cross to Port Royal

After the affair at what the Yankees thought was Dr. Ashton's aptly named Bleak Hill Plantation, Conger decided to divide the command. He and Baker took four men and a corporal and searched south toward the Rappahannock. Lieutenant Doherty and the rest of the column went through King George Court House to follow up on Major O'Beirne's previous path. They would all meet in Port Conway later that day. As it turned out, the two parties converged at Belle Grove Plantation, the home of Carolinus Taylor, just before the ferry. Taylor fed part of the column, while the rest foraged at a farm across the road.

"I am beat, Baker," Conger said, as he limped around the camp painfully. "Why don't you and Doherty go down to the ferry and make inquiries? I am going to rest a while here." Conger and most of the troopers were asleep before Baker and Doherty and the half dozen worn out, luckless men with them cleared the horizon.

"Let's ask that Negro if he knows anything," Baker said.

Doherty stopped his horse, blocking the road. "Say, boy, what's your name? What do you do around here?"

"Dick Wilson, sir," came the answer. "I been shad fishing down to the landing."

"You would not have happened to see two strangers down by the ferry, yesterday," Baker inquired. "One was taller and lame, the other shorter and about twenty years of age?"

"Oh, yes, sir," came the answer. "They crossed around noon to Port Royal, after me and Mr. Rollins--he live in Port Conway, you know--come in from shad fishing."

"Where is this Rollins?"

"Oh, he the only man left in town, you cain't miss him. No one else there, most times."

Baker looked at Doherty and grinned. Doherty widened his eyes and nodded his head in joyful agreement. It was the most pleasant the two men had been to each other during the expedition. The good humor would not last.

After a short ride, the Federal officers found William Rollins sitting on his front porch, half asleep in the warm afternoon sun.

Baker got down from his horse. "Wake up, sir! Wake up!" He shook Rollins out of his lethargy. "How do you do?"

"Howdy yourself and see how you like it," Rollins said. Baker ignored what he thought to be a smart-aleck reply, not realizing it was a common response to such a greeting in the Antebellum South.

"Who are you?" Baker asked.

"I am Rollins. I own the ferry landing."

"Well, Rollins, you have not by chance seen two strangers, one lame and the other a shorter, younger man? Come by yesterday? Took the ferry over to Port Royal?"

"Sure," Rollins said. "Around noon. They come in a two-horse wagon driven by a local colored man named Lucas. Oh, he ain't from around *here*. He come in from *upcountry*, near Dr. Stuart's place."

"Describe the two men for me, please," Baker insisted.

"Well . . . the one was about your height, had a game left leg. Looked all black and swollen-like. The troopers said it looked so bad that they thought he might have to have it cut off by a sawbones soon. Carried two crutches and a brace of pistols. T'other was shorter, little stockier, kinda child-like in his talk at times. Run on forever. Carried a carbine, like the fancy ones the U.S. Navy men use when they come up the river looking for Rebs. You know, load it once, shoot it all week. . . . How's that?"

"Take a look at these daguerreotypes for me?"

"Why not? I like tintypes, you know. Cain't get enough of 'em. Yeah, this is the short, young feller. This looks like t'other, but he don't have no moustache. Just a fortnight's beard. I think that's him, alright." Rollins had just identified Herold and Booth.

"What troopers?"

"Huh? . . ."

"You said troopers said the man's game leg looked so bad. . . ."

"Oh! . . . They was three Confederate soldiers here, too. Rode up after the two strangers. They all got pretty thick, after a while. Everyone crossed about one o'clock. One of the troopers was Willie Jett. Comes by often--or, at least, before the war he did. Probably will come by more now, since it is over, so they say."

Doherty turned to one of his men. "Corporal, go and get Colonel Conger. Wake and bring up the whole column. Leave no one behind.

Hurry! And you three, get into that rowboat and go across to Port Royal and bring back the ferry. Use your pistols, if necessary. Do not take 'no' for an answer!"

Soon afterwards, Conger came down at a gallop. The rest of the command under Sergeant Corbett came up ten minutes later at a walk. Conger went over all the ground covered earlier by Baker and Doherty.

"Oh, yeah, that was them," William Rollins insisted. "I recognize them likenessess for sure. The Reb trooper was Willie Jett. His daddy lives over to Westmoreland, I think."

"Now, Will," Bettie Rollins chipped in. She had come out as the man had gone to fetch Conger. "You know all three of those boys. The one was the Ruggles boy, Tibby, they call him. His daddy was a general in the Confederate army. The other one was his cousin, Fellow Bainbridge. They will not be hard to find. Willie Jett, for instance, is courting the Gouldman girl over at Bowling Green. He said he thought to go there and spark her a while, don'tcha know? Her people keep the Star Hotel."

"Aw . . . how do you know all that?" Rollins asked his wife, disbelievingly.

"Why, you men don't see nor hear anything, I swan," she scolded him back.

Conger was pleased with the results. He even got Rollins to sign a sort of "confession." Then he administered the *coup d' grace*. "Will you guide us to Bowling Green? Where is it?"

"Oh, 'bout fifteen, twenty miles south, Rollins said. Guess I could take you . . ."

"No, you don't!" Bettie Rollins snapped out. "Not and be able to live around here any more. What six kinds of fool are you?"

"She is right, I cannot do it."

"How about we place him under arrest and put a gun on him for public consumption?" Doherty suggested. "It has worked before, up in Maryland."

"How about that?" Conger asked.

"What do you think, Bettie?" Rollins looked over to his wife.

"Well, I do not like any of it," she said, "but I reckon these men *will* take you, no matter what. That is the best way. As a prisoner, but not really one."

During the conversation, Thornton had been running the ferry. The gunpoint escort proved unnecessary; he worked for all armies with equal alacrity. Anyway, they all paid the same--nothing. He brought the barge over for the first time at a little after three p.m. He could only ferry six men and horses at one time. Each passage took around thirty minutes. It was nearly six p.m. before the whole column was assembled on the south bank and ready to move. And it was getting dark again. Nearly twenty-four hours without much of a rest. But the quarry was in their sights. Conger and Baker, at least, could smell blood. Or was it the blood money?

3. The End of a Reverie

Back at the Garretts', the star attraction at noon dinner was not Booth, but brother Jack, who had returned from his visit to a nearby shoemaker.

"You know, Father, about that rumor that Lincoln has been assassinated?"

"It has been around a couple of days," Mr. Garrett remarked, "but I do not believe a word of it. No one has killed a president before. True, there was an attempt on Andy Jackson over thirty years ago. But no one has ever tried such since then. It is some idle report started by stragglers, I reckon."

"Well," Jack said, "hear what I learned over at Mr. Acres' while he was repairing my boots. There was another feller named Geavitt there. While we waited, he told me that he had seen a Richmond newspaper and, among the other news, was a story of how $140,000 was being offered up in Washington City for the arrest of the man who had killed the President of the United States."

Everyone looked at Jack. Mr. Boyd seemed especially interested, although he said nothing.

"Well," Willie said, "he had better not come thisaway or he will be gobbled up!"

"How much did you say had been offered?" Booth asked calmly.

"The man from Richmond said $140,000 for sure," Jack replied. "Why?"

"I would sooner suppose $500,000, or more *like* $500, 000," Booth mused.

Willie did not care how much the actual amount was. "I could use $100,000 dollars just now," he concluded. Everyone laughed, except Booth.

"Would you betray him? For that?" Booth quietly interjected.

"He had not better tempt me," Willie concluded, "for I haven't a dollar in the world."

"I suppose the assassin has been paid," said one of the daughters.

"Do you think so, Miss?" Booth queried with a wan smile. "By whom do you suppose he was paid?"

"Oh," she said off-handedly with a shrug, "I suppose by both the North and the South. There are a great many, North and South, who are anxious to be rid of Mr. Lincoln."

"It is my opinion," Booth said with some authority, "that he was not paid a cent, but did it for notoriety's sake and for the good of his country."

As dinner was completed and everyone arose from the table, Mrs. Garrett noted Booth wince as he stood on his crutches. "Mr. Boyd," she said, "would you like me to change the dressing on your wound?"

"Oh, no, ma'am, thank you. It does not give me the slightest pain," Booth lied.

"You really ought to see a doctor," Mr. Garrett said, looking very concerned. Willie had already told his father that he believed the limb was in need of amputation. He had seen many such wounds in the war.

"Really, I am doing fine, sir," Booth said amiably. "But thank you both for your concern."

In the front room headed for the veranda, Booth stopped at the map, now back up on the wall. He turned to Jack. "Do you, by chance, have a map of Virginia, proper?"

"No, sir, I do not. Why do you need a map?"

"I want to get the exact route to Orange Courthouse. From there I wish to go to Johnston's army and thence to Mexico."

"Why would you want to go to Orange Courthouse?"

"I have heard that a good many Marylanders are there. I hope to get a horse from them. I have been to Maryland, but the Federals are requiring everyone to take the oath, and I have sworn never to do that. So, I reckon, I will have to leave the country."

Jack pointed the route to Orange Courthouse on the wall map. Booth made some notes on a piece of paper and put it in his pocket. Jack left him at the map, noting to himself that Mr. Boyd must have been looking at it before, because the stray pencil marks on it were new.

A while later, Booth was back at his chair on the veranda, making notes in his diary:

April 25th

At present there is but one feeling on the subject of Lincoln's assassination--and no one dares to speak otherwise. After some thought I have come to a different conclusion. Seward is the man who for years has nursed and fostered and fed this irrepressible conflict, till it had grown to be the monster which is preying upon the country. Lincoln is the man who has aided, abetted, and encouraged the schemes of Seward, dragging down the Nation far lower than Seward ever anticipated. Lincoln was elected president under the Constitution in 1860. After four years of war during which crimes have been committed, by his permission and with his approval, which would have disgraced Nero, he stepped into his role as dictator.

This is plain fact . . . .

Jack Garrett was sitting on the steps. Hearing a noise, Jack looked toward the road and saw some men pass by on horseback.

"There go some of your party from yesterday, now. Headed for Port Royal, looks like."

Booth snapped out of his seeming lethargy of pain. He threw down the diary and got up out of his chair with amazing rapidity. "Go up and get my pistols!" he shouted.

"What do you want with your pistols?" Jack inquired, puzzled at the change that had overcome his porch companion.

Booth turned on Jack and spoke in a voice that Garrett had never heard before. It possessed all of the commanding qualities of a general officer on the battle field. "Go now and get my pistols!" Each word was distinct, projected from the depths of his soul, precise in its delivery. It was his old stage voice that resounded across the veranda.

Garrett ran into the house and up the stairs. He grabbed the belt with its weapons. Then he looked out the second story window and saw that the riders had passed without coming in. He put the belt back on the bed post and came down empty handed.

"They have gone past the gate," Jack said.

Booth listened for a minute, grunted in agreement, turned and reseated himself in his old place.

Within five minutes, a lone figure strode down the farm lane. He carried a cavalry carbine slung over his shoulder with a bit of soft cotton rope. "Who *is* that?" Jack wanted to know.

Booth jumped up again and said, "Oh ... that is one of *our* men."

"What do you mean?" Jack retorted, never having seen Herold before.

"Why, one of those who crossed over with me." Booth then asked young Richard to fetch his pistols and knife. Thrilled to be able to handle such fearsome weapons Richard quickly ran up the stairs and returned with them in hand. He gave them to Booth proudly, his heart beating wildly, more from the excitement of touching the weapons than the exertion of climbing the stairs two at a time. Booth strapped them on and tousled the boy's hair by way of a thank you.

4. A Tense Afternoon at Garrett's Farm

Booth stepped off the porch and met Herold in the yard. "How is it going, Davy?"

"Right as rain. Bainbridge and Lieutenant Ruggles are checking out the road to Port Royal behind us. Want to see if any Yanks are on our trail. We are supposed to get the Garretts or someone to take us to Orange Courthouse or Guinea's Station. Someone will meet us there. Mosby's headquarters are supposed to be around there. That feller, Stringbean, or whatever ["Stringfellow," Booth interjected, rolling his eyes] . . . oh . . . yeah, hah! String*fellow* has already passed through a couple of days ago, and the line is all clear for receiving us and moving us on."

But Herold was more excited about his sojourn with the three Confederates than in mundane matters like escape. "I stayed at a Mrs. Clark's with Bainbridge," he continued, breathlessly. "Her son was with Mosby, just like Jett and them. Like my new shoes? Got them in Bowling Green this morning. And say, Johnny they have the nicest little whorehouse down the road towards Bowling Green. It's called The Trappe, and there are a lot of horny gals there---a mother and her daughters. The old lady serviced me herself. Well, I . . ."

"Save it Dave," Booth cut him off abruptly. "We have to get you introduced and invited in for the night. Won't be easy. The old man is off until supper time; the sons are getting suspicious. They think they are on to us, but really don't know why, yet. Come with me, and I'll go to work on the oldest brother."

Jack Garrett was still sitting on the porch. As Booth and Herold approached, he stood up.

"This is my cousin, David Boyd," Booth said to him. "Davy, meet Jack Garrett."

"Hey," Herold said shaking hands. "Do you suppose that you all can entertain me for the night?"

"Well, I am not the proprietor of the house. My father is out and I do not know when he will return. I cannot take you in on my own account." By now, Garrett actually wished to get both men off the premises. He was very suspicious of Booth's conduct earlier that evening. This guest was way too edgy to suit Jack.

"Well, never mind," Herold said. "Mayn't I just take a seat on the steps and wait until your father comes back?" Garrett waved a silent assent with a motion of his hand, pointing to a place beside him on the steps. Booth opened his diary and made the final touches to his last entry-- something he had been working on all day:

. . . The people of the North are only fit for a despotical form of government. But so great has been the influence of the Founding Fathers on the minds of men, that no one has been found sufficiently bold to throw off openly the ideals of the Constitution and Bill of Rights which control them, grasp the scepter and destroy free institutions. Tragically, the position, which no bold man would strike for, Lincoln *sneaked* into, as he sneaked into Washington in 1861. It was just as he predicted in his Lyceum speech back in 1838--there he was, barricading and fortifying himself every day, by the trick of executive proclamation, and his refusal to work with Congress, except as a collective sycophant. I much doubt if a less subtle Andy Johnson can start where Lincoln left off. Congress will now strike back, in its turn. As for Seward, he being the most conservative of the cabinet, while I regret the ills that have befallen his family and household, I cannot but say he has reaped the whirlwind that he sowed.

What is to become of a nation when all the clever mountebanks and humbugging quacks are exalted to the high places? Such men have really no weight of character. How American all this is! Where is virtue, if vice is not to be held up in ignominy?

The Yankees are bad. But, if Virginia is any indication, the Southerners appear to be no better. It may be that they are simply dispirited and exhausted. But in any event, it is inexplicable and most disturbing to me. They have forsaken State Rights for the Yankee dictatorship. Even the hated John Brown is more of a hero here than I, who killed the American tyrant of the ages, shouting Virginia's sacred motto, for and on behalf of the Confederacy that we all hold most dear.

Booth placed his little stub of pencil back in its loop and closed his diary for the last time. He put it back in his coat pocket and leaned back on his elbows. He had hardly been comfortably settled in when the pounding of hooves coming up the drive caused everyone to stand up. Garrett recognized Lieutenant Ruggles. He had seen him from the second story bedroom window when Booth arrived the day before. The other was Fellow Bainbridge, as Booth and Herold knew. The two fugitives walked out to meet the riders.

"Well, boys," Booth exclaimed, "what is in the wind now?"

"Great Scott, fellers!" Ruggles yelled, loudly enough that Jack Garrett overheard every word. "We hear tell that they are about forty Federal cavalry crossing the Rappahannock down at the ferry. Y'all had better get out of the way! We are cutting out before they take us, too."

"Take to the woods," Bainbridge advised. "Hide yourselves! They will never find you in those ravines!"

"Yes," Ruggles confirmed, "get there as quickly as y'all can! Lose no time in starting!"

"I'll do as you say, boys," Booth pledged. "Ride on! Good bye! It will never do for you to be found in *my* company!"

Then he grabbed Ruggles' leg and said in a low voice so that Garrett could not overhear, "Rest assured of one thing, good friend, John Wilkes Booth will never be taken alive!" With that the two Confederate soldiers turned and spurred their mounts back to the road. They turned south for Bowling Green.

Immediately, Booth and Herold started for the woods west of the house. "I'm damned if I will take their oath," Booth shouted over his shoulder at Jack for effect. But he knew that Jack Garrett, and through him the whole family, would be harder to deal with than ever. And how in the Hell could the Yankees have found them so fast? Booth questioned himself silently. They were all confused up in Maryland, the last we heard. Damn! Booth and Herold could not move very fast, as Booth was loaded down with the pistols, his knife, and the laborious impediment of his crutches. They disappeared into the woods, Herold having to wait for Booth to get there.

Within five minutes, however, Herold was back. "What do you think of the idea that Federal cavalry is crossing to Port Royal?" Herold asked Jack Garrett.

"I don't reckon I believe it much," Garrett responded. "Cain't figure where they would come from. No Yankees reported over thataway before. Hey, le's ask the colored boy." He pointed to a black youth coming up the lane. "He lives in Port Royal. His name is Jim. He used to belong to P. H. Pendleton in town. His daddy works for my pa here."

"Hey, Jim," Garrett called out. "Hear anything about Yankee cavalry crossing the ferry?"

"Sure have, Mist' Jack. They was getting organized in the street for a ride. Coming thisaway, I reckon. I told those two Reb horsemen about it, too." With that Jim continued towards the fields behind the house.

"Well, there you have it," Jack said. He looked at Herold intently. "Say, since you have come here my suspicions have been greatly aroused. All is not right with you Boyds. It would please me no end if y'all would leave here. We are peaceable citizens and don't want to get into any difficulty with the Federal authorities."

Herold laughed casually. "Don't make yourself alarmed about us," he said. "We will not get you into any trouble. Say, you wouldn't happen to have anything to eat?"

"No, nothing will be cooked until supper, and I 'low as how you will not get any of *that* unless you promise to leave here." Garrett was interrupted by the pounding of hooves on the highway. A large body of men was tearing up the road from Port Royal. Before Herold or Garrett could properly react, a cavalry detachment thundered by in a cloud of dust, accompanied by the creaking of leather and the clanging of sabers. They did not even pause as they passed the main gate. Indeed, it would turn out later that they had not even seen it. Jack Garrett made them out to be more like thirty men rather than forty. But they were Yankees, nonetheless, and going Hell-bent for leather toward Bowling Green.

"There goes the cavalry," remarked Garrett.

"Well, that is all," Herold muttered.

"Why are you so uneasy about these soldiers, if you are what you say you are?"

"I will tell you the truth," Herold said, rapidly cooking up another "stretcher" in his overly active mind. "Over there in Maryland the other night, we went on a spree and had a row with some soldiers, and, as we ran away, we shot at them, and, I reckon, must have hurt somebody."

"Y'all gotta leave," Garrett insisted once again. Two horsemen, trying to catch up with those who had passed a few minutes earlier, punctuated Garrett's plea.

"Is there any place to buy a horse around here?"

"No, the armies have pretty well stripped this region years ago. Everyone needs what little stock they have."

"Cain't we hire a conveyance?"

"Well, there is an old colored man named Edward Freeman over the main road there. He keeps a conveyance and often hires out."

"What do you reckon it would cost to get him to take us to Orange Courthouse?"

"Ol' Ned Freeman is mighty fond of specie," Garrett informed Herold. "He might do it for five or six dollars. But he probably will not go beyond Guinea Station."

"I do not have any specie," Herold said, reaching into his wallet, "but here is a Secretary Chase note. I will give this to get us there." Herold handed Garrett a ten dollar greenback. Herold took a small stick lying on the ground and stepped into a dusty part of the yard. He made a few calculations, stood there a moment rechecking his figures, and turned back to Garrett.

"I make that as about seven dollars and thirty cents in specie."

"I will go over and do what I can to get Freeman to take you," Garrett said, impressed by Herold's monetary effort in the dirt. "I do mightily want you all to leave, and soon." With that he started down the lane to Freeman's.

5. The Yankees By-Pass Garrett's Farm

"All right, Rollins, lead off to Bowling Green," Conger ordered. He waved his pistol at the beleaguered guide for public consumption. It seemed like the whole town had turned out to see the Union cavalry ferried across and reassembled in the main street.

"Colonel Conger, by your leave, sir," Doherty remonstrated. He knew that the men had been in the saddle nearly twenty-four hours. They were muttering among themselves, as soldiers do, and their horses were tired and growing unresponsive. "Do you plan to halt the troop for the night, sir?"

"Hell, no!" Conger said. "Any delay now, Lieutenant, may cost us our prize."

"The men and horses are worn out, sir. They need sleep. Surely, Booth cannot escape us now."

"There will be time to rest when we capture our fugitives, Lieutenant. They have encountered friends, who will assist them in many ways. Tomorrow morning may find them on fresh horses and able to outride us."

"That is my point sir. If we camp now and start early, before dawn, our men and horses will be fresh, too."

"Dammit, Lieutenant! The men and horses have not gone two miles since noon. The men have been sitting on their asses all afternoon waiting for everyone to cross that two-bit ferry! The horses have been eating up the lawns of half the houses in Port Royal."

"The men are grumbling, Colonel, and may cause trouble if we do not stop for a brief rest."

"That is your affair, *Lieutenant*. You are responsible for the behavior of the troop."

Doherty did not miss the emphasis that Conger gave the word, "Lieutenant." It sounded more disparaging each time he said it. He was truly pulling rank. Doherty, resignedly mumbled, "yes, sir," and looked at the column dejectedly, as if to say silently, I have done what I could. Sorry, men. The soldiers glared back from horseback at Conger and Baker, the sources of their misery.

"Column south, Sergeant," Doherty said to Corbett.

Corbett turned and commanded, "Forward!" He brought his arm up and down twice, signaling for a trot, to keep up with the already departed Conger and Baker. Rollins rode next to Conger, who still had his pistol in hand. The column groaned audibly, men and horses alike, as it moved on.

Those lazy bastards, Conger thought as he rode. They gripe about tired. They ought to have to walk and ride with my legs and feel the hurt I have had to put up with the whole way. That Doherty is a pain in the rump. Too aware of the feelings of his men. A good officer has to rise above his men, not be one of them.

About three miles below Port Royal, Conger saw the Freeman homestead near the road.

"Baker, take a man and go question that colored wench in the yard, yonder."

The column never halted; the interest in the Freeman place drew everyone's attention to the opposite side of the road from the Garrett farm. But, then, they were acting on a hot tip regarding Bowling Green, not Garrett's Farm. Little did they know that their quarry was within a couple of hundred yards of the road at that very minute, watching them pass by on the highway.

"Well, her man was not at home," Baker reported as he galloped up to the head of the column. "I asked her if she had seen any strange white men. She had not."

"Thank you, Lieutenant Baker," Conger said. "By the way, Mr. Rollins here informs me that there is a place up ahead before we get to Bowling Green. It is sort of a road house. We will check it out before going on. There are women there, if you catch my drift. I have heard it said that Booth cannot pass one by."

He and Baker both chuckled at Booth's womanizing reputation, perhaps a bit enviously.

"Colonel!" It was Doherty. "Look up ahead! Dust in the road! There they are! Two men, up on the ridge! Sergeant Corbett says that they have been dogging us since Port Royal!"

"Send out a squad and run them down!" Conger yelled.

"Not if you want to make Bowling Green tonight, sir. Our horses cannot make much more than a slow trot. Those boys are going at a full gallop." Doherty smugly noted that his prediction had come to pass. The men and horses were spent.

"He is right, Colonel," Baker agreed, quietly.

"Well, never mind," Conger said after a pause, "finding this feller, Jett, in Bowling Green is more important."

He, too, was finally realizing that they all, men and animals, had to save what strength they had left for the capture of Booth down the road in Bowling Green. And so Ruggles and Bainbridge, those intrepid videttes for Booth and Herold (if it were them, no one ever found out), who were on the ridge ahead, out-ran the weary cavalry, escaping in the growing gloom of darkness that settled over the woods and roads.

6. The Confederates Make Contact

When Jack Garrett came back from visiting Freeman's, he had three men with him. They found that Booth had rejoined Herold and that both were awaiting Jack on the veranda.

"What luck?" Herold asked.

"Well, Freeman was not at home. His missus told me that the cavalry was Yankee, all right. Wearing bluecoats. A couple of them stopped and asked her if she had seen any strange white men. She had not. But they are looking for someone, for sure. I 'low that I will have to take you down, myself. Otherwise you will never get out of here. When do you want to leave?"

"Tomorrow morning will be fine," Booth replied coolly. "Who are these men?"

"They are from Mosby," Jack said. "Without paroles. I told them they could come over and eat supper with us. They will be moving on later. This one is a neighbor, W. D. Newbill. The others are a cousin, Bill Lightfoot, and . . ."

Before the usual handshaking amenities could be observed, the whole crowd was called in to supper. It was consumed with a minimum of conversation, the atmosphere strained by the presence of the newcomers. Booth and the three Mosby men eyed each other cautiously. Somehow, Booth seemed to divine their true purpose, to kill him to prevent his capture by Union soldiers, if it came to that.

Mrs. Garrett tried to get a conversation going by asking Newbill about his family and his Confederate service. This provided an opening for Herold, who, as usual, could not keep his mouth shut for very long. The monologue sounded like utter nonsense, especially to Jack, Willie, and the three Mosby men, who had seen much seriousness in the service of the Confederacy. A few of the other Garretts actually thought him right smart for liquor.

"Yep," Herold bragged," I was in the Confederate army, all right. I was a member of the Thirtieth Virginia Volunteers. Company C, it was, Captain Robinson."

"I am quite well acquainted with the Thirtieth and all of its companies," Jack asserted," but I do not know of any Captain Robinson. I am certain there was none by that name."

"To tell you the truth," Herold responded, "I was there only one week. I was out on picket and in the first night was wounded. See?" He rolled up his sleeve to reveal an ugly scar. "The Yanks took me prisoner and sent me north. I was compelled to take the oath of allegiance. I been running the blockade ever since."

"Harrumph, some stuff!" muttered Willie. Newbill snorted a rude chuckle. Mrs. Garrett scowled at everyone, silently demanding manners be observed on all sides.

After supper, all the men went out to the porch. "How are you going to send us?" Booth wanted to know.

"I have not decided, yet," Jack Garrett answered. "Probably on horseback."

"Well, that is the very thing," Booth said, "send us horseback."

Garrett was getting paranoid. He immediately thought Booth's query about method was designed to ascertain how many horses the Garretts had. Perhaps he and Herold would steal a couple and flee in the dark.

"Never mind," Jack came back. "I will determine how you go before morning."

"Can we go to Guinea's rather than Orange Courthouse?" Booth asked.

"Why would you wish to go there instead of Orange?" Jack wanted to know.

"We have heard that a Maryland artillery battery is there which has not yet disbanded. If we can get there, we will be safe. Might even get horses . . . Well Davy, I think we might ought to turn in. Big day tomorrow, don't you know?"

"Where are you thinking of sleeping?" Jack said off-handedly.

Booth was taken back a bit. "Why, in the house," he said incredulously.

"No, gentlemen, you cannot sleep in the house tonight," Jack said resolutely.

"Well, sir, I daresay that anywhere would better than going up stairs with you!"

Herold entered the conversation, seeking to mollify Booth and Jack Garrett, who seemed headed for harsh words and a possible fight. "Well, we will sleep *under* the house, then."

"You cannot sleep under the house," Jack said, scoffing. "The dogs will bite you."

"Well," Herold pondered, "what is in that barn then?" He pointed over to the tobacco barn west of the house.

"Nothing but hay and fodder. And some furniture from Fredericksburg stored there since the battle."

"We will sleep in there then," Herold concluded, triumphantly.

As he and Booth set off to the tobacco barn, Jack turned to Willie Garrett and muttered quietly, "We had better lock them in for the night. I am very suspicious of those two. They might try and steal our horses and escape. Pa thinks they might be guerillas who have done something to cause them to fear arrest. He wants us to keep a sharp eye on them tonight."

"I hate to say this," Lightfoot muttered, "but I am of a mind, sorta like that ol' boy in our regiment, when he was asked what he thought of Maryland after we crossed the Potomac at Shepardstown after the fight at Gettysburg, 'To Hell with Maryland,' he said. 'I tell you, she is the most loyal state in your damned Union. You may bet your life on that!'"

"Yeah," Jack Garrett concurred. "We had a saying about Maryland, too--'We do not want her, y'all can keep her, she is the damnedyankees' Maryland, now!' We should have never tried to liberate her, either in '62 or in '63. No gratitude, I tell you, no gratitude at all."

"Well, be that as it may, Colonel Mosby wants them to come down to Hanover Junction or Ashland tomorrow. We cannot allow them to leave independently," Newbill warned. "They might stumble onto that Federal cavalry column that passed through here. Can you lock them in? Without creating a ruckus? And we really need to get that wagon from Old Freeman--and him, too, as driver, if we can. Booth cain't ride a mile."

"I gave his missus Herold's ten dollars. Freeman will be ready to move tomorrow. Willie, is that big padlock around somewhere?"

"I picked it up from the cowshed this evening. Greased it up a mite, so it will work smoothly."

Pleased with the arrangements, the Mosby men bade their farewells and left. They would hide out at their own homes until tomorrow, when they would return to help move Booth and Herold to the Hanover Junction area. They never told the Garretts about the deadlier possibilities of their assignment, the elimination of Booth and Herold. The two Garrett boys went quietly down to the barn. The barn walls were built with wide separations between the vertical boards, which allowed air to circulate and cure the tobacco as it hung from poles laid over multiple cross beams. Jack now laid his ear to one of these crevices to see if he could hear anything of the fugitive's possible plans. Meanwhile, Willie carefully clicked a large padlock on the door hasps.

Jack and Willie returned to the house for the nightly family worship. After prayers, Jack came over to Willie, as he crawled into bed upstairs. "I still do not trust those men. We had better take blankets and sleep out in one of the corn cribs, where we can guard the horses, personal like."

"Good idea," Willie agreed. They took their blankets, a Confederate-issue Enfield rifled musket, and quietly went back down stairs. They left the house silently, not telling anyone what they were doing or where they were going.

7. At the Trappe

"This is the Carter place," Rollins told Conger. "Some call it the Halfway House because it is roughly halfway between Bowling Green and Port Royal. But it is known locally as the Trappe." The windows blazed brightly and invitingly in the murkiness of the forest.

"The Trappe? Why?"

"Go on in and you will see," came the response.

"You are not going in?"

"*Hell*, no! My old lady would rawhide me good, if she ever heard I went in there!"

"Oh, for crying out loud! C'mon, Baker," Conger said. Both men dismounted and walked up to the house. Conger was limping badly. With his old wounds, he really was not up to this ride, but he bit his lower lip and stiffly mounted the stairs to the porch.

The door swung open and Mrs. Carter stepped out. Her bustier emphasized her ample bosom, which was just barely covered by a skimpy cloak that could hardly be called a robe. "Well, well, hel-lo, gentlemen," she purred.

"Hey! It is a whorehouse!" a trooper in the column yelled with glee. The whole column woke up. They were not *that* tired, after all.

"As you were!" Doherty commanded. Then, he said softly to Sergeant Corbett, "Watch the men. And especially Rollins. Do not let him get away."

Corbett was a self-castrated eunuch. He had performed the job with a pair of scissors in a religious frenzy, and had, inadvertently, nearly killed himself. He did it as an act of contrition after he had been tormented by the lustful thoughts two prostitutes had aroused in him while he was proselytizing on a Boston Street corner. He hated the lure of "Jezebels," as he called the kind of women whoremongering soldiers had appreciated since the beginning of time.

"You can trust me, sir!" he said with conviction. "I will keep the men pure in deed, if not in thought. And Mr. Rollins will be here when you return."

Doherty dismounted--way too quickly, thought the censorious Corbett--and followed Conger and Baker into the Trappe.

Corbett's would not be an easy task. "Hello, boys!" said one well-endowed young thing, so scantily clad that her better qualities literally fell out of the open second story window she was leaning through. "Come on up!"

"Have I got something special for you," a girl called invitingly from the porch.

"O-o-o-o! You're cute," another cooed from the doorway as Doherty brushed past. Doherty deftly sidestepped her grasping arms.

"Watch out, Lieutenant. Them Southern breastworks can be hard to take," a trooper shouted out of the darkness. The whole column laughed and howled, one of them making a pretty passable bird call, while another enthusiastically made a vulgar kissing sound. Even the horses had perked up, snorting, shaking their heads, and swishing their tails. A scowling Corbett rode forward to block any contact between the girls and the column. From inside the house, from one of the girls, came a plaintive, wailing tune:

The man that has good whiskey
And giveth his neighbor none,
Shan't have any of my good whiskey
When his good whiskey is gone
When . . .

"Now, all together, boys," she called out, merrily, and the whole troop sang movingly, off-key:

. . . When his good whiskey is gone

Inside, Conger was trying to elicit the usual information about Booth and his allies. But Mrs. Carter and several more of her girls were interested in matters of a more prurient nature.

"Did you see some men ride by here yesterday or today?"

"Aw, come on, honey, have a drink," Mrs. Carter said, taking Conger by the arm.

"Please, madam!" Conger snapped. "I wish merely to secure information. It is very important." Then he cleverly put new meaning into the conversation. "The men we seek brutally ravished a young lady and we are in pursuit of them."

"Maybe we should tell," hinted one girl.

"Well, go ahead," said Mrs. Carter dejectedly. "It is just like Yankees not to appreciate the finer things in life." Several of the girls tittered concupiscently.

"Do you know something, Miss?" Doherty asked one of them.

"Well, four men stopped here yesterday."

"Were they all mounted?"

"They certainly were," Mrs. Carter interjected. She and the girls laughed.

"Please, ladies," Lieutenant Baker scolded. "What about their horses?"

"Well," one girl said, "there were four men and three horses. Two of them rode in twain."

"One of them have crutches and a game leg?" Conger asked, taking control, once again.

"Oh, no," the women chorused.

"But, they all came back today around noon. Said they had stayed at Bowling Green," the talkative girl said. "One of them was Willie Jett. He said something about spending the night at Clarke's place below Bowling Green."

"Oh, no, Janie," another said. "It was that other private who said that. There were two privates, one lieutenant, and the young man in regular clothes." Obviously the ladies were well-schooled in the finer aspects of military rank and apparel.

"Yes," Janie confirmed, "that is right! And they came back by today *without* that Jett feller."

"You sure they were the same men both times?" Conger pressed.

"Yes, except that the sweet one, Willie Jett, did not come back today. The rest all did. Went toward Port Royal."

"Are you *sure* that you would not like to let the men have a drink, or *something?* They look pretty done in," pleaded Mrs. Carter. She winked at Doherty, who actually blushed.

"Too done in for what *you* have in mind, madam, I assure you. Come on," Conger said with disgust, turning and limping toward the door.

"Let us get the Hell out of here!" He gave Doherty a dirty look as he passed toward the door.

"Damnedyankees," Mrs. Carter muttered under her breath. Baker looked back sharply. "Good bye, gentlemen," she said charmingly. "Sorry we could not do more for you, tonight." Her smile was naughty. Her lips trembled ever so slightly, as she ran her tongue over them. "God!" Doherty thought, "She is a *real* humdinger!"

"'Bye, fellas," the girl in the window yelled out, waving her hand so enthusiastically that everything about her bounced invitingly.

"Good bye, beautiful!" one trooper called out.

"I love you, darling!" a blond-haired youngster avowed.

"*Wait* for me, my sweet!" a corporal begged, arms spread wide.

"I will be back!" another trooper yelled.

"Lieutenant!" Conger screamed to Doherty, "Look to this group of rowdies, *sir*, if you will, and bring them under discipline!"

Doherty could hardly keep from laughing. "Si-lence," his voice broke. Regaining his composure, he ordered, "No talking in ranks! Sergeant reform the column! Column of twos!"

"What do you think?" Baker asked Conger. "Obviously Booth did not get to here. He has got to be somewhere between here and the ferry."

"We go for the sure thing. I bet Jett is still at his girlfriend's place, the Star Hotel. And he will know where Booth is. Let's go get him, now, tonight."

The girls jumped up and down and waved on the porch and from the windows, as the cavalrymen headed for Bowling Green in silence. When the last trooper, far from the gaze of the officers up front, was about to pass beyond the halo of light, he turned in his saddle and threw the girls a grandiose kiss. Then, followed by the squealing of the girls, they disappeared into the darkness, cursing John Wilkes Booth and Colonel Conger for ruining what could have been a great evening.

8. Asleep In the Barn

"John, they have locked us in! Le's shoot the hasps off and get the Hell out of here." Herold was on the verge of panic.

"Relax, Dave," Booth reassured him. "Nothing will happen. We are safe in here. No one can come in, either. The locked door makes this building appear unoccupied."

"But what if they send for the Federal cavalry?"

"They will *not*, I tell you. The Garretts are true to The Cause. They have fought for it and put their hearts and souls into it. They have to live here. They would not ruin their lives to turn us in."

Herold was not so sure, but he kept his doubts hidden. Those people would turn us over in a second, if there was a buck in it, he thought. *I* would turn *them* in for a reward, and you can lay to that, for sure.

The inside of the barn was roomy and drafty, the latter by design. It was designed to keep curing tobacco constantly exposed to the air. But it was not as spacious as it seemed from the outside. A good section of the barn was packed with the furniture of people who had lost their homes in Fredericksburg and the surrounding area to the Yankee invasion. The floor was straw covered in sections, and some fodder for the cattle and horses kept dry in another part of the building.

Booth and Herold scraped some straw together and laid out their blankets, generously provided by the Garretts. Booth marveled how Herold, panic-stricken one moment, could fall asleep, in what seemed like seconds, in the next. But he could not. Booth stared at the rafters, the hanging cobwebs fairly seemed to glow in the dim half-light of the tobacco barn. Odd, . . . it almost looked like falling snow . . .

Once I was pure as the snow--but I fell:
Fell, like the snowflakes, from heaven to Hell:
Fell, to be trampled as the filth of the street;
Fell, to be scoffed, to be spit on, and beat.
Pleading,
Cursing,
Dreading to die,
Selling my soul to whoever would buy,
Dealing in shame for a morsel of bread,
Hating the living and fearing the dead.
Merciful God! Have I fallen so low?
And yet I was once like this beautiful snow!

Once I was fair as the beautiful snow,
With an eye like its crystals, a heart like its glow:
Once I was loved for my innocent grace,
Flattered and sought for the charm of my face.
Father,
Mother,
Sisters all,

God, and myself, I have lost by my fall.
The veriest wretch that goes shivering by
Will take a wide sweep, lest I wander too nigh;
For all that is on or about me, I know
There is nothing that's pure but the beautiful snow.

How strange it should be that this beautiful snow
Should fall on a sinner with nowhere to go.
How strange it should be, when the night comes again,
If the snow and the ice struck my desperate brain!
Fainting,
Freezing,
Dying alone,
Too wicked for prayer, too weak for my moan
To be heard in the crash of the crazy town
Gone mad in its joy at the snow's coming down;
To lie and to die in my terrible woe,
With a bed and a shroud of the beautiful snow! . . .

9. The Yankees at Bowling Green

"Yonder is Bowling Green," Rollins told Conger. "The Star Hotel ain't much, but it is that bigger building in the center, there. It is owned by Mrs. Julia Gouldman. She is the one my wife thinks has a daughter what is sweet on Willie Jett--or him on her."

Across the square were the burned-out remnants of the Caroline County Courthouse, which had once dwarfed the Star Hotel, until the black infantry of Grant's IX Corps had torched it in May 1864. It had been a terrifying sight for the citizens of Bowling Green, five thousand freed slaves in blue uniform, armed to the teeth, singing "John Brown's Body lies a' moldering in the grave, as we go marching on!" The Colored Troops (as the Union government denominated them, officially) had verbally insulted the residents, mostly women and children, in the "grossest manner," according to a correspondent of the New York *Daily News*.

The soldiers threw away their army rations and took more palatable civilian food, leaving none to feed the population. Townspeople said that three rapes occurred, but the army denied that any had been reported. None were punished. One of the victims had committed suicide. So, at least, the story went. Baker and Doherty doubted that a town so thoroughly treed would challenge the Booth pursuit column, but Conger was taking no chances.

"Sergeant Corbett. Stay here with all of the number twos and fours." Conger was indicating, in a military way, that he wanted the left file to stay on the edge of town. The men had counted off by fours back at Belle Plain before they had started. "The rest of you come with me. Shut up, Lieutenant!"

Conger's rude comment prevented Lieutenant Doherty from protesting that the Colonel was issuing orders directly to his men, rather than through him. Nonetheless, Corbett looked at Doherty for confirmation. Doherty nodded. Corbett took the left file off the road and dismounted. He posted sentries to prevent anyone from leaving town. The rest of the column followed Rollins into the Gouldman House, as the business was called, in the style of the times, despite the dilapidated sign, which read, "Star Hotel," that appeared over the front veranda.

"Surround the building," Conger said to the troopers. A look at Lieutenant Doherty warned that no argument would be allowed. "Give me enough time to get around back, Baker, and then wake them up." But as Conger and several troopers moved to the back of the hotel, a dog began to bark loudly from within. By the time they got to the back door a bewildered black man was standing in it, half awake.

"We are looking for some men and believe they are in this house," Conger said.

"What do you mean, waking all these folks up?" It was a big, brassy black woman who elbowed her way between Conger and the black man, effectively blocking the door. And she was wide awake.

"Do not sass me, Auntie," Conger growled, drawing his revolver." I am not in the mood. Is there a man with a broken leg in here?"

"Well, they is some men here, but no one is lame," the woman said.

"Is there a man named Jett in here?"

"Yessir. He come to see his gal."

"Which room is he in?"

"First right, up the main stairs, sir."

Conger pushed the two blacks aside with his gun hand and met Baker and Doherty, who had just broken through the front door, in the main hall at the foot of the stairs. A white woman came into the room. She held a candle in her hand. Everything was yellow and ghostly in the light it threw.

"I am Mrs. Julia Gouldman," she said. "My husband is away, and I am here alone with my children and a visitor, Mr. Jett. He is a friend of my daughter, you know. Is there anything wrong?"

"Where is this Mr. Jett, ma'am?" Baker asked.

"He is upstairs in the first room on the right, sleeping with my son, who is recovering from a war wound. What is wrong?"

"Lead us up," Baker ordered.

But Conger thought better of it. "No, you stay here, lady. I will have that candle and go up myself."

A befuddled Mrs. Gouldman handed over the candlestick, reluctantly. "Do not hurt my son!" she begged.

Conger went up slowly and quietly, hugging the wall, revolver in one hand, candlestick in the other. The door on the right was not locked. Well-oiled, too! Not a creak as he opened the door. Conger fairly leaped into the room. Two men were in the bed across the room. One of them sat up. Conger cocked his pistol and leveled it at him.

"Willie Jett?"

"Y-y-yes, sir," Jett replied.

"Get up and get dressed. I want you."

Jett arose and began to put on his clothes. Meanwhile, there was a pounding of boots on the stairs. Baker and Doherty came into the room. Mrs. Gouldman and a couple of troopers followed them in, a few moments later.

"Is there some room where we can talk to this young man privately?" Conger questioned Mrs. Goldman.

"Any room up here is fine. None are occupied but this one. The war has not been good for business."

"Take him next door," Conger said to Baker and Doherty. "Do not let him escape." Jett was literally shaking in his boots by now.

Conger followed the trio into the empty room. "All right, you little jackanapes," Conger snarled, in a low voice to keep Mrs. Gouldman from hearing. "Where is Booth? Where is Herold?"

"C-can I speak to you alone?" He asked Conger." I-I think I know what you want."

Conger motioned for Baker and Doherty to leave.

"Upon my honor as a gentleman," Jett began, "I will tell you all I know, if you will shield me from complicity in this whole matter."

His honor as a gentleman! Conger thought. He nearly choked. If he did not know so much, I would shoot him just for the pleasure of it. It was these damned Southern *Gentlemen* who caused this war. Honor! He mentally grabbed a hold on himself.

"Yes, if we get Booth," he said. Hell, let Stanton sort out who would be tried and who would go free, Conger figured silently. What Jett does not know of the future will not matter.

"Booth is at the Richard Garrett place, about three miles this side of Port Royal. My lieutenant and another soldier took him there yesterday evening."

"Why . . . we just came past there earlier!"

"Oh? I supposed you were up from Richmond."

"No, we are out of the District. Who are those other men you spoke of--your companions?"

Jett hesitated.

"Come on, either you spill all of it or you will swing outside this hotel, in front of God and everybody. You would not want your girl to see you kick, now, would you?"

"They are Lieutenant Tibby Ruggles and Private Fellow Bainbridge."

"Alright, you are under arrest. You will lead us to Booth and Herold. If they are there and we fail to get them, it will be *my* fault. But if they are *not* there, especially Booth, it will be *your* neck. And that is a promise!"

Jett's horse was brought up from the stable. Conger limped out onto the porch and saw that once again, Doherty's men were asleep and disorganized.

"Get your troop organized and ready to ride, *Lieutenant!*" Conger ordered.

But before Doherty could move, Conger changed his mind. He turned to the bugler and ordered him to sound "Boots and Saddles." The commotion aroused the whole town, and Conger led the column north past the silent citizens, staring down from bedroom windows and gawking from their verandas.

"We go in style," he explained to Baker, "to overawe these damned Rebels."

But Doherty wondered silently if such bravado would not tip off an informant who might get to Booth before them. Any old horse in town could beat these broken down cavalry nags back to Garrett's. Worse yet, there was a Confederate army signal tower on the roof of the Star Hotel. If a signalman were still in town, no telling what might be awaiting them on the road back towards Port Royal . . .

The column picked up Sergeant Corbett and the men left outside Bowling Green and headed for Port Royal again. Conger warned Jett and

Rollins not to miss the turnoff to Garrett's farm, lest they forfeit their lives to a short rope and a long drop.

10. Initial Confrontation at the Garrett House

"This is Garrett's," Willie Jett said.

"Are you sure?" Conger asked, the implicit tone of warning in his voice. "I am not fooling. I will hang the man who misleads me."

"He is right, Colonel," Rollins said. "This is Garrett's main gate. I swear it."

"What is the layout? Jett, you have seen it before."

"They is an old tobacco barn straight ahead, and the family's house to the left as you go in. That is all I know. Lots of locust and apple trees in the yard."

"Doherty," Conger said, "detail four men to keep these two under guard. They had better be here when this is all over with, too."

Taking Baker with him, Conger rode into the farm yard. The two men had hardly entered when the hounds started baying and yelping at this undesired invasion of their territory. The two detectives soon returned, having confirmed the truth of Jett's description of the farm's layout.

"Hold on a little longer, men. Booth's in there, for sure! Lieutenant Doherty, have your men follow me and surround the house. Move quietly, no noise, no talking!"

Doherty gave the signal to move forward, allowing himself a wry grin. Well, I am in command again. Hell, genius, he thought, silently deriding Conger, you already have the dogs up. The house will soon follow. Would not be surprised if Booth and Herold are already headed for the woods.

Baker spryly leaped up on the porch and banged on the door with his revolver butt. Out in the yard, one of the more aggressive dogs yipped off in pain as a well-placed kick from a cavalry boot found its mark. The remainder of the pack still raised a ruckus, but from a safe distance.

"Open up in there! Be quick about it!" Baker shouted.

There was a rustling noise and the sound of wood scraping against wood. A window next to the door was raised. Old Richard Garrett stuck his head out to see what the matter was. Baker grabbed his arm and put his pistol to the man's head.

"We are Federal officers," Baker snarled.

"Open the door! Get a light and be right quick about it!" The new voice belonged to Conger, who had just arrived on the porch.

Garrett did as he was ordered. He opened the door, a lighted candle in his hand.

"Where are they? What do you mean by sheltering the murderers of the President?" Conger shot his questions so quickly that none could have been answered.

Garrett was bewildereded and frightened. He had a tendency to stutter, and the affliction seized upon him in all its magnitude now. His response was a tongue-tied, "wha' . . . wha' . . . I . . . I . . . ."

"Where are the two men who have been staying here the past two days?" Conger yelled.

"Th-th-they are no, no . . . not he-here," Garrett stammered.

"Do not tell me that," Conger warned, cocking his pistol. "They *are* here!"

Garrett, his body convulsed with tremblings, could do nothing but attempt to stutter out more gibberish.

Conger turned to a trooper, "Soldier go get a rope! I aim to put this old miscreant to the top of one of these trees, and right now!"

In the midst of this exchange, Mrs. Garrett called out from behind a door down the hall, "Father, here are your clothes, dress yourself!" Nineteenth century propriety could be asserted at the oddest times.

"Search this place, Lieutenant!" Conger raged.

"But there are unclad women about, sir!" Doherty objected. More of that Victorian propriety intervened, once again.

"Do not hang him, sir, please," the voice of Mrs. Garrett begged. Lucinda Holloway also pleaded for mercy. The youngest Garrett girl began to sob and moan, "Papa, oh, Papa!" in the midst of her tears.

Conger dragged Garrett out of the house and made him stand on a chopping block. A rope was thrown over a tree limb above his head and fastened to his neck. Half a dozen men stood ready to hoist him up so that he would slowly strangle.

"Colonel!" The voice was from Corporal Oliver Lonkey, who had been detailed to guard the back of the house. "Hold on, sir! I have someone here from behind the house that can help out."

Into the midst of federals came a man, dressed in Rebel gray, escorted by a trooper in Union blue.

"I heard the uproar and came up to help out," said the Confederate soldier. "This man nearly shot me. I am Jack Garrett. This is my father. Do not hurt him. Give him time. He is tongue-tied and cannot talk hurriedly. What do you gentlemen want with the two men the corporal says you are looking for?"

"That is none of your business, Reb," Conger said icily. "We know they are here. We have Jett out at the road and he says he left them here. We mean to have them. If you do not tell us instantly, we will hang you and the old man and burn this house to the ground. Now make haste, my patience is wearing mighty thin."

"Please, don't hurt my father. Father, it is best to tell them. Gentlemen, if you want to know where those men are, I will take you to the place. They did not sleep in the house tonight, but are in an outhouse."

In those days, an outhouse could be any building away from the main home, not specifically a privy, as is commonly thought today. So, Jack Garrett pointed to the darkened barn-like structure off to the west.

"My brother and I locked them in last night--they cannot get out."

"What brother?"

"Willie. He and I have been sleeping in the corncrib to guard our horses. We were afraid the men might try to steal them. Some of your men have him out back there. He has the key."

"Baker, take that boy," he pointed to young Richard, who had come down to watch the proceedings, "and go get the key from brother Willie. Jack Garrett and I will meet you at the barn. Bring everyone along, including Willie. Doherty, leave a half dozen men under Sergeant Wendell to guard the house. And keep the old man on the block, ready to swing. The rest of you surround the tobacco barn. Doherty, you and Sergeant Corbett, get them moving. Now!"

11. Herold Surrenders

"Dave, they are here."

"Huh? Humph. What is the matter? Is it time to go?"

"A cavalryman has just ridden around the barn. I could hear his saber clanking. There! He stopped and looked in at the back corner! There he goes, back up towards the house!"

"What? Oh, no. Oh my God! Aw-w-w, mother! . . . We had better give up."

"I will suffer death first," Booth swore. "Come on. They are still up at the house. The door is still locked. Let us see if we cannot break through the wall and take to the woods."

Both men went to the back wall of the barn away from the house.

"Look for a weak or loose board," Booth said.

"I cain't find any," Herold whined.

Booth sat down and began to kick at one wood panel with his good leg. "Here, Davy, help me! Let us kick together!"

The board moved but a few inches, not yielding enough to let either man through.

"John, I cannot kick hard enough left footed. Cain't we switch sides?"

"Be careful of my broken leg. Now, kick!"

But left-footed or right-footed, the panel yielded only a few inches more to Herold's desperate battering. Still not enough to pass either man through.

Herold began to thrash about angrily in the straw, kicking at the blankets that had once covered him.

"Sh-h-h," Booth cautioned him quietly. "Someone is coming down. Do not make any noise. Maybe they will go off, thinking we are not here."

This hope filled fragment of naïveté was quickly blown away, when Lieutenant Baker yelled out, "You men had better come out of there. We know who you are. I want you to surrender. If you do not, I will burn the barn down in fifteen minutes."

Herold looked at Booth. Even through the darkness, Booth knew his companion's eyes were wide with fear. Booth wondered if these were Confederates who had come to rescue them or Yankees who had come to arrest them. The actor thought a moment, lining out his part, as it were. Then he spoke, putting on a bold front, "Who are you?"

Conger whispered quietly in Baker's ear. "Do not, by any remark made to him, allow him to know who we are. You need not tell him who we are. If he thinks we are Rebels, or thinks we are his friends, we will take advantage of it. We will not lie to him about it, but we need not answer any questions that have any reference to that subject. Simply insist on his coming out . . . if he will."

Lieutenant Baker nodded. "Never mind who *we* are. We know who *you* are and you had better come out and deliver yourselves up."

The outside of the barn grew bright, as the weary troopers of the Sixteenth New York gathered brush and loose boards and began to build numerous small fires. Some of the men gathered around the flames to warm themselves. Others actually fell asleep. Conger was furious. He turned to Lieutenant Doherty, who was petulantly standing aside, as usual, letting Conger and his minion, Baker, run things.

"Lieutenant Doherty," he shouted, "you damned cowardly scoundrel"--this unfairly to a man who had served with distinction in four crack combat units since 1861--"can you not control your men? Damn it!

If you do not keep those cowards in their places here, those fellows in the barn will get away. Get their asses back in position now!"

The two officers went down opposite sides of the barn, rousting out the tired soldiers from their fires and blankets and placing them back in line. "You, Sergeant Corbett," Conger said, placing a stick on the ground near the rear of one wall and standing him next to it, "do not leave your post Sergeant, on any condition."

"Yessir," Corbett intoned.

Returning to the front door, Lieutenant Doherty said, "I think we ought to wait for daylight. They are trapped and cannot go anywhere."

"Hell, no! We are going to flush them out, here and now." Although Conger did not say it, he was not about to share the reward money with any possible reinforcements the dawn might bring. It was bad enough to split with twenty-eight others of all ranks.

Colonel Conger grabbed hold of Jack Garrett. There was a rustling and creaking about the main door. Booth heard the lock snap open. "Now listen carefully, Reb," Conger whispered threateningly in his ear, resting his revolver along Garrett's shoulder with the barrel pointed at his neck. "You are going to go in there to your friends and demand their arms and bring them out. If you fail, we will burn this barn down on top of them."

Baker opened the door and Conger gave Garrett a rude shove. He stumbled into the dark maw of the building, momentarily blind from the blackness of the interior. Baker shouted after him, "We are going to send in this man, on whose premises you are, to get your arms, and you must come out and deliver yourselves up."

"Gentlemen," Garrett almost whispered as he talked. "The cavalry are after you. You are the ones. You had better give yourselves up."

"You have implicated me," Booth snarled. "You damn Judas! Get out of here! You have betrayed me!"

Lieutenant Baker, hearing the oaths Booth threw at Garrett, spoke up once again. "We sent this young man, in whose custody we find you. Give him your arms and surrender or we shall burn the barn and have a bonfire *and* a shooting match."

"There are nearly fifty armed men out there," said Garrett, amazed at Booth's hesitation in the face of such odds. "Escape is impossible. Be reasonable and surrender yourself."

Booth glowered at Garrett, who could just make out the hatred in those piercing, hazel eyes, glowing like those of a wild, enraged cat.

"The word surrender is not in my vocabulary," Booth snapped. "I have never learned the meaning of that. You vile traitor! I have half a mind to kill you right here!" He reached to his belt. Garrett thought he was going for one of his revolvers and beat a hasty retreat.

"Captain, let me out. I will do anything I can for you, but I cain't risk my life in here. Lemme out!"

"Sir," Garrett said to Colonel Conger, once safely outside, "he will not give up. I will not go back in there again. He has threatened to kill me."

"How do you know he was going to harm you?" Conger said with incredulity in his voice.

"He reached for his pistol in the hay behind him, and I came out. My life is very dear to me. I would not like to risk it in that barn again."

Then Garrett looked at the lit candle that Lieutenant Baker had been holding in his hand during the negotiations. "You had etter put that out or he will shoot you by its light," Garrett said.

Baker placed the candle down in the dirt near the door, so that its glow would illuminate the front of the barn. He wanted no one to slip out in the dark. But in the romantic fashion of thousands of men who had died on both sides during that bloodiest of all American wars, he refused to stand in the darkness. Honor demanded that he stand within the arc of light, to be seen by all, friend and foe alike. He placed Jack and Willie nearby, but separated, each with a guard, ordered to shoot them down at the first shot fired from the barn.

"Come, come, gentlemen," Baker called out. "Time's awastin'. Surrender now. I will give you no more than ten minutes. Then, we torch the barn."

"Gentlemen," Booth yelled back; or, rather, his voice boomed back, so resonant and full of timbre that it could be heard clear to the highway, as it reverberated out on the night zephyrs. There was no fear in it. Rather, it rang with the note of command. "Give me time for reflection! You have spoiled my plans; I was going to Mexico to make my fortune."

"Your fortune has already been assured. Come out!"

"Now, now, gentlemen, if I have done anything, I did it for the good of my country; at least I pray that I did so."

After some pause, Booth spoke again. "I am alone; there is no one in here with me."

"No, sir. We know that *two* men went in there and two must come out," Baker asserted firmly.

"Oh, God, Johnny!" pleaded Herold, in quiet desperation. "I do not want to die. Le's give it up. Please!"

"I am not going to surrender only to be mocked and hanged later. Come on, Davy! Let us give them one last, good fight, just like Richard III."

"What the Hell has some English king from hundreds of years ago got to do with this? I want to go out and save *me*--in the here and now!"

"Surrender, *boy*, if you must. But as for me, I will die like a *man!*"

"Please, Johnny," Herold pleaded. The term "boy" had cut through his soul like a knife, but fear and self preservation overrode all other emotions in Herold's panic-stricken mind.

"Alright Davy. I will do what I can to save you." Booth raised his voice aloud again. Again Baker was impressed with its force and clarity. "There is a man here who wishes very much to surrender."

Then Booth turned on Herold and snapped loud enough for Baker to hear, "Leave *me*, will you? You little rat! Go! I would not have you to stay with me. Get out before I shoot you and blow my own brains out!"

Herold did not catch on to the ruse Booth had created for him. "I *am* going! I do not intend to be burnt alive!" Herold ran up and shook the door, which had the lock slipped through the hasp again. "Let me out! I know nothing of this man in here."

"Let him out, Captain," Booth said resignedly. "This young man is innocent." He thought for a moment, and then spoke again, "I want you to take careful notice of one thing. The gentleman whose place this place, Mr. Garrett, nor any of his family, knows who I am, or what I have done."

Lieutenant Doherty, attempting to assume a larger role for himself after Conger's previous rebuke, yelled back to Herold, "Bring out the arms and you can come out."

"I have no arms," Herold cried out, then beginning to sob.

"But you *have*," Lieutenant Baker insisted, jockeying for a more commanding position, as befitted a cousin of the head of the National Detective Police. "You brought a carbine across the river. You must hand it out!"

Booth interjected loudly here. "He has no arms. They are mine and *I* have them."

Baker yelled back, angrily, "This man carried a carbine, and he must hand it out!"

"Upon the word and honor of a gentleman, he has no arms. The arms are mine, and I shall keep them."

"Please, God!" Herold prayed again. "He will shoot me! Merciful Jesus! Please let me come out!"

"We had better let him out," Doherty said to Baker.

"No," Baker replied. "Wait until Colonel Conger comes--here he is!"

"I got one of the Garrett boys piling up pine boards and twigs at the rear corner next to the straw inside. Never mind the arms," Conger ordered, gasping in pain from his exertions. which had caused his unhealed wounds to be aggrivated. "If we can get one of the men out, let us do it, and wait no longer. I am going back to supervise preparations for the fire."

Richard Garrett ran up to Conger as he went to the back of the barn. "I cain't pile up no more wood and sticks, Mister. He said he would shoot me if'n I did."

"That's all right, sonny," Conger reassured him. "We have got enough to do the job up right."

Back at the front door, the competition between Doherty and Baker intensified. "I will take that man out myself!" Lieutenant Doherty said, as Conger disappeared around the corner once again. He motioned to a trooper by the door who then took the lock out of the hasp and opened the door slightly.

"Whoever you are, put out your hands! Let me see your hands!" Doherty ordered. Herold did as he was told, and Doherty grabbed him and pulled the badly frightened, tear-stained boy out into the night.

"I am not Booth!" he whined. Nobody paid any attention to his blubbering. Herold was relieved of his gloves, pocketknife, and a piece of a page out of an atlas. It was part of a map of Virginia from a school book. Manacles were then placed on his wrists.

Doherty grabbed him by the collar. "Come and stand up by the house," he said, pulling Herold along. Herold continued whimpering, sometimes crying like a child.

"Let me go away," Herold pleaded.

"Not on your tintype, sonny boy," Doherty said, gruffly.

"Let me go around here, then. I will not leave. I will not go away."

"No, sir," Doherty said, again.

"Who is that man in the barn?" Herold asked, feigning a wide-eyed innocence.

Doherty could not believe his ears. "Why, you know very well who it is."

"No, I do not, Herold insisted. He told me his name was Boyd."

"It is Booth and you know it," Doherty retorted.

"No, I did not know it. I did not know that it was Booth."

Lieutenant Doherty called out to a trooper at the Garrett house, "Millington! Tie this fool to a tree with your picket rope. If he keeps on whimpering, gag him."

"No, don't. Let me stay loose, I will not run."

"Who was in the barn with you? Was it Booth?" Doherty tried one more time.

"Yes," Herold owned up. "Booth is in the barn."

"Tie him up!" Doherty ordered.

"That is not fair, sir! I told you what you wanted. . . . . Ahh! Not so tight!" Herold complained as Trooper John Millington lashed him to a tree beside the Garrett's front porch.

"Shut up, Reb," came the trooper's insensitive reply.

Herold kept trying. "You know, I always liked Mr. Lincoln's jokes. . . ." The rest Doherty could not hear as he rushed back toward the tobacco barn, still shaking his head in amazement.

12. The Death of John Wilkes Booth

Back at the barn, Doherty's temporary absence left the field to Baker. He called out to Booth, "You had better come out, too, and surrender. You have five minutes or we fire the barn!"

Evidently, Booth still was not sure if he faced Yankees or possibly a Confederate unit come to rescue him. "Tell me who you are and what you want of me, he demanded. It may be I am being taken by friends."

"It makes no difference who *we* are," Baker said. "We want *you*. We have fifty well-armed men around this barn. You cannot escape and we do not wish to kill you."

Booth paused to ponder a bit. "Captain, this is a hard case, I swear. I am a cripple; I have got but one leg. Give me a chance. Draw up your men in line of battle twenty yards from the door and I will fight your whole command."

"We are not here to *fight* you," an exasperated Baker retorted. "We are here to *take* you. You are now free to come out and surrender."

"Give me a little time to consider," Booth stalled.

"Very well," Baker said with a sigh. "You can have two more minutes."

Booth took most of the allotted time before he answered. "Captain, I believe you to be a brave and honorable man. I have had half a dozen chances to shoot you. I have a bead drawn on you now, and could pull the trigger, but I do not wish to do it. Withdraw your men from the door, any distance, and I will come out. Give me this chance for my life, Captain, for I will not be taken alive."

"Your time is up!" snapped Lieutenant Baker. "We shall wait no longer. We shall fire the barn."

"Well then, my brave boys, you may prepare a stretcher for me .. . One more stain on the glorious old banner!" Booth said, referring to his love of the pre-war Old Glory and Lincoln's defiling of it, as stated in his "To Whom It May Concern" letter, which he had locked up some time ago in his brother-in-law's safe.

Colonel Conger came around the corner of the barn. "Are you ready?" he asked.

"Yes," Baker said.

Conger limped back around the corner to the rear of the barn, where he picked up a six inch twisted straw fuse and lit it with a match. The acrid smell of sulfur drifted in the night air. Conger waited a moment for the fuse to flare up and get going. Then he threw it through the crack into the hay and straw on the other side. The dry straw flashed so quickly, it was as if it exploded. The flames raced along the length of the barn where the straw and fodder were piled. The open walls of the tobacco barn let in massive amounts of air, which fueled the blaze and sucked the flames all the way to the rafters. It followed the trail of straw under the dry, wooden furniture piled in the back of the barn. The loosely stacked, prized pieces, so meticulously rescued from the war, now fell victim to its *Götterdämmerung*. The very cobwebs seemed to breathe fire, as they disappeared in a waft of super-heated air.

Before the blaze was set, the soldiers had all been easily visible around their lights and bonfires to Booth in the darkened barn. Now the situation was reversed. Booth was in the spotlight he cherished so much while on stage. He spun around as agilely as his crutches would allow, carbine in hand, working the lever. He moved along the wall, peering through the ventilation cracks between the boards, looking for the man who set the fire. But the pace and ferocity of the flames seemed to blind him, temporarily. He leaned back from the fierce heat and bumped a small table in the middle of the floor. Throwing the carbine down, he grabbed the table by one leg, as if he would flip it over and extinguish the blaze with its top. But the fire was too far gone to submit to half measures. Already the roof was catching. Smoke rolled along the ridge pole and out through the openings in the walls. Booth consigned the table to the flames.

Now fully aware of the fire's intensity, Booth turned back toward the front door. Conger raced around the barn to meet him in front. Booth threw down one crutch and drew a revolver. The other was holstered on his belt next to the sheathed Bowie knife. It was his moment in the sun, the thing he had treasured all his life. He drew himself up to full height. His hair blew in the wind created by the miniature firestorm behind him. The light flickered all around, crowning him with a ghostly aura, outlining his tousled hair like the halo highlighting a holy figure in some medieval painting. His alabaster forehead glowed red from the reflected fire, his pupils glistened like lumps of coal, his lips drawn tightly in a grim, determined frown.

Outside, the soldiers temporarily scattered from the flames. Their officers stood transfixed by the drama unfolding before them. Booth threw down his second crutch. He was standing free on his own legs for the last time. The Booth of old. The premier actor of his day. The greatest scene-stealer of the era. This was in his finest hour, his final role, standing bravely without a sign of fear at the tremendous odds arraigned against him. He was the last Confederate hero, the embodiment of Richard III at Bosworth Field, fighting gamely to the end. He sprang forward, oblivious to the sudden pain that shot up his leg, his revolver ready for action.

He remembered something he had said to his sister, Asia, when she asked him why he had to have the east-facing bedroom in the garret. No setting sun for me. It is too melancholy--let me see him rise.

But he would not see his beloved rising sun. His father had pronounced his fate years before. The good do not always win, he had said. So, too, had Asia. I am not to drown, hang, or burn, although my sister has believed I am a predestined martyr of some sort, Johnny remembered. And it was his own stated desire as a youth that he should die with the satisfaction of knowing he had done something never before accomplished by any other man; something no other man would do. But he was damned if he would die strangling at the end of a Yankee noose in a dank prison courtyard, as had his friend John Yates Beall before him, or swing in front of a sensation-seeking public, like old Osawatomie John Brown.

A shot rang out. Booth pitched forward on his face. Baker fumbled with the lock, tearing it out of the hasp and desperately throwing it aside. He sprang into the barn, closely followed by Doherty, who had just returned from securing Herold. Conger and Jack Garrett piled in after them. Baker grabbed Booth's gun hand and wrenched the revolver away. Jack Garrett leaped toward the fire.

"Save my property! Help put out the fire," he shouted.

"You men," Conger shouted at the soldiers congregating at the door. "Get in here and put out the flames!"

Conger then looked at the dying Booth, held up in Baker's arms. The wound at the back of his neck was visible. "He has shot himself," Conger asserted, more than a little astonished.

"No, he did not either," Baker retorted firmly.

"It is Booth, all right," Doherty interjected. "I know him, personally, from a theater party."

Conger produced a photograph and the reward poster, with its written description of Lincoln's assailant. They confirmed Doherty's statement.

"It *is* John Wilkes Booth, the famous actor," said Baker, as if he could not trust Doherty. Standing nearby, Richard Garrett realized for the first time who the wounded, alleged Confederate soldier, Boyd, really was. He ran to spread the news to his family.

"Whereabouts is he shot?" Conger asked. "In the neck or the head?" Baker indicated the location of the wound, just below Booth's right ear. It was as if he had placed the revolver behind his ear and it slipped as he jerked on the trigger. A perfect suicide. Oddly, the bullet had entered Booth's head at about the same spot as the one he had put in Lincoln. Their trajectories, of course were ninety degrees apart--Lincoln's traveling through the brain, Booth's severing his own spinal cord. But the entry wounds were remarkably similar.

"Yes, sir," Conger said with finality, "he shot himself!"

"No, he did not!" Baker refused to yield the point. "Someone shot him, and whoever did it goes back to the City under arrest."

A shot whizzed by, followed by a series of popping noises. Davy Herold's abandoned box of Spencer cartridges was burning up.

"Well," Conger said, "let us carry him out of here. This whole place will soon be burning."

The three officers grabbed Booth like a sack of potatoes and hauled him out of the path of the advancing fire. They were followed by Garrett and the soldiers who had vainly tried to control the flames.

But Baker was not yet willing to stop the argument. "What on earth did *you* shoot him for?" he said to Conger accusingly.

"Damn it! *I* did *not* shoot him!"

Baker looked at the Colonel a moment. Maybe it would be better, if Conger did do the shooting, not to spread it about. Baker knelt and placed Booth's head and shoulders in his lap. He motioned for a bucket of water that had been drawn for putting out the fire, before it was decided to let the holocaust burn itself out. Baker splashed water in Booth's still pale, handsome face. His eyes blinked. They opened up with a shocked look, as if he wondered how these soldiers could have followed him into the very depths of Hell. If Yankees were here, it surely could not be Heaven!

He was still alive! Baker took a military-issue, collapsible, metal cup from his pocket and filled it with water. He poured it into Booth's open mouth. The actor coughed and spewed it back, nearly hitting Baker in the face.

"Tell mother," Booth began. He paused, thought a moment, and repeated it. "Tell mother . . . ." Booth's head slumped to one side as he passed out, again. Baker took his kerchief from around his neck, dampened it in the bucket, and gently bathed Booth's forehead.

His eyelids began to flicker again, batting furiously at first and then locking wide open. Booth was staring intently, although it seemed as if he could not focus on any one object or idea. Conger got down on one knee. He did not want to miss a word of possible confession. His boss, Colonel Lafayette C. Baker, and Baker's boss, Secretary of War Stanton, would want to hear it all.

Booth concentrated on him. "Tell mother . . . I die . . . for my country," Booth whispered. Conger had put his ear close as Booth's lips moved.

Conger thought a moment and repeated the sentence. "Tell mother I died for my country. Is that what you say?"

"Yes," came the hoarse reply. "I did . . . what . . . I thought . . . best. "

Baker repeated the phrase again and asked, Booth, "Do I get it correctly?" Booth half-nodded his head affirmatively.

"Captain," Booth cried out painfully, as loudly as he could. Conger bent down to hear Booth's hoarse whisper. "It is hard . . . that this . . . man's property should . . . be destroyed . . . . He does . . . not . . . know who . . . I am." The Garretts had been saved from being hanged by the Federal juggernaut, although there would be plenty of tough days of jail and interrogation to follow for Jack and Willie.

Conger and Baker looked at each other, and then at the remnants of the still blazing barn. The heat was intense. Baker motioned to some nearby soldiers watching the little scene before them. The soldiers picked up Booth and moved him to the safety of the long porch of the Garrett house. In response to a request from Baker, and with the help of the children, Lucinda Holloway and Mrs. Garrett brought a mattress out.

Booth was placed on it, protesting all the while, "No, no! Let . . . me die . . . here! Let me . . . die here!"

"The damned Rebel is still living!" Doherty exclaimed. "Sergeant! Send a man into Port Royal and bring out a doctor! Miss," he said to Lucinda Holloway, "do you perchance have a pillow for his head?"

Miss Holloway put the pillow under Booth's head. "Would you like some wine? Some water?" Booth refused everything. Presently, however he changed his mind and stuck out his tongue. Miss Holloway took her handkerchief, wetted it in water and a bit of wine, and placed it on his extended tongue. She then moistened his lips.

Booth then saw Willie Jett, standing among the soldiers. "Did that . . . man . . . betray me?" he inquired haltingly. Booth's eyes seemed briefly to flash as of old. Then they grew dull again. No answer followed.

"Turn me," Booth begged.

Conger and Baker rolled him to his left. Booth cried out in agony. "No! . . . Other way!" The two officers obliged and revolved him to his right.

Booth again groaned in pain. "On my . . . face!"

"You cannot lie on your face," Conger protested. They rolled Booth again on to his back.

"Press . . . your hand . . . down on . . . throat."

Conger did as he was instructed.

"Hard . . . er!"

Conger pressed again with more force. Booth tried to cough. He wanted to clear his throat. To make it function again--the most melodious and famous throat on the American stage. He had much to say. But he could not. He was losing muscular control.

"Open your mouth and put out your tongue," Conger said. "I'll see if it bleeds." Booth complied. Conger looked down his throat then used his finger to clear any obstruction. Nothing. No blood.

"The bullet has not gone through any part of it there," Conger told him.

Lieutenant Doherty reached down where Booth had been rolled and picked up an object that had fallen out of his coat pocket. "What is this? Great Scott, gentlemen! It is a diary! Look!" Doherty thumbed through it rapidly. "It covers events for the last year or so."

Conger and Baker gathered around to see the prize Doherty had found. Conger rudely snatched the little volume from the lieutenant's hand.

It names names, it reveals the whole conspiracy! This is fabulous!

"My God!" Baker breathed out in a whisper.

Booth's physical suffering was intense, but when he realized that his diary was in the hands of the enemy, his agony was beyond bearing. "Oh . . . kill me . . . kill me . . . quick!" he pleaded.

"Oh, no, Booth. We do not want you to die," Baker said. "You were shot against orders."

"We don't want to kill you. We want you to get well," Conger affirmed, an evil smirk spreading across his face as he looked through the dairy once more. "My God," he said quietly to himself. "We have them all! Everyone! It is all in Booth's own hand!"

"I . . . care not . . . to . . . outlive my . . . country," Booth choked, as if he were some Civil War version of Nathan Hale.

"I daresay that neither your country nor its traitorous leaders will out-live you, sir." Conger was still simpering with the irony of it all, when he stepped from the veranda and collared Sergeant Andrew Wendell. "Who shot this man, Sergeant?"

"Sergeant Corbett claims he did it sir. But the men do not believe him. He is kind of a queer sort, full of Hell-fire and damnation, don'tcha know? Glory seeker--and I don't mean the glory of God, like he always claims, either."

"Go get him. Bring him up here, now!"

By this time the trooper sent to Port Royal returned with Dr. Charles Urquhart, Jr. He examined the wound. "He is mortally wounded, gentlemen," he said to the three Union officers.

"I cannot . . . stand it! I . . . want . . . to die!" Booth screamed, summoning all the strength he had for the occasion.

"You will, sir," Dr. Urquhart said gently, placing his hand on Booth's shoulder reassuringly. "But in God's good time."

There was a rustle of men approaching through the grass and trees.

Sergeant Wendell called out to Conger, "Here is Sergeant Corbett, sir."

Corbett stood at attention; shoulders squared, back straight, eyes front, hands along his legs, his thumbs pointing down the yellow stripes on his trousers.

"Corbett, what in Hell did you shoot for?"

The sergeant never blinked. "Providence directed me, sir."

"Let me see your pistol, Sergeant."

Corbett handed over his Remington .44 caliber Army model sidearm. Conger sniffed the barrel. Nothing. He pulled back the hammer and examined the cylinders. All of them were loaded. The weapon had not been fired.

Conger stood looking at the man before him for some time. "Well," he said finally, shaking his head in disbelief, "I guess He did or you could not have hit Booth through that crack in the barn." He handed the pistol back to the religionistic Sergeant. "You may go, Corbett."

Corbett saluted smartly, and Conger returned it half-heartedly. The men know Corbett very well, he mused to himself. Very well indeed.

"How long will he live, Doctor?" Conger inquired aloud as he returned to the porch.

"As little as a half hour . . . maybe an hour or more. But he does not have long. He will not see noon," Urquhart said as he watched Booth twitch and sigh in lengthening intervals. In the east, the first light of dawn painted the sky an eerie red that highlighted the yellow flames and billowing smoke rising from the still-burning barn.

Conger motioned to Baker. They went through Booth's pockets and removed everything they could find. Conger placed the small items, including the diary, in his coat pockets. He wrapped the two holstered revolvers and the sheathed Bowie knife in Booth's belt, and tied the bundle to his McClellan cavalry saddle. Then he picked up Booth's carbine.

"I am going on ahead to report," he said to Baker. "You await Booth's death and follow along. We want our story to get to your cousin and Stanton before Doherty, or anyone else, can poison the well, so to speak. We must secure the fame and the reward due us."

"How long should we wait for Booth to, die? What if he lives?" Baker wanted to know.

"Wait an hour," Conger decided, after pondering a bit. "If he is still alive, send over to Belle Plain for a military surgeon from one of the gun ships. If he dies, get the best conveyance available and bring him on to the City."

Baker returned to the corpse--for, in truth, Booth was little more than a still-talking, dead man. "Miss," Baker said to Lucinda Holloway, who was still kneeling beside Booth and regularly moistening his lips, "could you rub his forehead and temples with your fingers, ever so gently? It might relieve some of his agony."

Miss Holloway nodded her head, yes. She crawled over, took Booths head in her lap, and tenderly began caressing his head.

"Lift . . . my . . . hands," Booth rasped.

Baker looked at him quizzically, "Hands?"

Lucinda Holloway repeated, "Yes, his hands."

Baker lifted them so Booth could see the palms of the appendages that had snuffed out the life of the leader of the Union twelve days earlier. Momentarily, halo-like, Lucy Hale's ring twinkled in the pale light of the dying fire. Booth seemed transfixed by the sight.

"Useless," he mumbled. "Useless."

At least that is what Baker heard. Some of the troopers, standing farther away, thought that he said, "Lucy, Lucy." But as one of them said dismissively later, "Who the Hell is Lucy?"

With that, the death rattle drifted up his throat, and he heard from afar the gypsy's curse one last time, "You are born under an unlucky star. You have got in your hand a thundering crowd of enemies--not one friend--you will make a bad end. . . .You cannot escape it."

All that we see or seem, is but a dream within a dream.

The voice drifted into silence. A peaceful fog came over mind. His neck and head stiffened and relaxed. Dr. Urquhart checked his pulse, looked up at Baker, and shook his head slowly, side to side. With a scalpel, he deftly snipped a curl from Booth's head and unobtrusively pressed it into Miss Holloway's hand. His fingers passed over the staring, hazel eyes, hiding them forever behind those pallid lids rimmed with perfect, black lashes. Then the good doctor closed Booth's jaw for the last time. The voice that had mesmerized America with its love of Shakespeare, and hatred of the cause of forced Union, would be heard nevermore.

Lucinda Holloway silently shed a tear as she slowly lowered his head to the porch and got up, still carrying her lock of Booth's hair, to join the Garrett family, watching from near the front door.

Doherty and Conger questioned the family to confirm that the man lying dead on the porch was the same one who had stayed with them the last day and half. They all said it was, but denied knowing him by any other name than John W. Boyd, until Richard had told them differently just moments before.

Out in the yard, Old Man Garrett was allowed to climb down from the improvised gibbet, at last. His health would never be the same again. The dank, chill air of this night just passed, like the cold hand of death that now held John Wilkes Booth in its grasp, had penetrated to his very soul and would hold tightly to him.

It was April 26, destined to be remembered in much of the South thereafter as Confederate Memorial Day.

PART VII

EPILOGUE (1865)

But if you falter one little bit, sir, stumble over one word, fail to do your
duty for the first time in your life, you will hang higher than Haman!
--Edwin McM. Stanton to Louis Weichmann, late April 30, 1865

That is awfully complex . . . a lot to ask of anyone.
--Nettie Slater to George N. Sanders, late April 1865

I am thinking of going off the crook.
Aw, bull shit! You could not earn an *honest* living.
--Conversation between Charles A. Dunham (AKA Sandford
Conover, James Watson Wallace) and George N. Sanders, late April 1865

1. Back to the Rappahannock

"What happened, Bill?"

Lieutenant Tibby Ruggles and his cousin, Fellow Bainbridge, stood in the shadows across the highway from the Garrett farm. Beside them stood W. D. Newbill. The other Mosby man, who had eaten at Garrett's the night before, had not yet shown up.

Private William B. Lightfoot of the 9th Virginia Volunteer Cavalry, once Willie Jett's parent unit before he went with Mosby's irregulars, looked over his shoulder toward the smoldering fire of the tobacco barn, its smoke darkly eminent in the growing light of dawn, as the sky's brightening backdrop changed from fire red to light gray. Like the others, Lightfoot was an unparoled soldier who was part of the covering force that was to escort first, Lincoln, then Harney, then Booth to safety and block any the Federal pursuit. Most important, his nondescript face was unknown to the Federal officers and soldiers over at Garrett's.

"Lordy. It is flat spooky over there," Lightfoot reported. "The whole barn has collapsed; all but the center pole. I been told that is where Booth leaned when he was palavering with the Bluebellies. That post is singed a mite by the fire but is still as sound as Hogan's goat."

"My God, but that *is* strange," Newbill opined.

"The sawbones out of Port Royal, ol' Doc Urquhart, just declared Booth dead," Lightfoot continued. "Ain't surprised--blood all over the Garrett's porch. But the Bluebellies couldn't wait. They emptied his pockets about twenty minutes ago. Remember that Yank officer, the feller in civilian clothes, who rode off alone a while back? He is a colonel, according to one of the troopers. He had Booth's effects in his pockets and saddlebags. The carbine he carried was Booth's--came from the barn."

"Oh, yeah?" Tibby Ruggles did not seem too interested.

"Did you know that Booth kept a diary?" Lightfoot continued, one eyebrow raised. "At least he had some sort of day book or appointment book. That colonel and that other one, a lieutenant, dressed in civilian clothes, too--they looked at it and appeared real interested in what it said."

Ruggles' nonchalant countenance changed immediately. He was really interested in this news. "We better send *that* out along the line, he said. If Booth kept any record of what went into planning the kidnapping, or the gun powder plots, or his assassination scheme. . . ."

". . . a lot of good people might be hanged," Fellow Bainbridge completed his cousin's thoughts.

"Wait a minute, some of the Yankees are coming over thisaway," Lightfoot said.

"Reckon they saw you?" Ruggles asked

"Naw! They was too busy with Booth to notice me. Besides half the neighborhood was standing over there at one time or another."

"Le's all sashay on out of here, kinda cautious and slow-like," Bainbridge said. "We hain't any of us got paroles. No need to spend any time in a Yankee prison."

"And then you, Lightfoot, go home and get your horse. Then you can go south and inform Mosby that he and his men can go in for their paroles," Ruggles said. "They will not be needed to get Booth to safety. Herold can cut his own deal, if he can. I am not going to risk any lives saving the likes of him! We will have a hard enough time getting into a Yankee provost marshal for paroles of our own."

As the Confederate soldiers melted into the pine forest, Jack Garrett and Sergeant Wendell, accompanied by two troopers, crossed the road to the house of Garrett's black neighbor, Edward Freeman. Unlike the previous afternoon, Freeman was at home, as promised.

"Uncle Ned," Garrett said, "we would like to use your horse and wagon."

"They is no '*would like*' about it, Sergeant Wendell interjected. We are impressing your horse, wagon, and you, *boy.*"

"He is an old man," Garrett said with firmness. "Use the term 'uncle,' not 'boy.'"

Wendell was not impressed with the short lecture in condescending Southern proprieties when addressing black people. "Just help the damned black hitch up, you Rebel traitor," Wendell snapped, "I have my orders."

Ironic, Garrett thought, as he helped old Freeman harness his emaciated horse to a dilapidated wagon that must be as old as the old man himself. This is the same rig we had hoped yesterday evening to hire to be rid of the Boyds--that is, Booth and Herold--by this same hour this morning. Only Booth and Herold were not going to Guinea Station, Ashland or Hanover Junction, now. One was going to the City to be autopsied and the other to be hanged.

The wagon fairly creaked and groaned as Freeman and Garrett brought it across to pick up Booth's body. Doherty had already sewed Booth's remains up in a saddle blanket using one of Mrs. Garrett's darning needles--a crude job to say the least. A couple of the bigger cavalrymen picked up the body as they would have a chunk of meat and threw it into the bed of Edward Freeman's would-be vehicle. It landed with an unceremonious thud.

"I have ordered the men to cook breakfast," Lieutenant Doherty said to Baker.

"I think that we ought to get started without delay," Baker came back. "That ferry crossing will take some time."

"We will have to forage half the men off this farm and the rest off another place down the road. I have sent Sergeant Corbett off to find a likely farm now. It will take a couple of hours."

"I tell you what; I will take Jett, a couple of troopers to escort him, and what's left of Booth. We will start out now, ahead of you and the rest of the command. With a little luck you can join us on the road and we will all wind up in Belle Plain by this evening. You can escort the two Garrett boys, Jack and Willie, and Herold to the *John S. Ide*. They are all under arrest. Tie them to their saddles. Take care they do not get away."

Doherty looked at Baker questioningly, as if he smelled at rat. But Baker was right. They might as well start part of the command crossing as soon as possible. Besides he still had Herold, and possession was nine-tenths of the law when rewards were involved. "Go ahead," he agreed.

With that, Baker, Jett, two troopers, and old Ned Freeman, carrying the one-time toast of the American theater in a humble, rickety wagon that announced its coming a half mile ahead of its abject appearance by its infernal squeaking, set out for Belle Plain. At the Port Royal Ferry, Jim Thornton and his black oarsmen took them across at one time, in the company of another passenger, Wellford Mason, back from his trip south to alert the underground of Booth's coming. He had met Lightfoot below Garrett's on the Bowling Green Road. As Mason had a parole, he agreed to pass brazenly through the Union cavalry to inform Hoomes Williamson and Tom Harbin of the morning's events and Booth's demise. He would also speak of the existence of Booth's diary. Lightfoot, lacking a parole, was directed to do the same with Mosby, Mason knowing that the road to Ashland was clear of roving Yankee patrols.

"Hey, Uncle Ned! Who you got there?" he asked the old black man, motioning to the back of Freeman's wagon. "Dead Yank?" He grinned. Mason knew Freeman from childhood. Like so many travelers in that neck of the woods, he had often slaked his thirst at Freeman's well, occasionally leaving tobacco or whiskey in exchange.

Baker was in no mood to spread the word that he had what was left of the man who had killed Lincoln. One never knew what lay ahead on these poorly traveled Southern highways.

"Yeah, a dead Yank, sure enough," he butted in.

"No kidding?"

Mason took a good long look at what little of Booth he could see. He recognized the unusual footwear, a riding boot and slipper, from the man he had stood next to a few days before on the ferry. He rode off to report to Hoomes Williamson: mission accomplished.

Lightfoot was correct. Booth was definitely dead. But that other Yank officer, the one who had Booth's diary, was long gone north. They would never catch him before he reached the Potomac.

2. The Eerie Trip to Belle Plain

Baker watched the suspicious ex-Confederate soldier, for that is what he thought of the inquisitive Mason, mount and ride off from Port Conway.

"Take the shortest way to Belle Plain," he said to Freeman.

"Yessah," replied the old man.

Freeman clucked to his horse, which strained at the traces. Baker, Jett, and the troopers fell in behind. After two or three miles, Baker began to look back along their trail, impatiently expecting Doherty's column to come up. Nothing was to be seen. No dust, no clanking of equipments, no noise but the springtime chatter of hundreds of unseen birds, disturbed out of their normal song by the yelping of the ungreased wheels of Freeman's wagon.

"This road does not appear to be well traveled," Baker remarked to Freeman, spurring his mount up parallel to the wagon seat. "Is this the right road?"

"Massa, I have been over this road many and many a time before the war, and I am sure it is the *shortest* way to Belle Plain."

Back at the ferry, Doherty had just crossed the Rappahannock with the first of his men. The squad was led by Corporal Herman Neugarten. Doherty motioned him over. Neugarten walked his horse over to the Lieutenant.

"Corporal Neugarten [he pronounced it in the English form, "Newgarden," not the German "Noygarten," as the corporal would have], have you seen any sign of Lieutenant Baker?"

"No, sir," came the reply. "They appear to have gone ahead."

Doherty went back to supervise the ferry operation. After a quarter of an hour, he reined in his steed in front of Neugarten and spoke again.

"Corporal, I am worried about this division of the column. I want you to ride up ahead and contact Lieutenant Baker. Tell him to stop and await the rest of the column. Then you return to me at once and report."

"Yes, sir!" Neugarten turned his mount and spurred him up the road toward Belle Plain. After a half hour or so, Doherty noticed that Neugarten had not returned. After an hour, he became even more worried. What had happened to Baker? Had he been ambushed? That unreliable know-it-all had been interfering with his command of the column throughout the whole expedition.

Meanwhile, unknown to Doherty, Neugarten caught up to Baker about four miles down the road.

"So, Lieutenant Doherty wants me to stop and wait for him, eh? Well, Corporal, you just join this little band and we will let the rest of the column catch up to *us*."

"But sir, Lieutenant Doherty wanted me to report back to him once I delivered the message."

"I am in charge here. Do as you are told, Corporal."

Baker began to smell treachery. That damned Doherty had left him; hung him out to dry. Here he was with the dead assassin of the President, a Rebel prisoner, three grumpy men, a broken down horse and wagon driven by a useless old black man, surrounded by enemies in the midst of Rebel territory. It grew hot and sultry. The sun became unbearable. Occasionally, men in gray passed by, asking the same questions as the Reb back at the ferry. "What's that, a dead Yank?" When Baker answered in the affirmative, "Yes, a deserter," he would say, they would joke and laugh as they passed on. Baker thought it best to play along. He laughed, too.

My God, Baker thought. I have been in the saddle for two days and nights. I want to sleep, but am too anxious to try it. Jett would be out of here like a shot, if I dozed off. That narrow spot between the trees looks like a good spot for an ambush. This road is too full of twists and turns to be the one we took when following Booth. Even at night, I can tell the difference.

Neugarten spoke up. "Sir, I think that we should have taken the left fork way back a piece."

Baker rode up along side of the wagon. "Now you look here, *boy*," he threatened Freeman, "if you have betrayed me I will kill you this instant."

"Naw suh," Freeman pledged, with what Baker took, in his current state of mind, as a deceptive smile. "This is the right road. You just be patient, now. Don't worry. Ol' Freeman goin' take you to Belle Plain by the *shortest* way possible, you can lay on it, suh."

"For God's sake!" Baker muttered to himself, once again. "Will I ever see the City again?"

Now a new problem arose. Baker noticed that Freeman's old horse was beginning to tire. Each hill became more difficult than the last. Baker finally had Neugarten throw the old wagon driver a picket rope and help pull. Freeman was obviously as hot, tired, hungry, and thirsty as the soldiers and he were, but Baker knew that the horses were suffering even more.

Suddenly there was a terrible crash. The front axle shot out from under the wagon. The king pin had broken loose. Freed from his load, Freeman's old horse charged unexpectedly forward, almost running over Neugarten's startled mount, which quickly side-stepped and snorted in momentary panic. Booth's body slid forward and out of the wagon bed in a heap. Blood seeped from the poorly sewn sack on to the ground. The disturbed corpse emitted a foul odor that caused Freeman to cry out in horror. Baker felt himself about to throw up, but his stomach was too empty for him to do much more than wretch dryly a couple of times.

"All right!" Baker ordered. "Let us put everything back together!" He and the two privates dismounted. The troopers had lifted the ancient wagon bed so that Freeman could roll the wheels and axle back in place. Then the tired old black man crawled under the bed to reset the king pin.

"Oh, my Lord," he hollered. "The tainted blood of the killer of Lincoln has run onto my hand! Lord have mercy on this poor old soul!"

"Cut it out!" Baker shouted, having grown weary of the vicissitudes of this nightmare trip. "Stop your damn noise this minute! That will not harm you! It will wash off!" His patience with the old black man was hanging by a very fine thread!

Freeman actually was crying. The tears rolled down his dusty cheeks, in little rivulets that glistened in the sun. "Oh! It will never wash off, no, never! It is the blood of a murderer," he whined with a certainty that honored Shakespeare's portrayal of Lady Macbeth.

Suddenly, there was a rush as Willie Jett put heels to his mount and dashed past the distracted guards and into the woods. He was gone before Neugarten, the only mounted man, could stop him. The Corporal spun his horse and spurred after him in pursuit. He returned shortly, alone.

"I could not track him in the thick underbrush, sir."

"Never mind, Corporal," Baker snapped. "Get down and give us a hand."

King pin back in place, Booth's putrid body back in the bed, the weary little cavalcade pushed on. More hills, more ravines, more former Confederate soldiers. More questions. More laughter at rude humor that cut to the core of Baker's pious Yankee soul. Then night began to fall. The coolness of the late evening acted to rejuvenate man and beast alike. Baker hoped that the impending darkness would act to lessen the traffic and act as a shield against prying eyes.

"There the Potomac!" Freeman shouted. "See? I tol' you we would take the shortest route! God A'mighty! The Lord be praised!"

Even Baker raised a shout of jubilation. Then he realized that their troubles were not over. They were at the Potomac, all right, but there was no wharf. Freeman had led them to the old landing. Sometime during the war the Federal army's engineers had moved the whole wharf to a new location at Aquia Creek, three quarters of a mile away. Of course, no one ever though to consult with Freeman about the move. Through the dusk, Baker could see the lights of the *John S. Ide*, lying at the dock. But it was blocked from their location by a huge bluff. There was no river road. Baker started to raise a huzzah, but stopped. What if Rebels got to them first? He would have to ride back a ways and find a way around.

"Now look here, old man," Baker said tightly. "You take the body into those trees and reeds over there and await my return. And you had better keep quiet. He turned to the two privates. See to it that body is here, when I get back. Neugarten, come with me."

Baker and Neugarten rode two miles before they found a way around the ridge. Baker urged his tired buckskin horse on to the new landing. Poor beast! It was already quivering when Baker got off at the wharf. Neugarten's was not much better. Doherty and his troopers had been there for hours.

"Why did you not return to me as I ordered?"

"Sorry, sir." Neugarten shrugged helplessly and looked at Baker.

Lieutenant Doherty stepped between Baker and the corporal. "Now look here. I resent your giving orders to my men without my explicit permission. I command this unit. I told Neugarten to rejoin the column. If you do not have the sense to stay on the correct road, then you have to take the consequences. I will not risk a single man of this column just for your sake in enemy territory. You are damn lucky that you made the 6 p.m. deadline, or we would have had to leave you here, on your own. By the way," Doherty asked, "where *is* the old man with Booth's body?"

"He is about a mile downstream," Baker said wearily. "We can take a boat and go down and fetch the body. The horse and the old Negro are too done in to come around the bluffs, as we did." Baker looked around. "What has happened to Colonel Conger?"

"He took the regularly scheduled steamer to the District some time ago," Doherty said. "Wait a minute! Where is Jett? The Reb who led us to the farm? And the men assigned to guard him?"

"Jett escaped during the day, when we stopped to repair that piece of junk these damned Southerners refer to as a wagon. The troopers are with the old man and the wagon below here."

"Conger will not be happy about that!"

"Jett will not go far," Baker came back. "Besides, we will have to come back to get his fellow conspirators, Ruggles and Bainbridge."

Baker proved correct. Jett would be retaken in a couple of weeks by another column and testify on behalf of the government at the trial of the conspirators. The same fate befell Ruggles and Bainbridge, although they never testified against anyone publicly. Along with hundreds of others, Harbin, Baden, Newbill and Lightfoot would come in to the provost marshall's post at Ashland Station and get their paroles, unsuspected of their roles in trying to save Booth.

But their commander, John Singleton Mosby, had problems of his own. The Yankees were unsure of why he had refused to come in with the rest of his men, when offered the same terms as Robert E. Lee at Appomattox. They placed a two thousand dollar reward on his head, fearing future mischief by the Gray Ghost of the Confederacy. Finally, when an indictment of Lee for treason, contrary to the Appomattox terms, fell through, and Lee applied for a pardon, Mosby followed his chief and successfully obtained a parole. Both men acted with the full support of General U. S. Grant.

And old Freeman? Doherty gave him a niggardly two dollars for the trip. Before he got home, the old black man had to abandon his worn-out wagon on the side of the road, where it was left to rot. Fortunately, he had Davy Herold's ten dollar "Secretary Chase note" that Jack Garrett had given him earlier.

But John Wilkes Booth still had many miles to travel. His rapidly putrefying body, or what was left of it, apart from the horrible stench, was placed into a small boat, rowed out and lifted up to the deck on the fantail of the *John S. Ide*.

3. Back in Washington

Lt. Colonel Everton Conger arrived in Lafayette C. Baker's office across from Willard's Hotel late on the afternoon of the 26th. The head of the National Detective Police was chatting with several of his men in the lobby when Conger stepped in, carrying Booth's carbine and pistols in his arms.

"Conger! How goes it?"

"Fine, sir! May I see you in your office . . . privately?" Conger asked.

"Certainly!" Baker escorted Conger in and closed the door. Conger dropped Booth's weapons on Baker's desk with a resounding thud. "Well, sir," he said in a low voice almost a whisper, "we got Booth and Herold."

Baker leaped up and cheered. "We must tell Stanton immediately." He opened the door to the lobby and shouted to the clerk, "Bring me a carriage! At once!" Then he turned back to Conger and shut the door, again.

"Where were they?"

"Right where you said they would be. Hiding at a farm owned by some feller named Garrett about two or three miles below Port Royal on the Rappahannock. I have some bad news, though. Booth is dead. Shot during the fray. A sergeant in the 16th New York Cavalry claims to have done it. He is some kind of religious nut. Men chaff him all the time. I checked his pistol and he had not fired a shot. Nor had anyone else. Booth seems to have killed himself."

Meanwhile, Conger was in the process of emptying his pockets of the smaller items taken from the body.

"Where are Byron and the escort?"

"I left them behind. Doherty, who was a prissy pain in the ass the entire way, I might add, wanted to rest his men and horses. I told Lieutenant Baker to bring on the body and prisoners--we have several besides Herold--when he could find a conveyance. I do not know when they will get here, after dark, I suppose."

Baker examined several of the papers and looked at the diary.

There was a rap at the door. "The carriage is ready, sir."

"Well, grab all of this stuff and let's go over and see the Secretary of War. Here, I will carry that diary. By God! Stanton is gonna *love* this!"

Baker had the carriage driver take his time going to Stanton's house, so as not to attract undue attention. But his excitement made the short trip seem agonizingly slow. The Secretary had been feeling ill and thus was at home, a rare occasion, particularly this early in the day. The servant answered their ring and showed them into Stanton's study. The Secretary was resting on a couch, despondent at the way the search for Booth was preceding, despairing of hearing any good information at all.

"We have got Booth!" Baker shouted gleefully, no longer able to restrain his enthusiasm.

For a moment, Stanton just lay there. Finally, he put his hands to his eyes. Beyond that he said nothing, nor did he move. Then he got up, quite deliberately, and put on his coat. Meanwhile, Baker and Conger were in the process of depositing Booth's effects on a nearby table. They ignored the Secretary's lack of enthusiasm.

But Stanton soon brought them up short. "Do not say that you have Booth, unless you know it."

"Well. At any rate, I will show you proof which ought to be sufficient to satisfy anybody."

"What proof do you have, Colonel?"

"The papers that were found on Booth, sir."

Stanton looked at the bank drafts and the diary. Immediately, his face shone with glee.

"He will make a fine defendant at a public trial and hanging." In his mind, Stanton could hear the strains of "Hail to the Chief," being played in his honor.

"There is one minor problem, sir," Baker intoned. "Booth is dead. We only have Herold and some miscellaneous Rebs captive."

"What? Who killed him? By God! I will have someone's hide for this!"

"It was a sergeant in the 16th New York Cavalry, sir, the escort. Well, he *claims* to have shot Booth. Actually it seems more probable that Booth shot himself." Conger then proceeded to tell the story of the sergeant with the unfired revolver, who claimed to have shot Booth.

"I will have him court-martialed," Stanton promised. "For violation of direct orders. If he wants the credit, I will let him take it . . . in the guardhouse!"

"Actually," Baker said, "that is exactly what Colonel Conger and I have been hashing out on the way over, sir. We have what we think will be a better idea. Hear us out, if you please"

"Yes, sir," Conger seconded. "We think that this Sergeant Corbett ought to receive the credit for killing Booth--but in a complementary way. Why do we not make him into a sort of national hero? 'The Man Who Killed the Man Who Shot Lincoln.' That sort of thing."

Stanton mulled the notion over. It made sense. It would belay any repercussions. A devoutly religious man called by God to avenge the nation's loss. Yes, it was actually quite brilliant. A truly "Baker" solution . . . well . . . now . . . a "Stanton" solution, to a potentially sticky problem.

"I like it," Stanton pronounced with finality. "We have the diary, anyhow; we do not need Booth."

He looked at Booth's revolvers, especially the one with the empty cylinder.

"Gentlemen," the Secretary finally said, with a twinkle in his eye, "perhaps we *had* better give Sergeant Corbett full credit for the shooting of Booth. The full treatment-- commendation, confrontation with the press, perhaps a tour to select cities--something along that line. But, *before* our hero meets the American people, let us *recharge* the empty chamber, and, by all means *clean* the barrel of Booth's pistol." He laughed. Baker and Conger smiled and then began to laugh, too. Soon all three were wiping the tears from their eyes.

"Now, gentlemen," said Stanton, all business once more, "Let us get down to cases. I want you to take Major Eckert, my aide, and meet that steamboat, what did you call her, Colonel?" "The *John S. Ide*, sir," replied Conger. "Yes, of course, the *Ide*--meet her at Alexandria. Take the prisoners off and transfer them to the tug you use to get down there. I will have the navy send one over from the arsenal landing. Take them to the monitors anchored off the Navy Yard. Turn them over to the Marines aboard there. We want none of the captives to communicate with each other, nor to any persons not authorized in writing by me. Take Booth's body over there too, set it up on deck and I will have it autopsied in the morning. My God, but he must be a mite ripe by now, the weather being so warm and all. Whew! I will write you a pass to get through the guards on the *Saugus* and *Montauk*."

At 10:30 p.m., the *John S. Ide* docked at Alexandria, signaled ashore by the dockmaster. Lafayette Baker climbed aboard and nearly stumbled across the sleeping form of his cousin. In the process, he jostled several sleeping cavalry men who gave voice to groggy complaints of the most uncomplimentary sort.

Baker nudged his cousin with his foot. Byron slept on, as if dead. Baker bent over and shook him awake. "Come on, Byron," he said, "I will find you a better place to sleep."

Within an hour, the prisoners and Booth's corpse were in the hands of the Navy.

"Now, Byron, we will go and see the Secretary of War. He is waiting in his office for you."

"At midnight?"

"Sure. You know Stanton. 'Do it now,' he always says. He cannot get enough of eyewitness accounts of Booth's demise," Conger added.

At the War Department, Stanton eagerly listened to Byron Baker's account of his adventures hunting and capturing Booth and Herold, and the transport of Booth's corpse to the steamer. At the end of the story telling, Stanton brought out Booth's Spencer carbine.

"Are you not accustomed to handling a carbine? If so, what is the matter with this? It cannot be discharged!"

Byron Baker took the weapon and opened the breech by pulling the trigger guard down. "Ah! Here is the problem! A cartridge has gotten out of position--it seems to have turned in the breech, jamming the mechanism. Look at the marks on the casing. No wonder Booth threw it down without firing a shot and took up his pistol in the barn!"

"You should have seen him standing there in the light of the burning barn," Conger said. "Standing there like he owned the world, like he was some sort of hero out of the pages of Sir Walter Scott!"

"That damned fool," Byron Baker said, derisively.

"Easy, Gentlemen," Stanton interjected. "Out of each act, no matter how evil, some good must come. His assassination has made Abraham Lincoln the quintessential martyr to this Great War. Everyone has joined to mourn him as the Great Emancipator and the Savior of the Union. In many ways, Booth was not merely the last Confederate hero. He was the last Union hero, too, in an unspoken sense. In large measure, his evil act has elevated President Lincoln to be the most revered of all our former chief executives, overshadowing even the heretofore universally venerated George Washington. The Republican Party will owe Booth silent obeisance for decades to come. Lincoln's death has smashed the pre-war Southern dominance of our government, the Slave Power Conspiracy, for all time. Even more so than the war itself. People will vote without thinking, just as they (and their grandfathers) shot--well into the next generations."

4. The Autopsy and a National Hero

Early the next morning, two young naval officers escorted a heavily veiled woman on board the USS*Montauk*, where John Wilkes Booth's moldering body was laid out for the coming autopsy and formal identification. One of the officers produced a knife and cut the binding that Lieutenant Doherty had so laboriously stitched twenty-four hours earlier to hold the corpse for transport. The odor of decay was overwhelming, and the three moved to the windward side to escape it as much as possible. Once the officers had undone as much of the sewing as was necessary to reveal the head, they pulled the blanket back. There he was, the once proud star of the American theater, face still recognizable and pale, hair coal black, but duller than usual.

"Oh! A-a-a-h-h! Ai-e-e-e! John! . . . No . . . no . . . no!" the woman wailed as she fell across the vile blanket in which Booth lay. Her body was racked violently with emotion. She sucked in great gulps of air between her tears of grief, which fell until she was so drained that she was left with a harrowing headache, which pounded from her forehead to behind her blood-shot eyes. She moaned as the officers pulled her back. One held her tightly in his arms as she sobbed uncontrollably on his shoulder. The other, the one with the knife, cut a lock of the famous hair (there would be so many stories involving a lock of the actor's famous hair that later commentators would wonder aloud that it was a marvel Booth was not bald when buried), and pulled the blanket back over the remains of Booth's head. He handed the curled strand to the lady with the now tear-stained veil.

"Th-thank you s-so m-much," Lucy Hale managed to blubber out.

Then the three left the gunboat the way they came. When Stanton heard of the incident later in the day he threw one of his prize-winning fits of rage. He then issued an order that no one could come aboard any of the gunboats acting as prison ships without an order signed by him and Secretary of the Navy Gideon Welles. He disguised the identity of Lucy Hale by circulating the story that the visitor was a former mistress of Booth, who had charmed the two officers into doing what they knew was prohibited. For those who doubted that, he also claimed that one of the visitors was an assistant surgeon who would help with the autopsy and wanted to see the body before proceeding. The woman was a friend, who had no business being there and was overcome by the condition of the cadaver.

About mid-morning, a correctly authorized party boarded the *Montauk* to conduct the autopsy and the identification of the dead man as John Wilkes Booth. Led by Surgeon General of the Army Joseph K. Barnes, it included Major Thomas T. Eckert (Stanton's representative), Judge Advocate General Joseph Holt, the Honorable John A. Bingham (designated to be a prosecutor of the co-conspirators), William G. Moore (a War Department clerk), Colonel Lafayette C. Baker, Lieutenant L.

Byron Baker, Lt. Colonel Everton J. Conger, Dr. John Frederick May (who had operated on Booth's neck previously), Charles Dawson (a clerk at the National Hotel where Booth resided), John L. Smith (a deputy U.S. Marshal, married to George Andrew Atzerodt's sister, Katerina, and soon to help preside over his own brother-in-law's hanging to prove his loyalty to the remnants of the Lincoln regime), and photographer Alexander Gardner and his assistant, T. H. O'Sullivan.

The first to look at the body in the presence of this august crowd was Dr. May. At first he claimed he could not recognize the corpse as that of Booth. But at his request, a couple of brave souls held it up in a sitting position, and Dr. May said it was indeed the actor, especially after he examined a scar at the base of his neck, a scar that occurred as a result of an actress ("Charlotte Cushman, I believe it was," May said, unwittingly repeating the lie Booth told him a couple of years before) hugging him too hard during a performance and breaking open a half-healed incision from an operation May had performed. Others backed him up. Then Surgeon General Barnes conducted the autopsy and removed the three vertebrae from Booth's neck, through which the fatal bullet had passed. He suggested that Booth go six feet under posthaste.

Stanton was already seeing to the burial. But it had to be done with secrecy, so that none could find Booth and deface him or exalt him. This was a job for Lafayette C. Baker.

"He does not care where we put it," Baker said to cousin Byron, "only let it be put where it will not be found until Gabriel blows his last trumpet." Byron, of course, knew that Stanton had already determined the exact spot--he did not operate in any other way. "I want you to go with me," Lafe Baker said. "By the way, I made brigadier general. Stanton's appointment, without the approval of Congress, yet. He dated it from the 26th, when Booth was killed."

Byron Baker extended his hand. "Congratulations! It is a great triumph for our family, something we all have thought was long over due."

"Thank you, Cousin! By the bye, Stanton told me that another party of twenty-five cavalry from Colonel Olcutt's office (he is a Provost Marshal who General Augur imported from New York to work the Lincoln murder), got to Garrett's about two hours after you left. Under a Major H. W. Smith--the man who led the party that arrested Mrs. Surratt and Seward's assassination, Paine. Thank God, for their slow steamboat from here to Port Royal! I hear he lost two or three hours at Point Lookout, trying to get a better craft. You know, we got that reward by the skin of our teeth. He would have out-ranked everyone, including Conger, who is technically a civilian. You did a good job getting Booth's body out of there in a hurry."

Full of mutual admiration, the Bakers reported to the *Montauk* that afternoon. They made quite a to-do about loading a length of chain and a heavy cannon ball. The banks of both sides of the Eastern Branch of the Potomac were filled with on-lookers. Everyone wanted to know where Booth would be buried. Lafayette Baker and his intrepid cousin grabbed the body, sewn back up in its bloody shroud, and unceremoniously dumped it into the bottom of their row boat.

With Byron at the oars, they rowed down stream to the marsh at Giesboro Point on the east bank. Here, in the reeds, bogs, and swamps, were beds of quicksand where the Army disposed of condemned horses and mules. It was so putrid that the corpse smelled good by comparison. That stunt pretty well cleared out the crowds. The reeds hid the Bakers and their cargo from the morbidly curious.

"Throw in the cannon ball and then the chain. Let it drag over the gunwale," Lafe Baker said. "Do not be too gentle about it. I want those people closest to hear the splash and the rattle of the chain."

Byron did as he was ordered. Then the Bakers sat there in the boat until sundown, manfully trying not to be sick from the stench.

"Row over to the arsenal, Byron," the head of the National Detectives ordered. "Up to the landing at the tip of the peninsula."

Once there, the Baker's unloaded the body and left it in a corner of a pier building. Later, Dr. George Loring Porter, an assistant surgeon at the post, would pick up the body with the post's civilian storekeeper, E. M. Stebbins, and four soldiers. They transported it to one of the gun rooms at the Old Penitentiary. There a hole had already been dug by others. The four soldiers lowered Booth's body into a gun case already in the bottom of the hole, then laid in a glass jar which enclosed a paper on which was written the deceased's name, and shut the lid, which had the name "Booth" painted upon it.

They shoveled the hole full, tamped the soil down, put the excess dirt in the wagon, and concealed all traces of their efforts. Then Mr. Stebbins locked the door to the room and deposited the keys with Secretary Stanton. It was just two weeks, almost to the hour, since Booth had shot his way into American History. There everything rested, until President Andrew Johnson allowed Edwin Booth to claim the body and transfer it to the family plot in Baltimore's Greenmount Cemetery in 1869.

A few days later, Judge Advocate General Holt called Colonel Conger into his office. Holt was tying up loose ends in the Booth case, preparatory to prosecuting it before a military court.

"About this shooting of John Wilkes Booth in the barn," Holt began, "did you give the soldiers any orders *not* to shoot?"

"No, sir, I did not think that was necessary."

"I wish you would prepare a specification against this Sergeant Boston Corbett."

Holt then dismissed Conger and went on with his work. Because of his earlier conversation with Secretary Stanton on making Corbett a national hero, Conger ignored the incident.

A week later an acting assistant general from Holt's office called on Conger at the headquarters of the National Detective Police. He looked at the man sitting there in civilian clothes.

"Is your name Conger?"

"Yes, I am *Colonel* Conger," he said pointedly, not familiar of any military regulation that permitted to shavetails to ignore custom in referring to officers of higher rank, whether in or out of the service. "Try saying 'sir' when addressing superior officers, Lieutenant!"

"Sir! The Judge Advocate General wants to know if you have prepared specifications against Sergeant Boston Corbett, sir"

"No, I have not."

"Well, sir, the Judge Advocate wants to know why you have not complied with his order."

"I did not exactly understand that what he said was an order. It was given to me verbally at the time of the inquiry as to Booth's death and identity, and I did not understand what the Judge Advocate wanted."

"You will hear again from the Judge Advocate on this matter, sir."

Sure enough, a written order followed on the heels of the Lieutenant's departure. Conger was very disturbed at this upsetting of the Corbett-as-hero picture that he, Stanton, and General Baker had drawn up. After a day of thinking on it, Conger decided to confront Holt in person.

"Sir," Conger said when he was admitted to the inner sanctum of Holt's office, "I would like to talk to Secretary Stanton concerning the Corbett case."

"Your orders are very clear, Colonel."

"I still believe that Corbett did not disobey any direct command, sir."

"Do you wish to see the Secretary today?"

"If I cannot see him today, I would like to call on him at home tonight, if that would be more convenient, sir."

"It is alright for you to see the Secretary now, Colonel."

Conger proceeded directly to Stanton's office and obtained immediate admittance. As Stanton was wont to do, he sat scribbling on papers on his desk, ignoring Conger's presence a while.

Then, without looking up, Stanton said, "You wanted to see me Everton?" Stanton and Conger knew each other before the war and Stanton often addressed him familiarly, when no one else was present.

"Yes, Mr. Secretary."

"What do you want from me?"

"I have a written order from General Holt to prepare at once charges against Sergeant Boston Corbett. I cannot comply with that order, sir."

"Why not?"

"Secretary Stanton, you know as well as I do that it was with a feeling of great relief that the American people learned that Booth was dead. Not only that, there is a feeling of glorification of the man who professed to have killed him, and now I am to prefer charges against him. I will not do it. It goes against common sense and what, I thought, was our prior verbal agreement. We both know that Booth shot himself. There was no disobedience of orders by anyone concerned with the taking of Booth."

"Have you got that order, Everton?" Stanton put out his hand.

"Yes, sir." Conger handed the paper to the Secretary.

"I will take care of it. Sometimes General Holt and I do not act in concert, but we always seek the same goals: Union, Freedom, and Equality. And the political supremacy of the Republican Party."

"Yes, sir. Thank you, sir."

That was the last Conger ever heard of castigating Corbett for killing Booth.

5. The Convoluted Jailhouse Interview of David Herold

The day after Davy Herold was lodged safely aboard the U.S.S. *Montauk*, lying moored off the Navy Yard, midstream in the Eastern Branch of the Potomac, Special Judge Advocate John A. Bingham came to interview him. The *Montauk* was an iron monitor; a class of ships build after the pattern of the original U.S.S. *Monitor*, which had fought the Confederate iron-clad, C.S.S. *Virginia* to a stand-still in Hampton Roads in the spring of 1862.

Unlike the longer and bigger double-turreted models that followed, the *Montauk* kept the *Monitor's* single turret with its two massive Dahlgren guns, one an 11 inch smoothbore and the other a 15 inch smoothbore. There were a few improvements in the *Montauk* from the original *Monitor*. The pilot house was removed from the forecastle deck and placed squarely on top of the turret, giving the captain more control of the gun laying. And there was a glacis, or armored ring, around the base of the turret where it emerged from the deck to prevent an enemy shell from hitting this vulnerable spot head on.

But there was no improving certain disadvantages that the older iron ships had. The *Montauk* only had a freeboard ranging from an inch and a half aft to two and a half inches forward. This meant that the whole area below decks was under water. Combined with the oppressive humidity of the Washington area, the living quarters were stifling and the walls and ceilings constantly dripped condensed moisture. So, the Lincoln conspirators chained up below dwelt in everlasting dampness, just like the ship's 68 man crew.

Herold's chains clanked against the iron floor as he turned to face the approaching footsteps. A Marine guard led Bingham and a stenographer into where Herold lay, chained to the bulkhead. Both men stooped over as they walked. Since they were not very tall, it was indicative of how little headroom existed between decks. There was a clatter as another Marine dropped two small, three-legged stools for the Judge Advocate and his assistant to sit on while the interview was conducted. Both Marines withdrew--chained as he was, there was no way Herold could move fast enough to cause the interviewers any trouble.

Bingham was from Cadiz, Ohio, the heart of the Western Reserve. As such he accurately typified his Yankee forebears. He was a humorless, antislavery zealot, and a former congressman just reelected. He was renowned for his combative style of debate and famous for his bitter invective and biting sarcasm. He was a formidable prosecutor and would later go on in Congress to write much of the first section of the Fourteenth Amendment and support Military Reconstruction. But in Davy Herold, he met his match in deviousness. Herold never knew when to give up and he filled Bingham full of as much buncome as the market would bear. This was Herold's hour. He would get no chance to testify in court, it was prohibited under the law of the time as hearsay tainted with self-interest, so Bingham let him run on. The Congressman would get the last laugh, so to speak, at Herold's hanging in July.

Bingham started Herold off with questions that brought forth details of his life heretofore. Davy essentially told Bingham the same story he had regaled the Mudd's with at breakfast ten days before; who he worked for, how he broke his ankle, whom he knew in Southern Maryland, and his prowess as a hunter of small game. Then, Bingham got to the point.

"When, if at all, did you first become acquainted with J. Wilkes Booth?"

"I do not remember the time exactly. I think it was when I was a clerk with William S. Thompson, druggist, corner of 15th St. and New York Ave., two years ago this spring . . ."

Bingham gave a start. That was caddy-corner right across the street from the White House!

". . . the time when Booth had a ball taken from his neck by some surgeon in Washington. I met Mr. Booth, off and on, sometimes once a week, or maybe two or three times. We would always stand and have a chat."

Bingham wanted to know if Herold had sent or received letters from Booth, but that line of questioning only drew a reference to Herold's receiving a half dozen complimentary theater tickets from the actor, and an admission that he had gone behind the scenes for a visit, once.

"I have been to his hotel to see him, I have been to his room," Herold offered.

Bingham leaned forward, "What hotel and what room?"

Herold grew vague again. "At the National. I do not recollect the room. I met him on the street."

Bingham wanted none of that. "How often did you visit him at the National Hotel?"

"I do not think I went to his room more than five or six times."

"When was it?"

"I do not know. It was in the winter time and this spring. I went there to see him about some coal oil. He said he was in the coal oil business."

"Whom did you meet in his rooms?"

Herold remembered John McCullough, G. A. Atzerodt, and a lady. "I do not know who she was."

Bingham focused in on the topic of Atzerodt. "How often did you meet Atzerodt at his rooms?"

"When Atzerodt was stopping at the Pennsylvania House, I was there nearly every day for about two weeks."

But Bingham's effort to pin down whether Atzerodt and Booth had discussed anything together about President Lincoln got no favorable response.

Herold claimed that he had been down into the country on April 14 to sell a horse. In reality he had been down the day before and had slept over at Joseph Huntt's. He admitted to being at Lloyd's to have a drink or two and paying his existing bar tab. Then he owned up that the horse deal was actually to have taken place nine or ten days before. That left the whole question unanswered as to when he was in the lower counties and what for. Bingham shook his head in confusion and disbelief.

Herold's story of coming back into the City and meeting the injured Booth at Soper's Hill was an imaginative combination of unadorned veracity, half truths, and outright prevarication. He said that he met Booth, who had sprained his leg in a fall with his hired bay horse. The actor talked Herold into going back down country with him. Booth already had his carbine. Herold had already heard that Booth had shot Lincoln from a man he met at a crossroads near Bryantown, but Booth denied that he had committed the assassination.

Then, in some sort of mysterious manner, Herold continued, Booth had gone and got his leg set and received a pair of crutches, while Herold had gone into Bryantown and confirmed that Booth had killed Lincoln. Booth told Herold that he had used as an alias the name of Tyson. Herold could not remember the doctor's name who had worked on Booth. He confronted Booth with the Lincoln murder, once more, and Booth owned up to it. Herold claimed that he wanted to flee, but, Booth with his glib tongue, backed by his pistols, knife, and carbine frightened him into staying.

"He told me that I must go with him. His leg was broken. He said if I ran away, he would shoot me, and that parties in Washington would implicate me."

Herold then rattled on in a totally incomprehensible manner that earned him the reputation of being addle-pated. He confused Samuel Cox with John Hughes, and combined them into one person named Thomas. He gave Canter's name and said that at least two unnamed free blacks had assisted him and Booth with food and directions. He asserted that he and Booth had hidden in Zekiah Swamp for a couple of days, instead of nearly a week, but never mentioned their jaunts over to Adams' place in Newport. He admitted that they had crossed the Potomac from Nanjemoy Creek and had met a lady, who refused them help, and a man, who had sold them fourteen or fifteen biscuits and three slices of bacon. But he called none by their correct names, until he came to Dr. Stuart. By now Booth had adopted the pseudonym of Boyd, Herold said.

The would-be druggist told of how he and Booth had slept at the house of "a free darkey," as he put it, and then had gone on to Port Conway and met the three Confederate cavalrymen. He got Willie Jett's name and role correctly, but did not mention Tibby Ruggles at all and called Fellow Bainbridge, "Bennington." He was not sure that they knew who Booth really was. He did remember leaving Booth at Garrett's Farm and of going on to a Mrs. Clarke's for the night with Bennington, but never mentioned Mrs. Carter and her daughters at the Trappe.

"Do you want to go back where you came from?" Bennington had asked.

Herold replied, "No, I am not at all anxious to do so. But the gentleman that the Captain [Jett] left there will be anxious for me to come back, and I am almost afraid to stay away from him."

The rest of the tale involving the fight at the barn was pretty accurate; after all, it could be confirmed by the soldiers. The only "crime" that Herold admitted to was confirming to Jett that Booth's alias, Boyd, was his real name.

Almost in passing, Herold had said that Booth had at least thirty-five accomplices in Washington. Bingham wanted to know more.

"Did he tell you who these thirty-five men in Washington, or any of them, were?"

"He did not. He mentioned one or two names. I recollect the name of Ed Henson or Hanson. He said that five men ought to have met him. He also mentioned the name of . . . I do not know. He said there was a letter he wrote, and they all signed their names to it--I mean the five-- giving their reasons for doing such things. He told me this the day before we crossed into Virginia."

"What was this letter about?"

"I do not know."

"What did he say he did with this letter?"

"He left it behind, I believe."

"Where?"

"I do not know. He said it would be published. He must have sent it through the post office. I do not know to whom it was sent. He said it would be in the *Intelligencer*."

Herold then agreed that he knew John H. Surratt, Jr., and had last met him through several young men, one of whom he knew worked in the War Department. He gave the full names of all of them. Again, they knew nothing except that they all had met and had a drink together. He was shown nine photographs and recognized John Surratt, George Atzerodt, Edman Spangler, and Mike O'Laughlen. He had never seen the others. He denied that any of them, including himself, had ever had any evil intentions against the person of Abraham Lincoln.

John Bingham looked at his clerk and shook his head. He knew that Herold was in the plot at all levels from kidnapping to murder, but he could make neither heads nor tails of this mish-mash. They would have to hang Herold with the testimony of others, who wished to save their hides more than he did. Bingham led the way out of the monitor's hold into a refreshing burst of clean air. He felt the sudden need for a bath and a clean set of clothes.

6. Weichmann Turns Himself In and Cuts a Deal

Louis J. Weichmann was shaking with fear and anticipation, as he entered the forbidding office at the head of the stairs on the second floor of the War Department. This was not in the War Office building, where Weichmann worked under Brevet Major D. H. L. Gleason, for Brevet Major General William Hoffman, in the Commissary of Prisons. That was to the west across 17th Street. This was the *real* War Department, the nerve center of the vast Union war machine, in popular jargon, the honest-to-God "Lunatic Asylum," right next to the west wing of the White House. It was the place whose telegraph room President Lincoln had visited daily to keep track of the progress of the war. It was at the end of the path from the White House, the spot where John Wilkes Booth had suggested back in March that the conspirators seize Lincoln and transport him to Richmond.

A round-shouldered, balding man sat at the desk that faced the doorway, as Weichmann entered the Secretary's office. An acting assistant adjutant general, the army's fancy name for a glorified clerk with shoulder boards, had told Weichmann to stand quietly at the head of the desk until he was spoken to. The Secretary of War would get to him in due time. Weichmann wondered when "due time" would be. He stood for a minute. The Secretary continued to scratch on the papers in front of him, seemingly oblivious to Weichmann's presence.

Another minute passed. To Weichmann it was more like an eon. The Secretary busied himself with another stack of papers, grabbed a couple of them and wrote a hastily scribbled endorsement on their backs. All official papers in those days were answered in that manner--folded length-wise and the comment for the next reviewing officer written on the back, across the short way. When Stanton wrote an endorsement, it generally meant that the original letter was on its way back to the original issuing officer with an approval or disapproval, unless it went to the

White House, once occupied by Lincoln, now by President Andrew Johnson.

Stanton rode roughshod over all, including President Lincoln, whom he had once characterized as "the original gorilla," and now he would do the same with Johnson. On the antecedents of the New President, Stanton agreed with the acerbic assessment of another Republican, who had once questioned the presence on the ticket in 1864 of this Tennessean, the only Southern U.S. Senator who had remained loyal to the Union, with a gruff, "why couldn't we have got an *American* for the job?" But Lincoln had insisted and the opposition fell by the way.

Finally, after three or four minutes, Edwin McMasters Stanton glared menacingly over his wire-rimmed glasse at the poor, distraught, uncomfortable soul standing before him. He said nothing, he just stared. Weichmann, in great distress, looked back at the Secretary, and then lowered his eyes to break contact, not realizing that the myopic Stanton could see little without peering directly through the thick lenses he wore. Weichmann noticed that the Secretary of War was a man of just under medium height, fairly stout, plainly dressed, and had thinning dark hair and a scraggly beard, both with broad bands of white running through them. He vainly perfumed his beard, as much from a desire to filter out the vile smells that drifted through official Washington, as anything else.

Stanton did not smile; at least few ever saw him smile, much less laugh. He gave short interviews and gave a quick "yes" or "no" to all bribes, requests, and pleadings. There was no appeal; Lincoln rarely overruled his war minister, whom he had fondly dubbed "Mars." It was not hard for Weichmann to see him as one journalist had: "the unloved Secretary of War." But Stanton was not running a popularity contest. He was fighting a war for the very essence of what he saw as the most important entity in the world, the Union without slavery. No one was about to stand in the way of this victory, as Weichmann was very soon to discover.

"I understand you work for me in one of the departments," Stanton said kindly, without looking up.

"Yessir," Weichmann said, "Commissary General of Prisons, Major Gleason under General Hoffman."

"Then," Stanton's voice turned icy as he stared at Weichmann through his thick spectacles, "what do you mean associating with Rebel spies, kidnappers, and murders?"

"Sir, I . . ." Weichmann could feel his sphincters draw up. A chill seized his spine. He hoped that he would not soil himself.

"I have a report here from Colonel J. A. Foster. Do you know him, Mr. Wickman?" Stanton had intentionally mispronounced Weichmann's name. Like the machine-gun fired questions which gave him no time to answer, it was all a part of the strategy designed to unnerve Weichmann and distract him from the real point of the interrogation. Stanton had an inordinate streak of cruelty in his soul at times like this. He enjoyed making his victims squirm.

"It is Weichmann, sir, I . . ."

"Colonel Foster is one of my provost marshals, an investigator, a sort of military prosecutor and policeman, all rolled into one. He has looked into your record and finds it highly improbable that you are ignorant of the doings of your friends and associates, John Wilkes Booth and John Surratt. Indeed, you have as much of our sainted President's blood on your hands as does that arch fiend, the murderer, Booth! Colonel Foster finds it most incriminating, as do I, that you live at the boarding house run by Mrs. Mary Surratt.

"Moreover, Colonel Foster says that you tried to induce your fellow clerks into the plot, promising them thousands of dollars. He has the testimony of a clerk in your office, Gilbert J. Raynor, I believe. I see large amounts of franked envelopes from the Commissary General of Prisons were found in your room--stolen no doubt. Did you not have to take an oath of loyalty to the Union before you were employed?"

"Yes, sir, I. . . ."

"You appear to have done your best to violate that oath--not very inspiring when one finds that you were once a student for the priesthood. Now I am not a papist, but I find it hard to believe that even the Whore of Babylon encourages dishonesty among its priests. Well?"

"Sir, I . . ."

"Are you acquainted with one David E. Herold?"

"Yes, sir. Well, sort of. I met him some three times. The first was at Surrattsville a couple of years ago, the last about eight or ten weeks past."

"Are you the person who drove Mrs. Surratt into the country to set up Booth's escape route on April 14?"

"No, sir."

"What!?"

"Well, I *did* drive Mrs. Surratt, but not to help Booth. She had business with a Mr. Nothey over past due payments on some land her husband sold him years ago. I took her down on April 11, too, for the same reason."

"You deny that she delivered a package from Booth to a confederate there?"

"Well, she did take a few things down for Mr. Booth. But we did not know what they were--at least, *I* did not. They were all wrapped up in a paper."

"Humph! Mighty convenient, if you ask me. You know a man named Lewis Payne, or Wood, or Kinchloe?"

"Well, this fellow Wood did visit Mrs. Surratt's boarding house twice. He did not stay long--a couple of days. And later he came back. Claimed to be a Baptist preacher, name of Paine, but I never believed him. Not honest enough for a Leveler."

Stanton ignored Weichmann's unsubtle attempt to do to Protestantism what the Secretary had unfairly done to Catholicism. "How did you make the acquaintance of the assassin, John Wilkes Booth?"

"We, Johnny Surratt and I, were walking on the street one evening and a man from down country introduced us. We met solely by chance, I assure you."

"Bah! You were introduced quite intentionally by Dr. Samuel Alexander Mudd from Charles County, and Booth became a regular visitor at the Surratt boarding house, and Booth and Surratt had numerous private interviews. When did you last see Booth?"

"Well, I reckon it was about 2 or 2:30 in the evening of April 14, when he gave Mrs. Surratt that package."

"How about Mrs. Slater?"

"Who?"

"You deny that you are acquainted with Sarah Slater? How about Augustus Spencer Howell? Do you know what this is?" Stanton threw the Confederate decoding apparatus that Spencer Howell had taught him to use back in February. "It was found in Booth's effects, but Howell says that it is yours. He gave it to you. He also says you gave him confidential government papers concerning the numbers of Confederate prisoners of war we hold and where."

"Well, I do know Mr. Howell. If you have seen him, you know he has the air and look about him of a natural-born exaggerator. He stayed at the boarding house a couple of months ago. But only for a few days. He was the one traveling with Mrs. Slater. I never really *met* her; I just saw her and was told who she was."

"By whom?"

"Why, by Mr. Howell and Johnny Surratt. And Mrs. Surratt told me that Mr. Howell was a blockade runner."

"When did you last see this *Johnny* Surratt?"

"Well, we had dinner at Kloman's oyster house at the first of this month--before he went to Canada. He boasted of having been down to Richmond and having seen Judah P. Benjamin and Jefferson Davis. They assured him Richmond would not be evacuated. Poor ol' Johnny," continued Weichmann piously, "he has been rather dissipated for some time. Why, he had even been to a house of ill fame!"

"For crying out loud," Stanton said exasperatedly to no one in particular, "this is almost too much to believe."

"Please, Mr. Stanton. I am a loyal man. I told Major Gleason, my direct superior, of the evil intents of Booth and Surratt to kidnap President Lincoln months ago, before the Second Inaugural. Just ask him."

"Oh, I already *have*, you can lay to that! Both he and a fellow officer, Joseph N. Clark of the Adjutant General's Office, have reported everything you told Major Gleason to me, *and* their suspicions that you were directly involved in an assassination plot against the President and the Cabinet. This *before* it actually happened!"

"But I went in to Police Chief Richards and accompanied his men to Surrattsville and Montreal to try and find Surratt."

"All that was accomplished at Surrattsville was for that arch-traitor John M. Lloyd to send the cavalry down the wrong road after Booth. You did nothing to help. But we have taken care of him! By the way, you did not *come* to the Police Station; you had to be *dragged in* by your fellow boarder, John Holohan. And that only after the Metropolitan Police ordered you two to appear. You have heard of Brooke Stabler?"

"The stable manager?"

"That is the man. He says he saw you about dawn on the day after Lincoln's murder. He says that you were--where is that report? (Stanton rummaged about on the desk a minute). Oh, yes, here it is! Stabler says that you--he did not know your name but knew you as a War Department clerk that went around with Booth and Surratt and their friends--that *you* tried to keep him from doing his duty as a law-biding citizen. You wanted him to keep mum on Surratt and Booth and their acquaintanceship with each other and with you. Said that you rode out with Booth often--hum-m-m . . . that *is* interesting--also says that you were nervous and excited, trembled all over, and even wanted a drink of whiskey. You do not look much like a drinking man to me, I daresay. Interesting, this occurred right after the police raided the Surratt boardinghouse . . ."

"But I *did* go into the police . . ."

"Real *cozy* relationship you had with Richards and his men, I will say! Detective McDevitt took care of you like you were his own son.

Arrested you, but never threw you in a cell. Let you sleep on the jailhouse floor without manacles. Fed you breakfast at his own home. Took you to Baltimore to find George Andrew Atzerodt, but it was another wild goose chase. Just like that free trip to Montreal. I had to order Richards to get you back here, and empty-handed at that! Well, I have seen to it that there will be no more interference from the Metropolitan Police, you can rest assured of that."

"Sir, I have here a letter from Bishop John McGill who is sponsoring my continued religious education at St. Mary's Seminar at Baltimore, to begin this fall."

Stanton glanced at the proffered letter, taking in its contents quickly, especially noting that Bishop McGill was from Richmond. Then he stood up, glared at Weichmann, while leaning forward with both fists dug deeply into the blotter on his desk.

"You are a disgrace to you country, sir! I have half a mind to put the rope around your neck, myself! Ah! General Baker! Come in, sir. Put the bracelets on this vermin and take him to the Old Capitol. The charge is treason!"

"Please, Mr. Stanton, hear me out! I want to cooperate . . ."

"Just a minute, General . . . Cooperate, huh? All right, Mr. Weichmann, that is the magic word. You *will*, sir. If you do, if you say everything we tell you to, if you convince the military tribunal--there is not going to be a civilian trial here; after all, Mr. Lincoln was commander in chief--if you hold your composure and bring the public to our side, if you deny any coercion on my part or on that of any of my officers, I will see to it that you do *not* hang. But if you falter one little bit, sir, stumble over one word, fail to do your duty for the first time in your life, you will hang higher than Haman! As God is my witness! You are going to be one very believable and, if necessary, one *lying* son of a bitch! Is that understood, young man?"

Weichmann nodded weakly. He felt faint. He felt sick. He felt violated. He was afraid. Afraid of losing his freedom, his life. He would teach John Surratt and Booth to exclude him from their plans and treat him like a pariah. He would teach them to put his life in jeopardy. Let those who must go to the gallows. Even Mrs. Surratt and Anna, if needs be. He wanted to live--at all costs!

"To the Old Capitol, General!" Stanton snapped. "We do not want our new-found key witness, Mr. Weichmann, to go astray."

If the terrified Weichmann could have but looked back into the Secretary's office, as Baker hauled him off, he would have been shocked to have seen him with his head bowed on his desk, sobbing softly. This job pained and exhausted him, *almost* as much as it pleased him.

7. Sarah Slater Destroys the Evidence

Confederate Secretary of War James A. Seddon recognized talent when he saw it. And "it" stood before his desk at the War Department, in the form of a beautiful young lady. In her early twenties (in fact, she had just turned twenty-two, four days before she had arrived in Seddon's office), light complexioned, with black eyes and raven-colored hair, the slim, delicate-looking young woman was built to please. The Secretary looked at her intently, perhaps too intently, a shade too long. She blushed and lowered her eyes demurely. Her fingers played with the ribbons of her fashionable, petite straw hat, the one with a heavy veil attached to conceal her features from the prying eyes of the lecherous soldiers and civilian contractors, with which Richmond's muddy streets still teemed in mid-January 1865. What an accomplished actress! Seddon marveled.

The Secretary perused the letter that Major Isaac Carrington, the Provost Marshal of Richmond had forwarded to him, along with its bearer:

House of Representatives
January 16, 1865
Sir;
We have the honor to ask for a passport for Mrs. Nettie Slater of Salisbury, North Carolina, to pass the military lines of the Confederate States. She is a resident of Salisbury, but her mother is a French lady residing in the City of New York, and her daughter desires to return to her mother, where she can be more comfortably situated.

She has lost her only brother in the Confederate Army, and we have no hesitation in vouching for her loyalty and her high social position and hope that she will meet with no difficulty in passing the lines of our army.
We have the honor to be,
B. S. Gaither, M[ember of] C[ongress]
J. G. Ramsay, M[ember of] C[ongress]

On the back of the letter, which had been folded vertically, the long way, was Major Carrington's reason for sending her to the Secretary:

Resp'y referred to the Hon. Sec. of War.

My only reason for hesitating in giving this pass is that the husband of the applicant is in the Confederate service. The representations of the Hon. Mssrs. Gaither & Ramsay make a case for exception to the general rule.

I. H. Carrington
Jan'y 16/65 P[rovost] M[arshal]

There must be more to this woman than met the eye, Seddon figured. If he only knew! For example, she had three brothers, not one, two of whom had deserted the Confederate service, one of *them* also being charged with enticing others of his unit to leave with him. But that was just the beginning.

Nettie Slater was born Sarah Antoinette Gilbert (pronounced in the French manner, with a soft, sibilant 'g') in Middletown, Connecticut, in 1843. Her parents came from the French West Indies, and the family spoke French as well as English; in Nettie's case, without a foreign accent in either. Her father manufactured pills, and bore the honorary title of 'Doctor.' He also taught French in a local high school. Her mother ran a rooming house, and evidently, along with her other household duties, Nettie provided little 'extras' for the boarders. In any case, she was known to "enjoy a doubtful reputation," as was said, discreetly, about such things in those days. In the late 1850's the family removed to Hartford where Nettie gave birth to a son out of wedlock.

The event adversely affected the Gilbert family. Her mother took Nettie's boy and her elder daughter and moved to New York City. Disgusted with the whole affair, her father and brothers departed for Kinston, North Carolina. Initially, Nettie followed her mother. But eventually she, too, went to Kinston, and then to New Bern, where she married a local dance instructor, Rowan Slater. The son of a respectable New Bern family, Rowan was looked down upon unfairly as rather effeminate, because of his profession.

The Civil War caused the young Slaters to move to Goldsboro, where Rowan became a Confederate purchasing agent, dancing not being of prime concern for the war generation, as it had been in antebellum days. Eventually, Rowan joined the army, and Nettie never saw him again. After the surrender of Lee's army at Appomattox, Slater would look for his wife, but he would find nothing of her but a death notice. In this, however, he was more successful than the crowd of Yankee detectives that Union Secretary of War Stanton sent out after her. They found nothing at all.

But Seddon, of course, did not know any of this. He would not have cared if he had. He merely suspected that the outwardly sweet, young, sensitive creature standing before him was not as pure as she seemed.

"How would you like to make a little easy money," Seddon asked, "on your feet, not on your back?"

"Really, sir!" she gasped. "I did not come her to be insulted by low, vile creatures such as yourself, posing as government bureaucrats. I *thought* you were a gentleman. I see that I am much mistaken"

"Save the theatrics, Mrs. Slater. I am not here to censure you. I have a proposition for you which will also be of some value to the Confederate government, your past notwithstanding. Actually, it would take someone with what I suspect is your background to pull this off. I want to employ you as a courier for the Confederate War Department, and possibly the State Department. Hear me out," he insisted, with a wave of his hand, as she began to remonstrate. "The job is to carry dispatches from Richmond to Montreal by way of New York City. Each time you accomplish your assigned task, you will be paid in gold. A day or two with your New York family *en route* would seem in order. Are you interested?"

Sarah Slater smiled. Her new career would not last long, she knew, because the Confederacy was on its last pegs. *She* could see that, even if men like Seddon seemed oblivious to the truth of it. She would make three trips for Seddon and Judah P. Benjamin (she had never had sex with a circumcised man like the Rebel Secretary of State before--there was a little something missing in it, she thought), traveling variously with Gus S. Howell and John H. Surratt, Jr. Howell was very business-like, but Surratt was panting the entire way whenever they traveled together, like a rutting, buck elk.

However, John Surratt did not possess the nerve to act on his fantasies. Nettie, like Benjamin's assistant, L. Quinton Washington, recognized him for what he was, "unusually mutton-headed for his role," as Washington had once indelicately put it. And so, lovely Nettie, very much assured of herself, soon had Surratt literally eating out of her hand. When she and Surratt had arrived in Montreal April 4, 1865, Nettie gave her messages to General Edwin G. Lee and moved in with John Surratt. But Yankee pursuit, with Surratt's old chum Louis Weichmnann assisting the Federal officers, caused the twosome to part ways in order to foil potential arrest.

Returning quietly to her mother's residence in New York City, Nettie was dismayed to be arrested in the general sweep of all suspected

Confederate agents. Giving her name as Antionette Gilbert and appealing to the French Embassy, she managed to gain release from the Carrol Annex of the Old Capitol Prison in a matter of days. The April journey with John Surratt was to have been her last trip for the Confederates.

Nettie was startled to hear a knock at her mother's door in New York City, some three weeks later. She peered out through the door glass from behind the dainty lace curtain. A man stood on the stoop. He was middle-aged, tending toward stout, with a black beard and moustache. Was that food stuck on his beard? His suit was unkempt and had streaks of dust on it. It must not have been brushed in weeks. He saw her gaze and waved his hand playfully but carefully in front of his chest, so passersby might not see.

"Yes?" Nettie said, opening the door, ever so slightly.

"Mrs. Slater? I am George N. Sanders. From your friends in Montreal? May I come in? It is most awkward and uncultured, not to say dangerous, to be talking here, so near the street."

"Do you have some identification, sir?"

"Come Retribution."

"Complete Victory. Do come inside, Mr. Sanders."

"Much obliged, ma'am, I'm sure."

Sanders removed his hat and followed her into a parlor, where she motioned him to sit down opposite her.

"We wish to engage your services for another, *one* more, I *assure* you, very dangerous, but *essential*, undertaking, Mrs. Slater."

"But I have done with the Confederacy, sir. Besides, it looks rather like a Lost Cause, now. And I do not relish another, more prolonged stay in the Old Capitol."

"It may be even *more* lost as a cause, unless you can accomplish *the* Secret Service action of the war. I will pay you, say, $25,000 in gold. Half now, the remainder when you have completed your assignment."

"I am to . . ."

"Gain entry to the office of Secretary of War Edwin McMasters Stanton and find the diary of John Wilkes Booth. You will leave the diary there, but you must excise any page that implicates any Confederate official or implies that the Confederate States of American had anything to do with Lincoln's death."

"This appears to be frightfully complex . . . a great deal to ask of anyone."

"If you bring me the pages intact, there will be a bonus."

"How much?"

"Half again as much."

"How do you know I will not hand it over to the Yankees? Or hold some of the pages for blackmail?"

"Because they will hang you. They have no scruples as regards stretching a lady's neck these days. And if you do not play square with me, we will dispose of you in such a manner that no one will ever miss you . . . or your family. But we would much rather *pay* you and keep our end of the deal. You have worked well for us in the past. Thirty-seven thousand five hundred dollars would make for a very fine pension."

"Seventy-five thousand, if I get the pages to you."

"Seventy-five?" Sanders gave his hostess a weary smile. "Mrs. Slater, you took the first payment out of the funds you were to have given General Edwin Gray Lee in Montreal, I believe. We will call your account closed on that little matter, after the discharge of your newly assigned task in the District."

Nettie Slater sighed. "Very well."

"Very well, indeed. Here is my hand on it." As his massive hand enveloped hers, she was aware that he was passing her something. It was a key. She looked at him, questioningly. "I am told it is a copy of that which opens the ironclad safe in Mr. Stanton's office. I daresay you might find some use for it?"

Some days later, a newly hired French-speaking char woman entered Secretary of War Stanton's office. It was late. Very few people were at the War Department at this hour. The Secretary himself was out for the evening, gone home to take rest from the never-ending eccentricities of ending the war that occurred daily. As with most things pertaining to security matters during the War Between The States, on both sides, War Department safeguards were at best lax, and at worst, nonexistent. There were no sentries present; the war was all but over, anyway.

Nettie Slater made a half-hearted swipe with her feather duster across Stanton's desk. She appeared to be listening to noises, or the lack of them, in that hall, rather than cleaning up. She set her bucket, mop, and broom down, strategically placing it so that any intruder would trip over it upon entering. She then lithely stepped over to the heavy safe in the corner.

She took George Sander's key from her blouse, where it had hung concealed between her breasts from a cord around her neck. She had little faith that it would work. It was, after all, cut from a wax impression of the original. She wondered who had got it, how, and when. But then, she was given to understand that many keys to this and other vaults in various departments had been cut early in the war for emergency uses.

She put the key in the lock. It would not turn. She pushed it in harder and twisted. Nothing. Then she pulled the key out slowly, keeping pressure on it, turning it in its slot. Still nothing. She took it out and dressed the rough edges with a metal fingernail file. She reinserted the key in the lock. Finally, after jockeying it around for what seemed like an interminable amount of time, the lock gave way. The door creaked open, noisily. She listened. A door opened and closed far down the corridor. She listened again. No one in the hallway. She looked into the cavernous iron box. There it was! The little brown leather book with the red lining. She picked it up and breathed rapidly in her excitement.

As Nettie Slater examined the diary, she knew one thing for sure--there was no way this material could be made public without resulting in the hanging of many prominent men of, at least up to now, spotless reputations. But, as Sanders had warned her, she could not destroy the diary completely. Too many people had seen it. She could, however, purge it of its most cogent revelations and then let Stanton, the Bakers, and Conger fight it out in the Congress, the courts, and the newspapers as to what it had originally contained.

Nettie looked around to confirm her privacy. Slowly the bogus charwoman took a pen knife and began to cut page after page from the little leather book. The little knife, sharp as a surgeon's scalpel, excised over two dozen pages, leaf after leaf. Then she stopped and placed the little book back into Stanton's massive safe. The public could see it now. It was harmless. Only two innocuous entries were left. At worst, the diary now showed Booth to be an honest, true believer in the Confederacy and his act as that of a revolutionary, or counter- revolutionary, as she surmised Stanton and the upcoming military court would prefer to view it. At best, it showed the assassin to be a paranoid mental case, acting on his own volition without the knowledge of the Confederate government, and in the end, regretting his very move against Lincoln.

The next day, a very sick-to-his-stomach Edwin Stanton stared at Booth's diary with its missing pages. Some one had defaced it, *his* diary, the document that was going to send the high and low, among the Confederate conspirators who had acted against Lincoln, to the gallows. He had already stumbled over Nettie Slater's booby-trap of bucket, broom, and mop, when he had entered the office that morning. He had kicked water all over the floor. The newly hired charwoman who had left behind the tools of her trade was not to be found. It was going to be a long day for Edwin Stanton. There was a knock on the door jamb.

"Here is Louis Weichmann, sir."

"All right, Weichmann," Stanton growled, after his aide left the room." I want you to tell me *everything* you know about this so-called French Woman. Leave nothing out, by God! Remember, the noose awaits he who falters."

Despite Stanton's efforts, Nettie Slater was seen briefly only once afterward in 1868, during a reunion of Confederate agents in Lexington, Kentucky. After that, she disappeared forever into the great void of history.

8. George Sanders Changes History

George Sanders walked into the St. Lawrence Hotel in Montreal and surveyed the room. He readily spied the man he sought standing near the entrance to the hotel bar. Sanders casually made his way over to Charles A. Dunham, a man who could best be described as a shadowy figure in the Confederate society in Canada, an *éminence grise,* as the French aptly say.

As Sanders was aware, Dunham was a noted con-man. Born in Croton, New York, the son of a successful tanner, Dunham had studied law, but had failed to pass his bar exam. Instead he found he had a natural talent for swindling. He seemed to specialize in finding heirs to alleged fortunes for a price. Of course, he pocketed the funds paid him and the fortunes never materialized. His real talent lay in adopting multiple identities and disguises to match. He also wrote numerous letters of varying truth or the lack of it. After Dunham finished with a "client," the unfortunate mark never knew which end was up. The best of investigators could not begin to fathom his expert and confusing trails.

For men like Sanders and Dunham, the American Civil war was an economic windfall--politically and ideologically for Sanders, less nobly so for Dunham. The latter first tried to raise a Union regiment, with himself as colonel. He soon claimed that he had recruited five hundred men. After a period of time, the enrolling authorities looked into his claims and found thirty-six recruits. Dunham was sacked and his men parceled out to other regiments. From there on, he was involved in numerous schemes that necessitated his crossing the lines between North and South, and publishing fake articles under assumed names about his adventures.

The Confederates were very suspicious of Dunham during his first visit to their capitol, and as a result, he spent several months in Castle Thunder, Provost Marshal General John H. Winder's horrible prison in Richmond which housed disloyal and suspicious characters, designed to be so degrading as to elicit quick confessions from its inmates in return for their release from the wretched place. But Dunham had used his time in Richmond, in prison or out, to learn much about the Confederacy. More important, he hung around various departments, purloining official copies of letterhead stationary. It was said that he could make it appear as if the Confederate government was operating out of any desk on the North American continent.

Sanders first saw Dunham hanging around the Niagara Peace Conference in 1864. He was supposedly a news reporter, using his expert knowledge to write articles on Confederate operations out of Canada. Like all reporters of the time, that which he could not divine, he simply made up out of whole cloth. Later, police picked him up while he was snooping around the U. S-Canadian border in the vicinity of St. Albans, Vermont, just after its banks had been liberated of their money by a group of Confederate raiders. He was arrested, but, encouraged by an informer, Canadian authorities soon found that he was harmless and turned him loose. His savior was none other than George N. Sanders.

Sanders began to see great potential in Dunham, who was at the time writing articles for the *New York Tribune,* under the by-line of Sanford Conover. As usual, that which Dunham did not know, he fabricated. He also testified as an expert in the Canadian trial of the St. Albans raiders, authenticating the signatures of Confederate high officials, in this case, Secretary of War James A. Seddon. His testimony got the prisoners released, claiming that Confederate documents introduced to show them to be military men, and not mere robbers, were legitimate. This time, he used the name James Watson Wallace. By now, Sanders, who testified at the trial the same day as Dunham-Conover-Wallace, recognized that Dunham's incomparable talents, the big lie, forgery, aliases, false claims, and thievery, could be utilized on behalf of the Confederate cause.

"Well, sir, good afternoon, Mr. Dunham," Sanders said, as he greeted his collegue in the St. Lawrence House lobby. "Or should I say, Wallace, or Conover? What handle are you going by, now?"

"Easy, now, Mr. Sanders. I have done good work for you and The Cause."

"For a *price*, yes. But never out of *conviction*, I daresay. Speaking of price, how would you like to earn a lifetime's pension, utilizing your expert skills as a story-teller and natural-born prevaricator?"

"From whom?"

"The Confederacy, of course."

"You mean the *defunct* Confederacy?"

"In all but money. We are talking gold, by the way, not paper."

"What is the balram?"

"Say, $25,000?"

"Treble it."

"I cannot go above $50,000 in coin of the realm."

"I am thinking of going off the crook."

"Aw, spare me the theatrics! You could not earn an *honest* living."

"All right, all right! You have made your point. What is the bunco?"

"To save the reputation of the Confederate States of America and its loyal servants, high and low."

"All that? It ought to be worth *at least* a million."

"Come now! This game is a natural for a man of your abilities! You ought to do it *gratis* for the sake of the Stars and Bars. Think of the publicity and the enhancement of your reputation. Your future services will be in demand, world-wide."

"None of that! I will do it for $100,000 in gold. No funny money, Yankee or Confederate."

"Done! Here is the big thing. I want you to admit to the truth to the Confederate expatriates here in Montreal in writing; namely, that you are a fraud, even though what you said at the trial of the so-called Booth conspirators about Confederate official involvement in the Lincoln abduction and assassination was true. Deny that you have ever used the pseudonym of Sanford Conover and sign the thing James W. Wallace. Then go back to the District, and when the Yankees confront you say you were forced to confess in your letter at the threat of your life."

"How about at gunpoint? I can tell them as Charles Dunham that I never testified before any commission or trial as Sanford Conover, even though I did."

"Yeah, that will do fine. The Rebs left up here in exile will do the rest. The will lambaste you in the press as the liar you are. Since they believe it, their arguments will carry much weight."

"All right, Sanders, I get the drift. By the time I get through with this, no one will know who I am, what I said, or who my aliases are."

"That is the spirit! I have a list of paid-off witnesses you can call upon, some fraudulent, some beyond reproach. But the Yanks will not know who is who. We are going to feed them Dr. James B. Merritt, too. He will tell the same tales as you. When we get done, even the witnesses telling the truth, that the Confederate government was behind Booth and his gang, will not be believed. We are not going to let the truth get in the way of history. After all, history is way too important to be left up to the historians."

"What if I get copped? This will all come under the title of perjury."

"Oh, Hell, Dunham, what is a little jail time between friends . . . for $100,000?"

Dunham did what he was paid for. The Confederacy, and its servants, especially Jefferson Davis and John Surratt, were saved by his duplicitous tales of their guilt. No one knew what to believe. The Confederates denied all; Dunham-Conover-Wallace lied, and told the truth, and lied, again and again. But it was not enough to save the immediate conspirators. The Federal solicitors decided to prosecute only those associated directly with John Wilkes Booth *before* the fact of the assassination. Mary E. Surratt, David E. Herold, G. Andrew Atzerodt, and Lewis T. Powell were all hanged. Dr. Samuel A. Mudd, Samuel B. Arnold, and Michael O'Laughlen received prison terms for life. Edman Spangler got a six-year term.

In private, Edwin McMasters Stanton went positively berserk, raging against the leaders of the Rebellion and the incompetency of his own minions. But publicly, he kept his composure. Without Booth's diary, in its complete form, he had no proof of what was the true story. Without the French Woman or George N. Sanders, he had no witnesses to replace the diary. Exasperated, Stanton finally had Dunham arrested, tried, convicted, and sentenced to a long jail term for perjury. But the elusive con-artist managed to escape his captors and disappear into the same oblivion that Clio had reserved for Nettie Slater.

But unlike the never-to-be-seen-again French Woman, Dunham would reappear on the public scene some twenty years later. Now an allegedly prosperous New Jersey lawyer, acquainted since the Civil War with Dr. Francis J. Tumblety, a suspect in the notorious Jack the Ripper murders that had recently plagued London's East End, Dunham described for the yellow press Tumblety's weird proclivities for collecting and preserving wombs and other female body parts, and his all-consuming hatred of women, which stemmed from Tumblety's own failed marriage to a prostitute whose past was unknown to him until after the ceremony.

Tumblety was not a stranger to Lafayette C. Baker or Secretary of War Stanton. He had been arrested in St. Louis during the John Wilkes Booth pursuit where he had been operating an herbal medicine scam using the alias Dr. J. H. Blackburn. This, at a time when the War Department was searching for Dr. *Luke* Blackburn for attempting to spread yellow fever into Yankee cities, miliary posts, and even the Lincoln White

House. Evidently, three weeks in the Old Capitol Prison in 1865 did not intimidate Dunham into maintaining his anonimity in 1888. There is some suspicion that he contacted the press in the Ripper story, not the other way around.

Dunham's last wartime employer, Sanders, went back to Europe after the war. Like John Surratt, he had a $25,000 price tag on his head, courtesy of President Andrew Johnson, and a group of Yankees had tried unsuccessfully to abduct him during that long summer of 1865. He was involved in the revolt of the Paris Commune in 1872. He was on the losing side of that rebellion, too. Shortly after, he returned to the United States and lived out his life in obscurity.

And why not? Stanton was long dead, never achieving the presidency he sought, death snatching him away just as President U. S. Grant appointed him to the U.S. Supreme Court, by way of consolation. John Surratt had walked free after a hung jury, luckily being tried in a civil court. Jefferson Davis had been released. He had suffered several years in jail at Fortress Monroe, having never been brought to trial, with a dignity and nobility that moved even the harshest of Northerners to pity him and to post his bail bond. He would spend the rest of his life defending The Cause he had served so well, this time, in print, as a state rights movement.

President Andrew Johnson, more and more the obstinate defender of the secessionists he had once condemned, until he was impeached by enraged Radical Republicans, had beaten his own removal from office by one vote. In revenge, during his last days as President, he had pardoned Dr. Mudd, Edman Spangler, and Samuel Arnold, and nearly everyone else in the Confederacy, except Jefferson Davis. Congress would give amnesty to all who remained unpardoned in 1872, except for Jefferson Davis. He would not have accepted a pardon had it been offered. Davis believed that he never had done anything wrong--that the public knew of, anyhow. The aftermath of the Civil War, the era of Reconstruction, was fast becoming unpopular, the North proving, in fact, to be more anti African-American as Booth had ever seemed.

In the end, just as Sanders had wanted, everyone was convinced that a lone gunman, that maddest of the "Mad Booths of Maryland," had killed the now-sainted Abraham Lincoln, on his own twisted volition. And there the story has remained, ingrained in the national psyche, for all time.

Clio could and would live with that; and so have the American people, happy in their ignorance, ever since.

The End

END NOTES; OR, THE HISTORY BEHIND THE FICTION

PREFACE: GETTING RIGHT WITH BOOTH

The Celtic saying is central to Douglas Monroe, *The 21 Lessons of Merlyn--A Study in Druid Magic and Lore* (St. Paul, Mn.: Llewellyn Publications, 1992).

Joseph Bradley, Sr., is quoted in Francis Wilson, *John Wilkes Booth: Fact and Fiction of Lincoln's Assassination* (Boston: Houghton Mifflin, 1929), vii. The quotations from Booth's diary are in John Rhodehamel and Louise Taper (eds.), *"Right or Wrong, God Judge Me": The Writings of John Wilkes Booth* (Urbana: University of Illinois Press, 1997), 154. Characterizations of Booth are from Lloyd Lewis, *The Assassination of Lincoln: History and Myth* (Lincoln, Neb.: Bison Books, 1994, original 1929), 131; William Hanchett, "The Lincoln Murder Conspiracies," in Gabor S. Boritt and Norman O. Furness (eds.), *The Historian's Lincoln: Pseudohistory, Psychohistory, and History* (Urbana: University of Illinois Press, 1988), 329, and Stanley Kimmel, *The Mad Booths of Maryland* (2 ed., rev. and enlarged, New York: Dover Publications, 1969); and Edward Steers, Jr., *Blood on the Moon: The Assassination of Abraham Lincoln* (Lexington: University of Kentucky Press, 2001), 2.

For a sample of Boothian fiction, consult Steven G. Miller, "John Wilkes Booth and the Lincoln Assassination in Recent Fiction," *Surratt Courier*, 29 (June 2004), 4-9, which lists twenty-nine pieces of fiction from the period 1983 to 2003 alone. The best one-volume biography of Lincoln is David Donald, *Lincoln* (New York: Simon & Schuster, 1995). For his earlier essay, see Donald, "Getting Right With Lincoln," *Lincoln Reconsidered* (New York: Vantage, 1956); which is complemented by T. Harry Williams, "Abraham Lincoln: Principle and Pragmatism in Politics," *Mississippi Valley Historical Review*, 40 (June 1953), 89-108.

For ideas as to what a Lincolnian Reconstruction *might* have entailed or actually *did* entail, depending on one's viewpoint, see William Hesseltine, *Lincoln's Plan of Reconstruction* (Tuscaloosa: Confederate Publishing Co., 1960); and Harold Hyman, *Lincoln's Reconstruction: Neither Failure of Vision Nor Vision of Failure* (Ft. Wayne, IN: Louis A. Warren Lincoln Library and Museum, 1980).

Lincoln's most recent critic is Lerone Bennett, Jr., *Forced into Glory: Abraham Lincoln's White Dream* (Chicago: Johnson Publishing Co., 1999). Bennett and another Lincoln critic, M. E. Bradford, both see

Lincoln as a skillful manipulator of language, saying one thing and doing another. See Bradford, "Against Lincoln: An Address at Gettysburg," in Boritt and Furness (eds.), *The Historian's Lincoln* , 107-15.

For other, more positive views of Lincoln's Emancipation activities, see Caesar A. Roy, "Was Lincoln the Great Emancipator?" *Civil War Times Illustrated*, 33 (May/June 1994), 46-49; LaWanda Cox, *Lincoln and Black Freedom: A Study in Presidential Leadership* (Columbia: University of South Carolina Press, 1981); and William K. Klingman, *Abraham Lincoln and the Road to Emancipation* (New York: Viking, 2001). The whole process has been dramatized in a popular vein in William Safire, *Freedom: A Novel of Abraham Lincoln and the Civil War* (Graden City, N.Y.: Doubleday & Company, 1987).

A scholarly look at just how much Lincoln changed American government is the theme in Thomas J. DiLorenzo, "The Great Centralizer: Abraham Lincoln and the War Between the States," *Independent Review*, 3 (No. 2, Fall 1998), 243-71. This was expanded and became the basis for DiLorenzo's book, *The Real Lincoln: A New Look at Abraham Lincoln, His Agenda, and an Unnecessary War* (Roseville, CA.: Prima Publishing, 2002).

A fuller, more polemical statement of the same thesis carried to its fullest implications is Greg Loren Durand, "America's Caesar: The Decline and Fall of Republican Government in the United States of America" at www.crownrights.com/caesar. A full bibliography of anti-Lincoln articles of varying venom appear in "King Lincoln Archive," www.lewrockwell.com.

Bennett is taken apart in Michael Burkhimer, "The Lincoln Assassination as a Rebuttal to the Bennett Thesis," *Surratt Courier*, 26 (October 2001), 4-9. Critics of the viewpoint of DiLorenzo (and by implication those who support him) include Geoff Metcalf, "Lincoln: Tyrant or Champion . . . or Both?" at www.worldnewsdaily. com/news/article #27512, who straddles the line and actually winds up supporting DiLorenzo more than debunking him; and Metcalf's ensuing interviews with Richard Ferrier and David Quackenbush, who accuse DiLorenzo of everything from misquoting sources to outright lying. See *ibid*., # 27396, #27346. DiLorenzo defends himself in *ibid*., #27225. The nastiness of the name-calling exchange tends to vindicate DiLorenzo's contention that he "must be hitting a responsive chord. . . ." A somewhat more measured debate is Thomas DiLorenzo and Gerald Prokopowicz. "Abraham Lincoln: Savior or Tyrant?" *North & South*, 7 (January 2004), 44-55.

William L. Richter

A contrary, measured scholarly view to Booth's and others' concept of Lincoln as a grasping king or Roman emperor is in Herman Belz, *Lincoln and the Constitution: The Dictatorship Question Reconsidered* (Ft. Wayne, IN: Louis A. Warren Lincoln Library and Museum, 1984). Also of interest is Jude Wanniski, "Defending Abraham Lincoln," in www.townhall.com/columnists/judewaniski/jw20020625.shtml. A nice short commentary is Frederick Harch, "Lincoln the Tyrant," Journal of the Lincoln Assassination, 19 (December 2005), 42-47.

An essential place to start any examination of John Wilkes Booth is Blaine V. Houmes, *Abraham Lincoln Assassination Bibliography: A Compendium of Reference Materials* (Clinton, Md.: Surratt Society, 1997). See also, Constance Head, "John Wilkes Booth in American Fiction," *Lincoln Herald*, 82 (Winter 1980), 455-62; and her "John Wilkes Booth as a Hero Figure," *Journal of American Culture*, 5 (Fall 1982), 22-28, which argues that a fictional account might allow the reader to reach the real Booth, in a manner which non-fiction never can. This point is argued without reference to Booth in Jill Lepore, "Just the Facts, Ma'am: Fake Memoirs, Factual Fictions, and the History of History," *New Yorker*, 83 (March 24, 2008), 79-83. The perennial interest in Booth is explored in Gene Smith, "The Booth Obsession," *American Heritage*, 52 (September 1992), 105-19.

The "other" Lincoln is in M. E. Bradford, "The Lincoln Legacy: A Long View," in Bradford, *Remembering Who We Are: Observations of a Southern Conservative* (Athens: University of Georgia Press, 1985), 143-56; Bradford, "Dividing the House: The Gnosticism of Lincoln's Political Rhetoric," *Modern Age*, 23 (Winter 1979), 10-24; Thomas Fleming, "Lincoln's Tragic Heroism," *National Review*, 41 (December 8, 1989), 38-40. The quotes on Lincoln by politicians of the time are from Donald, *Lincoln Reconsidered*, 3-4.

Whether Lincoln was the common man's advocate in his economic policies, emphasizing the potential of everyone to advance from laborer or farmer to entrepreneur (Gabor S. Boritt, "Lincoln and the economics of the American Dream," in Boritt and Furness [eds.], *The Historian's Lincoln*, 87-106), or started the Gilded Age of greed and exploitation of the common man by corporations, like the railroads which Lincoln represented as an attorney before the war (Mark W. Summers, *The Plundering Generation: Corruption and the Crisis of the Union* [New York: Oxford University Press, 1987), *Railroads, Reconstruction, and the Gospel of Prosperity: Aid Under the Radical Republicans* [Princeton: Princeton University Press, 1984], and his *The Era of Good Stealings*

[New York: Oxford University Press, 1993]), is open to much question. See M. E. Bradford, "Against Lincoln: An Address at Gettysburg," in Boritt and Furness (eds.), *The Historian's Lincoln*, 107-15, and Phillip S. Paludan, "Commentary on 'Lincoln and the Economics of the American Dream'," *ibid.*, 116-23.

For Bradford's view of the millennial Lincoln, see his "Lincoln, the Declaration, and Secular Puritanism: A Rhetoric for Continuing Revolution," *A Better Guide than Reason: Federalists & Anti-Federalists* (New Brunswick, N.J.: Transaction Publishers, 1994), 185-203, especially 187 (grapes of wrath), 188 (what is believed to be), 198 (Allen Tate), 199-200. The comparison of Lincoln and Jesus Christ is in Steers, *Blood on the Moon*, 292.

For a critiques of Bradford and Fleming, see Harry V. Jaffa, *Crisis of the House Divided: An Interpretation of the Issues in the Lincoln-Douglas Debates* (Garden City, N. Y., Doubleday, 1959); and Jaffa, *A New Birth of Freedom: Abraham Lincoln and the Coming of the Civil War* (Lanham, Md. : Rowman & Littlefield Publishers, 2000); and, for a shorthand version, Jaffa, "Lincoln's Character Assassins," *National Review*, 42 (January 22, 1990), 34-38. Bradford's answer to Jaffa is in "The Heresy of Equality: Bradford Replies to Jaffa," *Modern Age*, 20 (Winter 1876), 62-77. Also, for a more present-minded viewpoint, see Suzanne Garment, "The NEH Becomes a Storm Center Once Again," *Wall Street Journal* (October 31, 1981); and Eric Foner, "Lincoln, Bradford, and the Conservatives," *New York Times* (February 13, 1982), A-24.

A common theme both during the Civil War and now is to point out that Lincoln's opponents were racists and bigots of a high order and to thus ignore the real problems that his presidency entertained. This is the tale of "Father Abraham" that Bennett criticized in *Forced into Glory*, and that modern critics of Bennett employ in lambasting his book, maintaining that any Lincoln statement to the contrary, of which Bennett found many, is circumstantial or out of character. A good synopsis of this attack is in Michael Burkhimer, "The Lincoln Assassination as a Rebuttal to the Bennett Thesis," *Surratt Courier*, 26 (October 2001), 4-9.

The revision of heroes and villains in American history is from C. Vann Woodward, "The Fall of the American Adam," *American Academy of the Arts and Sciences Bulletin*, 35 (1981), 26-34. See also, Jack Kemp, "Getting Lincoln Right," in http://jewish world review.com/cols/kemp1.asp (May 16, 2001).

Machiavelli's thinking on conspiracies is from Claudia Roth Pierpont, "The Florentine: The Man Who Taught Rulers How to Rule," *New Yorker*, 83 (September 15, 2008), 87-93, especially 92.

Whether Yankee occupation practices in the conquered South were measured and more-or-less controlled or vicious and running rampant is argued by Mark Grimsley, *The Hard Hand of War: Union Military Policy Toward Southern Civilians, 1861-1865* (New York: Cambridge University Press, 1995); and Walter Brian Cisco, *War Crimes Against Southern Civilians* (Gretna, La.: Pelican Publishing Company, 2007).

On Americans liking their presidential assassins insane, see James W. Clarke, "Conspiracies, Myths, and the Will to Believe: The Importance of Context," in Boritt and Furness (eds.), *The Historian's Lincoln*, 365-73.

Book 1: The Abductors

PART I: PROLOGUE (1864)

1. The Diary
For lists of Booth's possessions, see William Hanchett, "Booth's Diary," *Journal of the Illinois Historical Society*, 72 (Feb. 1979), 39-56; George S. Bryan, *The Great American Myth: The True Story of Lincoln's Murder* (Introduction by William Hanchett, Chicago: Americana House, 1990, orig. 1940), 266; Jeannine Clarke Dodels, "The Last Days of John Wilkes Booth," (Undated, unpublished ms. in the possession of the author through the kind permission of Professor Dodels), 27-28; Steers, *Blood on the Moon*, 265.

The accidental puncture of Seward's hematoma, which ironically may have saved his life, is revealed in Walter Burke, "A New Twist to the Seward Stabbing," in David Dillon (ed.), *The Lincoln Assassination: From the Pages of the* Surratt Courier, *1986-1999* (13 Parts, Clinton, Md.: The Surratt Society, 2000), II, 23.

A good brief characterization of Stanton is in Roy Z. Chamlee, Jr., *Lincoln's Assassins: A Complete Account of their Capture, Trail, and Punishment* (Jefferson N.C.: McFarland & Company Inc., Publishers, 1990), 35-44, 159. Stanton's gruff manner in daily matters, is from George Alfred Townsend, *Washington: Outside and Inside.* (Hartford: James Betts & Co., 1873), 359-60. The Secretary's course in the wake of Lincoln's assassination is examined in Beverly Bone, "Edwin Stanton in the Wake of the Lincoln Assassination," *Lincoln Herald*, 82 (Winter 1980), 508-21. See also, Hamilton Gay Howard, *Civil War Echoes: Character Sketches and Secrets* (Washington: Howard Publishing Co., 1907), 226-36; and Otto Eisenschiml, "Stanton's Reign of Terror," in his *In the Shadow of Lincoln's Death* (New York: Wilfred Funk, 1940), 191-213.

2. A Raid on Richmond
The classic work on the Kilpatrick-Dahlgren Raid is Virgil Carrington Jones, *Eight Hours Before Richmond* (New York: Holt, 1957). A more modern approach is Duane Schultz, *The Dahlgren Affair: Terror and Conspiracy in the Civil War* (New York: W. W. Norton & Company, 1998). Other accounts of varying length include, Emory Thomas, "The Kilpatrick-Dahlgren Raid, Part I," *Civil War Times Illustrated*, 16 (February 1978), 4-9, 46-48, and "Part II," *ibid.*, (April 1978), 26-33; Bruce Catton, "A Boy Named Martin," in *The Army of the*

Potomac: A Stillness at Appomattox (Garden City, N.Y.: Doubleday, 1953), 1-18; Edward G. Longacre, "To Burn the Hateful City: The Kilpatrick-Dahlgren Raid on Richmond, (February 28-March 4, 1864)," in *Mounted Raids of the Civil War* (South Brunswick, N.J.: A. S. Barnes, 1975), 225-57; and Stephen W. Sears, "Raid on Richmond," *MHQ: The Quarterly Journal of Military History*, 11 (Autumn 1998), 88-96. See also, Sears, *Controversies & Commanders: Dispatches from the Army of the Potomac* (Boston: Houghton Mifflin, 1999), 225-51.

Getting a balanced picture of the role of Union Secretary of War Edwin McMasters Stanton has been most difficult. Stanton's life and career were praised lavishly upon his death, which caused his numerous personal and political enemies, led by Jeremiah Black, to launch a counterattack. The anti-Stanton theme received a big boost with the 1911 appearance of cabinet colleague, Secretary of the Navy Gideon Wells's *Diary*, the best version of which is Howard Beale (ed.), *The Diary of Gideon Wells* (3 vols., New York: Norton, 1960). Other critics, whose methods and research have been widely questioned (see *e.g.*, William Hanchett, "The Historian as Gamesman: Otto Eisenschiml, 1880-1963," *Civil War History*, 36 [March 1990], 5-16) include, Otto Eisenschiml, *Why Was Lincoln Murdered?* (New York: Grossett & Dunlap, 1937), and Theodore Roscoe, *The Web of Conspiracy* (Englewood Cliffs, N.J.: Prentice-Hall, 1959), who see Stanton as being behind Lincoln's untimely death. Stanton receives his due in George C. Gorham, *Life and Public Services of Edwin M. Stanton* (2 vols., Boston: Houghton Mifflin and Company, 1899); Frank A. Flower, *Edwin McMasters Stanton, The Autocrat of Rebellion, Emancipation, and Reconstruction* (Akron, Ohio: Saalfield Pub. Co., 1905); Fletcher Pratt, *Stanton: Lincoln's Secretary of War* (New York: Norton, 1953); and Benjamin P. Thomas and Harold M. Hyman, *Stanton: The Life and Times of Lincoln's Secretary of War* (New York: Knopf, 1962).

An excellent personal description of Stanton is in William E. Doster, *Lincoln and Episodes of the Civil War* (New York: G.P. Putnam's Sons, 1915), 112-33.

General H. Judson Kilpatrick is usually panned in most studies as a comical, rash character. See Edward G. Longacre, "Judson Kilpatrick," *Civil War Times Illustrated*, 10 (April 1971), 24-33; and Stephen Z. Starr, *The Union Cavalry in the Civil War* (3 vols., Baton Rouge: Louisiana State University Press, 1985), particularly volume 2, *passim*; and Samuel J. Martin, *"Kill Cavalry": Sherman's Merchant of Terror. The Life of Union General Hugh Judson Kilpatrick* (Madison N.J.: Fairleigh Dickinson University Press, 1996), who moreover paints him as a coward, which others do not. See also, Howard, *Civil War Echoes: Character Sketches and Secrets*, 214-22.

The Wistar Raid mentioned in Stanton's interview of Kilpatrick is treated in David George, Jr., "'Black Flag Warfare': Lincoln and the Raid Against Richmond and Jefferson Davis," *The Pennsylvania Magazine of History and Biography*, 115 (July 1991), 291-318.

3. The Dahlgren Papers

On General Meade, see George Meade (ed.),*The Life and Letters of General George Gordon Meade* (2 vols., New York: Charles Scribner's Sons, 1913); George Agassiz (ed.), *Meade's Headquarters, 1863-1865: Letters of Colonel Theodore Lyman from Wilderness to Appomattox* (Boston: Atlantic Monthly Press, 1922). For what Patrick knew, see David S. Sparks (ed.), *Inside Lincoln's Army: The Diary of Marsena Rudolph Patrick, Provost Marshal General, Army of the Potomac* (New York: Thomas Yoseloff, 1964). Dahlgren's father defended his son to the end, see Rear Adm. John A. Dahlgren, *Memoir of Ulric Dahlgren* (Philadelphia: J. B. Lippincott, 1872). For the Union Bureau of Military Information, see Edwin C. Fishel, *The Secret War for Union: The Untold Story of Military Intelligence in the Civil War* (Boston: Houghton Mifflin, 1996).

The big problem is the authenticity of the Dahlgren papers, which Jones, Catton, and Longacre more or less accepted, Thomas suspicioned, and Schultz has openly denied. The controversy is presented in David F. Riggs, "The Dahlgren Papers Reconsidered," *Lincoln Herald*, 83 (Summer 1981), 659-67; James W. McPherson, "A Failed Richmond Raid and Its Consequences," *Columbiad: A Quarterly Review of the War Between the States*, 2 (Winter 1999), 130-133; Stephen W. Sears, "The Dahlgren Papers Revisited," *ibid.*, 3 (Summer 1999), at www.thehistorynet.com/Columbiad. James O. Hall, "The Dahlgren Papers: A Yankee Plot to Kill President Davis," *Civil War Times Illustrated*, 22 (November 1983), 30-39, makes the best case for their authenticity. See also, James O. Hall, "Gunning for Davis," *Civil War Times Illustrated*, 37 (February 1999), 66-68.

4. The Confederate Response

The Southern view of the incident is set forth in R. L. T. Beale, "Part Taken by the Ninth Virginia Cavalry in Repelling the Dahlgren Raid," *Southern Historical Society Papers* , 3 (1877), 219-21, and J. Wm. Jones (ed.), "The Kilpatrick-Dahlgren Raid against Richmond," *ibid.*, 13 (1885), 515-60; Lee's view is set forth in letter no. 640, in Clifford

Dowdey and Louis H. Manarin (eds.), *The Wartime Papers of R. E. Lee* (New York: Branhall House, 1961), 678-79.

The change in wartime Confederate policy resulting from the Dahlgren papers is put forth in William A. Tidwell, James O. Hall and David Winfred Gaddy, "Dahlgren's Raid and Its Aftermath," *Come Retribution: The Confederate Secret Service and the Assassination of Lincoln* (Jackson: University Press of Mississippi, 1988), 19, 241-52. The pro-Southern sympathies of the native-born population of Washington, D.C., is high-lighted in Ralph W. Donnelly, "District of Columbia Confederates," *Military Affairs*, 23 (1959-1960), 207-208.

The Richmond Unionists' removal and hiding of young Dahlgren's body is described in Meriwether Stuart, "Colonel Ulric Dahlgren and Richmond's Underground, April 1864," *Virginia Magazine of History and Biography*, 72 (April 1964), 152-204.

Lincoln's complicity in the Richmond Raid is examined with adverse consequences to the President's reputation in David George, Jr., "'Black Flag Warfare': Lincoln and the Raid Against Richmond and Jefferson Davis," 291-318.

5. The Secret Service Plan of 1864
    The Confederate secret plans for 1864 are described in William A. Tidwell, "The Confederate Secret Service in Canada," *April '65: Confederate Covert Action in the Civil War* (Kent, Ohio: The Kent State University Press, 1995), 107-59; Tidwell, Hall, and Gaddy, "Confederate Operations in Canada," *Come Retribution*, 171-211. The reception of *Come Retribution*, with its thesis that the Confederate government actively sought the abduction of Lincoln in response to the Dahlgren papers, has been mixed. See William Hanchett's analysis of some of the reviews in his "The Lincoln Assassination Revisited," *North & South*, 3 (September 2000), 33-39. James E. T. Lange and Katherine DeWitt, Jr., "Who Ordered Lincoln's Death?" *ibid.*, 1 (No. 6, 1998), 16-33, conclude that Judah P. Benjamin was behind turning abduction into murder, an arguable proposition as the discussion in "The Lincoln Assassination: Do the Pieces Fit?" *ibid.*, 2 (April 1999), 26-34, demonstrates. See also, William A. Tidwell to Editor, *ibid.*, 2 (June 1999), 5, on the mechanics of what Benjamin and Davis had to do to authorize of monies spent in secret operations. Both had to know and approve.

See also, George Fort Milton, *Abraham Lincoln and the Fifth Column* (New York: Vanguard, 1942); John W. Headly, *Confederate Operations in Canada and New York* (New York: Time-Life Books, 1984), and James D. Horan, *Confederate Agent: A Discovery in History*

(New York: Crown Publishers, 1954). Most intriguing in this light is the fine work of Larry Starkey, *Wilkes Booth Came to Washington* (New York: Random House, 1976), who views the whole assassination as the "Ultimate Border Incident."

The desire of Generals Lee and Stonewall Jackson, in particular, for a military offensive into the North is detailed in James A. Kegel, *North with Lee and Jackson: The Lost Story of Gettysburg* (Mechanicsburg, Pa.: Stackpole Books, 1996), a drive that was compromised by the more cautious, even indecisive, approach of President Davis, as is shown in Steven E. Woodward, *Davis and Lee at War* (Lawrence: University Press of Kansas, 1995).

Bragg's misgivings are the fictitious voicing of a theme in Kevin Phillips, *The Cousins' Wars: Religion, politics, and the Triumph of Anglo-America* (New York: Basic Books, 1999), 407-57. It is probably way too wise an inquiry for the real Bragg to have made, but a pertinent one, nonetheless. The standard work on Bragg, is Grady McWhiney, and Judith Hallock, *Braxton Bragg and Confederate Defeat* (2 vols., Tuscaloosa: University of Alabama Press, 1969, 1991), an updating and revising of Don Carlos Seitz, *Braxton Bragg, General of the Confederacy* (Freeport, N.Y.: Books for Libraries Press, 1971, orig. 1924).

PART II: THE BOOTHS (1821-1860)

1. The Robinarch

The significance of Abraham Lincoln's 1838 Speech before the Young Men's Lyceum is laid out in Edmund Wilson, *Patriotic Gore: Studies in the Literature of the American Civil War* (New York: Oxford University Press, 1962), 106-108. A more recent look ad the speech is Major L. Wilson, "Lincoln and Van Buren in the Steps of the Fathers: Another Look at the Lyceum Address," *Civil War History*, 29 (September 1983), 197-211. Also important are the materials in George B. Forgie, "Lincoln's Tyrants," in Boritt and Furness (eds.), *The Historian's Lincoln*, 285-312. Forgie wonders whether Jefferson Davis and others of the same era saw a similar threat to American institutions as did Lincoln, and reacted just as dictatorially as he has been accused of doing.

See also, the comments by M. E. Bradford, "The Lincoln Legacy: A Long View," 153-55; Thomas Fleming, "Lincoln's Tragic Heroism," 38-40; and Bennett, *Forced into Glory*, 201-204.

The speech itself is in Roy P. Basler *et al.* (eds.), *The Collected Works of Abraham Lincoln* (9 vols., New Brunswick, N.J.: Rutgers University Press, 1953), I, 108-15.

For Lincoln's physical characteristics and their effect on his health, see Edward J. Kempf, "Abraham Lincoln's Organic and Emotional Neurosis," in Norman Kiell (ed.), *Psychological Studies of Famous Americans: The Civil War Era* (New York: Twayne Publishers, 1964), 67-87.

On Lincoln's import on American political thought, then and now, see M. E. Bradford, "Lincoln, the Declaration, and Secular Puritanism: A Rhetoric for Continuing Revolution," in his *A Better Guide than Reason,* 185-203, which covers some of the same ground as Phillips, *Cousin's Wars*, *passim.*

2. He Was Called John Wilkes for a Reason

The views of the English Opposition Politicians of the eighteenth century, generally called Whigs, and of the King's Men, generally called Tories, are explained in Bernard Bailyn, *Ideological Origins of the American Revolution* (Cambridge: Harvard University Press, 1967). The best treatment of Algernon Sidney is Caroline Robbins, "Algernon Sidney's *Discourses Concerning Government*: Textbook of Revolution," *William and Mary Quarterly*, Series 3, 4 (1947), 267-96; see also, Alan Craig Houston, *Algernon Sidney and the Republican Heritage in England and America.* (Princeton: Princeton University Press, 1991).

For the ideological naming of Booth males--the female progeny escaped such, generally, although sister Asia Frigga went through the usual male naming process (Asia for the continent upon which mankind first walked and Frigga for the Norse goddess of marriage and home)-- see, Terry Alford (ed.), *John Wilkes Booth: A Sister's Memoir by Asia Booth Clarke* (Jackson: University Press of Mississippi, 1996), 5.

See also, Gene Smith, *American Gothic: The Story of America's Legendary Theatrical Family--Junius, Edwin, and John Wilkes Booth* (New York: Simon & Schuster, 1992), 17-43; and Kimmel, *Mad Booths of Maryland*, 340-41; David Miller DeWitt, *The Assassination of Abraham Lincoln* (New York: Macmillan, 1909), 1-2, George Alfred Townsend, *The Life, Crime, and Capture of John Wilkes Booth* (New York: Dick & Fitzgerald, 1865), 19-27; Wilson, *John Wilkes Booth,* 1-25.

3. Bastards All

Smith, *American Gothic*, 17-23, 33-36, 43. Kimmel, *Mad Booths of Maryland*, Parts I & II, gives the fullest treatment of Booth family relations in England and America. Also of interest, Deidre Barber Kincaid, ""Mary Ann Doolittle: The 'Flower Girl' Myth of the Booths' Mother," *Surratt Courier*, 29 (March 2004), 3-5.

4. Madder than a Hatter
For the antics of Junius Brutus Booth, Sr., consult Smith, *American Gothic*, 24-32; Kimmel, *Mad Booths of Maryland*, 13-92; Effie Ellsler Weston (ed.), *The Stage Memories of John A. Ellsler* (Cleveland: The Rowfant Club, 1950), 15-17, 70-85, and Lewis, *The Assassination of Lincoln*, 131-43. Even if apocryphal, these tales did create the real aura that preceded and followed the Elder Booth, and even his sons, everywhere. The craziness seemed to continue each generation, see David Rankin Barbee, "Lincoln and Booth" (Unpublished ms. in the David Rankin Barbee [DRB] papers, Georgetown University [GU], 392-411.

5. The Old Man's Guardians
Kimmel, *The Mad Booths of Maryland*, 13-145, is best here. See also, Smith, *American Gothic*, 24-25, 36-40; Ellsler, *Stage Memories*, 81-82. On Tudor Hall, see Dorothy Fox, "Childhood Home of an American Arch-Villain," *Civil War Times Illustrated*, 29 (March-April 1990), 12, 14, 18, 66-67; Ella V. Mahoney, *Sketches of Tudor Hall and the Booth Family* (Baltimore: Franklin Printing Co., 1925).

6. Down on "The Farm"
Alford (ed.), *John Wilkes Booth: A Sister's Memoir by Asia Booth Clarke*, 31-101, *passim*; Asia Booth Clarke, *The Elder and Younger Booth* (Boston: James R. Osgood, 1882), 65-68; Smith, *American Gothic*, 44-76. On the Old Capitol Prison, see Robertson, James I. "Old Capitol: Eminence to Infamy," *Maryland Historical Magazine*, 65 (Winter 1970), 394-412; Joan L. Chaconas, "Old Capitol Prison," in Michael W. Kauffman (ed.), *In Pursuit of . . . : Continuing Research in the Field of the Lincoln Assassination* (Clinton, Md.: Surratt Society, 1990), 115-16; Virginia Lomax, *The Old Capitol and Its Inmates* (New York: E.J. Hale & Son, 1867); and James J. Williamson, *Prison Life in the Old Capitol and Reminiscences of the Civil War* (West Orange, N. J.: N. Pub., 1911).

7. His Father's Son
Alford (ed.), *John Wilkes Booth: A Sister's Memoir by Asia Booth Clarke*, 31-101, *passim*. John Wilkes Booth to T. William O'Laughlen, January 25, April 30 (I got my eye, tell th[em] to kiss my), August 8 (whent to a Champaign), November 8, 1854 and January 25 (very pleasant place, Bac[c]hus I believe), June 18 (I will do nothing), November 12, 1855, in Rhodehamel and Taper (eds.), *Writings of John Wilkes Booth*, 37-44. See also, Barbee, "Lincoln and Booth," 207-28,

DRB papers, GU. On the medieval aspects of antebellum Southern life, see Rollin G. Osterweis, *Romanticism and Realism in the Old South* (New Haven: Yale University Press, 1949).

8. Billy Bow-Legs
Alford (ed.), *John Wilkes Booth: A Sister's Memoir by Asia Booth Clarke*, 31-101, *passim*. On Booth's education, such as it was, see James O. Hall, "John Wilkes Booth at School," *Surratt Courier*, 16 (July 1991), 3-4; Rhodehamel and Taper (eds.), *Writings of John Wilkes Booth*, 37n.1; Roscoe, *Web of Conspiracy*, 32-33. For what it is worth, William H. Seward, Abraham Lincoln's Secretary of War had the same nickname, "Billy Bowlegs," as as Booth while a youth. See Shelby Foote, *The Civil War* (3 vols., New York: Vintage Press, 1874), I, 18.

9. A Mother's Omen and the Gypsy Curse
Alford (ed.), *John Wilkes Booth: A Sister's Memoir by Asia Booth Clarke*, 33-34, 40-44, 66.

10. The Reluctant Farmer
Alford (ed.), *John Wilkes Booth: A Sister's Memoir by Asia Booth Clarke*, 46-50, 71-73; John Wilkes Booth to T. William O'Laughlen, August 8, 1854, in Rhodehamel and Taper (eds.), *Writings of John Wilkes Booth*, 38-39 and footnotes.

11. The Aspiring Actor
On Edwin going to Australia, see Kimmel, *Mad Booths of Maryland*, Part II. For Mary Ann Holmes Booth's appearance in Boston, see Terry Alford, "Mary Ann Holmes--Actress?" *Surratt Courier*, 16 (May 1991), 5-6; on John Wilkes Booth's theater studies and debut, Alford (ed.), *John Wilkes Booth: A Sister's Memoir by Asia Booth Clarke*, 50-51, 76-77.

PART III: ANTEBELLUM (1821-1860)

1. The Proselyte and the Drunkard
The best thumbnail sketch of Mary Surratt is Laurie Verge, "A Portrait of Mary Surratt," Kauffman (ed.), *In Pursuit of . . .* , 47-52, also reprinted more recently in *Surratt Courier*, 31 (March 2006), 4-7. The most comprehensive biography is Elizabeth Stegner Trindal, *Mary Surratt: An American Tragedy* (Gretna: Pelican Publishing Co., 1996). For the materials in this section see 13-26.

The description of the tavern as an eight room building is from Townsend, *Washington: Outside and Inside*, 707-708. The present-day attached kitchen is commonly referred to as a storeroom in Antebellum and Civil War era accounts. See *e.g.*, Testimony of John Lloyd, Benn Pitman (comp.), *The Assassination of President Lincoln and the Trial of the Conspirators* (Cincinnati: Moore, Wilstach & Baldwin, 1865), 85 and R. Sutton, *et al* (comps.), *The Reporter: Containing . . . Trial of John H. Surratt, on an Indictment for Murder of President Lincoln* (Washington: Sutton, 1867), III, 246-58. But see the testimony of George Kallenbach, in James O. Hall, "Hiding the Shooting Irons," Dillon (ed.), *The Lincoln Assassination: From the Pages of the* Surratt Courier, I, 19-21, which identifies the attached kitchen as it is now.

As their titles and subtitles imply, most Mary Surratt biographies (with the refreshing exception of Kate Clifford Larson, *The Assassin's Accomplice: Mary Surratt and the Plot to Kill Abraham Lincoln* [New York: Basic Books, 2008]) are concerned with her guilt in the Lincoln plots, abduction and assassination, and wonder if her punishment fit the crime, or if, indeed, she committed any crime. See Guy W. Moore, *The Case of Mrs. Surratt: Her Controversial Trial and Execution for Conspiracy in the Lincoln Assassination* (Norman: University of Oklahoma Press, 1954); and Helen Jones Campbell, *The Case for Mrs. Surratt* (New York: G. P. Putnam's Sons, 1943), which is helped, or hindered, depending upon one's point of view, by its strong use of dialogue to set the scene. See also, Laurie Verge, "John P. Brophy," Kauffman (ed.), *In Pursuit of . . .* , 189-94, who believes that evidence of her innocence lay in Stanton's office safe; and the analysis of Frank Russo, "An Interesting Look at Mrs. Surratt's Guilt or Innocence," *Surratt Society News*, 9 (March 1984), 5-6, who postulates that when she denied her guilt it was cleverly done after her confession to Father J. A. Walter, which prohibited him from ever revealing what she had actually confessed to. Definitive modern statements of Mary Surratt's guilt are in Clark Larsen, "A Policeman's Perspective," Dillon (ed.), *The Lincoln Assassination: From the Pages of the* Surratt Courier, VI, 17-20; and James O. Hall, *The Surratt Family and John Wilkes Booth* (Clinton, Md.: Surratt Society, ca. 1993), 16-17, 21-23.

See also, Thomas Reed Turner, "Mrs. Mary Surratt," in his *Beware the People Weeping: Public Opinion and the Assassination of Abraham Lincoln* (Baton Rouge: Louisiana State University Press, 1982), 155-81; Otto Eisenschiml, "The Woman in the Case," in his *Why Was Lincoln Murdered?* (Boston: Little, Brown and Company, 1937), 270-95; Chamlee, *Lincoln's Assassins*, 98-103; Roscoe, *Web of Conspiracy*, 44-

50; J. E. Buckingham, *Reminiscences and Souvenirs of the Assassination of Abraham Lincoln* (Washington: Rufus H. Darby, 1894), 43-45; Hall, *The Surratt Family and John Wilkes Booth*, 1-8. James E. T. Lange and Katherine DeWitt, Jr., "The Law of Conspiracy," Dillon (ed.), *The Lincoln Assassination: From the Pages of the* Surratt Courier, VI, 3-4, explain how one can become ensnared in a plot without actually being there to effect it.

A nice compromise; Mary Surratt knew of the kidnapping plot but not the shift to assassination. See Laurie Verge, "Mrs. Surratt: Did She or Didn't She?" (Unpublished paper delivered to the Surratt Society, March 29, 2003).

2. The Belle of Prince George's County
Joseph George, Jr., "'A True Childe of Sorrow': Two Letters of Mary E. Surratt," *Maryland Historical Magazine*, 80 (Winter 1985), 402-405. A typescript of the letters, which we have interpreted differently than Professor George, is available in the vertical file at the James O. Hall Library, Surratt House Museum, Clinton, Maryland. See also, Kenneth J. Zanca, "Was Mrs. Surratt Married in the Church?" *Surratt Courier*, 28 (January 2003), 5-7, and the commentary by Alfred Isaacson, "More on the Surratt Wedding," *Surratt Courier*, 28 (March 2003), 6-7.

3. St. Ignatius and His Disciple
Factual materials taken from Trindal, *Mary Surratt*, 19-39, and xeroxed article by J. G. S. on the Rt. Rev. Joseph Finotti, from the vertical file at the James O. Hall Library, Surratt House Museum.

4. The Seventh Commandment
Most scholars doubt the affair, but its rumor titillated citizens of Southern Maryland for years. See Article by Johnny Bouquet, "Johnny Bouquet's Walks: 'Maryland, My Maryland,'" *New York Times*, May 8, 1881, p. 10, and appended note from James O. Hall to Laurie Verge, February 11, 1990, vertical file, James O. Hall Library, Surratt House Museum.

5. Heartbreak and Scholarship
See comment by John C. Brennan, January 14, 1989, the vertical file at the James O. Hall Library, Surratt House Museum. The letters are all in Mary Surratt's file, *ibid.*, by date. See also, Trindal, *Mary Surratt*, 41-44; Joseph George, Jr., "'A True Childe of Sorrow': Two Letters of

Mary Surratt," 402-405; and "New Surratt Letters Discovered," *Surratt Courier*, 13 (October 1988), 5-6.

6. Two School Chums
Louis J. Weichmann, *A True Story of Abraham Lincoln and of the Conspiracy of 1865* (Edited by Floyd E. Risvold. New York: Alfred A. Knopf, 1975), 11-17. For an early essay on Weichmann and the part he played in the Lincoln conspiracies, which has become a fairly standard treatment of the subject, see Osborn H. Oldroyd, *The Assassination of Abraham Lincoln: Flight, Pursuit, Capture, and Punishment of the Conspirators* (Washington: O. H. Oldroyd, 1901), 153-93.

Technically, Weichmann's family spelled the name Wiechmann, but its spelling and pronunciation have been butchered for so long that even he changed it to Weichmann. For a modern author who refuses to follow this convention, see Steers, *Blood on the Moon*, 80, *et seq.*

On Isaac Surratt, see Joseph E. "Rick" Smith III and William L. Richter. "Isaac in Texas—A Theoretical Look at the Other Surratt," *Surratt Courier*, 33 (November), 3-7.

7. High Society
For Booth's career prior up to his Richmond appearances, see Gordon Samples, *Lust for Fame: The Stage Career of John Wilkes Booth* (Jefferson, N.C.: McFarland & Company, Inc., 1982), 19-46. On Booth's allergies and relation with the Beal's, see John Wilkes Booth to Edwin Booth, Sept. 10, 1858, and the advertisements selling the livestock and the renting of The Farm in Rhodehamel and Taper (eds.), *Writings of John Wilkes Booth*, 44-46 and footnotes; Barbee, "Lincoln and Booth," 229-54, DRB papers, GU.

8. A Public Hanging
The general story line follows Glenn Tucker, "John Wilkes Booth at the John Brown Hanging," *Lincoln Herald*, 78 (Spring 1976), 3-11. John Brown's statements and the hanging are from Stephen B. Oates, *To Purge this Land with Blood: A Biography of John Brown* (New York: Harper & Row, 1970), 351-52. See also, Louis, *The Assassination of Lincoln*, 147-49; Alford (ed.), *John Wilkes Booth: A Sister's Memoir by Asia Booth Clarke*, 81, 88-89.

See letters from Mary Devlin Booth to Edwin Booth, November 28, 1859 (Your news regarding); December 28, 1859 (I grieve), in L. Terry Oggel (ed.), *The Letters and Notebooks of Mary Devlin Booth* (New York: Greenwood Press, 1987), 22-23, 27-29.

My story of the meeting of Booth and Beall is imagined from William A. Tidwell, "John Wilkes Booth and John Yates Beall," *Surratt Courier*, 25 (November 2000), 3-5. Beall's influence in Booth's life is real (see, *e.g.*, J. Ninian Beall, "Why Booth Killed Lincoln," Columbia Historical Society of Washington, D.C., *Records*, 48-49 [1946-1947], 127-41), but too much has been made of it. It was peripheral, not central.

9. The Political Philosophy of John Wilkes Booth I: The Fugitive Slave Issue
The argument here generally follows the materials presented in Arthur Bestor, "State Sovereignty and Slavery: A Reinterpretation of Proslavery Constitutional Doctrine, 1846-1860," *Journal of the Illinois State Historical Society*, 53 (1960), 117-80. See also, William L. Richter, "Out of the Sahara of the Bozart: The Political Thought of John Wilkes Booth" (Unpublished paper delivered to the Surratt Society, April 1, 2006).

On state rights before the secession movement, much of which occurred in the North rather than the South, see Thomas J. DiLorenzo, *The Real Lincoln*, 85-129, and DiLorenzo, "Yankee Confederates: New England Secession Movements Prior to the War between the States," in David Gordon (ed.), *Secession, State and Liberty* (New Brunswick, N. J.: Transaction Publishers, 1998), 135-53; James M. Banner, Jr., *To the Hartford Convention: The Federalists and the Origins of Party Politics in Massachusetts, 1789-1815* (New York: Knopf, 1970); William W. Freehling, *Prelude to Civil War: The Nullification Crisis in South Carolina, 1816-1836* (New York: Harper & Row, 1965); Thomas D. Morris, *Free Men All: The Personal Liberty Laws of the North, 1780-1861* (Baltimore: The Johns Hopkins University Press, 1974).

Interestingly, Lincoln himself made some pro-secession statements as a Congressman during the Mexican War, which he vehemently opposed. See Herbert Mitgang, "The Mexican War Dove," *New Republic*, 156 (February 11, 1967), 24, as quoted in a longer piece on secession's place in U. S. and world history by Reo M. Christensen, "Secession? Certainly!" in Christensen, *Heresies Right and Left: Some Political Assumptions Reexamined* (New York: Harper & Row, 1973), 51-70.

In 1860, the South would personalize its concern with the fugitive issue, preferring to see Lincoln's oral pledges to return escaped slaves as duplicity rather than separate from Radical Republican promises to end the system. See Bennett, *Forced into Glory*, 288-91.

10. The Political Philosophy of John Wilkes Booth II: Slavery in the Territories

Bestor, "State Sovereignty and Slavery: A Reinterpretation of Proslavery Constitutional Doctrine, 1846-1860," 117-80, and Richter, "Out of the Sahara of the Bozart: The Political Thought of John Wilkes Booth." The most comprehensive work on the Dred Scott decision is Don Fehrenbacher, *The Dred Scott Case: Its Significance in American Law and Politics* (New York: Oxford University Press, 1978). See also, F. H. Hodder, "Some Phases of the Dred Scott Case," *Mississippi Valley Historical Review*, 16 (June 1929), 3-22; and Bennett, *Forced into Glory*, 260-63, where he voices the opinion that Lincoln's concern with the constitutional issued raised by Dred Scott was an expression for white migration to the west free of any black competition, slave or free. This is not totally fair, because in his "House Divided" speech, Lincoln revealed that he feared that the U.S. Supreme Court would expand the Dred Scott decision to make slavery legal within all of the states, even the free ones. See Roy Basler (ed.), *The Collected Works of Abraham Lincoln* (9 vols., New Brunswick: Rutgers University Press, 1953), II, 464-65, for Lincoln's expert analysis of Dred Scott. See also, Alexander Gigante, "Slavery and a House Divided," at http://afroamhistory.about.com/library/prm/blhousedivided.htm.

11. A Country Doctor

On the youth of Dr. Mudd and the life in southeastern Maryland, see Nettie Mudd, *The Life of Samuel A. Mudd* . . . (New York: Neale Publishing, 1908, reprinted 1962), 23-29; Eldon C. Weckesser, *His Name Was Mudd: The Life of Dr. Samuel A. Mudd, Who Treated the Fleeing John Wilkes Booth* (Jefferson, N.C.: McFarland & Co., Inc., 1991), 55-67; Samuel Carter III, *The Riddle of Dr. Mudd* (New York: G. P. Putnam's Sons, 1974), 11-41 Hal Higdon, The Union vs. Dr. Mudd (Chicago: Follett Publishing Company, 1964), 17-21. All of these volumes, to one degree or another, see Dr. Mudd as an essentially loyal man unfairly prosecuted for his role in setting Booth's leg.

Most Mudd biographers use "Frank" for Mrs. Mudd's nickname. We have chosen, however, to use "Frankie," because it sounds more femine, and according to its use in a letter from Margaret Bearden to Dr. Richard Mudd, January 12, 1962.

On the secession movement, see Dwight L. Dumond, *The Secession Movement, 1860-1861* (New York: Octagon Books, 1963, orig. 1931); William L. Barney, *The Road to Secession: A New Perspective on the Old South* (New York: Praeger, 1972); Steven A. Channing, *Crisis of*

Fear: Secession in South Carolina (New York: Norton, 1970); Daniel Crofts, *Reluctant Confederates: Upper South Unionists in the Secession Crisis* (Chapel Hill: University of North Carolina Press, 1989); David Gordon (ed.), *Secession, State, & Liberty*; Paul C. Nagel, *One Nation Indivisible: The Union in American Thought, 1776-1861* (New York: Oxford University Press, 1964); Ulrich B. Phillips, *The Course of the South to Secession: An Interpretation* (New York: Appleton-Century, 1939); David M. Potter, *Lincoln and His Party in the Secession Crisis* (New Haven: Yale University Press, 1962, 2nd rev. ed.); and Kenneth M. Stampp, *And the War Came: The North and the Secession Crisis, 1860-1861* (Baton Rouge: Louisiana State University Press, 1950).

The suspension of civil liberties is usually excused as Lincoln rationalized it--it was necessary to save the Union and the Constitution. Adherents to this theory point out that only some 13,500 persons suffered arbitrary arrest and most arrests came to enforce conscription--which ignores what happened in Maryland, especially in 1861. Others find the total arrests to be more like 18,000 to 30,000. See John A. Marshall, *American Bastille: A History of the Illegal Arrests and Imprisonment of American Citizens during the Late Civil War* (New York: De Capo, 1970, orig. 1869); Frank L. Klement, *Dark Lanterns: Secret Political Societies, Conspiracies, and Treason Trials in the Civil War* (Baton Rouge: Louisiana State University Press, 1984); Harold M. Hyman and William M. Wiecek, *Equal Justice under Law: Constitutional Development, 1835-1875* (New York: Harper & Row, 1982); Mark E. Neely, Jr., *The Fate of Liberty: Abraham Lincoln and Civil Liberties* (New York: Oxford University Press, 1991); and Herman Belz, *Lincoln and the Constitution: The Dictatorship Question Reconsidered*. For a deeper, different view, consult James Ostrowski, "Was the Union Army's Invasion of the Confederate States a Lawful Act? An Analysis of President Lincoln's Legal Arguments Against Secession," in Gordon (ed.), *Secession State and Liberty*, 155-90.

12. The Conditional Unionist

For the background to Booth's undelivered speech, see Jeannine Clarke Dodels, "Water on Stone: A Study of John Wilkes Booth's 1860 Political Draft Preserved at the Players' Club NY" (unpublished paper, a copy of which was graciously given to us by the author). The account in Rhodehamel and Taper (eds.), *Writings of John Wilkes Booth*, 47-53, relies heavily on this paper. Booth's speech is published in several places, *ibid.*, 55-64, being one of the best sources, amplified by explanatory footnotes, *ibid.*, 64-69. See also, Dodels, "John Wilkes Booth's Secession

Crisis Speech of 1860," in Arthur Kincaid (ed.), *John Wilkes Booth, Actor: The Proceedings of a Conference Weekend in Bel Air, Maryland, May 1988* (North Leigh, Oxfordshire: Privately Published, 1988), 48-51.

On Lincoln's rejection of various peace efforts in 1861, see Richard N. Current, *Lincoln and the First Shot* (Philadelphia: J. B. Lippincott and Co., 1963); Jeffrey R. Hummel, "Why Did Lincoln Choose War?" *North & South*, 4 (September 2001), 38-44; David Rankin Barbee, "How Lincoln Rejected Peace Overtures in 1861," *Tyler's Quarterly Historical and Genealogical Magazine*, 15 (Jan. 1934), 137-44; Robert Gray Gunderson, *Old Gentlemen's Convention: The Washington Peace Conference of 1861* (Madison: University of Wisconsin Press, 1961), 21, 34, 83, 85, 88-89, 99-100, 102.

There have been many recent explorations of why the South seceded (race and slavery are the most favored topics, then and now), or was secession legal (still a sectional argument). This discussion is best illustrated by the excellent on-going debate in *North & South* magazine. See Kent Masterson Brown, "Secession: A Constitutional Remedy for the Breach of the Organic Law," 3 (August 2000), 12-21; John Y. Simon, "'Rebellion Thus Sugar-coated,'" 3 (September, 2000), 10-16; James M. McPherson, "What Caused the Civil War?" 4 (November 2000), 12-22; and Charles B. Dew, "Apostles of Secession," 4 (April 2001), 24-38, which provides a fine introduction for his book, *Apostles of Secession: Southern Secession Commissioners and the Causes of the Civil War* (Charlottesville: University Press of Virginia, 2001).

All in all, many of these essays confirm what premier historian of the South Ulrich B. Phillips called the "Central Theme of Southern History" (*American Historical Review*, 24 [October 1928], 30-43), that the South would always act politically to remain a "white man's country." For a statement from Alexander Stephens, now Vice President of the Confederacy, that slavery was the cause of the war and the "cornerstone" of the Southern social divide between whites and blacks, see the discussion on Bennett, *Forced into Glory*, 341-43. But nothing yet beats the plain reasoning in Mel Bradford, "All to Do Over: The Revolutionary Precedent and the Secession of 1861," in Bradford, *A Better Guide than Reason*, 153-68. See also, Eugene D. Genovese, *The World the Slaveholders Made: Two Essays in Interpretation* (New York: Vintage, 1971), 99-102.

On the events surrounding Ft. Sumter, see Albert Castel, "Fort Sumter--1861," *Civil War Times Illustrated*, 15 (October 1976), [Special Issue]; Robert Hendrickson, *Sumter: The First Day of the Civil War* (Chelsea, MI: Scarborough House, 1990); Roy Meredith, *Storm over*

Sumter (New York: Simon & Schuster, 1957); W. A. Swanberg, *First Blood: The Story of Fort Sumter* (New York: Charles Scribner's Sons, 1957).

PART IV: THE MAELSTROM (1861-1864)

1. Judah P. Benjamin I: His Women
Considering that he destroyed most of his personal and political papers, there has been a lot of work done on Benjamin, a testimony to this interesting character and his importance to attempting to achieve Rebel independence. He was the only person to serve in three positions under Jefferson Davis: Attorney General (February 25, 1861), Secretary of War (September 17, 1861), and Secretary of State (February 22, 1862). See Pierce Butler, *Judah P. Benjamin* (Philadelphia: George W. Jacobs & Company, 1906), good for its quotes of old letters and documents; Robert Douthat Meade, *Judah P. Benjamin: Confederate Statesman* (New York: Oxford University Press, 1943), which set a new standard for its time; Simon I. Niemon, *Judah Benjamin* (Indianapolis: Bobbs-Merrill, 1963); Martin Rywell, *Judah Benjamin: Unsung Rebel Prince* (Asheville, N.C.: Stephens Press, 1948), short, but poignant; and Eli N. Evans, *Judah P. Benjamin: The Jewish Confederate* (New York: The Free Press, 1988), by far the best of the lot, who examines his subject from the viewpoint of being a Jew, a Southerner, an American, and a cosmopolitan citizen of the western world. None of them see Benjamin as a conspirator against Lincoln's person, in any way, shape or form.
There are numerous shorter essays on Benjamin's role in the Confederacy, but the best for our purposes are Hudson Strode, "Judah P. Benjamin's Loyalty to Jefferson Davis," *Georgia Review*, 20 (1966), 251-60, the title of which reveals Benjamin's key to Davis' trust; Robert Douthat Meade, "Judah P. Benjamin," *Civil War Times Illustrated*, 10 (June 1971), 10-20, a good general survey; Meade, "The Relations between Judah P. Benjamin and Jefferson Davis," *Journal of Southern History*, 5 (1939), 468-78; and Eli N. Evans, "In Search of Judah P. Benjamin," in Evans, *The Lonely Days Were Sundays* (Jackson: University Press of Mississippi, 1993), 17-34, a moving essay, actually an interview of author Evans, which places Judaism in its Southern context.
The best and most recent one-volume studies of the Confederate President are William J. Cooper, *Jefferson Davis: American* (New York: Knopf, 2000); and Herman Hattaway and Richard E. Beringer, *Jefferson Davis, Confederate President* (Manhattan: University Press of Kansas, 2002).

2. Judah P. Benjamin II: Ideological Heart of the Confederacy
    Any of the Benjamin biographies covers the ground of this
chapter. The conclusion is our interpretation of Evans, "In Search of
Judah P. Benjamin," 17-34.

3. Dr. Mudd Bares His Soul--and His Neck
    The letter appears in print in Mudd, *The Life of Mudd*, 341-46.
See also, comments in Carter, *Riddle of Mudd*, 41-55. The pro-
Confederate proclivities of Mudd and his neighbors is detailed in William
A. Tidwell, "Charles County: Confederate Cauldron," *Maryland
Historical Magazine*, 91 (Spring 1996), 16-27. More generally, see Harry
Wright Newman, *Maryland and the Confederacy* (Annapolis, MD: Harry
Wright Newman, 1976); Carolyn S. Billups, "Maryland--A Southern
Perspective," *Surratt Courier*, 23 (November 1998), 4-7. The Rev. Fr.
Vincinanza is identified in Michael Kauffman to William L. Richter,
September 5, 2002.

4. John Surratt--Confederate Postmaster
    Alfred Isaacson (ed.), "Some Letters of Anna Surratt," *Maryland
Historical Magazine*, 54 (September 1959), 310-13; Trindal, *Mary
Surratt*, 57-73; Campbell, *Case for Mrs. Surratt*, 35-47; Weichmann, *A
True Story*; 18-19; Roscoe, *Web of Conspiracy*, 50-56; James O. Hall,
"You Have Mail . . . ," *Surratt Courier*, 25 (July 2000), 8-9, shows how
the Rebel mail system worked; and David Winfred Gaddy, "The Surratt
Tavern--A Confederate 'Safe House'?" Kauffman (ed.), *In Pursuit of . . .* ,
129-30, illustrates that Confederate authorities were well aware of the
Surratt Tavern as one of their key places on the "secret line." The outfit
that ran the secret line is discussed in Edmund H. Cummings, "The Signal
Corps in the Confederate States Army," *Southern Historical Society
Papers*, 16 (January-December 1888), 93-107; Tidwell, Hall, Gaddy,
Come Retribution, 31-222.
    For Surratt's own account, full of contempt for his Union
adversaries, see Gerald McMurtry (ed.), "[John H. Surratt's] Lecture on
the Lincoln Conspiracy," *Lincoln Herald*, 51 (Dec. 1949), 20-33, 39,
which is also in Clara E. Laughlin, *The Death of Lincoln: The Story of
Booth's Plot, His Deed and the Penalty* (New York: Doubleday, Page &
Co., 1909), 222-49. The old mill is described in Laurie Verge, "The
Surratt Mill," Kauffman (ed.), *In Pursuit of . . . ,* 125-27.

On Isaac Surratt, see Joseph E. "Rick" Smith III and William L. Richter. "Isaac in Texas—A Theoretical Look at the Other Surratt," *Surratt Courier*, 33 (November), 3-7.

There were a great many witnesses willing to come forward and testify as to the loyalty of Mary Surratt and her brother, Zad Jenkins. See Pitman (comp.), *The Assassination of President Lincoln and the Trial of the Conspirators*, 135-38. There were as many willing to defend the character of Lou Weichmann and impeach the loyalty of Mrs. Surratt and Jenkins, *ibid.*, 127, 138-39, 141-43. This same pattern was repeated during the John Surratt trial in 1867, see Sutton, *et al. (comps.), The Reporter: Containing . . . Trial of John H. Surratt, on an Indictment for Murder of President Lincoln,* IV, *passim.*

For the preferred use Pitman version of the court martial testimony, see John C. Brennan, "The Three Versions of the Testimony in the 1865 Conspiracy Trial," and "More on the Three Versions of the 1865 Trial Testimony," in Kauffman (ed.), *In Pursuit of . . . ,* 175-84, 185-88. Another viewpoint, defending the Poore version as best, can be found in Steers, *Blood on the Moon*, xii-xiii.

5. Lewis Powell Wounded and Captured

Betty J. Ownsbey, *Alias "Paine": Lewis Thornton Powell, the Mystery Man of the Lincoln Conspiracy* (Jefferson, N.C.: McFarland & Company, Publishers, 1993), 15-17. See also, Betty J. Ownsbey, "The Military Career of an Assassin," *North & South*, 2 (November 1998), 48-58; Betty O. Gregory, "Lewis Powell: Mystery Man of the Conspiracy," Kauffman (ed.), *In Pursuit of . . . ,* 15-21; Jerry H. Maxwell, "The Bizarre Case of Lewis Paine," *Lincoln Herald*, 81 (Winter 1979), 223-33; Leon O. Prior, "Lewis Payne, Pawn of John Wilkes Booth," *Florida Historical Quarterly*, 43 (July 1964), 1-20; Buckingham, *Reminiscences and Souvenirs of the Assassination of Abraham Lincoln* , 39-43; and Vaughn Shelton, *Mask for Treason: The Lincoln Murder Trial* (Harrisburg, Pa.: Stackpole Books, 1965). Ownsbey demolishes much of Shelton's convoluted notion that Powell was actually two men, himself and a cousin, the latter of whom had a death wish. There is much of value in his volume beyond this, but one must be patient to dig it out. Roscoe, *Web of Conspiracy*, 65-67, is full of the usual misinterpretations of the "ignorant brute" Lewis Powell. Gregory and Maxwell provide the best short accounts, but nothing surpasses Ownsbey's fine volume.

6. Powell as a Union Hospital Orderly

Ownsbey, *Alias "Paine": Lewis Thornton Powell,* 17-20. For the numerous blacks who served with the Army of Northern Virginia in various support roles such as teamsters, hospital orderlys, and such, see Ervin L. Jordan, *Black Confederates and Afro-Yankees in Civil War Virginia* (Charlottsville: University of Virginia, 1995), 223-24.

7. Lewis Powell Meets Maggie Branson
    Ownsbey, *Alias "Paine": Lewis Thornton Powell,* 15-16, 18; Ownsbey, "The Elusive Branson Sisters of Baltimore," Dillon (ed.), *The Lincoln Assassination: From the Pages of the* Surratt Courier, V, 13-16.

8. Lewis Powell Meets Lewis Payne
    Ownsbey, *Alias "Paine": Lewis Thornton Powell,* 21, 158-60. On Powell's health, see Ownsbey, "Lewis Thornton Powell's Many Medical Problems," Dillon (ed.), *The Lincoln Assassination: From the Pages of the* Surratt Courier, V, 9-11.

9. Colonel Mosby, General Lee, and Secretary Seddon
    James A. Ramage, *Gray Ghost: The Life and Legend of Col. John Singleton Mosby* (Lexington: The University Press of Kentucky, 1999), 131-46, Tidwell, Hall, and Gaddy, *Come Retribution,* 132-54. Lee's consistent views on the counterproductive use of most detachments of partisan rangers, specifically exempting Mosby's command, are presented in letters no. 606 and no. 649, in Dowdey and Manarin (eds.), *Wartime Papers of R. E. Lee,* 650-51, 688-89; and document no. 73 in Douglas Southall Freeman (ed.), *Lee's Dispatches . . .* (New York: G. P. Putnam's Sons, 1915), 131-32, and footnote, 132-134. See also, Roy L. Curry, "James A. Seddon: A Southern Prototype," *Virginia Magazine of History and Biography,* 63 (April 1955), 123-50; and Rembert Patrick, *Jefferson Davis and His Cabinet* (Baton Rouge: Louisiana State University Press, 1944), 132-48.

10. Powell Becomes a Partisan Ranger
    Ownsbey, *Alias "Paine": Lewis Thornton Powell,* 21-27, 160. Hugh C. Keen and Horace Mewborn, *43rd Battalion Virginia Cavalry, Mosby's Command* (2nd ed., Lynchburg, Va.: H. E. Howard, 1993), 11-21; Ramage, *Gray Ghost: The Life and Legend of Col. John Singleton Mosby,* 96-104. See also, testimony in Pitman (comp.), *The Assassination of President Lincoln and the Trial of the Conspirators,* 166.

PART V: THE THESPIAN (1861-1864)

1. I Am--Myself, Alone
The chapter title is a mimicking of Shakespeare's *Henry VI* (Part III, Act 5 Scene 6), which the English annotator, Colley Cibber, moved to Act 1, Scene 2, of his more exciting, condensed version of *Richard III*-- the one used by the Booths and others of the era.

Booth's launching of his independent career as a star, what acting at that time entailed, what he brought to the stage, and what the critics had to say are described in Samples, *Lust for Fame*, 52-122. Booth's letters at this time are filled with booking details. See various documents in Rhodehamel and Taper (eds.), *Writings of John Wilkes Booth*, 69-106, in a section that they entitle aptly, "'A Star of the First Magnitude': John Wilkes on Stage, 1861-1864." In general, see, Kimmel, *The Mad Booths of Maryland*, 149-85, *passim*; Barbee, "Lincoln and Booth," 255-312, DRB papers, GU; and Joseph George, Jr., "The Night John Wilkes Booth Played before Abraham Lincoln," *Lincoln Herald*, 59 (Summer 1957), 11-15. Also of interest is the written introduction and the portraits and *cartes de visite* of the photographic study of the actor in Richard J. S. Gutman and Kellie O. Gutman, *John Wilkes Booth Himself* (Dover, Mass.: Hired Hand Press, 1979). See also, Weichmann, *A True Story*; 36-42, although his story has been nullified somewhat by more recent research.

2. Davy Herold Finds Acting a Dangerous Business
The meeting with Herold and the doctor's appointment for the surgery is in Michael W. Kauffman, "David Edgar Herold: The Forgotten Conspirator," Kauffman (ed.), *In Pursuit of . . . ,* 23-28; Laurie Verge, "That Trifling Boy . . . ," *Surratt Courier*, 27 (January 2002), 4-9; Kimmel, *Mad Booths of Maryland*, 173-74; Dr. John F. May, "The Mark of the Scalpel," *Records of the Columbia Historical Society*, 13 (1910), 49-68; and Joseph K. Barnes, "The Booth Autopsy," in Laurie Verge (ed.), *The Body in the Barn: The Controversy Over the Death of John Wilkes Booth* (Clinton, Md.: The Surratt Society, 1993), 67-68. Booth's penchant for accidents is detailed in Arthur F. Loux, "The Accident-Prone John Wilkes Booth," *Lincoln Herald*, 85 (Winter 1983), 283-68. See also, Smith, *American Gothic*, 85-88.

3. The Original French Connection
For his invitation to play in St. Joseph, see Thomas Harbine *et al.* to John Wilkes Booth, January 4, 1864, in Rhodehamel and Taper (eds.), *Writings of John Wilkes Booth*, 95. His methods of concealing and

carrying drugs is described in, Alford (ed.), *John Wilkes Booth: A Sister's Memoir by Asia Booth Clarke*, 85-86. See also, Tidwell, Hall, and Gaddy, *Come Retribution*, 259-60, for more on Booth's drug smuggling.

The French trip is covered in F. Lauriston Bullard, "When--If Ever--Was John Wilkes Booth in Paris?" *Lincoln Herald*, 50 (June 1948), 28-34; and Bullard, "A Plausible Solution of the Mystery of John Wilkes Booth's Alleged Visit to Paris," *ibid.*, 52 (October 1950), 41-43. See also, Samples, *Lust For Fame*, 116-23. For the meeting with Kimball, see John Wilkes Booth to Moses Kimball, January 2, 1864, in Rhodehamel and Taper (eds.), *Writings of John Wilkes Booth*, 93-94 and footnotes. The pro-Confederate leanings of the DeBars are in *ibid.*, 87n1. Also of interest is Smith, *American Gothic*, 90.

Although it admittedly has some other shortcomings (Edward Steers, Jr. and Joan Chaconas, "Dark Union: Bad History," *North & South*, 7 [January 2004], 12-30), the illegal trade between the North and the South during the War is discussed in Leonard F. Gutteridge and Ray A. Neff, *Dark Union: The Secret Web of Profiteers, Ploiticians, and Booth Conspirators that Led to Lincoln's Death* (Hoboken, NJ: Weilet, 2003). See also, Charles Higham, *Murdering Mr. Lincoln: A New Detection of the Nineteenth Century's Greatest Crime* (Beverly Hills: New Millenium Press, 2004), passim, especially xvii, 66,109, 122, 123-24, 149, 170, 174, 178, 193, 196.

4. Experiencing a Yankee Tyrant First-Hand

For Booth and Andrew Johnson's supposed meeting, see Howard, *Civil War Echoes: Character Sketches and Secrets*, 83-84. Booth's appearances in Nashville are in Charles E. Holding, "John Wilkes Booth Stars in Nashville," *Tennessee Historical Quarterly*, 23 (March 1964), 73-79. Booth's troubles with the Yankee military authorities is presented Samples, *Lust For Fame*, 134-41; Kimmel, *Mad Booths of Maryland*, 175.

On Booth's life in 1864, in general, see Constance Head, "John Wilkes Booth: Prologue to Assassination," *Lincoln Herald*, 85 (Winter 1983), 254-79.

5. A-Whoring We Will Go

For the Booths and the New York Draft Riots, see Kimmel, *Mad Booths of Maryland*, 175. In the hypothetical conversation between Booth and Johnson, Johnson's views as paraphrased here are presented best in Hans L. Trefousse, *Andrew Johnson: A Biography* (New York: Norton, 1989), 128-75. The rest is pure fiction--probably.

6. Occupied New Orleans

New Orleans during Booth's visit is described in Samples, *Lust For Fame*, 142-48. See also, John S. Kendall, *The Golden Age of the New Orleans Theater* (Baton Rouge: Louisiana State University Press, 1952).

Booth suffered greatly from bronchitis at this time, probably from his ill-advised winter trip from Leavenworth to St. Louis, and therein lies a problem--Booth's health. Since the beginning, it has been common to blame Booth's desire to assassinate Lincoln on some physical or mental infirmity. American assassins have never been viewed as sane, ever since Richard Lawrence tried to kill Andrew Jackson in 1835, up to when John W. Hinckley, Jr., tried to do the same to Ronald W. Reagan in 1981. In Lawrence's case, mental deficiency might be valid. The hapless Lawrence fired two pistols at President Jackson, at point blank range. The caps exploded but the powder charges did not. The odd against this happening once, much less twice, are phenomenal. But for the rest of America's assassins, insanity is a knee-jerk reaction that often has covered-up important reasons why the act took place.

Booth is no exception. Although not the first to question Booth's health, medical Dr. Ralph Brooks raised a firestorm ("Insane? Or, Ill?" Dillon (ed.), *The Lincoln Assassination: From the Pages of the* Surratt Courier, XIII, 3-6) by asserting that the possibility that John Wilkes Booth was ill with paresis (the third stage of syphilis). This affected his drinking, which was heavy, and his mind, filling him with delusions of grandeur. The whole thing was compounded by Booth's growing voice problems, that seemed to defy any cure. In the third stage of syphilis, the organism treponema pallidum swarms through the body affecting many organs. Included in these are the brain and the larynx. Booth knew he was doomed and went out in a blaze of delusional glory.

The Brooks article brought immediate response. David W. Gaddy thought that the idea merited consideration ("Repercussions on a Recent Article," *ibid.*, XIII, 7). But he was pretty much alone in his open view. Edward Steers, Jr., thought Brooks' foray nothing but supposition without any fact, whatever. He found no evidence of syphilis or constant, incurable hoarseness ("Historical Malpractice," *ibid.*, XIII, 9-11). Booth had erysipelas in August 1864 and an occasional cold, that was all. Deirdre Barber Kincaid thought such forays into speculation as Brooks' merely served to hide Booth real reason for killing Lincoln--it was a political act by an idealistic young man that grew out of the war and real differences in what the United States was all about ("Insane--or Underresearched?" *ibid.*, XIII, 13-14).

For a look at Civil War sexually transmitted diseases, see Thomas P. Lowry, *The Story the Soldiers Wouldn't Tell: Sex in the Civil War* (Mechanicsburg, Pa.: Stackpole Books, 1994), and, closer to home for Booth, Lowry, *The Civil War Bawdy Houses of Washington, D.C.* (Fredericksburg, Va.: Sergeant Kirkland's, 1997), which emphasizes a provost marshal's register of seventy-three houses, including how many women worked in each and rating them from first to fourth class. Who says the government does not provide needed services for the people?

Syphilis aside, Booth has been seen as somehow deluded from the beginning. His first biographer, Francis Wilson, *John Wilkes Booth*, 136-49, worried about Booth's "morbid thirst for notoriety," as did Constance Head ("J.W.B.: I am Myself Alone," Kauffman (ed.), *In Pursuit of. . .*, 41-46). Others wondered about his feelings of inadequacy in his competition with his brother Edwin (Philip Weissman, "Why Booth Killed Lincoln: A Psychoanalytic Study," *Psychoanalysis and the Social Sciences*, 5 [1958], 99-115), or living up to his father's reputation, built at the cost of ignoring the boy at home (George W. Wilson, "John Wilkes Booth: Father Murderer," *American Imago*, 1 [1940], 49-60), or his over-indulgent childhood, which produced a what one observer had called a "killer narcissist"--a child devoid of values, a condition avoided on by more conditional love during childhood (Barbara Lerner, "The Killer Narcissists," *National Review On-line*, May 19, 1999, at townhall.com). And it all started with his mother's nightmare of the raised bloody arm and the gypsy curse of a short violent life (Christopher New, *America's Civil War*, March 1993, at erols.com/candidus/wilkes-1).

But nothing will bring the Booth advocates out of the woodwork faster than an accusation of hoarseness threatening his acting career and causing him to advance from failing actor to erstwhile presidential assassin. Booth family biographer Stanley Kimmel first made chronic throat problems a central explanation of John Wilkes Booth's motives for killing Lincoln in his *Mad Booths of Maryland*, 179-81, 184-85. The assertion had no basis in fact. Nowadays, even casual mention of it as in John B. Horner, "John Wilkes Booth as Oil Speculator," *Surratt Courier*, 25 (June 2000), 3-7, will draw forth a response like Arthur Kincaid, "Redefining 'Mediocrity' and 'Genius'," *ibid.*, 26 (January 2001), 3-7, condemning the mere thought that Booth had voice problems beyond the occasional cold, brought on by the drafty, barn-like theaters he played in.

7. The Destructionists

This conversation is made up from materials in Tidwell, "Sage and the Destructionists," *April '65*, 77-105, and is designed to show the depth of Confederate secret action at this stage of the war, which affected Booth at least peripherally. See also, Tidwell, Hall, and Gaddy, "The Department of 'Dirty Tricks' and the Secret Service," *Come Retribution*, 155-170. There is strong suspicion that such devices spoken of by Sage sunk the Union steamer *Sultana* near Memphis with the greatest American loss of of life in any water disaster including the *Titanic*. See William O. Bryant, *Cahaba Prison and the Sultana Disaster* (Tuscaloosa: University of Alabama Press, 1990); and D. H. Rule, "*Sultana:* The Case for Sabotage," *North & South*, 5 (December 2001), 76-87. Rule tells of Union soldiers finding a defused coal bomb on his desk in Richmond after the war, *ibid.*, 84.

8. Back Bay (Boston)
The land purchases are in John Wilkes Booth to Joseph Simonds, Philadelphia, April 3, 1863, Rhodehamel and Taper (eds.), *Writings of John Wilkes Booth*, 86-87 and footnotes. On Simonds, see Ernest C. Miller, *John Wilkes Booth, Oilman* (New York: The Exposition Press, 1947), 26, 34 The rest is from Clara Morris, "Some Recollections of John Wilkes Booth," *McClure's Magazine*, 11 (February 1901), 299-304, reprinted in Dillon (ed.), *The Lincoln Assassination: From the Pages of the* Surratt Courier, V, 3-4. See also, Richard and Kellie Gutman, "Boston: A Home for John Wilkes Booth," *Surratt Society News*, 10 (September 1985), 1, 6-8.

9. The Sunflowers
For Booth's destruction of compromising letters or removed signatures and refused to let other read them, see Morris, "Some Recollections of John Wilkes Booth," 299-304. See also, Samples, *Lust for Fame,* 129-32, 149-54. See also, Smith, *American Gothic*, 82-98. On Booth and women in general, see Barbee, "Lincoln and Booth," 363-91, DRB papers, GU.
The Isabel Sumner letters, June 7, 1864 (How shall I write you); June 17, 1864; July 14, 1864 (You see, Indeed I Thought you); July 24, 1864 (Have I in any way); August 16, 1864; August 27?, 1864 are in Rhodehamel and Taper (eds.), *Writings of John Wilkes Booth*, 106-109 (introductory text), 110-11, 113-14, 114-15, 115-16, 116-17, 117.
10. Dramatic Oil Company
For Booth's summer in Pennsylvania's oil fields, see John J. McLaurin, *Sketches in Crude Oil: Some Accidents and Incidents of the Petroleum Development in All Parts of the Globe* (Harrisburg, Pa.: McLaurin, 1896), 96-97; Hildegarde Dolson, "John Wilkes Booth Wants a

Gusher," in *The Great Oildorado: The Gaudy and Turbulent Years of the First Oil Rush: Pennsylvania, 1859-1880* (New York: Random House, 1959), 1465-76; Ellsler (ed.), *Stage Memories*, 125-28; Ernest C. Miller, *John Wilkes Booth, Oilman* , *passim*; Horner, "John Wilkes Booth as Oil Speculator," 3-7. Relevant letters include John Wilkes Booth to John Adam Ellsler, January 23, 1864; June 11, 1864; June 17, 1864 in Rhodehamel and Taper (eds.), *Writings of John Wilkes Booth*, 96-98, 111-13, 113, and footnotes.

11. A Window at Meadeville
　　　On the Meadeville incident, see Weichmann, *A True Story*, 42-44; and Samples, *Lust for Fame,* 158-61. On the possible poison plot, see the extensive explanation of DeWitt, *Assassination of Abraham Lincoln*, 259-63.

　　　Booth's disappearances mystified his partners, who believed that he did not concentrate on the matters at hand, and denied that they knew anything of his plotting against Lincoln. See Miller, *John Wilkes Booth, Oilman*, 48-58.

PART VI: PRELIMINARIES (1864-1865)

1. Booth Meets Four Rebels in Boston
　　　This incident is purely fictional in its make-up, but not its occurrence. See Tidwell, *April '65*, 137; and Tidwell, Hall and Gaddy, *Come Retribution*, 19, 262-63. As DeWitt notes, *The Assassination of Abraham Lincoln,* 9-10, Booth could be satisfied with drug-running until the Confederates lost the battle of Gettysburg. Then, more had to be done, as the situation had become more critical for the South's independence. Marshal Kane's arrest is in an excellent piece by Charles B. Clark, "Suppression and Control of Maryland, 1861-1865: A Study of Federal-State Relations During Civil Conflict," *Maryland Historical Magazine*, 54 (September 1959), 257. Booth's activities in the railroad sabotage is suggested in William Hanchett, *John Wilkes Booth and the Terrible Truth about the Civil War* (Racine: Lincoln Fellowship of Wisconsin, Historical Bulletin No. 49), 9-10, utilizing research first developed by Arthur Loux. For more on the railroad sabotage (which many saw as a pro-Union action to keep Federal troops out of Baltimore and lessen pro-Confederate rioting in the streets) that led up to the U.S. Supreme Court case, *ex parte* Merryman (17 F. Cas. [1861] at 144), see Nelson D. Lankford, *Cry Havoc! The Crooked Road to Civil War, 1861* (New York: Viking, 2007), 150-53.

2. Arnold and O'Laughlen: First Recruits
   For the so-called Baltimore Plot, see John Mason Potter, *Thirteen Desperate Days* (New York: Ivan Obolensky, 1964). See also, Laurie Verge, "The Baltimore Plot," in Kauffman (ed.), *In Pursuit of . . . ,* 137-40; James O. Hall, "The Baltimore Plot," *Surratt Courier,* 27 (February 2002), 4-7; Louis A Warren, "The First Attempt to Assassinate Lincoln," *Lincoln Lore* (March 6, 1933), 1; Richard Betterly, Seize Mr. Lincoln: The 1861 Baltimore Plot," *Civil War Times Illustrated,* 25 (February 1987), 14-21; Edward Stanley Lanis, "Allen Pinkerton and the Baltimore 'Assassination' Plot against Lincoln," *Maryland Historical Magazine,* 45 (March 1950), 1-13.

   In general, see Tidwell, Hall, and Gaddy, *Come Retribution,* 21, 263-64.; Percy E. Martin, "Baltimorean in Big Trouble: Samuel Arnold, A Lincoln Conspirator, *History Trails,* 25 (Winter 1990-91), 5-8; Percy E. Martin, "The Six Hour War of Samuel Arnold," *Surratt Courier,* 33 (July 2008), 3-6; Michael W. Kauffman (ed.), *Memoirs of a Lincoln Conspirator* [Samuel B. Arnold] (Bowie, Md.: Heritage Press, 1995), 31-47; Roscoe, *Web of Conspiracy,* 58-61. Also of interest is the letter from John C. Brennan to Terry Alford, September 16, 1992, (copy in vertical file under "O'Laughlen," Surratt House Museum) in which he speculates that T. William O'Laughlen was the real O'Laughlen interested in the Lincoln abduction, but was restrained from acting with the conspirators by family considerations (wife and children). So, he sent and sent his younger brother, Mike, instead, along with a loan of $500 to the project. The blood oath is from Felix G. Stidger, *Treason History of the Sons of Liberty* (Chicago: Felix G. Stidger, 1903), appendix. On Mike O'Laughlen, see Frederick Hatch, "Michael O'Laughlen: A Biography," *Journal of the Lincoln Assassination,* 17 (April 2003), 11-13.

3. Meeting in Richmond I: The Genesis of Abducting Lincoln
   In general, see Tidwell, Hall and Gaddy, *Come Retribution,* 19, 271-327, *passim.*
On the North Anna Campaign, see Gordon C. Rhea*, To the North Anna River: Grant and Lee, May 13-25, 1864* (Baton Rouge: Louisiana State University Press, 2000), 255-354; for the fight at Deep Bottom, Bryce Sudarow, "Glory Denied: First Deep Bottom," *North & South,* 3 (September 2000), 17-32, and his "'Nothing But a Miracle Could Save Us': Second Battle of Deep Bottom, Virginia, August 14-20, 1864," *ibid.,* 4 (January 2001), 12-32; on Early in the Shenandoah Valley, Edward J. Stackpole, *Sheridan in the Shenandoah: Jubal Early's Nemesis*

(Harrisburg, Pa.: Stackpole, 1961); for B. T. Johnson's plan to abduct Lincoln which failed at the Confederate defeat at Ft. Stevens, then his overextended attempt on Pt. Lookout, see John C. Brennan, "General Bradley T. Johnson's Plan to Abduct President Lincoln," *Chronicles of St. Mary's,* 22 (Nov. and Dec. 1974), 413-25; B. T. Johnson, "My Ride Around Baltimore in 1864," *Cavalry Journal,* (Sept 1869), 413-24; and his "My Ride Around Baltimore," *ibid.,* (Sept 1889), 250-60.

    The plan to liberate Confederate Prisoners held at Camp Hoffman on Old Point Lookout, is in letter no. 816, in Dowdey and Manarin (eds.), *Wartime Papers of R. E. Lee,* 806-808; and Freeman (ed.), Document No. 149, *Lee's Dispatches,* 269-71.

    4. Meeting in Richmond II: Scouting Out the Possibilities
    The best general study of the Confederate behind-the-lines activity is Jane Singer, *The Confederate Dirty War : Arson, Bombings, Assassination and Plots for Chemical and Germ Attacks on the Union* (Jefferson, N.C.: McFarland & Company, 2005). See also, Higham, Murdering Mr. Lincoln, 93-158; Tidwell, Hall, and Gaddy, *Come Retribution,* 19, 20, 21, 22, 24, 271-327, *passim*; Tidwell, *April '65,* 73-74, 132, 158-59; Alan Axelrod, *The War Between the Spies: A History of Espionage during the Civil War* (New York: The Atlantic Monthly Press, 1992), 211-32; and Nancy D. Baird, "The Yellow Fever Plot," *Civil War Times Illustrated,* 13 (November 1974), 16-23. See also, Thomas N. Conrad, *A Confederate Spy* (New York: J. S. Ogilvie Pub. Co., 1892); Horan, *Confederate Agent: A Discovery in History;* Steers, *Blood on the Moon,* 39-59; Percy E. Martin, "John 'Bull' Frizzell," Kauffman (ed.), *In Pursuit of . . . ,* 91-96.

    It was a rough war for Mosby, who was wounded several times, see Ramage, *Gray Ghost: The Life and Legend of Col. John Singleton Mosby,* 55, 88, 113-14, 196-97, 201 (wounded too much), 234-35, 369n.10.

    On Samuel Ruth, see Albert Castel, "Samuel Ruth: Union Spy," *Civil War Times Illustrated,* 14 (February 1976), 36-45, and Meriwether Stuart, "Samuel Ruth and General R. R. Lee: Disloyalty and the Line of Supply to Fredericksburg," *Virginia Magazine of History and Biography,* 71 (January 1963), 35-109. See also, Angus J. Johnson, "Disloyalty on Confederate Railroads in Virginia," *ibid.,* 63 (1955), 410-26.

    The use of blacks in the Confederate forces, wider than previously supposed, is treated in Jordan, *Black Confederates and Afro-Yankees in Civil War Virginia*; Richard Rollins (ed.), *Black Southerners in Gray: Essays on Afro-Americansin Confederate Armies* (Redondo

Beach, CA: Rank and File Publications,1994); and Robert Durden, *The Gray and the Black* (Baton Rouge: LSU Press, 1972).

5. Wat Bowie Scouts Out the Mail Line
Tidwell, Hall, and Gaddy, *Come Retribution*, 21; James O. Hall, "Appointment in Samara: The Strange Death of Walter Bowie," *North & South*, 1 (February 1998), 76-80. In actuality, Bowie was probably killed by a shotgun blast, see Harnett T. Kane, "Scholar in Blackface," in his *Spies for the Blue and Gray* (Garden City, N.Y.: Hanover House. 1954), 157-69; Ramage, *Gray Ghost: The Life and Legend of Col. John Singleton Mosby,* 229-31. See also, Lafayette C. Baker, *History of the United States Secret Service* (Philadelphia: L. C. Baker, 1867), 181-93; Jacob Mogelever, *Death to Traitors: The Story of General Lafayette C. Baker, Lincoln's Forgotten Secret Service Chief* (New York: Doubleday & Company, 1960), 172-74.

6. George N. Sanders: The Professional Revolutionary
In general, on Confederate agents and activities in Canada, see the very interesting article by Randall A. Haines, "Evidence of a Canadian Connection with Confederate Agents in the Lincoln Assassination." *Surratt Courier*, 29 (July 2004), 3-7. More specifically, see Tidwell, Hall, and Gaddy, *Come Retribution*, 20, 21, 328-34; "Booth in Canada," box 4, folder 221, DRB papers, GU. For Sanders, see Merle E. Curti, "George Nicholas Sanders," in Dumas Malone (ed.), *Dictionary of American Biography* (New York: Charles Scribner's Sons, 1935), XIV, 334-35. On Reid Sanders, see Meriwether Stuart, "Operation Sanders: Wherein Old Friends and Ardent Pro-Southerners Prove to be Union Secret Agents," *Virginia Magazine of History and Biography*, 81 (April 1973), 157-99. The Hudson's Bay Claims are treated in John S. Galbraith, "George N. Sanders: 'Influence' Man for the Hudson's Bay Company," *Oregon Historical Quarterly*, 53 (September 1952), 159-76. A newer, sadly as yet unpublished massive study on one of the primcipal characters in the Confederate Canadian operations is Randall A. Haines, "The Notorious George N. Sanders: His Career and role in the Lincoln Assassination" (unpublished ms. in the James O. Hall Library, Surratt Museum, 1994). Published (and a sort of combination of Gutteridge and Neff, *Dark Union,* and Haines, "The Notorious George N. Sanders"), is Higham, *Murdering Mr. Lincoln,* who puts Sanders at the center of the Lincoln assassination plot as its prime architect. For materials in this section, which were written before Higham published his tome and confirmed by his separate research, see *ibid.*, especially 1-51.

William L. Richter

On the attempts to introduce slavery north of the Ohio River in the early nineteenth century, see Paul Finkelmann, "Slavery and the Northwest Ordinance: A Study in Ambiguity," and "Evading the Ordinance: The Persistence of Bondage in Indiana and Illinois," in his *Slavery and the Founders: Race and Liberty in the Age of Jefferson* (Armonk, N. Y.: M. E. Sharpe, 1996), 34-79. In general, see Phillips, *Cousins' Wars*, 317-510; and R. Carlyle Buley, *The Old Northwest: Pioneer Period, 1815-1840* (2 vols., Bloomington: Indiana University Press, 1950), I, 58-93.

7. The Golden Circle
On the dichotomies of President Lincoln's stated policies and those actually enacted see Lerone Bennett, *Forced into Glory*, 143, 254-58, 353, 375, 393, 414 (better come to an agreement), 141-25, 539-46, 554-55, 590. In general, see Phillips, *Cousins' Wars*, 317-510; Merle E. Curti, "'Young America,'" *American Historical Review*, 32 (October 1926), 34-55.

On the Knights of the Golden Circle and Southern filibustering expeditions, consult Robert E. May, *The Southern Dream of a Caribbean Empire, 1854-61* (Baton Rouge: Louisiana State University Press, 1973), 3, 20, 49, 91-94, 148-55; Olliger Crenshaw, "The Knights of the Golden Circle," *American Historical Review*, 47 (1941), 23-50; C. A. Bridges, "The Knights of the Golden Circle: A Filibustering Fantasy," *Southwestern Historical Quarterly*, 287-302; and Joe A. Stout, Jr., *The Liberators: Filibustering Expeditions into Mexico, 1848-1862, and the Last Gasp of Manifest Destiny* (Los Angeles: Westernlore Press, 1973). Both Booth and neighbor T. William O'Laughlen (if not his brother Mike, too, later a co-conspirator against Lincoln) were rumored to be members of the Golden Circle.

On Bickley, see James O. Hall, "A Magnificent Charlatan: George Washington Lafayette Bickley Made a Career of Deceit," *Civil War Times Illustrated*, 18 (February 1980), 40-42; Edward Steers, Jr., "Who's Buried in Grant's Tomb?" *Surratt Courier*, 26 (April 2001), 5-7.

The Golden Circle's influence as regards secession and the Civil War is set out in an excellent article by David Keehn, "Strong Arm of Secession: The Knights of the Golden Circle in the Secession Crisis of 1861," *North & South*, 10 (June 2005), 42-57. Keehn discounts the influence of the flamboyant Bickley in favor of others such as Elkanah Greer, G. W. Chilton, Ben McCulloch and Virginius Groener, who are generally ignored by modern historians. See also, Roy S. Dunn, "The KGC in Texas, 1860-1861," *Southwestern Historical Quarterly*, 70 (April

1967, 543-573, and Higham, *Murdering Mr. Lincoln*, 23, 28, 40, 47, 55-56, 65, 107, 113. A really good summary of the Knights in the Old Northwest during the Civil War is in Bruce Catton, *Glory Road* (New York: Doubleday, 1952), 111-24, *passim*.

8. Sic Semper Tyrannus

Merle E. Curtis [sic], "George Sanders--American Patriot of the Fifties," *South Atlantic Quarterly*, 27 (January 1928), 79-87; Randall A. Haines, "The Revolutionist Charged with Complicity in Lincoln's Death," *Surratt Courier*, 13 (September 1988), 5-8, *ibid.*, (October 1988), 7-9; Adam Mayer, "St. Lawrence Hall in Montreal," *Civil War Times Illustrated*, 31 (January-February 1993), 44-46, 74 (goose is cooked). See also, Higham, *Murdering Mr. Lincoln*, 21-51.

9. Dinner with P. C. Martin

Tidwell, Hall, and Gaddy, *Come Retribution*, 21-22, 24-25. Barbee, "Lincoln and Booth," 513-550, DRB papers, GU, sees the Maryland connection as crucial. Maryland planters conceived the kidnap scheme as a solution to their own problems with Lincoln's policy (actually Congress' through the Confiscation Acts) of permitting their runaway slaves to be held without compensation as seizable contraband of war, which they saw correctly as the beginnings of emancipation.

For part of the money trail, see Jim Kushlan, "A Paper Link to a Conspiracy," *Civil War Times Illustrated*, 30 (September-October 1991), 15. See also, Weichmann, *A True Story*; 42-53.

General Robert E. Lee was not impressed with the strategic abilities of the Right Reverend Doctor Kensey Johns Stewart, despite his relationship to the Lee family by marriage. See dispatch no. 170 in Freeman (ed.), *Lee's Dispatches*, 302-304.

In this chapter and several above, we chose to believe Sanford Conover's revelation during the military commission that Booth's code-name was "Pet." See Pitman, *The Assassination of President Lincoln and the Trial of the Conspirators*, 31. For more on the moniker, "Pet," see George A. Townsend's notes, "A Talk with Louis Weichmann," in verticle file, Surratt House Museum.

On Confederate Activities emanating out of the Canadian operation, see Jim Kushlan (ed.), "Rebel Secret Agents and Saboteurs in Canada," *Civil War Times Illustrated*, 40 (June 2001), [Special Issue]; Klement, *Dark Lanterns: Secret Political Societies, Conspiracies and Treason trials in the Civil War*, and Higham, *Murdering Mr. Lincoln*, 116, 161-62.

10. Part of the Family

    James O. Hall, "John M. Lloyd: Star Witness," Kauffman (ed.), *In Pursuit of . . . ,* 97-100; Laurie Verge, "That Man Lloyd," Dillon (ed.), *The Lincoln Assassination: From the Pages of the* Surratt Courier, V, 23-24; Campbell, *Case for Mrs. Surratt*, 47-54; Trindal, *Mary Surratt*, 69-71; Weichmann, *A True Story*; 18-27; Helen Jones Campbell, *Confederate Courier* [A Life of John H. Surratt, Jr.] (New York: St. Martin's Press, 1964), 27-28, 31-32.

    On Davy Herold, see Michael W. Kauffman, "David Edgar Herold: The Forgotten Conspirator," 23-28; Laurie Verge, "That Trifling Boy . . . ," *Surratt Courier*, 27 (January 2002), 4-9; Buckingham, *Reminiscences and Souvenirs of the Assassination of Abraham Lincoln*, 29-33; Roscoe, *Web of Conspiracy*, 56-58; "David E. Herold," box 5, folder 246, DRB papers, GU.

    We think the life of Mary Surratt illustrates the thesis Laurie Verge has presented in her article, "Into the Fray: The Changing Role of Women During the Civil War," *Surratt Courier*, 22 (March 1997), 4-8, that the role of women changed greatly during the war, becoming more assertive and self-reliant--in a much over-used word, "liberated." For a more recent assertion of this social change see, Larson, *Assassin's Accomlice*, xvii, referencing Elizabeth Leonard, "Mary Walker, Mary Surratt, and Some Thoughts on Gender in the Civil War," in Catherine Clinton and Nina Silber (eds.), *Battle Scars,: Gender and Sexuality in the Civil War* (New York: Oxford University Press, 2006), 104-19.

    Throughout her life, if her handwriting is any indication, Mary Surratt gave evidence of being a very ambitious, angry at the lackluster performance of her husband, combined with a greatly crushed her social ego and lack of sexual fulfillment, which resulted in a tough "go to Hell" attitude that was very evident to the Yankees who searched her tavern, and arrested and interrogated her in prison.

11. Lou Weichmann, Confederate Spy

    Trindal, *Mary Surratt*, 53-84, *passim*; Oldroyd, *Assassination of Abraham Lincoln*, 153-93, *passim*; Weichmann, *A True Story*; 27-29; Daniel Weinberg, "Job Wanted," *Surratt Courier*, 25 (August 2000), 3.

PART VII: THE PLOT THICKENS (1865)

1. Booth Meets Dr. Mudd

    Whether Booth lost his wardrobe in a storm, as he believed, or his ship was destroyed by Capt. Martin's partner in the blockade running business to collect the $32,000 insurance money is uncertain. But Capt. Martin's death was essential to his partner, Alexander "Sandy" Keith, Jr., to collect. The latter view is a part of Ann Larabee, *The Dynamite Fiend: The Chilling Tale of a Confederate Spy, Con Artist, and Mass Murderer*, by (New York: Palgrave MacMillan, 2005). On the rest of the section, see Mudd, *Life of Mudd*, 29; Steers, *His Name Is Still Mudd* (Gettysburg, PA.: Thonas Publications, 1997), 39-48, 60-69; Carter, *Riddle of Mudd*, 70-85; Edward Steers, Jr., "The Deceptive Doctor," *Columbiad: A Quarterly Review of the War Between the States*, 2 (Summer 1998), 114-28, Rhodehamel and Taper (eds.), *Writings of John Wilkes Booth*, 123-24 and footnotes; Roscoe, *Web of Conspiracy*, 63-64. See also, article in *Cincinnati Enquirer*, April 18, 1892, copy in vertical file under G. A. Townsend, James O. Hall Library, Surratt House Museum; and Gary R. Planck, "The Name Is Mudd," *Lincoln Herald*, 81 (Winter 1979), 222.

The guilt or innocence of Dr. Mudd's involvement with the Confederacy and John Wilkes Booth is a never-ending argument. Led by his grandson, Dr. Richard D. Mudd, Dr. Samuel A. Mudd's case has gone through legal appeal in the Department of the Army, a mock trial at the University of Richmond's School of Law (with some of the fanciest names in American legal community participating), and extensive letter-writing campaigns to governors, congressmen and presidents, resulting in several requests to order that the Army set aside the original guilty verdict that was pardoned by President Andrew Johnson. So far, the Army has refused to act.

It is the contention of this author that all of the accused conspirators, from Jefferson Davis to Dr. Mudd, were guilty of complicity in either the abduction plot, or the assassination, or both. We believe that Mudd was a skillful prevaricator (why not, his life was at stake) and he was aided by his friends and neighbors, all of whom hated emancipation and the perceived Yankee tyranny that Maryland and the occupied South endured. The same pro-Southern cover-up occurred later in the civilian criminal trial of John Surratt, Jr.

We believe that the pro-Mudd forces tend to ignore Mudd's earlier contacts with Booth and his alleged ignorance of who Booth was, using a false beard story to explain this problem. We believe that conspirator Lewis Thornton Powell was correct when he asserted to his trail lawyer that many of the co-conspirators had not been caught or even identified. We also believe, in the end, that the persistent, pro-Mudd advocates, led by his current lineage, will win the modern public relations game, but not the historical argument. See, *e.g.*, the comments by Mary

Mudd McHale, "A Response re: Dr. Mudd," *Surratt Courier*, 26 (December 2001), 3-4.

For a sample of what has occurred in the case of Dr. Samuel A. Mudd consult the following, more or less in order of their presentation to the public: "The Verdict is in. . . : A Review of the case of Dr. Samuel A. Mudd," *Surratt Courier*, 18 (September 1992), 4-6, a review to date; John Paul Jones (ed.), *Dr. Mudd and the Lincoln Assassination: The Case Reopened* . . . (Mechanicsburg, Pa.: Combined Books, 1995), which has the Richmond University proceedings and numerous independent essays, pro and con Dr. Mudd; John E. McHale, Jr., *Dr. Samuel A. Mudd and the Lincoln Assassinatio*n (Parsippany, J. J. : Dillon Press, 1995), written by a relative who ably presents the Pro-Mudd side of the argument in a very readable format, pointing out the inconsistencies of those questioning Mudd's innocence. McHale and the Mudd side have been backed up by Michael W. Kauffman, *American Brutus: John Wilkes Booth and the Lincoln Conspiracies* (New York: Random House, 2004), 334-97 *passim*. Steers, *His Name Is Still Mudd*, leads the way in the anti-Mudd case and reprints numerous relevant documents from then and now. See also Steers, *Blood on the Moon*, 3, 144-54, 238-39.

Finally, there is the flurry of articles from both sides appearing in the *Surratt Courier*, and reprinted in Dillon (ed.), *The Lincoln Assassination: From the Pages of the* Surratt Courier, VIII, the latter of which is cited here. See John E. McHale, "Legal Aspects of the Dr. Mudd Case," 3-10; Edward Steers, Jr., "Dr. Samuel A. Mudd: 'His Prevarications Were Painful,'" 11-15; James O. Hall, "Dr. Mudd--Again--Part I," 17-20; Hall, "Dr. Mudd and Booth's Photograph [Part II]," 21-28, who takes up where Steers left off; John E. McHale, "A Response," 29-30. James E. T. Lange, "Some 'Muddy' Legal Issues," *Surratt Courier*, 24 (October 1998), 5-8, make a vain attempt to drive the last historical nail in the coffin of the pro-Mudd case, as demonstrated by Richard Willing, "A Point in Dr. Mudd's Favor?" *ibid.*, 26 (December 2001), 5-6.

Just how many Confederate spies existed in Maryland is impossible to fathom, but some revealing work by David Winfred Gaddy demonstrates just how public, yet concealed, such activity was, often even to the spy's family. See his series of articles, "The Surratt Tavern--A Confederate 'Safe House'?" Kauffman (ed.), *In Pursuit of . . .*, 129-30; "Gray Cloak and Dagger," *Civil War Times Illustrated*, 14 (July 1975), 20-27; "William Norris and the Confederate Signal and Secret Service," *Maryland Historical Magazine*, 70 (Summer 1975), 167-88; and "John Williamson Palmer: Confederate Agent," *Maryland Historical Magazine*, 83 (Summer 1988), 98-110. Most illustrative as to how secret such activity could be is in his "Confederate Spy Unmasked: An Afterward," *Manuscripts*, 30 (Spring 1978), 94. See also, Daniel L. Sutherland, "'Altamont' of the *Tribune*: John Williamson Palmer in the Civil War," *Maryland Historical Magazine*, 78 (Spring 1983), 54-66.

In the end, you pays your money and takes your choice. In our opinion, Mudd was really lucky he did not hang.

2. Old Blaze and the Blue Hen's Chickens

Ramage, *Gray Ghost: The Life and Legend of Col. John Singleton Mosby*, 97, 223-27, 264-65; Ownsbey, *Alias "Paine": Lewis Thornton Powell,* 27-28; Hugh C. Keen and Horace Mewborn, *43rd Battalion Virginia Cavalry, Mosby's Command*, 218-22, 305-306, 360-61.

3. To Whom It May Concern: Booth Secedes from the Union

The letter has appeared in whole or in part in numerous studies. See *e.g.*, Alford (ed.), *John Wilkes Booth: A Sister's Memoir by Asia Booth Clarke*, 105-110; Rhodehamel and Taper (eds.), *Writings of John Wilkes Booth*, 124-30 and footnotes; Laughlin, *Death of Lincoln*, 20-24, Buckingham, *Reminiscences and Souvenirs of the Assassination of Abraham Lincoln*, 53-57.

In addition to an improved Union military picture, represented by Sherman's victory at Atlanta and Sheridan's successful Shenandoah Valley Campaign, Lincoln and the Republicans used the Confederacy's sputtering behind-the-lines campaign from Canada as part of their successful 1864 election campaign. The Republicans attacked the Democratic Party's peace platform as dictated by Confederate agents (it was not); revealed the depths of the so-called Northwest Conspiracy through the Indian Treason Trials, which gutted its northern leadership and produced the later U.S. Supreme Court case, *ex parte* Milligan; and issued a separate definitive report on the activities of Confederate agents in these secret Peace or Copperhead societies (based on the old Golden Circle, now called the Order of American Knights, with its militant wing, the Sons of Liberty). See Benjamin J. Swett, "The Chicago Conspiracy," *Atlantic Monthly*, (July 1865), 108-20; Swett, "Conspiracies of the Rebellion, *North American Review*, 144 (February 1887), 179-89; Mark E. Neely, Jr., "Treason in Indiana: A Review Essay," *Lincoln Lore*, (February and March, 1974), 1-4, 1-3; William Zornow, "Treason as a Campaign Issue in the Re-election of Lincoln," *Abraham Lincoln Quarterly*, 5 (June 1949), 348-63; Davis, "The Turning Point that Wasn't: The Confederates and the Election of 1864," *Myths and Realities of the Confederate Defeat*, 127-47; and Larry E. Nelson, *Bullets, Ballots, and*

Rhetoric: Confederate Policy for the United States Presidential Contest of 1864 (University, Ala.: University of Alabama Press, 1980).
On the election of 1864 in general, see James M. McPherson, *The Battle Cry of Freedom: The Civil War Era* (New York: Ballantine, 1989), 713-718, 721, 743, 765, 770-83, 788-90, 803-806. Bennett, *Forced into Glory*, 432-34, sees the election of 1864 as the first time that Lincoln actually had a political party--not the Republicans, but the Union Party of Conservative Republicans and War Democrats that had neutralized Radical Republican opposition to Lincoln by exploiting the treason issue, reinforced by battlefield victories. For other viewpoints, consult David E. Long, *The Jewel of Liberty: Abraham Lincoln's Re-election and the End of Slavery* (Mechanicsburg, PA: Stackpole, 1994); Robert L. Morris, "The Lincoln-Johnson Plan for Reconstruction and the Republican Convention of 1864," *Lincoln Herald*, 71 (Spring 1969), 33-39; John C. Waugh, *Reelecting Lincoln: The Battle for the 1864 Presidency* (New York: Crown, 1997); Hans L. Trefousse, *The Radical Republicans: Lincoln's Vanguard for Racial Justice* (New York: Alfred A. Knopf, 1969); Williams, "Lincoln and the Radicals," in Grady McWhiney (ed.), *Grant, Lee, Lincoln, and the Radicals* (Evanston: Northwestern University Press, 1964), 92-117; David H. Donald, "Devils Facing Zionwards," *ibid.*, 72-91; and Williams, *Lincoln and the Radicals* (Madison: University of Wisconsin Press, 1941).

4. Family Politics I: John and Asia
Alford (ed.), *John Wilkes Booth: A Sister's Memoir by Asia Booth Clarke*, 79, 82-84, 86-89

5. Family Politics II: John vs. June, Ned, and Sleepy
Alford (ed.), *John Wilkes Booth: A Sister's Memoir by Asia Booth Clarke*, 81, 88-89, 113, 116, 119, 121; Smith, *American Gothic*, 102-103.
Wilson, *John Wilkes Booth*, 38-61, remarks on Booth's "secession froth," and doubts that Ned or any family member would have thought enough of Johnny's letters or plots do much more than ridicule them. Booth's concept of Lincoln as Tyrant was a common theme North and South, even within the Republican Party. See *e.g.*, James W. Clarke, *American Assassins: The Darker Side of Politics* (Princeton: Princeton University Press, 1982), 26-27; Frank Klement, "A Small Town Editor Criticizes Lincoln: A Study in Editorial Abuse," *Lincoln Herald*, 54 (Summer 1952), 27-32, 60; and especially, Joseph George, Jr., "'Abraham Africanus I': President Lincoln Through the Eyes of a Copperhead

Editor," *Civil War History*, 14 (September 1968), 226-41. For the constant hostility of John Wilkes Booth and others toward those who occupied Maryland for the Union, see Clark, "Suppression and Control of Maryland," 241-71, quote from 267.

For the attempt to burn New York City the night of the play, see Axelrod, *War Between the Spies*, 233-52; and Singer, *Confederate Dirty War*, 55-75, especially 61.

On Booth's theme, "When Lincoln Shall Be King," the work of DiLorenzo, "The Great Centralizer: Abraham Lincoln and the War Between the States," 243-71, and *The Real Lincoln*, 54-84, are instructive. On the idea that Lincoln was a tool of New England, see Phillips, *Cousin's Wars*, passim, for an expanded, modern thesis of a similar nature.

6. Booth Meets Tom Harbin
Mudd, *Life of Mudd*, 29; Steers, *His Name Is Still Mudd*, 39-48, 60-69; Steers, "The Deceptive Doctor," 114-28; Steers, *Blood on the Moon*, 78-79; Townsend in *Cincinnati Enquirer*, April 14, 1892, copy in vertical file under G. A. Townsend, Surratt House Museum. On Harbin, see John Stewart, *Confederate Spies at Large: The Lives of Lincoln Assassination Conspirator Thomas Harbin and Charlie Russell* (Jefferson, N.C.: McFarland Co., Publishers, 2007), and Joseph E. "Rick," Smith, III with William L. Richter. *In the Shadows of the Lincoln Assassination: The Life of Confederate Spy Thomas H. Harbin* (Laurel, Md.: Burgundy Press, 2008), 93-99.

7. For the Sake of a One-eyed Horse
Carter, *Riddle of Mudd*, 70-85; Steers, "The Deceptive Doctor," 114-28. The contents of the letter that Frankie Mudd destroyed are forever lost to imagination. Ours was stimulated by combining and editing the letters in Lowry, *The Story the Soldiers Wouldn't Tell*, 37-38, 160, 169, to produce the intimate lines of Booth's lady love.

8. Meeting in Richmond III: Powell and the Baltimoreans
Ownsbey, *Alias "Paine": Lewis Thornton Powell* , 35-40. Descriptions of condidtions and locations in wartime Richmond can be found in Emory Thomas, "Wartime Richmond," *Civil War Times Illustrated*, 16 (June 1977), 1-50.

9. Powell Goes on a Special Mission
Ownsbey, *Alias "Paine": Lewis Thornton Powell,* 36-37.

10. Booth Meets John Surratt

Weichmann, *A True Story*; 29-36. Descriptions of condidtions and locations in wartime Washington can be found in Stanley Kimmel, *Mr. Lincoln's Washington* (New York: Bramhall House, 1957); and Margaret Leech, *Reveille in Washington, 1860-1865* (New York: Harper & Brothers, Publishers, 1941).

11. Surratt Joins the Plot

Weichmann, *A True Story*; 66-78. For more on Surratt's Civil War activities with the Confederate underground, see William L. Richter, *Confederate Freedom Fighter: The Story of John H. Surratt & the Plots Against Lincoln* (Laurel, Md.: Burgundy Press, 2008).

We disagree with the traditional account that John Surratt wished the public to believe, that he joined Booth very reluctantly. See McMurtry (ed.), "[John H. Surratt's] Lecture on the Lincoln Conspiracy," 24-25; Oldroyd, *Assassination of Abraham Lincoln*, 153-93, *passim*. A fine dramatization of this view is Glenn Koons, "Booth Reveals His Plan to Surratt," *Surratt Society News*, 9 (February 1984), 5-8. Surratt knew Mudd and we believe that he was hot for action of any kind against the North, especially when its originator was vouched for by men like Mudd and Tom Harbin. More accurate to our mind is the account in DeWitt, *Assassination of Abraham Lincoln*, 24, where he claims that Surratt "welcomed the project with the utmost ardor."

On Atzerodt, see James O. Hall, and Edward Steers, Jr. "George Andrew Atzerodt," Kauffman (ed.), *In Pursuit of. . . ,* 29-32, Buckingham, *Reminiscences and Souvenirs of the Assassination of Abraham Lincoln*, 33-37; Roscoe, *Web of Conspiracy*, 61-63.

12. The Mechanics of Receiving Lincoln in Richmond

Tidwell, Hall, and Gaddy, *Come Retribution*, 22-24, 317-20, 293-95, 346-62.

On the torpedoes used by Lt. Kennon and the Confederate navy, see R.O. Crowley, "Making the Infernal Machines," *Civil War Times Illustrated*, 12 (June 1973), 24-35; and Dean Snyder, "Torpedoes for the Confederacy," *Civil War Times Illustrated*, 24 (March 1985), 40-45.

13. Restructuring the Secret Service Command

Tidwell, Hall, and Gaddy, *Come Retribution*, 22, 24, 346-47, 357; Tidwell, *April '65*, 156, 159; H. V. Canan, "Confederate Military Intelligence," *Maryland Historical Magazine*, 59 (March 1964), 34-51.

On Norris and his importance, see David Winfred Gaddy, "William Norris and the Confederate Signal and Secret Service," 167-88. For Brig. Gen. Edwin G. Lee, see Alexandra Lee Levin, "The Canada Contact: Edwin Gray Lee," *Civil War Times Illustrated*, 18 (June 1979), 4-8, 42-47.

Problems in Canada with the Secret Service's top command are set forth in Oscar A. Kinchen, *Confederate Operations in Canada and the North* (North Quincy, Mass.: Christopher Publishing House, 1970). William C. Davis, "The Conduct of 'Mr. Thompson'," *Civil War Times Illustrated*, 9 (May 1970), 4-7, 43-47; Peggy Robbins, "The Greatest Scoundrel [Jacob Thompson]," *Civil War Times Illustrated*, 31 (November/December 1992), 54-59, 89-90. A more general discussion of problematical behind-the-lines activities on both sides is Edwin C. Fishel, "The Mythology of Civil War Intelligence," *Civil War History*, 10 (December 1964), 344-67. See also, Donald E. Markle, *Spies and Spymasters of the Civil War* (New York: Hippocrene Books, 1994).

14. Recruiting His Theater Pals Unsuccessfully
Pitman (comp.), *The Assassination of President Lincoln and the Trial of the Conspirators* , 44-45; DeWitt, *Assassination of Abraham Lincoln*, 23-26; Weichmann, *A True Story*; 57-60. See also, "Samuel K. Chester," box 4, folder 224, DRB papers, GU.

PART VIII: FIRST ATTEMPT (1865)

1. The Port Tobacco Connection
Trindal, *Mary Surratt,* 92; Weichmann, *A True Story*; 30, 70-72. For a sketch of Andrew Atzerodt, see James O. Hall and Edward Steers, Jr., "George Andrew Atzerodt," Kauffman (ed.), *In Pursuit of . . .* , 29-32. Martin's story is in R. Sutton, *et al* (comps.), *The Reporter: Containing . . . Trial of John H. Surratt, on an Indictment for Murder of President Lincoln,* III, 193-94.

2. The January Kidnap Fiasco
In general, see DeWitt, *Assassination of Abraham Lincoln*, 25-27; Oldroyd, *Assassination of Abraham Lincoln*, 153-93, *passim*; Roscoe, *Web of Conspiracy*, 72-75, 485-86; Weichmann, Weichmann, *A True Story*; 73-74. Richard Mitchell Smoot, *The Unwritten History of the Assassination of Abraham Lincoln* (Clinton, Mass.: W. J. Coulter, 1908), 7-9, discusses the boat deal, which is expanded on in "Some Damaging Evidence," *Surratt Courier*, 39 (June 2005), 3-5 and commented on in

Frederick Hatch, "The Unwritten History of the Assassination of
Abraham Lincoln," *Journal of the Lincoln Assassination*, 19 (December
2005); for Martin's story and Smoot's testimony at the John H. Surratt
trial, see Edwards Pierrepont, *To the Jury on the Trial of John H. Surratt
for the Murder of President Lincoln* (Washington: Government Printing
Office, 1867), 23, 51-52; R. Sutton, *et al* (comps.), *The Reporter:
Containing . . . Trial of John H. Surratt, on an Indictment for Murder of
President Lincoln*, III, 175-77. For a good acount of Smoot's activities in
the Confederate underground, see John M. Wearmouth and Roberta J.
Wearmouth, *Thomas A. Jones: Chief Agent of the Confederate Secret
Service in Maryland* (Port Tobacco, MD: Stones Throw Publishing,
2000), 149-53.

3. Powell Becomes Cousin Lewis
    Powell's guerilla activities are in Ownsbey, *Alias "Paine": Lewis
Thornton Powell*, 158-73; Ramage, *Gray Ghost: The Life and Legend of
Col. John Singleton Mosby*, 223-27. On Harry Gilmore's men, see John
Bakeless, "Catching Harry Gilmore," *Civil War Times Illustrated*, 10
(April 1971), 24-33.

4. Powell Meets John Surratt and Loves Mary Branson
    Ownsbey, *Alias "Paine": Lewis Thornton Powell*, 35-36;
Ownsbey, "The Elusive Branson Sisters of Baltimore," 5-8. See also, H.
B. Smith, *Between the Lines: Secret Service stories Told Fifty Years After*
(New York: Booz Bros., 1911), 304-10, for Maggie Branson's
interrogation after the Lincoln Assassination. See also, Pitman (comp.),
The Assassination of President Lincoln and the Trial of the Conspirators,
160-61; Weichmann, *A True Story*, 73-77.

5. War to the Knife . . .
    This conversation is paraphrased from Benjamin's actual speech
at Richmond's African Church as printed in the *Richmond Dispatch*,
February 10, 1865. See also, Bennett, *Forced into Glory*, 610-15 ("root
hog or die!" from Hampton Roads Peace Conference).

6. . . . Knife to the Hilt
    Richmond Dispatch, February 10, 1865. For criticisms, see J. B.
Jones, *A Rebel War Clerk's Diary at the Confederate States Capital* (Ed.
by Howard Swiggett, 2 vols., New York: Old Hickory Bookshop, 1935),

II, 451 (desperate), 457 (ridiculous); and Edward Younger (ed.), *Inside the Confederate Government: The Diary of Robert Garlick Hill Kean, Head of the Bureau of War* (Westport, Conn.: Greenwood Press, 1973), 182-84, 197, 204-205; Cooper, *Jefferson Davis*, 506-21. See also, Thomas P. Lowery, "Opposition to Negro Equality," *North & South*, 3 (June 2000), 9, 80-81. For more on a general view of republicanism (note the lower case "r") as a key issue in secession, beyond that accredited to Benjamin here, see Joseph R. Stromberg, "Republicanism, Federalism, and Secession, 1790 to 1865," in Gordon (ed.), *Secession, State and Liberty*, 99-133.

7. The New Rebel Safe House
      Trindal, *Mary Surratt*, 85-96; Campbell, *Case for Mrs. Surratt*, 55-62; Campbell, *Confederate Courier*, 49-51; Otto Eisenschiml, "Mrs. Surratt's Boarding House," in his *In the Shadow of Lincoln's Death* , 91-98; James O. Hall, "Miss Dean," *Surratt Society News*, 4 (September 1979), 4; Laurie Verge, "Who Was Annie Ward?" *Surratt Courier*, 33 (July 2008), 6-7; Hall, "The Other Boardinghouse Residents--Mary Apollonia Dean and the Holohan Family," Kauffman (ed.), *In Pursuit of . . .*, 65-68; and Hall, *The Surratt Family and John Wilkes Booth*, 8-10. A look at the boardinghouse from a more recent perspective is Harold O. Wang, "A Visit to the Surratt Boardinghouse," Kauffman (ed.), *In Pursuit of . . .*, 121-24.

8. Booth Gets Richmond's Approval
      Tidwell, Hall, and Gaddy, *Come Retribution*, 26-27. There is no reason to refer to the gang as "Cartoon Assassins," as does Lewis, *The Assassination of Lincoln*, 158-74. They were each picked to perform a special part in the abduction process, as we have Surratt say here. The similarity between General Bradley Johnson's Plan to kidnap Lincoln and Booth's later plot is noted in John C. Brennan, "The Confederate Plan to Abduct Lincoln," Kauffman (ed.), *In Pursuit of . . .*, 141-49. On Lincoln's cavalry escort, see Robert W. McBride, "Lincoln's Bodyguard: The Union Light Guard of Ohio, with Some Personal Recollections of Abraham Lincoln," *Indiana Historical Society Publications*, 5 (1911), 5-39. This section was written six years ago without the recent, expert analysis of Larson, *Assassin's Accomplice*, 43-95, who confirms our assessment of Mary Surratt's active participation in the Lincoln Assassination, from providing (in Andrew Johnson's words), "The nest that hatched the rotten egg," to private encouragement and material support (230).

9. Booth Finally Goes to War Despite His Mother's Objections
     See Rhodehamel and Taper (eds.), *Writings of John Wilkes Booth*, 130-31 and footnotes; Alford (ed.), *John Wilkes Booth: A Sister's Memoir by Asia Booth Clarke*,

10. Gus Howell and the French Woman
     Trindal, Mary Surratt, 92, 96-98, Campbell, *Case for Mrs. Surratt*, 74; Weichmann, *A True Story*; 85-86.

11. Powell Visits Mrs. Surratt
     Ownsbey, *Alias "Paine": Lewis Thornton Powell*, 40-42; Trindal, Mary Surratt, 98-99; Alford (ed.), *John Wilkes Booth: A Sister's Memoir by Asia Booth Clarke*, 85 (Virginia--Virginia); Rhodehamel and Taper (eds.), *Writings of John Wilkes Booth*, 131-134 and footnotes; Oldroyd, *Assassination of Abraham Lincoln*, 153-93, *passim*; Weichmann, *A True Story*; 78-87.

12. Confederate Campaign of 1865
     Tidwell, Hall, and Gaddy, *Come Retribution*, 25-26, 362-402.
     On the realities of what faced Lee as Jefferson Davis' military advisor (1861), then as commanding general, first of the Army of Northern Virginia (1862) and then of the entire confederacy (1865), consult, Joseph L. Harsh, "'As Stupid a Fellow as I Am . . .': On the Real Military Genius of Robert E. Lee," *North & South*, 3 (June 2000), 60-71.
     As is correctly pointed out by John C. Breckinridge's biographer (William C. Davis, *John C. Breckinridge: Statesman, Soldier, Symbol* [Baton Rouge: Louisiana State University Press,1974], 489-588, *passim*; and "John C. Breckinridge and Confederate Defeat," in his *The Lost Cause: Myths and Realities of the Confederate Defeat* [Lawrence: University Press of Kansas, 1996], 148-58), and Jefferson Davis' most recent biographer (Cooper, *Jefferson Davis*, 498), there are no records that implicate any of the men in this chapter in any abduction or, especially, assassination plot against President Lincoln. Evans, *Judah P. Benjamin*, 349-71, in a chapter aptly subtitled "Lingering Suspicion," holds with Cooper--there are no records--even though he admits that Benjamin destroyed all of his papers to prevent "a legacy of mischief' (398). General Lee's most recent chronicler, Michael Fellman, *The Making of Robert E. Lee* (New York: Random House, 2000), never mentions the Kilpatrick-Dahlgren Raid, much less anything to do with Lincoln's abduction or execution. But he does note that Lee was a strong Southern sectionalist, who became more so during and after the war, and who was

dedicated to restoring white political control of the South. Secretary Breckinridge's knowledge of Harney's gunpowder plot is arguable, although one wonders if jail is all he fears in post-war Union retribution, since he knew of the campaign of 1865--as did Lee.

The danger of interpreting Lee as anything but the perfect man portrayed in Douglas Southall Freeman, *R. E. Lee* (4 vols., New York: Charles Scribner's Sons, 1934-1935) is demonstrated by Thomas Connelly, *The Marble Man: Robert E. Lee and His Image in American Society* (New York: Knopf, 1977), and especially Alan T. Nolan, *Lee Considered: General Robert E. Lee and Civil War History* (Chapel Hill: University of North Carolina Press, 1991). For a typical critical review of Nolan (despite the title's implication), see Doug Bandow, "The Marble Man," *National Review*, 43 (October 21, 1991), 48-49. But one ought to read without preconceived notions Nolan's chapter, "Those People--The Magnanimous Adversary," 107-11, in which he concludes that Lee was less disposed to Yankee conduct in the South than one might suppose, when estimating what Lee might or might not have done to bring about a Southern victory.

See the letter from William A. Tidwell to Editor, *North & South*, 2 (June 1999), 5, on the mechanics of what Secretary Benjamin and President Davis had to do to approve of monies spent in secret operations. Both had to know and approve. One wonder how much the others knew and hid. See also, Tidwell, "Was Booth Part of a Confederate Conspiracy?" in Richard Bak, *The Day Lincoln Was Shot: An Illustrated Chronicle* (Dallas: Taylor Publishing Co., 1998), 63-68, especially 68, for the critical role Washington military staff and Lincoln and his cabinet play in Union coordination of Northern armies.

PART IX: ANOTHER FAILURE (1865)

1. Louis Weichmann Tells Major Gleason

Weichmann, *A True Story*; 109-10; Chamlee, *Lincoln's Assassins*,113-16; Oldroyd, *Assassination of Abraham Lincoln*, 153-93, *passim*. D. H. L. Gleason, "Conspiracy Against Lincoln," *Magazine of History*, 13 (February 1911), 59-65, for the major's story, inflated as to his role in revealing the plot against Lincoln ahead of time, something he really never did. Information of Gleason's life, military career, and injuries can be found in Benjamin Crowninshield, *A History of the First Regiment of Massachusetts Cavalry Volunteers* (Boston: Houghton, Mifflin, 1891), 323.

See William Hanchett, "The War Department and Booth's Abduction Plot," *Lincoln Herald*, 82 (Winter 1980), 499-508. Hanchett's belief pretty much obviates the theses set forth in Robert Lockwood Mills, *It Didn't Happen the Way You Think: The Lincoln Assassination--What the Experts Missed* (New Canaan, Conn.: Write Ideas, 1993), 124-31, and Eisenschiml, "Premonitions vs. Secret Service Reports," *Why Was Lincoln Murdered?* 40-53, that Stanton knew that there was a plot to kidnap the President and intentionally failed to stop it, hoping to inflame North-South passions and block Lincoln's soft-hearted approach to Reconstruction, which was supported by Seward.

2. Wilkes Booth in Love

We agree with Constance Head, "John Wilkes Booth: Prologue to Assassination," 260, that there has to be something to his relationship with Lucy, beyond mere exploitation. See also, "Miss Bessie [*sic*] Hale and Booth," box 4, folder 218, DRB papers, GU. Just when Booth and Lucy met is open to question. We have stuck with a traditional late date, the fall of 1864. But a much earlier date of February 1862 is put forth in Richmond Morcum, "They All Loved Lucy," *American Heritage*, 21 (October 1970), 12-15. For what it is worth, Booth's home in Washington, the National Hotel, was the frequented by Northerners, as opposed to Southerners, and Down-east Yankee abolitionists at that.

3. Lucy Lambert Hale

Of course, if the thesis put forth in Izola Forrester is true, that Booth was married or, at lest, had a common law relationship before the war and his family home was in the Shenandoah Valley, all notions that Booth had noble pursuits in mind for his romance of Lucy Hale may be bunk. See Forrester, *This One Mad Act. The Unknown Story of John Wilkes Booth and His Family* (Boston: Hale, Cushman, and Flint, 1937). Forrester's work is backed up by another author claiming descent from the same Booth marriage, Theodore J. Nottingham. See his *The Curse of Cain: The Untold Story of John Wilkes Booth* (Nicholasville, Ky.: Appaloosa Books, 1997). The characterization of Hale in New Hampshire history is from J. Denis Robinson, "Hail Hale, the Hype's All Here," *As I Please*, 2 (No. 4, March 1. 1998) at seacoastnh.com.

4. Powell Beats Up Annie

Ownsbey, *Alias "Paine": Lewis Thornton Powell* , 45-50; H. B. Smith, *Between the Lines*, 255-58. See also, Pitman (comp.), *The*

Assassination of President Lincoln and the Trial of the Conspirators, 160-61

5. Powell Visits Mrs. Surratt Again
Ownsbey, *Alias "Paine": Lewis Thornton Powell,* 51-53; Oldroyd, *Assassination of Abraham Lincoln*, 153-93, *passim*; Weichmann, *A True Story*; 96-114.

6. Booth Attends A March Ball
The ball events are in "Booth and Bob Lincoln," Chicago *Daily Inter-Ocean*, June 18, 1878. For the so-called Battle of Kilpatrick's Pants, see William Preston Mangum II, "Kill Cavalry's Nasty Surprise," *America's Civil War*, 9 (November 1996), 42-48, friends said he was missing only boots, hat, and coat. Booth's tirade on Lincoln is from box 3, DRB papers, GU. The changing Lincoln visiage, in reality as well as in the public eye, is the theme of Harold Holzer, "The Changing Wartime Image of Lincoln," in Bak, *The Day Lincoln Was Shot*, 28-37.

7. Weichmann Gets Nosy
Weichmann, *A True Story*; 97-98.

8. An Evening at Gautier's
Kauffman (ed.), *Memoirs of a Lincoln Conspirator* [Samuel B. Arnold], 38-47. See also, Arnold's later statement, in Laurie Verge (ed.), *From War Department Files: Statements Made by the Alleged Lincoln Conspirators Under Examination, 1865* (Clinton, Md.: Surratt Society, 1980), 20-22. Booth's various alternate plans and their holes as pointed out by others are in Roscoe, *Web of Conspiracy*, 69-87; Hanchett, "The War Department and Booth's Abduction Plot," 499-508, *passim*. Lincoln's trips to the War Department often invlved checking the flow of telegraph messages from the various military fronts. See David Homer Bates, *Lincoln in the Telegraph Office* (New York: D. Appleton-Century Co., 1907).

9. Booth Plots a Kidnapping
Weichmann, *A True Story*; 114-15. On the trunk, see Thomas G. Shaffer, "The Gospel According to John Matthews," Dillon (ed.), *The Lincoln Assassination: From the Pages of the* Surratt Courier, 25-32.

10. The Kidnapping that Failed

Tidwell, Hall, and Gaddy, *Come Retribution*, 27. The most accurate story is William Hanchett, "The Ambush on the Seventh Street Road," Kauffman (ed.), *In Pursuit of . . .*, 151-161. For Surratt's account of the affair, see McMurtry (ed.), "[John H. Surratt's] Lecture on the Lincoln Conspiracy," 25-28; and Edward Steers, Jr., "John Surratt, Jr., Speaks at the Cooper Institute," Kauffman (ed.), *In Pursuit of . . .*, 283-84. See also, Ownsbey, *Alias "Paine": Lewis Thornton Powell*, 60-62; Roscoe, *Web of Conspiracy*, 84-86; Weichmann, *A True Story*; 96-114. The weather is in DRB papers, box 7, GU.

11. Aftermath of the Kidnap Attempt

Ownsbey, *Alias "Paine": Lewis Thornton Powell*, 62-64; Oldroyd, *Assassination of Abraham Lincoln*, 153-93, *passim*; Hanchett, "The War Department and Booth's Abduction Plot," 499-508, *passim*. See also, Ramage *Gray Ghost: The Life and Legend of Col. John Singleton Mosby*, 277, where Mosby called in his command from the Northern Neck after the failure of the March abduction attempt.

12. Herold Goes to Tee Bee

Laurie Verge, "That Trifling Boy . . . ," *Surratt Courier*, 27 (January 2002), 4-9; Weichmann, *A True Story*; 118-19. See also, Laurie Verge and James O. Hall, "The Hidden Guns," Kauffman (ed.), *In Pursuit of . . .*, 253-55. Thompson's and Norton's accounts are in R. Sutton, *et al. (comps.), The Reporter: Containing . . . Trial of John H. Surratt, on an Indictment for Murder of President Lincoln*, III, 239-42, 390-95.

13. A Grand Finale and a Stunning Exit

"Booth and Bob Lincoln," Chicago *Daily Inter-Ocean*, June 18, 1878.

Book 2: The Assassins

PART I: REGROUPING (1865)

1. Lincoln on Black Confederate Soldiers
   This whole incident is described in the *National Intelligencer*, March 18, 1865, including full speeches by the participants. For this and another version of Lincoln's speech, see Basler (ed.), *Collected Works*, VIII, 360-62.

   Historically, the use of blacks in the Confederate forces is treated in Jordan, *Black Confederates and Afro-Yankees in Civil War Virginia*; Richard Rollins (ed.), *Black Southerners in Gray*; and Robert Durden, *The Gray and the Black*.

2. A Pair of Slippers
   Weichmann, *A True Story*; 85-86, 122-24. Sutton, *et al. (comps.)*, *The Reporter: Containing . . . Trial of John H. Surratt, on an Indictment for Murder of President Lincoln*, IV, 141-43. Watson is identified in Steers, *Blood on the Moon*, 88-89.

3. A Room for James C. Kincheloe
   Ownsbey, *Alias "Paine": Lewis Thornton Powell* , 65-69; Weichmann, *A True Story*; 120-22, 173; Tidwell, Hall, and Gaddy, *Come Retribution*, 415; Rhodehamel and Taper (eds.), *Writings of John Wilkes Booth*, 142-44 and footnotes; Kauffman (ed.), *Memoirs of a Lincoln Conspirator* [Samuel B. Arnold], 8-11; Laurie Verge, "Who Was Annie Ward?" *Surratt Courier*, 33 (July 2008), 6-7; Percy E. Martin, "Samuel Bland Arnold Revisited," Kauffman (ed.), *In Pursuit of . . .* , 33-39; Martin, "Baltimorean in Big Trouble, Samuel Arnold, A Lincoln Conspirator," 5-8; the "Sam" letter is also in T. M. Harris, *Assassination of Lincoln: A History of the Great Conspiracy Trial of the Conspirators by a Military Commission, and a Review of the Trial of John H. Surratt* (Boston: American Citizen Company, 1892), 72, Frederick Hatch,"The 'Sam' Letter," *Journal of the Lincoln Assassination*, 19 (August 2005), 22-26; and Weichmann, *A True Story*; 124-25. See also, R. Sutton, *et al* (comps.), *The Reporter: Containing . . . Trial of John H. Surratt, on an Indictment for Murder of President Lincoln,* III, 195.

4. Tying Up Loose Ends
   For Harney's "Gunpowder Plot," see Tidwell, Hall, and Gaddy, *Come Retribution*, 27; Tidwell, *April '65*, 160-96, *passim*. On

Stringfellow, see Bakeless, *Spies of the Confederacy* , 22; Laurie Verge
and James O. Hall, "Could It Have Been Mrs. Surratt?" Dillon (ed.), *The
Lincoln Assassination: From the Pages of the* Surratt Courier*, I, 23;
Axelrod, *The War between the Spies*, 145-59; and John F. Stanton, "'Hold
the Boat, Tom'," *Surratt Society News*, 8 (September 1983), 3-4. See also,
Weichmann, *A True Story*; 126-27.

   5. John Surratt Goes to Montreal
      Weichmann, *A True Story*; 127. For Surratt's account, see
McMurtry (ed.), "[John H. Surratt's] Lecture on the Lincoln Conspiracy,"
28-33, 39. On the flight and last days of the Confederate government, see
Michael B. Ballard, *A Long Shadow: Jefferson Davis and the Final Days
of the Confederacy* (Jackson: University Press of Mississippi, 1986); John
H. Brubaker, III, *The Last Capitol: Danville, Virginia, and the Final Days
of the Confederacy* (Danville, Va.: Danville Museum of Fine Arts and
History, 1979); Rembert W. Patrick, *The Fall of Richmond* (Baton Rouge:
Louisiana State University Press, 1960); James C. Clark, *Last Train
South: The Flight of the Confederate Government from Richmond*
(Jefferson, N.C.: McFarland Company, Inc., 1984).

   6. The Confederate Sympathies of Dr. Mudd
      See testimony in Pitman (comp.), *The Assassination of President
Lincoln and the Trial of the Conspirators*, 168-217.

   7. Mudd's trip to Giesboro
      Pitman (comp.), *The Assassination of President Lincoln and the
Trial of the Conspirators*, 168-217.

   8. Aboard the *Malvern*
      Edward H. Ripley, *The Capture and Occupation of Richmond,
April 3rd, 1865* (New York: G. P. {Putnam's Sons, 1907), 21-26. See also,
Edward H. Ripley, *Vermont General: The Unusual War Experiences of
Edward Hastings Ripley, 1862-1865* (Ed. by Otto Eisenschiml, New
York: The Devin-Adair Company, 1960). Lincoln's last line, which he
used often, is in Baker, *History of the United States Secret Service*, 475.

   9. Mrs. Surratt's Trip of April 11
      Trindal, *Mary Surratt*, 90, 116, 287-88; Campbell, *Case for Mrs.
Surratt*, 53, 82-84; Eisenschiml, "Mrs. Surratt's Boarding House," and his,
"The Woman in the Case," in *Why Was Lincoln Murdered?* 102, 280;
Weichmann, *A True Story*, 133-34, 171; Moore, *Case of Mary Surratt*, 77-

78, 80-81; Turner, "Mrs. Mary Surratt," in *Beware the People Weeping*, 155; Harris, *Assassination of Lincoln*, 196-97; Hall, "John M. Lloyd: Star Witness," Kauffman (ed.), *In Pursuit of . . .*, 97; Oldroyd, *Assassination of Abraham Lincoln*, 153-93, *passim*. See also, Pitman (comp.), *The Assassination of President Lincoln and the Trial of the Conspirators* , 85-87, 121; R. Sutton, *et al. (comps.), The Reporter: Containing . . . Trial of John H. Surratt, on an Indictment for Murder of President Lincoln*, III, 248-58, *ibid.*, IV, 143-46; Laurie Verge, "The Surratt's Neighbors," Kauffman (ed.), *In Pursuit of . . .*, 89-90; Hall, *The Surratt Family and John Wilkes Booth*, 17. The Lloyd-Offutt affaire is spoken of in Elizabeth Stegner Trindal, "Two Men Who Held the Noose," *Surratt Courier*, 28 (July 2003), 3-5. Nothey signed his name with an "x" on his statement to the Federal authorities about the matter in "Mary Surratt," box 7, folder 359, DRB papers, GU. Hence his illiteracy.

   10. Lincoln Confiscates 'Dixie"
         Laughlin, *Death of Lincoln*, 259-61. See also, "Booth's Movements, April 9-13, 1865," box 4, folder 211, DRB papers, GU.

   11. Lincoln's Final Speech
         The speech is in Basler (ed.), *Collected Works*, VIII, 399-405. See also, DeWitt, *Assassination of Abraham Lincoln*, 39-40; "Booth's Movements, April 9-13, 1865," box 4, folder 211, DRB papers, GU; Noah Brooks, *Washington in Lincoln's Time* (Ed. by Herbert Mitgang, New York: Rinehart & Company, Inc., 1958), 225-28. Bennett, *Forced into Glory*, 588-89, 606-609, 619, sees Lincoln's references, to permitting ("let in," was Lincoln's condescending phrase) some blacks (the educated and soldiers) to vote, as more foot-dragging on the equal rights issue--exactly what Radical Republicans in Congress believed, but the complete opposite of what Booth thought.
         Most studies are more complementary to Lincoln. See Peyton McCrary, *Abraham Lincoln and Reconstruction: The Louisiana Experiment* (Princeton: Princeton University Press, 1978); William C. Harris, *With Charity for All: Lincoln and the Restoration of the Union* (Lexington: University of Kentucky Press, 1997); Hesseltine, *Lincoln's Plan of Reconstruction;* C. Peter Ripley, *Slaves and Freedmen in Civil War Louisiana* (Baton Rouge: Louisiana State University Press, 1978); T. Harry Williams, "Abraham Lincoln: Principle and Pragmatism in Politics," *Mississippi Valley Historical Review*, 40 (June 1953), 89-108.

12. Meeting at the Herndon House

Tidwell, Hall, and Gaddy, *Come Retribution*, 27-29, discuss Booth altering his abduction operation to include Harney's assassination objective. See DeWitt, *Assassination of Abraham Lincoln*, 40-41, 44-45; Wilson, *John Wilkes Booth*, 93-97; E. A. Emerson, "How Wilkes Booth's Friend Described His Crime," *Literary Digest*, (Mar. 6, 1926), 58, 60. See also, "Booth's Movements, April 9-13, 1865," box 4, folder 211, DRB papers, GU.

Lincoln's trip to Richmond with his young son, Tad, is the subject of Harold Holzer, "'I Was Myself at the Front'," *Civil War Times Illustrated*, 29 (January/February 1991), 28-35.

Many, quoting barkeeper John Deery, thought that Booth was crazed by liquor during this period. See, *e.g.*, Miller, *John Wilkes Booth, Oilman*, 39-40; Shelton, *Mask for Treason*, 265-66. For the Burke's Station battle, see Ramage, *Gray Ghost: The Life and Legend of Col. John Singleton Mosby*, 278-79.

Martha Murphy's testimony is in Pitman, *The Assassination of President Lincoln and the Trial of the Conspirators*, 154; and R. Sutton, *et al. (comps.), The Reporter: Containing . . . Trial of John H. Surratt, on an Indictment for Murder of President Lincoln*, III, 214-16.

The idea of Booth attempting to shoot Lincoln on April 13, was first pointed out to us by Booth expert Michael W. Kauffman, who posits that Booth's entry in his diary of "the Ides" on that date with nothing following is key to the notion. See Richter to Kauffman, December 14, 2001, and Kauffman to Richter, December 17, 2001, e-mails in the author's possession. This notion of two assassination attempts seems born out at least circumstantially in other places, especially in Atzerodt's confession cited in the following chapter, below.

13. The Aborted Attempt of April 13

Wilson, *John Wilkes Booth*, 96-97; Atzerodt's "Lost Statement," is in Steers, *His Name Is Still Mudd*, 121-24; Joan L. Chaconas, "Unpublished Atzerodt Confession offered Here for the First Time," *Surratt Courier*, 13 (October 1988), 1-3. See also, Atzerodt's statement, *Verge (ed.), From War Department Files*, 59-62.

14. Booth Spends a Night with Ella Starr Turner

The Etta Letter (Roscoe, *Web of Conspiracy*, 318) and No. 5's letter (Pitman, *The Assassination of President Lincoln and the Trial of the Conspirators*, 42; and R. Sutton, *et al. [comps.], The Reporter: Containing . . Trial of John H. Surratt, on an Indictment for Murder of*

William L. Richter

President Lincoln, III, 404), are seen as a fake or unimportant to most chroniclers. But Larry Starkey, *Wilkes Booth Came to Washington,* 120-27, makes the trip to New York City a key to his thesis that Booth was going to ditch all of his companions and after arriving at Surrattsville, head north the forty miles to Baltimore and catch the train for New York there. He posits that he had a relay of horses, but he might have been able to push the bay mare the whole way (killing her in the process, perhaps) and arrive within the nine hours necessary. After being in New York City for half a day, Booth could catch the "Midnight Special" that traveled to Montreal via St. Albans, where coincidentally, John Surratt dallied, as if waiting for someone. It might also explain the fake beard that Dr. Mudd and his wife claimed that they saw later on Booth as a disguise. He was going to disguise himself, all right, but to pass north, not south down the secret line. Booth's broken leg caused him to abort the flight to New York and permitted Davy Herold to catch up with him before Surrattsville. The two then fled on the only route available, the one all of Booth's clues left behind in Washington pointed to.

15. Herold Stays Overnight at Huntt's
Laurie Verge, "That Trifling Boy . . . ," *Surratt Courier,* 27 (January 2002), 4-9. See Herold's confession in *Verge (ed.), From War Department Files,* 1-19. Smoot, *Unwritten History,* 9-10, says that he heard of the horses at Huntt's from Atzerodt.

PART II: THE ASSASSINATION (1865)

1. Booth's Friday Morning
DeWitt, *Assassination of Abraham Lincoln,* 41-42; Wilson, *John Wilkes Booth,* 255; and Philip Van Doren Stern, *The Man Who Killed Lincoln: The Story of John Wilkes Booth and His Part in the Assassination* (New York: Literary Guild of America, Inc., 1939). For the note to Johnson, see Rhodehamel and Taper (eds.), *Writings of John Wilkes Booth,* 146 and footnotes. See also, "Booth's Movements, April 14, 1865," box 4, folder 215, DRB papers, GU; and testimony of Charles Wood, R. Sutton, *et al. (comps.), The Reporter: Containing . . . Trial of John H. Surratt, on an Indictment for Murder of President Lincoln,* III, 381-383.

2. A Fateful Letter and a Pair of Binoculars
DeWitt, *Assassination of Abraham Lincoln,* 42; Trindal, *Mary Surratt,* 116-17; Campbell, *Case for Mrs. Surratt,* 84-86; Eisenschiml,

"The Woman in the Case," 284-85; Moore, *Case of Mrs. Surratt*, 78, 81-83; Harris, *Assassination of Lincoln*, 197-98, 202; Laughlin, *Death of Lincoln*, 322-23; Weichmann, *A True Story*, 163-72, 263-64; John C. Brennan, "John Wilkes Booth's Field Glasses," *Surratt Society News*, 7 (October 1982), 5-6.

3. Booth's Friday Afternoon
For the letter, see Rhodehamel and Taper (eds.), *Writings of John Wilkes Booth*, 144-46 and footnotes. The color of Booth's mount is in Townsend, *Washington: Outside and Inside*, 714. See also, "Booth's Movements, April 14, 1865," box 4, folder 215, DRB papers, GU. Booth's statements to the Circle on the theater as art form are paraphrased from the comments of Kevin Spacey, *Parade Magazine* (October 24, 1999), 6.

4. The Letter to the *National Intelligencer:* Booth Opts for Assassination
The text of the letter appears in several places. See *e.g.*, Rhodehamel and Taper (eds.), *Writings of John Wilkes Booth*, 147-53 and footnotes. But Matthews burned the original document and it has become traditional to say, as he claimed, that it was much the same as Booth's earlier "To Whom It May Concern" letter that was ensconced in John Sleeper Clarke's safe in Philadelphia.
Although we are not willing to go as far as Thomas G. Shaffer, "The Gospel According to John Matthews," Dillon (ed.), *The Lincoln Assassination: From the Pages of the* Surratt Courier, I, 25-32, and accuse Matthews of making up the existence of the *National Intelligencer* letter out of whole cloth, he has a point that Matthews could not have memorized such a lengthy piece in a panicked glance or two. This having been said, we agree with Terry Alford, "John Matthews: A Vindication of the Historical Consensus," Dillon (ed.), *The Lincoln Assassination: From the Pages of the* Surratt Courier, I, 43-47, and Deirdre Barber, "Further Thoughts on John Matthews," *ibid.*, I 41-42, that such a letter existed, although Robert L. Mills, "John Matthews A Liar?" *ibid.*, I 39, is not so sure. In the end, Shaffer accuses Alford of over-kill and criticizing him for points he never made (see Thomas G. Shaffer, "A Final Say on John Matthews," *ibid.*, I, 49-50). But much of their argument really begs the question as Laurie Verge states in her appended paragraphs to "A Final Say." There was a letter, Booth told Herold about it while they hid in the swamp (see Verge [ed.], *From War Departmnt Files*, 1-19) and John Matthews received it, but what it said, no one really knows.

Actor or not, we do not believe that Matthews could "wing it" and remember the intricacies of Booth's political mind. We do agree with James O. Hall, "That Letter to the *National Intelligencer*," Dillon (ed.), *The Lincoln Assassination: From the Pages of the* Surratt Courier, I, 33-38, that Matthews remembered the *gist* of the latter and reconstructed it years later, relying on the by then public "to Whom it May Concern" letter that Booth had stored in "Sleepy" Clarke's safe.

We have taken the privilege of writing what we thought Booth might have said, under the notion he would not have to write the same letter twice--or four times, if the account in Samples, *Lust for Fame*, 162-66 is accurate. We have relied on Algernon Sidney, *Discourses Concerning Government*. (Edited by Thomas G. West. Indianapolis: Library Classics, 1990); DiLorenzo, "The Great Centralizer: Abraham Lincoln and the War Between the States," 243-71, his *The Real Lincoln: A New Look at Abraham Lincoln, His Agenda, and an Unnecessary War* ; and Younger (ed.), *Inside the Confederate Government: The Diary of Robert Garlick Hill Kean*, pp. 215-23, particularly the section on how the Lincoln Administration violated the Constitution as it stood in 1860. See also, Edward Hyams, "Abraham Lincoln: A Victim of Faction," in his *Killing No Murder: A Study of Assassination as a Political Means* (London: Panther Modern Society, 1970), 68-69.

We have signed the letter with all of the names of the conspirators, suspecting that Matthews was not about to implicate John Surratt after the fact, only those killed or executed for the deed.

5. Booth Prepares for his Biggest Role

See Rhodehamel and Taper (eds.), *Writings of John Wilkes Booth*, 147-53 especially footnotes. See also, "Booth's Movements, April 14, 1865," DRB papers, GU.

According to tradition, Booth left the name of John H. Surratt, Jr., off the *National Intelligencer* letter, as pointed out in Trindal, *Mary Surratt*, 260, but, unlike Trindal, we believe that he was in Washington and a part of the final assassination conspiracy (e.g., Richter, *Confederate Freedom Fighter*, 158-64, 178-81). We do not believe the E. G. Lee story that John was scouting out Elmira with an eye to freeing Confederates held prisoner at this late time of the war. In his 1867 trial, the Federal government claimed that he boarded the same train as General Grant and tried to shoot him, only to be foiled by the locked door. As to the letter, Booth trusted Surratt and O'Laughlen but not necessarily Powell, and definitely not Herold or Atzerodt, so he set them all up in the *Intelligencer* letter, so they could not testify against him, as he did to Arnold earlier with the Sam Letter. James E. T. Lange and Katherine DeWitt, Jr., "The Law of Conspiracy," *Surratt Courier*, 23 (January 1998), 6-8, and John C. Brennan, "Why Wern't the Defendants Permitted to Testify in Their Own Defense?" in Kauffman (ed.), *In Pursuit of . . . ,* 243-44, explain how one can become ensnared in a plot without actually being there to effect it and how self testimony was viewed then as hearsay. See also, Philip Van Doren Stern, "A Vivid Scene--and Then Mystery," *New York Times Magazine,* (May 8, 1938), 3, 18; Eisenschiml, "The Plots Against Grant, Stanton, and Johnson," *Why Was Lincoln Murdered?* 162-74; and the testimony in *Surratt Trial, passim.*

For Surratt's story of flight, concealment, and trial, see definitive study by Andrew C. A. Jampoler, *The Last Lincoln Conspirator: John Surratt's Flight from the Gallows* (Annapolis: Naval Institute Press, 2008). An earlier account is Mark Wilson Seymour (ed.), *The Pursuit and Arrest of John H. Surratt: Dispatches from the Official Record of the Assassination of Abraham Lincoln* (Austin: Proofmark Civil War Library, 2000). See also, John C. Brennan, "John H. Surratt's 'Pilgrim' Interview," Kauffman (ed.), *In Pursuit of . . . ,* 53-64, Alexandria Lee Levin, "Who Hid John H. Surratt, the Lincoln Conspiracy Case Figure?" *Maryland Historical Magazine,* 18 (June 1979), 175-84; and John F. Doyle, "The Case of John Harrison Surratt, Jr.," *Surratt Courier,* 25 (March 2000), 3-7; Hall, *The Surratt Family and John Wilkes Booth,* 16. The later life, trial and career of John Surratt can be followed in the articles in "Capture & Trial of John Harrison Surratt, Jr.," Dillon (ed.), *The Lincoln Assassination: From the Pages of the* Surratt Courier, X, 1-46.

John Surratt, Jr., has been memorialized by Campbell's, *Confederate Courier.* For a good short summary of the John Surratt story, see Alfred Issacson, "John Surratt and the Lincoln Assassination Plot," *Maryland Historical Magazine,* 52 (December 1957), 315-42, for which he was mercilessly pummeled by Otto Eisenschiml, "A 'Study' of John Surratt?" *Journal of the Illinois State Historical Society,* 52 (Spring 1959), 181-89. Issacson's attempt to defend himself was similarly belittled in Isaacson and Eisenschiml, "Final Two Chapters in the Surratt Controversy," *ibid.,* 52 (Summer 1959), 279-90.

Just how important John H. Surratt, Jr., was to the plots against Lincoln is hard to fathom. He may have been more critical than Booth, as only he knew all of the co-conspirators intimately, many even from before the war. Booth only knew Arnold and O'Laughlen well, and Herold, casually. Surratt also knew O'Laughlen before the war, but not Arnold. On Surratt's importance, see James E. T. Lange and Katherine DeWitt, Jr., "One Who Got Away: John Harrison Surratt," *North & South,* 4 (January

2000), 51-56. This makes one wonder if the usual idea of Booth rounding out his gang (see, *e.g.*, Barbee, "Lincoln and Booth," 551-77, DRB papers, GU) might ought to be changed to Surratt doing it. For a standard treatment of Surratt, see Alfred Isaacson, "John Surratt and the Lincoln Assassination Plot," *Maryland Historical Magazine*, 52 (December 1957), 315-42.

Booth's penchant to whistle, hum, or sing forbidden songs, often to the embarrassment of his companions, is in DeWitt, *Assassination of Abraham Lincoln*, 9. The song is from Williamson, *Prison Life in the Old Capitol*, 78. The departure of the Grants is explained in Eisenschiml, "Grant Suddenly Leaves Washington," in his *Why Was Lincoln Murdered?* 54-64, with the caveat that Booth surely would have attacked the occupants of the theater box with more verve and not been deterred had the General been there. It is doubtful that theater security would have been much better. See also, Steers, *Blood on the Moon*, 16-22, on Lincoln's security--or lack of it.

6. Meeting at the Canterbury Music Hall

Ownsbey, *Alias "Paine": Lewis Thornton Powell* , 73-75, basing her account on Powell's checking out of the Herndon House and an account of Lt. Benjamin Vanderpoel of the 59th New York Volunteer infantry at the Trial of John Surratt. Vanderpoel knew Booth and saw him and characters recognizable as Powell, Atzerodt, and Herold at the Canterbury, see R. Sutton, *et al. (comps.), The Reporter: Containing . . . Trial of John H. Surratt, on an Indictment for Murder of President Lincoln,* III, 211-14. This makes the traditional Herndon House meeting a possibility for the night before (Thursday) and gives credence to the notion of two attempts on Lincoln's life on consecutive nights, the Ides or Maundy Thursday (April 13), as Booth wrote in his diary, and Good Friday (April 14). The John H. Surratt trial lawyers and Vanderpoel erroneously said the meeting was at the Metropolitan, up the street. But Paine's assignation with Mary Gardner hints otherwise.

For a copy of the words to "John Harrolson," see Lowry, *The Story the Soldiers Wouldn't Tell*, 51-52. The story of Mrs. Lincoln's unfortunate public conduct in Virginia is related in Brendan H. Egan, Jr., "Mary Lincoln at City Point," *Surratt Courier*, 26 (November 2001), 4-7.

7. Booth's Friday Evening Dinner

"Booth and Bob Lincoln," Chicago *Daily Inter-Ocean*, June 18, 1878.

8. Mrs. Surratt's Trip of April 14

Trindal, *Mary Surratt*, 116-19, 258; Campbell, *Case for Mrs. Surratt*, 84-90; Eisenschiml, "Mrs. Surratt's Boarding House," 102-103; Eisenschiml, "The Woman in the Case," 284-85; Moore, *Case of Mrs. Surratt*, 78, 81-83; Turner, "Mrs. Mary Surratt," 155; Oldroyd, *Assassination of Abraham Lincoln*, 153-93, *passim*; Weichmann, *A True Story*, 163-74, 263-64; Harris, *Assassination of Lincoln*, 202; Hall, "John M. Lloyd: Star Witness," Kauffman (ed.), *In Pursuit of . . .*, 97-99; James O. Hall, "Why John M. Lloyd Was in Upper Marlboro," *ibid.*, 229-32; James O. Hall and Laurie Verge, "About Those Guns," *ibid.*, 253-56; Hall, *The Surratt Family and John Wilkes Booth*, 17-19. A manuscript copy letter Weichmann wrote to John Nothey on Mary Surratt's behalf with Zad Jenkins' coaching is in the vertical file at the Surratt House Museum, with an appended comment by James O. Hall. See also, Pitman (comp.), *The Assassination of President Lincoln and the Trial of the Conspirators*, 85-87, 121, 125-26; R. Sutton, *et al. (comps.), The Reporter: Containing . . . Trial of John H. Surratt, on an Indictment for Murder of President Lincoln*, III, 246-58.

9. Booth Arrives at the Theater

Baker, *History of the United States Secret Service*, 484, was convinced about the time calling. See also, R. Sutton, *et al* (comps.), *The Reporter: Containing . . . Trial of John H. Surratt, on an Indictment for Murder of President Lincoln*, III, 128-46, 166-70; "Sergeant Joseph M. Dye," box 5, folder 300, DRB papers, GU. Booth's statement of coming fame, in the bar, originally coming from Eleanor Ruggles, *Prince of Players* (New York: Norton, 1953), 179, is seen as apocryphal by most modern historians--but it surely fits his mood.

For more on the varied tales about Peanut John Burroughs, see Joan L. Chaconas, "Will the Real 'Peanuts' Burroughs Please Rise?!" Dillon (ed.), *The Lincoln Assassination: From the Pages of the* Surratt Courier, V, 17-21.

10. Lewis Paine Prepares for the Fray

Ownsbey, *Alias "Paine": Lewis Thornton Powell*, 73.

11. Booth Kills Lincoln

Lincoln's final day is detailed in Oldroyd, *The Assassination of Abraham Lincoln*, 7-29; Jim Bishop, *The Day Lincoln Was Shot* (New York: Harper & Bros., 1955); W. Emerson Reck, *A. Lincoln: His Last 24*

Hours (Jefferson, N.C.: McFarland & Co., Inc., 1987); and Bak, *The Day Lincon Was Shot*, 71-104. The wound Lincoln suffered is analyzed in John K. Lattimer, *Kennedy and Lincoln: Medical and Ballistic Comparisons of Their Assassinations* (New York: Harcourt, Brace, Jovanovich, 1980). The possibility of Lincoln surviving his wound with better contemporary or modern medical care is the subject between Dr. Lattimer (no) and Dr. Richard A. R. Fraser, who found Lincoln's medical care close to incompetent. See Art Candenquist, "The Lattimer-Fraser Debate," Dillon (ed.), *The Lincoln Assassination: From the Pages of the* Surratt Courier, II 25-26. Dr. Blaine V. Houmes, "The Wound of Abraham Lincoln," *ibid.*, II, 27-30, believes that Lincoln's wound would have been fatal, regardless of the medical technology available at any time in history.

For an excellent, up-to-date, magazine-length description of Booth's final day, see Michael W. Kauffman, "John Wilkes Booth and the Murder of Abraham Lincoln," *Blue and Gray Magazine*, 7 (April 1990), 8-25, 46-62. More dated, but still with some validity, is Robert H. Fowler, "Album of the Lincoln Murder: Illustrating how It Was Planned, Committed and Avenged, "*Civil War Times Illustrated*, 4 (July 1965), 1-4, 7, 10-11, 15-16, 21-22, 25-26. See also, "Booth's Movements, April 14, 1865," DRB papers, GU.

For a brief, point-by-point chapter-length discussion of Booth's last hours, see Kimmel, *Mad Booths of Maryland*, 215-23; a more detailed account with some on Lincoln, is in Smith, *American Gothic*, 133-59; and Dorothy Meserve Kunhardt and Philip B. Kunhardt, Jr., "Assassination!" *American Heritage*, 16 (April 1965), 5-35, and by the same authors, *Twenty Days: A Narrative in Text and Pictures of the Assassination of Abraham Lincoln and the Twenty Days that Followed--the Nation in Mourning, the Long Trip Home to Springfield* (New York: Harper & Row, Publishers, 1965). Dated, but interesting, is Townsend, *The Life, Crime, and Capture of John Wilkes Booth*, 5-10.

See also, DeWitt, *Assassination of Abraham Lincoln*, 7-28, 46-50; Wilson, *John Wilkes Booth*, 106-17, 128-29; Buckingham, *Reminiscences and Souvenirs of the Assassination of Abraham Lincoln*, 7-17, 73-76; McKinley, "Death to Tyrants!" in his *Assassination in America* (New York: Harper & Row, 1977), 18; Laughlin, *The Death of Lincoln*, 68-99, which is shortened for popular consumption in Clara E. Laughlin, "The Last Twenty-four Hours of Lincoln's Life." *Ladies Home Journal*, 20 (February 1909), 12ff.; Steers, *Blood on the Moon*, 117-130.

On the couple that accompanied the Lincoln's to the theater, see R. Gerald McMurtry, "Major Rathbone and Miss Harris: Guests of the

Lincolns in the Ford's Theater Box," *Lincoln Lore* (August 1971), 1-3; Frank Rathbun, "The Rathbone Connection," Kauffman (ed.), *In Pursuit of . . . ,* 213-20.

The word "sockdolagizing" means rendering a final, finishing blow. One can wonder along with Laurie Verge, "A Random Thought," *Surratt Courier*, 22 (April 1997), 6, if this line not only brought forth a good laugh, but had a symbolic significance related to Booth's act of shooting Lincoln. Booth's entry into the foyer and the route he used to access the Lincoln box is detailed in Michale W. Kauffman, "Door Number 7 or Door Number 8?" *Surratt Courier*, 33 (February 2008), 3-4. The reaction of Harry Hawk is in Tom Bogar, "Why Harry Hawk Ran Off the Stage So Fast," *Surratt Courier*, 32 (August 2007), 3-4.

For the episode with William Withers, see Richard Sloan, "John Wilkes Booth's Other Victim," *American Heritage*, 41 (Feb-Mar 1991), 114-16; and his "Jennie Gourlay and William Withers," *The Lincolnian*, 13 (November-December 1996), 2, 7. Joan L. Chaconas, "William Withers' Wound," Dillon (ed.), *The Lincoln Assassination: From the Pages of the* Surratt Courier, II, 13-14, points out that at the military commission proceedings, Withers merely said that he was knocked down. The wound story appeared years later. See also, Paul Killina, "Non-Combatant's Service," Dillon (ed.), *The Lincoln Assassination: From the Pages of the* Surratt Courier, V, 29-30.

Numerous persons saw the murder and wrote about it, in later years. Their stories are collected in Timothy Good (ed.), *We Saw Lincoln Shot: One Hundred Eyewitness Accounts* (Jackson: University Press of Mississippi, 1995). See also, Joan L. Chaconas, "Witnesses to the Assassination," Dillon (ed.), *The Lincoln Assassination: From the Pages of the* Surratt Courier, II, 3-8.

The lack of security puzzles modern Americans, who see conspiracy behind it, but it probably did not bother people at the time as much. For a good synopsis of what the government ought to have known, but did not, see Roscoe, *Web of Conspiracy*, 2-29, and, of course, Eisenschiml, *Why Was Lincoln Murdered?, passim.* A more measured approach is James O. Hall, "The Mystery of Lincoln's Guard," Kauffman (ed.), *In Pursuit of . . . ,* 233-38. Arthur F. Loux, "The Mystery of the Telegraphic Interruption," *Lincoln Herald*, 81 (Winter 1979), 234-37, finds nothing conspiratorial about that episode. Instead, the line was intentionally shut down (and it was only one company out of several plus the military line, hence ineffective) to prevent possible communication with feared co-conspirators and to hold the information back from Federal soldiers occupying the South. See also, Loux, "The Telegraph

Interruption," Dillon (ed.), *The Lincoln Assassination: From the Pages of the* Surratt Courier, III, 7-9; and James O. Hall, "The First War Department Telegram About Lincoln's Assassination," *ibid.*, III, 11-12.

PART III: TENUOUS ESCAPES (1865)

1. A Quick Stop at Mrs. Surratt's
On the escape in general, see James L. Swanson, *Manhunt: The 12-Day Chase for Lincoln's Killer* (New York: HarperCollins, 2006); and especially Michael W. Kauffman, "Booth's Escape Route: Lincoln's Assassin on the Run," *Blue and Gray Magazine*, 7 (June 1990), 9-21, 38-51; and Bak, *The Day Lincoln Was Shot, 105-40.* Kauffman makes the point (p. 12) that so many fail to recognize--that no one really knows where Booth went between Ford's Theater and the Navy Yard Bridge. Trindal, *Mary Surratt*, 287; Harris, *Assassination of Lincoln*, 199; Roscoe, Web of Conspiracy, 233-35; Turner, "Mrs. Mary Surratt," 157; Eisenschiml, "Mrs. Surratt's Boarding House," 107; Susan Jackson was not asleep as Lette Jenkins thought, her testimony is in Sutton, *et al. (comps.), The Reporter: Containing . . . Trial of John H. Surratt, on an Indictment for Murder of President Lincoln,* IV, 14-15; Smoot, *Unwritten History*, 11-14. Mrs. Surratt's use of "Pet" is from the transcribed copy of George A. Townsend's notes, "Talk with Louis Weichmann," vertical file, Surratt House Museum.

2. A Busy Night at the Navy Yard Bridge
Kauffman, "Booth's Escape Route: Lincoln's Assassin on the Run," 12-13; and Fowler, "Album of the Lincoln Murder," 29, 32-33, 35-38, 42, 46, 48-49; Roscoe, *Web of Conspiracy*, 137-39, 149-53; Laughlin, *Death of Lincoln*, 119-20. See also, Joan L. Chaconas and James O. Hall, "Crossing the Navy Yard Bridge," *Surratt Courier*, 21 (September 1996), 5-7; Pitman (comp.), *The Assassination of President Lincoln and the Trial of the Conspirators* , 84.
Fletcher knew that Herold and Atzerodt were friends and that Atzerodt had to cross the navy Yard Bridge to get home. So he went down to see if either had passed. See R. Sutton, *et al. (comps.), The Reporter: Containing . . . Trial of John H. Surratt, on an Indictment for Murder of President Lincoln,* III, 201-206.
Moonrise was at 10:10 p.m., according to an employee of the Naval Observatory, see Sutton, *et al. (comps.), The Reporter: Containing . . . Trial of John H. Surratt, on an Indictment for Murder of President Lincoln,* IV, 29. But another opined that it rose at 8:40 p.m., then returned

to the stand to change his testimony to have moonrise occur *about* 10:10 p.m., *ibid.*, 324, 330.

3. Carnage at Seward's

Ownsbey, *Alias "Paine": Lewis Thornton Powell* , 70-88; Chamlee, *Lincoln's Assassins*, 1-3; DeWitt, *Assassination of Abraham Lincoln*, 50-52; Roscoe, *Web of Conspiracy*, 108-14, 140-49; Patricia Carley Johnson, (ed.), "'I Have Supped Fully on Horrors'," *American Heritage*, 10 (October 1959), 60-65, 96-100. See also, Pitman (comp.), *The Assassination of President Lincoln and the Trial of the Conspirators,* 154-59; Sutton, *et al. (comps.), The Reporter: Containing . . . Trial of John H. Surratt, on an Indictment for Murder of President Lincoln,* III, 216-19, 222-25; Townsend, *The Life, Crime, and Capture of John Wilkes Booth*, 10-12.

James O. Hall, "Senator Atchison and Presidential Succession," *Surratt Courier*, 16 (July 1991), 2-3; and James E. T. Lange and Katherine DeWitt, Jr., "Further Notes on Presidential Succession," *ibid.*, 16 (September 1991), point out that presidential succession was not as cut and dried at this time in American history as it is today. If the President and Vice President died, the Secretary of State had call a new election to fill their spots. If the Secretary were also dead, then no back-up procedure had been envisioned. Theoretically, this would have caused some chaos in the Federal government, and possibly in the Army's field command, hopefully giving General Lee and the Confederate government time to institute their already-envisioned Campaign of 1865. See also, John C. Brennan, "Why the Attempt to Assassinate Secretary of State William H. Seward," Dillon (ed.), *The Lincoln Assassination: From the Pages of the* Surratt Courier, II, 17-22.

4. O'Laughlen Misses Stanton

National Intelligencer, July 9, 1965, reprinted in Dillon (ed.), *The Lincoln Assassination: From the Pages of the* Surratt Courier, III, 23-25; Eisenschiml, "The Plots Against Grant, Stanton, and Johnson," *Why Was Lincoln Murdered?* 162-74; Roscoe, *Web of Conspiracy*, 114-16; Pitman (comp.), *The Assassination of President Lincoln and the Trial of the Conspirators,* 221-32; Sutton, *et al. (comps.), The Reporter: Containing . . . Trial of John H. Surratt, on an Indictment for Murder of President Lincoln,* IV, 145-46.

Historian Michael W. Kauffman has aptly noted the religious contradictions of the assasination, as well as the fluctuation of the Roman Ides from day to day depending upon the month, in his commentary on the annual Booth Escape Route Tour sponsored by the Surratt Society during the summer months.

See also, the letter from John C. Brennan to Terry Alford, September 16, 1992, (copy in vertical file under "O'Laughlen," Surratt House Museum) in which he speculates that Booth never paid back the $500 William O'Laughlen had advanced him for the abduction in August 1864. The loan was the business Mike came to Washington to see Booth about, says Brennan, possibly accompanied by the more assertive William, not to kill Stanton. Mike kept his mouth shut on this to the end.

5. Booth Breaks a Leg

Kauffman, "Booth's Escape Route: Lincoln's Assassin on the Run," 13, 17 (sidebar).

There is much confusion on where Booth's leg was broken and what bone was broken. The standard version is that he broke it jumping from Lincoln's box to the stage. But if he had, he never could have mounted his flighty horse. In all likelihood, Booth wrenched his back jumping to the stage, hence his fall to the floor and constant complaints to Dr. and Mrs. Mudd about his back bothering him. Where did he break his left leg? Kauffman is probably correct, it happened on the road to Surrattsville, noted for its deep mud, numerous pot holes, and ever-constant, wretched ruts worn by the wheels of passing wagons. Kauffman's theory is expanded upon by Joseph E. "Rick," Smith III, "Break a Leg," *Surratt Courier*, 28 (June 2003), 4-6.

At the autopsy, Dr. John F. May described the broken leg as his right leg not the left, but James O. Hall dismisses this, saying that May got mixed up between his left and Booth's. Dr. Mudd called the break one to the large leg bone (the tibia), while Surgeon General Joseph K. Barnes called it one to the small bone (the fibula). Jay Winik, *April 1865: The Month that Saved America* (New York: HarperCollins, 2001), 253, votes with Mudd and calls the broken bone the shinbone, which he believes was broken in Booth's jump to the stage. This seems doubtful, as the difference is between painful movement or incapacity.

Worse yet, Mrs. Eliza Rogers, a friend of the Booth family who saw the coffin opened in 1869 when the body was returned to the Booth family, said that the left keg was broken through *both* bones, which had by-passed each other in the coffin and protruded through the rotted leg in compound fracture. This had led to some suspecting that Federal cavalrymen brutalized Booth as he was dragged from the barn. So the battle rages. See Terry Shulman, "What Really Happened to the Assassin?" *Civil War Times Illustrated*, 31 (July/August 1992), 50-51. For the sake of argument, we assume that Booth sprained some muscles or slipped a disk in his back when he hit the stage in Ford's, broke his left leg when his horse fell with him at Soper's Hill, and the injury was to the fibula or small leg bone. The reader may agree or disagree at his or her own pleasure.

On crossing to the Uniontown side of the Navy Yard Bridge, see particularly, Douglas Truran to the Surratt Society, July 6, 1992, and enclosures, copy in vertical file, James O. Hall Library, Surratt House Museum. See also, Laughlin, *Death of Lincoln*, 120-21; Pitman (comp.), *The Assassination of President Lincoln and the Trial of the Conspirators*, 85.

6. On to Surrattsville

For the broken-down wagon, see James O. Hall, *John Wilkes Booth's Escape Route* (Clinton, Md.: Surratt Society, 2000), 5. See also, Laughlin, *Death of Lincoln*, 212-22; Pitman (comp.), *The Assassination of President Lincoln and the Trial of the Conspirators* , 85, 129. On Lloyd's wife being sent away, see Baker, *History of the United States Secret Service*, 483. See also, Barbee, "Lincoln and Booth," 823-52, *passim*, DRB papers, GU. Locating Soper's Hill on the road to Upper Marlboro, Barbee believes that Booth and Herold never went by Surrattsville, making his interpretation unique among historians.

7. John Fletcher Identifies a Horse
Chamlee, *Lincoln's Assassins*, 16-18.

8. The Boardinghouse Search

Trindal, *Mary Surratt*, 119-20; Moore, *Case of Mrs. Surratt*, 16-18, 83-85; Weichmann, *A True Story*, 174-79; Harris, *Assassination of Lincoln*, 198-99, 203; Roscoe, *Web of Conspiracy*, 230-33; Oldroyd, *Assassination of Abraham Lincoln*, 153-93, *passim*; Turner, "Mrs. Mary Surratt," 156; Laughlin, *Death of Lincoln*, 158-62; Gary R. Planck, "Lincoln's Assassination: The 'Forgotten' Investigation: A. C. Richards, Superintendent of the Metropolitan Police," *Lincoln Herald*, 82 (Winter 1980), 521-39; James O. Hall, "Why Was Mrs. Surratt's Home Raided on the Night of April 14-15, 1865?" Kauffman (ed.), *In Pursuit of . . .* , 239-42.

John Holohan claimed that he answered the door on this occasion, Sutton, *et al. (comps.), The Reporter: Containing . . . Trial of John H. Surratt, on an Indictment for Murder of President Lincoln,* IV, 88-89. For Detective Clarvoe's story, see *ibid.*, 100-104; McDevitt 's tale is in *ibid.*, 115-18. See also, Joseph George, Jr. (comp.), "Townsend Interviews Weichmann," Dillon (ed.), *The Lincoln Assassination: From the Pages of the* Surratt Courier, IX, 17-22.

9. Booth Finds a Doctor

Kauffman, "Booth's Escape Route: Lincoln's Assassin on the Run,"13-14, 17; Mudd, *Life of Mudd*, 30; Carter, *Riddle of Mudd*, 212-33; Edward Steers, Jr., "The Deceptive Doctor," 114-28; Higdon, *The Union vs. Dr. Mudd*, 9-11; Roscoe, *Web of Conspiracy*, 170-79; Laughlin, *Death of Lincoln*, 123-24. See also, Pitman (comp.), *The Assassination of President Lincoln and the Trial of the Conspirators* , 87-90; Barbee, "Lincoln and Booth," 823-52, *passim*, DRB papers, GU.

10. All Those God Damned Booths are Crazy

"Booth and Bob Lincoln," Chicago *Daily Inter-Ocean*, June 18, 1878. Just whether the assassination was sudden impulse, as believed by Constance Head, "Insights on John Wilkes Booth from His Sister Asia's Correspondence," *Lincoln Herald*, 82 (Winter 1980), 540-44, or the romance was, is arguable. Actually, historians disagree which Hale daughter was Booth's true-love, Lucy or her sister Elizabeth (Bessie). The trend began with Lucy, went over to Bessie in the mid-twentieth century, and has swung back to Lucy. See Morcum, "They All Loved Lucy," 12-15. George S. Bryan, *The Great American Myth*, 243, questions the validity of Lucy's marriage promise. But Asia refused to give up on the impending marriage story. See, *e.g.*, Asia Booth Clarke to Jean Anderson Sherwood, Philadelphia, May 22, 1965, James O. Hall, Laurie Verge, and Joan V. Bradgon. "A Sister's Thoughts: A Letter from Asia Booth Clarke," Kauffman (ed.), *In Pursuit of . . . ,* 107-110.

11. Lafayette C. Baker Takes on the Pursuit

Baker's own account, *History of the United States Secret Service*, is scarred by half-truths and heavy reliance on the work of others, rather than his own experience. Better is his biography by Jacob Mogelever, *Death to Traitors*, 332-36, for the material in this chapter; 29-331, for Baker's life and career before the Lincoln Assassination. More on Baker is in C. Wyatt Evans, "Lafayette Baker and Security in the Civil War North," *North & South*, 11 (September 2008), 44-51. Luther Byron Baker's account is L. B. Baker, "An Eyewitness Account of the Death and Burial of J. Wilkes Booth," *Journal of the Illinois State Historical Society*, 39 (Dec. 1946), 425-46. For the bell incident, see folder 147, box 3, DRB Papers, GU.

12. Breakfast at Dr. Mudd's
Mudd, *Life of Mudd*, 30-31; Laughlin, *Death of Lincoln*, 124-25. Some of Herold's conversation is from his later confession in *Verge (ed.), From War Department Files*, 1-19. See also, Kauffman, "Booth's Escape Route: Lincoln's Assassin on the Run," 17; Laurie Verge, "That Trifling Boy . . . ," *Surratt Courier*, 27 (January 2002), 4-9.

13. Lloyd Misleads the Pursuit and Cuts a Deal
Chamlee, *Lincoln's Assassins*, 24-25, 46-48, 126-27; Weichmann, *A True Story*; 181; Roscoe, *Web of Conspiracy*, 200-202; Hall, "John M. Lloyd: Star Witness," 97-99; Trindal, *Mary Surratt*, 263-64; Moore, *Case of Mrs. Surratt*, 79; Campbell, *Case for Mrs. Surratt*, 92-97; Eisenschiml, "The Woman in the Case," 285-86, 293; Turner, "Mrs. Mary Surratt," 162; James O. Hall, "Corn and the Cavalry," *Surratt Society News*, 6 (September 1981), 3-4. See also, Pitman (comp.), *The Assassination of President Lincoln and the Trial of the Conspirators*, 127, 141; R. Sutton, *et al. (comps.), The Reporter: Containing . . . Trial of John H. Surratt, on an Indictment for Murder of President Lincoln,* III, 246-58. The questioning of Lloyd is described in, "He Almost Saved Lincoln," *Boston Sunday Globe*, December 12, 1897, copy in vertical file, Surratt House Museum. Finding the carbine between the walls is in James O. Hall, "Hiding the Shooting Irons," Dillon (ed.), *The Lincoln Assassination: From the Pages of the* Surratt Courier, I, 19-21.

14. Looking for a Conveyance
Mudd, *Life of Mudd*, 31-32; Kauffman, "Booth's Escape Route: Lincoln's Assassin on the Run," 17.

15. The Uncommunicative Patient
Mudd, *Life of Mudd*, 31-32; Laughlin, *Death of Lincoln*, 125; Kauffman, "Booth's Escape Route: Lincoln's Assassin on the Run," 17.

16. Dr. Mudd at Bryantown
The account that makes the most sense to us is Edward Steers, Jr., "Dr. Mudd's Sense of Timing: The Trip to Bryantown," Dillon (ed.), *The Lincoln Assassination: From the Pages of the* Surratt Courier, VIII, 33-36. But not all are convinced. See John E. McHale, "A Letter in Response," *ibid.*, VIII, 37-38; and Clark Larsen, "Response to Response *in re* Mudd," *ibid.*, VIII, 39-42. See also, William A. Tidwell, "April 15, 1865," *Surratt Courier*, 22 (April-May-June 1997), 6-10, 5-10, 4-9;

Kauffman, "Booth's Escape Route: Lincoln's Assassin on the Run," 17-18.

Advocates of Dr. Mudd's innocence often maintain that he was shown a picture of Edwin Booth, not John Wilkes, hence the denial he had seen *that* man at his house. This argument is belittled by critics who point out that the correct picture was shown the hapless doctor. We have taken the coward's way out and allowed Lt. Dana to get his Booths mixed up, *verbally*. But Mudd knew which Booth was at question, picture or not.

See the exchange between John E. McHale (on Mudd's behalf) and James O. Hall and Edward Steers, Jr., (against Mudd), which hit hard against the doctor's strict parsing of his answers to the Federal detectives' questions: Dillon (ed.), *The Lincoln Assassination: From the Pages of the* Surratt Courier, VIII, 1-30. See also, Steers, "The Wrong Picture," *ibid.,* VIII, 31-32, and Steers, *Blood on the Moon*, xiii. A nice summary of he whole argument is Andrew Ferguson, "Last Battle of the Civil War [The Guilt or Innocence of Dr. Mudd]," *Weekly Standard*, 8 (December 30, 2002), [1-13].

17. Dr. Mudd Confronts Booth

Mudd, *Life of Mudd*, 32-33. The attitude of Southerners in general was not as sad as current Lincoln legend often supposes. See Martin Abbott, "Southern Reaction to Lincoln's Assassination," *Abraham Lincoln Quarterly*, 7 (Sept. 1952), 110-27. Expressed sorrow often depended on how close to Yankee military reaction or possible pardon the pro-Confederate speakers were.

18. Seeking William Bertle

William A. Tidwell, "April 15, 1865," *Surratt Courier*, 22 (April-May-June 1997), 6-10, 5-10, 4-9.

19. Oswell Swann Guides Booth to Captain Cox

Kauffman, "Booth's Escape Route: Lincoln's Assassin on the Run," 18-19; James O. Hall, "Oswell Swann and the Fugitive Assassins," Kauffman (ed.), *In Pursuit of . . . ,* 171-73; Laurie Verge and James O. Hall "Crossing the Zekiah," Dillon (ed.), *The Lincoln Assassination: From the Pages of the* Surratt Courier, IV, 7-8; Laughlin, *Death of Lincoln*, 128-30; Steers, *Blood on the Moon*, 150-51, 156-58, 160, footnotes on 316-316. See also, William A. Tidwell, "April 15, 1865," *Surratt Courier*, 22 (April-May-June 1997), 6-10, 5-10, 4-9; and Otto Eisenschiml, "The Conspirators Who Went Free," *Why Was Lincoln*

Murdered? 296-307; Barbee, "Lincoln and Booth," 823-52, *passim*, DRB papers, GU.

20. Trying to Fool Swann
Tidwell, Hall, and Gaddy, *Come Retribution*, 446-48; Eisenschiml, "The Conspirators Who Went Free," *Why Was Lincoln Murdered?* 296-307. Mary Swann's statement to the Federals and her later pension is in box 5, folder 238, DRB papers GU. See also, Barbee, "Lincoln and Booth," 823-52, *passim*, DRB papers, *ibid.*

PART IV: FIRST ARRESTS (1865)

1. Tom Jones Takes Over
Kauffman, "Booth's Escape Route: Lincoln's Assassin on the Run," 19; Chamlee, *Lincoln's Assassins,* 139-42; Thomas A. Jones, *J. Wilkes Booth: An Account of His Sojourn in Southern Maryland . . . and His Death in Virginia* (Chicago: Laird & Lee, 1893), 1-82. For a good acount of Jones' activities in the Confederate underground, plus the text of his book, see Wearmouth and Wearmouth, *Thomas A. Jones: Chief Agent of the Confederate Secret Service in Maryland.*

2. Baker's Handbill
Mogelever, *Death to Traitors*, 336-38; Chamlee, *Lincoln's Assassins*, 61; Roscoe, *Web of Conspiracy*, 198-207. The confusion of the initial pursuit is in Turner, "Pursuit," in *Beware the People Weeping,* 100-11. Baker's handbill appeared in the Washington *Daily Morning Chronicle*, April 17, 1965, for the first time.

3. The Confederates Withdraw from Maryland
William A. Tidwell, "April 15, 1865," *Surratt Courier*, 22 (April-May-June 1997), 6-10, 5-10, 4-9. Historians, agreeing with the defense at the military commission trial, find No. 5's letter to be a fiction, and inadmissible as evidence. See Pitman, *The Assassination of President Lincoln and the Trial of the Conspirators,* 42 (letter), and 66-69 (court discussion). That may be so, but the prosecution and the court found otherwise. We find it interesting, as it seems to admit to the thesis of Larry Starkey, *Wilkes Booth Came to Washington*, 120-27 that Booth intended to take the Midnight Special from New York City to Canada. It also jibes with the Etta letter, which suggests the same thing. An intense government investigation connected neither letter to its authors. Besides, if they be fiction, so is this novel.

4. O'Laughlen Turns Himself In; Arnold Taken at Ft. Monroe and Confesses

Chamlee, *Lincoln's Assassins*, 67-69, 72; Percy E. Martin, "The Hookstown Connection," and "The Surprising Speed in the Identification of Two Baltimore Conspirators," Kauffman (ed.), *In Pursuit of . . . ,* 117-19, 167-69; Martin, "Baltimorean in Big Trouble: Samuel Arnold, A Lincoln Conspirator," 5-8; Kauffman (ed.), *Memoirs of a Lincoln Conspirator* [Samuel B. Arnold], 47-56; Smith, *Between the Lines*, 290-96; Harris, Assassination of Lincoln, 71-77; Roscoe, *Web of Conspiracy*, 235-37; Pitman (comp.), *The Assassination of President Lincoln and the Trial of the Conspirators,* 121-22, 232-43. Randall knew that Arnold was friendly with Booth. Even before the "Sam" letter was known, he urged McPhail to check Arnold out as soon as the news that Booth had killed Lincoln arrived in Baltimore. See Steers, *Blood on the Moon*, xii, 171.

5. Edman Spangler, Fall Guy

Michael Kauffman, "Edman Spangler: A Life Rediscovered," Dillon (ed.), *The Lincoln Assassination: From the Pages of the* Surratt Courier, XI, 33-36, 1-7; Roscoe, *Web of Conspiracy*, 64-65, 235-37; Laughlin, *Death of Lincoln*, 317-21; Anne Catherine Pierce, "A Letter from Spangler," Kauffman (ed.), *In Pursuit of . . . ,* 277-78; Pitman (comp.), *The Assassination of President Lincoln and the Trial of the Conspirators* , 97-112. An interesting sidelight on Spangler's involvement is in R. Gerald McMurtry, "Did 'Coughdrop Joe' Ratto Hold Booth's Horse?" *Lincoln Lore* (January 1969), 2-3.

6. The Arrest of Mary Surratt

Trindal, *Mary Surratt*, 123-28; Campbell, *Case for Mrs. Surratt*, 1-15, *passim*; Harris, *Assassination of Lincoln*, 198-99; Moore, *Case of Mrs. Surratt*, 18-20; Weichmann, *A True Story*, 184-85, 264, 266-67; Chamlee, *Lincoln's Assassins*, 79-80; Roscoe, *Web of Conspiracy*, 242-45; Laughlin, *Death of Lincoln*, 161-62. See also, Pitman (comp.), *The Assassination of President Lincoln and the Trial of the Conspirators*, 121-22; R. Sutton, *et al. (comps.), The Reporter: Containing . . . Trial of John H. Surratt, on an Indictment for Murder of President Lincoln,* III, 278-82, 284-91, 374-77; "Mary Surratt," box 7, folder 359, DRB papers, GU.

7. The Arrest of Powell

Ownsbey, *Alias "Paine": Lewis Thornton Powell* , 89-100; Chamlee, *Lincoln's Assassins*, 80-81; Laughlin, *Death of Lincoln*, 162-63;

Weichmann, *A True Story*; 185-86; "Mary Surratt," box 7, folder 359, DRB papers, GU. See also, Pitman (comp.), *The Assassination of President Lincoln and the Trial of the Conspirators*, 121-22.

8. Mary Surratt in Jail

Trindal, *Mary Surratt*, 129--41; Campbell, *Case for Mrs. Surratt*, 98-112; Eisenschiml, "Mrs. Surratt's Boarding House," 104-109; Eisenschiml, "The Woman in the Case," 287-88; Chamlee, *Lincoln's Assassins*, 82-89, 174-88; Roscoe, *Web of Conspiracy*, 246-50.

Military interrogations of Mary Surratt are in Verge (ed.), *From War Department Files*, 33-52. Anna's interrogation produced even less than those of her mother but, then, she really did not know that much, *ibid*. 53-57. The general thesis that Mary Surratt never broke under interrogation is a theme in Larson, *Assassin's Accomplice*, 97-117.

The suspicion that everyone, but Atzerodt, kept their mouths shut and took their punishments without implicating others is the conclusion of Brennan, "The Confederate Plan to Abduct Lincoln," 141-49. The most hostile attack on Mrs. Surratt came in the memoirs of a trail commissioner. See Harris, *Assassination of Lincoln*, 192-209.

The final sentiments attributed to Mary Surratt are from Myra Lockett Avery, *Dixie After the War* (New York: Doubleday, Page and Co., 1906), 82; and Dinah Faber, "Could It Have Been Mary?" *Surratt Courier*, 27 (May 2002), 5-6.

9. New Home in the Swamp

The actual description of the swamp came from the report of Major James O'Beirne, who coordinated the search, and is in Oldroyd, *Assassination of Abraham Lincoln*, 67. It is also described in a similar fashion by George Alfred Townsend, *Katy of Catoctin; or, the Chain-breakers* (New Ed., Cambridge, Md.: Tidewater Publishers, 1959), 531, who had explored the region personally after the war. See also, Jones, *J. Wilkes Booth*, 83-89; Kauffman, "Booth's Escape Route: Lincoln's Assassin on the Run," 19-20.

For the creepy, crawly creatures in the Zekiah (only poisonous copperheads, amongst the many non-poisonous snakes), see Randal Berry, "'See Any Snakes out There?': Booth and Herold's Four Nights in the Pine Thicket," *Surratt Courier*, 33 (October 2008), 3-4.

Very important is a new interpretation suggested by Joseph E. "Rick," Smith, III, "The Owens Statement," *Surratt Courier*, 32 (October 2007), 3-6, which uses a statement by a black employee of Austin L. Adams to suggest the Booth and Herold spent some of their time at the

Adams' Tavern at Newport and in the woods nearby. Smith expands on his thesis with "What is Horse Faking" *ibid.*, 33 (April 2008), 4-6, which is later ampliphied again in his, "More on the Fate of the Horses," *ibid.*, 33 (May 2008), 4-5. See also Bruce Catton, *Army of the Potomac: Glory Road*, 246, quoting Crowninshield, *History of the First Massachusetts Cavalry*, 294-95, on how people of the time altered horse appearance to prevent original owners from detecting a stolen animal.

10. Tom Jones Meets Billy Williams
   Jones, *J. Wilkes Booth*, 89-95.

11. The Arrest of Andrew Atzerodt
   Brendan Egan, "The Capture of Atzerodt," *Surratt Courier*, 26 (March 2001), 4-7; Thomas P. Lowery, "Profile: A Mystery Solved," *North & South*, 4 (No. 4, 2001), 10-12, for how Atzerodt got past the roadblock at Tennalytown; Chamlee, *Lincoln's Assassins*, 20-22, 29, 69-71; Eisenschiml, "The Plots Against Grant, Stanton, and Johnson," *Why Was Lincoln Murdered?* 162-74; Harris, *Assassination of Lincoln*, 68-71; Roscoe, *The Web of Conspiracy,* 116-120; 254-67; Edward Steers, Jr., "The Suspicious Character in Room 126," *The Lincolnian*, 1 (September-October 1982), 5-6; Pitman (comp.), *The Assassination of President Lincoln and the Trial of the Conspirators* , 144-54; Laughlin, *Death of Lincoln*, 167-69. See also, Percy E. Martin, "Adventures with Mr. Hall on the Trail of George Atzerodt," Kauffman (ed.), *In Pursuit of . . . ,* 279-82, for a possible location of George Andrew Atzerodt's, until now, lost grave.

12. Boredom in the Swamp
   Jones, *J. Wilkes Booth*, 96-97; Rhodehamel and Taper (eds.), *Writings of John Wilkes Booth*, 154 and footnotes; Hanchett, "Booth's Diary," 40. For various newspaper columns on the baseness of Booth's assassination, see box 3, DRB papers, GU. The weather is in box 7, *ibid.* A bass monkey is a plate framework used on the old wooden sailing ships to store stacked pyramids of cannon balls. It shrunk when cold and the cannon balls would roll off. Hence the phrase Booth used to describe the weather.

13. The Arrest and Statements of Dr. Samuel A. Mudd
   Mudd, *Life of Mudd*, 33-34, Steers, *His Name Is Still Mudd*, 28-38. Mudd's statements are in Verge (ed.), *From War Department Files*, 25-31, and in Steers, *His Name Is Still Mudd*, 106-115, 125-130;

Weckesser, *His Name Was Mudd*, 210-13; Laughlin, *Death of Lincoln*, 126-27, 214-21. See also, David C. Dillon (ed.), *John Wilkes Booth: The FBI Files* (Clinton, MD: Surratt Society, 2002), *passim*.

14. Baker's Pictorial Reward Poster
Mogelever, *Death to Traitors*, 338-44; Roscoe, *Web of Conspiracy*, 222-23, 327-51; Baker, "An Eyewitness Account of the Death and Burial of J. Wilkes Booth," 425-46. O'Bierne's role is described in Townsend, *The Life, Crime, and capture of John Wilkes Booth*, 49-56. See also, Turner, "Capture," in *Beware the People Weeping,* 112-14, 116, and Barbee, "Lincoln and Booth," 911-58, *passim*, DRB papers, GU.

15. Jones Moves Booth and Herold to the Potomac
Jones, *J. Wilkes Booth*, 98-106; George Alfred Townsend, "How Wilkes Booth Crossed the Potomac," *Century Magazine*, (April 1884), 822-32; Eisenschiml, "The Conspirators Who Went Free," *Why Was Lincoln Murdered?* 296-307; Kauffman, "Booth's Escape Route: Lincoln's Assassin on the Run," 21, 38.

16. Booth and Herold at the Potomac
Jones, *J. Wilkes Booth*, 107-111 Jones' instructions to Booth and Herold are modified by the account in John Stanton, "Mrs. Quesenberry and John Wilkes Booth," *King George Journal*, week of March 31, 2008. See also, Kauffman, "Booth's Escape Route: Lincoln's Assassin on the Run," 21, 38; Stanton, Mrs. Quesenberry and John Wilkes Booth"; Barbee, "Lincoln and Booth," 823-52, *passim*, DRB papers, GU. See also, William A. Tidwell, "Booth Crosses the Potomac: An Exercise in Historical Research," *Civil War History*, 36 (No. 4, 1990), 325-33. An older version is George Alfred Townsend, "How Wilkes Booth Crossed the Potomac," *Century Magazine*, (April 1884), 822-32. We have followed a different narrative, posited by researcher and Surratt House docent, Rick Smith, "The Owens Statement," *Surratt Courier*, 32 (October 2007), 3-6. It seems that Tom Jones' story on moving Booth and Herold to the Potomac may have been a blind to conceal the activities of other Confederate operatives, especially Ausrtin L. Adams and his wife and also his black employee, James Owens, and young Samuel Cox, Jr., who moved Booth and Herold on their D.C.-rented horses to the river. Both Smith and Frederick Hatch, "They Shot Horses, Didn't They? Booth and Herold in the Woods," *Journal of the Lincoln Assassination*, 21 (December 2007), 42-46, doubt that Booth and Herold's horses were shot

and dumped in the swamp or the Potomac (as suggested by others). They were kept and/or sold, their identities and color having been altered by dyes and shoe-polish.

17. Booth Detours to Indiantown

Roscoe, *Web of Conspiracy*, 357-61; Laughlin, *Death of Lincoln*, 138; Tidwell, "Booth Crosses the Potomac: An Exercise in Historical Research," 325-33; Rhodehamel and Taper (eds.), *Writings of John Wilkes Booth*, 154-55 and footnotes; Hanchett, "Booth's Diary," 41-42; Kauffman, "Booth's Escape Route: Lincoln's Assassin on the Run," 38. Winfield M. Thompson, "Booth Loses His Way on the River," *Boston Globe*, April 24, 1915 (Part 15 of a 30 part series), maintains that the treacherous current and eddys carried the two men up to Nanjemoy, when they stopped paddling and hunkered down in the boat to escape notice by sailors in the passing gunboats. We think it was an intentional decision, based on Booth's discussions in Canada. For the arrest of Thomas Conrad, see John F. Stanton, "The Arrest of Thomas Nelson Conrad and Fannie Byrd Dade," *Surratt Courier*, 29 (October 2004), 3-4.

18. The Confessions of Andrew Atzerodt

Atzerodt's "Lost Statement," is in Steers, *His Name Is Still Mudd*, 121-24; Joan L. Chaconas, "Unpublished Atzerodt Confession Offered Here for the First Time," Dillon (ed.), *The Lincoln Assassination: From the Pages of the* Surratt Courier, III, 19-21; *National Intelligencer*, July 9, 1965, reprinted in *ibid.*, III, 23-25; and *Baltimore American*, January 18, 1869, reprinted in *ibid.*, III, 27-28. Others from Verge (ed.), *From War Department Files*, 59-62. See also, Laughlin, *Death of Lincoln*, 283-85; and "Affidavit of Capt. Frank Monroe, U.S.M.C.," *Verge (ed.), From War Department Files*, 59. We think, Atzerodt said correctly that Herold was afraid to kill Vice President Johnson on April 13, but said it to cover his own fear. Herold was to be sent to Huntt's all along, and Surratt was to kill Johnson. Arzerodt, true to form, refused to act on April 14. Another look at others possibly involved in Booth's plots is Philip Van Doren Stern, "The Unknown Conspirator," *American Heritage* , 8 (February 1957), 51-59, 103.

PART V: INTO VIRGINIA (1865)

1. Herold Finds Mrs. Quesenberry

Kauffman, "Booth's Escape Route: Lincoln's Assassin on the Run," 40; Barbee, "Lincoln and Booth," 853-83, *passim*, DRB papers,

GU. Many of the pertinent original sources of Booth's sourjourn in Virginia can be found in James O. Hall (comp.), *On the Way to Garrett's Barn: John Wilkes Booth and David Herold in the Northern Neck of Virginia, April 22-26, 1865* . . . . Ed. by David C. Dillon (Clinton, MD: Surratt Society, 2001). See also, J. E. "Rick" Smith III and William L. Richter, "'I Told Him He Must Go Away':" Elizbeth Rouse Quesenberry and the Escape of Lincoln's Assassin," *Surratt Courier*, 33 (September 2008), 4-7; and Smith with Richter. *In the Shadows of the Lincoln Assassination: The Life of Confederate Spy Thomas H. Harbin*, 123-32.

2. Tom Harbin Helps Booth
Laughlin, *Death of Lincoln*, 139; Kauffman, "Booth's Escape Route: Lincoln's Assassin on the Run," 40; Barbee, "Lincoln and Booth," 853-83, *passim*, DRB papers, GU

3. Dr. Stuart's Unexpected Dinner Guests
Kauffman, "Booth's Escape Route: Lincoln's Assassin on the Run," 40, 42. Dr. Stuart's statement to Federal authorities is in Roscoe, *Web of Conspiracy*, 542-43. See also Eisenschiml, "The Conspirators Who Went Free," 296-307; Barbee, "Lincoln and Booth," 853-83, *passim*, DRB papers, GU. Dr. Stuart's Statement, May 6, 1865, is in Roscoe, *Web of Conspiracy*, 542-43. As in many accounts, his name is misspelled "Stewart."

4. William Lucas' Two Unwanted Overnight Visitors
Kauffman, "Booth's Escape Route: Lincoln's Assassin on the Run," 42. Roscoe, *Web of Conspiracy*, 361-64; Rhodehamel and Taper (eds.), *Writings of John Wilkes Booth*, 157-59 and footnotes. See also, James O. Hall, "Two Pages From Booth's Diary: Dr. Richard Stuart Meets John Wilkes Booth," Dillon (ed.), *The Lincoln Assassination: From the Pages of the* Surratt Courier, IV 11-12.

5. Charlie Lucas Takes Booth and Herold to Port Conway
Roscoe, *Web of Conspiracy*, 364- 67; Kauffman, "Booth's Escape Route:
Lincoln's Assassin on the Run," 42-43; Barbee, "Lincoln and Booth," 853-83, *passim*,
DRB Papers, UG.

6. Baker Put on Booth's Trail

Mogelever, *Death to Traitors*, 338-45; Baker, "An Eyewitness Account of the Death and Burial of J. Wilkes Booth," 425-46. An excellent treatment of Baker's methods and Wood's role is Curtis Carroll Davis, "In Pursuit of Booth Once More: A New Claimant Heard From," *Maryland Historical Magazine*, 79 (Fall 1984), 220-34.

See also, Chamlee, *Lincoln's Assassins*, 146; Otto Eisenschiml, "Baker Directs the Pursuit," *Why Was Lincoln Murdered?*, 116-29; Larsen, "A Policeman's Perspective," 4-7, who understands Baker's letting others do his work for him, and the importance of the cavalry escort to protect Byron Baker and Conger while *they* found Booth; which is not the presentation on Steers, *Blood on the Moon*, 195-200. The report of William P. Wood is in box 5, DRB papers, GU. See also, Barbee, "Lincoln and Booth," 911-58, *passim*, DRB papers, *ibid.*

For an alternative interpretation of how Baker found out where Booth was, see John F. Stanton, "The Arrest of Thomas Nelson Conrad and Fannie Byrd Dade," *Surratt Courier*, 29 (October 2004), 3-4, who posits that Conrad and/or one of his agents was a double agent. But how they knew Booth was at Indiantown or Port Royal is not explained.

7. The Three Rebels

M. B. Ruggles, "Pursuit and Death of John Wilkes Booth: Major Ruggles's Narrative," *Century Magazine*, 39 (January 1890), 443-46, reprinted in Prentiss Ingraham, "The Pursuit and Death of John Wilkes Booth," Dillon (ed.), *The Lincoln Assassination: From the Pages of the Surratt Courier*, IV, 23-31, which also includes an account by Lt. Bainbridge, 26-27; Kauffman, "Booth's Escape Route: Lincoln's Assassin on the Run," 43-44; Barbee, "Lincoln and Booth," 853-83, *passim*, DRB papers, GU; Pitman (comp.), *The Assassination of President Lincoln and the Trial of the Conspirators*, 90-91.

8. Across the Rappahannock to Port Royal

Kate H. Mason, "A True Story of the Capture and Death of John Wilkes Booth," *Northern Neck Historical Magazine*, 13 (December 1963), 1237-39. The condition of Booth's leg, while pitiful to behold, evidently was not necessarily as bad as a casual observer might assume. But his suffering was real and extreme, because of his outdoors living and moving about. See statement of Surgeon General C. R. Reynolds to David Rankin Barbee, March 30, 1936, "Autopsy and Identification of Body," box 4, folder 812, DRB papers, GU. Rollins claimed that Booth had shaved off his moustache, contrary to the picture, Steers, *Blood on the Moon*, 318n20.

9. Byron Baker and Everton Conger Meet Lt. Doherty
Mogelever, *Death to Traitors*, 346-47; Davis, "In Pursuit of Booth Once More: A New Claimant Heard From," 220-34; Roscoe, *Web of Conspiracy*, 367-70; Steven G. Miller, "More on Capt. Doherty . . . ," Dillon (ed.), *The Lincoln Assassination: From the Pages of the* Surratt Courier, IV, 55-57. See also, Otto Eisenchiml, "The End of the Trail," *Why Was Lincoln Murdered?,* 130-52. See also, Joan L. Chaconas, "Lieutenant Edward P. Doherty," Dillon (ed.), *The Lincoln Assassination: From the Pages of the* Surratt Courier, 53-54; and Frederick Hatch, "Biography: Everton J. Conger," *Journal of the Lincoln Assassination,* 17 (August 2003), 33.

10. Refuge at Garrett's Farm
An excellent account is Dodels, "The Last Days of John Wilkes Booth," 1-4. See also Betsy Fleet (ed.), "A Chapter of Unwritten History: Richard Baynham Garrett's Account of the Flight and Death of John Wilkes Booth," *Virginia Magazine of History and Biography*, 71 (October 1963), 388-407; "Statement of John M. Garrett," *Surratt Courier*, 20 (March 1995), 4-9; "Deposition of William H. Garrett," *ibid.*, 24 (May 1999), 5-7, both reprinted in "Mr. Booth Visits the Garrett Family," Dillon (ed.), *The Lincoln Assassination: From the Pages of the* Surratt Courier, IV, 33-39; Kauffman, "Booth's Escape Route: Lincoln's Assassin on the Run," 44-45; Barbee, "Lincoln and Booth," 884-910, *passim*, DRB papers, GU. The diary entry is in Rhodehamel and Taper (eds.), *Writings of John Wilkes Booth*, 155 and footnotes; and Hanchett, "Booth's Diary," 42. There is some dispute as to the exact arrangement of the fences and gates at Garrett's Farm, see David C. Dillon, "Where Were the Garrett Farm Gates?" *Surratt Courier*, 28 (August 2003), 3-6.

11. Last Night in Bed
Kauffman, "Booth's Escape Route: Lincoln's Assassin on the Run,"45-46.

12. Looking for Booth Along the North Bank of the Rappahannock
William L. Reuter, *The King Can Do No Wrong* (New York: Pageant Press, Inc., 1958), 31; Mogelever, *Death to Traitors*, 348-49; Baker, "An Eyewitness Account of the Death and Burial of J. Wilkes Booth," 425-46; Doherty's Report and various communications relative to

the Search for Booth and command arrangements are reprinted in "Official Report on the Capture of John Wilkes Booth, *Surratt Courier*, 25 (May 2000), 3-7. See also, Steven G. Miller (ed.), "A Trooper's Account of the Death of Booth," Dillon (ed.), *The Lincoln Assassination: From the Pages of the* Surratt Courier, IV, 45-50. Miller also has the complete list of the men who trailed Booth. See his "Rollcall for the Garrett's Farm Patrol," Dillon (ed.), *The Lincoln Assassination: From the Pages of the* Surratt Courier, IV, 41-44.

The harsher aspects of Federal searches are revealed in Michael R. Bradley, "In the Crosshairs: Southern Civilians Targeted by the U.S. Army," *North & South*, 10 (March 2008), 46-61. This is in marked contrast to the more exculpatory interpretation of Mark Grimsley, *The Hard Hand of War: Union Military Policy toward Southern Civilians* (New York: Cambridge University Press, 1995).

PART VI: LAST DAY (1865)

1. Happy Morning at Garrett's Farm

Dodels, "Last Days of John Wilkes Booth," 4-7; Kauffman, "Booth's Escape Route: Lincoln's Assassin on the Run," 45. The field glasses Booth demonstrated to the Garrett children are described in detail in John C. Brennan, "John Wilkes Booth's Field Glasses," 5-6. See also, Fleet (ed.), "A Chapter of Unwritten History: Richard Baynham Garrett's Account," 388-407; "Statement of John M. Garrett," 4-9; "Deposition of William H. Garrett," 5-7; Barbee, "Lincoln and Booth," 884-910, *passim*, DRB papers, GU

2. The Yankees Cross to Port Royal

Mogelever, *Death to Traitors*, 349-51; Reuter, *The King Can Do No Wrong,* 32-33; Laughlin, *Death of Lincoln*, 145; Kauffman, "Booth's Escape Route: Lincoln's Assassin on the Run," 48; Baker, "An Eyewitness Account of the Death and Burial of J. Wilkes Booth," 425-46; Doherty's "Official Report on the Capture of John Wilkes Booth, *Surratt Courier*, 25 (May 2000), 3-7. Rollin's confession, dated April 25, 1865, is in box 3, DRB papers, GU.

3. The End of a Reverie

Dodels, "Last Days of John Wilkes Booth," 7-8; Kauffman, "Booth's Escape Route: Lincoln's Assassin on the Run," 46, 48; statement of Miss Halloway, in Wilson, *John Wilkes Booth*, 208-22; Fleet (ed.), "A

Chapter of Unwritten History: Richard Baynham Garrett's Account," 388-407; "Statement of John M. Garrett," 4-9.

4. A Tense Afternoon at Garrett's Farm
Dodels, "The Last Days of John Wilkes Booth," 8-11; Kauffman, "Booth's Escape Route: Lincoln's Assassin on the Run," 48; Statement of Miss Halloway, in Wilson, *John Wilkes Booth*, 208-22; Fleet (ed.), "A Chapter of Unwritten History: Richard Baynham Garrett's Account," 388-407; "Statement of John M. Garrett," 4-9; "Deposition of William H. Garrett," 5-7.
Booth's Diary entries are from Bayly Ellen Marks and Mark Norton Schatz (eds.), *Between North and South: A Maryland Journalist Views the Civil War, The Narrative of William Wilkins Glenn, 1861-1869* (Rutherford, N. J.: Fairleigh Dickinson University Press, 1976), 196-97 (people of the North [with some modification]), 224 (Yankees are bad), 250 (what is to become), 253 (How American).
Just whether Davy Herold got new shoes or his old ones mended is not really known. He seemed to have a foot problem that caused him to limp, while at the Garrett farm. It seemed to go away after his lengthy incarceration. See John C. Brennan, "Hobbledehoy David Edgar Herold," Dillon (ed.), *The Lincoln Assassination: From the Pages of the* Surratt Courier, IV, 3-5; Laurie Verge, "That Trifling Boy . . . ," *Surratt Courier*, 27 (January 2002), 4-9.

5. The Yankees By-Pass Garrett's Farm
Mogelever, *Death to Traitors*, 351-52; Reuter, *The King Can Do No Wrong*, 35-36; Baker, "An Eyewitness Account of the Death and Burial of J. Wilkes Booth," 425-46; "Statement of John M. Garrett," 4-9. No one knows if the Rebel riders were Ruggles and Bainbridge or someone else, see David C. Dillon, "Who Were the Horsemen on the Hill?" *Surratt Courier*, 27 (June 2002), 4-7.

6. The Confederates Make Contact
Roscoe, *Web of Conspiracy*, 375-80; Dodels, "The Last Days of John Wilkes Booth," 11-12. Jack Garrett's scorn of Maryland was commonplace farther south by 1863. See Clark, "Suppression and Control of Maryland," 269. On the Confederate attempt to control Booth's escape, see Smith with Richter. *In the Shadows of the Lincoln Assassination: The Life of Confederate Spy Thomas H. Harbin*, 132-40.

7. At the Trappe

Reuter, *The King Can Do No Wrong,* 36-37. The song is from Williamson, *Prison Life in the Old Capitol*, 82.

8. Asleep In the Barn

"Statement of John M. Garrett," 4-9. James O. Hall, "Beautiful Snow," *Surratt Courier*, 11 (February 1986), 3-4, discusses and presents a reprint of the poem.

9. The Yankees at Bowling Green

Mogelever, *Death to Traitors*, 351-53; Reuter, *The King Can Do No Wrong*, 37-40; Chamlee, *Lincoln's Assassins*, 153-54, Kauffman, "Booth's Escape Route: Lincoln's Assassin on the Run," 48; Baker, "An Eyewitness Account of the Death and Burial of J. Wilkes Booth," 425-46; Doherty's "Official Report on the Capture of John Wilkes Booth," *Surratt Courier*, 25 (May 2000), 3-7. On the Rebel signal system that existed in Northern Virginia, and the possibility that a tower stood atop of the Starr Hotel, see William A. Tidwell, "The Confederate Signal System in the Northern Neck: An Object Lesson in Careful Reading," *Surratt Courier*, 20 (February 1995), 4-5.

10. Initial Confrontation at the Garrett House

Dodels, "The Last days of John Wilkes Booth," 12-15; Mogelever, *Death to Traitors*, 353-55; Reuter, *The King Can Do No Wrong,* 41-43; Chamlee, *Lincoln's Assassins*, 154; Roscoe, *Web of Conspiracy*, 381-83; Laughlin, *Death of Lincoln*, 147; Townsend, *Life, Crime, and Death of John Wilkes Booth*, 30-31; Kauffman, "Booth's Escape Route: Lincoln's Assassin on the Run," 48; Barbee, "Lincoln and Booth," 959-84, *passim*, DRB papers, GU.

See also, Statement of Miss Halloway, in Wilson, *John Wilkes Booth*, 208-22; Baker, "An Eyewitness Account of the Death and Burial of J. Wilkes Booth," 425-46; Doherty's "Official Report on the Capture of John Wilkes Booth," *Surratt Courier*, 25 (May 2000), 3-7; Fleet (ed.), "A Chapter of Unwritten History: Richard Baynham Garrett's Account," 388-407; Miller (ed.), "A Trooper's Account of the Death of Booth," 5-9; "Statement of John M. Garrett," 4-9; and Steven G. Miller (ed.), "Boston Corbett's Long-Forgotten Story of Wilkes Booth's Death," *Surratt Courier*, 26 (May 2001), 5-7; *ibid.*, 26 (June 2001), 4-6.

11. Herold Surrenders
Dodels, "The Last Days of John Wilkes Booth," 15-22; Mogelever, *Death to Traitors*, 355-57; Reuter, *The King Can Do No Wrong,* 43-46; Chamlee, *Lincoln's Assassins*, 153-54; Roscoe, *Web of Conspiracy*, 383-87; Laughlin, *Death of Lincoln*, 150; Townsend, *Life, Crime, and Death of John Wilkes Booth*, 35; Kauffman, "Booth's Escape Route: Lincoln's Assassin on the Run," 49; Barbee, "Lincoln and Booth," 959-84, *passim*, DRB papers, GU.

See also, Statement of Miss Halloway, in Wilson, *John Wilkes Booth*, 208-22; Baker, "An Eyewitness Account of the Death and Burial of J. Wilkes Booth," 425-46; Doherty's "Official Report on the Capture of John Wilkes Booth," 3-7; Fleet (ed.), "A Chapter of Unwritten History: Richard Baynham Garrett's Account," 388-407; Miller (ed.), "A Trooper's Account of the Death of Booth," 5-9; "Statement of John M. Garrett," 4-9; Miller (ed.), "Boston Corbett's Long-Forgotten Story of Wilkes Booth's Death," *Surratt Courier*, 26 (June 2001), 4-6.

12. The Death of John Wilkes Booth
Dodels, "The Last Days of John Wilkes Booth," 22-28; Mogelever, *Death to Traitors*, 357-60; Reuter, *The King Can Do No Wrong,* 46-51; Chamlee, *Lincoln's Assassins*, 155-57; Roscoe, *Web of Conspiracy*, 387-98; Oldroyd, *Assassination of Abraham Lincoln*, 70-78; Laughlin, *Death of Lincoln*, 147-53; Townsend, *Life, Crime, and Death of John Wilkes Booth*, 32-39; Kauffman, "Booth's Escape Route: Lincoln's Assassin on the Run," 49-50; Barbee, "Lincoln and Booth," 959-84, *passim*, DRB papers, GU.

See also, Conger's and Baker's testimony, R. Sutton, *et al. (comps.), The Reporter: Containing. . Trial of John H. Surratt, on an Indictment for Murder of President Lincoln,* III, 260-73; Doherty's "Official Report on the Capture of John Wilkes Booth," *Surratt Courier*, 25 (May 2000), 3-7; Baker, "An Eyewitness Account of the Death and Burial of J. Wilkes Booth," 425-46; Statement of Miss Halloway, in Wilson, *John Wilkes Booth*, 208-22; Otto Eisenschiml, "Death Visits Garrett's Farm," *Why Was Lincoln Murdered?*, 153-61.

Rob Wick, "Why Did Everton Conger Burn Down Richard Garrett's Tobacco Barn?" *Surratt Courier*, 33 (May 2008), 6-7, Theorizes that Conger was suffering from the extended ride to find Booth and wanted to get the ordeal over with posthaste. While not in disagreement with this analysis, we think that Conger's fear of the arrival of more federal troops and the subsequent dilution of the reward money also had great influence on his decision to speed up events by setting the barn on fire.

See also, Wilson, *ibid.*, 171-93; Miller (ed.), "A Trooper's Account of the Death of Booth,"5-9; Fleet (ed.), "A Chapter of Unwritten History: Richard Baynham Garrett's Account," 388-407, more easily accessed in Richard Baynham Garrett, "End of a Manhunt," *American Heritage*, 17 (June 1966), 40-43, 105. Richard Garrett returned the lock of hair to Edwin Booth, some years later.

Booth's standard last words, "useless, useless," may be a figment of Byron Baker's imagination. At least that is what Northerners *wanted* Booth to say, to make some sort of apology. J. Denis Robinson, "The 'New' Dying Words of John Wilkes Booth," *As I Please*, 2 (No. 5; April 20, 1998) at seacoastnh.com, believes that Booth was looking at the ring Lucy had given him, when Lt. Baker raised his hands. He uttered "Lucy, Lucy," but his tongue was nearly paralyzed so the words came out as Baker thought it ought. He suggests one hold the tip of one's tongue and try it. Maybe Robinson and we are guilty of what we accused Baker of-- hearing what *we* want. It should have happened that way, even if it did not. Booth's trouble in making himself understood is directly related to his difficulty in breathing, which led eventually to his asphyxiation. No matter what his last words were, Dr. Blaine V. Houmes, "The Last Words of John Wilkes Booth . . . Or Were They?" *Surratt Courier*, 32 (June 2007), 3-7, believes that Booth could talk in some fashion after being shot as his vocal cords were undamaged.

John K. Lattimer, *Kennedy and Lincoln*, 61-84, makes much of the fact that Booth could not have shot himself, because the "long-barreled" 1860 Colt's Army revolver was too heavy for Booth to manipulate to get his thumb on the trigger without using both hands. He was encumbered with the Spencer carbine or his crutch in his left hand. Moreover, Booth could not duplicate the angle of the bullet's path if he fired the gun normally. He illustrates his points clearly in pictures (p.79).

We went to the Arizona Historical Society and procured such a sidearm to try it out. If one holds the gun as Lattimer said one ought, his story is correct. But, that is not the way a real shooter would do it. Rather than holding the weapon with our elbow at our side, we held it as any man familiar with firearms, like Booth was, with our elbow out to the side and above our shoulder height. The revolver is held as normal, but with the barrel down and the handgrip up. It is possible in this manner to not only duplicate Booth's angle of wound, but almost any angle ones wishes to produce. The barrel is long, but not *that* long. Try it and see.

As to the need to use both hands, the curator, a man about Booth's height (5'9"), manipulated the weapon easily in one hand to change from his trigger finger to his thumb--without even waiting for our suggestion. "How about this way?" he asked. Again, moving the elbow out away from one's side and holding it at shoulder height or above allows one to produce almost any angle of bullet path.

Lattimer also vetoes the notion that Booth could have committed suicide because the autopsy mentioned no powder burns or collateral damage a close shot would incur (pp. 78-83). He shot pork necks, kept them out for thirty hours, as Booth's body was before autopsy, to reach his conclusion. The problem here is that Booth's decaying body was already blackened and distended so badly that initially the first witness to see him (Dr. John F. May, who had removed the boil from his neck two years earlier), had trouble identifying his horrible visage. See May, "The Mark of the Scalpel," 49-68. According to the Pima County (Arizona) medical examiner, under the right conditions, the body can blacken within twenty-four hours. It was very warm at the end of April 1865, and Booth's body was already in bad shape later on the day he was killed.

With the humidity present around Virginia and Maryland, the body tends to swell with retained fluids as it decays. Body decomposition does alter the shape and character of wounds. It is quite possible that experienced surgeons like Barnes and Woodward did not mention any marks of suicide, like powder burns, not because they missed them, but because that is what Stanton told them to do. In any case, the possibility of suicide is neither ruled in nor out in the autopsy reports. As to the assertion that Booth's collar would have caught fire had he shot himself, one wonders if a gun barrel pressed tight to the body might absorb such fire. Maybe his shirt had no collar (a common style in those days) to catch fire. It is another one of those things that was not mentioned in the autopsies. But DeWitt, *Assassination of Abraham Lincoln*, 90, emphasizes that Col. Conger thought that Booth "had the appearance of a man who put a pistol to his head and shot himself--shooting a little too low."

According to Lt. Baker (75), he had to twist the gun out of Booth's iron grasp, when he entered the barn after the shot rang out. But a man shot through the spinal cord as Booth was, according to the autopsy report (Dr. J. Janvier Woodward, of the Army Medical Museum) and pictures of his vertebrae (pp. 69-70), cannot hold anything. (See also, the autopsy report of Surgeon General J. K. Barnes, in Verge (ed.), *The Body in the Barn*, 67-68). According to the Pima County medical examiner, under the conditions described in the autopsy reports, Booth immediately would have been paralyzed, totally, from the neck (4th vertebrae) down, as

Barnes had reported. He would not have been rigid, but completely flaccid in his muscles and nerves--nothing functioning as it should. Booth had to have dropped anything with any weight as the bullet severed his spinal cord. Lt. Baker either lied or exaggerated, possibly wanting to look like a daring man of action, or more worthy of a bigger share of the reward.

Whether Booth shot himself or someone else shot him, many questioned whether Sgt. Corbett actually did it. Otto Eisenschiml, "Who Shot Booth?" in *O. E.: Historian Without an Armchair* (Indianapolis: Bobbs-Merrill, 1963), 159-66, concludes that Conger shot Booth to stop him from incriminating Stanton or other unnamed persons of note, in or out of the Federal government. We doubt that. Booth shot himself in the back of the head to save his pretty face (Lattimer, *Kennedy and Lincoln*, 75). His weapon slipped and the shot cut his spinal cord instead of blowing his brains out--the final piece of the bad luck that had attended all of his efforts since January 1865. The standard version is Blaine V. Houmes and Steven G. Miller, "The Death of John Wilkes Booth: Suicide by Cop?" *American Journal of Forensic Psychiatry*, 25 (No. 2, 2004), 25-36.

On Boston Corbett, see Richard F. Snow, "Boston Corbett," *American Heritage*, 30 (June-July 1980), 48-49; and Laurie Verge, "The Killer of John Wilkes Booth," Kauffman (ed.), *In Pursuit of . . . ,* 111-12. Corbett's own intriguing tale is in Steven G. Milled (ed.), "Boston Corbett's Long-Forgotten Story of Wilkes Booth's Death," *Surratt Courier*, 26 (May 2001), 5-7; *ibid.*, 26 (June 2001), 4-6.

The notion that Booth survived the barn holocaust became popular over the years following the assassination. It received a real boost with the publication of Finis L. Bates, *Escape and Suicide of John Wilkes Booth, Assassin of President Lincoln* (Memphis: Pilcher Printing Co., 1907), and is instrumental to those who claim to be direct descendents of Booth, Forrester, *This One Mad Act.,* and Nottingham *The Curse of Cain..* They are all torn apart, Bates specifically, in a 1907 letter written by Reverend Richard B. Garrett, see "A Garrett Speaks Out," Dillon (ed.), *The Lincoln Assassination: From the Pages of the* Surratt Courier, XI, 13-14; and an article by William G. Shepherd, "Shattering the Myth of John Wilkes Booth's Escape: An Adventure in Journalism," *Harper's Magazine*, 68 (Nov. 1924), 702-19. See also, "The Booth 'Mummy'," Dillon (ed.), *The Lincoln Assassination: From the Pages of the* Surratt Courier, XII, 1-17; Mark L. Siegel, "The Flight of John Wilkes Booth and the Corpse Brought from Garrett's Farm," *Lincoln Herald*, 84 (Winter 1982), 210-17.

But the argument continues. Otto Eisenschiml, "Was Booth Killed at Garrett's Farm? *Why Was Lincoln Murdered?*, 147-55, believes that the lack of tattoo marks on the 1903 corpse rules out Bate's story. It was Booth who died in 1865. Nate Orlowek (see Timothy Crouse, "A Conspiracy Theory to End All Conspiracy Theories: Did John Wilkes Booth Act Alone?" *Rolling Stone*, 216 [July 1, 1976], 42-42-44, 47, 91-- 92, 94) has spent a lifetime believing that Booth got away. A complete discussion of where things stand currently is in the Surratt House Museum publication, Verge (ed.), *The Body in the Barn*. The most recent study is C. Wyatt Evans, *The Legend of John Wilkes Booth: Myth, Memory, and a Mummy* (Lawrence: University Press of Kansas, 2004). See also, Erich L. Ewald, (ed.), "The Butcher's Tale" The Primary Documentation of 'Chris Ritter's' Confrontation with Louis Weichmann," Dillon (ed.), *The Lincoln Assassination: From the Pages of the* Surratt Courier, XI, 5-10, and two statements by Richard B. Garrett that Booth was dead and he saw him die, *ibid.*, XI, 11-14.

The official government position is still that Booth died in the barn. See Dillon (comp.), *John Wilkes Booth: The FBI Files, passim.* But just recently, Booth's distant relatives have asserted that they believe the actor was not in the Garrett barn and hope that modern DNA research will prove their argument to be beyond reproach. See Edward Collmore, "On the Trail of the Assassin," *Philadelphia Inquirer*, April 26, 2008, A1-A11.

Confederate Memorial Day is celebrated on April 26 in Mississippi, Alabama, Florida, and Georgia. But it is celerated in May 10 in the Carolinas, and in Virginia on May 30, while in the rest of the South it is celebrated on June 3.

PART VII: EPILOGUE (1865)

1. Back to the Rappahannock
Mogelever, *Death to Traitors*, 360-61; Oldroyd, *Assassination of Abraham Lincoln*, 78. The Lightfoot story is in Lloyd Lewis, *Myths After Lincoln* (New York: The Press of the Readers Club, 1922), 245-46; Mason, "A True Story of the Capture and Death of John Wilkes Booth," 1237-39; Miller (ed.), "Boston Corbett's Long-Forgotten Story of Wilkes Booth's Death," *Surratt Courier*, 26 (June 2001), 4-6.

2. The Eerie Trip to Belle Plain
Mogelever, *Death to Traitors*, 361-63; Oldroyd, *Assassination of Abraham Lincoln*, 78-79. See also, Ramage, *Gray Ghost: The Life and Legend of Col. John Singleton Mosby*, 283-88; Tidwell, *April '65*, 160-96,

passim; Tidwell, Hall, and Gaddy, *Come Retribution*, 468-70; Baker, "An Eyewitness Account of the Death and Burial of J. Wilkes Booth," 425-46; Doherty's "Official Report on the Capture of John Wilkes Booth," *Surratt Courier*, 25 (May 2000), 3-7. See also, Edward P. Doherty, "Pursuit and Death of John Wilkes Booth: Captain Doherty's Narrative," *Century Magazine*, (January. 1890), 446-49, reprinted in Prentiss Ingraham, "The Pursuit and Death of John Wilkes Booth," Dillon (ed.), *The Lincoln Assassination: From the Pages of the* Surratt Courier, IV, 23-31; Eisenschiml, "The Conspirators Who Went Free," 296-307.

3. Back in Washington
Mogelever, *Death to Traitors*, 363-66; Turner, *Beware the People Weeping*, 115, 212ff.

4. The Autopsy and a National Hero
Oldroyd, *Assassination of Abraham Lincoln*, 79, lists the members of the autopsy and inquest, and 80-83, describes the burial. See also, James O. Hall, "The Body on the Monitor," in Verge (ed.), *The Body in the Barn.*, 69-72; Mogelever, *Death to Traitors*, 366-69; Reuter, *The King Can Do No Wrong,* 53-55; Roscoe, *Web of Conspiracy*, 398-99; Laughlin, *Death of Lincoln*, 154-57. See also, "Autopsy and Identification of the Body," Box 4, Folder 182, DRB papers, GU; and George Loring Porter, "How Booth's Body Was Hidden," *Magazine of History*, 38 (1929), 19-35; Steers, *Blood on the Moon*, 261-62. The identification of John L. Smith is from Michael Kauffman to William L. Richter, September 5, 2002.

The likelihood that Booth would have been bald, had everyone who claimed to have obtained a lock of hair done so, is credited to Booth historian James O. Hall in Joan Chaconas, "Booth Escape Tour Summary," *Surratt Society News*, 2 (June 1977), 4.

5. The Convoluted Jailhouse Interview of David Herold
Roscoe, *Web of Conspiracy*, 153-56. Bingham's interview of Herold is reprinted in Verge (ed.), *From War Department Files*, 1-19. In his interview, Herold mentioned that Booth presented himself to the doctor who set his leg as "Tyson," the same name Dr. Mudd used ("Tyser" or "Tyson") in his earlier statememts to the investigators. It is the one place that their stories mesh. Mudd supporters claim that this shows that the doctor told the truth, while those who doubt Mudd see it as a prearranged story, made up before Booth and Herold left Mudd's farm. See Laurie Verge, "That Trifling Boy . . . ," *Surratt Courier*, 27 (January

2002), 4-9; and Richard Willing, "A Point in Dr. Mudd's Favor?" *Surratt Courier*, 26 (December 2001), 5--6.

    6. Weichmann Turns Himself in and Cuts a Deal
        An excellent personal description of Stanton and his personality is in William E. Doster, *Lincoln and Episodes of the Civil War*, 112-33.
        Much of the material on Weichmann's trip with the police to Baltimore and Canada is in Planck, "Lincoln's Assassination: The 'Forgotten' Investigation," 521-39, Chamlee, *Lincoln's Assassins*, 73-78. See also, Pitman (comp.), *The Assassination of President Lincoln and the Trial of the Conspirators* , 139-40; Sutton, *et al. (comps.), The Reporter: Containing . . . Trial of John H. Surratt, on an Indictment for Murder of President Lincoln,* IV, 88-100, 106-115; Trindal, *Mary Surratt*, 212-22, 272, 288-89; Moore, *Case of Mrs. Surratt*, 85-89; Turner, "Mrs. Mary Surratt," 159, 160-62; Weichmann, *A True Story*, 179-80, 217-33, 269; Roscoe, *Web of Conspiracy,* 239-42; Eisenschiml, "The Woman in the Case," 290-92.
        The clerks in Weichmann's place of employ all talked freely to clear themselves and implicate him. See various items in "Louis J. Weichmann," box 7, folder 364, DRB papers, GU.
        Weichmann's testimony is in Pitman, *The Assassination of President Lincoln and the Trial of the Conspirators*, 113-21; and R. Sutton, *et al. (comps.), The Reporter: Containing . . . Trial of John H. Surratt, on an Indictment for Murder of President Lincoln,* III, 301-54. Olivia Jenkins contradicts him in *ibid.,* IV, 136-41, and Lewis J. Carland testifies that Weichmann admitted his prevarications to him, *ibid.,* 187-91. See also, Joseph George, Jr., "Support at Last: The Efforts of John P. Brophy," Dillon (ed.), *The Lincoln Assassination: From the Pages of the Surratt Courier*, VI, 23-26; *id.,* "Trial of Mrs. Surratt: John P. Brophy's Rare Pamphlet," *Lincoln Herald*, 93 (Spring 1991), 17-22; and Laurie Verge, "John P. Brophy," Kauffman (ed.), *In Pursuit of . . . ,* 189-94.
        On whether [yes] and how much Weichmann lied [a lot], see Thomas R. Turner, "Did Weichmann Turn State's Evidence to Save Himself? A Critique of *A True History of the Assassination of Abraham Lincoln,*" *Lincoln Herald*, 81 (Winter 1979), 265-67; and Joseph George, Jr., "Nature's First Law: Louis J. Weichmann and Mrs. Surratt," *Civil War History*, 28 (No. 2, 1982), 101-127. One assumes that most of what Weichmann left out was his active role in the abduction plot, securing passwords for the bridges, and the giving of information on Confederate prisoners held in the North.

For more on Weichmann's veracity and later life, see the various articles by Erich L. Ewald in Dillon (ed.), *The Lincoln Assassination: From the Pages of the* Surratt Courier, IX, 1-13, 23-30.

7. Sarah Slater Destroys the Evidence
James O. Hall, "The Saga of Sarah Slater [orig., "Lady in the Veil," *Maryland Independent* (Waldorf), June 25, July 2, 1975]," Kauffman (ed.), *In Pursuit of . . . ,* 69-88; Hall, "Veiled Lady: The Saga of Sara Slater," *North & South,* 3 (August 2000), 34-44; Tonia J. Smith, "[Sara Slater]," (August 17, 1997), at users.nbn.net/tj1. The newest and most intriguing interpretation of Sarah Slater is John F. Stanton, "Some Thoughts on Sarah Slater," *Surratt Courier,* 32 (February 2007), 3-6, which we have used partially. Her appearance at the Kentucky spy reunion is in John F. Stanton to Laurie Verge, February 20, 2008, e-mail in the author's possession, and amplified in Stanton's "Anne Olivia Floyd: 1826-1905," *Surratt Courier,* 33 (June 2008), 5-8, especially 7-8, Sarah Slater's short stay in the Old Capitol prison is in Lomax, *Old Capitol and Its Inmates,* 153-54, as confirmed in Michael W. Kauffman, *American Brutus,* 327, 336.

What exactly the missing pages held (if anything) is not known. There have been many attempts to find the real missing pages, besides the meager fictional effort in this novel. The most notable occurred in 1975, when Schick Sunn Classic Pictures produced a sensational film, "The Lincoln Conspiracy." It was followed by a best-selling book, David Balsiger and Charles E. Sellier, Jr., *The Lincoln Conspiracy* (Los Angeles: Schick Sunn Classic Productions, 1977). Both accounts claimed to rely on new, recently discovered evidence, some 6,000 Edwin McMasters Stanton papers, including Booth's original letter to the *National Intelligencer* and Booth's lost diary entries. These discoveries allegedly implicate many big men in the North in government, finance, mercantile interests, and the military forces by name.

Historians hoped to see the originals, but the owner withdrew them from the public. All that is left is an oral tape that her agent made of them, and later transcribed. The Surratt Society has published the purported transcripts of the letter and missing diary, even though their historical analysts have proclaimed them fraudulent. See Hanchett, "Booth's Diary," 39-56, *passim;* James O. Hall, "That Letter to the *National Intelligencer,"* 4-8; and Laurie Verge, "Those Missing Pages from the 'Diary' of John Wilkes Booth," Dillon (ed.), *The Lincoln Assassination: From the Pages of the* Surratt Courier, IV, 13-20.

The official government position is still that Booth's Diary has never been in any other form than its mutilated present condition. See Dillon (comp.), *John Wilkes Booth: The FBI Files, passim.*

8. George Sanders Changes History

On Sanders and the cover-up of Confederate participation in Lincoln's demise, see Tidwell, *April '65*, 148-54. For a history of how effective the cover-up was and how it became the standard view of the assassination see, William Hanchett, "Lincoln's Murder: The Simple Conspiracy Theory," *Civil War Times Illustrated*, 30 (November/December 1991), 28-35, 70.

The standard treatment of the charges against the Confederacy as perjured or the machinations of the evil mind of Union Secretary of War Edwin McM. Stanton are in Dewitt, *Assassination of Abraham Lincoln, passim*; Turner, *Beware the People Weeping*, 125-37, and Seymour J. Frank, "The Conspiracy to Implicate the Confederate Leaders in Lincoln's Assassination," *Mississippi Valley Historical Review*, 40 (Mar. 1954), 629-56.

For the testimony of Richard Montgomery, Sanford Conover (Dunham), and Dr. James B. Merritt, see Pitman (comp.), *The Assassination of President Lincoln and the Trial of the Conspirators* , 24-37. At least one trial commission officer believed the three told the truth, Harris, *Assassination of Lincoln*, 163-78, although W. W. Cleary, one of the Confederate mission in Canada denied it all for himself and the others, "The Attempt to Fasten the Assassination of President Lincoln on President Davis and Other Innocent Parties," *Southern Historical Society Papers*, 9 (July and Aug. 1881), 313-25. William C. Davis, "The Conduct of 'Mr. Thompson'," 4-7, 43-47, however, condemns the head of the commission as monetarily crooked, as Davis and Benjamin feared. Let us be more generous, however, and assume that some of the missing money went to Slater, Montgomery, Dunham, and Merritt.

Dunham's later career is detailed in Stewart Evans and Paul Gainey, *Jack the Ripper: First American Serial Killer* (New York: Kodansha International, 1995), 194-210. Of interest here is an article in the *Rochester (N.Y.) Democrat and Republican*, December 3, 1888. For what it is worth, Tumblety was known to frequent the Tremont House in Boston, one of Booth's haunts while in town during the war. We would like to thank Michael W. Kauffman for bringing this source to our attention.

Both Davis and his vice president wrote multi-volume tomes defending their actions as Confederate officials and converted state rights advocates. See Jefferson Davis, *Rise and Fall of the Confederate Government* (2 vols., New York: Thomas Yoseloff, 1958); Alexander H. Stephens, *A Constitutional View of the Late War between the States* (2 vols., Philadelphia: National Publishing Company, 1870).

William L. Richter

BIBLIOGRAPHY

KEY

BIB = Verge, Laurie (ed.). *The Body in the Barn: The Controversy Over the Death of John Wilkes Booth* (Clinton, Md.: The Surratt Society, 1993).

IPO = Kauffman, Michael W. (ed.). *In Pursuit of . . . : Continuing Research in the Field of the Lincoln Assassination* (Clinton, Md.: The Surratt Society, 1990).

Aaron, Daniel. "What Can You Learn from a Historical Novel?" *American Heritage*, 43 (Oct 1992), 54-62.

Abbott, Martin. "Southern Reaction to Lincoln's Assassination," *Abraham Lincoln Quarterly*, 7 (Sept. 1952), 110-27.

Agassiz, George (ed.), *Meade's Headquarters, 1863-1865: Letters of Colonel Theodore Lyman from Wilderness to Appomattox* (Boston: Atlantic Monthly Press, 1922).

Alford, Terry (ed.), *John Wilkes Booth: A Sister's Memoir by Asia Booth Clarke* (Jackson: University Press of Mississippi, 1996).

Alford, Terry. "Mary Ann Holmes--Actress?" *Surratt Courier*, 16 (May 1991), 5-6.

Anderson, Dwight G. *Abraham Lincoln: The Quest for Immortality* (New York: Knopf, 1982).

Andrews, David C. "A Bit of Americana," *IPO*, 247-50.

Arnold, Samuel Bland. *Memoirs of a Lincoln Conspirator* (Ed. by Michael W. Kauffman, Bowie, Md.: Heritage Press, 1995).

Axelrod, Alan. *War Between the Spies: A History of Espionage during the Civil War* (New York: The Atlantic Monthly Press, 1992).

Bailyn, Bernard. *Ideological Origins of the American Revolution* (Cambridge: Harvard University Press, 1967).

Baird, Nancy D. " Yellow Fever Plot," *Civil War Times Illustrated*, 13 (November 1974), 16-23.

Bak, Richard. *Day Lincoln Was Shot: An Illustrated Chronicle* (Dallas: Taylor Publishing Co., 1998).

Bakeless, John. "Catching Harry Gilmore," *Civil War Times Illustrated*, 10 (April 1971), 24-33.

Bakeless, John. *Spies of the Confederacy* (Philadelphia: J. B. Lippincott Company, 1970).

Baker, L. B. "An Eyewitness Account of the Death and Burial of J. Wilkes Booth," *Journal of the Illinois State Historical Society*, 39 (Dec. 1946), 425-46.

Baker, Lafayette C. *History of the United States Secret Service* (Philadelphia: L. C. Baker, 1867).

Ballard, Michael B. *A Long Shadow: Jefferson Davis and the Final Days of the Confederacy* (Jackson: University Press of Mississippi, 1986).

Balsiger, David and Charles E. Sellier, Jr., *The Lincoln Conspiracy* (Los Angeles: Schick Sunn Classic Productions, 1977).

Bandow, Doug. "Marble Man," *National Review*, 43 (October 21, 1991), 48-49.

Banner, James M., Jr., *To the Hartford Convention: The Federalists and the Origins of Party Politics in Massachusetts, 1789-1815* (New York: Knopf, 1970).

Barbee, David Rankin. "How Lincoln Rejected Peace Overtures in 1861," *Tyler's Quarterly Historical and Genealogical Magazine*, 15 (Jan. 1934), 137-44.

Barbee, David Rankin. "Lincoln and Booth" (Unpublished ms. in the David Rankin Barbee papers, Georgetown University).

Baringer, William. *Lincoln's Rise to Power* (Boston: Little, Brown and Company, 1937).

Barnes, Joseph K. "Booth Autopsy," *BIB*, 67-68.

Barney, William L. *Road to Secession: A New Perspective on the Old South* (New York: Praeger, 1972).

Basler, Roy P. et al. (eds.), *The Collected Works of Abraham Lincoln* (9 vols., New Brunswick, N.J.: Rutgers University Press, 1953).

Bates, David Homer. *Lincoln in the Telegraph Office* (New York: D. Appleton-Century Co., 1907).

Bates, Finis L. *Escape and Suicide of John Wilkes Booth, Assassin of President Lincoln* (Memphis: Pilcher Printing Co., 1907).

Bauer, Charles J. *So I Killed Lincoln: John Wilkes Booth* (New York: Vantage Press, 1976).

Beale, Howard K. (ed.), *The Diary of Gideon Wells* (3 vols., New York: Norton, 1960).

Beale, R. L. T. "Part Taken by the Ninth Virginia Cavalry in Repelling the Dahlgren Raid," *Southern Historical Society Papers* , 3 (1877), 219-21.

Beall, J. Ninian. "Why Booth Killed Lincoln," *Columbia Historical Society of Washington, D.C., Records*, 48-49 (1946-1947), 127-41.

Belz, Herman. *Lincoln and the Constitution: The Dictatorship Question Reconsidered* (Ft. Wayne, IN: Louis A. Warren Lincoln Library and Museum, 1984).

Bennett, Lerone, Jr.. *Forced into Glory: Abraham Lincoln's White Dream* (Chicago: Johnson Publishing Co., 1999).

Bernard, Kenneth A. "Herman Melville, the Civil War and the Assassination," *Lincoln Herald*, 81 (Winter 1979), 268-69.

Berry, Randal. "'See Any Snakes out There?': Booth and Herold's Four Nights in the Pine Thicket," *Surratt Courier*, 33 (October 2008), 3-4.

Bestor, Arthur. "State Sovereignty and Slavery: A Reinterpretation of Proslavery Constitutional Doctrine, 1846-1860," *Journal of the Illinois State Historical Society*, 53 (1960), 117-80.

Betterly, Richard. "Seize Mr. Lincoln: The 1861 Baltimore Plot," *Civil War Times Illustrated*, 25 (February 1987), 14-21.

Billups, Carolyn S. "Maryland--A Southern Perspective," *Surratt Courier*, 23 (November 1998), 4-7.

Bingham, John. *Argument of . . .* (Washington: Government Printing Office, 1965).

Birkhimer, Michael. "Lincoln Assassination as a Rebuttal to the Bennett Thesis," *Surratt Courier*, 26 (October 2001), 4-9.

Bishop, Jim. *Day Lincoln Was Shot* (New York: Harper & Bros., 1955).

Bogar, Tom. "Why Harry Hawk Ran Off the Stage So Fast," *Surratt Courier*, 32 (August 2007), 3-4.

Bone, Beverly. "Edwin Stanton in the Wake of the Lincoln Assassination," *Lincoln Herald*, 82 (Winter 1980), 508-21.

"Booth and Bob Lincoln," *Chicago Daily Inter-Ocean*, June 18, 1878.

Boritt, Gabor S, and Norman O. Furness (eds.). *Historian's Lincoln: Pseudohistory, Psycohistory, and History* (Urbana: University of Illinois Press, 1988).

Bouquet, Johnny. "Johnny Bouquet's Walks: 'Maryland, My Maryland,'" *New York Times*, May 8, 1881, p. 10.

Bradford, M. E. "Dividing the House: The Gnosticism of Lincoln's Political Rhetoric," *Modern Age*, 23 (Winter 1979), 10-24.

Bradford, M. E. "A Fire Bell in the Night: The Southern Conservative View," *Modern Age*, 17 (Winter 1973), 9-15.

Bradford, M. E. "A Writ of Fire and Sword: The Politics of Oliver Cromwell," *Occasional Review*, 3 (summer 1975), 61-80.

[Bradford, M. E.] "For the Chair of NEH: A Southern Candidate Recalls His Struggle," *Humanities in the South*, 56 (1982), 11-13.

Bradford, M. E. "Heresy of Equality: Bradford Replies to Jaffa," *Modern Age*, 20 (Winter 1876), 62-77.

Bradford, M. E. *A Better Guide than Reason: Federalists & Anti-Federalists* (New Brunswick, N.J.: Transaction Publishers, 1994).

Bradford, M. E. *Remembering Who We Are: Observations of a Southern Conservative* (Athens: University of Georgia Press, 1985).

Bradley, Michael R. "In the Crosshairs: Southern Civilians Targeted by the U.S. Army," *North & South*, 10 (March 2008), 46-61.

Brennan, John C. "A Book Review of Escape and Suicide of John Wilkes Booth, Finus L. Bates (1907)," *BIB*, 57-66.

Brennan, John C. "A Great Heap of Rubbish," *Surratt Courier*, 18 (May 1993), 4-5.

Brennan, John C. "Confederate Spy--Captain Thomas Nelson Conrad," *Surratt Society News*, 2 (June 1977).

Brennan, John C. "General Bradley T. Johnson's Plan to Abduct President Lincoln," *Chronicles of St. Mary's*, 22 (Nov. and Dec. 1974), 413-25.

Brennan, John C. "John H. Surratt's 'Pilgrim Interview'," *IPO*, 53-64.

Brennan, John C. "John Wilkes Booth's Field Glasses," *Surratt Society News*, 7 (October 1982), 5-6.

Brennan, John C. "More on the Three Versions of the 1865 Trial Testimony," *Surratt Courier*, 11 (February 1986), 5-7.

Brennan, John C. "Why Weren't the Defendants Permitted to Testify in Their Own Defense?" *IPO*, 243-44.

Brennan, John C. "Confederate Plan to Abduct President Lincoln," *IPO*, 141-49.

Brennan, John C. "Three Versions of the Testimony in the 1865 Trial Testimony," *IPO*, 185-88.

Brennan, John C. *Pictorial Primer Having to Do with the Assassination of Abraham Lincoln and with the Assassin, John Wilkes Booth* (Laurel, Md.: Minuteman Press, 1979).

Bridges, C. A. "Knights of the Golden Circle: A Filibustering Fantasy," *Southwestern Historical Quarterly*, 44 (1940-41), 287-302.

Brooks, Noah. *Washington in Lincoln's Time* (Ed. by Herbert Mitgang, New York: Rinehart & Company, Inc., 1958).

Brown, Kent Masterson. "Secession: A Constitutional Remedy for the Breach of the Organic Law," *North & South*, 3 (August 2000), 12-21.

Brubaker, John H. III. *Last Capitol: Danville, Virginia, and the Final Days of the Confederacy* (Danville, Va.: Danville Museum of Fine Arts and History, 1979).

Bryan, George S. *Great American Myth* (Introduction by William Hanchett, Chicago: Americana House, Inc., 1990, orig. 1940).

Bryant, William O. *Cahaba Prison and the Sultana Disaster* (Tuscaloosa: University of Alabama Press, 1990).

Buckingham, J. E. *Reminiscences and Souvenirs of the Assassination of Abraham Lincoln* (Washington: Rufus H. Darby, 1894).

Buley, R. Carlyle. *Old Northwest: Pioneer Period, 1815-1840* (2 vols., Bloomington: Indiana University Press, 1950).

Bullard, F. Lauriston. "A Plausible Solution of the Mystery of John Wilkes Booth's Alleged Visit to Paris," *Lincoln Herald*, 52 (October 1950), 41-43.

Bullard, F. Lauriston. "When--If Ever--Was John Wilkes Booth in Paris?" *Lincoln Herald*, 50 (June 1948), 28-34.

Bulloch, James D. *Secret Service of the Confederate States in Europe* (2 vols., New York: Thomas Yoseloff. 1959).

Burke, Walter. "A New Twist to the Seward Stabbing," *Surratt Courier*, 15 (September 1990), 4.

Burkhimer, Michael. "What Do You Deem the Most Important Events in Your Services [Guarding the Lincoln Conspirators]?" *Surratt Courier,* 17 (April 2002), 5-7.

Burnett, Henry L. *Controversy between President Johnson and Judge Holt* (Pamphlet, New York: D. Appleton. 1891).

Burnett, Henry L. *Some Incidents in the Trial of President Lincoln's Assassins* (Pamphlet, New York: D. Appleton. 1891).

Butler, Pierce. *Judah P. Benjamin* (Philadelphia: George W. Jacobs & Company, 1906).

Campbell, Daniel. "Job Wanted," *Surratt Courier*, 25 (August 2000), 3.

Campbell, Helen Jones. *Case for Mrs. Surratt* (New York: G. P. Putnam's Sons, 1943).

Campbell, Helen Jones. *Confederate Courier [A Life of John H. Surratt, Jr.]* (New York: St. Martin's Press, 1964).

Canan, H. V. "Confederate Military Intelligence," *Maryland Historical Magazine*, 59 (March 1964), 34-51.

Carter, Samuel, III. *Riddle of Dr. Mudd* (New York: G. P. Putnam's Sons, 1974).

Castel, Albert. "Fort Sumter--1861," *Civil War Times Illustrated*, 15 (October 1976), [Special Issue].

Castel, Albert. "Samuel Ruth: Union Spy," *Civil War Times Illustrated*, 14 (February 1976), 36-45.

Cate, Wirt Armistead. "Ford, the Booths, and Lincoln's Assassination," *Emory University Quarterly*, 5 (March 1949), 11-19.

Catton, Bruce. *Army of the Potomac: Glory Road* (Garden City, NY.: Doubleday, 1952).

Catton, Bruce. *Army of the Potomac: A Stillness at Appomattox* (Garden City, N.Y.: Doubleday, 1953).

Chaconas Joan L. and James O. Hall. "Crossing the Navy Yard Bridge," *Surratt Courier*, 21 (September 1996), 5-7.

Chaconas, Joan L. "Assassins: Their Attempts, Foiled and Otherwise," *Surratt Society News*, 6 (June 1981), 4-6.

Chaconas, Joan L. "Booth Escape Tour Summary," *Surratt Society News*, 2 (June 1977), 4.

Chaconas, Joan L. "George Alfred Townsend's Papers," *IPO*, 101-106.

Chaconas, Joan L. "Historic Fort McNair," *The Lincolnian*, 1 (January-February 1983), 1-3.

Chaconas, Joan L. "Old Capitol Prison," *IPO*, 115-16.

Chaconas, Joan L. "Unpublished Atzerodt Confession offered Here for the First Time," *Surratt Courier*, 13 (October 1988), 1-3.

Chamlee, Roy Z., Jr., *Lincoln's Assassins: A Complete Account of their Capture, Trail, and Punishment* (Jefferson N.C.: McFarland & Company Inc., Publishers, 1990).

Channing, Steven A. *Crisis of Fear: Secession in South Carolina* (New York: Norton, 1970).

Chitty, Arthur Ben. "Booth Myth Defended," *BIB*, 7-10.

Christensen, Reo M. *Heresies Right and Left: Some Political Assumptions Reexamined* (New York: Harper & Row, 1973).

Clampitt, John W. "Trial of Mrs. Surratt," *North American Review*, (Sept. 1888), 223-40.

Clark, Charles B. "Suppression and Control of Maryland, 1861-1865: A Study of Federal-State Relations During Civil Conflict," *Maryland Historical Magazine*, 54 (September 1959)," 241-71.

Clark, James C. *Last Train South: The Flight of the Confederate Government from Richmond* (Jefferson, N.C.: McFarland Company, Inc., 1984).

Clarke, Asia Booth. *Elder and Younger Booth* (Boston: James R. Osgood, 1882).

Clarke, James W. *American Assassins: The Darker Side of Politics* (Princeton: Princeton University Press, 1982), 26-27.

Cleary, W. W. "Attempt to Fasten the Assassination of President Lincoln on President Davis and Other Innocent Parties," *Southern Historical Society Papers*, 9 (July and Aug. 1881), 313-25.

Cochran, Hamilton. "Booth's Other Pistol," *Civil War Times Illustrated*, 13 (January 1975), 20-24.

Collmore, Edward. "On the Trail of the Assassin," *Philadelphia Inquirer*, April 26, 2008, A1-A11.

Connelly, Thomas. *Marble Man: Robert E. Lee and His Image in American Society* (New York: Knopf, 1977).

Conrad, Thomas N. *A Confederate Spy* (New York: J. S. Ogilvie Pub. Co., 1892).

Cooper, William J. *Jefferson Davis: American* (New York: Knopf, 2000).

Cox, LaWanda. *Lincoln and Black Freedom: A Study in Presidential Leadership* (Columbia: University of South Carolina Press, 1981).

Crenshaw, Olliger. "Knights of the Golden Circle," *American Historical Review*, 47 (1941), 23-50.

Crofts, Daniel. *Reluctant Confederates: Upper South Unionists in the Secession Crisis* (Chapel Hill: University of North Carolina Press, 1989).

Crook, William H. "Lincoln as I Knew Him," *Harper's Monthly*, (Feb. 1907), 107-14.

Crook, William H. "Lincoln's Last Day," *Harper's Monthly*, (Sept. 1907), 519-30.

Crouse, Timothy. "A Conspiracy Theory to End All Conspiracy Theories: Did John Wilkes Booth Act Alone?" *Rolling Stone*, 216 (July 1, 1976), 42-42-44, 47, 91--92, 94.

Crowley, R. O. "Making the Infernal Machines," *Civil War Times Illustrated*, 12 (June 1973), 24-35.

Cumming, Carman. *Devil's Game: The Civil War Intrigues of Charles A. Dunham* (Urbana: University of Illinois Press, 2008).

Cummings, Edmund H. "Signal Corps in the Confederate States Army," *Southern Historical Society Papers*, 16 (January-December 1888), 93-107.

Current, Richard N. *Lincoln and the First Shot* (Philadelphia: J. B. Lippincott and Co., 1963).

Curry, Roy L. "James A. Seddon: A Southern Prototype," *Virginia Magazine of History and Biography*, 63 (April 1955), 123-50.

Curti, Merle E. "George Nicholas Sanders," in Dumas Malone (ed.), *Dictionary of American Biography* (New York: Charles Scribner's Sons, 1935), XIV, 334-35.

Curti, Merle E. "'Young America,'" *American Historical Review*, 32 (October 1926), 34-55.

Curtis [sic], Merle E. "George Sanders--American Patriot of the Fifties," *South Atlantic Quarterly*, 27 (January 1928), 79-87.

Davis, Curtis Carroll. "In Pursuit of Booth Once More: A New Claimant Heard From," *Maryland Historical Magazine*, 79 (Fall 1984), 220-34.

Davis, Curtis Carroll. "Civil War's Most Over-Rated Spy," *West Virginia History*, 27 (October 1965), 1-9.

Davis, Curtis Carroll. "Companions of Crisis: The Spy Memoir as a Social Document," *Civil War History*, 10 (December 1964), 385-400.

Davis, Jefferson. *Rise and Fall of the Confederate Government* (2 vols., New York: Thomas Yoseloff, 1958).

Davis, William C. "Behind the Lines," *Civil War Times Illustrated*, 20 (Nov. 1981), 26-28.

Davis, William C. "Caveat Emptor," *Civil War Times Illustrated*, 16 (Aug. 1977), 33-37.

Davis, William C. "Conduct of 'Mr. Thompson'," *Civil War Times Illustrated*, 9 (May 1970), 4-7, 43-47.

Davis, William C. *John C. Breckinridge: Statesman, Soldier, Symbol* (Baton Rouge: Louisiana State University Press, 1974).

Davis, William C. "Lincoln Conspiracy--Hoax?" *Civil War Times Illustrated*, 16 (Nov. 1977), 47-49.

Davis, William C. *Lost Cause: Myths and Realities of the Confederate Defeat* (Lawrence: University Press of Kansas, 1996).

Denton, Lawrence M. *A Southern Star For Maryland: Maryland and the Secession Crisis* (Baltimore: Publishing Concepts, 1997).

Dew, Charles B. "Apostles of Secession," *North & South*, 4 (April 2001), 24-38.

Dew, Charles B. *Apostles of Secession: Southern Secession Commissioners and the Causes of the Civil War* (Charlottesville: University Press of Virginia, 2001).

DeWitt, David Miller. *Assassination of Abraham Lincoln* (New York: Macmillan, 1909).

Dillon, David (ed.). *The Lincoln Assassination: From the Pages of the Surratt Courier, 1986-1999* (13 Parts, Clinton, Md.: The Surratt Society, 2000).

Dillon, David C. (ed.). *John Wilkes Booth: The FBI Files* (Clinton, MD: Surratt Society, 2002).

Dillon, David C. "Where Were the Garrett Farm Gates?" *Surratt Courier*, 28 (August 2003), 3-6.

Dillon, David C. "Who Were the Horsemen on the Hill?" *Surratt Courier*, 27 (June 2002), 4-7.

DiLorenzo, Thomas J. and Gerald Prokopowicz. "Abraham Lincoln: Savior or Tyrant?" *North & South*, 7 (January 2004), 44-55.

DiLorenzo, Thomas J. " Great Centralizer: Abraham Lincoln and the War Between the States," Independent Review, 3 (No. 2, Fall 1998), 243-71.

DiLorenzo, Thomas J. *Real Lincoln: A New Look at Abraham Lincoln, His Agenda, and an Unnecessary War* (Roseville, CA.: Prima Publishing, 2002).

Dodels, Jeannine Clarke. " Last Days of John Wilkes Booth," (Undated, unpublished ms).

Doherty, Edward P. "Official Report on the Capture of John Wilkes Booth," *Surratt Courier*, 25 (May 2000), 3.ff

Doherty, Edward P. "Pursuit and Death of John Wilkes Booth: Captain Doherty's Narrative," *Century Magazine*, (January. 1890), 446-49.

Dolson, Hildegarde. *Great Oildorado: The Gaudy and Turbulent Years of the First Oil Rush, Pennsylvannia, 1859-1880* (New York: Random House, 1959).

Donald, David. *Lincoln* (New York: Simon & Schuster, 1995).

Donnelly, Ralph W. "District of Columbia Confederates," *Military Affairs*, 23 (1959-60), 207-208.

Doster, William E. *Lincoln and Episodes of the Civil War* (New York: G.P. Putnam's Sons, 1915).

Dowdey, Clifford and Louis H. Manarin (eds.). *Wartime Papers of R. E. Lee* (New York: Branhall House, 1961).

Doyle, John F. "Case of John Harrison Surratt, Jr.," *Surratt Courier*, 25 (March 2000), 3-7.

Dumond, Dwight L. *Secession Movement, 1860-1861* (New York: Octagon Books, 1963, orig. 1931).

Dunn, Roy S. "The KGC in Texas, 1860-1861," *Southwestern Historical Quarterly*, 70 (April 1987, 543-573).

Durden, Robert. *Gray and the Black* (Baton Rouge: LSU Press, 1972).

Egan, Brendan H., Jr. "Mary Lincoln at City Point," *Surratt Courier*, 26 (November 2001), 4-7.

Eisenschiml, Otto E. "Addenda to Lincoln's Assassination," *Journal of the Illinois State Historical Society*, 43 (Summer and Autum 1950), 91-99, 204-19.

Eisenschiml, Otto E. "Did He, Too, Try to Kill Lincoln?" *Lincoln Herald*, 48 (June 1946), 30-33.

Eisenschiml, Otto. *In the Shadow of Lincoln's Death* (New York: Wilfred Funk, 1940).

Eisenschiml, Otto E. *O.E. Historian without an Armchair* (Indianapolis: Bobbs-Merrill, 1963). E468/E42

Eisenschiml, Otto E. *Reviewers Reviewed: A Challenge to Historical Critics* (Pamphlet, Ann Arbor: William L. Clements Library, 1940). E457.5/E573

Eisenschiml, Otto. "A 'Study' of John Surratt?" *Journal of the Illinois State Historical Society*, 52 (Spring 1959), 181-89

Eisenschiml, Otto. *Why Was Lincoln Murdered?* (New York: Grossett & Dunlap, 1937).

Eisenschiml, Otto E. and Alfred Isaacson. "Final Two Chapters in the Surratt Controversy," *Journal of the Illinois State Historical Society*, 52 (Summer 1959), 279-90.

Ellsler, John A. Stage *Memories of John A. Ellsler*. Edited by Effie Ellsler Weston. (Cleveland: The Rowfant Club, 1950).

[Emerson, E. A.] "How Wilkes Booth's Friend Described His Crime," *Literary Digest*, (Mar. 6, 1926).

Entwisle, Elaine and Laurie Verge. "For M'Lady," *Surratt Society News*, 6 (August 1981), 5-6.

Evans, C. Wyatt. "Lafayette Baker and Security in the Civil War North," *North & South*, 11 (September 2008), 44-51.

Evans, C. Wyatt. *The Legend of John Wilkes Booth: Myth, Memory, and a Mummy* (Lawrence: University Press of Kansas, 2004).

Evans, Eli N. *Judah P. Benjamin: The Jewish Confederate* (New York: The Free Press, 1988).

Evans, Eli N. *Lonely Days Were Sundays* (Jackson: University Press of Mississippi, 1993).

Evans, Stewart and Paul Gainey, *Jack the Ripper: First American Serial Killer* (New York: Kodansha International, 1995).

Ewald, Erich L. "Butcher's Tale: The Primary Documentation of 'Chris Ritter's' Confrontation with Louis J. Weichmann," *Surratt Courier*, 17 (April 1992), 4-8.

Ewald, Erich L. "Talespinner and the Witness: A Legion of Questions and a Phalanx of Speculations Concerning Chris Ritter and Louis J. Weichmann," *Surratt Courier*, 18 (March 1993), 5-9.

Ewald, Erich L. "Witness and the Young Boy: New Information Regarding the Testimony of Louis J. Weichmann," *Surratt Courier*, 16 (October 1991), 4-9.

Faber, Dinah (ed.). "Could It Have Been Mary?" *Surratt Courier*, 27 (May 2002), 5-7.

Fehrenbacher, Don. *Dred Scott Case: Its Significance in American Law and Politics* (New York: Oxford University Press, 1978).

Feis, William B. et al. "Lincoln Assassination: Do the Pieces Fit?" *North & South*, 2 (No. 4, April 1999), 26-34.

Fellman, Michael. *Making of Robert E. Lee* (New York: Random House, 2000).

Ferguson, Andrew. "Last Battle of the Civil War [The Guilt or Innocence of Dr. Mudd]," *Weekly Standard*, 8 (December 30, 2002), [1-13].

Ferguson, W. J. *I saw Booth Shoot Lincoln* (Austin: Pemberton, 1969, repr.)

Fields, Barbara Jeanne. *Slavery and Freedom on the Middle Ground: Maryland during the Nineteenth Century* (New Haven: Yale University Press, 1985).

Finkelmann, Paul. *Slavery and the Founders: Race and Liberty in the Age of Jefferson* (Armonk, N. Y.: M. E. Sharpe, 1996).

Fishel, Edwin C. "Mythology of Civil War Intelligence," *Civil War History*, 10 (December 1964), 344-67.

Fishel, Edwin C. *Secret War for Union: The Untold Story of Military Intelligence in the Civil War* (Boston: Houghton Mifflin, 1996).

Fleet, Betsy (ed.). "A Chapter of Unwritten History: Richard Baynham Garrett's Account of the Flight and Death of John Wilkes Booth," *Virginia Magazine of History and Biography*, 71 (October 1963), 388-407.

Fleming, Thomas. "Lincoln's Tragic Heroism," *National Review*, 41 (December 8, 1989), 38-40.

Flower, Frank A. Edwin McMasters *Stanton, The Autocrat of Rebellion, Emancipation, and Reconstruction* (Akron, Ohio: Saalfield Pub. Co., 1905).

Foner, Eric. "Lincoln, Bradford, and the Conservatives," *New York Times* (February 13, 1982), A-24.

Forrester, Izola. *This One Mad Act. The Unknown Story of John Wilkes Booth and His Family* (Boston: Hale, Cushman, and Flint, 1937).

Fowler, Robert H. "Album of the Lincoln Murder: Illustrating How It Was Planned, Committed and Avenged, "*Civil War Times Illustrated*, 4 (July 1965) [Special Issue].

Fowler, Robert H. "New Evidence in [the] Lincoln Murder Conspiracy," *Civil War Times Illustrated*, 3 (Feb. 1965), 4-6, 8-11.

Fowler, Robert H. "Was Stanton behind Lincoln's Murder?" *Civil War Times*, 3 (Aug. 1961), 4-13, 16-23.

Fox, Dorothy. "Childhood Home of an American Arch-Villain," *Civil War Times Illustrated*, 29 (March-April 1990), 12, 14, 18, 66-67.

Frank, Seymour J. "Conspiracy to Implicate the Confederate Leaders in Lincoln's Assassination," *Mississippi Valley Historical Review*, 40 (Mar. 1954), 629-56.

Freehling, William W. *Prelude to Civil War: The Nullification Crisis in South Carolina, 1816-1836* (New York: Harper & Row, 1965).

Freehling, William W. *The Road to Disunion* (2 vols., New York: Oxford University Press, 1990-2007).

Freeman, Douglas Southall (ed.). *Lee's Dispatches: Unpublished Letters of General Robert E. Lee, C.S.A., to Jefferson Davis and the War Department of the Confederate States of America, 1862-1865, from the Private Collection of Wymberly Jones DeRenne* (New York: G.P. Putnam's Sons, 1915.

Freeman, Douglas Southall. *R. E. Lee* (4 vols., New York: Charles Scribner's Sons, 1934-1935).

Gaddy, David Winfred. "Confederate Spy Unmasked: An Afterward," *Manuscripts*, 30 (Spring 1978), 94.

Gaddy, David Winfred. "Gray Cloak and Dagger," *Civil War Times Illustrated*, 14 (July 1975), 20-27.

Gaddy, David Winfred. "John Williamson Palmer: Confederate Agent," *Maryland Historical Magazine*, 83 (Summer 1988), 98-110.

Gaddy, David Winfred. "Surratt Tavern--A Confederate 'Safe House'?" *IPO*, 129-30.

Gaddy, David Winfred. "William Norris and the Confederate Signal and Secret Service," *Maryland Historical Magazine*, 70 (Summer 1975), 167-88.

Galbraith, John S. "George N. Sanders: 'Influence' Man for the Hudson's Bay Company," *Oregon Historical Quarterly*, 53 (September 1952), 159-76.

Garment, Suzanne. "NEH Becomes a Storm Center Once Again," *Wall Street Journal* (October 31, 1981).

Garrett, Richard Baynham. "A Chapter of Unwritten History. . . . Account of the Flight and Death of John Wilkes Booth," ed. By Betsy Fleet, *Virginia Magazine of History and Biography*, 71 (Oct 1973), 386-407.

Garrett, Richard Baynham. "End of a Manhunt," *American Heritage*, 17 (June 1966), 40-43, 105.

Gay, William H. "Lincoln's Assassination: How Nashville Heard the News," *Tennessee Historical Magazine*, (April 1919), 38-39.

Genovese, Eugene D. *World the Slaveholders Made: Two Essays in Interpretation* (New York: Vintage, 1971).

George, David, Jr., "'Black Flag Warfare': Lincoln and the Raid Against Richmond and Jefferson Davis," *The Pennsylvania Magazine of History and Biography*, 115 (July 1991), 291-318.

George, Joseph, Jr. "'Abraham Africanus I': President Lincoln Through the Eyes of a Copperhead Editor," *Civil War History*, 14 (September 1968), 226-41.

George, Joseph, Jr. "Nature's First Law: Louis J. Weichmann and Mrs. Surratt," *Civil War History*, 28 (No. 2, 1982), 101-127.

George, Joseph, Jr. "New Surratt Letters Discovered," *Surratt Courier*, 13 (October 1988), 5-6.

George, Joseph, Jr. "Old Abe Must Go Up the Spout': Henry von Steinaecker and the Lincoln of the Lincoln Conspiracy Trial," *Lincoln Herald*, 94 (Winter 1992), 148-56.

George, Joseph, Jr. "Support at Last: The Efforts of John P. Brophy," *Surratt Courier*, 16 (April 1991), 4-6.

George, Joseph, Jr. "Trial of Mrs. Surratt John P. Brophy's Rare Pamphlet," *Lincoln Herald*, 93 (Spring 1991), 17-22.

George, Joseph, Jr. (ed.). "Scene of the Trial," *Surratt Courier*, 24 (February 1999), 4-7.

George, Joseph, Jr. "Night John Wilkes Booth Played before Abraham Lincoln," *Lincoln Herald*, 59 (Summer 1957), 11-15.

Gleason, D. H. L. "Conspiracy Against Lincoln," *Magazine of History*, 13 (February 1911), 59-65.

Good Timothy (ed.). *We Saw Lincoln Shot: One Hundred Eyewitness Accounts* (Jackson: University Press of Mississippi, 1995).

Gordon, David (ed.). *Secession, State and Liberty* (New Brunswick, N. J.: Transaction Publishers, 1998).

Gorham, George C. *Life and Public Services of Edwin M. Stanton* (2 vols., Boston: Houghton Mifflin and Company, 1899).

Gray, John. "Fate of the Lincoln Conspirators: The Account of the Hanging, Given by Lieutenant Colonel Christian Rath, the Executioner," 11 *McClure's Magazine*, 37 (1911), 626-36.

Grossmann, Edwina Booth. *Edwin Booth: Recollections by his Daughter* (New York: The Century Co., 1894).

Gunderson, Robert Gray. *Old Gentlemen's Convention: The Washington Peace Conference of 1861* (Madison: University of Wisconsin Press, 1961).

Gutman, Richard and Kellie O. Gutma. "Boston: A Home for John Wilkes Booth," *Surratt Society News*, 10 (September 1985), 1, 6-8.

Gutman, Richard J. S. and Kellie O. Gutman. *John Wilkes Booth Himself* (Dover, Mass.: Hired Hand Press, 1979).

Gutteridge, Leonard F. and Ray A. Neff, *Dark Union: The Secret Web of Profiteers, Politicians, and Booth Conspirators that Led to Lincoln's Death* (Hoboken, NJ: Weilet, 2003).

Haines, Randall A. "Revolutionist with Complicity in Lincoln's Death," Pt. 1, *Surratt Courier*, 13 (September 1988), 5-8.

Haines, Randall A. "Revolutionist with Complicity in Lincoln's Death," Pt. 2, *Surratt Courier*, 13 (October 1988), 7-10.

Haines, Randall A. "Evidence of a Canadian Connection with Confederate Agents in the Lincoln Assassination." *Surratt Courier*, 29 (July 2004), 3-7.

Haines, Randall A. "The Notorious George N. Sanders: His Career and role in the Lincoln Assassination" (unpublished ms. in the James O. Hall Library, Surratt Museum, 1994).

Hall, James O. "A Clarification," *IPO*, 171-74.

Hall, James O. "A Magnificent Charlatan: George Washington Lafayette Bickley Made a Career of Deceit," *Civil War Times Illustrated*, 18 (February 1980), 40-42.

Hall, James O. "Appointment in Samara: The Strange Death of Walter Bowie," *North & South*, 1 (February 1998), 76-80.

Hall, James O. "Baltimore Plot," *Surratt Courier*, 27 (February 2002), 4-7.

Hall, James O. "Beautiful Snow," *Surratt Courier*, 11 (February 1986), 3-4.

Hall, James O. "Corn and the Cavalry," *Surratt Society News*, 6 (September 1981), 3-4.

Hall, James O. "Body on the Monitor," *BIB*, 69-72.

Hall, James O. "Case of David E. George," *BIB*, 47-52.

Hall, James O. "Dahlgren Papers: A Yankee Plot to Kill President Davis," *Civil War Times Illustrated*, 22 (November 1983), 30-39.

Hall, James O. "Death of Thomas Jones," *Surratt Society News*, 6 (August 1981), 4-5

Hall, James O. "Gunning for Davis," *Civil War Times Illustrated*, 37 (February 1999), 66-68.

Hall, James O. "Hartranft Letterbooks," *IPO*, 265-68.

Hall, James O. "John Wilkes Booth at School," *Surratt Courier*, 16 (July 1991), 3-4.

Hall, James O. *John Wilkes Booth's Escape Route* (Clinton, Md.: Surratt Society, 2000).

Hall, James O. "Miss Dean," *Surratt Society News*, 4 (September 1979), 4.

Hall, James O. "Mystery of Lincoln's Guard," *IPO*, 233-38.

Hall, James O. "Other Boardinghouse Residents--Mary Apollonia Dean and the Holohan Family," *IPO*, 65-68.

Hall, James O. "Saga of Sarah Slater [orig., "Lady in the Veil," *Maryland Independent* (Waldorf), June 25, July 2, 1975]," *IPO*, 69-88.

Hall, James O. "Senator Atchison and Presidential Succession," *Surratt Courier*, 16 (July 1991), 2-3.

Hall, James O. "Spy Harrison," *Civil War Times Illustrated*, 24 (Feb. 1986), 19-25.

Hall, James O. "That Letter to the National Intelligencer," Surratt Courier, 18 (November 1993), 4-8.

Hall, James O. "Unsolved Mysteries Revisited," *BIB*, 13-18.

Hall, James O. "Veiled Lady: The Saga of Sara Slater," *North & South*, 3 (August 2000), 34-44.

Hall, James O. "Why John M. Lloyd Was in Upper Marlboro," *IPO*, 229-32.

Hall, James O. "Why Was Mrs. Surratt's Home Raided on the Night of April 14-15, 1865?" *IPO*, 239-42.

Hall, James O. "You Have Mail . . . ," *Surratt Courier*, 25 (July 2000), 8-9.

Hall, James O. and Edward Steers, Jr. "George Andrew Atzerodt," *IPO*, 29-32.

Hall, James O. and Laurie Verge. "About Those Guns." *IPO*, 253-56.

Hall, James O., Laurie Verge, and Joan V. Bradgon. "A Sister's Thoughts: A Letter from Asia Booth Clarke," *IPO*, 107-110.

Hall. James O. "John M. Lloyd: Star Witness," *IPO*, 97-100.

Hanchett, William. "Ambush on the Seventh Street Road," *IPO*, 151-63.

Hanchett, William. "Booth's Diary," *Journal of the Illinois Historical Society*, 72 (Feb. 1979), 39-56.

Hanchett, William. "Historian as Gamesman: Otto Eisenschiml, 1880-1963," *Civil War History*, 36 (March 1990), 5-16.

Hanchett, William. *John Wilkes Booth and the Terrible Truth about the Civil War* (Racine: Lincoln Fellowship of Wisconsin, Historical Bulletin No. 49).

Hanchett, William. "Lincoln Assassination Revisited," *North & South*, 3 (September 2000), 33-39.

Hanchett, William. *Lincoln Murder Conspiracies* (Urbana: University of Illinois Press, 1983).

Hanchett, William. "Lincoln's Murder: The Simple Conspiracy Theory," *Civil War Times Illustrated*, 30 (November/December 1991), 28-35, 70.

Hanchett, William. "War Department and Booth's Abduction Plot," *Lincoln Herald*, 82 (Winter 1980), 499-508.

Harold M. Hyman and William M. Wiecek, *Equal Justice under Law: Constitutional Development, 1835-1875* (New York: Harper & Row, 1982).

Harris, Joel Chandler. *On the Wing of Occasions: Being the Authorized Version of Certain Curious Episodes of the Late Civil War Including the Hitherto Suppressed Narrative of the Kidnapping of President Lincoln* (New York: Doubleday, Page & Co., 1900).

Harris, T. M. *Assassination of Lincoln: A History of the Great Conspiracy Trial of the Conspirators by a Military Commission, and a Review of the Trial of John H. Surratt* (Boston: American Citizen Company, 1892).

Harris, William C. *With Charity for All: Lincoln and the Restoration of the Union* (Lexington: University of Kentucky Press, 1997).

Harsh, Joseph L. "'As Stupid a Fellow as I Am . . .': On the Real Military Genius of Robert E. Lee," *North & South*, 3 (June 2000), 60-71.

Hasson, Richard. "More on John Surratt," *Surratt Society News*, 6 (August 1981), 3.

Hatch, Frederick. "'Sam' Letter," *Journal of the Lincoln Assassination*, 19 (August 2005), 22-26.

Hatch, Frederick. "Biography: Everton J. Conger," *Journal of the Lincoln Assassination*, 17 (August 2003), 33.

Hatch, Frederick. "Lincoln the Tyrant?" *Journal of the Lincoln Assassination*, 19 (December 2005), 42-47.

Hatch, Frederick. "Michael O'Laughlen: A Biography," *Journal of the Lincoln Assassination*, 17 (April 2003), 11-13.

Hatch, Frederick. "They Shot Horses, Didn't They? Booth and Herold in the Woods," *Journal of the Lincoln Assassination*, 21 (December 2007), 42-46.

Hattaway, Herman and Richard E. Beringer, *Jefferson Davis, Confederate President* (Manhattan: University Press of Kansas, 2002).

Hazelton, Joseph H. "Assassination of President Lincoln," *The Lincolnian*, 4 (March April 1986), 6.

Head, Constance. "Insights on John Wilkes Booth from His Sister Asia's Correspondence," *Lincoln Herald*, 82 (Winter 1980), 540-44.

Head, Constance. "J.W.B.: I am Myself Alone," *IPO*, 41-46.

Head, Constance. "John Wilkes Booth as a Hero Figure, " *Journal of American Culture*, 5 (Fall 1982), 22-28.

Head, Constance. "John Wilkes Booth in American Fiction," *Lincoln Herald*, 82 (Winter 1980), 455-62.

Head, Constance. "John Wilkes Booth: Prologue to Assassination, *Lincoln Herald*, 85 (Winter 1983), 254-79.

Headly, John W. *Confederate Operations in Canada and New York* (New York: Time-Life Books, 1984).

Hebblewaite, Frank. "A Clarification," *BIB*, 11-12.

Hendrickson, Robert. *Sumter: The First Day of the Civil War* (Chelsea, MI: Scarborough House, 1990).

Hesseltine, William B. *Lincoln's Plan of Reconstruction* (Tuscaloosa: Confederate Publishing Co., 1960).

Higdon, Hal. *Union vs. Dr. Mudd* (Chicago: Follett Publishing Company, 1964).

Higham, Charles. *Murdering Mr. Lincoln: A New Detection of the Nineteenth's Century's Most Famous Crime* (Beverly Hills: New Millenium Press, 2004).

Hodder, F. H. "Some Phases of the Dred Scott Case," *Mississippi Valley Historical Review*, 16 (June 1929), 3-22;

Holding, Charles E. "John Wilkes Booth Stars in Nashville," *Tennessee Historical Quarterly*, 23 (March 1964), 73-79.

Holt, Joseph and James Speed. "New Facts about Mrs. Surratt," *North American Review*, (July 1880), 82-94.

Holzer, Harold. "'I Was Myself at the Front'," *Civil War Times Illustrated*, 29 (January/February 1991), 28-35.

Horan, James D. *Confederate Agent: A Discovery in History* (New York: Crown Publishers, 1954).

Horner, "John B. John Wilkes Booth as Oil Speculator," *Surratt Courier*, 25 (June 2000), 3-7.

Houmes, Blaine V. "The Last Words of John Wilkes Booth . . . Or Were They?" *Surratt Courier*, 32 (June 2007), 3-7.

Houmes, Blaine V. *Abraham Lincoln Assassination Bibliography: A Compendium of Reference Materials* (Clinton, Md.: Surratt Society, 1997).

Houmes, Blaine V. and Steven G. Miller, "The Death of John Wilkes Booth: Suicide by Cop?" *American Journal of Forensic Psychiatry*, 25 (No. 2, 2004), 25-36.

Houston, Alan Craig. *Algernon Sidney and the Republican Heritage in England and America* (Princeton: Princeton University Press, 1991).

Howard, Hamilton Gay. *Civil War Echoes: Character Sketches and Secrets* (Washington: Howard Publishing Co., 1907).

Hummel, Jeffrey R. "Why Did Lincoln Choose War?" *North & South*, 4 (September 2001), 38-44.

Hyams, Edward. *Killing No Murder: A Study of Assassination as a Political Means* (London: Panther Modern Society, 1970).

Hyman, Harold M. "Hitting the Fan(s) Again: or, Sic Semper Conspiracies," *Reviews in American History*, 12 (September 1984), 388-92.

Hyman, Harold M. *A More Perfect Union: The Impact of the Civil War and Reconstruction on the Constitution* (Boston: Houghton Mifflin, 1975).

Hyman, Harold M. *With Malice Toward Some: Scholarship (or Something Less) on the Lincoln Murder* (Pamphlet, Springfield: Abraham Lincoln Association, 1978).

Hyman, Harold. *Lincoln's Reconstruction: Neither Failure of Vision Nor Vision of Failure* (Ft. Wayne, IN: Louis A. Warren Lincoln Library and Museum, 1980).

Isaacson, Alfred. "John Surratt and the Lincoln Assassination Plot," *Maryland Historical Magazine*, 52 (December 1957), 315-42.

Isaacson, Alfred. "More on the Surratt Wedding," *Surratt Courier*, 28 (March 2003), 6-7.

Isaacson, Alfred (ed.). "Some Letters of Anna Surratt," *Maryland Historical Magazine*, 54 (September 1959), 310-13.

Isaacson, Alfred and Otto Eisenschiml, "Final Two Chapters in the Surratt Controversy," *Journal of the Illinois State Historical Society*, 52 (Summer 1959), 279-90.

Jaffa, Harry V. *Crisis of the House Divided: An Interpretation of the Issues in the Lincoln-Douglas Debates* (Garden City, N. Y., Doubleday, 1959).

Jaffa, Harry V. "Lincoln's Character Assassins," *National Review*, 42 (January 22, 1990), 34-38.

Jaffa, Harry V. *A New Birth of Freedom: Abraham Lincoln and the Coming of the Civil War* (Lanham, Md.: Rowan & Littlefield Publishers, 2000).

James, Marquis. *They Had Their Hour* (Indianapolis: Bobbs-Merrill, 1934).

Jampoler, Andrew C. A. *The Last Lincoln Conspirator: John Surratt's Flight from the Gallows* (Annapolis: Naval Institute Press, 2008).

Johnson, Angus J. "Disloyalty on Confederate Railroads in Virginia," *Virginia Magazine of History and Biography*, 63 (October 1955), 410-26.

Johnson, B. T. "My Ride Around Baltimore in 1864," *Cavalry Journal*, (Sept 1869), 413-24.

Johnson, B. T. "My Ride Around Baltimore," *Cavalry Journal*, (Sept 1889), 250-60.

Johnson, Patricia Carley (ed.). "'I Have Supped Fully on Horrors'," *American Heritage*, 10 (October 1959), 60-65, 96-100.

Jones, J. B. *A Rebel War Clerk's Diary at the Confederate States Capital* (Ed. by Howard Swiggett, 2 vols., New York: Old Hickory Bookshop, 1935).

Jones, J. Wm. (ed.), The Kilpatrick-Dahlgren Raid against Richmond," *Southern Historical Society Papers*, 13 (1885), 515-60.

Jones, John Paul (ed.). *Dr. Mudd and the Lincoln Assassination: The Case Reopened* (Mechanicsville, Pa.: Combined Books, 1995).

Jones, Thomas A. *J. Wilkes Booth: An Account of His Sojourn in Southern Maryland . . . and His Death in Virginia* (Chicago: Laird & Lee, 1893).

Jones, Virgil Carrington. *Eight Hours Before Richmond* (New York: Holt, 1957).

Jordan, Ervin L. *Black Confederates and Afro-Yankees in Civil War Virginia* (Charlottesville: University of Virginia, 1995).

Jude Wanniski, "Defending Abraham Lincoln," www.townhall.com/columnists/judewaniski/jw20020625.

Kallina, Paul. "Non-Combatant's Service," *Surratt Courier*, 16 (May 1991), 4.

Kane, Harnett T. *Spies for the Blue and Gray* (Garden City, N.Y.: Hanover House. 1954).

Kauffman, Michael W. *American Brutus: John Wilkes Booth and the Lincoln Conspiracies* (New York: Random House, 2004).

Kauffman, Michael W. "Booth, Republicanism and the Lincoln Assassination" (Special Scholarship Thesis, University of Virginia, 1980).

Kauffman, Michael W. "David Edgar Herold: The Forgotten Conspirator," *IPO*, 23-28.

Kauffman, Michael W. "Fort Lesley McNair and the Lincoln Conspirators," *Lincoln Herald*, 80 (Winter 1978), 176-88.

Kauffman, Michael W. (ed.), *In Pursuit of . . . : Continuing Research in the Field of the Lincoln Assassination* (Clinton, Md.: Surratt Society, 1990).

Kauffman, Michael W. (ed.). *Memoirs of a Lincoln Conspirator [Samuel B. Arnold]* (Bowie, Md.: Heritage Press, 1995).

Kauffman, Michael W. "Booth's Escape Route: Lincoln's Assassin on the Run," *Blue and Gray Magazine*, 7 (June 1990)[Special Issue].

Kauffman, Michael W. "Door Number 7 or Door Number 8?" *Surratt Courier*, 33 (February 2008), 3-4.

Kauffman, Michael W. "John Wilkes Booth and the Murder of Abraham Lincoln," *Blue and Gray Magazine*, 7 (April 1990[Special Issue].

Kauffman, Michael W. "Reward Money and Its Current Value," *Surratt Courier*, 22 (June 1997), 3.

Keen, Hugh C. and Horace Mewborn, *43rd Battalion Virginia Cavalry, Mosby's Command* (2nd ed., Lynchburg, Va.: H. E. Howard, 1993).

Keehn, David. "Strong Arm of Secession: The Knights of the Golden Circle in the Secession Crisis of 1861," *North & South*, 10 (June 2005), 42-57.

Keesler, Robert L. "More on that Surratt Picture," *IPO*, 257-64.

Kegel, James A. *North with Lee and Jackson: The Lost Story of Gettysburg* (Mechanicsburg, Pa.: Stackpole Books, 1996).

Kemp, Jack. "Getting Lincoln Right," in http://jewish world review.com/cols/kemp1.asp (May 16, 2001).

Kendall, John S. *Golden Age of the New Orleans Theater* (Baton Rouge: Louisiana State University Press, 1952).

Kiell, Norman (ed.), *Psychological Studies of Famous Americans: The Civil War Era* (New York: Twayne Publishers, 1964).

Kimmel, Stanley. *Mad Booths of Maryland* (2 ed., rev. and enlarged, New York: Dover Publications, 1969).

Kimmel, Stanley. *Mr. Lincoln's Washington* (New York: Bramhall House, 1957).

Kincaid, Arthur (ed.). *John Wilkes Booth, Actor: The Proceedings of a Conference Weekend in Bel Air, Maryland, May 1988* (North Leigh, Oxfordshire: Privately Published, 1988).

Kincaid, Arthur. " Pages from a Diary." *Surratt Courier*, 18 (April 1993), 4-5.

Kincaid, Arthur. "Redefining 'Mediocrity' and 'Genius'," *Surratt Courier*, 26 (January 2001), 3-7.

Kincaid, Arthur. "Unlocked Book Revisited," *Surratt Courier*, 16 (September 1991), 3-6.

Kincaid, Deirdre Barber. "A Rebuttal," *Surratt Courier*, 24 (September 1999), 3.

Kincaid, Deirdre Barber. "Mary Ann Doolittle: The 'Flower Girl' Myth of the Booths' Mother," *Surratt Courier*, 29 (March 2004), 3-5.

Kinchen, Oscar A. *Confederate Operations in Canada and the North* (North Quincy, Mass.: Christopher Publishing House, 1970).

Klement, Frank L. *Dark Lanterns: Secret Political Societies, Conspiracies and Treason trials in the Civil War* (Baton Rouge: Louisiana State University Press, 1984).

Klement, Frank. "A Small Town Editor Criticizes Lincoln: A Study in Editorial Abuse," *Lincoln Herald*, 54 (Summer 1952), 27-32, 60.

Klingman, William K. *Abraham Lincoln and the Road to Emancipation* (New York: Viking, 2001).

Koons, Glenn. "Booth Reveals His Plan to Surratt," *Surratt Society News*, 9 (February 1984), 5-8.

Kunhardt, Dorothy Meserve and Philip B. Kunhardt, Jr. *Twenty Days: A Narrative in Text and Pictures of the Assassination of Abraham Lincoln and the Twenty Days that Followed--the Nation in Mourning, the Long Trip Home to Springfield* (New York: Harper & Row, Publishers, 1965).

Kunhardt, Dorothy Meserve and Philip B., Jr. "Assassination!" *American Heritage*, 16 (April 1965), 5-35.

Kushlan, Jim (ed.). "Rebel Secret Agents and Saboteurs in Canada," *Civil War Times Illustrated*, 40 (June 2001), [Special Issue].

Kushlan, Jim. "A Paper Link to a Conspiracy," *Civil War Times Illustrated*, 30 (September-October 1991), 15.

Lange, James E. T. "Some 'Muddy' Legal Issues," *Surratt Courier*, 24 (October 1998), 5-8.

Lange, James E. T. and Katherine DeWitt, Jr. "Further Notes on Presidential Succession," *Surratt Courier*, 16 (September 1991), 2-3.

Lange, James E. T. and Katherine DeWitt, Jr. "Hanson Hiss Article a Fraud," *Surratt Courier*, 19 (November 1994), 3-5.

Lange, James E. T. and Katherine DeWitt, Jr. "One Who Got Away: John Harrison Surratt," *North & South*, 4 (January 2000), 51-56.

Lange, James E. T. and Katherine DeWitt, Jr. "Who Ordered Lincoln's Death?" *North & South*, 1 (No. 6, 1998), 16-33.

Lange, James E. T. and Katherine DeWitt, Jr. "Law of Conspiracy," *Surratt Courier*, 23 (January 1998), 6-8.

Lanis, Edward Stanley. "Allen Pinkerton and the Baltimore 'Assassination' Plot against Lincoln," *Maryland Historical Magazine*, 45 (March 1950), 1-13.

Larabee, Ann. *The Dynamite Fiend: The Chilling Tale of a Confederate Spy, Con Artist, and Mass Murderer* (New York: Palgrave MacMillan, 2005).

Larsen, Clark. "A Policeman's Perspective," *Surratt Courier*, 23 (October 1998), 4-7.

Larson, Kate Clifford. *The Assassin's Accomplice: Mary Surratt and the Plot to Kill Abraham Lincoln*. (New York: Basic Books, 2008).

Lattimer, John K. *Kennedy and Lincoln: Medical and Ballistic Comparisons of Their Assassinations* (New York: Harcourt, Brace, Jovanovich, 1980).

Laughlin, Clara E. "Last Twenty-four Hours of Lincoln's Life." *Ladies Home Journal*, 20 (February 1909), 12ff.

Laughlin, Clara E. *Death of Lincoln: The Story of Booth's Plot, His Deed and the Penalty* (New York: Doubleday, Page & Co., 1909).

Leech, Margaret. *Reveille in Washington, 1860-1865* (New York: Harper & Brothers, Publishers, 1941).

Leonardi, Dell. *Reincarnation of John Wilkes Booth: A Study in Hypnotic Regression* (Old Greenwich, Conn.: Devin-Adair, 1975).

Lepore, Jill. "Just the Facts, Ma'am: Fake Memoirs, Factual Fictions, and the History of History," The New Yorker, 83 (March 24, 2008), 78-83.

Lerner, Barbara. "Killer Narcissists," *National Review* On-line, May 19, 1999, at townhall.com.

Levin, Alexandra Lee. "Canada Contact: Edwin Gray Lee," *Civil War Times Illustrated*, 18 (Winter 1979), 4-6, 8, 42-47.

Levin, Alexandria Lee. "Who Hid John H. Surratt, the Lincoln Conspiracy Case Figure?" *Maryland Historical Magazine*, 18 (June 1979), 175-84.

Lewis, Lloyd. "This Is to Certify," *Liberty*, (Feby. 4, 1928).

Lewis, Lloyd. "Four Who Were Hanged," *Liberty*, (Feby. 11, 1928).

Lewis, Lloyd. *Assassination of Lincoln: History and Myth* (Lincoln, Neb.: Bison Books, 1994, original 1929).

Lewis, Lloyd. *Myths After Lincoln* (New York: The Press of the Readers Club, 1922).

Lomax, Virginia. *Old Capitol and Its Inmates* (New York: E.J. Hale & Son, 1867).

Long, David E. *Jewel of Liberty: Abraham Lincoln's Re-election and the End of Slavery* (Mechanicsburg, PA: Stackpole, 1994).

Longacre, Edward G. "Judson Kilpatrick," *Civil War Times Illustrated*, 10 (April 1971), 24-33.

Longacre, Edward G. *Mounted Raids of the Civil War* (South Brunswick, N.J.: A. S. Barnes, 1975.

Loux, Arthur F. "Accident-Prone John Wilkes Booth," *Lincoln Herald*, 85 (Winter 1983), 283-68.

Loux, Arthur F. "Mystery of the Telegraphic Interruption," *Lincoln Herald*, 81 (Winter 1979), 234-37.

Lowry, Thomas P. *Civil War Bawdy Houses of Washington, D.C.* (Fredericksburg, Va.: Sergeant Kirkland's, 1997).

Lowery, Thomas P. "Opposition to Negro Equality," *North & South*, 3 (June 2000), 9, 80-81.

Lowry, Thomas P. *Story the Soldiers Wouldn't Tell: Sex in the Civil War* (Mechanicsburg, Pa.: Stackpole Books, 1994).

MacNair, James D. "Further Thoughts," *BIB*, 43-46.

Mahoney, Ella V. *Sketches of Tudor Hall and the Booth Family* (Baltimore: Franklin Printing Co., 1925).

Markle, Donald E. *Spies and Spymasters of the Civil War* (New York: Hippocrene Books, 1994).

Marks, Bayly Ellen and Mark Norton Schatz (eds.), *Between North and South: A Maryland Journalist Views the Civil War, The Narrative of William Wilkins Glenn, 1861-1869* (Rutherford, N. J.: Fairleigh Dickinson University Press, 1976).

Marshall, John A. *American Bastille: A History of the Illegal Arrests and Imprisonment of American Citizens during the Late Civil War* (2 vols., New York: De Capo, 1970).

Martin, Percy E. "Adventures With Mr. Hall on the Trail of George Atzerodt," IPO, 279-82.

Martin, Percy E. "Baltimorean in Big Trouble," Samuel Arnold, A Lincoln Conspirator," *History Trails*, 25 (Winter 1990-91), 5-8.

Martin, Percy E. "Hookstown Connection," IPO, 117-20.

Martin, Percy E. "John 'Bull' Frizzell," IPO, 91-96.

Martin, Percy E. "Samuel Bland Arnold Revisited," IPO, 33-41.

Martin, Percy E. "The Six Hour War of Samuel Arnold," *Surratt Courier*, 33 (July 2008), 3-6.

Martin, Percy E. "The Surprising Speed of Identification of Two Baltimore Conspirators," IPO, 167-70.

Martin, Samuel J. *"Kill Cavalry": Sherman's Merchant of Terror. The Life of Union General Hugh Judson Kilpatrick* (Madison N.J.: Fairleigh Dickinson University Press, 1996).

Mason, Kate H. "A True Story of the Capture and Death of John Wilkes Booth," *Northern Neck Historical Magazine*, 13 (December 1963), 1237-39.

Masters, Edgar Lee. *Lincoln, the Man.* (New York: Dodd, Meade & Company, 1931).

Maxwell, Jerry H. "Bizarre Case of Lewis Paine," *Lincoln Herald*, 81 (Winter 1979), 223-33.

May, John F. "Mark of the Scalpel," *Records of the Columbia Historical Society*, 13 (1910), 49-68.

May, Robert E. *Southern Dream of a Caribbean Empire, 1854-61* (Baton Rouge: Louisiana State University Press, 1973).

Mayer, Adam. "St. Lawrence Hall in Montreal," *Civil War Times Illustrated*, 31 (January-February 1993), 44-46, 74.

McBride, Robert W. "Lincoln's Bodyguard: The Union Light Guard of Ohio, with Some Personal Recollections of Abraham Lincoln," *Indiana Historical Society Publications*, 5 (1911), 5-39.

McCarty, Burke. *Suppressed Truth about the Assassination of Abraham Lincoln* (Haverill, Mass.: Arya Varta Publishing Co., 1964).

McCrary, Peyton. *Abraham Lincoln and Reconstruction: The Louisiana Experiment* (Princeton: Princeton University Press, 1978)

McHale, John E. "A Response," The *Surratt Courier*, 23 (September 1998), 4-5.

McHale, John E., Jr. *Dr. Samuel A. Mudd and the Lincoln Assassination* (Parsippany, J. J. : Dillon Press, 1895).

McHale, Mary Mudd. "A Response re: Dr. Mudd," *Surratt Courier*, 26 (December 2001), 3-4.

McKinley, James. *Assassination in America* (New York: Harper & Row, 1977).

McLaurin, John J. *Sketches in Crude Oil: Some Accidents and Incidents of the Petroleum Development in All Parts of the Globe* (Harrisburg, Pa.: McLaurin, 1896).

McLoughlin, Emmett. *An Inquiry into the Assassination of Abraham Lincoln* (New York: Lyle Stuart, Inc., 1963).

McMurtry, R. Gerald (ed.). "[John H. Surratt's] Lecture on the Lincoln Conspiracy," *Lincoln Herald*, 51 (Dec. 1949), 20-33, 39.

McMurtry, R. Gerald. "Did 'Coughdrop Joe' Ratto Hold Booth's Horse?" *Lincoln Lore* (January 1969), 2-3.

McMurtry, R. Gerald. "Major Rathbone and Miss Harris: Guests of the Lincolns in the Ford's Theater Box," *Lincoln Lore* (August 1971), 1-3.

McPherson, James M. "A Failed Richmond Raid and Its Consequences," *Columbiad: A Quarterly Review of the War Between the States*, 2 (Winter 1999), 130-133.

McPherson, James M. "What Caused the Civil War?" *North & South*, 4 (November 2000), 12-22.

McPherson, James M. *Battle Cry of Freedom: The Civil War Era* (New York: Ballantine, 1989).

McWhiney, Grady (ed.). *Grant, Lee, Lincoln, and the Radicals* (Evanston: Northwestern University Press, 1964).

McWhiney, Grady and Judith Hallock, *Braxton Bragg and Confederate Defeat* (2 vols., Tuscaloosa: University of Alabama Press, 1969, 1991.

Meade, George (ed.).*The Life and Letters of General George Gordon Meade* (2 vols., New York: Charles Scribner's Sons, 1913).

Meade, Robert Douthat. "Judah P. Benjamin," *Civil War Times Illustrated*, 10 (June 1971), 10-20.

Meade, Robert Douthat. *Judah P. Benjamin: Confederate Statesman* (New York: Oxford University Press, 1943).

Meade, Robert Douthat. "Relations between Judah P. Benjamin and Jefferson Davis," *Journal of Southern History*, 5 (1939), 468-78.

Meredith, Roy. *Storm over Sumter* (New York: Simon & Schuster, 1957).

Metcalf, Geoff. "Lincoln: Tyrant or Champion . . . or Both?" at www.worldnewsdaily.com/news/article #27512

Miller, Ernest C. *John Wilkes Booth, Oilman* (New York: The Exposition Press, 1947).

Miller, Steven G. "[First Sergeant] Wilson D. Kenzie, the Linchpin of the Booth Escape Theories," *BIB*, 25-34.

Miller, Steven G. "Did Lieutenant William C. Allen Witness the Shooting of J. Wilkes Booth?" *BIB*, 35-42.

Miller, Steven G. "More on Capt. Doherty. . . ," *Surratt Courier*, 15 (September 1990), 5-7.

Miller, Steven G. "Rollcall for the Garrett's Farm Patrol," *Surratt Courier*, 19 (September 1994), 3-5.

Miller, Steven G. "Who Was the Boy at the Hanging of the Lincoln Conspirators?" *Surratt Courier*, 17 (March 1993), 4-5.

Miller, Steven G. "Why I Believe Booth Died at Garrett's Farm," *BIB*, 19-24.

Miller, Steven G. (ed.). "A Trooper's Account of the Death of Booth," *Surratt Courier*, 20 (May 1995), 5-9.

Miller, Steven G. (ed.). "Boston Corbett's Long-Forgotten Story of Wilkes Booth's Death," *Surratt Courier*, 26 (May 2001), 5-7; ibid., 26 (June 2001), 4-6.

Mills, Robert Lockwood. *It Didn't Happen the Way You Think: The Lincoln Assassination—What the Experts Missed* (New Canaan, Conn.: Write Ideas, 1993).

Milton, George Fort. *Abraham Lincoln and the Fifth Column* (New York: Vanguard, 1942).

Mitgang, Herbert. "Mexican War Dove," *New Republic*, 156 (February 11, 1967), 24.

Mogelever, Jacob. *Death to Traitors: The Story of General Lafayette C. Baker, Lincoln's Forgotten Secret Service Chief* (New York: Doubleday & Company, 1960).

Monroe, Douglas. *Twenty-one Lessons of Merlyn--A Study in Druid Magic and Lore* (St. Paul, Mn.: Llewellyn Publications, 1992).

Moore, Guy W. "Questions and Answers," *IPO*, 269-78.

Moore, Guy W. "Researching the Case of Mrs. Surratt Thirty Years Ago," *IPO*, 285-92.

Moore, Guy W. *Case of Mrs. Surratt: Her Controversial Trial and Execution for Conspiracy in the Lincoln Assassination* (Norman: University of Oklahoma Press, 1954).

Morcum, Richmond. "They All Loved Lucy," *American Heritage*, 21 (October 1970), 12-15.

Morris, Clara. "Some Recollections of John Wilkes Booth," *McClure's Magazine*, (February 1901), 299-304.

Morris, Robert L. "Lincoln-Johnson Plan for Reconstruction and the Republican Convention of 1864," *Lincoln Herald*, 71 (Spring 1969), 33-39.

Morris, Thomas D. *Free Men All: The Personal Liberty Laws of the North, 1780-1861* (Baltimore: The Johns Hopkins University Press, 1974).

Mudd, Nettie. *Life of Samuel A. Mudd . . .* (New York: Neale Publishing, 1908, reprinted 1962).

Nagel, Paul C. *One Nation Indivisible: The Union in American Thought, 1776-1861* (New York: Oxford University Press, 1964).

Neely, Mark E., Jr. "Treason in Indiana: A Review Essay," *Lincoln Lore*, (February and March, 1974), 1-4, 1-3.

Neely, Mark E., Jr. "Lincoln Theme since Randall's Call: The Promises and Perils of Professionalism," *Papers of the Abraham Lincoln Association*, 1 (1979), 10-70.

Neely, Mark E., Jr.. *Fate of Liberty: Abraham Lincoln and Civil Liberties* (New York: Oxford University Press, 1991).

Nelson, Larry E. *Bullets, Ballots, and Rhetoric: Confederate Policy for the United States Presidential Contest of 1864* (University, Ala.: University of Alabama Press, 1980).

New, Christopher. "America's Civil War," March 1993, at erols.com/candidus/wilkes-1.

Newman, Harry Wright. *Maryland and the Confederacy* (Annapolis, MD: Harry Wright Newman, 1976).

Nichols, Roy Franklin. "United States vs. Jefferson Davis," *American Historical Review*, 31 (Jany. 1926), 266-84.

Niemon, Simon I. *Judah Benjamin* (Indianapolis: Bobbs-Merrill, 1963).

Nolan, Alan T. *Lee Considered: General Robert E. Lee and Civil War History* (Chapel Hill: University of North Carolina Press, 1991).

Nottingham. Theodore J. *Curse of Cain: The Untold Story of John Wilkes Booth* (Nicholasville, Ky.: Appaloosa Books, 1997).

Oates, Stephen B. *To Purge this Land with Blood: A Biography of John Brown* (New York: Harper & Row, 1970).

Oggel, L. Terry (ed.). *Letters and Notebooks of Mary Devlin Booth* (New York: Greenwood Press, 1987).

Oldroyd, Osborn H. *Assassination of Abraham Lincoln: Flight, Pursuit, Capture, and Punishment of the Conspirators* (Washington: O. H. Oldroyd, 1901).

Orlowek, Nate. "Why We Believe Booth Died in 1903," *BIB*, 3-6.

Osterweis, Rollin G. *Romanticism and Realism in the Old South* (New Haven: Yale University Press, 1949).

O'Toole, G.J.A. *Cosgrove Report: Being a Private Inquiry of a Pinkerton Detective into the Death of President Lincoln* (New York: Rawson, Wade, 1979).

Ownsbey, Betty J. "Lewis Powell: Mystery Man of the Conspiracy," *IPO*, 15-22.

Ownsbey, Betty J. "Elusive Brannon Sisters," *Surratt Courier*, 19 (November 1994), 5-8.

Ownsbey, Betty J. "Military Career of an Assassin," *North & South*, 2 (November 1998), 48-58.

Ownsbey, Betty J. *Alias "Paine": Lewis Thornton Powell, the Mystery Man of the Lincoln Conspiracy* (Jefferson, N.C.: McFarland & Company, Publishers, 1993).

Patrick, Rembert W. *Fall of Richmond* (Baton Rouge: Louisiana State University Press, 1960).

Patrick, Rembert. *Jefferson Davis and His Cabinet* (Baton Rouge: Louisiana State University Press, 1944).

Pegram William M. "An Historical Identification: John Wilkes Booth-- What Became of Him?" *Maryland Historical Magazine*, 8 (1913), 327-31.

Pierpont, Claudia Roth. "TheFlorentine: The Man Who Taught Rulers How to Rule," *New Yorker*, 83 (September 15, 2008), 87-93.

Phillips, Kevin. *The Cousins' Wars: Religion, Politics, and the Triumph of Anglo-America* (New York: Basic Books, 1999).

Phillips, Ulrich B. "Central Theme of Southern History," *American Historical Review*, 24 (October 1928), 30-43.

Pierrepont, Edwards. *To the Jury on the Trial of John H. Surratt for the Murder of President Lincoln* (Washington: Government Printing Office, 1867).

Pitman, Benn (comp.), T*he Assassination of President Lincoln and the Trial of the Conspirators* (Cincinnati: Moore, Wilstach & Baldwin, 1865).

Planck, Gary R. "Lincoln's Assassination: The 'Forgotten' Investigation: A. C. Richards, Superintendent of the Metropolitan Police," *Lincoln Herald*, 82 (Winter 1980), 521-39.

Planck, Gary R. "Name Is Mudd," *Lincoln Herald*, 81 (Winter 1979), 222.

Porter, George Loring. "How Booth's Body Was Hidden," *Magazine of History*, 38 (1929), 19-35.

Potter, David M. *Lincoln and His Party in the Secession Crisis* (New Haven: Yale University Press, 1962, 2nd rev. ed.).

Potter, John Mason. *Thirteen Desperate Days* (New York: Ivan Obolensky, 1964).

Poulter, Keith (ed.), "Lincoln Assassination: Do the Pieces Fit?" *North & South*, 2 (April 1999), 26-34.

Pratt, Fletcher. *Stanton: Lincoln's Secretary of War* (New York: Norton, 1953).

Prior, Leon O. "Lewis Payne, Pawn of John Wilkes Booth," *Florida Historical Quarterly*, 43 (July 1964), 1-20.

Ramage, James A. *Gray Ghost: The Life and Legend of Col. John Singleton Mosby* (Lexington: The University Press of Kentucky, 1999).

Randall, James G. *Constitutional Problems Under Lincoln* (Rev. ed., Urbana: University of Illinois Press, 1964).

Rathbun, Frank. "Rathbone Connection," *IPO*, 213-20.

Reck, W. Emerson. A. *Lincoln: His Last 24 Hours* (Jefferson, N.C.: McFarland & Co., Inc., 1987).

Reuter, William L. *King Can Do No Wrong* (New York: Pageant Press, Inc., 1958).

Rhea, Gordon C. *To the North Anna River: Grant and Lee, May 13-25, 1864* (Baton Rouge: Louisiana State University Press, 2000).

Rhodehamel, John and Louise Taper (eds.). *"Right or Wrong, God Judge Me": The Writings of John Wilkes Booth* (Urbana: University of Illinois Press, 1997).

Richter, William L. *Confederate Freedom Fighter: The Story of John H. Surratt & the Plots Against Lincoln* (Laurel, Md.: Burgundy Press, 2008).

Richter, William L. "How Did Anakin Skywalker become Darth Vader?: The Deconstruction of Abraham Lincoln" (Unpublished paper delivered to the Surratt Society, April 2, 2005).

Richter, William L. "Out of the Sahara of the Bozart: The Political Thought of John Wilkes Booth" (Unpublished paper delivered to the Surratt Society, April 1, 2006).

Riggs, David F. "Dahlgren Papers Reconsidered," *Lincoln Herald*, 83 (Summer 1981), 659-67.

Ripley, C. Peter. *Slaves and Freedmen in Civil War Louisiana* (Baton Rouge: Louisiana State University Press, 1978).

Ripley, Edward H. *Capture and Occupation of Richmond, April 3rd, 1865* (New York: G. P. Putnam's Sons, 1907).

Ripley, Edward H. *Vermont General: The Unusual War Experiences of Edward Hastings Ripley, 1862-1865* (Ed. by Otto Eisenschiml, New York: The Devin-Adair Company, 1960).

Robbins, Caroline. "Algernon Sidney's Discourses Concerning Government: Textbook of Revolution," *William and Mary Quarterly*, Series 3, 4 (1947), 267-96.

Robbins, Peggy. "Greatest Scoundrel [Jacob Thompson]," *Civil War Times Illustrated*, 31 (November/December 1992), 54-59, 89-90.

Robertson, James I. "Old Capitol: Eminence to Infamy," *Maryland Historical Magazine*, 65 (Winter 1970), 394-412.

Robinson, J. Denis. "Hail Hale, the Hype's All Here," As I Please, 2 (No. 4, March 1. 1998) at seacoastnh.com.

Robinson, J. Denis. "'New' Dying Words of John Wilkes Booth," As I Please, 2 (No. 5; April 20, 1998) at seacoastnh.com.

Rollins, Richard (ed.). *Black Southerners in Gray: Essays on Afro-Americansin Confederate Armies* (Redondo Beach, CA: Rank and File Publications,1994).

Roscoe, Theodore. "They Tried to Stop Booth," *Collier's Magazine*, (Dec. 27, 1924).

Roscoe, Theodore. *Web of Conspiracy* (Englewood Cliffs, N.J.: Prentice-Hall, 1959).

Roy, Caesar A. "Was Lincoln the Great Emancipator?" *Civil War Times Illustrated*, 33 (May/June 1994), 46-49.

Ruggles, M. B. "Pursuit and Death of John Wilkes Booth: Major Ruggles's Narrative," *Century Magazine*, 39 (Jany. 1890), 443-46.

Rule, D. H. "Sultana: The Case for Sabotage," *North & South*, 5 (December 2001), 76-87.

Russo, Frank. "An Interesting Look at Mrs. Surratt's Guilt or Innocence," *Surratt Society News*, 9 (March 1984), 5-6.

Rychlik, Jan. "Cardinal Antonelli and Rufus King--Two Men Against John Surratt," *Surratt Courier*, 23 (November 1998), 3-4.

Rywell, Martin. *Judah Benjamin: Unsung Rebel Prince* (Asheville, N.C.: Stephens Press, 1948).

Safire, William. *Freedom: A Novel of Abraham Lincoln and the Civil War* (Graden City, N.Y.: Doubleday & Company, 1987).

Samples, Gordon. *Lust for Fame: The Stage Career of John Wilkes Booth* (Jefferson, N.C.: McFarland & Company, Inc., 1982).

Schultz, Duane. *Dahlgren Affair: Terror and Conspiracy in the Civil War* (New York: W. W. Norton & Company, 1998).

Sears, Stephen W. "Raid on Richmond," *MHQ: The Quarterly Journal of Military History*, 11 (Autumn 1998), 88-96.

Sears, Stephen W. "Dahlgren Papers Revisited," *MHQ: The Quarterly Journal of Military History,* 3 (Summer 1999), at www.thehistorynet.com/Columbiad

Sears, Stephen W. *Controversies & Commanders: Dispatches from the Army of the Potomac* (Boston: Houghton Mifflin, 1999).

Seitz, Don Carlos. *Braxton Bragg, General of the Confederacy* (Frreeport, N.Y.: Books for Libraries Press, 1971, orig. 1924).

Seymour, Mark Wilson (ed.). *Pursuit and Arrest of John H. Surratt: Dispatches from the Official Record of the Assassination of Abraham Lincoln* (Austin: Proofmark Civil War Library, 2000).

Shelton, Vaughn. *Mask for Treason: The Lincoln Murder Trial* (Harrisburg, Pa.: Stackpole Books, 1965).

Shepherd, William G. "Shattering the Myth of John Wilkes Booth's Escape: An Adventure in Journalism," *Harper's Magazine*, 68 (Nov. 1924), 702-19.

Shulman, Terry. "What Really Happened to the Assassin?" *Civil War Times Illustrated*, 31 (July/August 1992), 50-51.

Sidney, Algernon. *Discourses Concerning Government*. Edited by Thomas G. West. Indianapolis: Library Classics, 1990.

Siegel, Mark L. "Flight of John Wilkes Booth and the Corpse Brought from Garrett's Farm," *Lincoln Herald*, 84 (Winter 1982), 210-17.

Simon, John Y. "'Rebellion Thus Sugar-coated,'" *North & South*, 3 (September, 2000), 10-16.

Singer, Jane. *The Confederate Dirty War : Arson, Bombings, Assassination and Plots for Chemical and Germ Attacks on the Union* (Jefferson, N.C.: McFarland & Company, 2005).

Sloan, Richard (ed.). "Mummy's Examination," *BIB*, 53-56.

Sloan, Richard. "Jennie Gourlay and William Withers," *The Lincolnian,* 13 (November-December 1996), 2, 7.

Sloan, Richard. "Assassin's Ride," *Surratt Society News*, 10 (October 1985), 4.

Sloan, Richard. "John Wilkes Booth's Other Victim," *American Heritage*, 41 (Feb-Mar 1991), 114-16.

Smith, Gene. "Booth Obsession," *American Heritage*, 52 (September 1992), 105-119.

Smith, Gene. *American Gothic: The Story of America's Legendary Theatrical Family--Junius, Edwin, and John Wilkes Booth* (New York: Simon & Schuster, 1992).

Smith, Henry Bascom. *Between the Lines: Secret Service stories Told Fifty Years After* (New York: Booz Bros., 1911).

Smith, Joseph E. "Rick," III. "Break a Leg," *Surratt Courier*, 28 (June 2003), 4-6.

Smith, Joseph E. "Rick," III. "More on the Fate of the Horses," *Surratt Courier*, 33 (May 2008), 4-5.

Smith, Joseph E. "Rick," III. "The Owens Statement," *Surratt Courier*, 32 (October 2007), 3-6.

Smith, Joseph E. "Rick," III. "What is Horse Faking?" *Surratt Courier*, 33 (April 2008), 4-6.

Smith, Joseph E. "Rick," III and William L. Richter. "Isaac in Texas— A Theoretical Look at the Other Surratt,"

Smith, J. E. "Rick," III and William L. Richter, "'I Told Him He Must Go Away':" Elizbeth Rouse Quesenberry and the Escape of Lincoln's Assassin," *Surratt Courier*, 33 (September 2008), 4-7.

Smith, Joseph E. "Rick," III and William L. Richter. "Isaac in Texas— A Theoretical Look at the Other Surratt," *Surratt Courier*, 33 (November), 3-7.

Smith, Joseph E. "Rick," III, with William L. Richter. *In the Shadows of the Lincoln Assassination: The Life of Confederate Spy Thomas H. Harbin* (Laurel, Md.: Burgundy Press, 2008).

Smith, Tonia J. "[Sara Slater]," (August 17, 1997), at users.nbn.net/tj1.

Smoot, Richard Mitchell. *Unwritten History of the Assassination of Abraham Lincoln* (Clinton, Mass.: W. J. Coulter, 1908).

Snow, Richard F. "Boston Corbett," *American Heritage*, 30 (June-July 1980), 48-49.

Snyder, Dean. "Torpedoes for the Confederacy," *Civil War Times Illustrated*, 24 (March 1985), 40-45.

"Some Damaging Evidence," *Surratt Courier*, 39 (June 2005), 3-5.

Sparks, David S. (ed.), *Inside Lincoln's Army: The Diary of Marsena Rudolph Patrick, Provost Marshal General, Army of the Potomac* (New York: Thomas Yoseloff, 1964).

Speed, James. "Assassins of Lincoln," *North American Review*, 145 (Sept. 1888), 314-19.

Stackpole, Edward J. *Sheridan in the Shenandoah: Jubal Early's Nemesis* (Harrisburg, Pa.: Stackpole, 1961).

Stampp, Kenneth M. *And the War Came: The North and the Secession Crisis, 1860-1861* (Baton Rouge: Louisiana State University Press, 1950).

Stanton, John F. "Anne Olivia Floyd: 1826-1905," *Surratt Courier*, 33 (June 2008), 5-8.

Stanton, John F. "Arrest of Thomas Nelson Conrad and Fannie Byrd Dade," *Surratt Courier*, 29 (October 2004), 3-4.

Stanton, John F. "'Hold the Boat, Tom'," *Surratt Society News*, 8 (September 1983), 3-4.

Stanton, John F. "Mrs. Quesenberry and John Wilkes Booth," *King George Journal*, week of March 31, 2008.

Stanton, John F. "Some Thoughts on Sarah Slater," *Surratt Courier*, 32 (February 2007), 3-6.

Starkey, Larry. *Wilkes Booth Came to Washington* (New York: Random House, 1976).

Starr, Stephen Z. *Union Cavalry in the Civil War* (3 vols., Baton Rouge: Louisiana State University Press, 1985).

Steers, Edward, Jr. "Deceptive Doctor," *Columbiad: A Quarterly Review of the War Between the States*, 2 (Summer 1998), 114-28.

Steers, Edward, Jr. "Dr. Mudd's Sense of Timing: The Trip into Bryantown," *Surratt Courier*, 24 (September 1999), 4-8.

Steers, Edward, Jr. *Escape and Capture of John Wilkes Booth* (Gettysburg: Thomas Publications, 1992).

Steers, Edward, Jr. *His Name Is Still Mudd* (Gettysburg, PA.: Thonas Publications, 1997).

Steers, Edward, Jr. "John Surratt Speaks at the Cooper Institute," *IPO*, 283-84.

Steers, Edward, Jr. "John T. Ford and Friends," *The Lincolnian*, 1 (July August 1983), 1-4.

Steers, Edward, Jr. "A Remarkable Voice from the Past: Mrs. Nettie Mudd Monroe Speaks of Her Father as 'the Prisoner of Shark Island'," *Surratt Courier*, 26 (November 2001), 3-7.

Steers, Edward, Jr. "Sic Semper Terrible!" *Surratt Courier*, 24 (August 1999), 5.

Steers, Edward, Jr. "Suspicious Character in Room 126," *The Lincolnian*, 1 (September-October 1982), 5-6.

Steers, Edward, Jr. "Who's Buried in Grant's Tomb?" *Surratt Courier*, 26 (April 2001), 5-7.

Steers, Edward, Jr. "Wrong Picture," *Surratt Courier*, 23 (October 1998), 3-4.

Steers, Edward, *Jr. Blood on the Moon: The Assassination of Abraham Lincoln* (Lexington: University of Kentucky Press, 2001).

Stephens, Alexander H. *A Constitutional View of the Late War between the States* (2 vols., Philadelphia: National Publishing Company, 1870).

Stern, Philip Van Doren. "A Vivid Scene--and Then Mystery," *New York Times Magazine*, (May 8, 1938), 3, 18.

Stern, Philip Van Doren. "Unknown Conspirator," *American Heritage*, 8 (February 1957), 51-59, 103.

Stern, Philip Van Doren. *Man Who Killed Lincoln: The Story of John Wilkes Booth and His Part in the Assassination* (New York: Literary Guild of America, Inc., 1939).

Stewart, John. *Confederate Spies at Large: The Lives of Lincoln Assassination Conspirator Tom Harbin and Charlie Russell* (Jefferson, N.C.: McFarland Co., Inc., Publishers, 2007).

Stidger, Felix G. *Treason History of the Sons of Liberty* (Chicago: Felix G. Stidger, 1903).

Stout, Joe A., Jr. *Liberators: Filibustering Expeditions into Mexico, 1848-1862, and the Last Gasp of Manifest Destiny* (Los Angeles: Westernlore Press, 1973).

Strode, Hudson. "Judah P. Benjamin's Loyalty to Jefferson Davis," *Georgia Review*, 20 (1966), 251-60.

Stuart, Meriwether. "Colonel Ulric Dahlgren and Richmond's Underground, April 1864," *Virginia Magazine of History and Biography*, 72 (April 1964), 152-204.

Stuart, Meriwether. "Operation Sanders: Wherein Old Friends and Ardent Pro-Southerners Prove to be Union Secret Agents," *Virginia Magazine of History and Biography*, 81 (April 1973), 157-99.

Stuart, Meriwether. "Samuel Ruth and General R. R. Lee: Disloyalty and the Line of Supply to Fredericksburg," *Virginia Magazine of History and Biography*, 71 (January 1963), 35-109.

Sudarow, Bryce. "Glory Denied: First Deep Bottom," *North & South*, 3 (September 2000), 17-32.

Sudarow, Bryce. "'Nothing But a Miracle Could Save Us': Second Battle of Deep Bottom, Virginia, August 14-20, 1864," *North & South*, 4 (January 2001), 12-32.

Summers, Mark W. *Era of Good Stealings* (New York: Oxford University Press, 1993).

Summers, Mark W. *Plundering Generation: Corruption and the Crisis of the Union* (New York: Oxford University Press, 1987).

Summers, Mark W. *Railroads, Reconstruction, and the Gospel of Prosperity: Aid Under the Radical Republicans* (Princeton: Princeton University Press, 1984).

Surratt, John H. "Lecture on the Lincoln Conspiracy," ed. by R. Gerald McMurtry, *Lincoln Herald*, 51 (Dec. 1949), 20-33, 39.

Sutherland, Daniel E. "'Altamont' of the Tribune: John Williamson Palmer in the Civil War," *Maryland Historical Magazine*, 78 (Spring 1983), 54-66.

Sutton, R. et al (comps.), *The Reporter: Containing . . . Trial of John H. Surratt, on an Indictment for Murder of President Lincoln* (Vols. III and IV, Washington: Sutton, 1867).

Swanberg, W. A. *First Blood: The Story of Fort Sumter* (New York: Charles Scribner's Sons, 1957).

Swett, Benjamin J. "Chicago Conspiracy," *Atlantic Monthly*, (July 1865), 108-20.

Swett, Leonard. "Conspiracies of the Rebellion," *North American Review*, 144 (February 1887), 179-89.

Taylor, W. H. "A New Story of the Assassination of Lincoln," *Leslie's Weekly*, 106 (Mar. 26, 1908), 302.

Thomas, Benjamin P. and Harold M. Hyman, *Stanton: The Life and Times of Lincoln's Secretary of War* (New York: Knopf, 1962).

Thomas, Emory. "Wartime Richmond," *Civil War Times Illustrated*, 16 (June 1977), 1-50.

Thomas, Emory. "Kilpatrick-Dahlgren Raid, Part I," *Civil War Times Illustrated*, 16 (February 1978), 4-9, 46-48, and "Part II," ibid. , (April 1978), 26-33.

Thompson, George Raynor. "Civil War Signals," *Military Affairs*, 8 (Winter 1954), 188-201.

Thompson, Winfield M. "Booth Loses His Way on the River," *Boston Globe*, April 24, 1915 (Part 15 of a 30 part series).

Tice, Douglas O. "'Bread or Blood': The Richmond Bread Riot," *Civil War Times Illustrated*, 12 (February 1974), 12-19.

Tidwell, William A. "April 15, 1865," *Surratt Courier*, 22 (April-May-June 1997), 6-10, 5-10, 4-9.

Tidwell, William A. "Booth Crosses the Potomac: An Exercise in Historical Research," *Civil War History*, 36 (No. 4, 1990), 325-33.

Tidwell, William A. "John Wilkes Booth and John Yates Beall," *Surratt Courier*, 25 (November 2000), 3-5.

Tidwell, William A. "Lincoln's Assassination," *North & South*, 2 (June 1999), 5.

Tidwell, William A. "Charles County: Confederate Cauldron," *Maryland Historical Magazine*, 91 (Spring 1996), 16-27.

Tidwell, William A. "Confederate Signal System in the Northern Neck: An Object Lesson in Careful Reading," *Surratt Courier*, 20 (February 1995), 4-5.

Tidwell, William A. *April '65: Confederate Covert Action in the Civil War* (Kent, Ohio: The Kent State University Press, 1995).

Tidwell, William A., James O. Hall and David Winfred Gaddy, *Come Retribution: The Confederate Secret Service and the Assassination of Lincoln* (Jackson: University Press of Mississippi, 1988).

Townsend, George Alfred. "How Wilkes Booth Crossed the Potomac," *Century Magazine*, (April 1884), 822-32.

Trefousse, Hans L. *Andrew Johnson: A Biography* (New York: Norton, 1989).

Trefousse, Hans L. *Radical Republicans: Lincoln's Vanguard for Racial Justice* (New York: Alfred A. Knopf, 1969).

Trefousse, Hans Louis. "Belated Revelations of the Assassination Committee," *Lincoln Herald*, 58 (Spring-Summer 1956), 13-16.

Trefousse, Hans Louis. "Lincoln's Assassination: A Disaster for the Radicals," *Lincoln Herald*, 82 (Winter 1980), 498.

Trindal, Elizabeth Stegner. "Two Men Who Held the Noose," *Surratt Courier*, 28 (July 2003), 3-5.

Trindal, Elizabeth Stegner. *Mary Surratt: An American Tragedy* (Gretna: Pelican Publishing Co., 1996).

Trindal, Mary E. "History at Its Worst," *Surratt Courier*, 16 (June 1991), 5-6.

Tucker, Glenn. "John Wilkes Booth at the John Brown Hanging," *Lincoln Herald*, 78 (Spring 1976), 3-11.

Turner, Thomas R. "Did Weichmann Turn State's Evidence to Save Himself? A Critique of A True History of the Assassination of Abraham Lincoln," *Lincoln Herald*, 81 (Winter 1979), 265-67.

Turner, Thomas Reed. *Beware the People Weeping: Public Opinion and the Assassination of Abraham Lincoln* (Baton Rouge: Louisiana State University Press, 1982).

Van Swaringen, Doris. "Surratt Tavern Public Rooms," *Surratt Society News*, 4 (September 1979), 3.

"Verdict is in. . . : A Review of the case of Dr. Samuel A. Mudd," *Surratt Courier*, 18 (September 1992), 4-6.

Verge, Laurie. "Baltimore Plot," *IPO*, 137-40.

Verge, Laurie (ed.). *Body in the Barn: The Controversy Over the Death of John Wilkes Booth* (Clinton, Md.: The Surratt Society, 1993).

Verge, Laurie (ed.). *From War Department Files: Statements Made by the Alleged Lincoln Conspirators Under Examination, 1865* (Clinton, Md.: Surratt Society, 1980).

Verge, Laurie. "Into the Fray: The Changing Role of Women During the Civil War," *Surratt Courier*, 22 (March 1997), 4-8.

Verge, Laurie. "John P. Brophy," *IPO*, 189-94.

Verge, Laurie. "Killer of John Wilkes Booth," *IPO*, 111-12.

Verge, Laurie. "115 Years Ago--The Spring of 1860," *IPO*, 9-13.

Verge, Laurie. "A Portrait of Mary Elizabeth Surratt," *Surratt Courier*, 31 (March 2006), 4-7.

Verge, Laurie. "Surratt Mill," *IPO*, 125-28.

Verge, Laurie. "Surratt's Neighbors," *IPO*, 89-90.

Verge, Laurie. "That Trifling Boy . . . ," *Surratt Courier*, 27 (January 2002), 4-9.

Verge, Laurie. "Those Missing Pages from the 'Diary' of John Wilkes Booth," Dillon (ed.), *The Lincoln Assassination: From the Pages of the* Surratt Courier, IV, 13-20.

Verge, Laurie. "What Happened to the [Surratt] Children?" *Surratt Society News*, 9 (July-August 1984), 4-5.

Verge, Laurie. "Who Was Annie Ward?" *Surratt Courier*, 33 (July 2008), 6-7.

Verge, Laurie and James O. Hall, "Could It Have Been Mrs. Surratt?" *Surratt Courier*, 24 (September 1999), 3-4.

Walton, John M., Jr. "Mr. Stanton's Conscience," *Surratt Society News*, 6 (August 1981), 3-4.

Wamsley, J. E. "Last Meeting of the Confederate Cabinet," *Mississippi Valley Historical Review*, 6 (December 1919), 336-49.

Wang, Harold O. "A Visit to the Surratt Boardinghouse," *IPO*, 121-24.

Warren, Louis A. "First Attempt to Assassinate Lincoln," *Lincoln Lore* (March 6, 1933), 1.

Waugh, John C. *Reelecting Lincoln: The Battle for the 1864 Presidency* (New York: Crown, 1997).

Wearmouth, John M. and Roberta J. Wearmouth, *Thomas A. Jones: Chief Agent of the Confederate Secret Service in Maryland* (Port Tobacco, MD: Stones Throw Publishing, 2000).

Weckesser, Eldon C. *His Name Was Mudd: The Life of Dr. Samuel A. Mudd, Who Treated the Fleeing John Wilkes Booth* (Jefferson, N.C.: McFarland & Co., Inc., 1991).

Weichmann, Louis J. *A True Story of Abraham Lincoln and of the Conspiracy of 1865* (Edited by Floyd E. Risvold. New York: Alfred A. Knopf, 1975).

Weinberg, Daniel. "Job Wanted," *Surratt Courier*, 25 (August 200), 3.

Weissman, Philip. "Why Booth Killed Lincoln: A Psychoanalytic Study," *Psychoanalysis and the Social Sciences*, 5 (1958), 99-115.

Wert, Jeffry D. *Mosby's Rangers* (New York: Simon and Schuster, 1990).

Weston, Effie Ellsler (ed.), *The Stage Memories of John A. Ellsler* (Cleveland: The Rowfant Club, 1950).

Whellams, David. "Jefferson Davis Comes to Canada," *Surratt Courier*, 19 (April 1993), 5-8.

Wick, Rob. "Why Did Everton Conger Burn Down Richard Garrett's Tobacco Barn?" Surratt Courier, 33 (May 2008), 6-7.

Williams, Benjamin. "Trial of Mrs. Surratt and the Lincoln Assassination Plot," *Alabama Lawyer*, 25 (1964), 22-31.

Williams, T. Harry. "Abraham Lincoln: Principle and Pragmatism in Politics," *Mississippi Valley Historical Review*, 40 (June 1953), 89-108.

Williams, T. Harry. *Lincoln and the Radicals* (Madison: University of Wisconsin Press, 1941).

Williams, Walter. "Secession or Nullification," (April 10, 2002) www.townhall.com/columnists

Williamson, James J. *Prison Life in the Old Capitol and Reminiscences of the Civil War* (West Orange, N. J.: N. Pub., 1911).

Willing, Richard. "A Point in Dr. Mudd's Favor?" *Surratt Courier*, 16 (December 2001), 5-6.

Willing. "A Point in Dr. Mudd's Favor?" *Surratt Courier*, 16 (December 2001), 5-6.

Wilson, Francis. *John Wilkes Booth: Fact and Fiction of Lincoln's Assassination* (Boston: Houghton Mifflin, 1929).

Wilson, George W. "John Wilkes Booth: Father Murderer," *American Imago*, 1 (1940), 49-60.

Wilson, Major L. "Lincoln and Van Buren in the Steps of the Fathers: Another Look at the Lyceum Address," *Civil War History*, 29 (September 1983), 197-211.

Winik, Jay. April 1865: *The Month that Saved America* (New York: HarperCollins, 2001).

Woods, Rufus. *Weirdest Story in American History: The Escape of John Wilkes Booth* (Wenatchee, Wash.: Rufus Woods, 1944).

Woodward, C. Vann. "Fall of the American Adam," *American Academy of the Arts and Sciences Bulletin*, 35 (1981), 26-34.

Woodward, Steven E. *Davis and Lee at War* (Lawrence: University Press of Kansas, 1995).

Wright, J. W. A. "Mysterious Fate of Blockade Runners." *Overland Monthly and Out West Magazine*, 7 (1886), 298-303.

Yerby, Frank. "How and Why I Write the Costume Novel," *Harper's Magazine*, 219 (October 1959), 145-50.

Younger, Edward (ed.). *Inside the Confederate Government: The Diary of Robert Garlick Hill Kean, Head of the Bureau of War* (Westport, Conn.: Greenwood Press, 1973).

Zaid, Mark S. "A Rebuttal," *Surratt Courier*, 20 (May 1995), 4-5.

Zanca, Kenneth J. "Was Mrs. Surratt Married in the Church?" *Surratt Courier*, 28 (January 2003), 5-7.

Zornow, William. "Treason as a Campaign Issue in the Re-election of Lincoln," *Abraham Lincoln Quarterly*, 5 (June 1949), 348-63.